The Complete Novels of
J. Meade Falkner

The Complete Novels of J. Meade Falkner

Tales of Adventure & Mystery

Moonfleet

———

The Lost Stradivarius

———

The Nebuly Coat

———

J. Meade Falkner

LEONAUR

The Complete Novels of J. Meade Falkner
Tales of Adventure & Mystery
Moonfleet
_____

The Lost Stradivarius
_____

The Nebuly Coat
by J. Meade Falkner
FIRST EDITION

First published under the titles
Moonfleet
The Lost Stradivarius
The Nebuly Coat

Leonaur is an imprint of Oakpast Ltd
Copyright in this form © 2013 Oakpast Ltd

ISBN: 978-1-78282-249-3 (hardcover)
ISBN: 978-1-78282-250-9 (softcover)

http://www.leonaur.com

Publisher's Notes

The views expressed in this book are not necessarily
those of the publisher.

Contents

Moonfleet

Contents

We thought there was no more behind But such a day tomorrow as today And to be a boy eternal.
                              Shakespeare

To All Mohunes of Fleet
and Moonfleet in Agro Dorcestrensi
Living or Dead

Says the Cap'n to the Crew,
We have slipped the Revenue,
I can see the cliffs of Dover on the lee:
Tip the signal to the Swan,
And anchor broadside on,
And out with the kegs of Eau-de-Vie,
Says the Cap'n:
Out with the kegs of Eau-de-Vie.
Says the Lander to his men,
Get your grummets on the pin,
There's a blue light burning out at sea.
The windward anchors creep,
And the Gauger's fast asleep,
And the kegs are bobbing one, two, three,
Says the Lander:
The kegs are bobbing one, two, three.

But the bold Preventive man
Primes the powder in his pan
And cries to the Posse, Follow me.
We will take this smuggling gang,
And those that fight shall hang
Dingle dangle from the execution tree,
Says the Gauger:
Dingle dangle with the weary moon to see.

Chapter 1: In Moonfleet Village

So sleeps the pride of former days—More

The village of Moonfleet lies half a mile from the sea on the right or west bank of the Fleet stream. This rivulet, which is so narrow as it passes the houses that I have known a good jumper clear it without a pole, broadens out into salt marshes below the village, and loses itself at last in a lake of brackish water. The lake is good for nothing except sea-fowl, herons, and oysters, and forms such a place as they call in the Indies a lagoon; being shut off from the open Channel by a monstrous great beach or dike of pebbles, of which I shall speak more hereafter. When I was a child I thought that this place was called Moonfleet, because on a still night, whether in summer, or in winter frosts, the moon shone very brightly on the lagoon; but learned afterwards that 'twas but short for 'Mohune-fleet', from the Mohunes, a great family who were once lords of all these parts.

My name is John Trenchard, and I was fifteen years of age when this story begins. My father and mother had both been dead for years, and I boarded with my aunt, Miss Arnold, who was kind to me in her own fashion, but too strict and precise ever to make me love her.

I shall first speak of one evening in the fall of the year 1757. It must have been late in October, though I have forgotten the exact date, and I sat in the little front parlour reading after tea. My aunt had few books; a Bible, a Common Prayer, and some volumes of sermons are all that I can recollect now; but the Reverend Mr. Glennie, who taught us village children, had lent me a story-book, full of interest and adventure, called the *Arabian Nights Entertainment*. At last the light began to fail, and I was nothing loath to leave off reading for several reasons; as, first, the parlour was a chilly room with horse-hair chairs and sofa, and only a coloured-paper screen in the grate, for my aunt did not allow a fire till the first of November; second, there was a rank smell of molten tallow in the house, for my aunt was dipping winter candles on frames in the back kitchen; third, I had reached a part in

13

the *Arabian Nights* which tightened my breath and made me wish to leave off reading for very anxiousness of expectation. It was that point in the story of the *Wonderful Lamp*, where the false uncle lets fall a stone that seals the mouth of the underground chamber; and immures the boy, Aladdin, in the darkness, because he would not give up the lamp till he stood safe on the surface again.

This scene reminded me of one of those dreadful nightmares, where we dream we are shut in a little room, the walls of which are closing in upon us, and so impressed me that the memory of it served as a warning in an adventure that befell me later on. So I gave up reading and stepped out into the street. It was a poor street at best, though once, no doubt, it had been finer. Now, there were not two hundred souls in Moonfleet, and yet the houses that held them straggled sadly over half a mile, lying at intervals along either side of the road. Nothing was ever made new in the village; if a house wanted repair badly, it was pulled down, and so there were toothless gaps in the street, and overrun gardens with broken-down walls, and many of the houses that yet stood looked as though they could stand but little longer.

The sun had set; indeed, it was already so dusk that the lower or sea-end of the street was lost from sight. There was a little fog or smoke-wreath in the air, with an odour of burning weeds, and that first frosty feeling of the autumn that makes us think of glowing fires and the comfort of long winter evenings to come. All was very still, but I could hear the tapping of a hammer farther down the street, and walked to see what was doing, for we had no trades in Moonfleet save that of fishing. It was Ratsey the sexton at work in a shed which opened on the street, lettering a tombstone with a mallet and graver. He had been mason before he became fisherman, and was handy with his tools; so that if anyone wanted a headstone set up in the church-yard, he went to Ratsey to get it done. I lent over the half-door and watched him a minute, chipping away with the graver in a bad light from a lantern; then he looked up, and seeing me, said:

'Here, John, if you have nothing to do, come in and hold the lantern for me, 'tis but a half-hour's job to get all finished.'

Ratsey was always kind to me, and had lent me a chisel many a time to make boats, so I stepped in and held the lantern watching him chink out the bits of Portland stone with a graver, and blinking the while when they came too near my eyes. The inscription stood complete, but he was putting the finishing touches to a little sea-piece carved at the top of the stone, which showed a schooner boarding

14

a cutter. I thought it fine work at the time, but know now that it was rough enough; indeed, you may see it for yourself in Moonfleet churchyard to this day, and read the inscription too, though it is yellow with lichen, and not so plain as it was that night. This is how it runs:

Sacred to the Memory of David Block
Aged 15, who was killed by a shot
fired from the *Elector* Schooner, 21 June 1757.
Of life bereft (by fell design),
I mingle with my fellow clay.
On God's protection I recline
To save me in the Judgement Day.
There too must you, cruel man, appear,
Repent ere it be all too late;
Or else a dreadful sentence fear,
For God will sure revenge my fate.

The Reverend Mr. Glennie wrote the verses, and I knew them by heart, for he had given me a copy; indeed, the whole village had rung with the tale of David's death, and it was yet in every mouth. He was only child to Elzevir Block, who kept the Why Not? inn at the bottom of the village, and was with the *contrabandiers*, when their ketch was boarded that June night by the Government schooner. People said that it was Magistrate Maskew of Moonfleet Manor who had put the Revenue men on the track, and anyway he was on board the *Elector* as she overhauled the ketch. There was some show of fighting when the vessels first came alongside, of one another, and Maskew drew a pistol and fired it off in young David's face, with only the two gunwales between them.

In the afternoon of Midsummer's Day the *Elector* brought the ketch into Moonfleet, and there was a posse of constables to march the smugglers off to Dorchester Jail. The prisoners trudged up through the village ironed two and two together, while people stood at their doors or followed them, the men greeting them with a kindly word, for we knew most of them as Ringstave and Monkbury men, and the women sorrowing for their wives. But they left David's body in the ketch, so the boy paid dear for his night's frolic.

'Ay, 'twas a cruel, cruel thing to fire on so young a lad,' Ratsey said, as he stepped back a pace to study the effect of a flag that he was chiselling on the Revenue schooner, 'and trouble is likely to come to the other poor fellows taken, for Lawyer Empson says three of them

15

will surely hang at next Assize. I recollect', he went on, 'thirty years ago, when there was a bit of a scuffle between the *Royal Sophy* and the *Marnhull*, they hanged four of the *contrabandiers*, and my old father caught his death of cold what with going to see the poor chaps turned off at Dorchester, and standing up to his knees in the river Frome to get a sight of them, for all the countryside was there, and such a press there was no place on land. There, that's enough,' he said, turning again to the gravestone. 'On Monday I'll line the ports in black, and get a brush of red to pick out the flag; and now, my son, you've helped with the lantern, so come down to the Why Not? and there I'll have a word with Elzevir, who sadly needs the talk of kindly friends to cheer him, and we'll find you a glass of Hollands to keep out autumn chills.'

I was but a lad, and thought it a vast honour to be asked to the Why Not?—for did not such an invitation raise me at once to the dignity of manhood. Ah, sweet boyhood, how eager are we as boys to be quit of thee, with what regret do we look back on thee before our man's race is half-way run! Yet was not my pleasure without alloy, for I feared even to think of what Aunt Jane would say if she knew that I had been at the Why Not?—and beside that, I stood in awe of grim old Elzevir Block, grimmer and sadder a thousand times since David's death.

The Why Not? was not the real name of the inn; it was properly the Mohune Arms. The Mohunes had once owned, as I have said, the whole of the village; but their fortunes fell, and with them fell the fortunes of Moonfleet. The ruins of their mansion showed grey on the hillside above the village; their almshouses stood halfway down the street, with the quadrangle deserted and overgrown; the Mohune image and superscription was on everything from the church to the inn, and everything that bore it was stamped also with the superscription of decay. And here it is necessary that I say a few words as to this family badge; for, as you will see, I was to bear it all my life, and shall carry its impress with me to the grave.

The Mohune shield was plain white or silver, and bore nothing upon it except a great black 'Y'. I call it a 'Y', though the Reverend Mr. Glennie once explained to me that it was not a 'Y' at all, but what heralds call a *cross-pall*. *Cross-pall* or no *cross-pall*, it looked for all the world like a black 'Y', with a broad arm ending in each of the top corners of the shield, and the tail coming down into the bottom. You might see that cognizance carved on the manor, and on the stonework and woodwork of the church, and on a score of houses in the village, and it hung on the signboard over the door of the inn. Everyone knew the

Mohune 'Y' for miles around, and a former landlord having called the inn the Why Not? in jest, the name had stuck to it ever since.

More than once on winter evenings, when men were drinking in the Why Not?, I had stood outside, and listened to them singing 'Ducky-stones', or 'Kegs bobbing One, Two, Three', or some of the other tunes that sailors sing in the west. Such songs had neither beginning nor ending, and very little sense to catch hold of in the middle. One man would crone the air, and the others would crone a solemn chorus, but there was little hard drinking, for Elzevir Block never got drunk himself, and did not like his guests to get drunk either. On singing nights the room grew hot, and the steam stood so thick on the glass inside that one could not see in; but at other times, when there was no company, I have peeped through the red curtains and watched Elzevir Block and Ratsey playing backgammon at the trestle-table by the fire.

It was on the trestle-table that Block had afterwards laid out his son's dead body, and some said they had looked through the window at night and seen the father trying to wash the blood-matting out of the boy's yellow hair, and heard him groaning and talking to the lifeless clay as if it could understand. Anyhow, there had been little drinking in the inn since that time, for Block grew more and more silent and morose. He had never courted customers, and now he scowled on any that came, so that men looked on the Why Not? as a blighted spot, and went to drink at the Three Choughs at Ringstave.

My heart was in my mouth when Ratsey lifted the latch and led me into the inn parlour. It was a low sanded room with no light except a fire of seawood on the hearth, burning clear and lambent with blue salt flames. There were tables at each end of the room, and wooden-seated chairs round the walls, and at the trestle table by the chimney sat Elzevir Block smoking a long pipe and looking at the fire. He was a man of fifty, with a shock of grizzled hair, a broad but not unkindly face of regular features, bushy eyebrows, and the finest forehead that I ever saw. His frame was thick-set, and still immensely strong; indeed, the countryside was full of tales of his strange prowess or endurance.

Blocks had been landlords at the Why Not? father and son for years, but Elzevir's mother came from the Low Countries, and that was how he got his outland name and could speak Dutch. Few men knew much of him, and folks often wondered how it was he kept the Why Not? on so little custom as went that way. Yet he never seemed to lack for money; and if people loved to tell stories of his strength, they would speak also of widows helped, and sick comforted with unknown gifts, and hint that some of them came from Elzevir Block for all he was so grim and silent.

He turned round and got up as we came in, and my fears led me to think that his face darkened when he saw me.

'What does this boy want?' he said to Ratsey sharply.

'He wants the same as I want, and that's a glass of Ararat milk to keep out autumn chills,' the sexton answered, drawing another chair up to the trestle-table.

'Cows' milk is best for children such as he,' was Elzevir's answer, as he took two shining brass candlesticks from the mantel-board, set them on the table, and lit the candles with a burning chip from the hearth.

'John is no child; he is the same age as David, and comes from helping me to finish David's headstone. 'Tis finished now, barring the paint upon the ships, and, please God, by Monday night we will have it set fair and square in the churchyard, and then the poor lad may rest in peace, knowing he has above him Master Ratsey's best handiwork, and the parson's verses to set forth how shamefully he came to his end.'

I thought that Elzevir softened a little as Ratsey spoke of his son, and he said, 'Ay, David rests in peace. 'Tis they that brought him to his end that shall not rest in peace when their time comes. And it may come sooner than they think,' he added, speaking more to himself than to us. I knew that he meant Mr. Maskew, and recollected that some had warned the magistrate that he had better keep out of Elzevir's way, for there was no knowing what a desperate man might do. And yet the two had met since in the village street, and nothing worse come of it than a scowling look from Block.

'Tush, man!' broke in the sexton, 'it was the foulest deed ever man did; but let not thy mind brood on it, nor think how thou mayest get thyself avenged. Leave that to Providence; for He whose wisdom lets such things be done, will surely see they meet their due reward. "*Vengeance is Mine; I will repay, saith the Lord*".' And he took his hat off and hung it on a peg.

Block did not answer, but set three glasses on the table, and then took out from a cupboard a little round long-necked bottle, from which he poured out a glass for Ratsey and himself. Then he half-filled the third, and pushed it along the table to me, saying, 'There, take it, lad, if thou wilt; 'twill do thee no good, but may do thee no harm.'

Ratsey raised his glass almost before it was filled. He sniffed the liquor and smacked his lips. 'O rare milk of Ararat!' he said, 'it is sweet and strong, and sets the heart at ease. And now get the backgammon-board, John, and set it for us on the table.' So they fell to the game, and I took a sly sip at the liquor, but nearly choked myself, not being used to strong waters, and finding it heady and burning in the throat. Neither man spoke, and there was no sound except the constant rattle of the dice, and the rubbing of the pieces being moved across the board. Now and then one of the players stopped to light his pipe, and at the end of a game they scored their totals on the table with a bit of chalk. So I watched them for an hour, knowing the game myself, and being interested at seeing Elzevir's backgammon-board, which I had heard talked of before.

It had formed part of the furniture of the Why Not? for generations of landlords, and served perhaps to pass time for cavaliers of the Civil Wars. All was of oak, black and polished, board, dice-boxes, and men, but round the edge ran a Latin inscription inlaid in light wood, which I read on that first evening, but did not understand till Mr. Glennie translated it to me. I had cause to remember it afterwards, so I shall set it down here in Latin for those who know that tongue, *Ita in vita ut in lusu alae pessima jactura arte corrigenda est*, and in English as Mr. Glennie translated it, *As in life, so in a game of hazard, skill will make something of the worst of throws.*

At last Elzevir looked up and spoke to me, not unkindly, 'Lad, it is time for you to go home; men say that Blackbeard walks on the first nights of winter, and some have met him face to face betwixt this house and yours.' I saw he wanted to be rid of me, so bade them both goodnight, and was off home, running all the way thither, though not from any fear of Blackbeard, for Ratsey had often told me that there was no chance of meeting him unless one passed the churchyard by night.

Blackbeard was one of the Mohunes who had died a century back, and was buried in the vault under the church, with others of his family, but could not rest there, whether, as some said, because he was always looking for a lost treasure, or as others, because of his exceeding wickedness in life. If this last were the true reason, he must have been bad indeed, for Mohunes have died before and since his day wicked enough to bear anyone company in their vault or elsewhere. Men would have it that on dark winter nights Blackbeard might be seen with an old-fashioned lanthorn digging for treasure in the graveyard; and those who professed to know said he was the tallest of men, with full black beard, coppery face, and such evil eyes, that any who once met their gaze must die within a year. However that might be, there were few in Moonfleet who would not rather walk ten miles round than go near the churchyard after dark; and once when Cracky Jones, a poor doited body, was found there one summer morning, lying dead on the grass, it was thought that he had met Blackbeard in the night.

Mr. Glennie, who knew more about such things than anyone else, told me that Blackbeard was none other than a certain Colonel John Mohune, deceased about one hundred years ago. He would have it that Colonel Mohune, in the dreadful wars against King Charles the First, had deserted the allegiance of his house and supported the cause of the rebels. So being made Governor of Carisbrooke Castle for the Parliament, he became there the king's jailer, but was false to his trust. For the king, carrying constantly hidden about his person a great diamond which had once been given him by his brother King of France, Mohune got wind of this jewel, and promised that if it were given him he would wink at His Majesty's escape.

Then this wicked man, having taken the bribe, plays traitor again, comes with a file of soldiers at the hour appointed for the king's flight, finds His Majesty escaping through a window, has him away to a stricter ward, and reports to the Parliament that the king's escape is only prevented by Colonel Mohune's watchfulness. But how true, as Mr. Glennie said, that we should not be envious against the ungodly, against the man that walketh after evil counsels. Suspicion fell on Colonel Mohune; he was removed from his governorship, and came back to his home at Moonfleet. There he lived in seclusion, despised by both parties in the State, until he died, about the time of the happy Restoration of King Charles the Second.

But even after his death he could not get rest; for men said that he had hid somewhere that treasure given him to permit the king's escape, and that not daring to reclaim it, had let the secret die with him, and so must needs come out of his grave to try to get at it again. Mr. Glennie would never say whether he believed the tale or not, pointing out that apparitions both of good and evil spirits are related in Holy Scripture, but that the churchyard was an unlikely spot for Colonel Mohune to seek his treasure in; for had it been buried there, he would have had a hundred chances to have it up in his lifetime. However this may be, though I was brave as a lion by day, and used indeed to frequent the churchyard, because there was the widest view of the sea to be obtained from it, yet no reward would have taken me thither at night. Nor was I myself without some witness to the tale, for having to walk to Ringstave for Dr. Hawkins on the night my aunt broke her leg, I took the path along the down which overlooks the churchyard at a mile off; and thence most certainly saw a light moving to and fro about the church, where no honest man could be at two o'clock in the morning.

Chapter 2: The Floods

Then banks came down with ruin and rout,
Then beaten spray flew round about,
Then all the mighty floods were out,
And all the world was in the sea—Jean Ingelow

On the third of November, a few days after this visit to the Why Not?, the wind, which had been blowing from the south-west, began about four in the afternoon to rise in sudden strong gusts. The rooks had been pitch-falling all the morning, so we knew that bad weather was due; and when we came out from the schooling that Mr. Glennie gave us in the hall of the old almshouses, there were wisps of thatch, and even stray tiles, flying from the roofs, and the children sang:

Blow wind, rise storm,
Ship ashore before morn.

It is heathenish rhyme that has come down out of other and worse times; for though I do not say but that a wreck on Moonfleet beach was looked upon sometimes as little short of a godsend, yet I hope none of us were so wicked as to *wish* a vessel to be wrecked that we might share in the plunder. Indeed, I have known the men of Moonfleet risk their own lives a hundred times to save those of shipwrecked mariners, as when the *Darius*, East Indiaman, came ashore; nay, even poor nameless corpses washed up were sure of Christian burial, or perhaps of one of Master Ratsey's headstones to set forth sex and date, as may be seen in the churchyard to this day.

Our village lies near the centre of Moonfleet Bay, a great bight twenty miles across, and a death-trap to up-channel sailors in a south-westerly gale. For with that wind blowing strong from south, if you cannot double the Snout, you must most surely come ashore; and many a good ship failing to round that point has beat up and down the bay all day, but come to beach in the evening. And once on the beach, the sea has little mercy, for the water is deep right in, and the waves curl over full on the pebbles with a weight no timbers can withstand. Then if poor fellows try to save themselves, there is a deadly under-tow or rush back of the water, which sucks them off their legs, and carries them again under the thundering waves. It is that back-suck of the pebbles that you may hear for miles inland, even at Dorchester, on still nights long after the winds that caused it have sunk, and which makes people turn in their beds, and thank God they are not fighting with the sea on Moonfleet beach.

But on this third of November there was no wreck, only such a wind as I have never known before, and only once since. All night long the tempest grew fiercer, and I think no one in Moonfleet went to bed; for there was such a breaking of tiles and glass, such a bang-ing of doors and rattling of shutters, that no sleep was possible, and we were afraid besides lest the chimneys should fall and crush us. The wind blew fiercest about five in the morning, and then some ran up the street calling out a new danger—that the sea was breaking over the beach, and that all the place was like to be flooded. Some of the women were for flitting forthwith and climbing the down; but Master Ratsey, who was going round with others to comfort people, soon showed us that the upper part of the village stood so high, that if the water was to get thither, there was no knowing if it would not cover Ridgedown itself.

But what with its being a spring-tide, and the sea breaking clean over the great outer beach of pebbles—a thing that had not happened for fifty years—there was so much water piled up in the lagoon, that it passed its bounds and flooded all the sea meadows, and even the lower end of the street. So when day broke, there was the churchyard flooded, though 'twas on rising ground, and the church itself standing up like a steep little island, and the water over the door-sill of the Why Not?, though Elzevir Block would not budge, saying he did not care if the sea swept him away. It was but a nine-hours' wonder, for the wind fell very suddenly; the water began to go back, the sun shone bright, and before noon people came out to the doors to see the floods and talk over the storm. Most said that never had been so fierce a wind, but some of the oldest spoke of one in the second year of Queen Anne, and would have it as bad or worse. But whether worse or not, this storm was a weighty matter enough for me, and turned the course of my life, as you shall hear.

I have said that the waters came up so high that the church stood out like an island; but they went back quickly, and Mr. Glennie was able to hold service on the next Sunday morning. Few enough folks came to Moonfleet Church at any time; but fewer still came that morning, for the meadows between the village and the churchyard were wet and miry from the water. There were streamers of seaweed tangled about the very tombstones, and against the outside of the churchyard wall was piled up a great bank of it, from which came a salt rancid smell like a guillemot's egg that is always in the air after a south-westerly gale has strewn the shore with wrack.

This church is as large as any other I have seen, and divided into two parts with a stone screen across the middle. Perhaps Moonfleet was once a large place, and then likely enough there were people to fill such a church, but never since I knew it did anyone worship in that part called the nave. This western portion was quite empty beyond a few old tombs and a Royal Arms of Queen Anne; the pavement too was damp and mossy; and there were green patches down the white walls where the rains had got in. So the handful of people that came to church were glad enough to get the other side of the screen in the chancel, where at least the pew floors were boarded over, and the panelling of oak-work kept off the draughts.

Now this Sunday morning there were only three or four, I think, beside Mr. Glennie and Ratsey and the half-dozen of us boys, who crossed the swampy meadows strewn with drowned shrew-mice and moles. Even my aunt was not at church, being prevented by a migraine, but a surprise waited those who did go, for there in a pew by himself sat Elzevir Block. The people stared at him as they came in, for no one had ever known him go to church before; some saying in the village that he was a Catholic, and others an *infidel*. However that may be, there he was this day, wishing perhaps to show a favour to the parson who had written the verses for David's headstone. He took no notice of anyone, nor exchanged greetings with those that came in, as was the fashion in Moonfleet Church, but kept his eyes fixed on a prayer-book which he held in his hand, though he could not be following the minister, for he never turned the leaf.

The church was so damp from the floods, that Master Ratsey had put a fire in the brazier which stood at the back, but was not commonly lighted till the winter had fairly begun. We boys sat as close to the brazier as we could, for the wet cold struck up from the flags, and besides that, we were so far from the clergyman, and so well screened by the oak backs, that we could bake an apple or roast a chestnut without much fear of being caught. But that morning there was something else to take off our thoughts; for before the service was well begun, we became aware of a strange noise under the church. The first time it came was just as Mr. Glennie was finishing 'Dearly Beloved', and we heard it again before the second lesson.

It was not a loud noise, but rather like that which a boat makes jostling against another at sea, only there was something deeper and more hollow about it. We boys looked at each other, for we knew what was under the church, and that the sound could only come from the Mohune Vault. No one at Moonfleet had ever seen the inside of that vault; but Ratsey was told by his father, who was clerk before him, that it underlay half the chancel, and that there were more than a score of Mohunes lying there. It had not been opened for over forty years, since Gerald Mohune, who burst a blood-vessel drinking at Weymouth races, was buried there; but there was a tale that one Sunday afternoon, many years back, there had come from the vault so horrible and unearthly a cry, that parson and people got up and fled from the church, and would not worship there for weeks afterwards.

We thought of these stories, and huddled up closer to the brazier, being frightened at the noise, and uncertain whether we should not turn tail and run from the church. For it was certain that something was moving in the Mohune vault, to which there was no entrance except by a ringed stone in the chancel floor, that had not been lifted for forty years.

However, we thought better of it, and did not budge, though I could see when standing up and looking over the tops of the seats that others beside ourselves were ill at ease; for Granny Tucker gave such starts when she heard the sounds, that twice her spectacles fell off her nose into her lap, and Master Ratsey seemed to be trying to mask the one noise by making another himself, whether by shuffling with his feet or by thumping down his prayer-book. But the thing that most surprised me was that even Elzevir Block, who cared, men said, for neither God nor Devil, looked unquiet, and gave a quick glance at Ratsey every time the sound came. So we sat till Mr. Glennie was well on with the sermon. His discourse interested me though I was only a boy, for he likened life to the letter 'Y', saying that 'in each man's life must come a point where two roads part like the arms of a "Y", and that everyone must choose for himself whether he will follow the broad and sloping path on the left or the steep and narrow path on the right. For,' said he, 'if you will look in your books, you will see that the letter "Y" is not like the Mohune's, with both arms equal, but has the arm on the left broader and more sloping than the arm on the right; hence ancient philosophers hold that this arm on the left represents the easy downward road to destruction, and the arm on the right the narrow upward path of life.' When we heard that we all fell to searching our prayer-books for a capital 'Y'; and Granny Tucker, who knew not A from B, made much ado in fumbling with her book, for she would have people think that she could read. Then just at that moment came a noise from below louder than those before, hollow and grating like the cry of an old man in pain. With that up jumps Granny Tucker, calling out loud in church to Mr. Glennie—

'O Master, however can'ee bide there preaching when the Moons be rising from their graves?' and out from the church.

That was too much for the others, and all fled, Mrs. Vining crying, 'Lordsakes, we shall all be throttled like Cracky Jones.'

So in a minute there were none left in the church, save and except Mr. Glennie, with me, Ratsey, and Elzevir Block. I did not run: first, not wishing to show myself coward before the men; second, because I thought if Blackbeard came he would fall on the men rather than on a boy; and third, that if it came to blows, Block was strong enough to give account even of a Mohune. Mr. Glennie went on with his sermon, making as though he neither heard any noise nor saw the people leave the church; and when he had finished, Elzevir walked out, but I stopped to see what the minister would say to Ratsey about the noise in the vault. The sexton helped Mr. Glennie off with his gown, and then seeing me standing by and listening, said—

'The Lord has sent evil angels among us; 'tis a terrible thing, Master Glennie, to hear the dead men moving under our feet.'

'Tut, tut,' answered the minister, 'it is only their own fears that make such noises terrible to the vulgar. As for Blackbeard, I am not here to say whether guilty spirits sometimes cannot rest and are seen wandering by men; but for these noises, they are certainly Nature's work as is the noise of waves upon the beach. The floods have filled the vault with water, and so the coffins getting afloat, move in some eddies that we know not of, and jostle one another. Then being hollow, they give forth those sounds you hear, and these are your evil angels. 'Tis very true the dead do move beneath our feet, but 'tis because they cannot help themselves, being carried hither and thither by the water. Fie, Ratsey man, you should know better than to fright a boy with silly

25

talk of spirits when the truth is bad enough.'

The parson's words had the ring of truth in them to me, and I never doubted that he was right. So this mystery was explained, and yet it was a dreadful thing, and made me shiver, to think of the Mohunes all adrift in their coffins, and jostling one another in the dark. I pictured them to myself, the many generations, old men and children, man and maid, all bones now, each afloat in his little box of rotting wood; and Blackbeard himself in a great coffin bigger than all the rest, coming crashing into the weaker ones, as a ship in a heavy sea comes crashing down sometimes in the trough, on a small boat that is trying to board her. And then there was the outer darkness of the vault itself to think of, and the close air, and the black putrid water nearly up to the roof on which such sorry ships were sailing.

Ratsey looked a little crestfallen at what Mr. Glennie said, but put a good face on it, and answered—

'Well, master, I am but a plain man, and know nothing about floods and these eddies and hidden workings of Nature of which you speak; but, saving your presence, I hold it a fond thing to make light of such warnings as are given us. 'Tis always said, "When the Moons move, then Moonfleet mourns"; and I have heard my father tell that the last time they stirred was in Queen Anne's second year, when the great storm blew men's homes about their heads. And as for frighting children, 'tis well that heady boys should learn to stand in awe, and not pry into what does not concern them—or they may come to harm.' He added the last words with what I felt sure was a nod of warning to myself, though I did not then understand what he meant. So he walked off in a huff with Elzevir, who was waiting for him outside, and I went with Mr. Glennie and carried his gown for him back to his lodging in the village.

Mr. Glennie was always very friendly, making much of me, and talking to me as though I were his equal; which was due, I think, to there being no one of his own knowledge in the neighbourhood, and so he had as lief talk to an ignorant boy as to an ignorant man. After we had passed the churchyard turnstile and were crossing the sludgy meadows, I asked him again what he knew of Blackbeard and his lost treasure.

'My son,' he answered, 'all that I have been able to gather is, that this Colonel John Mohune (foolishly called Blackbeard) was the first to impair the family fortunes by his excesses, and even let the almshouses fall to ruin, and turned the poor away. Unless report strangely belies him, he was an evil man, and besides numberless lesser crimes, had on his hands the blood of a faithful servant, whom he made away with because chance had brought to the man's ears some guilty secret of the master. Then, at the end of his life, being filled with fear and remorse (as must always happen with evil livers at the last), he sent for Rector Kindersley of Dorchester to confess him, though a Protestant, and wished to make amends by leaving that treasure so ill-gotten from King Charles (which was all that he had to leave) for the repair and support of the almshouses. He made a last will, which I have seen, to this effect, but without describing the treasure further than to call it a diamond, nor saying where it was to be found. Doubtless he meant to get it himself, sell it, and afterwards apply the profit to his good purpose, but before he could do so death called him suddenly to his account. So men say that he cannot rest in his grave, not having made even so tardy a reparation, and never will rest unless the treasure is found and spent upon the poor.'

I thought much over what Mr. Glennie had said and fell to wondering where Blackbeard could have hid his diamond, and whether I might not find it some day and make myself a rich man. Now, as I considered that noise we had heard under the church, and Parson Glennie's explanation of it, I was more and more perplexed; for the noise had, as I have said, something deep and hollow-booming in it, and how was that to be made by decayed coffins. I had more than once seen Ratsey, in digging a grave, turn up pieces of coffins, and sometimes a tarnished name-plate would show that they had not been so very long underground, and yet the wood was quite decayed and rotten. And granting that such were in the earth, and so might more easily perish, yet when the top was taken off old Guy's brick grave to put his widow beside him, Master Ratsey gave me a peep in, and old Guy's coffin had cracks and warps in it, and looked as if a sound blow would send it to pieces. Yet here were the Mohune coffins that had been put away for generations, and must be rotten as tinder, tapping against each other with a sound like a drum, as if they were still sound and air-tight. Still, Mr. Glennie must be right; for if it was not the coffins, what should it be that made the noise?

So on the next day after we heard the sounds in church, being the Monday, as soon as morning school was over, off I ran down street and across meadows to the churchyard, meaning to listen outside the church if the Mohunes were still moving. I say outside the church, for I knew Ratsey would not lend me the key to go in after what he had said about boys prying into things that did not concern them; and besides that, I do not know that I should care to have ventured inside alone, even if I had the key.

When I reached the church, not a little out of breath, I listened first on the side nearest the village, that is the north side; putting my ear against the wall, and afterwards lying down on the ground, though the grass was long and wet, so that I might the better catch any sound that came. But I could hear nothing, and so concluded that the Mohunes had come to rest again, yet thought I would walk round the church and listen too on the south or sea side, for that their worships might have drifted over to that side, and be there rubbing shoulders with one another. So I went round, and was glad to get out of the cold shade into the sun on the south. But here was a surprise; for when I came round a great buttress which juts out from the wall, what should I see but two men, and these two were Ratsey and Elzevir Block. I came upon them unawares, and, lo and behold, there was Master Ratsey lying also on the ground with his ear to the wall, while Elzevir sat back against the inside of the buttress with a spy-glass in his hand, smoking and looking out to sea.

Now, I had as much right to be in the churchyard as Ratsey or Elzevir, and yet I felt a sudden shame as if I had been caught in some bad act, and knew the blood was running to my cheeks. At first I had it in my mind to turn tail and make off, but concluded to stand my ground since they had seen me, and so bade them 'Good morning'. Master Ratsey jumped to his feet as nimbly as a cat; and if he had not been a man, I should have thought he was blushing too, for his face was very red, though that came perhaps from lying on the ground. I could see he was a little put about, and out of countenance, though he tried to say 'Good morning, John', in an easy tone, as if it was a common thing for him to be lying in the churchyard, with his ear to the wall, on a winter's morning. 'Good morning, John,' he said; 'and what might you be doing in the churchyard this fine day?'

I answered that I was come to listen if the Mohunes were still moving.

'Well, that I can't tell you,' returned Ratsey, 'not wishing to waste thought on such idle matters, and having to examine this wall whether the floods have not so damaged it as to need under-pinning; so if you have time to gad about of a morning, get you back to my workshop and fetch me a plasterer's hammer which I have left behind, so that I can try this mortar.'

I knew that he was making excuses about underpinning, for the wall was sound as a rock, but was glad enough to take him at his word and beat a retreat from where I was not wanted. Indeed, I soon saw how he was mocking me, for the men did not even wait for me to come back with the hammer, but I met them returning in the first meadow. Master Ratsey made another excuse that he did not need the hammer now, as he had found out that all that was wanted was a little pointing with new mortar. 'But if you have such time to waste, John,' he added, 'you can come tomorrow and help me to get new thwarts in the *Petrel*, which she badly wants.'

So we three came back to the village together; but looking up at Elzevir once while Master Ratsey was making these pretences, I saw his eyes twinkle under their heavy brows, as if he was amused at the other's embarrassment.

The next Sunday, when we went to church, all was quiet as usual, there was no Elzevir, and no more noises, and I never heard the Mohunes move again.

Chapter 3: A Discovery

Some bold adventurers disdain
The limits of their little reign,
And unknown regions dare descry;
Still, as they run, they look behind,
They hear a voice in every wind
And snatch a fearful joy.—Gray

I have said that I used often in the daytime, when not at school, to go to the churchyard, because being on a little rise, there was the best view of the sea to be had from it; and on a fine day you could watch the French privateers creeping along the cliffs under the Snout, and lying in wait for an Indiaman or up-channel trader. There were at Moonfleet few boys of my own age, and none that I cared to make my companion; so I was given to muse alone, and did so for the most part in the open air, all the more because my aunt did not like to see an idle boy, with muddy boots, about her house.

For a few weeks, indeed, after the day that I had surprised Elzevir and Ratsey, I kept away from the church, fearing to meet them there again; but a little later resumed my visits, and saw no more of them. Now, my favourite seat in the churchyard was the flat top of a raised stone tomb, which stands on the south-east of the church. I have heard Mr. Glennie call it an altar-tomb, and in its day it had been a fine monument, being carved round with festoons of fruit and flowers; but had suffered so much from the weather, that I never was able to read the lettering on it, or to find out who had been buried beneath. Here I chose most to sit, not only because it had a flat and convenient top, but because it was screened from the wind by a thick clump of yew-trees.

These yews had once, I think, completely surrounded it, but had either died or been cut down on the south side, so that anyone sitting on the grave-top was snug from the weather, and yet possessed a fine prospect over the sea. On the other three sides, the yews grew close and thick, embowering the tomb like the high back of a fireside chair; and many times in autumn I have seen the stone slab crimson with the fallen waxy berries, and taken some home to my aunt, who liked to taste them with a glass of sloe-gin after her Sunday dinner. Others beside me, no doubt, found this tomb a comfortable seat and look-out; for there was quite a path worn to it on the south side, though all the times I had visited it I had never seen anyone there.

So it came about that on a certain afternoon in the beginning of February, in the year 1758, I was sitting on this tomb looking out to sea. Though it was so early in the year, the air was soft and warm as a May day, and so still that I could hear the drumming of turnips that Gaffer George was flinging into a cart on the hillside, near half a mile away. Ever since the floods of which I have spoken, the weather had been open, but with high winds, and little or no rain. Thus as the land dried after the floods there began to open cracks in the heavy clay soil on which Moonfleet is built, such as are usually only seen with us in the height of summer. There were cracks by the side of the path in the sea-meadows between the village and the church, and cracks in the churchyard itself, and one running right up to this very tomb.

It must have been past four o'clock in the afternoon, and I was for returning to tea at my aunt's, when underneath the stone on which I sat I heard a rumbling and crumbling, and on jumping off saw that the crack in the ground had still further widened, just where it came up to the tomb, and that the dry earth had so shrunk and settled that there was a hole in the ground a foot or more across. Now this hole reached under the big stone that formed one side of the tomb, and falling on my hands and knees and looking down it, I perceived that there was under the monument a larger cavity, into which the hole opened. I believe there never was boy yet who saw a hole in the ground, or a cave in a hill, or much more an underground passage, but longed incontinently to be into it and discover whither it led. So it was with me; and seeing that the earth had fallen enough into the hole to open a way under the stone, I slipped myself in feet foremost, dropped down on to a heap of fallen mould, and found that I could stand upright under the monument itself.

Now this was what I had expected, for I thought that there had been below this grave a vault, the roof of which had given way and let the earth fall in. But as soon as my eyes were used to the dimmer light, I saw that it was no such thing, but that the hole into which I had crept was only the mouth of a passage, which sloped gently down in the direction of the church. My heart fell to thumping with eagerness and surprise, for I thought I had made a wonderful discovery, and that this hidden way would certainly lead to great things, perhaps even to Blackbeard's hoard; for ever since Mr. Glennie's tale I had constantly before my eyes a vision of the diamond and the wealth it was to bring me. The passage was two paces broad, as high as a tall man, and cut through the soil, without bricks or any other lining; and what surprised me most was that it did not seem deserted nor mouldy and cob-webbed, as one would expect such a place to be, but rather a well-used thoroughfare; for I could see the soft clay floor was trodden with the prints of many boots, and marked with a trail as if some heavy thing had been dragged over it.

So I set out down the passage, reaching out my hand before me lest I should run against anything in the dark, and sliding my feet slowly to avoid pitfalls in the floor. But before I had gone half a dozen paces, the darkness grew so black that I was frightened, and so far from going on was glad to turn sharp about, and see the glimmer of light that came in through the hole under the tomb. Then a horror of the darkness seized me, and before I well knew what I was about I found myself wriggling my body up under the tombstone on to the churchyard grass, and was once more in the low evening sunlight and the soft sweet air.

Home I ran to my aunt's, for it was past tea-time, and beside that I knew I must fetch a candle if I were ever to search out the passage; and to search it I had well made up my mind, no matter how much I was scared for this moment. My aunt gave me but a sorry greeting when I came into the kitchen, for I was late and hot. She never said much when displeased, but had a way of saying nothing, which was much worse; and would only reply yes or no, and that after an interval, to anything that was asked of her. So the meal was silent enough, for

31

she had finished before I arrived, and I ate but little myself being too much occupied with the thought of my strange discovery, and finding, beside, the tea lukewarm and the victuals not enticing.

You may guess that I said nothing of what I had seen, but made up my mind that as soon as my aunt's back was turned I would get a candle and tinder-box, and return to the churchyard. The sun was down before Aunt Jane gave thanks for what we had received, and then, turning to me, she said in a cold and measured voice:

'John, I have observed that you are often out and about of nights, sometimes as late as half past seven or eight. Now, it is not seemly for young folk to be abroad after dark, and I do not choose that my nephew should be called a gadabout. "What's bred in the bone will come out in the flesh", and 'twas with such loafing that your father began his wild ways, and afterwards led my poor sister such a life as never was, till the mercy of Providence took him away.'

Aunt Jane often spoke thus of my father, whom I never remembered, but believe him to have been an honest man and good fellow to boot, if something given to roaming and to the contraband.

'So understand', she went on, 'that I will not have you out again this evening, no, nor any other evening, after dusk. Bed is the place for youth when night falls, but if this seem to you too early you can sit with me for an hour in the parlour, and I will read you a discourse of Doctor Sherlock that will banish vain thoughts, and leave you in a fit frame for quiet sleep.'

So she led the way into the parlour, took the book from the shelf, put it on the table within the little circle of light cast by a shaded candle, and began. It was dull enough, though I had borne such tribulations before, and the drone of my aunt's voice would have sent me to sleep, as it had done at other times, even in a straight-backed chair, had I not been so full of my discovery, and chafed at this delay. Thus all the time my aunt read of spiritualities and saving grace, I had my mind on diamonds and all kinds of mammon, for I never doubted that Blackbeard's treasure would be found at the end of that secret passage. The sermon finished at last, and my aunt closed the book with a stiff 'goodnight' for me. I was for giving her my formal kiss, but she made as if she did not see me and turned away; so we went upstairs each to our own room, and I never kissed Aunt Jane again.

There was a moon three-quarters full, already in the sky, and on moonlight nights I was allowed no candle to show me to bed. But on that night I needed none, for I never took off my clothes, having resolved to wait till my aunt was asleep, and then, ghosts or no ghosts, to make my way back to the churchyard. I did not dare to put off that visit even till the morning, lest some chance passer-by should light upon the hole, and so forestall me with Blackbeard's treasure.

Thus I lay wide awake on my bed watching the shadow of the tester-post against the whitewashed wall, and noting how it had moved, by degrees, as the moon went farther round. At last, just as it touched the picture of the Good Shepherd which hung over the mantelpiece, I heard my aunt snoring in her room, and knew that I was free. Yet I waited a few minutes so that she might get well on with her first sleep, and then took off my boots, and in stockinged feet slipped past her room and down the stairs. How stair, handrail, and landing creaked that night, and how my feet and body struck noisily against things seen quite well but misjudged in the effort not to misjudge them! And yet there was the note of safety still sounding, for the snoring never ceased, and the sleeper woke not, though her waking then might have changed all my life. So I came safely to the kitchen, and there put in my pocket one of the best winter candles and the tinder-box, and as I crept out of the room heard suddenly how loud the old clock was ticking, and looking up saw the bright brass band marking half past ten on the dial.

Out in the street I kept in the shadow of the houses as far as I might, though all was silent as the grave; indeed, I think that when the moon is bright a great hush falls always upon Nature, as though she was taken up in wondering at her own beauty. Everyone was fast asleep in Moonfleet and there was no light in any window; only when I came opposite the Why Not? I saw from the red glow behind the curtains that the bottom room was lit up, so Elzevir was not yet gone to bed. It was strange, for the Why Not? had been shut up early for many a long night past, and I crossed over cautiously to see if I could make out what was going forward. But that was not to be done, for the panes were thickly steamed over; and this surprised me more as showing that there was a good company inside. Moreover, as I stood and listened I could hear a mutter of deep voices inside, not as of roisterers, but of sober men talking low.

Eagerness would not let me wait long, and I was off across the meadows towards the church, though not without sad misgivings as soon as the last house was left well behind me. At the churchyard wall my courage had waned somewhat: it seemed a shameless thing to come to rifle Blackbeard's treasure just in the very place and hour that

33

Blackbeard loved; and as I passed the turnstile I half-expected that a tall figure, hairy and evil-eyed, would spring out from the shadow on the north side of the church. But nothing stirred, and the frosty grass sounded crisp under my feet as I made across the churchyard, stepping over the graves and keeping always out of the shadows, towards the black clump of yew-trees on the far side.

When I got round the yews, there was the tomb standing out white against them, and at the foot of the tomb was the hole like a patch of black velvet spread upon the ground, it was so dark. Then, for a moment, I thought that Blackbeard might be lying in wait in the bottom of the hole, and I stood uncertain whether to go on or back. I could catch the rustle of the water on the beach—not of any waves, for the bay was smooth as glass, but just a lipper at the fringe; and wishing to put off with any excuse the descent into the passage, though I had quite resolved to make it, I settled with myself that I would count the water wash twenty times, and at the twentieth would let myself down into the hole. Only seven wavelets had come in when I forgot to count, for there, right in the middle of the moon's path across the water, lay a lugger moored broadside to the beach.

She was about half a mile out, but there was no mistake, for though her sails were lowered her masts and hull stood out black against the moonlight. Here was a fresh reason for delay, for surely one must consider what this craft could be, and what had brought her here. She was too small for a privateer, too large for a fishing-smack, and could not be a revenue boat by her low freeboard in the waist; and 'twas a strange thing for a boat to cast anchor in the midst of Moonfleet Bay even on a night so fine as this. Then while I watched I saw a blue flare in the bows, only for a moment, as if a man had lit a squib and flung it overboard, but I knew from it she was a *contrabandier*, and signalling either to the shore or to a mate in the offing.

With that, courage came back, and I resolved to make this flare my signal for getting down into the hole, screwing my heart up with the thought that if Blackbeard was really waiting for me there, 'twould be little good to turn tail now, for he would be after me and could certainly run much faster than I. Then I took one last look round, and down into the hole forthwith, the same way as I had got down earlier in the day. So on that February night John Trenchard found himself standing in the heap of loose fallen mould at the bottom of the hole, with a mixture of courage and cowardice in his heart, but overruling all a great desire to get at Blackbeard's diamond.

Out came tinder-box and candle, and I was glad indeed when the light burned up bright enough to show that no one, at any rate, was standing by my side. But then there was the passage, and who could say what might be lurking there? Yet I did not falter, but set out on this adventurous journey, walking very slowly indeed—but that was from fear of pitfalls—and nerving myself with the thought of the great diamond which surely would be found at the end of the passage. What should I not be able to do with such wealth? I would buy a nag for Mr. Glennie, a new boat for Ratsey, and a silk gown for Aunt Jane, in spite of her being so hard with me as on this night. And thus I would make myself the greatest man in Moonfleet, richer even than Mr. Maskew, and build a stone house in the sea-meadows with a good prospect of the sea, and marry Grace Maskew and live happily, and fish. I walked on down the passage, reaching out the candle as far as might be in front of me, and whistling to keep myself company, yet saw neither Blackbeard nor anyone else.

All the way there were footprints on the floor, and the roof was black as with smoke of torches, and this made me fear lest some of those who had been there before might have made away with the diamond. Now, though I have spoken of this journey down the passage as though it were a mile long, and though it verily seemed so to me that night, yet I afterwards found it was not more than twenty yards or thereabouts; and then I came upon a stone wall which had once blocked the road, but was now broken through so as to make a ragged doorway into a chamber beyond. There I stood on the rough sill of the door, holding my breath and reaching out my candle arm's-length into the darkness, to see what sort of a place this was before I put foot into it. And before the light had well time to fall on things, I knew that I was underneath the church, and that this chamber was none other than the Mohune Vault.

It was a large room, much larger, I think, than the schoolroom where Mr. Glennie taught us, but not near so high, being only some nine feet from floor to roof. I say floor, though in reality there was none, but only a bottom of soft wet sand; and when I stepped down on to it my heart beat very fiercely, for I remembered what manner of place I was entering, and the dreadful sounds which had issued from it that Sunday morning so short a time before. I satisfied myself that there was nothing evil lurking in the dark corners, or nothing visible at least, and then began to look round and note what was to be seen. Walls and roof were stone, and at one end was a staircase closed by a great flat stone at top—that same stone which I had often seen, with a ring in it, in the floor of the church above. All round the sides were stone shelves, with divisions between them like great bookcases, but instead of books there were the coffins of the Mohunes.

Yet these lay only at the sides, and in the middle of the room was something very different, for here were stacked scores of casks, kegs, and runlets, from a storage butt that might hold thirty gallons down to a breaker that held only one. They were marked all of them in white paint on the end with figures and letters, that doubtless set forth the quality to those that understood. Here indeed was a discovery, and instead of picking up at the end of the passage a little brass or silver casket, which had only to be opened to show Blackbeard's diamond gleaming inside, I had stumbled on the Mohune's vault, and found it to be nothing but a cellar of gentlemen of the contraband, for surely good liquor would never be stored in so shy a place if it ever had paid the excise.

As I walked round this stack of casks my foot struck sharply on the edge of a butt, which must have been near empty, and straightway came from it the same hollow, booming sound (only fainter) which had so frightened us in church that Sunday morning. So it was the casks, and not the coffins, that had been knocking one against another; and I was pleased with myself, remembering how I had reasoned that coffin-wood could never give that booming sound.

It was plain enough that the whole place had been under water: the floor was still muddy, and the green and sweating walls showed the flood-mark within two feet of the roof; there was a wisp or two of fine seaweed that had somehow got in, and a small crab was still alive and scuttled across the corner, yet the coffins were but little disturbed. They lay on the shelves in rows, one above the other, and numbered twenty-three in all: most were in lead, and so could never float, but of those in wood some were turned slantways in their niches, and one had floated right away and been left on the floor upside down in a corner when the waters went back.

First I fell to wondering as to whose cellar this was, and how so much liquor could have been brought in with secrecy; and how it was I had never seen anything of the contraband-men, though it was clear that they had made this flat tomb the entrance to their storehouse, as I had made it my seat. And then I remembered how Ratsey had tried to scare me with talk of Blackbeard; and how Elzevir, who had never been seen at church before, was there the Sunday of the noises; and how he had looked ill at ease whenever the noise came, though he was bold as a lion; and how I had tripped upon him and Ratsey in the churchyard; and how Master Ratsey lay with his ear to the wall: and putting all these things together and casting them up, I thought that Elzevir and Ratsey knew as much as any about this hiding-place.

These reflections gave me more courage, for I considered that the tales of Blackbeard walking or digging among the graves had been set afloat to keep those that were not wanted from the place, and guessed now that when I saw the light moving in the churchyard that night I went to fetch Dr. Hawkins, it was no corpse-candle, but a lantern of smugglers running a cargo. Then, having settled these important matters, I began to turn over in my mind how to get at the treasure; and herein was much cast down, for in this place was neither casket nor diamond, but only coffins and double-Hollands. So it was that, having no better plan, I set to work to see whether I could learn anything from the coffins themselves; but with little success, for the lead coffins had no names upon them, and on such of the wooden coffins as bore plates I found the writing to be Latin, and so rusted over that I could make nothing of it.

Soon I wished I had not come at all, considering that the diamond had vanished into air, and it was a sad thing to be cabined with so many dead men. It moved me, too, to see pieces of banners and funeral shields, and even shreds of wreaths that dear hearts had put there a century ago, now all ruined and rotten—some still clinging, water-sodden, to the coffins, and some trampled in the sand of the floor. I had spent some time in this bootless search, and was resolved to give up further inquiry and foot it home, when the clock in the tower struck midnight. Surely never was ghostly hour sounded in more ghostly place.

Moonfleet peal was known over half the county, and the finest part of it was the clock bell. 'Twas said that in times past (when, perhaps, the chimes were rung more often than now) the voice of this bell had led safe home boats that were lost in the fog; and this night its clangour, mellow and profound, reached even to the vault. *Bim-bom* it went, *bim-bom*, twelve heavy thuds that shook the walls, twelve resonant echoes that followed, and then a purring and vibration of the air, so that the ear could not tell when it ended.

I was wrought up, perhaps, by the strangeness of the hour and place, and my hearing quicker than at other times, but before the tremor of the bell was quite passed away I knew there was some other sound in the air, and that the awful stillness of the vault was broken. At first I could not tell what this new sound was, nor whence it came, and now it seemed a little noise close by, and now a great noise in the distance. And then it grew nearer and more defined, and in a moment I knew it was the sound of voices talking. They must have been a long way off at first, and for a minute, that seemed as an age, they came no nearer. What a minute was that to me! Even now, so many years after, I can recall the anguish of it, and how I stood with ears pricked up, eyes starting, and a clammy sweat upon my face, waiting for those speakers to come. It was the anguish of the rabbit at the end of his burrow, with the ferret's eyes gleaming in the dark, and gun and lurcher waiting at the mouth of the hole. I was caught in a trap, and knew beside that contraband-men had a way of sealing prying eyes and stilling babbling tongues; and I remembered poor Cracky Jones found dead in the churchyard, and how men *said* he had met Blackbeard in the night.

These were but the thoughts of a second, but the voices were nearer, and I heard a dull thud far up the passage, and knew that a man had jumped down from the churchyard into the hole. So I took a last stare round, agonizing to see if there was any way of escape; but the stone walls and roof were solid enough to crush me, and the stack of casks too closely packed to hide more than a rat. There was a man speaking now from the bottom of the hole to others in the churchyard, and then my eyes were led as by a loadstone to a great wooden coffin that lay by itself on the top shelf, a full six feet from the ground.

When I saw the coffin I knew that I was respited, for, as I judged, there was space between it and the wall behind enough to contain my little carcass; and in a second I had put out the candle, scrambled up the shelves, half-stunned my senses with dashing my head against the roof, and squeezed my body betwixt wall and coffin. There I lay on one side with a thin and rotten plank between the dead man and me, dazed with the blow to my head, and breathing hard; while the glow of torches as they came down the passage reddened and flickered on the roof above.

Chapter 4: In the Vault

Let us hob and nob with Death—Tennyson

Though nothing of the vault except the roof was visible from where I lay, and so I could not see these visitors, yet I heard every word spoken, and soon made out one voice as being Master Ratsey's. This discovery gave me no surprise but much solace, for I thought that if the worst happened and I was discovered, I should find one friend with whom I could plead for life.

'It is well the earth gave way', the sexton was saying, 'on a night when we were here to find it. I was in the graveyard myself after midday, and all was snug and tight then. 'Twould have been awkward enough to have the hole stand open through the day, for any passer-by to light on.'

There were four or five men in the vault already, and I could hear more coming down the passage, and guessed from their heavy footsteps that they were carrying burdens. There was a sound, too, of dumping kegs down on the ground, with a swish of liquor inside them, and then the noise of casks being moved.

'I thought we should have a fall there ere long,' Ratsey went on, 'what with this drought parching the ground, and the trampling at the edge when we move out the side stone to get in, but there is no mischief done beyond what can be easily made good. A gravestone or two and a few spades of earth will make all sound again. Leave that to me.'

'Be careful what you do,' rejoined another man's voice that I did not know, 'lest someone see you digging, and scent us out.'

'Make your mind easy,' Ratsey said; 'I have dug too often in this graveyard for any to wonder if they see me with a spade.'

Then the conversation broke off, and there was little more talking, only a noise of men going backwards and forwards, and of putting down of kegs and the hollow gurgle of good liquor being poured from breakers into the casks. By and by fumes of brandy began to fill the air, and climb to where I lay, overcoming the mouldy smell of decayed wood and the dampness of the green walls. It may have been that these fumes mounted to my head, and gave me courage not my own, but so it was that I lost something of the stifling fear that had gripped me, and could listen with more ease to what was going forward. There was a pause in the carrying to and fro; they were talking again now, and someone said—

'I was in Dorchester three days ago, and heard men say it will go hard with the poor chaps who had the brush with the *Elector* last summer. Judge Barentyne comes on Assize next week, and that old fox Maskew has driven down to Taunton to get at him before and coach him back; making out to him that the Law's arm is weak in these parts against the contraband, and must be strengthened by some wholesome hangings.'

'They are a cruel pair,' another put in, 'and we shall have new gibbets on Ridgedown for leading lights. Once I get even with Maskew,
the other may go hang, ay, and they may hang me too.'

'The Devil send him to meet me one dark night on the down
alone,' said someone else, 'and I will give him a pistol's mouth to look
down, and spoil his face for him.'

'No, thou wilt not,' said a deep voice, and then I knew that Elzevir
was there too; 'none shall lay hand on Maskew but I. So mark that, lad,
that when his day of reckoning comes, 'tis *I* will reckon with him.'

Then for a few minutes I did not pay much heed to what was said,
being terribly straitened for room, and cramped with pain from lying so long in one place. The thick smoke from the pitch torches too
came curling across the roof and down upon me, making me sick and
giddy with its evil smell and taste; and though all was very dim, I could
see my hands were black with oily smuts. At last I was able to wriggle
myself over without making too much noise, and felt a great relief in
changing sides, but gave such a start as made the coffin creak again at
hearing my own name.

'There is a boy of Trenchard's,' said a voice that I thought was
Parmiter's, who lived at the bottom of the village—'there is a boy of
Trenchard's that I mistrust; he is for ever wandering in the graveyard,
and I have seen him a score of times sitting on this tomb and looking
out to sea. This very night, when the wind fell at sundown, and we
were hung up with sails flapping, three miles out, and waited for the
dark to get the sweeps, I took my glass to scan the coast-line, and lo,
here on the tomb-top sits Master Trenchard. I could not see his face,
but knew him by his cut, and fear the boy sits there to play the spy
and then tells Maskew.' 'You're right,' said Greening of Ringstave, for I
knew his slow drawl; 'and many a time when I have sat in The Wood,
and watched the Manor to see Maskew safe at home before we ran a
cargo, I have seen this boy too go round about the place with a hang-
dog look, scanning the house as if his life depended on't.'

'Twas very true what Greening said; for of a summer evening I
would take the path that led up Weatherbeech Hill, behind the Man-
or; both because 'twas a walk that had a good prospect in itself, and
also a sweet charm for me, namely, the hope of seeing Grace Maskew.
And there I often sat upon the stile that ends the path and opens on
the down, and watched the old half-ruined house below; and sometimes saw white-frocked Gracie walking on the terrace in the evening
sun, and sometimes in returning passed her window near enough to

wave a greeting.

And once, when she had the fever, and Dr. Hawkins came twice a day to see her, I had no heart for school, but sat on that stile the live-long day, looking at the gabled house where she was lying ill. And Mr. Glennie never rated me for playing truant, nor told Aunt Jane, guessing, as I thought afterwards, the cause, and having once been young himself. 'Twas but boy's love, yet serious for me; and on the day she lay near death, I made so bold as to stop Dr. Hawkins on his horse and ask him how she did; and he bearing with me for the eagerness that he read in my face, bent down over his saddle and smiled, and said my playmate would come back to me again.

So it was quite true that I had watched the house, but not as a spy, and would not have borne tales to old Maskew for anything that could be offered. Then Ratsey spoke up for me and said—''Tis a false scent. The boy is well enough, and simple, and has told me many a time he seeks the churchyard because there is a fine view to be had there of the sea, and 'tis the sea he loves. A month ago, when the high tide set, and this vault was so full of water that we could not get in, I came with Elzevir to make out if the floods were going down inside, or what eddy 'twas that set the casks tapping one against another. So as I lay on the ground with my ear glued close against the wall, who should march round the church but John Trenchard, Esquire, not treading delicately like King Agag, or spying, but just come on a voyage of discovery for himself. For in the church on Sunday, when we heard the tapping in the vault below, my young gentleman was scared enough; but afterwards, being told by Parson Glennie—who should know better—that such noises were not made by ghosts, but by the Mohunes at sea in their coffins, he plucks up heart, and comes down on the Monday to see if they are still afloat. So there he caught me lying like a zany on the ground.

You may guess I stood at attention soon enough, but told him I was looking at the founds to see if they wanted underpinning from the floods. And so I set his mind at ease, for 'tis a simple child, and packed him off to get my dubbing hammer. And I think the boy will not be here so often now to frighten honest Parmiter, for I have weaved him some pretty tales of Blackbeard, and he has a wholesome scare of meeting the colonel. But after dark I pledge my life that neither he nor any other in the town would pass the churchyard wall, no, not for a thousand pounds.'

I heard him chuckling to himself, and the others laughed loudly too, when he was telling how he palmed me off; but 'he laughs loudest who laughs last', thought I, and should have chuckled too, were it not for making the coffin creak. And then, to my surprise, Elzevir spoke: 'The lad is a brave lad; I would he were my son. He is David's age, and will make a good sailor later on.'

They were simple words, yet pleasing to me; for Elzevir spoke as if he meant them, and I had got to like him a little in spite of all his grimness; and beside that, was sorry for his grief over his son. I was so moved by what he said, that for a moment I was for jumping up and calling out to him that I lay here and liked him well, but then thought better of it, and so kept still.

The carrying was over, and I fancy they were all sitting on the ends of kegs or leaning up against the pile; but could not see, and was still much troubled with the torch smoke, though now and then I caught through it a whiff of tobacco, which showed that some were smoking.

Then Greening, who had a singing voice for all his drawl, struck up with—

Says the Cap'n to the crew,
We have slipt the revenue,

—but Ratsey stopped him with a sharp 'No more of that; the words aren't to our taste tonight, but come as wry as if the parson called *Old Hundred* and I tuned up with *Veni.*' I knew he meant the last verse with a hanging touch in it; but Greening was for going on with the song, until some others broke in too, and he saw that the company would have none of it.

'Not but what the labourer is worthy of his hire,' went on Master Ratsey; 'so spile that little breaker of Schiedam, and send a rummer round to keep off midnight chills.'

He loved a glass of the good liquor well, and with him 'twas always the same reasoning, namely, to keep off chills; though he chopped the words to suit the season, and now 'twas autumn, now winter, now spring, or summer chills.

They must have found glasses, though I could not remember to have seen any in the vault, for a minute later fugleman Ratsey spoke again—

'Now, lads, glasses full and bumpers for a toast. And here's to Blackbeard, to Father Blackbeard, who watches over our treasure better than he did over his own; for were it not the fear of him that keeps off idle feet and prying eyes, we should have the gaugers in, and our store ransacked twenty times.'

So he spoke, and it seemed there was a little halting at first, as of men not liking to take Blackbeard's name in Blackbeard's place, or raise the Devil by mocking at him. But then some of the bolder shouted 'Blackbeard', and so the more timid chimed in, and in a minute there were a score of voices calling 'Blackbeard, Blackbeard', till the place rang again.

Then Elzevir cried out angrily, 'Silence. Are you mad, or has the liquor mastered you? Are you Revenue-men that you dare shout and roister? or *contrabandiers* with the lugger in the offing, and your life in your hand. You make noise enough to wake folk in Moonfleet from their beds.'

'Tut, man,' retorted Ratsey testily, 'and if they waked, they would but pull the blankets tight about their ears, and say 'twas Blackbeard piping his crew of lost Mohunes to help him dig for treasure.'

Yet for all that 'twas plain that Block ruled the roost, for there was silence for a minute, and then one said, 'Ay, Master Elzevir is right; let us away, the night is far spent, and we have nothing but the sweeps to take the lugger out of sight by dawn.'

So the meeting broke up, and the torchlight grew dimmer, and died away as it had come in a red flicker on the roof, and the footsteps sounded fainter as they went up the passage, until the vault was left to the dead men and me. Yet for a very long time—it seemed hours—after all had gone I could hear a murmur of distant voices, and knew that some were talking at the end of the passage, and perhaps considering how the landslip might best be restored. So while I heard them thus conversing I dared not descend from my perch, lest someone might turn back to the vault, though I was glad enough to sit up, and ease my aching back and limbs. Yet in the awful blackness of the place even the echo of these human voices seemed a kindly and blessed thing, and a certain shrinking loneliness fell on me when they ceased at last and all was silent. Then I resolved I would be off at once, and get back to the moonlight bed that I had left hours ago, having no stomach for more treasure-hunting, and being glad indeed to be still left with the treasure of life.

Thus, sitting where I was, I lit my candle once more, and then clambered across that great coffin which, for two hours or more, had been a mid-wall of partition between me and danger. But to get out of the niche was harder than to get in; for now that I had a candle to light me, I saw that the coffin, though sound enough to outer view, was wormed through and through, and little better than a rotten shell. So it was that I had some ado to get over it, not daring either to kneel upon it or to bring much weight to bear with my hand, lest it should go through. And now having got safely across, I sat for an instant on that narrow ledge of the stone shelf which projected beyond the coffin on the vault side, and made ready to jump forward on to the floor below. And how it happened I know not, but there I lost my balance, and as I slipped the candle flew out of my grasp.

Then I clutched at the coffin to save myself, but my hand went clean through it, and so I came to the ground in a cloud of dust and splinters; having only got hold of a wisp of seaweed, or a handful of those draggled funeral trappings which were strewn about this place. The floor of the vault was sandy; and so, though I fell crookedly, I took but little harm beyond a shaking; and soon, pulling myself together, set to strike my flint and blow the match into a flame to search for the fallen candle. Yet all the time I kept in my fingers this handful of light stuff; and when the flame burnt up again I held the thing against the light, and saw that it was no wisp of seaweed, but something black and wiry. For a moment, I could not gather what I had hold of, but then gave a start that nearly sent the candle out, and perhaps a cry, and let it drop as if it were red-hot iron, for I knew that it was a man's beard.

Now when I saw that, I felt a sort of throttling fright, as though one had caught hold of my heartstrings; and so many and such strange thoughts rose in me, that the blood went pounding round and round in my head, as it did once afterwards when I was fighting with the sea and near drowned. Surely to have in hand the beard of any dead man in any place was bad enough, but worse a thousand times in such a place as this, and to know on whose face it had grown. For, almost before I fully saw what it was, I knew it was that black beard which had given Colonel John Mohune his nickname, and this was his great coffin I had hid behind.

I had lain, therefore, all that time, cheek by jowl with Blackbeard himself, with only a thin shell of tinder wood to keep him from me, and now had thrust my hand into his coffin and plucked away his beard. So that if ever wicked men have power to show themselves after death, and still to work evil, one would guess that he would show himself now and fall upon me. Thus a sick dread got hold of me, and had I been a woman or a girl I think I should have swooned; but being only a boy, and not knowing how to swoon, did the next best thing, which was to put myself as far as might be from the beard, and make for the outlet. Yet had I scarce set foot in the passage when I stopped, remembering how once already this same evening I had played the coward, and run home scared with my own fears.

So I was brought up for very shame, and beside that thought how I had come to this place to look for Blackbeard's treasure, and might have gone away without knowing even so much as where he lay, had not chance first led me to be down by his side, and afterwards placed my hand upon his beard. And surely this could not be chance alone, but must rather be the finger of Providence guiding me to that which I desired to find. This consideration somewhat restored my courage, and after several feints to return, advances, stoppings, and panics, I was in the vault again, walking carefully round the stack of barrels, and fearing to see the glimmer of the candle fall upon that beard.

There it was upon the sand, and holding the candle nearer to it with a certain caution, as though it would spring up and bite me, I saw it was a great full black beard, more than a foot long, but going grey at the tips; and had at the back, keeping it together, a thin tissue of dried skin, like the false parting which Aunt Jane wore under her cap on Sundays. This I could see as it lay before me, for I did not handle or lift it, but only peered into it, with the candle, on all sides, busying myself the while with thoughts of the man of whom it had once been part.

In returning to the vault, I had no very sure purpose in mind; only a vague surmise that this finding of Blackbeard's coffin would somehow lead to the finding of his treasure. But as I looked at the beard and pondered, I began to see that if anything was to be done, it must be by searching in the coffin itself, and the clearer this became to me, the greater was my dislike to set about such a task. So I put off the evil hour, by feigning to myself that it was necessary to make a careful scrutiny of the beard, and thus wasted at least ten minutes. But at length, seeing that the candle was burning low, and could certainly last little more than half an hour, and considering that it must now be getting near dawn, I buckled to the distasteful work of rummaging the coffin. Nor had I any need to climb up on to the top shelf again, but standing on the one beneath, found my head and arms well on a level with the search.

And beside that, the task was not so difficult as I had thought; for in my fall I had broken off the head-end of the lid, and brought away the whole of that side that faced the vault. Now, any lad of my age, and perhaps some men too, might well have been frightened to set about such a matter as to search in a coffin; and if any had said, a few hours before, that I should ever have courage to do this by night in the Mohune vault, I would not have believed him. Yet here I was, and had advanced along the path of terror so gradually, and as it were foot by foot in the past night, that when I came to this final step I was not near so scared as when I first felt my way into the vault. It was not the first time either that I had looked on death; but had, indeed, always a leaning to such sights and matters, and had seen corpses washed up from the *Darius* and other wrecks, and besides that had helped Ratsey to case some poor bodies that had died in their beds.

The coffin was, as I have said, of great length, and the side being removed, I could see the whole outline of the skeleton that lay in it. I say the outline, for the form was wrapped in a woollen or flannel shroud, so that the bones themselves were not visible. The man that lay in it was little short of a giant, measuring, as I guessed, a full six and a half feet, and the flannel having sunk in over the belly, the end of the breast-bone, the hips, knees, and toes were very easy to be made out. The head was swathed in linen bands that had been white, but were now stained and discoloured with damp, but of this I shall not speak more, and beneath the chin-cloth the beard had once escaped. The clutch which I had made to save myself in falling had torn away this chin-band and let the lower jaw drop on the breast; but little else was disturbed, and there was Colonel John Mohune resting as he had been laid out a century ago. I lifted that portion of the lid which had been left behind, and reached over to see if there was anything hid on the other side of the body; but had scarce let the light fall in the coffin when my heart gave a great bound, and all fear left me in the flush of success, for there I saw what I had come to seek.

On the breast of this silent and swathed figure lay a locket, attached to the neck by a thin chain, which passed inside the linen bandages. A whiter portion of the flannel showed how far the beard had extended, but locket and chain were quite black, though I judged that they were made of silver. The shape of this locket was not unlike a crown-piece, only three times as thick, and as soon as I set eyes upon it I never doubted but that inside would be found the diamond.

It was then that a great pity came over me for this thin shadow of man; thinking rather what a fine, tall gentleman Colonel Mohune had once been, and a good soldier no doubt besides, than that he had wasted a noble estate and played traitor to the king. And then I reflected that it was all for the bit of flashing stone, which lay as I hoped within the locket, that he had sold his honour; and wished that the jewel might bring me better fortune than had fallen to him, or at any rate, that it might not lead me into such miry paths. Yet such thoughts did not delay my purpose, and I possessed myself of the locket easily enough, finding a hasp in the chain, and so drawing it out from the linen folds. I had expected as I moved the locket to hear the jewel rattle in the inside, but there was no sound, and then I thought that the diamond might cleave to the side with damp, or perhaps be wrapped in wool. Scarcely was the locket well in my hand before I had it undone, finding a thumb-nick whereby, after a little persuasion, the back, though rusted, could be opened on a hinge. My breath came very fast, and I shook so that I had a difficulty to keep my thumbnail in the nick, yet hardly was it opened before exalted expectation gave place to deepest disappointment.

For there lay all the secret of the locket disclosed, and there was no diamond, no, nor any other jewel, and nothing at all except a little piece of folded paper. Then I felt like a man who has played away all his property and stakes his last crown—heavy-hearted, yet hoping against hope that luck may turn, and that with this piece be may win back all his money. So it was with me; for I hoped that this paper might have written on it directions for the finding of the jewel, and that I might yet rise from the table a winner. It was but a frail hope, and quickly dashed; for when I had smoothed the creases and spread out the piece of paper in the candle-light, there was nothing to be seen except a few verses from the Psalms of David. The paper was yellow, and showed a lattice of folds where it had been pressed into the locket; but the handwriting, though small, was clear and neat, and there was no mistaking a word of what was there set down. 'Twas so short, I could read it at once:

The days of our age are threescore years and ten;
And though men be so strong that they come
To fourscore years, yet is their strength then
But labour and sorrow, so soon passeth it
Away, and we are gone. —Psalm 90, 21

And as for me, my feet are almost gone;
My treadings are wellnigh slipped. —73, 6

But let not the waterflood drown me; neither let
The deep swallow me up. —69, 11

So, going through the vale of misery, I shall

Use it for a well, till the pools are filled
With water. —84, 14

For thou hast made the North and the South:
Tabor and Hermon shall rejoice in thy name. —89, 6

So here was an end to great hopes, and I was after all to leave the vault no richer than I had entered it. For look at it as I might, I could not see that these verses could ever lead to any diamond; and though I might otherwise have thought of ciphers or secret writing, yet, remembering what Mr. Glennie had said, that Blackbeard after his wicked life desired to make a good end, and sent for a parson to confess him, I guessed that such pious words had been hung round his neck as a charm to keep the spirits of evil away from his tomb. I was disappointed enough, but before I left picked up the beard from the floor, though it sent a shiver through me to touch it, and put it back in its place on the dead man's breast. I restored also such pieces of the coffin as I could get at, but could not make much of it; so left things as they were, trusting that those who came there next would think the wood had fallen to pieces by natural decay. But the locket I kept, and hung about my neck under my shirt; both as being a curious thing in itself, and because I thought that if the good words inside it were strong enough to keep off bad spirits from Blackbeard, they would be also strong enough to keep Blackbeard from me.

When this was done the candle had burnt so low, that I could no longer hold it in my fingers, and was forced to stick it on a piece of the broken wood, and so carry it before me. But, after all, I was not to escape from Blackbeard's clutches so easily; for when I came to the end of the passage, and was prepared to climb up into the churchyard, I found that the hole was stopped, and that there was no exit.

I understood now how it was that I had heard talking so long after the company had left the vault; for it was clear that Ratsey had been as good as his word, and that the falling in of the ground had been repaired before the contraband-men went home that night. At first I made light of the matter, thinking I should soon be able to dislodge this new work, and so find a way out. But when I looked more narrowly into the business, I did not feel so sure; for they had made a sound job of it, putting one very heavy burial slab at the side to pile earth against till the hole was full, and then covering it with another. These were both of slate, and I knew whence they came; for there were a dozen or more of such disused and weather-worn covers laid up against the north side of the church, and every one of them a good burden for four men. Yet I hoped by grouting at the earth below it to be able to dislodge the stone at the side; but while I was considering how best to begin, the candle flickered, the wick gave a sudden lurch to one side, and I was left in darkness.

Thus my plight was evil indeed, for I had nothing now to burn to give me light, and knew that 'twas no use setting to grout till I could see to go about it. Moreover, the darkness was of that black kind that is never found beneath the open sky, no, not even on the darkest night, but lurks in close and covered places and strains the eyes in trying to see into it. Yet I did not give way, but settled to wait for the dawn, which must, I knew, be now at hand; for then I thought enough light would come through the chinks of the tomb above to show me how to set to work. Nor was I even much scared, as one who having been in peril of life from the contraband-men for a spy, and in peril from evil ghosts for rifling Blackbeard's tomb, deemed it a light thing to be left in the dark to wait an hour till morning. So I sat down on the floor of the passage, which, if damp, was at least soft, and being tired with what I had gone through, and not used to miss a night's rest, fell straightway asleep.

How long I slept I cannot tell, for I had nothing to guide me to the time, but woke at length, and found myself still in darkness. I stood up and stretched my limbs, but did not feel as one refreshed by wholesome sleep, but sick and tired with pains in back, arms, and legs, as if beaten or bruised. I have said I was still in darkness, yet it was not the blackness of the last night; and looking up into the inside of the tomb above, I could see the faintest line of light at one corner, which showed the sun was up.

For this line of light was the sunlight, filtering slowly through a crevice at the joining of the stones; but the sides of the tomb had been fitted much closer than I reckoned for, and it was plain there would never be light in the place enough to guide me to my work. All this I considered as I rested on the ground, for I had sat down again, feeling too tired to stand. But as I kept my eye on the narrow streak of light I was much startled, for I looked at the south-west corner of the tomb, and yet was looking towards the sun. This I gathered from the tone of the light; and although there was no direct outlet to the air, and only a glimmer came in, as I have said, yet I knew certainly that the sun was low in the west and falling full upon this stone.

Here was a surprise, and a sad one for me, for I perceived that I had slept away a day, and that the sun was setting for another night. And yet it mattered little, for night or daytime there was no light to help me in this horrible place; and though my eyes had grown accustomed to the gloom, I could make out nothing to show me where to work. So I took out my tinder-box, meaning to fan the match into a flame, and to get at least one moment's look at the place, and then to set to digging with my hands.

But as I lay asleep the top had been pressed off the box, and the tinder got loose in my pocket; and though I picked the tinder out easily enough, and got it in the box again, yet the salt damps of the place had soddened it in the night, and spark by spark fell idle from the flint.

And then it was that I first perceived the danger in which I stood; for there was no hope of kindling a light, and I doubted now whether even in the light I could ever have done much to dislodge the great slab of slate. I began also to feel very hungry, as not having eaten for twenty-four hours; and worse than that, there was a parching thirst and dryness in my throat, and nothing with which to quench it. Yet there was no time to be lost if I was ever to get out alive, and so I groped with my hands against the side of the grave until I made out the bottom edge of the slab, and then fell to grubbing beneath it with my fingers. But the earth, which the day before had looked light and loamy to the eye, was stiff and hard enough when one came to tackle it with naked hands, and in an hour's time I had done little more than further weary myself and bruise my fingers.

Then I was forced to rest; and, sitting down on the ground, saw that the glimmering streak of light had faded, and that the awful blackness of the previous night was creeping up again. And now I had no heart to face it, being cowed with hunger, thirst, and weariness; and so flung myself upon my face, that I might not see how dark it was, and groaned for very lowness of spirit. Thus I lay for a long time, but afterwards stood up and cried aloud, and shrieked if anyone should haply hear me, calling to Mr. Glennie and Ratsey, and even Elzevir, by name, to save me from this awful place. But there came no answer, except the echo of my own voice sounding hollow and far off down in the vault. So in despair I turned back to the earth wall below the slab, and scrabbled at it with my fingers, till my nails were broken and the blood ran out; having all the while a sure knowledge, like a cord twisted round my head, that no effort of mine could ever dislodge the great stone. And thus the hours passed, and I shall not say more here, for the remembrance of that time is still terrible, and besides, no words could ever set forth the anguish I then suffered, yet did slumber come sometimes to my help; for even while I was working at the earth, sheer weariness would overtake me, and I sank on to the ground and fell asleep.

And still the hours passed, and at last I knew by the glimmer of light in the tomb above that the sun had risen again, and a maddening thirst had hold of me. And then I thought of all the barrels piled up in the vault and of the liquor that they held; and stuck not because 'twas spirit, for I would scarce have paused to sate that thirst even with molten lead. So I felt my way down the passage back to the vault, and recked not of the darkness, nor of Blackbeard and his crew, if only I could lay my lips to liquor. Thus I groped about the barrels till near the top of the stack my hand struck on the spile of a keg, and drawing it, I got my mouth to the hold.

What the liquor was I do not know, but it was not so strong but that I could swallow it in great gulps and found it less burning than my burning throat. But when I turned to get back to the passage, I could not find the outlet, and fumbled round and round until my brain was dizzy, and I fell senseless to the ground.

Chapter 5: The Rescue

Shades of the dead, have I not heard your voices
Rise on the night-rolling breath of the gale?—Byron

When I came to myself I was lying, not in the outer blackness of the Mohune vault, not on a floor of sand; but in a bed of sweet clean linen, and in a little whitewashed room, through the window of which the spring sunlight streamed. Oh, the blessed sunshine, and how I praised God for the light! At first I thought I was in my own bed at my aunt's house, and had dreamed of the vault and the smugglers, and that my being prisoned in the darkness was but the horror of a nightmare. I was for getting up, but fell back on my pillow in the effort to rise, with a weakness and sick languor which I had never known before. And as I sunk down, I felt something swing about my neck, and putting up my hand, found 'twas Colonel John Mohune's black locket, and so knew that part at least of this adventure was no dream.

Then the door opened, and to my wandering thought it seemed that I was back again in the vault, for in came Elzevir Block. Then I held up my hands, and cried—

'O Elzevir, save me, save me; I am not come to spy.'

But he, with a kind look on his face, put his hand on my shoulder, and pushed me gently back, saying—

'Lie still, lad, there is none here will hurt thee, and drink this.'

He held out to me a bowl of steaming broth, that filled the room with a savour sweeter, ten thousand times, to me than every rose and lily of the world; yet would not let me drink it at a gulp, but made me sip it with a spoon like any baby. Thus while I drank, he told me where I was, namely, in an attic at the Why Not?, but would not say more then, bidding me get to sleep again, and I should know all afterwards. And so it was ten days or more before youth and health had their way, and I was strong again; and all that time Elzevir Block sat by my bed, and nursed me tenderly as a woman. So piece by piece I learned the story of how they found me.

'Twas Mr. Glennie who first moved to seek me; for when the second day came that I was not at school, he thought that I was ill, and went to my aunt's to ask how I did, as was his wont when any ailed. But Aunt Jane answered him stiffly that she could not say how I did.

'For', says she, 'he is run off I know not where, but as he makes his bed, must he lie on't; and if he run away for his pleasure, may stay away for mine. I have been pestered with this lot too long, and only bore with him for poor sister Martha's sake; but 'tis after his father that the graceless lad takes, and thus rewards me.'

With that she bangs the door in the parson's face and off he goes to Ratsey, but can learn nothing there, and so concludes that I have run away to sea, and am seeking ship at Poole or Weymouth.

But that same day came Sam Tewkesbury to the Why Not? about nightfall, and begged a glass of rum, being, as he said, 'all of a shake', and telling a tale of how he passed the churchyard wall on his return from work, and in the dusk heard screams and wailing voices, and knew 'twas Blackbeard piping his lost Mohunes to hunt for treasure. So, though he saw nothing, he turned tail and never stopped running till he stood at the inn door. Then, forthwith, Elzevir leaves Sam to drink at the Why Not? alone, and himself sets off running up the street to call for Master Ratsey; and they two make straight across the sea-meadows in the dark.

'For as soon as I heard Tewkesbury tell of screams and wailings in the air, and no one to be seen,' said Elzevir, 'I guessed that some poor soul had got shut in the vault, and was there crying for his life. And to this I was not guided by mother wit, but by a surer and a sadder token. Thou wilt have heard how thirteen years ago a daft body we called Cracky Jones was found one morning in the churchyard dead. He was gone missing for a week before, and twice within that week I had sat through the night upon the hill behind the church, watching to warn the lugger with a flare she could not put in for the surf upon the beach. And on those nights, the air being still though a heavy swell was running, I heard thrice or more a throttled scream come shivering across the meadows from the graveyard. Yet beyond turning my blood cold for a moment, it gave me little trouble, for evil tales have hung about the church; and though I did not set much store by the old yarns of Blackbeard piping up his crew, yet I thought strange things might well go on among the graves at night. And so I never budged, nor stirred hand or foot to save a fellow-creature in his agony.

'But when the surf fell enough for the boats to get ashore, and Greening held a lantern for me to jump down into the passage, after we had got the side out of the tomb, the first thing the light fell on at the bottom was a white face turned skyward. I have not forgot that, lad, for 'twas Cracky Jones lay there, with his face thin and shrunk, yet all the doited look gone out of it. We tried to force some brandy in his mouth, but he was stark and dead; with knees drawn up towards his head, so stiff we had to lift him doubled as he was, and lay him by the churchyard wall for some of us to find next day. We never knew how he got there, but guessed that he had hung about the landers some night when they ran a cargo, and slipped in when the watchman's back was turned. Thus when Sam Tewkesbury spoke of screams and waitings, and no one to be seen, I knew what 'twas, but never guessed who might be shut in there, not knowing thou wert gone amissing. So ran to Ratsey to get his help to slip the side stone off, for by myself I cannot stir it now, though once I did when I was younger; and from him learned that thou wert lost, and knew whom we should find before we got there.'

I shuddered while Elzevir talked, for I thought how Cracky Jones had perhaps hidden behind the self-same coffin that sheltered me, and how narrowly I had escaped his fate. And that old story came back into my mind, how, years ago, there once arose so terrible a cry from the vault at service-time, that parson and people fled from the church; and I doubted not now that some other poor soul had got shut in that awful place, and was then calling for help to those whose fears would not let them listen.

'There we found thee,' Elzevir went on, 'stretched out on the sand, senseless and far gone; and there was something in thy face that made me think of David when he lay stretched out in his last sleep. And so I put thee on my shoulder and bare thee back, and here thou art in David's room, and shalt find board and bed with me as long as thou hast mind to.' We spoke much together during the days when I was getting stronger, and I grew to like Elzevir well, finding his grimness was but on the outside, and that never was a kinder man. Indeed, I think that my being with him did him good; for he felt that there was once more someone to love him, and his heart went out to me as to his son David. Never once did he ask me to keep my counsel as to the vault and what I had seen there, knowing, perhaps, he had no need, for I would have died rather than tell the secret to any. Only, one day Master Ratsey, who often came to see me, said—

'John, there is only Elzevir and I who know that you have seen the inside of our bond-cellar; and 'tis well, for if some of the landers guessed, they might have ugly ways to stop all chance of prating. So keep our secret tight, and we'll keep yours, for "he that refraineth his lips is wise".'

I wondered how Master Ratsey could quote Scripture so pat, and yet cheat the revenue; though, in truth, 'twas thought little sin at Moonfleet to run a cargo; and, perhaps, he guessed what I was thinking, for he added—

'Not that a Christian man has aught to be ashamed of in landing a cask of good liquor, for we read that when Israel came out of Egypt, the chosen people were bid trick their oppressors out of jewels of silver and jewels of gold; and among those cruel taskmasters, some of the wont must certainly have been the tax-gatherers.'

★★★★★★

The first walk I took when I grew stronger and was able to get about was up to Aunt Jane's, notwithstanding she had never so much as been to ask after me all these days. She knew, indeed, where I was, for Ratsey had told her I lay at the Why Not?, explaining that Elzevir had found me one night on the ground famished and half-dead, yet not saying where. But my aunt greeted me with hard words, which I need not repeat here; for, perhaps, she meant them not unkindly, but only to bring me back again to the right way.

She did not let me cross the threshold, holding the door ajar in her hand, and saying she would have no tavern-loungers in her house, but that if I liked the Why Not? so well, I could go back there again for her. I had been for begging her pardon for playing truant; but when I heard such scurvy words, felt the devil rise in my heart, and only laughed, though bitter tears were in my eyes. So I turned my back upon the only home that I had ever known, and sauntered off down the village, feeling very lone, and am not sure I was not crying before I came again to the Why Not?

Then Elzevir saw that my face was downcast, and asked what ailed me, and so I told him how my aunt had turned me away, and that I had no home to go to. But he seemed pleased rather than sorry, and said that I must come now and live with him, for he had plenty for both; and that since chance had led him to save my life, I should be to him a son in David's place. So I went to keep house with him at the Why Not? and my aunt sent down my bag of clothes, and would have made over to Elzevir the pittance that my father left for my keep, but he said it was not needful, and he would have none of it.

CHAPTER 6: AN ASSAULT

Surely after all,
The noblest answer unto such
Is perfect stillness when they brawl—Tennyson

I have more than once brought up the name of Mr. Maskew; and as I shall have other things to tell of him later on, I may as well relate here what manner of man he was. His stature was but medium, not exceeding five feet four inches, I think; and to make the most of it, he flung his head far back, and gave himself a little strut in walking. He had a thin face with a sharp nose that looked as if it would peck you, and grey eyes that could pierce a millstone if there was a guinea on the far side of it. His hair, for he wore his own, had been red, though it was now grizzled; and the colour of it was set down in Moonfleet to his being a Scotchman, for we thought all Scotchmen were red-headed. He was a lawyer by profession, and having made money in Edinburgh, had gone so far south as Moonfleet to get quit, as was said, of the memories of rascally deeds.

It was about four years since he bought a parcel of the Mohune Estate, which had been breaking up and selling piecemeal for a generation; and on his land stood the Manor House, or so much of it as was left. Of the mansion I have spoken before. It was a very long house of two storeys, with a projecting gable and doorway in the middle, and at each end gabled wings running out crosswise. The Maskews lived in one of these wings, and that was the only habitable portion of the place; for as to the rest, the glass was out of the windows, and in some places the roofs had fallen in. Mr. Maskew made no attempt to repair house or grounds, and the bough of the great cedar which the snows had brought down in '49 still blocked the drive.

The entrance to the house was through the porchway in the middle, but more than one tumble-down corridor had to be threaded before one reached the inhabited wing; while fowls and pigs and squirrels had possession of the terrace lawns in front. It was not for want of money that Maskew let things remain thus, for men said that he was rich enough, only that his mood was miserly; and perhaps, also, it was the lack of woman's company that made him think so little of neatness and order. For his wife was dead; and though he had a daughter, she was young, and had not yet weight enough to make her father do things that he did not choose.

Till Maskew came there had been none living in the Manor House for a generation, so the village children used the terrace for a playground, and picked primroses in the woods; and the men thought they had a right to snare a rabbit or shoot a pheasant in the chase. But the new owner changed all this, hiding gins and spring-guns in the coverts, and nailing up boards on the trees to say he would have the law of any that trespassed. So he soon made enemies for himself, and before long had everyone's hand against him. Yet he preferred his neighbour's enmity to their goodwill, and went about to make it more bitter by getting himself posted for magistrate, and giving out that he would put down the contraband thereabouts. For no one round Moonfleet was for the Excise; but farmers loved a glass of Schnapps that had never been gauged, and their wives a piece of fine lace from France. And then came the affair between the *Elector* and the ketch, with David Block's death; and after that they said it was not safe for Maskew to walk at large, and that he would be found some day dead on the down; but he gave no heed to it, and went on as if he had been a paid exciseman rather than a magistrate.

When I was a little boy the Manor woods were my delight, and many a sunny afternoon have I sat on the terrace edge looking down over the village, and munching red quarantines from the ruined fruit gardens. And though this was now forbidden, yet the Manor had still a sweeter attraction to me than apples or bird-batting, and that was Grace Maskew. She was an only child, and about my own age, or little better, at the time of which I am speaking. I knew her, because she went every day to the old almshouses to be taught by the Reverend Mr. Glennie, from whom I also received my schooling. She was tall for her age, and slim, with a thin face and a tumble of tawny hair, which flew about her in a wind or when she ran. Her frocks were washed and patched and faded, and showed more of her arms and legs than the dressmaker had ever intended, for she was a growing girl, and had none to look after her clothes. She was a favourite playfellow with all, and an early choice for games of 'prisoner's base', and she could beat most of us boys at speed. Thus, though we all hated her father, and had for him many jeering titles among ourselves; yet we never used an evil nickname nor a railing word against him when she was by, because we liked her well.

There were a half-dozen of us boys, and as many girls, whom Mr. Glennie used to teach; and that you may see what sort of man Maskew was, I will tell you what happened one day in school between him and the parson. Mr. Glennie taught us in the almshouses; for though there were now no bedesmen, and the houses themselves were fallen to decay, yet the little hall in which the inmates had once dined was still maintained, and served for our schoolroom. It was a long and lofty room, with a high wainscot all round it, a carved oak screen at one end, and a broad window at the other. A very heavy table, polished by use, and sadly besmirched with ink, ran down the middle of the hall with benches on either side of it for us to use; and a high desk for Mr. Glennie stood under the window at the end of the room. Thus we were sitting one morning with our summing-slates and grammars before us when the door in the screen opens and Mr. Maskew enters.

I have told you already of the verses which Mr. Glennie wrote for David Block's grave; and when the floods had gone down Ratsey set up the headstone with the poetry carved on it. But Maskew, through not going to church, never saw the stone for weeks, until one morning, walking through the churchyard, he lighted on it, and knew the verses for Mr. Glennie's. So 'twas to have it out with the parson that he had come to school this day; and though we did not know so much then, yet guessed from his presence that something was in the wind, and could read in his face that he was very angry. Now, for all that we hated Maskew, yet were we glad enough to see him there, as hoping for something strange to vary the sameness of school, and scenting a disturbance in the air. Only Grace was ill at ease for fear her father should say something unseemly, and kept her head down with shocks of hair falling over her book, though I could see her blushing between them. So in vapours Maskew, and with an angry glance about him makes straight for the desk where our master sits at the top of the room.

For a moment Mr. Glennie, being shortsighted, did not see who 'twas; but as his visitor drew near, rose courteously to greet him.

'Good day to you, Mister Maskew,' says he, holding out his hand.

But Maskew puts his arms behind his back and bubbles out, 'Hold not out your hand to me lest I spit on it. 'Tis like your snivelling cant to write sweet psalms for smuggling rogues and try to frighten honest men with your judgements.'

At first Mr. Glennie did not know what the other would be at, and afterwards understanding, turned very pale; but said as a minister he would never be backward in reproving those whom he considered in the wrong, whether from the pulpit or from the gravestone. Then Maskew flies into a great passion, and pours out many vile and insolent words, saying Mr. Glennie is in league with the smugglers and fattens on their crimes; that the poetry is a libel; and that he, Maskew, will have the law of him for calumny.

After that he took Grace by the arm, and bade her get hat and cape and come with him. 'For', says he, 'I will not have thee taught any more by a psalm-singing hypocrite that calls thy father murderer.' And all the while he kept drawing up closer to Mr. Glennie, until the two stood very near each other.

There was a great difference between them; the one short and blustering, with a red face turned up; the other tall and craning down, ill-clad, ill-fed, and pale. Maskew had in his left hand a basket, with which he went marketing of mornings, for he made his own purchases, and liked fish, as being cheaper than meat. He had been chaffering with the fishwives this very day, and was bringing back his provend with him when he visited our school.

Then he said to Mr. Glennie: 'Now, Sir Parson, the law has given into your fool's hands a power over this churchyard, and 'tis your trade to stop unseemly headlines from being set up within its walls, or once set up, to turn them out forthwith. So I give you a week's grace, and if tomorrow sennight yon stone be not gone, I will have it up and flung in pieces outside the wall.'

Mr. Glennie answered him in a low voice, but quite clear, so that we could hear where we sat: 'I can neither turn the stone out myself, nor stop you from turning it out if you so mind; but if you do this thing, and dishonour the graveyard, there is One stronger than either you or I that must be reckoned with.'

I knew afterwards that he meant the Almighty, but thought then that 'twas of Elzevir he spoke; and so, perhaps, did Mr. Maskew, for he fell into a worse rage, thrust his hand in the basket, whipped out a great sole he had there, and in a twinkling dashes it in Mr. Glennie's face, with a 'Then, take that for an unmannerly parson, for I would not foul my fist with your mealy chops.'

But to see that stirred my choler, for Mr. Glennie was weak as wax, and would never have held up his hand to stop a blow, even were he strong as Goliath. So I was for setting on Maskew, and being a stout lad for my age, could have had him on the floor as easy as a baby; but as I rose from my seat, I saw he held Grace by the hand, and so hung back for a moment, and before I got my thoughts together he was gone, and I saw the tail of Grace's cape whisk round the screen door.

A sole is at the best an ugly thing to have in one's face, and this sole was larger than most, for Maskew took care to get what he could for his money, so it went with a loud smack on Mr. Glennie's cheek, and then fell with another smack on the floor. At this we all laughed, as children will, and Mr. Glennie did not check us, but went back and sat very quiet at his desk; and soon I was sorry I had laughed, for he looked sad, with his face sanded and a great red patch on one side, and beside that the fin had scratched him and made a blood-drop trickle down his cheek. A few minutes later the thin voice of the almshouse clock said twelve, and away walked Mr. Glennie without his usual 'Good day, children', and there was the sole left lying on the dusty floor in front of his desk.

It seemed a shame so fine a fish should be wasted, so I picked it up and slipped it in my desk, sending Fred Burt to get his mother's gridiron that we might grill it on the schoolroom fire. While he was gone I went out to the court to play, and had not been there five minutes when back comes Maskew through our playground without Grace, and goes into the schoolroom. But in the screen at the end of the room was a chink, against which we used to hold our fingers on bright days for the sun to shine through, and show the blood pink; so up I slipped and fixed my eye to the hole, wanting to know what he was at. He had his basket with him, and I soon saw he had come back for the sole, not having the heart to leave so good a bit of fish. But look where he would, he could not find it, for he never searched my desk, and had to go off with a sour countenance; but Fred Burt and I cooked the sole, and found it well flavoured, for all it had given so much pain to Mr. Glennie.

After that Grace came no more to school, both because her father had said she should not, and because she was herself ashamed to go back after what Maskew had done to Mr. Glennie. And then it was that I took to wandering much in the Manor woods, having no fear of man-traps, for I knew their place as soon as they were put down, but often catching sight of Grace, and sometimes finding occasion to talk with her. Thus time passed, and I lived with Elzevir at the Why Not?, still going to school of mornings, but spending the afternoons in fishing, or in helping him in the garden, or with the boats. As soon as I got to know him well, I begged him to let me help run the cargoes, but he refused, saying I was yet too young, and must not come into mischief. Yet, later, yielding to my importunity, he consented; and more than one dark night I was in the landing-boats that unburdened the lugger, though I could never bring myself to enter the Mohune vault again, but would stand as sentry at the passage-mouth.

And all the while I had round my neck Colonel John Mohune's locket, and at first wore it next myself, but finding it black the skin, put it between shirt and body-jacket. And there by dint of wear it grew less black, and showed a little of the metal underneath, and at last I took to polishing it at odd times, until it came out quite white and shiny, like the pure silver that it was. Elzevir had seen this locket when he put me to bed the first time I came to the Why Not? and afterwards I told him whence I got it; but though we had it out more than once of an evening, we could never come at any hidden meaning. Indeed, we scarce tried to, judging it to be certainly a sacred charm to keep evil spirits from Blackbeard's body.

Chapter 7: An Auction

What if my house be troubled with a rat,
And I be pleased to give ten thousand ducats
To have it baned—Shakespeare

One evening in March, when the days were lengthening fast, there came a messenger from Dorchester, and brought printed notices for fixing to the shutters of the Why Not? and to the church door, which said that in a week's time the bailiff of the duchy of Cornwall would visit Moonfleet. This bailiff was an important person, and his visits stood as events in village history. Once in five years he made a per-ambulation, or journey, through the whole duchy, inspecting all the Royal property, and arranging for new leases. His visits to Moonfleet were generally short enough, for owing to the Mohunes owning all the land, the only duchy estate there was the Why Not? and the only duty of the bailiff to renew that five-year lease, under which Blocks had held the inn, father and son, for generations. But for all that, the business was not performed without ceremony, for there was a solemn show of putting up the lease of the inn to the highest bidder, though it was well understood that no one except Elzevir would make an offer.

So one morning, a week later, I went up to the top end of the village to watch for the bailiff's postchaise, and about eleven of the forenoon saw it coming down the hill with four horses and two postillions. Presently it came past, and I saw there were two men in it—a clerk sitting with his back to the horses, and in the seat opposite a little man in a periwig, whom I took for the bailiff. Then I ran down to my aunt's house, for Elzevir had asked me to beg one of her best winter candles for a purpose which I will explain presently. I had not seen Aunt Jane, except in church, since the day that she dismissed me, but she was no stiffer than usual, and gave me the candle readily enough. 'There,' she said, 'take it, and I wish it may bring light into your dark heart, and show you what a wicked thing it is to leave your own kith and kin and go to dwell in a tavern.' I was for saying that it was kith and kin that left me, and not I them; and as for living in a tavern, it was better to live there than nowhere at all, as she would wish me to do in turning me out of her house; but did not, and only thanked her for the candle, and was off.

When I came to the inn, there was the postchaise in front of the door, the horses being led away to bait, and a little group of villagers standing round; for though the auction of the Why Not? was in itself a trite thing with a foregone conclusion, yet the bailiff's visit always stirred some show of interest. There were a few children with their noses flattened against the windows of the parlour, and inside were Mr. Bailiff and Mr. Clerk hard at work on their dinner. Mr. Bailiff, who was, as I guessed, the little man in the periwig, sat at the top of the table, and Mr. Clerk sat at the bottom, and on chairs were placed their hats, and travelling-cloaks, and bundles of papers tied together with green tape. You may be sure that Elzevir had a good dinner for them, with hot rabbit pie and cold round of brawn, and a piece of blue vinny, which Mr. Bailiff ate heartily, but his clerk would not touch, saying he had as lief chew soap. There was also a bottle of Ararat milk, and a flagon of ale, for we were afraid to set French wines before them, lest they should fall to wondering how they were come by.

Elzevir took the candle, chiding me a little for being late, and set it in a brass candlestick in the middle of the table. Then Mr. Clerk takes a little rule from his pocket, measures an inch down on the candle, sticks into the grease at that point a scarf-pin with an onyx head that Elzevir lent him, and lights the wick. Now the reason of this was, that the custom ran in Moonfleet when either land or lease was put up to bidding, to stick a pin in a candle; and so long as the pin held firm, it was open to any to make a better offer, but when the flame burnt down and the pin fell out, then land or lease fell to the last bidder. So after dinner was over and the table cleared, Mr. Clerk takes out a roll of papers and reads a legal description of the Why Not?, calling it the Mohune Arms, an excellent messuage or tenement now used as a tavern, and speaking of the convenient paddocks or parcels of grazing land at the back of it, called Moons'-lease, amounting to sixteen acres more or less.

Then he invites the company to make an offer of rent for such a desirable property under a five years' lease, and as Elzevir and I are the only company present, the bidding is soon done; for Elzevir offers a rent of 12 a year, which has always been the value of the Why Not? The clerk makes a note of this; but the business is not over yet, for we must wait till the pin drops out of the candle before the lease is finally made out. So the men fell to smoking to pass the time, till there could not have been more than ten minutes' candle to burn, and Mr. Bailiff, with a glass of Ararat milk in his hand, was saying, 'Tis a curious and fine tap of Hollands you keep here, Master Block,' when in walked Mr. Maskew.

A thunderbolt would not have astonished me so much as did his appearance, and Elzevir's face grew black as night; but the bailiff and clerk showed no surprise, not knowing the terms on which persons in our village stood to one another, and thinking it natural that someone should come in to see the pin drop, and the end of an ancient custom. Indeed, Maskew seemed to know the bailiff, for he passed the time of day with him, and was then for sitting down at the table without taking any notice of Elzevir or me. But just as he began to seat himself, Block shouted out, 'You are no welcome visitor in my house, and I would sooner see your back than see your face, but sit at this table you shall not.' I knew what he meant; for on that table they had laid out David's body, and with that he struck his fist upon the board so smart as to make the bailiff jump and nearly bring the pin out of the candle.

'Heyday, sirs,' says Mr. Bailiff, astonished, 'let us have no brawling here, the more so as this worshipful gentleman is a magistrate and something of a friend of mine.' Yet Maskew refrained from sitting, but stood by the bailiff's chair, turning white, and not red, as he did with Mr. Glennie; and muttered something, that he had as lief stand as sit, and that it should soon be Block's turn to ask sitting-room of *him*.

I was wondering what possibly could have brought Maskew there, when the bailiff, who was ill at ease, said—'Come, Mr. Clerk, the pin hath but another minute's hold; rehearse what has been done, for I must get this lease delivered and off to Bridport, where much business waits.'

So the clerk read in a singsong voice that the property of the duchy of Cornwall, called the Mohune Arms, an inn or tavern, with all its land, tenements, and appurtenances, situate in the Parish of St. Sebastian, Moonfleet, having been offered on lease for five years, would be let to Elzevir Block at a rent of 12 *per annum*, unless anyone offered a higher rent before the pin fell from the candle.

There was no one to make another offer, and the bailiff said to Elzevir, 'Tell them to have the horses round, the pin will be out in a minute, and 'twill save time.' So Elzevir gave the order, and then we all stood round in silence, waiting for the pin to fall. The grease had burnt down to the mark, or almost below it, as it appeared; but just where the pin stuck in there was a little lump of harder tallow that held bravely out, refusing to be melted. The bailiff gave a stamp of impatience with his foot under the table as though he hoped thus to shake out the pin, and then a little dry voice came from Maskew, saying—

'I offer 13 a year for the inn.'

This fell upon us with so much surprise, that all looked round, seeking as it were some other speaker, and never thinking that it could be Maskew. Elzevir was the first, I believe, to fully understand 'twas he; and without turning to look at bailiff or Maskew, but having his elbows on the table, his face between his hands, and looking straight out to sea said in a sturdy voice, 'I offer 20.'

The words were scarce out of his mouth when Maskew caps them with 21, and so in less than a minute the rent of the Why Not? was near doubled. Then the bailiff looked from one to the other, not knowing what to make of it all, nor whether 'twas comedy or serious, and said—

'Kind sir, I warn ye not to trifle; I have no time to waste in April fooling, and he who makes offers in sport will have to stand to them in earnest.'

But there was no lack of earnest in one at least of the men that he had before him, and the voice with which Elzevir said 30 was still sturdy. Maskew called 31 and 41, and Elzevir 40 and 50, and then I looked at the candle, and saw that the head of the pin was no longer level, it had sunk a little—a very little. The clerk awoke from his indifference, and was making notes of the bids with a squeaking quill, the bailiff frowned as being puzzled, and thinking that none had a right to puzzle him. As for me, I could not sit still, but got on my feet, if so I might better bear the suspense; for I understood now that Maskew had made up his mind to turn Elzevir out, and that Elzevir was fighting for his home. *His* home, and had he not made it my home too, and were we both to be made outcasts to please the spite of this mean little man?

There were some more bids, and then I knew that Maskew was saying 91, and saw the head of the pin was lower; the hard lump of tallow in Aunt Jane's candle was thawing. The bailiff struck in: 'Are ye mad, sirs, and you, Master Block, save your breath, and spare your money; and if this worshipful gentleman must become innkeeper at any price, let him have the place in the Devil's name, and I will give thee the Mermaid, at Bridport, with a snug parlour, and ten times the trade of this.'

Elzevir seemed not to hear what he said, but only called out 100, with his face still looking out to sea, and the same sturdiness in his voice. Then Maskew tried a spring, and went to 120, and Elzevir capped him with 130, and 140, 150, 160, 170 followed quick. My breath came so fast that I was almost giddy, and I had to clench my hands to remind myself of where I was, and what was going on. The bidders too were breathing hard, Elzevir had taken his head from his hands, and the eyes of all were on the pin. The lump of tallow was worn down now; it was hard to say why the pin did not fall. Maskew gulped out 180, and Elzevir said 190, and then the pin gave a lurch, and I thought the Why Not? was saved, though at the price of ruin. No; the pin had not fallen, there was a film that held it by the point, one second, only one second. Elzevir's breath, which was ready to outbid whatever Maskew said, caught in his throat with the catching pin, and Maskew sighed out 200, before the pin pattered on the bottom of the brass candlestick.

The clerk forgot his master's presence and shut his notebook with a bang, 'Congratulate you, sir,' says he, quite pert to Maskew; 'you are the landlord of the poorest pothouse in the Duchy at 200 a year.'

The bailiff paid no heed to what his man did, but took his periwig

64

off and wiped his head. 'Well, I'm hanged,' he said; and so the Why Not? was lost.

Just as the last bid was given, Elzevir half-rose from his chair, and for a moment I expected to see him spring like a wild beast on Maskew; but he said nothing, and sat down again with the same stolid look on his face. And, indeed, it was perhaps well that he thus thought better of it, for Maskew stuck his hand into his bosom as the other rose; and though he withdrew it again when Elzevir got back to his chair, yet the front of his waistcoat was a little bulged, and, looking sideways, I saw the silver-shod butt of a pistol nestling far down against his white shirt. The bailiff was vexed, I think, that he had been betrayed into such strong words; for he tried at once to put on as indifferent an air as might be, saying in dry tones, 'Well, gentlemen, there seems to be here some personal matter into which I shall not attempt to spy. Two hundred pounds more or less is but a flea-bite to the Duchy; and if you, sir,' turning to Maskew, 'wish later on to change your mind, and be quit of the bargain, I shall not be the man to stand in your way. In any case, I imagine 'twill be time enough to seal the lease if I send it from London.'

I knew he said this, and hinted at delay as wishing to do Elzevir a good turn; for his clerk had the lease already made out pat, and it only wanted the name and rent filled in to be sealed and signed. But, 'No,' says Maskew, 'business is business, Mr. Bailiff, and the post uncertain to parts so distant from the capital as these; so I'll thank you to make out the lease to me now, and on May Day place me in possession.'

'So be it then,' said the bailiff a little testily, 'but blame me not for driving hard bargains; for the Duchy, whose servant I am,' and he raised his hat, 'is no daughter of the horse-leech. Fill in the figures, Mr. Scrutton, and let us away.'

So Mr. Scrutton, for that was Mr. Clerk's name, scratches a bit with his quill on the parchment sheet to fill in the money, and then Maskew scratches his name, and Mr. Bailiff scratches his name, and Mr. Clerk scratches again to witness Mr. Bailiff's name, and then Mr. Bailiff takes from his mails a little shagreen case, and out from the case comes sealing-wax and the travelling seal of the Duchy.

There was my aunt's best winter-candle still burning away in the daylight, for no one had taken any thought to put it out; and Mr. Bailiff melts the wax at it, till a drop of sealing-wax falls into the grease and makes a gutter down one side, and then there is a sweating of the parchment under the hot wax, and at last on goes the seal. 'Signed, sealed, and delivered,' says Mr. Clerk, rolling up the sheet and handing it to Maskew; and Maskew takes and thrusts it into his bosom underneath his waistcoat front—all cheek by jowl with that silver-hafted pistol, whose butt I had seen before.

The postchaise stood before the door, the horses were stamping on the cobble-stones, and the harness jingled. Mr. Clerk had carried out his mails, but Mr. Bailiff stopped for a moment as he flung the travelling cloak about his shoulders to say to Elzevir, 'Tut, man, take things not too hardly. Thou shalt have the Mermaid at 20 a year, which will be worth ten times as much to thee as this dreary place; and canst send thy son to Bryson's school, where they will make a scholar of him, for he is a brave lad'; and he touched my shoulder, and gave me a kindly look as he passed.

'I thank your worship', said Elzevir, 'for all your goodness; but when I quit this place, I shall not set up my staff again at any inn door.'

Mr. Bailiff seemed nettled to see his offer made so little of, and left the room with a sniff, 'Then I wish you good day.'

Maskew had slipped out before him, and the children's noses left the window-pane as the great man walked down the steps. There was a little group to see the start, but it quickly melted; and before the clatter of hoofs died away, the report spread through the village that Maskew had turned Elzevir out of the Why Not?

For a long time after all had gone, Elzevir sat at the table with his head between his hands, and I kept quiet also, both because I was myself sorry that we were to be sent adrift, and because I wished to show Elzevir that I felt for him in his troubles. But the young cannot enter fully into their elders' sorrows, however much they may wish to, and after a time the silence palled upon me. It was getting dusk, and the candle which bore itself so bravely through auction and lease-sealing burnt low in the socket. A minute later the light gave some flickering flashes, failings, and sputters, and then the wick tottered, and out popped the flame, leaving us with the chilly grey of a March evening creeping up in the corners of the room. I could bear the gloom no longer, but made up the fire till the light danced ruddy across pewter and porcelain on the dresser.

'Come, Master Block,' I said, 'there is time enough before May Day to think what we shall do, so let us take a cup of tea, and after that I will play you a game of backgammon.' But he still remained cast down, and would say nothing; and as chance would have it, though I wished to let him win at backgammon, that so, perhaps, he might get cheered, yet do what I would that night I could not lose. So as his luck grew worse his moodiness increased, and at last he shut the board with a bang, saying, in reference to that motto that ran round its edge, 'Life is like a game of hazard, and surely none ever flung worse throws, or made so little of them as I.'

CHAPTER 8: THE LANDING

Let my lamp at midnight hour
Be seen in some high lonely tower—Milton

Maskew got ugly looks from the men, and sour words from the wives, as he went up through the village that afternoon, for all knew what he had done, and for many days after the auction he durst not show his face abroad. Yet Damen of Ringstave and some others of the landers' men, who made it their business to keep an eye upon him, said that he had been twice to Weymouth of evenings, and held converse there with Mr. Luckham of the Excise, and with Captain Henning, who commanded the troopers then in quarters on the Nothe. And by degrees it got about, but how I do not know, that he had persuaded the Revenue to strike hard at the smugglers, and that a strong posse was to be held in readiness to take the landers in the act the next time they should try to run a cargo.

Why Maskew should so put himself about to help the Revenue I cannot tell, nor did anyone ever certainly find out; but some said 'twas out of sheer wantonness, and a desire to hurt his neighbours; and others, that he saw what an apt place this was for landing cargoes, and wished first to make a brave show of zeal for the Excise, and afterwards to get the whole of the contraband trade into his own hands. However that may be, I think he was certainly in league with the Revenue men, and more than once I saw him on the Manor terrace with a spy glass in his hand, and guessed that he was looking for the lugger in the offing. Now, word was mostly given to the lander, by safe hands, of the night on which a cargo should be run, and then in the morning or afternoon, the lugger would come just near enough the land to be made out with glasses, and afterwards lie off again out of sight till nightfall.

The nights chosen for such work were without moon, but as still as might be, so long as there was wind enough to fill the sails; and often the lugger could be made out from the beach, but sometimes 'twas necessary to signal with flares, though they were used as little as might be. Yet after there had been a long spell of rough weather, and a cargo had to be run at all hazards, I have known the boats come in even on the bright moonlight and take their risk, for 'twas said the Excise slept sounder round us than anywhere in all the Channel.

These tales of Maskew's doings failed not to reach Elzevir, and for some days he thought best not to move, though there was a cargo on the other side that wanted landing badly. But one evening when he had won at backgammon, and was in an open mood, he took me into confidence, setting down the dice box on the table, and saying—

'There is word come from the shippers that we must take a cargo, for that they cannot keep the stuff by them longer at St. Malo. Now with this devil at the Manor prowling round, I dare not risk the job on Moonfleet beach, nor yet stow the liquor in the vault; so I have told the *Bonaventure* to put her nose into this bay tomorrow afternoon that Maskew may see her well, and then to lie out again to sea, as she has done a hundred times before. But instead of waiting in the offing, she will make straight off up Channel to a little strip of shingle underneath Hoar Head.' I nodded to show I knew the place, and he went on—'Men used to choose that spot in good old times to beach a cargo before the passage to the vault was dug; and there is a worked-out quarry they called Pyegrove's Hole, not too far off up the down, and choked with brambles, where we can find shelter for a hundred kegs. So we'll be under Hoar Head at five tomorrow morn with the pack-horses. I wish we could be earlier, for the sun rises thereabout, but the tide will not serve before.'

It was at that moment that I felt a cold touch on my shoulders, as of the fresh air from outside, and thought beside I had a whiff of salt seaweed from the beach. So round I looked to see if door or window stood ajar. The window was tight enough, and shuttered to boot, but the door was not to be seen plainly for a wooden screen, which parted it from the parlour, and was meant to keep off draughts. Yet I could just see a top corner of the door above the screen and thought it was not fast. So up I got to shut it, for the nights were cold; but coming round the corner of the screen found that 'twas closed, and yet I could have sworn I saw the latch fall to its place as I walked towards it. Then I dashed forward, and in a trice had the door open, and was in the street. But the night was moonless and black, and I neither saw nor heard aught stirring, save the gentle sea-wash on Moonfleet beach beyond the salt meadows.

Elzevir looked at me uneasily as I came back.

'What ails thee, boy?' said he.

'I thought I heard someone at the door,' I answered; 'did you not feel a cold wind as if it was open?'

'It is but the night is sharp, the spring sets in very chill; slip the bolt, and sit down again,' and he flung a fresh log on the fire, that sent a cloud of sparks crackling up the chimney and out into the room.

'Elzevir,' I said, 'I think there was one listening at the door, and there may be others in the house, so before we sit again let us take candle and go through the rooms to make sure none are prying on us.'

He laughed and said, "Twas but the wind that blew the door open,' but that I might do as I pleased. So I lit another candle, and was for starting on my search; but he cried, 'Nay, thou shalt not go alone'; and so we went all round the house together, and found not so much as a mouse stirring.

He laughed the more when we came back to the parlour. "Tis the cold has chilled thy heart and made thee timid of that skulking rascal of the Manor; fill me a glass of Ararat milk, and one for thyself, and let us to bed.'

I had learned by this not to be afraid of the good liquor, and while we sat sipping it, Elzevir went on—

'There is a fortnight yet to run, and then you and I shall be cut adrift from our moorings. It is a cruel thing to see the doors of this house closed on me, where I and mine have lived a century or more, but I must see it. Yet let us not be too cast down, but try to make something even of this worst of throws.'

I was glad enough to hear him speak in this firmer strain, for I had seen what a sore thought it had been for these days past that he must leave the Why Not?, and how it often made him moody and downcast.

'We will have no more of innkeeping,' he said; 'I have been sick and tired of it this many a day, and care not now to see men abuse good liquor and addle their silly pates to fill my purse. And I have something, boy, put snug away in Dorchester town that will give us bread to eat and beer to drink, even if the throws run still deuce-ace. But we must seek a roof to shelter us when the Why Not? is shut, and 'tis best we leave this Moonfleet of ours for a season, till Maskew finds a rope's end long enough to hang himself withal. So, when our work is done tomorrow night, we will walk out along the cliff to Worth, and take a look at a cottage there that Damen spoke about, with a walled orchard at the back, and fuchsia hedge in front—'tis near the

Lobster Inn, and has a fine prospect of the sea; and if we live there, we will leave the vault alone awhile and use this Pyegrove's Hole for storehouse, till the watch is relaxed.'

I did not answer, having my thoughts on other things, and he tossed off his liquor, saying, 'Thou'rt tired; so let's to bed, for we shall get little sleep tomorrow night.'

It was true that I was tired, and yet I could not get to sleep, but tossed and turned in my bed for thinking of many things, and being vexed that we were to leave Moonfleet. Yet mine was a selfish sorrow; for I had little thought for Elzevir and the pain that it must be to him to quit, the Why Not?: nor yet was it the grief of leaving Moonfleet that so troubled me, although that was the only place I ever had known, and seemed to me then—as now—the only spot on earth fit to be lived in; but the real care and canker was that I was going away from Grace Maskew. For since she had left school I had grown fonder of her; and now that it was difficult to see her, I took the more pains to accomplish it, and met her sometimes in Manor Woods, and more than once, when Maskew was away, had walked with her on Weatherbeech Hill. So we bred up a boy-and-girl affection, and must needs pledge ourselves to be true to one another, not knowing what such silly words might mean.

And I told Grace all my secrets, not even excepting the doings of the contraband, and the Mohune vault and Blackbeard's locket, for I knew all was as safe with her as with me, and that her father could never rack aught from her. Nay, more, her bedroom was at the top of the gabled wing of the Manor House, and looked right out to sea; and one clear night, when our boat was coming late from fishing, I saw her candle burning there, and next day told her of it. And then she said that she would set a candle to burn before the panes on winter nights, and be a leading light for boats at sea. And so she did, and others beside me saw and used it, calling it 'Maskew's Match', and saying that it was the attorney sitting up all night to pore over ledgers and add up his fortune.

So this night as I lay awake I vexed and vexed myself for thinking of her, and at last resolved to go up next morning to the Manor Woods and lie in wait for Grace, to tell her what was up, and that we were going away to Worth.

Next day, the 16th of April—a day I have had cause to remember all my life—I played truant from Mr. Glennie, and by ten in the forenoon found myself in the woods.

There was a little dimple on the hillside above the house, green with burdocks in summer and filled with dry leaves in winter—just big enough to hold one lying flat, and not so deep but that I could look over the lip of it and see the house without being seen. Thither I went that day, and lay down in the dry leaves to wait and watch for Grace.

The morning was bright enough. The chills of the night before had given way to sunlight that seemed warm as summer, and yet had with it the soft freshness of spring. There was scarce a breath moving in the wood, though I could see the clouds of white dust stalking up the road that climbs Ridge down, and the trees were green with buds, yet without leafage to keep the sunbeams from lighting up the ground below, which glowed with yellow king-cups. So I lay there for a long, long while; and to make time pass quicker, took from my bosom the silver locket, and opening it, read again the parchment, which I had read times out of mind before, and knew indeed by heart.

'The days of our age are threescore years and ten', and the rest.

Now, whenever I handled the locket, my thoughts were turned to Mohune's treasure; and it was natural that it should be so, for the locket reminded me of my first journey to the vault; and I laughed at myself, remembering how simple I had been, and had hoped to find the place littered with diamonds, and to see the gold lying packed in heaps. And thus for the hundredth time I came to rack my brain to know where the diamond could be hid, and thought at last it must be buried in the churchyard, because of the talk of Blackbeard being seen on wild nights digging there for his treasure. But then, I reasoned, that very like it was the *contrabandiers* whom men had seen with spades when they were digging out the passage from the tomb to the vault, and set them down for ghosts because they wrought at night. And while I was busy with such thoughts, the door opened in the house below me, and out came Grace with a hood on her head and a basket for wild flowers in her hand.

I watched to see which way she would walk; and as soon as she took the path that leads up Weatherbeech, made off through the dry brushwood to meet her, for we had settled she should never go that road except when Maskew was away. So there we met and spent an hour together on the hill, though I shall not write here what we said, because it was mostly silly stuff. She spoke much of the auction and of Elzevir leaving the Why Not?, and though she never said a word against her father, let me know what pain his doing gave her. But most

71

she grieved that we were leaving Moonfleet, and showed her grief in such pretty ways, as made me almost glad to see her sorry. And from her I learned that Maskew was indeed absent from home, having been called away suddenly last night. The evening was so fine, he said (and this surprised me, remembering how dark and cold it was with us), that he must needs walk round the policies; but about nine o'clock came back and told her he had got a sudden call to business, which would take him to Weymouth then and there. So to saddle, and off he went on his mare, bidding Grace not to look for him for two nights to come.

I know not why it was, but what she said of Maskew made me thoughtful and silent, and she too must be back home lest the old servant that kept house for them should say she had been too long away, and so we parted. Then off I went through the woods and down the village street, but as I passed my old home saw Aunt Jane standing on the doorstep. I bade her 'Good day', and was for running on to the Why Not?, for I was late enough already, but she called me to her, seeming in a milder mood, and said she had something for me in the house. So left me standing while she went off to get it, and back she came and thrust into my hand a little prayer-book, which I had often seen about the parlour in past days, saying, 'Here is a Common Prayer which I had meant to send thee with thy clothes. It was thy poor mother's, and I pray may some day be as precious a balm to thee as it once was to that godly woman.' With that she gave me the 'Good day', and I pocketed the little red leather book, which did indeed afterwards prove precious to me, though not in the way she meant, and ran down street to the Why Not?

★★★★★★

That same evening Elzevir and I left the Why Not?, went up through the village, climbed the down, and were at the brow by sunset. We had started earlier than we fixed the night before, because word had come to Elzevir that morning that the tide called Gulder would serve for the beaching of the *Bonaventure* at three instead of five. 'Tis a strange thing the Gulder, and not even sailors can count closely with it; for on the Dorset coast the tide makes four times a day, twice with the common flow, and twice with the Gulder, and this last being shifty and uncertain as to time, flings out many a sea-reckoning.

It was about seven o'clock when we were at the top of the hill, and there were fifteen good miles to cover to get to Hoar Head. Dusk was upon us before we had walked half an hour; but when the night fell, it was not black as on the last evening, but a deep sort of blue, and the heat of the day did not die with the sun, but left the air still warm and balmy. We trudged on in silence, and were glad enough when we saw by a white stone here and there at the side of the path that we were nearing the cliff; for the Preventive men mark all the footpaths on the cliff with whitewashed stones, so that one can pick up the way without risk on a dark night. A few minutes more, and we reached a broad piece of open sward, which I knew for the top of Hoar Head.

Hoar Head is the highest of that line of cliffs, which stretches twenty miles from Weymouth to St. Alban's Head, and it stands up eighty fathoms or more above the water. The seaward side is a great sheer of chalk, but falls not straight into the sea, for three parts down there is a lower ledge or terrace, called the under-cliff.

'Twas to this ledge that we were bound; and though we were now straight above, I knew we had a mile or more to go before we could get down to it. So on we went again, and found the bridle-path that slopes down through a deep dip in the cliff line; and when we reached this under-ledge, I looked up at the sky, the night being clear, and guessed by the stars that 'twas past midnight. I knew the place from having once been there for blackberries; for the brambles on the under-cliff being sheltered every way but south, and open to the sun, grow the finest in all those parts.

We were not alone, for I could make out a score of men, some standing in groups, some resting on the ground, and the dark shapes of the pack-horses showing larger in the dimness. There were a few words of greeting muttered in deep voices, and then all was still, so that one heard the browsing horses trying to crop something off the turf. It was not the first cargo I had helped to run, and I knew most of the men, but did not speak with them, being tired, and wishing to rest till I was wanted. So cast myself down on the turf, but had not lain there long when I saw someone coming to me through the brambles, and Master Ratsey said, 'Well, Jack, so thou and Elzevir are leaving Moonfleet, and I fain would flit myself, but then who would be left to lead the old folk to their last homes, for dead do not bury their dead in these days.'

I was half-asleep, and took little heed of what he said, putting him off with, 'That need not keep you, Master; they will find others to fill your place.' Yet he would not let me be, but went on talking for the pleasure of hearing his own voice.

'Nay, child, you know not what you say. They may find men to dig a grave, and perhaps to fill it, but who shall toss the mould when Parson Glennie gives the "*earth to earth*"; it takes a mort of knowledge to make it rattle kindly on the coffin-lid.'

I felt sleep heavy on my eyelids, and was for begging him to let me rest, when there came a whistle from below, and in a moment all were on their feet. The drivers went to the packhorses' heads, and so we walked down to the strand, a silent moving group of men and horses mixed; and before we came to the bottom, heard the first boat's nose grind on the beach, and the feet of the seamen crunching in the pebbles. Then all fell to the business of landing, and a strange enough scene it was, what with the medley of men, the lanthorns swinging, and a frothy Upper from the sea running up till sometimes it was over our boots; and all the time there was a patter of French and Dutch, for most of the *Bonaventure's* men were foreigners. But I shall not speak more of this; for, after all, one landing is very like another, and kegs come ashore in much the same way, whether they are to pay excise or not.

It must have been three o'clock before the lugger's boats were off again to sea, and by that time the horses were well laden, and most of the men had a keg or two to carry beside. Then Elzevir, who was in command, gave the word, and we began to file away from the beach up to the under-cliff. Now, what with the cargo being heavy, we were longer than usual in getting away; and though there was no sign of sunrise, yet the night was greyer, and not so blue as it had been.

We reached the under-cliff, and were moving across it to address ourselves to the bridle-path, and so wind sideways up the steep; when I saw something moving behind one of the plumbs of brambles with which the place is beset. It was only a glimpse of motion that I had perceived, and could not say whether 'twas man or animal, or even frightened bird behind the bushes. But others had seen it as well; there was some shouting, half a dozen flung down their kegs and started in pursuit.

All eyes were turned to the bridle-path, and in a twinkling hunters and hunted were in view. The greyhounds were Damen and Garrett, with some others, and the hare was an older man, who leapt and bounded forward, faster than I should have thought any but a youth could run; but then he knew what men were after him, and that 'twas a race for life. For though it was but a moment before all were lost in the night, yet this was long enough to show me that the man was none other than Maskew, and I knew that his life was not worth ten minutes' purchase.

Now I hated this man, and had myself suffered something at his hand, besides seeing him put much grievous suffering on others; but I wished then with all my heart he might escape, and had a horrible dread of what was to come. Yet I knew all the time escape was impossible; for though Maskew ran desperately, the way was steep and stony, and he had behind him some of the fleetest feet along that coast. We had all stopped with one accord, as not wishing to move a step forward till we had seen the issue of the chase; and I was near enough to look into Elzevir's face, but saw there neither passion nor bloodthirstiness, but only a calm resolve, as if he had to deal with something well expected.

We had not long to wait, for very soon we heard a rolling of stones and trampling of feet coming down the path, and from the darkness issued a group of men, having Maskew in the middle of them. They were hustling him along fast, two having hold of him by the arms, and a third by the neck of his shirt behind. The sight gave me a sick qualm, like an overdose of tobacco, for it was the first time I had ever seen a man man-handled, and a fellow-creature abused. His cap was lost, and his thin hair tangled over his forehead, his coat was torn off, so that he stood in his waistcoat alone; he was pale, and gasped terribly, whether from the sharp run, or from violence, or fear, or all combined.

There was a babel of voices when they came up of desperate men who had a bitterest enemy in their clutch; and some shouted, 'Club him', 'Shoot him', 'Hang him', while others were for throwing him over the cliff. Then someone saw under the flap of his waistcoat that same silver-hafted pistol that lay so lately next the lease of the Why Not? and snatching it from him, flung it on the grass at Block's feet.

But Elzevir's deep voice mastered their contentions—

'Lads, ye remember how I said when this man's reckoning day should come 'twas I would reckon with him, and had your promise to it. Nor is it right that any should lay hand on him but I, for is he not sealed to me with my son's blood? So touch him not, but bind him hand and foot, and leave him here with me and go your ways; there is no time to lose, for the light grows apace.'

There was a little muttered murmuring, but Elzevir's will overbore them here as it had done in the vault; and they yielded the more easily, because every man knew in his heart that he would never see Maskew again alive. So within ten minutes all were winding up the bridle-path, horses and men, all except three; for there were left upon the brambly greensward of the under-cliff Maskew and Elzevir and I, and the pistol lay at Elzevir's feet.

Chapter 9: A Judgement

Let them fight it out, friend.
Things have gone too far,
God must judge the couple: leave them as they are—Browning

I made as if I would follow the others, not wishing to see what I must see if I stayed behind, and knowing that I was powerless to bend Elzevir from his purpose. But he called me back and bade me wait with him, for that I might be useful by and by. So I waited, but was only able to make a dreadful guess at how I might be of use, and feared the worst.

Maskew sat on the sward with his hands lashed tight behind his back, and his feet tied in front. They had set him with his shoulders against a great block of weather-worn stone that was half-buried and half-stuck up out of the turf. There he sat keeping his eyes on the ground, and was breathing less painfully than when he was first brought, but still very pale. Elzevir stood with the lanthorn in his hand, looking at Maskew with a fixed gaze, and we could hear the hoofs of the heavy-laden horses beating up the path, till they turned a corner, and all was still.

The silence was broken by Maskew: 'Unloose me, villain, and let me go. I am a magistrate of the county, and if you do not, I will have you gibbeted on this cliff-top.'

They were brave words enough, yet seemed to me but bad play-acting; and brought to my remembrance how, when I was a little fellow, Mr. Glennie once made me recite a battle-piece of Mr. Dryden before my betters; and how I could scarce get out the bloody threats for shyness and rising tears. So it was with Maskew's words; for he had much ado to gather breath to say them, and they came in a thin voice that had no sting of wrath or passion in it.

Then Elzevir spoke to him, not roughly, but resolved; and yet with melancholy, like a judge sentencing a prisoner:

'Talk not to me of gibbets, for thou wilt neither hang nor see men hanged again. A month ago thou satst under my roof, watching the flame burn down till the pin dropped and gave thee right to turn me out from my old home. And now this morning thou shalt watch that flame again, for I will give thee one inch more of candle, and when the pin drops, will put this thine own pistol to thy head, and kill thee with as little thought as I would kill a stoat or other vermin.'

Then he opened the lanthorn slide, took out from his neckcloth that same pin with the onyx head which he had used in the Why Not? and fixed it in the tallow a short inch from the top, setting the lanthorn down upon the sward in front of Maskew.

As for me, I was dismayed beyond telling at these words, and made giddy with the revulsion of feeling; for, whereas, but a few minutes ago, I would have thought nothing too bad for Maskew, now I was turned round to wish he might come off with his life, and to look with terror upon Elzevir.

It had grown much lighter, but not yet with the rosy flush of sunrise; only the stars had faded out, and the deep blue of the night given way to a misty grey. The light was strong enough to let all things be seen, but not to call the due tints back to them. So I could see cliffs and ground, bushes and stones and sea, and all were of one pearly grey colour, or rather they were colourless; but the most colourless and greyest thing of all was Maskew's face. His hair had got awry, and his head showed much balder than when it was well trimmed; his face, too, was drawn with heavy lines, and there were rings under his eyes. Beside all that, he had got an ugly fall in trying to escape, and one cheek was muddied, and down it trickled a blood-drop where a stone had cut him. He was a sorry sight enough, and looking at him, I remembered that day in the schoolroom when this very man had struck the parson, and how our master had sat patient under it, with a blood-drop trickling down his cheek too.

Maskew kept his eyes fixed for a long time on the ground, but raised them at last, and looked at me with a vacant yet pity-seeking look. Now, till that moment I had never seen a trace of Grace in his features, nor of him in hers; and yet as he gazed at me then, there was something of her present in his face, even battered as it was, so that it seemed as if she looked at me behind his eyes. And that made me the sorrier for him, and at last I felt I could not stand by and see him done to death.

When Elzevir had stuck the pin into the candle he never shut the slide again; and though no wind blew, there was a light breath moving in the morning off the sea, that got inside the lanthorn and set the flame askew. And so the candle guttered down one side till but little tallow was left above the pin; for though the flame grew pale and paler to the view in the growing morning light, yet it burnt freely all the time. So at last there was left, as I judged, but a quarter of an hour to run before the pin should fall, and I saw that Maskew knew this as well as I, for his eyes were fixed on the lanthorn.

At last he spoke again, but the brave words were gone, and the thin voice was thinner. He had dropped threats, and was begging piteously for his life. 'Spare me,' he said; 'spare me, Mr. Block: I have an only daughter, a young girl with none but me to guard her. Would you rob a young girl of her only help and cast her on the world? Would you have them find me dead upon the cliff and bring me back to her a bloody corpse?'

Then Elzevir answered: 'And had I not an only son, and was he not brought back to me a bloody corpse? Whose pistol was it that flashed in his face and took his life away? Do you not know? It was this very same that shall flash in yours. So make what peace you may with God, for you have little time to make it.'

With that he took the pistol from the ground where it had lain, and turning his back on Maskew, walked slowly to and fro among the bramble-plumps.

Though Maskew's words about his daughter seemed but to feed Elzevir's anger, by leading him to think of David, they sank deep in my heart; and if it had seemed a fearful thing before to stand by and see a fellow-creature butchered, it seemed now ten thousand times more fearful. And when I thought of Grace, and what such a deed would mean to her, my pulse beat so fierce that I must needs spring to my feet and run to reason with Elzevir, and tell him this must not be.

He was still walking among the bushes when I found him, and let me say my say till I was out of breath, and bore with me if I talked fast, and if my tongue outran my judgement.

'Thou hast a warm heart, lad,' he said, 'and 'tis for that I like thee. And if thou hast a chief place in thy heart for me, I cannot grumble if thou find a little room there even for our enemies. Would I could set thy soul at ease, and do all that thou askest. In the first flush of wrath, when he was taken plotting against our lives, it seemed a little thing enough to take his evil life. But now these morning airs have cooled me, and it goes against my will to shoot a cowering hound tied hand and foot, even though he had murdered twenty sons of mine. I have thought if there be any way to spare his life, and leave this hour's agony to read a lesson not to be unlearned until the grave. For such poltroons dread death, and in one hour they die a hundred times. But there is no way out: his life lies in the scale against the lives of all our men, yes, and thy life too. They left him in my hands well knowing I should take account of him; and am I now to play them false and turn him loose again to hang them all? It cannot be.'

Still I pleaded hard for Maskew's life, hanging on Elzevir's arm, and using every argument that I could think of to soften his purpose; but he pushed me off; and though I saw that he was loath to do it, I had a terrible conviction that he was not a man to be turned back from his resolve, and would go through with it to the end.

We came back together from the brambles to the piece of sward, and there sat Maskew where we had left him with his back against the stone. Only, while we were away he had managed to wriggle his watch out of the fob, and it lay beside him on the turf, tied to him with a black silk riband. The face of it was turned upwards, and as I passed I saw the hand pointed to five. Sunrise was very near; for though the cliff shut out the east from us, the west over Portland was all aglow with copper-red and gold, and the candle burnt low. The head of the pin was drooping, though very slightly, but as I saw it droop a month before, and I knew that the final act was not far off.

Maskew knew it too, for he made his last appeal, using such passionate words as I cannot now relate, and wriggling with his body as if to get his hands from behind his back and hold them up in supplication. He offered money; a thousand, five thousand, ten thousand pounds to be set free; he would give back the Why Not?; he would leave Moonfleet; and all the while the sweat ran down his furrowed face, and at last his voice was choked with sobs, for he was crying for his life in craven fear.

He might have spoken to a deaf man for all he moved his judge; and Elzevir's answer was to cock the pistol and prime the powder in the pan.

Then I stuck my fingers in my ears and shut my eyes, that I might neither see nor hear what followed, but in a second changed my mind and opened them again, for I had made a great resolve to stop this matter, come what might.

Maskew was making a dreadful sound between a moan and strangled cry; it almost seemed as if he thought that there were others by him beside Elzevir and me, and was shouting to them for help. The sun had risen, and his first rays blazed on a window far away in the west on top of Portland Island, and then there was a tinkle in the inside of the lanthorn, and the pin fell.

Elzevir looked full at Maskew, and raised his pistol; but before he had time to take aim, I dashed upon him like a wild cat, springing on his right arm, and crying to him to stop. It was an unequal struggle, a lad, though full-grown and lusty, against one of the powerfullest of men, but indignation nerved my arms, and his were weak, because he doubted of his right. So 'twas with some effort that he shook me off, and in the struggle the pistol was fired into the air.

Then I let go of him, and stumbled for a moment, tired with that bout, but pleased withal, because I saw what peace even so short a respite had brought to Maskew. For at the pistol shot 'twas as if a mask of horror had fallen from his face, and left him his old countenance again; and then I saw he turned his eyes towards the cliff-top, and thought that he was looking up in thankfulness to heaven.

But now a new thing happened; for before the echoes of that pistol-shot had died on the keen morning air, I thought I heard a noise of distant shouting, and looked about to see whence it could come. Elzevir looked round too, but Maskew forgetting to upbraid me for making him miss his aim, still kept his face turned up towards the cliff. Then the voices came nearer, and there was a mingled sound as of men shouting to one another, and gathering in from different places.

'Twas from the cliff-top that the voices came, and thither Elzevir and I looked up, and there too Maskew kept his eyes fixed. And in a moment there were a score of men stood on the cliff's edge high above our heads. The sky behind them was pink flushed with the keenest light of the young day, and they stood out against it sharp cut and black as the silhouette of my mother that used to hang up by the parlour chimney. They were soldiers, and I knew the tall mitre-caps of the 13th, and saw the shafts of light from the sunrise come flashing round their bodies, and glance off the barrels of their matchlocks.

I knew it all now; it was the Posse who had lain in ambush. Elzevir saw it too, and then all shouted at once. 'Yield at the king's command: you are our prisoners!' calls the voice of one of those black silhouettes, far up on the cliff-top.

'We are lost,' cries Elzevir; 'it is the Posse; but if we die, this traitor shall go before us,' and he makes towards Maskew to brain him with the pistol.

'Shoot, shoot, in the Devil's name,' screams Maskew, 'or I am a dead man.'

Then there came a flash of fire along the black line of silhouettes, with a crackle like a near peal of thunder, and a fut, fut, *fut*, of bullets in the turf. And before Elzevir could get at him, Maskew had fallen over on the sward with a groan, and with a little red hole in the middle of his forehead.

'Run for the cliff-side,' cried Elzevir to me; 'get close in, and they cannot touch thee,' and he made for the chalk wall. But I had fallen on my knees like a bullock felled by a pole-axe, and had a scorching pain in my left foot. Elzevir looked back. 'What, have they hit thee too?' he said, and ran and picked me up like a child. And then there is another flash and *fut, fut,* in the turf; but the shots find no billet this time, and we are lying close against the cliff, panting but safe.

CHAPTER 10: THE ESCAPE

How fearful And dizzy 'tis to cast one's eyes so low!
I'll look no more Lest my brain turn—Shakespeare

The while chalk was a bulwark between us and the foe; and though one or two of them loosed off their matchlocks, trying to get at us sideways, they could not even see their quarry, and 'twas only shooting at a venture. We were safe. But for how short a time! Safe just for so long as it should please the soldiers not to come down to take us, safe with a discharged pistol in our grasp, and a shot man lying at our feet.

Elzevir was the first to speak: 'Can you stand, John? Is the bone broken?'

'I cannot stand,' I said; 'there is something gone in my leg, and I feel blood running down into my boot.'

He knelt, and rolled down the leg of my stocking; but though he only moved my foot ever so little, it caused me sharp pain, for feeling was coming back after the first numbness of the shot.

'They have broke the leg, though it bleeds little,' Elzevir said. 'We have no time to splice it here, but I will put a kerchief round, and while I wrap it, listen to how we lie, and then choose what we shall do.'

I nodded, biting my lips hard to conceal the pain he gave me, and he went on: 'We have a quarter of an hour before the Posse can get down to us. But come they will, and thou canst judge what chance we have to save liberty or life with that carrion lying by us'—and he jerked his thumb at Maskew—'though I am glad 'twas not my hand that sent him to his reckoning, and therefore do not blame thee if thou didst make me waste a charge in air. So one thing we can do is to wait here until they come, and I can account for a few of them before they shoot me down; but thou canst not fight with a broken leg, and they will take thee alive, and then there is a dance on air at

81

Dorchester Jail.'

I felt sick with pain and bitterly cast down to think that I was like to come so soon to such a vile end; so only gave a sigh, wishing heartily that Maskew were not dead, and that my leg were not broke, but that I was back again at the Why Not? or even hearing one of Dr. Sherlock's sermons in my aunt's parlour.

Elzevir looked down at me when I sighed, and seeing, I suppose, that I was sorrowful, tried to put a better face on a bad business. 'Forgive me, lad,' he said, 'if I have spoke too roughly. There is yet another way that we may try; and if thou hadst but two whole legs, I would have tried it, but now 'tis little short of madness. And yet, if thou fear'st not, I will still try it. Just at the end of this flat ledge, farthest from where the bridle-path leads down, but not a hundred yards from where we stand, there is a sheep-track leading up the cliff. It starts where the under-cliff dies back again into the chalk face, and climbs by slants and elbow-turns up to the top. The shepherds call it the Zigzag, and even sheep lose their footing on it; and of men I never heard but one had climbed it, and that was lander Jordan, when the Excise was on his heels, half a century back. But he that tries it stakes all on head and foot, and a wounded bird like thee may not dare that flight. Yet, if thou art content to hang thy life upon a hair, I will carry thee some way; and where there is no room to carry, thou must down on hands and knees and trail thy foot.'

It was a desperate chance enough, but came as welcome as a patch of blue through lowering skies. 'Yes,' I said, 'dear Master Elzevir, let us get to it quickly; and if we fall, 'tis better far to die upon the rocks below than to wait here for them to hale us off to jail.' And with that I tried to stand, thinking I might go dot and carry even with a broken leg. But 'twas no use, and down I sank with a groan. Then Elzevir caught me up, holding me in his arms, with my head looking over his back, and made off for the Zigzag. And as we slunk along, close to the cliff-side, I saw, between the brambles, Maskew lying with his face turned up to the morning sky. And there was the little red hole in the middle of his forehead, and a thread of blood that welled up from it and trickled off on to the sward.

It was a sight to stagger any man, and would have made me swoon perhaps, but that there was no time, for we were at the end of the under-cliff, and Elzevir set me down for a minute, before he buckled to his task. And 'twas a task that might cow the bravest, and when I looked upon the Zigzag, it seemed better to stay where we were and fall into the hands of the Posse than set foot on that awful way, and fall upon the rocks below. For the Zigzag started off as a fair enough chalk path, but in a few paces narrowed down till it was but a whiter thread against the grey-white cliff-face, and afterwards turned sharply back, crossing a hundred feet direct above our heads. And then I smelt an evil stench, and looking about, saw the blown-out carcass of a rotting sheep lie close at hand.

'Faugh,' said Elzevir, ''tis a poor beast has lost his foothold.'

It was an ill omen enough, and I said as much, beseeching him to make his own way up the Zigzag and leave me where I was, for that they might have mercy on a boy.

'Tush!' he cried; 'it is thy heart that fails thee, and 'tis too late now to change counsel. We have fifteen minutes yet to win or lose with, and if we gain the cliff-top in that time we shall have an hour's start, or more, for they will take all that to search the under-cliff. And Maskew, too, will keep them in check a little, while they try to bring the life back to so good a man. But if we fall, why, we shall fall together, and outwit their cunning. So shut thy eyes, and keep them tight until I bid thee open them.'

With that he caught me up again, and I shut my eyes firm, rebuking myself for my faint-heartedness, and not telling him how much my foot hurt me. In a minute I knew from Elzevir's steps that he had left the turf and was upon the chalk. Now I do not believe that there were half a dozen men beside in England who would have ventured up that path, even free and untrammelled, and not a man in all the world to do it with a full-grown lad in his arms. Yet Elzevir made no bones of it, nor spoke a single word; only he went very slow, and I felt him scuffle with his foot as he set it forward, to make sure he was putting it down firm.

I said nothing, not wishing to distract him from his terrible task, and held my breath, when I could, so that I might lie quieter in his arms. Thus he went on for a time that seemed without end, and yet was really but a minute or two; and by degrees I felt the wind, that we could scarce perceive at all on the under-cliff, blow fresher and cold on the cliff-side. And then the path grew steeper and steeper, and Elzevir went slower and slower, till at last he spoke:

'John, I am going to stop; but open not thy eyes till I have set thee down and bid thee.'

I did as bidden, and he lowered me gently, setting me on all-fours upon the path; and speaking again:

'The path is too narrow here for me to carry thee, and thou must creep round this corner on thy hands and knees. But have a care to keep thy outer hand near to the inner, and the balance of thy body to the cliff, for there is no room to dance hornpipes here. And hold thy eyes fixed on the chalk-wall, looking neither down nor seaward.'

'Twas well he told me what to do, and well I did it; for when I opened my eyes, even without moving them from the cliff-side, I saw that the ledge was little more than a foot wide, and that ever so little a lean of the body would dash me on the rocks below. So I crept on, but spent much time that was so precious in travelling those ten yards to take me round the first elbow of the path; for my foot was heavy and gave me fierce pain to drag, though I tried to mask it from Elzevir. And he, forgetting what I suffered, cried out, 'Quicken thy pace, lad, if thou canst, the time is short.' Now so frail is man's temper, that though he was doing more than any ever did to save another's life, and was all I had to trust to in the world; yet because he forgot my pain and bade me quicken, my choler rose, and I nearly gave him back an angry word, but thought better of it and kept it in.

Then he told me to stop, for that the way grew wider and he would pick me up again. But here was another difficulty, for the path was still so narrow and the cliff-wall so close that he could not take me up in his arms. So I lay flat on my face, and he stepped over me, setting his foot between my shoulders to do it; and then, while he knelt down upon the path, I climbed up from behind upon him, putting my arms round his neck; and so he bore me 'pickaback'. I shut my eyes firm again, and thus we moved along another spell, mounting still and feeling the wind still freshening.

At length he said that we were come to the last turn of the path, and he must set me down once more. So down upon his knees and hands he went, and I slid off behind, on to the ledge. Both were on all-fours now; Elzevir first and I following. But as I crept along, I relaxed care for a moment, and my eyes wandered from the cliff-side and looked down. And far below I saw the blue sea twinkling like a dazzling mirror, and the gulls wheeling about the sheer chalk wall, and then I thought of that bloated carcass of a sheep that had fallen from this very spot perhaps, and in an instant felt a sickening qualm and swimming of the brain, and knew that I was giddy and must fall.

Then I called out to Elzevir, and he, guessing what had come over me, cries to turn upon my side, and press my belly to the cliff. And how he did it in such a narrow strait I know not; but he turned round, and lying down himself, thrust his hand firmly in my back, pressing me closer to the cliff. Yet it was none too soon, for if he had not held me tight, I should have flung myself down in sheer despair to get quit of that dreadful sickness.

'Keep thine eyes shut, John,' he said, 'and count up numbers loud to me, that I may know thou art not turning faint.' So I gave out, 'One, two, three,' and while I went on counting, heard him repeating to himself, though his words seemed thin and far off: 'We must have taken ten minutes to get here, and in five more they will be on the under-cliff; and if we ever reach the top, who knows but they have left a guard! No, no, they will not leave a guard, for not a man knows of the Zigzag; and, if they knew, they would not guess that we should try it. We have but fifty yards to go to win, and now this cursed giddy fit has come upon the child, and he will fall and drag me with him; or they will see us from below, and pick us off like sitting guillemots against the cliff-face.'

So he talked to himself, and all the while I would have given a world to pluck up heart and creep on farther; yet could not, for the deadly sweating fear that had hold of me. Thus I lay with my face to the cliff, and Elzevir pushing firmly in my back; and the thing that frightened me most was that there was nothing at all for the hand to take hold of, for had there been a piece of string, or even a thread of cotton, stretched along to give a semblance of support, I think I could have done it; but there was only the cliff-wall, sheer and white, against that narrowest way, with never cranny to put a finger into. The wind was blowing in fresh puffs, and though I did not open my eyes, I knew that it was moving the little tufts of bent grass, and the chiding cries of the gulls seemed to invite me to be done with fear and pain and broken leg, and fling myself off on to the rocks below.

Then Elzevir spoke. 'John' he said, 'there is no time to play the woman; another minute of this and we are lost. Pluck up thy courage, keep thy eyes to the cliff, and forward.'

Yet I could not, but answered: 'I cannot, I cannot; if I open my eyes, or move hand or foot, I shall fall on the rocks below.'

He waited a second, and then said: 'Nay, move thou must, and 'tis better to risk falling now, than fall for certain with another bullet in thee later on.' And with that he shifted his hand from my back and fixed it in my coat-collar, moving backwards himself, and setting to drag me after him.

Now, I was so besotted with fright that I would not budge an inch, fearing to fall over if I opened my eyes. And Elzevir, for all he was so strong, could not pull a helpless lump backwards up that path. So he gave it up, leaving go hold on me with a groan, and at that moment there rose from the under-cliff, below a sound of voices and shouting.

'Zounds, they are down already!' cried Elzevir, 'and have found Maskew's body; it is all up; another minute and they will see us.'

But so strange is the force of mind on body, and the power of a greater to master a lesser fear, that when I heard those voices from below, all fright of falling left me in a moment, and I could open my eyes without a trace of giddiness. So I began to move forward again on hands and knees. And Elzevir, seeing me, thought for a moment I had gone mad, and was dragging myself over the cliff; but then saw how it was, and moved backwards himself before me, saying in a low voice, 'Brave lad! Once creep round this turn, and I will pick thee up again. There is but fifty yards to go, and we shall foil these devils yet!'

Then we heard the voices again, but farther off, and not so loud; and knew that our pursuers had left the under-cliff and turned down on to the beach, thinking that we were hiding by the sea.

Five minutes later Elzevir stepped on to the cliff-top, with me upon his back.

'We have made something of this throw,' he said, 'and are safe for another hour, though I thought thy giddy head had ruined us.'

Then he put me gently upon the springy turf, and lay down himself upon his back, stretching his arms out straight on either side, and breathing hard to recover from the task he had performed.

★★★★★★

The day was still young, and far below us was stretched the moving floor of the Channel, with a silver-grey film of night-mists not yet lifted in the offing. A hummocky up-and-down line of cliffs, all projections, dents, bays, and hollows, trended southward till it ended in the great bluff of St. Alban's Head, ten miles away. The cliff-face was gleaming white, the sea tawny inshore, but purest blue outside, with the straight sunpath across it, spangled and gleaming like a mackerel's back.

The relief of being once more on firm ground, and the exultation of an escape from immediate danger, removed my pain and made me forget that my leg was broken. So I lay for a moment basking in the sun; and the wind, which a few minutes before threatened to blow me from that narrow ledge, seemed now but the gentlest of breezes, fresh

86

with the breath of the kindly sea. But this was only for a moment, for the anguish came back and grew apace, and I fell to thinking dismally of the plight we were in. How things had been against us in these last days! First there was losing the Why Not? and that was bad enough; second, there was the being known by the Excise for smugglers, and perhaps for murderers; third and last, there was the breaking of my leg, which made escape so difficult. But, most of all, there came before my eyes that grey face turned up against the morning sun, and I thought of all it meant for Grace, and would have given my own life to call back that of our worst enemy.

Then Elzevir sat up, stretching himself like one waking out of sleep, and said: 'We must be gone. They will not be back for some time yet, and, when they come, will not think to search closely for us hereabouts; but that we cannot risk, and must get clear away. This leg of thine will keep us tied for weeks, and we must find some place where we can lie hid, and tend it. Now, I know such a hiding-hole in Purbeck, which they call Joseph's Pit, and thither we must go; but it will take all the day to get there, for it is seven miles off, and I am older than I was, and thou too heavy a babe to carry over lightly.'

I did not know the pit he spoke of, but was glad to hear of some place, however far off, where I could lie still and get ease from the pain. And so he took me in his arms again and started off across the fields.

I need not tell of that weary journey, and indeed could not, if I wished; for the pain went to my head and filled me with such a drowsy anguish that I knew nothing except when some unlooked-for movement gave me a sharper twinge, and made me cry out. At first Elzevir walked briskly, but as the day wore on went slower, and was fain more than once to put me down and rest, till at last he could only carry me a hundred yards at a time. It was after noon, for the sun was past the meridian, and very hot for the time of year, when the face of the country began to change; and instead of the short sward of the open down, sprinkled with tiny white snail-shells, the ground was brashy with flat stones, and divided up into tillage fields.

It was a bleak wide-bitten place enough, looking as if 'twould never pay for turning, and instead of hedges there were dreary walls built of dry stone without mortar. Behind one of these walls, broken down in places, but held together with straggling ivy, and buttressed here and there with a bramble-bush, Elzevir put me down at length and said, 'I am beat, and can carry thee no farther for this present, though there is not now much farther to go. We have passed Purbeck Gates, and these walls will screen us from prying eyes if any chance comer pass along the down. And as for the soldiers, they are not like to come this way so soon, and if they come I cannot help it; for weariness and the sun's heat have made my feet like lead.

A score of years ago I would have laughed at such a task, but now 'tis different, and I must take a little sleep and rest till the air is cooler. So sit thee here and lean thy shoulder up against the wall, and thus thou canst look through this broken place and watch both ways. Then, if thou see aught moving, wake me up.—I wish I had a thimbleful of powder to make this whistle sound'—and he took Maskew's silver-butted pistol again from his bosom, and handled it lovingly,—'tis like my evil luck to carry fire-arms thirty years, and leave them at home at a pinch like this.' With that he flung himself down where there was a narrow shadow close against the bottom of the wall, and in a minute I knew from his heavy breathing that he was asleep.

The wind had freshened much, and was blowing strong from the west; and now that I was under the lee of the wall I began to perceive that drowsiness creeping upon me which overtakes a man who has been tousled for an hour or two by the wind, and gets at length into shelter. Moreover, though I was not tired by grievous toil like Elzevir, I had passed a night without sleep, and felt besides the weariness of pain to lull me to slumber. So it was, that before a quarter of an hour was past, I had much ado to keep awake, for all I knew that I was left on guard. Then I sought something to fix my thoughts, and looking on that side of the wall where the sward was, fell to counting the mole-hills that were cast up in numbers thereabout.

And when I had exhausted them, and reckoned up thirty little heaps of dry and powdery brown earth, that lay at random on the green turf, I turned my eyes to the tillage field on the other side of the wall, and saw the inch-high blades of corn coming up between the stones. Then I fell to counting the blades, feeling glad to have discovered a reckoning that would not be exhausted at thirty, but would go on for millions, and millions, and millions; and before I had reached ten in so heroic a numeration was fast asleep.

A sharp noise woke me with a start that set the pain tingling in my leg, and though I could see nothing, I knew that a shot had been fired very near us. I was for waking Elzevir, but he was already full awake, and put a finger on his lip to show I should not speak. Then he crept a few paces down the wall to where an ivy bush over-topped it, enough for him to look through the leaves without being seen. He dropped down again with a look of relief, and said, "Tis but a lad scaring rooks with a blunderbuss; we will not stir unless he makes this way."

A minute later he said: 'The boy is coming straight for the wall; we shall have to show ourselves'; and while he spoke there was a rattle of falling stones, where the boy was partly climbing and partly pulling down the dry wall, and so Elzevir stood up. The boy looked frightened, and made as if he would run off, but Elzevir passed him the time of day in a civil voice, and he stopped and gave it back.

'What are you doing here, son?' Block asked.

'Scaring rooks for Farmer Topp,' was the answer.

'Have you got a charge of powder to spare?' said Elzevir, showing his pistol. 'I want to get a rabbit in the gorse for supper, and have dropped my flask. Maybe you've seen a flask in walking through the furrows?'

He whispered to me to lie still, so that it might not be perceived my leg was broken; and the boy replied:

'No, I have seen no flask; but very like have not come the same way as you, being sent out here from Lowermoigne; and as for powder, I have little left, and must save that for the rooks, or shall get a beating for my pains.'

'Come,' said Elzevir, 'give me a charge or two, and there is half a crown for thee.' And he took the coin out of his pocket and showed it.

The boy's eyes twinkled, and so would mine at so valuable a piece, and he took out from his pocket a battered cowskin flask. 'Give flask and all,' said Elzevir, 'and thou shalt have a crown,' and he showed him the larger coin.

No time was wasted in words; Elzevir had the flask in his pocket, and the boy was biting the crown.

'What shot have you?' said Elzevir.

'What! have you dropped your shot-flask too?' asked the boy. And his voice had something of surprise in it.

'Nay, but my shot are over small; if thou hast a slug or two, I would take them.' 'I have a dozen goose-slugs, No. 2,' said the boy; 'but thou must pay a shilling for them. My master says I never am to use them, except I see a swan or buzzard, or something fit to cook, come over: I shall get a sound beating for my pains, and to be beat is worth a shilling.'

'If thou art beat, be beat for something more,' says Elzevir the tempter. 'Give me that firelock that thou carriest, and take a guinea.'

'Nay, I know not,' says the boy; 'there are queer tales afloat at Low-ermoigne, how that a posse met the contraband this morning, and shots were fired, and a gauger got an overdose of lead—maybe of goose slugs No. 2. The smugglers got off clear, but they say the hue and cry is up already, and that a head-price will be fixed of twenty pound. So if I sell you a fowling-piece, maybe I shall do wrong, and have the government upon me as well as my master.' The surprise in his voice was changed to suspicion, for while he spoke I saw that his eye had fallen on my foot, though I tried to keep it in the shadow; and that he saw the boot clotted with blood, and the kerchief tied round my leg.

"'Tis for that very reason,' says Elzevir, 'that I want the firelock. These smugglers are roaming loose, and a pistol is a poor thing to stop such wicked rascals on a lone hill-side. Come, come, *thou* dost not want a piece to guard thee; they will not hurt a boy.'

He had the guinea between his finger and thumb, and the gleam of the gold was too strong to be withstood. So we gained a sorry matchlock, slugs, and powder, and the boy walked off over the furrow, whistling with his hand in his pocket, and a guinea and a crown-piece in his hand.

His whistle sounded innocent enough, yet I mistrusted him, hav-ing caught his eye when he was looking at my bloody foot; and so I said as much to Elzevir, who only laughed, saying the boy was simple and harmless. But from where I sat I could peep out through the brambles in the open gap, and see without being seen—and there was my young gentleman walking carelessly enough, and whistling like any bird so long as Elzevir's head was above the wall; but when Elzevir sat down, the boy gave a careful look round, and seeing no one watching any more, dropped his whistling and made off as fast as heels would carry him. Then I knew that he had guessed who we were, and was off to warn the hue and cry; but before Elzevir was on his feet again, the boy was out of sight, over the hill-brow.

'Let us move on,' said Block; ''tis but a little distance now to go, and the heat is past already. We must have slept three hours or more, for thou art but a sorry watchman, John. 'Tis when the sentry sleeps that the enemy laughs, and for thee the posse might have had us both like daylight owls.'

With that he took me on his back and made off with a lusty stride, keeping as much as possible under the brow of the hill and in the shelter of the walls. We had slept longer than we thought, for the sun was westering fast, and though the rest had refreshed me, my leg had grown stiff, and hurt the more in dangling when we started again. Elzevir was still walking strongly, in spite of the heavy burden he carried, and in less than half an hour I knew, though I had never been there before, we were in the land of the old marble quarries at the back of Anvil Point.

Although I knew little of these quarries, and certainly was in evil plight to take note of anything at that time, yet afterwards I learnt much about them. Out of such excavations comes that black Purbeck Marble which you see in old churches in our country, and I am told in other parts of England as well. And the way of making a marble quarry is to sink a tunnel, slanting very steeply down into the earth, like a well turned askew, till you reach fifty, seventy, or perhaps one hundred feet deep. Then from the bottom of this shaft there spread out narrow passages or tunnels, mostly six feet high, but sometimes only three or four, and in these the marble is dug. These quarries were made by men centuries ago, some say by the Romans themselves; and though some are still worked in other parts of Purbeck, those at the back of Anvil Point have been disused beyond the memory of man.

We had left the stony village fields, and the face of the country was covered once more with the closest sward, which was just putting on the brighter green of spring. This turf was not smooth, but hummocky, for under it lay heaps of worthless stone and marble drawn out of the quarries ages ago, which the green vestment had covered for the most part, though it left sometimes a little patch of broken rubble peering out at the top of a mound. There were many tumble-down walls and low gables left of the cottages of the old quarrymen; grass-covered ridges marked out the little garden-folds, and here and there still stood a forlorn gooseberry-bush, or a stunted plum-or apple-tree with its branches all swept eastward by the up-Channel gales.

As for the quarry shafts themselves, they too were covered round the tips with the green turf, and down them led a narrow flight of steep-cut steps, with a slide of soap-stone at the side, on which the marble blocks were once hauled up by wooden winches. Down these steps no feet ever walked now, for not only were suffocating gases said to beset the bottom of the shafts, but men would have it that in the narrow passages below lurked evil spirits and demons. One who ought to know about such things, told me that when St. Aldhelm first came to Purbeck, he bound the old Pagan gods under a ban deep in these passages, but that the worst of all the crew was a certain demon called the Mandrive, who watched over the best of the black marble. And that was why such marble might only be used in churches or for graves, for if it were not for this holy purpose, the Mandrive would have power to strangle the man that hewed it.

It was by the side of one of these old shafts that Elzevir laid me down at last. The light was very low, showing all the little unevennesses of the turf; and the sward crept over the edges of the hole, and every crack and crevice in steps and slide was green with ferns. The green ferns shrouded the walls of the hole, and ruddy brown brambles overgrew the steps, till all was lost in the gloom that hung at the bottom of the pit.

Elzevir drew a deep breath or two of the cool evening air, like a man who has come through a difficult trial.

'There,' he said, 'this is Joseph's Pit, and here we must lie hid until thy foot is sound again. Once get to the bottom safe, and we can laugh at Posse, and hue and cry, and at the King's Crown itself. They cannot search all the quarries, and are not like to search any of them, for they are cowards at the best, and hang much on tales of the Mandrive. Ay, and such tales are true enough, for there lurk gases at the bottom of most of the shafts, like devils to strangle any that go down. And if they do come down this Joseph's Pit, we still have nineteen chances in a score they cannot thread the workings. But last, if they come down, and thread the path, there is this pistol and a rusty matchlock; and before they come to where we lie, we can hold the troop at bay and sell our lives so dear they will not care to buy them.'

We waited a few minutes, and then he took me in his arms and began to descend the steps, back first, as one goes down a hatchway. The sun was setting in a heavy bank of clouds just as we began to go down, and I could not help remembering how I had seen it set over peaceful Moonfleet only twenty-four hours ago; and how far off we were now, and how long it was likely to be before I saw that dear village and Grace again.

The stairs were still sharp cut and little worn, but Elzevir paid great care to his feet, lest he should slip on the ferns and mosses with which they were overgrown. When we reached the brambles he met them with his back, and though I heard the thorns tearing in his coat, he shoved them aside with his broad shoulders, and screened my dangling leg from getting caught. Thus he came safe without stumble to the bottom of the pit.

When we got there all was dark, but he stepped off into a narrow opening on the right hand, and walked on as if he knew the way. I could see nothing, but perceived that we were passing through endless galleries cut in the solid rock, high enough, for the most part, to allow of walking upright, but sometimes so low as to force him to bend down and carry me in a very constrained attitude. Only twice did he set me down at a turning, while he took out his tinder-box and lit a match; but at length the darkness became less dark, and I saw that we were in a large cave or room, into which the light came through some opening at the far end. At the same time I felt a colder breath and fresh salt smell in the air that told me we were very near the sea.

Chapter 11: The Sea-Cave

The dull loneness, the black shade,
That these hanging vaults have made:
The strange music of the waves
Beating on these hollow caves—Wither

He set me down in one corner, where was some loose dry silver-sand upon the floor, which others had perhaps used for a resting-place before. 'Thou must lie here for a month or two, lad,' he said; ''tis a mean bed, but I have known many worse, and will get straw tomorrow if I can, to better it.'

I had eaten nothing all day, nor had Elzevir, yet I felt no hunger, only a giddiness and burning thirst like that which came upon me when I was shut in the Mohune vault. So 'twas very music to me to hear a pat and splash of water dropping from the roof into a little pool upon the floor, and Elzevir made a cup out of my hat and gave a full drink of it that was icy-cool and more delicious than any smuggled wine of France.

And after that I knew little that happened for ten days or more, for fever had hold of me, and as I learnt afterwards, I talked wild and could scarce be restrained from jumping up and loosing the bindings that Elzevir had put upon my leg. And all that time he nursed me as tenderly as any mother could her child, and never left the cave except when he was forced to seek food. But after the fever passed it left me very thin, as I could see from hands and arms, and weaker than a baby; and I used to lie the whole day, not thinking much, nor troubling about anything, but eating what was given me and drawing a quiet pleasure from the knowledge that strength was gradually returning. Elzevir had found a battered sea-chest up on Peveril Point, and from the side of it made splints to set my leg—using his own shirt for bandages. The sand-bed too was made more soft and easy with some armfuls of straw, and in one corner of the cave was a little pile of driftwood and an iron cooking-pot. And all these things had Elzevir got by foraging of nights, using great care that none should see him, and taking only what would not be much missed or thought about; but soon he contrived to give Ratsey word of where we were, and after that the sexton fended for us.

There were none even of the landers knew what was become of us, save only Ratsey; and he never came down the quarry, but would leave what he brought in one of the ruined cottages a half-mile from the shaft. And all the while there was strict search being made for us, and mounted Excisemen scouring the country; for though at first the Posse took back Maskew's dead body and said we must have fallen over the cliff, for there was nothing to be found of us, yet afterwards a farm-boy brought a tale of how he had come suddenly on men lurking under a wall, and how one had a bloody foot and leg, and how the other sprung upon him and after a fierce struggle wrenched his master's rook-piece from his hands, rifled his pocket of a powder-horn, and made off with them like a hare towards Corfe.

And as to Maskew, some of the soldiers said that Elzevir had shot him, and others that he died by misadventure, being killed by a stray bullet of one of his own men on the hill-top; but for all that they put a head-price on Elzevir of 50, and 20 for me, so we had reason to lie close. It must have been Maskew that listened that night at the door when Elzevir told me the hour at which the cargo was to be run; for the Posse had been ordered to be at Hoar Head at four in the morning. So all the gang would have been taken had it not been for the *Gulder* making earlier, and the soldiers being delayed by tippling at the Lobster.

All this Elzevir learnt from Ratsey and told me to pass the time, though in truth I had as lief not heard it, for 'tis no pleasant thing to see one's head wrote down so low as 20. And what I wanted most to know, namely how Grace fared and how she took the bad news of her father's death, I could not hear, for Elzevir said nothing, and I was shy to ask him.

Now when I came entirely to myself, and was able to take stock of things, I found that the place in which I lay was a cave some eight yards square and three in height, whose straight-cut walls showed that men had once hewed stone therefrom. On one side was that passage through which we had come in, and on the other opened a sort of door which gave on to a stone ledge eight fathoms above high-water mark. For the cave was cut out just inside that iron cliff-face which lies between St. Alban's Head and Swanage. But the cliffs here are different from those on the other side of the Head, being neither so high as Hoar Head nor of chalk, but standing for the most part only an hundred or an hundred and fifty feet above the sea, and showing towards it a stern face of solid rock.

But though they rise not so high above the water, they go down a long way below it; so that there is fifty fathom right up to the cliff, and many a good craft out of reckoning in fog, or on a pitch-dark night, has run full against that frowning wall, and perished, ship and crew, without a soul to hear their cries. Yet, though the rock looks hard as adamant, the eternal washing of the wave has worn it out below, and even with the slightest swell there is a dull and distant booming of the surge in those cavernous deeps; and when the wind blows fresh, each roller smites the cliff like a thunder-clap, till even the living rock trembles again.

It was on a ledge of that rock-face that our cave opened, and sometimes on a fine day Elzevir would carry me out thither, so that I might sun myself and see all the moving Channel without myself being seen. For this ledge was carved out something like a balcony, so that when the quarry was in working they could lower the stone by pulleys to boats lying underneath, and perhaps haul up a keg or two by the way of ballast, as might be guessed by the stanchions still rusting in the rock.

Such was this gallery; and as for the inside of the cave, 'twas a great empty room, with a white floor made up of broken stone-dust trodden hard of old till one would say it was plaster; and dry, without those sweaty damps so often seen in such places—save only in one corner a land-spring dropped from the roof trickling down over spiky rock-icicles, and falling into a little hollow in the floor. This basin had been scooped out of set purpose, with a gutter seaward for the overflow, and round it and on the wet patch of the roof above grew a garden of ferns and other clinging plants.

The weeks moved on until we were in the middle of May, when even the nights were no longer cold, as the sun gathered power. And with the warmer days my strength too increased, and though I dared not yet stand, my leg had ceased to pain me, except for some sharp twinges now and then, which Elzevir said were caused by the bone setting. And then he would put a poultice made of grass upon the place, and once walked almost as far as Chaldron to pluck sorrel for a soothing mash.

Now though he had gone out and in so many times in safety, yet I was always ill at ease when he was away, lest he might fall into some ambush and never come back. Nor was it any thought of what would come to me if he were caught that grieved me, but only care for him; for I had come to lean in everything upon this grim and grizzled giant, and love him like a father. So when he was away I took to reading to beguile my thoughts; but found little choice of matter, having only my aunt's red Prayer-book that I thrust into my bosom the afternoon that I left Moonfleet, and Blackbeard's locket. For that locket hung always round my neck; and I often had the parchment out and read it; not that I did not know it now by heart, but because reading it seemed to bring Grace to my thoughts, for the last time I had read it was when I saw her in the Manor woods.

Elzevir and I had often talked over what was to be done when my leg should be sound again, and resolved to take passage to St. Malo in the *Bonaventure*, and there lie hid till the pursuit against us should have ceased. For though 'twas wartime, French and English were as brothers in the contraband, and the shippers would give us bit and sup, and glad to, as long as we had need of them. But of this I need not say more, because 'twas but a project, which other events came in to overturn.

Yet 'twas this very errand, namely, to fix with the *Bonaventure*'s men the time to take us over to the other side, that Elzevir had gone out, on the day of which I shall now speak. He was to go to Poole, and left our cave in the afternoon, thinking it safe to keep along the cliff-edge even in the daylight, and to strike across country when dusk came on. The wind had blown fresh all the morning from south-west, and after Elzevir had left, strengthened to a gale. My leg was now so strong that I could walk across the cave with the help of a stout blackthorn that Elzevir had cut me: and so I went out that afternoon on to the ledge to watch the growing sea. There I sat down, with my back against a protecting rock, in such a place that I could see up-Channel and yet shelter from the rushing wind.

The sky was overcast, and the long wall of rock showed grey with orange-brown patches and a darker line of sea-weed at the base like the under strake of a boat's belly, for the tide was but beginning to make. There was a mist, half-fog, half-spray, scudding before the wind, and through it I could see the white-backed rollers lifting over Peveril Point; while all along the cliff-face the sea-birds thronged the ledges, and sat huddled in snowy lines, knowing the mischief that was brewing in the elements.

It was a melancholy scene, and bred melancholy in my heart; and about sun-down the wind southed a point or two, setting the sea more against the cliff, so that the spray began to fly even over my ledge and drove me back into the cave. The night came on much sooner than usual, and before long I was lying on my straw bed in perfect darkness. The wind had gone still more to south, and was screaming through the opening of the cave; the caverns down below bellowed and rumbled; every now and then a giant roller struck the rock such a blow as made the cave tremble, and then a second later there would fall, splattering on the ledge outside, the heavy spray that had been lifted by the impact.

I have said that I was melancholy; but worse followed, for I grew timid, and fearful of the wild night, and the loneliness, and the darkness. And all sorts of evil tales came to my mind, and I thought much of baleful heathen gods that St. Aldhelm had banished to these underground cellars, and of the Mandrive who leapt on people in the dark and strangled them. And then fancy played another trick on me, and I seemed to see a man lying on the cave-floor with a drawn white face upturned, and a red hole in the forehead; and at last could bear the dark no longer, but got up with my lame leg and groped round till I found a candle, for we had two or three in store. 'Twas only with much ado I got it lit and set up in the corner of the cave, and then I sat down close by trying to screen it with my coat. But do what I would the wind came gusting round the corner, blowing the flame to one side, and making the candle gutter as another candle guttered on that black day at the Why Not? And so thought whisked round till I saw Maskew's face wearing a look of evil triumph, when the pin fell at the auction, and again his face grew deadly pale, and there was the bullet-mark on his brow.

Surely there were evil spirits in this place to lead my thoughts so much astray, and then there came to my mind that locket on my neck, which men had once hung round Blackbeard's to scare evil spirits from his tomb. If it could frighten them from him, might it not rout them now, and make them fly from me? And with that thought I took the parchment out, and opening it before the flickering light, although I knew all, word for word, conned it over again, and read it out aloud. It was a relief to hear a human voice, even though 'twas nothing but my own, and I took to shouting the words, having much ado even so to make them heard for the raging of the storm:

> *'The days of our age are threescore years and ten; and though men be so strong that they come to fourscore years: yet is their strength then but labour and sorrow; so soon passeth it away, and we are gone.*
> *'And as for me, my feet were almost . . .'*

At the 'almost' I stopped, being brought up suddenly with a fierce beat of blood through my veins, and a jump fit to burst them, for I had heard a scuffling noise in the passage that led to the cave, as if someone had stumbled against a loose stone in the dark. I did not know then, but have learnt since, that where there is a loud noise, such as the roaring of a cascade, the churning of a mill, or, as here, the rage and bluster of a storm—if there arise some different sound, even though it be as slight as the whistle of a bird, 'twill strike the ear clear above the general din. And so it was this night, for I caught that stumbling tread even when the gale blew loudest, and sat motionless and breathless, in my eagerness of listening, and then the gale lulled an instant, and I heard the slow beat of footsteps as of one groping his way down the passage in the dark.

I knew it was not Elzevir, for first he could not be back from Poole for many hours yet, and second, he always whistled in a certain way to show 'twas he coming and gave besides a pass-word; yet, if not Elzevir, who could it be? I blew out the light, for I did not want to guide the aim of some unknown marksman shooting at me from the dark; and then I thought of that gaunt strangler that sprang on marbleworkers in the gloom; yet it could not be the Mandrive, for surely he would know his own passages better than to stumble in them in the dark. It was more likely to be one of the hue and cry who had smelt us out, and hoped perhaps to be able to reconnoitre without being perceived on so awful a night. Whenever Elzevir went out foraging, he carried with him that silver-butted pistol which had once been Maskew's, but left behind the old rook-piece. We had plenty of powder and slugs now, having obtained a store of both from Ratsey, and Elzevir had bid me keep the matchlock charged, and use it or not after my own judgement, if any came to the cave; but gave as his counsel that it was better to die fighting than to swing at Dorchester, for that we should most certainly do if taken. We had agreed, moreover, on a pass-word, which was *Prosper the Bonaventure*, so that I might challenge betimes any that I heard coming, and if they gave not back this countersign might know it was not Elzevir.

So now I reached out for the piece, which lay beside me on the floor, and scrambled to my feet; lifting the deckle in the darkness, and feeling with my fingers in the pan to see 'twas full of powder.

The lull in the storm still lasted, and I heard the footsteps advancing, though with uncertain slowness, and once after a heavy stumble I thought I caught a muttereth oath, as if someone had struck his foot against a stone.

Then I shouted out clear in the darkness a 'Who goes there?' that rang again through the stone roofs. The footsteps stopped, but there was no answer. 'Who goes there?' I repeated. 'Answer, or I fire.'

'*Prosper the Bonaventure,*' came back out of the darkness, and I knew that I was safe. 'The devil take thee for a hot-blooded young bantam to shoot thy best friend with powder and ball, that he was fool enough to give thee'; and by this time I had guessed 'twas Master Ratsey, and recognized his voice. 'I would have let thee hear soon enough that 'twas I, if I had known I was so near thy lair; but 'tis more than a man's life is worth to creep down moleholes in the dark, and on a night like this. And why I could not get out the gibberish about the *Bonaventure* sooner, was because I matched my shin to break a stone, and lost the wager and my breath together. And when my wind returned 'tis very like that I was trapped into an oath, which is sad enough for me, who am sexton, and so to say in small orders of the Church of England as by law established.'

By the time I had put down the gun and coaxed the candle again to light, Ratsey stepped into the cave. He wore a sou'wester, and was dripping with wet, but seemed glad to see me and shook me by the hand. He was welcome enough to me also, for he banished the dreadful loneliness, and his coming was a bit out of my old pleasant life that lay so far away, and seemed to bring me once more within reach of some that were dearest.

CHAPTER 12: A FUNERAL

How he lies in his rights of a man!
Death has done all death can—Browning

We stood for a moment holding one another's hands; then Ratsey spoke. 'John, these two months have changed thee from boy to man. Thou wast a child when I turned that morning as we went up Hoar Head with the pack-horses, and looked back on thee and Elzevir below, and Maskew lying on the ground. 'Twas a sorry business, and has broken up the finest gang that ever ran a cargo, besides driving thee and Elzevir to hide in caves and dens of the earth. Thou shouldst have come with us that morn; not have stayed behind. The work was too rough for boys: the skipper should have piped the reefing-hands.'

It was true enough, or seemed to me true then, for I felt much cast down; but only said, 'Nay, Master Ratsey, where Master Block stays, there I must stay too, and where he goes I follow.'

Then I sat down upon the bed in the corner, feeling my leg began to ache; and the storm, which had lulled for a few minutes, came up again all the fiercer with wilder gusts and showers of spray and rain driving into the cave from seaward. So I was scarce sat down when in came a roaring blast, filling even our corner with cold, wet air, that quenched the weakling candle flame.

'God save us, what a night!' Ratsey cried.

'God save poor souls at sea,' said I.

'Amen to that,' says he, 'and would that every Amen I have said had come as truly from my heart. There will be sea enough on Moonfleet Beach this night to lift a schooner to the top of it, and launch her down into the fields behind. I had as lief be in the Mohune vault as in this fearsome place, and liefer too, if half the tales men tell are true of faces that may meet one here. For God's sake let us light a fire, for I caught sight of a store of driftwood before that sickly candle went out.'

It was some time before we got a fire alight, and even after the flame had caught well hold, the rush of the wind would every now and again blow the smoke into our eyes, or send a shower of sparks dancing through the cave. But by degrees the logs began to glow clear white, and such a cheerful warmth came out, as was in itself a solace and remedy for man's afflictions.

'Ah!' said Ratsey, 'I was shrammed with wet and cold, and half-dead with this baffling wind. It is a blessed thing a fire,' and he unbuttoned his pilot-coat, 'and needful now, if ever. My soul is very low, lad, for this place has strange memories for me; and I recollect, forty years ago (when I was just a boy like thee), old lander Jordan's gang, and I among them, were in this very cave on such another night. I was new to the trade then, as thou might be, and could not sleep for noise of wind and sea. And in the small hours of an autumn morning, as I lay here, just where we lie now, I heard such wailing cries above the storm, ay, and such shrieks of women, as made my blood run cold and have not yet forgot them.

And so I woke the gang who were all deep asleep as seasoned *contrabandiers* should be; but though we knew that there were fellow-creatures fighting for their lives in the seething flood beneath us, we could not stir hand or foot to save them, for nothing could be seen for rain and spray, and 'twas not till next morning that we learned the *Florida* had foundered just below with every soul on board. Ay, 'tis a queer life, and you and Block are in a queer strait now, and that is what I came to tell you. See here.' And he took out of his pocket an oblong strip of printed paper:

★★★★★★

G.R.

Whitehall, 15 May 1758

Whereas it hath been humbly represented to the king that on Friday, the night of the 16th of April last, *Thomas Maskew*, a justice of the peace, was most inhumanly murdered at Hoar Head, a lone place in the parish of Chaldron, in the County of Dorset, by one *Elzevir Block* and one *John Trenchard*, both of the parish of Moonfleet, in the aforesaid county: His Majesty, for the better discovering and bringing to justice these persons, is pleased to promise His Most Gracious *pardon* to any of the persons concerned therein, except the persons who actually committed the said murder; and, as a further encouragement, a *reward of fifty pounds* to any person who shall furnish such *information* as shall lead to the *apprehension* of the said *Elzevir Block*, and a *reward of twenty pounds* to any *person* who shall furnish such *information* as shall lead to the *apprehension* of the said *John Trenchard*. Such *information* to be given to *me*, or to the *governour* of *His Majesty's gaol* in Dorchester.

Holdernesse.

★★★★★★

'There—that's the bill,' he said; 'and a vastly fine piece it is, and yet I wish that 'twas played with other actors. Now, in Moonfleet there is none that know your hiding-place, and not a man, nor woman either, that would tell if they knew it ten times over. But fifty pounds for Elzevir, and twenty pounds for an empty pumpkin-top like thine, is a fair round sum, and there are vagabonds about this countryside scurvy enough to try to earn it. And some of these have set the Excisemen on *my* track, with tales of how it is I that know where you lie hid, and bring you meat and drink. So it is that I cannot stir abroad now, no,

101

not even to the church o' Sundays, without having some rogue lurking at my heels to watch my movements. And that is why I chose such a night to come hither, knowing these knaves like dry skins, but never thinking that the wind would blow like this. I am come to tell Block that 'tis not safe for me to be so much in Purbeck, and that I dare no longer bring food or what not, or these man-hounds will scent you out. Your leg is sound again, and 'tis best to be flitting while you may, and there's the *Eperon d'Or*, and *Chauvelais* to give you welcome on the other side.'

I told him how Elzevir was gone this very night to Poole to settle with the *Bonaventure*, when she should come to take us off; and at that Ratsey seemed pleased. There were many things I wished to learn of him, and especially how Grace did, but felt a shyness, and durst not ask him. And he said no more for a minute, seeming low-hearted and crouching over the fire. So we sat huddled in the corner by the glowing logs, the red light flickering on the cave roof, and showing the lines on Ratsey's face; while the steam rose from his drying clothes. The gale blew as fiercely as ever, but the tide had fallen, and there was not so much spray coming into the cave. Then Ratsey spoke again—

'My heart is very heavy, John, tonight, to think how all the good old times are gone, and how that Master Block can never again go back to Moonfleet. It was as fine a lander's crew as ever stood together, not even excepting Captain Jordan's, and now must all be broken up; for this mess of Maskew's has made the place too hot to hold us, and 'twill be many a long day before another cargo's run on Moonfleet Beach. But how to get the liquor out of Mohune's vault I know not; and that reminds me, I have something in my pouches for Elzevir an' thee'; and with that he drew forth either lapel a great wicker-bound flask. He put one to his lips, tilting it and drinking long and deep, and then passed it to me, with a sigh of satisfaction. 'Ah, that has the right smack. Here, take it, child, and warm thy heart; 'tis the true milk of Ararat, and the last thou'lt taste this side the Channel.'

Then I drank too, but lightly, for the good liquor was no stranger to me, though it was only so few months ago that I had tasted it for the first time in the Why Not? and in a minute it tingled in my fingertips. Soon a grateful sense of warmth and comfort stole over me, and our state seemed not so desperate, nor even the night so wild. Ratsey, too, wore a more cheerful air, and the lines in his face were not so deeply marked; the golden, sparkling influence of the flask had loosed his tongue, and he was talking now of what I most wanted to hear.

'Yes, yes, it is a sad break-up, and what will happen to the old Why Not? I cannot tell. None have passed the threshold since you left, only the Duchy men came and sealed the doors, making it felony to force them. And even these lawyer chaps know not where the right stands, for Maskew never paid a rent and died before he took possession; and Master Block's term is long expired, and now he is in hiding and an outlaw.

'But I am sorriest for Maskew's girl, who grows thin and pale as any lily. For when the soldiers brought the body back, the men stood at their doors and cursed the clay, and some of the fishwives spat at it; and old Mother Veitch, who kept house for him, swore he had never paid her a penny of wages, and that she was afear'd to stop under the same roof with such an evil corpse. So out she goes from the Manor House, leaving that poor child alone in it with her dead father; and there were not wanting some to say it was all a judgement; and called to mind how Elzevir had been once left alone with his dead son at the Why Not? But in the village there was not a man that doubted that 'twas Block had sent Maskew to his account, nor did I doubt it either, till a tale got abroad that he was killed by a stray shot fired by the Posse from the cliff. And when they took the hue-and-cry papers to the Manor House for his lass, as next of kin, to sign the requisition, she would not set her name to it, saying that Block had never lifted his hand against her father when they met at Moonfleet or on the road, and that she never would believe he was the man to let his anger sleep so long and then attack an enemy in cold blood. And as for thee, she knew thee for a trusty lad, who would not do such things himself, nor yet stand by whilst others did them.'

Now what Ratsey said was sweeter than any music in my ears, and I felt myself a better man, as anyone must of whom a true woman speaks well, and that I must live uprightly to deserve such praise. Then I resolved that come what might I would make my way once more to Moonfleet, before we fled from England, and see Grace; so that I might tell her all that happened about her father's death, saving only that Elzevir had meant himself to put Maskew away; for it was no use to tell her this when she had said that he could never think to do such a thing, and besides, for all I knew, he never did mean to shoot, but only to frighten him. Though I thus resolved, I said nothing of it to Master Ratsey, but only nodded, and he went on—

'Well, seeing there was no one save this poor girl to look to putting Maskew under ground, I must needs take it in hand myself; roughing together a sound coffin and digging as fair a grave for him as could be made for any lord, except that lords have always vaults to sleep in. Then I got Mother Nutting's fish-cart to carry the body down, for there was not a man in Moonfleet would lay hand to the coffin to bear it; and off we started down the street, I leading the wall-eyed pony, and the coffin following on the trolley. There was no mourner to see him home except his daughter, and she without a bit of black upon her, for she had no time to get her crapes; and yet she needed none, having grief writ plain enough upon her face.

'When we got to the churchyard, a crowd was gathered there, men and women and children, not only from Moonfleet but from Ringstave and Monkbury. They were not come to mourn, but to make gibes to show how much they hated him, and many of the children had old pots and pans for rough music. Parson Glennie was waiting in the church, and there he waited, for the cart could not pass the gate, and we had no bearers to lift the coffin. Then I looked round to see if there was any that would help to lift, but when I tried to meet a man's eye he looked away, and all I could see was the bitter scowling faces of the women. And all the while the girl stood by the trolley looking on the ground. She had a little kerchief over her head that let the hair fall about her shoulders, and her face was very white, with eyes red and swollen through weeping. But when she knew that all that crowd was there to mock her father, and that there was not a man would raise hand to lift him, she laid her head upon the coffin, hiding her face in her hands, and sobbed bitterly.'

Ratsey stopped for a moment and drank again deep at the flask; and as for me, I still said nothing, feeling a great lump in my throat; and reflecting how hatred and passion have power to turn men to brutes.

'I am a rough man,' Ratsey resumed, 'but tender-like withal, and when I saw her weep, I ran off to the church to tell the parson how it was, and beg him to come out and try if we two could lift the coffin. So out he came just as he was, with surplice on his back and book in hand. But when the men knew what he was come for, and looked upon that tall, fair girl bowed down over her father's coffin, their hearts were moved, and first Tom Tewkesbury stepped out with a sheepish air, and then Garrett, and then four others. So now we had six fine bearers, and 'twas only women that could still look hard and scowling, and even they said no word, and not a boy beat on his pan.

'Then Mr. Glennie, seeing he was not wanted for bearer, changed to parson, and strikes up with "I am the resurrection and the life". 'Tis a great text, John, and though I've heard it scores and scores of times, it never sounded sweeter than on that day. For 'twas a fine afternoon, and what with their being no wind, but the sun bright and the sea still and blue, there was a calm on everything that seemed to say "Rest in Peace, Rest in Peace". And was not the spring with us, and the whole land preaching of resurrection, the birds singing, trees and flowers waking from their winter sleep, and cowslips yellow on the very graves? Then surely 'tis a fond thing to push our enmities beyond the grave, and perhaps even *he* was not so bad as we held him, but might have tricked himself into thinking he did right to hunt down the contraband. I know not how it was, but something like this came into my mind, and did perhaps to others, for we got him under without a sign or word from any that stood there.

'There was not one sound heard inside the church or out, except Mr. Glennie's reading and my amens, and now and then a sob from the poor child. But when 'twas all over, and the coffin safe lowered, up she walks to Tom Tewkesbury saying, through her tears "I thank you, sir, for your kindness," and holds out her hand. So he took it, looking askew, and afterwards the five other bearers; and then she walked away by herself, and no one moved till she had left the churchyard gate, letting her pass out like a queen.'

'And so she is a queen,' I said, not being able to keep from speaking, for very pride to hear how she had borne herself, and because she had always shown kindness to me. 'So she is, and fairer than any queen to boot.'

Ratsey gave me a questioning look, and I could see a little smile upon his face in the firelight. 'Ay, she is fair enough,' said he, as though reflecting to himself, 'but white and thin. Mayhap she would make a match for thee—if ye were man and woman, and not boy and girl; if she were not rich, and thou not poor and an outlaw; and—if she would have thee.'

It vexed me to hear his banter, and to think how I had let my secret out, so I did not answer, and we sat by the embers for a while without speaking, while the wind still blew through the cave like a funnel.

Ratsey spoke first. 'John, pass me the flask; I can hear voices mounting the cliff of those poor souls of the *Florida*.'

With that he took another heavy pull, and flung a log on the fire, till sparks flew about as in a smithy, and the flame that had slumbered woke again and leapt out white, blue, and green from the salt wood.

Now, as the light danced and flickered I saw a piece of parchment lying at Ratsey's feet: and this was none other than the writing out of Blackbeard's locket, which I had been reading when I first heard footsteps in the passage, and had dropped in my alarm of hostile visitors. Ratsey saw it too, and stretched out his hand to pick it up. I would have concealed it if I could, because I had never told him how I had rifled Blackbeard's coffin, and did not want to be questioned as to how I had come by the writing. But to try to stop him getting hold of it would only have spurred his curiosity, and so I said nothing when he took it in his hands.

'What is this, son?' asked he.

'It is only Scripture verses,' I answered, 'which I got some time ago. 'Tis said they are a spell against Spirits of Evil, and I was reading them to keep off the loneliness of this place, when you came in and made me drop them.'

I was afraid lest he should ask whence I had got them, but he did not, thinking perhaps that my aunt had given them to me. The heat of the flames had curled the parchment a little, and he spread it out on his knee, conning it in the firelight.

''Tis well written,' he said, 'and good verses enough, but he who put them together for a spell knew little how to keep off evil spirits, for this would not keep a flea from a black cat. I could do ten times better myself, being not without some little understanding of such things,' and he nodded seriously; 'and though I never yet met any from the other world, they would not take me unprepared if they should come. For I have spent half my life in graveyard or church, and 'twould be as foolish to move about such places and have no words to meet an evil visitor withal, as to bear money on a lonely road without a pistol. So one day, after Parson Glennie had preached from Habakkuk, how that "the vision is for an appointed time, but at the end it shall speak and not lie: though it tarry, wait for it, because it will surely come, it will not tarry", I talked with him on these matters, and got from him three or four rousing texts such as spectres fear more than a burned child does the fire. I will learn them all to thee some day, but for the moment take this Latin which I got by heart: "*Abite a me in ignem eternum qui paratus est diabolo at angelis ejus.*" Englished it means: "*Depart from me into eternal fire prepared for the devil and his angels,*" but hath at least double that power in Latin.

'So get that after me by heart, and use it freely if thou art led to think that there are evil presences near, and in such lonely places as this cave.' I humoured him by doing as he desired; and that the rather because I hoped his thoughts would thus be turned away from the writing; but as soon as I had the spell by rote he turned back to the parchment, saying, 'He was but a poor divine who wrote this, for beside choosing ill-fitting verses, he cannot even give right numbers to them. For see here, "The days of our age are three-score years and ten; and though men be so strong that they come to four-score years, yet is their strength then but labour and sorrow, so soon passeth it away and we are gone", and he writes Psalm 90,21. Now I have said that Psalm with parson verse and verse about for every sleeper we have laid to rest in churchyard mould for thirty years; and know it hath not twenty verses in it, all told, and this same verse is the clerk's verse and cometh tenth, and yet he calls it twenty-first. I wish I had here a Common Prayer, and I would prove my words.'

He stopped and flung me back the parchment scornfully; but I folded it and slipped it in my pocket, brooding all the while over a strange thought that his last words had brought to me. Nor did I tell him that I had by me my aunt's prayer-book, wishing to examine for myself more closely whether he was right, after he should have gone.

'I must be away,' he said at last, 'though loath to leave this good fire and liquor. I would fain wait till Elzevir was back, and fainer till this gale was spent, but it may not be; the nights are short, and I must be out of Purbeck before sunrise. So tell Block what I say, that he and thou must flit; and pass the flask, for I have fifteen miles to walk against the wind, and must keep off these midnight chills.'

He drank again, and then rose to his feet, shaking himself like a dog; and walking briskly across the cave twice or thrice to make sure, as I thought, that the Ararat milk had not confused his steps. Then he shook my hand warmly, and disappeared in the deep shadow of the passage-mouth.

The wind was blowing more fitfully than before, and there was some sign of a lull between the gusts. I stood at the opening of the passage, and listened till the echo of Ratsey's footsteps died away, and then returning to the corner, flung more wood on the fire, and lit the candle. After that I took out again the parchment, and also my aunt's red prayer-book, and sat down to study them. First I looked out in the book that text about the '*days of our life*', and found that it was indeed in the ninetieth Psalm, but the tenth verse, just as Ratsey said, and not the twenty-first as it was writ on the parchment. And then I took the second text, and here again the Psalm was given correct, but the verse was two, and not six, as my scribe had it.

It was just the same with the other three—the number of the Psalm was right but the verse wrong. So here was a discovery, for all was painfully written smooth and clean without a blot, and yet in every verse an error. But if the second number did not stand for the verse, what else should it mean? I had scarce formed the question to myself before I had the answer, and knew that it must be the number of the word chosen in each text to make a secret meaning. I was in as great a fever and excitement now as when I found the locket in the Mohune vault, and could scarce count with trembling fingers as far as twenty-one, in the first verse, for hurry and amaze. It was 'fourscore' that the number fell on in the first text, 'feet' in the second, 'deep' in the third, 'well' in the fourth, 'north' in the fifth.

Fourscore—feet—deep—well—north.

There was the cipher read, and what an easy trick! and yet I had not lighted on it all this while, nor ever should have, but for Sexton Ratsey and his burial verse. It was a cunning plan of Blackbeard; but other folk were quite as cunning as he, and here was all his treasure at our feet. I chuckled over that to myself, rubbing my hands, and read it through again:

Fourscore—feet—deep—well—north.

'Twas all so simple, and the word in the fourth verse 'well' and not 'vale' or 'pool' as I had stuck at so often in trying to unriddle it. How was it I had not guessed as much before? and here was something to tell Elzevir when he came back, that the clue was found to the cipher, and the secret out. I would not reveal it all at once, but tease him by making him guess, and at last tell him everything, and we would set to work at once to make ourselves rich men. And then I thought once more of Grace, and how the laugh would be on my side now, for all Master Ratsey's banter about her being rich and me being poor!

Fourscore—feet-deep—well—north.

I read it again, and somehow it was this time a little less dear, and I fell to thinking what it was exactly that I should tell Elzevir, and how we were to get to work to find the treasure. 'Twas hid in a *well*—that was plain enough, but in what well?—and what did 'north' mean? Was it the *north well*, or to *north of the well*—or, was it fourscore feet *north* of the *deep well*? I stared at the verses as if the ink would change colour and show some other sense, and then a veil seemed drawn across the writing, and the meaning to slip away, and be as far as ever from my grasp. *Fourscore—feet—deep—well—north*: and by degrees exulting gladness gave way to bewilderment and disquiet of spirit, and in the gusts of wind I heard Blackbeard himself laughing and mocking me for thinking I had found his treasure. Still I read and re-read it, juggling with the words and turning them about to squeeze new meaning from them.

'Fourscore feet deep *in the north well*,'—' 'fourscore feet deep in the well *to north*'—'fourscore feet *north of the deep well*,'—so the words went round and round in my head, till I was tired and giddy, and fell unawares asleep.

It was daylight when I awoke, and the wind had fallen, though I could still hear the thunder of the swell against the rock-face down below. The fire was yet burning, and by it sat Elzevir, cooking something in the pot. He looked fresh and keen, like a man risen from a long night's sleep, rather than one who had spent the hours of darkness in struggling against a gale, and must afterwards remain watching because, forsooth, the sentinel sleeps.

He spoke as soon as he saw that I was awake, laughing and saying: 'How goes the night, Watchman? This is the second time that I have caught thee napping, and didst sleep so sound it might have taken a cold pistol's lips against thy forehead to awake thee.'

I was too full of my story even to beg his pardon, but began at once to tell him what had happened; and how, by following the hint that Ratsey dropped, I had made out, as I thought, a secret meaning in these verses. Elzevir heard me patiently, and with more show of interest towards the end; and then took the parchment in his hands, reading it carefully, and checking the errors of numbering by the help of the red prayer-book.

'I believe thou art right,' he said at length; 'for why should the figures all be false if there is no hidden trickery in it? If 't had been one or two were wrong, I would have said some priest had copied them in error; for priests are thriftless folk, and had as lief set a thing down wrong as right; but with all wrong there is no room for chance. So if he means it, let us see what 'tis he means. First he says 'tis in a well. But what well? and the depth he gives of fourscore feet is over-deep for any well near Moonfleet.'

I was for saying it must be the well at the Manor House, but before the words left my mouth, remembered there was no well at the manor at all, for the house was watered by a runnel brook that broke out from the woods above, and jumping down from stone to stone ran through the manor gardens, and emptied itself into the Fleet below.

'And now I come to think on it,' Elzevir went on, "tis more likely that the well he speaks of was not in these parts at all. For see here, this Blackboard was a spendthrift, squandering all he had, and would most surely have squandered the jewel too, could he have laid his hands on it. And yet 'tis said he did not, therefore I think he must have stowed it safe in some place where afterwards he could not get at it. For if 't had been near Moonfleet, he would have had it up a hundred times. But thou hast often talked of Blackbeard and his end with Parson Glennie; so speak up, lad, and let us hear all that thou know'st of these tales. Maybe 'twill help us to come to some judgement.'

So I told him all that Mr. Glennie had told me, how that Colonel John Mohune, whom men called Blackbeard, was a wastrel from his youth, and squandered all his substance in riotous living. Thus being at his last turn, he changed from royalist to rebel, and was set to guard the king in the castle of Carisbrooke. But there he stooped to a bribe, and took from his royal prisoner a splendid diamond of the crown to let him go; then, with the jewel in his pocket, turned traitor again, and showed a file of soldiers into the room where the king was stuck between the window bars, escaping.

But no one trusted Blackbeard after that, and so he lost his post, and came back in his age, a broken man, to Moonfleet. There he rusted out his life, but when he neared his end was filled with fear, and sent for a clergyman to give him consolation. And 'twas at the parson's instance that he made a will, and bequeathed the diamond, which was the only thing he had left, to the Mohune almshouses at Moonfleet. These were the very houses that he had robbed and let go to ruin, and they never benefited by his testament, for when it was opened there was the bequest plain enough, but not a word to say where was the jewel. Some said that it was all a mockery, and that Blackbeard never had the jewel; others that the jewel was in his hand when he died, but carried off by some that stood by. But most thought, and handed down the tale, that being taken suddenly, he died before he could reveal the safe place of the jewel; and that in his last throes he struggled hard to speak as if he had some secret to unburden.

All this I told Elzevir, and he listened close as though some of it was new to him. When I was speaking of Blackbeard being at Carisbrooke, he made a little quick move as though to speak, but did not, waiting till I had finished the tale. Then he broke out with: 'John, the diamond is yet at Carisbrooke. I wonder I had not thought of Carisbrooke before you spoke; and there he can get fourscore feet, and twice and thrice fourscore, if he list, and none to stop him. 'Tis Carisbrooke. I have heard of that well from childhood, and once saw it when a boy. It is dug in the Castle Keep, and goes down fifty fathoms or more into the bowels of the chalk below. It is so deep no man can draw the buckets on a winch, but they must have an ass inside a tread-wheel to hoist them up. Now, why this Colonel John Mohune, whom we call Blackbeard, should have chosen a well at all to hide his jewel in, I cannot say; but given he chose a well, 'twas odds he would choose Carisbrooke. 'Tis a known place, and I have heard that people come as far as from London to see the castle and this well.'

He spoke quick and with more fire than I had known him use before, and I felt he was right. It seemed indeed natural enough that if Blackbeard was to hide the diamond in a well, it would be in the well of that very castle where he had earned it so evilly.

'When he says the "well north",' continued Elzevir, ''tis clear he means to take a compass and mark north by needle, and at eighty feet in the well-side below that point will lie the treasure. I fixed yesterday with the *Bonaventure's* men that they should lie underneath this ledge tomorrow sennight, if the sea be smooth, and take us off on the spring-tide. At midnight is their hour, and I said eight days on, to give thy leg a week wherewith to strengthen. I thought to make for St. Malo, and leave thee at the *Eperon d'Or* with old Chauvelais, where thou couldst learn to patter French until these evil times have blown by. But now, if thou art set to hunt this treasure up, and hast a mind to run thy head into a noose; why, I am not so old but that I too can play the fool, and we will let St. Malo be, and make for Carisbrooke. I know the castle; it is not two miles distant from Newport, and at Newport we can lie at the Bugle, which is an inn addicted to the contraband. The king's writ runs but lamely in the Channel Isles and Wight, and if we wear some other kit than this, maybe we shall find Newport as safe as St. Malo.'

This was just what I wanted, and so we settled there and then that we would get the *Bonaventure* to land us in the Isle of Wight instead of at St. Malo. Since man first walked upon this earth, a tale of buried treasure must have had a master-power to stir his blood, and mine was hotly stirred. Even Elzevir, though he did not show it, was moved, I thought, at heart; and we chafed in our cave prison, and those eight days went wearily enough. Yet 'twas not time lost, for every day my leg grew stronger; and like a wolf which I saw once in a cage at Dorchester Fair, I spent hours in marching round the cave to kill the time and put more vigour in my steps. Ratsey did not visit us again, but in spite of what he said, met Elzevir more than once, and got money for him from Dorchester and many other things he needed.

It was after meeting Ratsey that Elzevir came back one night, bringing a long whip in one hand, and in the other a bundle which held clothes to mask us in the next scene. There was a carter's smock for him, white and quilted over with needlework, such as carters wear on the Down farms, and for me a smaller one, and hats and leather leggings all to match. We tried them on, and were for all the world carter and carter's boy; and I laughed long to see Elzevir stand there and practise how to crack his whip and cry 'Who-ho' as carters do to horses. And for all he was so grave, there was a smile on his face too, and he showed me how to twist a wisp of straw out of the bed to bind above my ankles at the bottom of the leggings. He had cut off his beard, and yet lost nothing of his looks; for his jaw and deep chin showed firm and powerful. And as for me, we made a broth of young walnut leaves and twigs, and tanned my hands and face with it a ruddy brown, so that I looked a different lad.

CHAPTER 13: AN INTERVIEW

No human creature stirred to go or come,
No face looked forth from shut or open casement,
No chimney smoked, there was no sign of home
From parapet to basement—Hood

And so the days went on, until there came to be but two nights more before we were to leave our cave. Now I have said that the delay chafed us, because we were impatient to get at the treasure; but there was something else that vexed me and made me more unquiet with every day that passed. And this was that I had resolved to see Grace before I left these parts, and yet knew not how to tell it to Elzevir. But on this evening, seeing the time was grown so short, I knew that I must speak or drop my purpose, and so spoke.

We were sitting like the sea-birds on the ledge outside our cave, looking towards St. Alban's Head and watching the last glow of sunset. The evening vapours began to sweep down Channel, and Elzevir shrugged his shoulders. 'The night turns chill,' he said, and got up to go back to the cave. So then I thought my time was come, and following him inside said:

'Dear Master Elzevir, you have watched over me all this while and tended me kinder than any father could his son; and 'tis to you I owe my life, and that my leg is strong again. Yet I am restless this night, and beg that you will give me leave to climb the shaft and walk abroad. It is two months and more that I have been in the cave and seen nothing but stone walls, and I would gladly tread once more upon the Down.'

'Say not that I have saved thy life,' Elzevir broke in; "twas I who brought thy life in danger; and but for me thou mightst even now be lying snug abed at Moonfleet, instead of hiding in the chambers of these rocks. So speak not of that, but if thou hast a mind to air thyself an hour, I see little harm in it. These wayward fancies fall on men as they get better of sickness; and I must go tonight to that ruined house of which I spoke to thee, to fetch a pocket compass Master Ratsey was to put there. So thou canst come with me and smell the night air on the Down.'

He had agreed more readily than I looked for, and so I pushed the matter, saying:

'Nay, master, grant me leave to go yet a little farther afield. You know that I was born in Moonfleet, and have been bred there all my life, and love the trees and stream and very stones of it. And I have set my heart on seeing it once more before we leave these parts for good and all. So give me leave to walk along the Down and look on Moonfleet but this once, and in this ploughboy guise I shall be safe enough, and will come back to you tomorrow night'

He looked at me a moment without speaking; and all the while I felt he saw me through and through, and yet he was not angry. But I turned red, and cast my eyes upon the ground, and then he spoke:

'Lad, I have known men risk their lives for many things: for gold, and love, and hate; but never one would play with death that he might see a tree or stream or stones. And when men say they love a place or town, thou mayst be sure 'tis not the place they love but some that live there; or that they loved some in the past, and so would see the spot again to kindle memory withal. Thus when thou speakest of Moonfleet, I may guess that thou hast someone there to see—or hope to see. It cannot be thine aunt, for there is no love lost between ye; and besides, no man ever periled his life to bid *adieu* to an aunt. So have no secrets from me, John, but tell me straight, and I will judge whether

113

this second treasure that thou seekest is true gold enough to fling thy life into the scale against it.'

Then I told him all, keeping nothing back, but trying to make him see that there was little danger in my visiting Moonfleet, for none would know me in a carter's dress, and that my knowledge of the place would let me use a hedge or wall or wood for cover; and finally, if I were seen, my leg was now sound, and there were few could beat me in a running match upon the Down. So I talked on, not so much in the hope of convincing him as to keep saying something; for I durst not look up, and feared to hear an angry word from him when I should stop. But at last I had spoken all I could, and ceased because I had no more. Yet he did not break out as I had thought, but there was silence; and after a moment I looked up, and saw by his face that his thoughts were wandering. When he spoke there was no anger in his voice, but only something sad.

'Thou art a foolish lad,' he said. 'Yet I was young once myself, and my ways have been too dark to make me wish to darken others, or try to chill young blood. Now thine own life has got a shadow on't already that I have helped to cast, so take the brightness of it while thou mayst, and get thee gone. But for this girl, I know her for a comely lass and good-hearted, and have wondered often how she came to have *him* for her father. I am glad now I have not his blood on my hands; and never would have gone to take it then, for all the evil he had brought on me, but that the lives of every mother's son hung on his life. So make thy mind at ease, and get thee gone and see these streams and trees and stones thou talkest of. Yet if thou'rt shot upon the Down, or taken off to jail, blame thine own folly and not me. And I will walk with thee to Purbeck Gates tonight, and then come back and wait. But if thou art not here again by midnight tomorrow, I shall believe that thou art taken in some snare, and come out to seek thee.'

I took his hand, and thanked him with what words I could that he had let me go, and then got on the smock, putting some bread and meat in my pockets, as I was likely to find little to eat on my journey. It was dark before we left the cave, for there is little dusk with us, and the division between day and night sharper than in more northern parts. Elzevir took me by the hand and led me through the darkness of the workings, telling me where I should stoop, and when the way was uneven. Thus we came to the bottom of the shaft, and looking up through ferns and brambles, I could see the deep blue of the sky overhead, and a great star gazing down full at us. We climbed the steps with the soap-stone slide at one side, and then walked on briskly over the springy turf through the hillocks of the coveted quarry-heaps and the ruins of the deserted cottages.

There was a heavy dew which got through my boots before we had gone half a mile, and though there was no moon, the sky was very clear, and I could see the veil of gossamers spread silvery white over the grass. Neither of us spoke, partly because it was safer not to speak, for the voice carries far in a still night on the Downs; and partly, I think, because the beauty of the starry heaven had taken hold upon us both, ruling our hearts with thoughts too big for words. We soon reached that ruined cottage of which Elzevir had spoken, and in what had once been an oven, found the compass safe enough as Ratsey had promised. Then on again over the solitary hills, not speaking ourselves, and neither seeing light in window nor hearing dog stir, until we reached that strange defile which men call the Gates of Purbeck. Here is a natural road nicking the highest summit of the hill, with walls as sharp as if the hand of man had cut them, through which have walked for ages all the few travellers in this lonely place, shepherds and sailors, soldiers and Excisemen. And although, as I suppose, no carts have been through it for centuries, there are ruts in the chalk floor as wide and deep as if the cars of giants used it in past times.

So here Elzevir stopped, and drawing from his bosom that silver-butted pistol of which I have spoken, thrust it in my hand. 'Here, take it, child,' he said, 'but use it not till thou art closely pressed, and then if thou *must* shoot, shoot low—it flings.' I took it and gripped his hand, and so we parted, he going back to Purbeck, and I making along the top of the ridge at the back of Hoar Head. It must have been near three when I reached a great grass-grown mound called Culliford Tree, that marks the resting-place of some old warrior of the past. The top is planted with a clump of trees that cut the skyline, and there I sat awhile to rest. But not for long, for looking back towards Purbeck, I could see the faint hint of dawn low on the sea-line behind St. Alban's Head, and so pressed forward knowing I had a full ten miles to cover yet.

Thus I travelled on, and soon came to the first sign of man, namely a flock of lambs being fed with turnips on a summer fallow. The sun was well up now, and flushed all with a rosy glow, showing the sheep and the roots they eat white against the brown earth. Still I saw no shepherd, nor even dog, and about seven o'clock stood safe on Weatherbeech Hill that looks down over Moonfleet.

There at my feet lay the Manor woods and the old house, and lower down the white road and the straggling cottages, and farther still the Why Not? and the glassy Fleet, and beyond that the open sea. I cannot say how sad, yet sweet, the sight was: it seemed like the mirage of the desert, of which I had been told—so beautiful, but never to be reached again by me. The air was still, and the blue smoke of the morning wood-fires rose straight up, but none from the Why Not? or Manor House. The sun was already very hot, and I dropped at once from the hill-top, digging my heels into the brown-burned turf, and keeping as much as might be among the furze champs. So I was soon in the wood, and made straight for the little dell and lay down there, burying myself in the wild rhubarb and burdocks, yet so that I could see the doorway of the Manor House over the lip of the hill.

Then I reflected what I was to do, or how I should get to speak with Grace: and thought I would first wait an hour or two, and see whether she came out, and afterwards, if she did not, would go down boldly and knock at the door. This seemed not very dangerous, for it was likely, from what Ratsey had said, that there was no one with her in the house, and if there was it would be but an old woman, to whom I could pass as a stranger in my disguise, and ask my way to some house in the village. So I lay still and munched a piece of bread, and heard the clock in the church tower strike eight and afterwards nine, but saw no one move in the house. The wood was all alive with singing-birds, and with the calling of cuckoo and wood-pigeon. There were deep patches of green shade and lighter patches of yellow sunlight, in which the iris leaves gleamed with a sheeny white, and a shimmering blue sea of ground-ivy spread all through the wood. It struck ten, and as the heat increased the birds sang less and the droning of the bees grew more distinct, and at last I got up, shook myself, smoothed my smock, and making a turn, came out on the road that led to the house.

Though my disguise was good, I fear I made but an indifferent bad ploughboy when walking, and found a difficulty in dealing with my hands, not knowing how ploughboys are wont to carry them. So I came round in front of the house, and gave a rat-tat on the door, while my pulse beat as loud inside of me as ever did the knocker without. The sound ran round the building, and backwards among the walks, and all was silent as before. I waited a minute, and was for knocking again, thinking there might be no one in the house, and then heard a light footstep coming along the corridor, yet durst not look through the window to see who it was in passing, as I might have done, but kept myself close to the door.

The bolts were being drawn, and a girl's voice asked, 'Who is there?' I gave a jump to hear that voice, knowing it well for Grace's, and had a mind to shout out my name. But then I remembered there might be some in the house with her besides, and that I must remain disguised. Moreover, laughing is so mixed with crying in our world, and trifling things with serious, that even in this pass I believe I was secretly pleased to have to play a trick on her, and test whether she would find me out in this dress or not. So I spoke out in our round Dorset speech, such as they talk it out in the vale, saying, 'A poor boy who is out of his way.'

Then she opened one leaf of the door, and asked me whither I would go, looking at me as one might at a stranger and not knowing who it was.

I answered that I was a farm lad who had walked from Purbeck, and sought an inn called the Why Not? kept by one Master Block. When she heard that, she gave a little start, and looked me over again, yet could make nothing of it, but said:

'Good lad, if you will step on to this terrace I can show you the Why Not? inn, but 'tis shut these two months or more, and Master Block away.'

With that she turned towards the terrace, I following, but when we were outside of ear-shot from the door, I spoke in my own voice, quick but low:

'Grace, it is I, John Trenchard, who am come to say goodbye before I leave these parts, and have much to tell that you would wish to hear. Are there any beside in the house with you?'

Now many girls who had suffered as she had, and were thus surprised, would have screamed, or perhaps swooned, but she did neither, only flushing a little and saying, also quick and low, 'Let us go back to the house; I am alone.'

So we went back, and after the door was bolted, took both hands and stood up face to face in the passage looking into one another's eyes. I was tired with a long walk and sleepless night, and so full of joy to see her again that my head swam and all seemed a sweet dream. Then she squeezed my hands, and I knew 'twas real, and was for kissing her for very love; but she guessed what I would be at, perhaps, and cast my hands loose, drawing back a little, as if to see me better, and saying, 'John, you have grown a man in these two months.' So I did not kiss her.

But if it was true that I was grown a man, it was truer still that she was grown a woman, and as tall as I. And these recent sufferings had taken from her something of light and frolic girlhood, and left her with a manner more staid and sober. She was dressed in black, with longer skirts, and her hair caught up behind; and perhaps it was the mourning frock that made her look pale and thin, as Ratsey said. So while I looked at her, she looked at me, and could not choose but smile to see my carter's smock; and as for my brown face and hands, thought I had been hiding in some country underneath the sun, until I told her of the walnut-juice. Then before we fell to talking, she said it was better we should sit in the garden, for that a woman might come in to help her with the house, and anyway it was safer, so that I might get out at the back in case of need. So she led the way down the corridor and through the living-part of the house, and we passed several rooms, and one little parlour lined with shelves and musty books. The blinds were pulled, but let enough light in to show a high-backed horsehair chair that stood at the table. In front of it lay an open volume, and a pair of horn-rimmed spectacles, that I had often seen on Maskew's nose; so I knew it was his study, and that nothing had been moved since last he sat there. Even now I trembled to think in whose house I was, and half-expected the old attorney to step in and hale me off to jail; till I remembered how all my trouble had come about, and how I last had seen him with his face turned up against the morning sun.

Thus we came to the garden, where I had never been before. It was a great square, shut in with a brick wall of twelve or fifteen feet, big enough to suit a palace, but then ill kept and sorely overgrown. I could spend long in speaking of that plot; how the flowers, and fruit-trees, pot-herbs, spice, and simples ran all wild and intermixed. The pink brick walls caught every ray of sun that fell, and that morning there was a hushed, close heat in it, and a warm breath rose from the strawberry beds, for they were then in full bearing. I was glad enough to get out of the sun when Grace led the way into a walk of medlar-trees and quinces, where the boughs interlaced and formed an alley to a brick summer-house. This summer-house stands in the angle of the south wall, and by it two fig-trees, whose tops you can see from the outside. They are well known for the biggest and the earliest bearing of all that part, and Grace showed me how, if danger threatened, I might climb up their boughs and scale the wall.

We sat in the summer-house, and I told her all that had happened at her father's death, only concealing that Elzevir had meant to do the

118

deed himself; because it was no use to tell her that, and besides, for all I knew, he never did mean to shoot, but only to frighten.

She wept again while I spoke, but afterwards dried her tears, and must needs look at my leg to see the bullet-wound, and if it was all soundly healed.

Then I told her of the secret sense that Master Ratsey's words put into the texts written on the parchment. I had showed her the locket before, but we had it out again now; and she read and read again the writing, while I pointed out how the words fell, and told her I was going away to get the diamond and come back the richest man in all the countryside.

Then she said, 'Ah, John! set not your heart too much upon this diamond. If what they say is true, 'twas evilly come by, and will bring evil with it. Even this wicked man durst not spend it for himself, but meant to give it to the poor; so, if indeed you ever find it, keep it not for yourself, but set his soul at rest by doing with it what he meant to do, or it will bring a curse upon you.'

I only smiled at what she said, taking it to be a girlish fancy, and did not tell her why I wanted so much to be rich—namely, to marry her one day. Then, having talked long about my own concerns as self-ishly as a man always does, I thought to ask after herself, and what she was going to do. She told me that a month past lawyers had come to Moonfleet, and pressed her to leave the place, and they would give her in charge to a lady in London, because, said they, her father had died without a will, and so she must be made a ward of Chancery. But she had begged them to let her be, for she could never live anywhere else than in Moonfleet, and that the air and commodity of the place suited her well. So they went off, saying that they must take direction of the Court to know whether she might stay here or not, and here she yet was. This made me sad, for all I knew of Chancery was that whatever it put hand on fell to ruin, as witness the Chancery Mills at Cerne, or the Chancery Wharf at Wareham; and certainly it would take little enough to ruin the Manor House, for it was three parts in decay already.

Thus we talked, and after that she put on a calico bonnet and picked me a dish of strawberries, staying to pull the finest, although the sun was beating down from mid-heaven, and brought me bread and meat from the house. Then she rolled up a shawl to make me a pillow, and bade me lie down on the seat that ran round the summer-house and get to sleep, for I had told her that I had walked all night, and must be back again at the cave come midnight She went back to the house, and that was the most sweet and peaceful sleep that ever I knew, for I was very tired, and had this thought to soothe me as I fell asleep—that I had seen Grace, and that she was so kind to me.

She was sitting beside me when I awoke and knitting a piece of work. The heat of the day was somewhat less, and she told me that it was past five o'clock by the sun-dial; so I knew that I must go. She made me take a packet of victuals and a bottle of milk, and as she put it into, my pocket the bottle struck on the butt of Maskew's pistol, which I had in my bosom. 'What have you there?' she said; but I did not tell her, fearing to call up bitter memories.

We stood hand in hand again, as we had done in the morning, and she said: 'John, you will wander on the sea, and may perhaps put into Moonfleet. Though you have not been here of late, I have kept a candle burning at the window every night, as in the past. So, if you come to beach on any night you will see that light, and know Grace remembers you. And if you see it not, then know that I am dead or gone, for I will think of you every night till you come back again.' I had nothing to say, for my heart was too full with her sweet words and with the sorrow of parting, but only drew her close to me and kissed her; and this time she did not step back, but kissed me again.

Then I climbed up the fig-tree, thinking it safer so to get out over the wall than to go back to the front of the house, and as I sat on the wall ready to drop the other side, turned to her and said goodbye.

'Goodbye,' cried she; 'and have a care how you touch the treasure; it was evilly come by, and will bring a curse with it.'

'Goodbye, goodbye,' I said, and dropped on to the soft leafy bottom of the wood.

CHAPTER 14: THE WELL-HOUSE

For those thou mayest not look upon
Are gathering fast round the yawning stone—Scott

It wanted yet half an hour of midnight when I found myself at the shaft of the marble quarry, and before I had well set foot on the steps to descend, heard Elzevir's voice challenging out of the darkness below. I gave back 'Prosper the Bonaventure', and so came home again to sleep the last time in our cave.

The next night was well suited to flight. There was a spring-tide with full moon, and a light breeze setting off the land which left the water smooth under the cliff. We saw the *Bonaventure* cruising in the

Channel before sundown, and after the darkness fell she lay close in and took us off in her boat. There were several men on board of her that I knew, and they greeted us kindly, and made much of us. I was indeed glad to be among them again, and yet felt a pang at leaving our dear Dorset coast, and the old cave that had been hospital and home to me for two months.

The wind set us up-Channel, and by daybreak they put us ashore at Cowes, so we walked to Newport and came there before many were stirring. Such as we saw in the street paid no heed to us but took us doubtless for some carter and his boy who had brought corn in from the country for the Southampton packet, and were about early to lead the team home again. 'Tis a little place enough this Newport, and we soon found the Bugle; but Elzevir made so good a carter that the landlord did not know him, though he had his acquaintance before. So they fenced a little with one another.

'Have you bed and victuals for a plain country man and his boy?' says Elzevir.

'Nay, that I have not,' says the landlord, looking him up and down, and not liking to take in strangers who might use their eyes inside, and perhaps get on the trail of the Contraband. ''Tis near the Summer Statute and the place over full already. I cannot move my gentlemen, and would bid you try the Wheatsheaf, which is a good house, and not so full as this.'

'Ay, 'tis a busy time, and 'tis these fairs that make things *prosper*,' and Elzevir marked the last word a little as he said it.

The man looked harder at him, and asked, 'Prosper what?' as if he were hard of hearing.

'*Prosper the Bonaventure,*' was the answer, and then the landlord caught Elzevir by the hand, shaking it hard and saying, 'Why, you are Master Block, and I expecting you this morn, and never knew you.' He laughed as he stared at us again, and Elzevir smiled too. Then the landlord led us in. 'And this is?' he said, looking at me.

'This is a well-licked whelp,' replied Elzevir, 'who got a bullet in the leg two months ago in that touch under Hoar Head; and is worth more than he looks, for they have put twenty golden guineas on his head—so have a care of such a precious top-knot.'

So long as we stopped at the Bugle we had the best of lodging and the choicest meat and drink, and all the while the landlord treated Elzevir as though he were a prince. And so he was indeed a prince among the *contrabandiers*, and held, as I found out long afterwards, for

121

captain of all landers between Start and Solent. At first the landlord would take no money of us, saying that he was in our debt, and had received many a good turn from Master Block in the past, but Elzevir had got gold from Dorchester before we left the cave and forced him to take payment.

I was glad enough to lie between clean sweet sheets at night instead of on a heap of sand, and sit once more knife and fork in hand before a well-filled trencher. 'Twas thought best I should show myself as little as possible, so I was content to pass my time in a room at the back of the house whilst Elzevir went abroad to make inquiries how we could find entrance to the Castle at Carisbrooke. Nor did the time hang heavy on my hands, for I found some old books in the Bugle, and among them several to my taste, especially a *History of Corfe Castle*, which set forth how there was a secret passage from the ruins to some of the old marble quarries, and perhaps to that very one that sheltered us.

Elzevir was out most of the day, so that I saw him only at breakfast and supper. He had been several times to Carisbrooke, and told me that the castle was used as a jail for persons taken in the wars, and was now full of French prisoners. He had met several of the turnkeys or jailers, drinking with them in the inns there, and making out that he was himself a carter, who waited at Newport till a wind-bound ship should bring grindstones from Lyme Regis. Thus he was able at last to enter the castle and to see well-house and well, and spent some days in trying to devise a plan whereby we might get at the well without making the man who had charge of it privy to our full design; but in this did not succeed.

There is a slip of garden at the back of the Bugle, which runs down to a little stream, and one evening when I was taking the air there after dark, Elzevir returned and said the time was come for us to put Blackbeard's cipher to the proof.

'I have tried every way,' he said, 'to see if we could work this secretly; but 'tis not to be done without the privity of the man who keeps the well, and even with his help it is not easy. He is a man I do not trust, but have been forced to tell him there is treasure hidden in the well, yet without saying where it lies or how to get it. He promises to let us search the well, taking one-third the value of all we find, for his share; for I said not that thou and I were one at heart, but only that there was a boy who had the key, and claimed an equal third with both of us. Tomorrow we must be up betimes, and at the castle gates by six o'clock for him to let us in. And thou shalt not be carter any more, but mason's boy, and I a mason, for I have got coats in the house, brushes and trowels and lime-bucket, and we are going to Carisbrooke to plaster up a weak patch in this same well-side.'

Elzevir had thought carefully over this plan, and when we left the Bugle next morning we were better masons in our splashed clothes than ever we had been farm servants. I carried a bucket and a brush, and Elzevir a plasterer's hammer and a coil of stout twine over his arm. It was a wet morning, and had been raining all night. The sky was stagnant, and one-coloured without wind, and the heavy drops fell straight down out of a grey veil that covered everything. The air struck cold when we first came out, but trudging over the heavy road soon made us remember that it was July, and we were very hot and soaking wet when we stood at the gateway of Carisbrooke Castle. Here are two flanking towers and a stout gate-house reached by a stone bridge crossing the moat; and when I saw it I remembered that 'twas here Colonel Mohune had earned the wages of his unrighteousness, and thought how many times he must have passed these gates. Elzevir knocked as one that had a right, and we were evidently expected, for a wicket in the heavy door was opened at once. The man who let us in was tall and stout, but had a puffy face, and too much flesh on him to be very strong, though he was not, I think, more than thirty years of age. He gave Elzevir a smile, and passed the time of day civilly enough, nodding also to me; but I did not like his oily black hair, and a shifty eye that turned away uneasily when one met it.

'Good-morning, Master Wellwright,' he said to Elzevir. 'You have brought ugly weather with you, and are drowning wet; will you take a sup of ale before you get to work?'

Elzevir thanked him kindly but would not drink, so the man led on and we followed him. We crossed a bailey or outer court where the rain had made the gravel very miry, and came on the other side to a door which led by steps into a large hall. This building had once been a banquet-room, I think, for there was an inscription over it very plain in lead: *He led me into his banquet hall, and his banner over me was love.*

I had time to read this while the turnkey unlocked the door with one of a heavy bunch of keys that he carried at his girdle. But when we entered, what a disappointment!—for there were no banquets now, no banners, no love, but the whole place gutted and turned into a barrack for French prisoners. The air was very close, as where men had slept all night, and a thick steam on the windows.

Most of the prisoners were still asleep, and lay stretched out on straw *palliasses* round the walls, but some were sitting up and making models of ships out of fish-bones, or building up crucifixes inside bottles, as sailors love to do in their spare time. They paid little heed to us as we passed, though the sleepy guards, who were lounging on their matchlocks, nodded to our conductor, and thus we went right through that evil-smelling white-washed room. We left it at the other end, went down three steps into the open air again, crossed another small court, and so came to a square building of stone with a high roof like the large dovecots that you may see in old stackyards.

Here our guide took another key, and, while the door was being opened, Elzevir whispered to me, 'It is the well-house,' and my pulse beat quick to think we were so near our goal.

The building was open to the roof, and the first thing to be seen in it was that tread-wheel of which Elzevir had spoken. It was a great open wheel of wood, ten or twelve feet across, and very like a mill-wheel, only the space between the rims was boarded flat, but had treads nailed on it to give foothold to a donkey. The patient beast was lying loose stabled on some straw in a corner of the room, and, as soon as we came in, stood up and stretched himself, knowing that the day's work was to begin. 'He was here long before my time,' the turnkey said, 'and knows the place so well that he goes into the wheel and sets to work by himself.' At the side of the wheel was the well-mouth, a dark, round opening with a low parapet round it, rising two feet from the floor.

We were so near our goal. Yet, were we near it at all? How did we know Mohune had meant to tell the place of hiding for the diamond in those words. They might have meant a dozen things beside. And if it was of the diamond they spoke, then how did we know the well was this one? there were a hundred wells beside. These thoughts came to me, making hope less sure; and perhaps it was the steamy overcast morning and the rain, or a scant breakfast, that beat my spirit down— for I have known men's mood change much with weather and with food; but sure it was that now we stood so near to put it to the touch, I liked our business less and less.

As soon as we were entered the turnkey locked the door from the inside, and when he let the key drop to its place, and it jangled with the others on his belt, it seemed to me he had us as his prisoners in a trap. I tried to catch his eye to see if it looked bad or good, but could not, for he kept his shifty face turned always somewhere else; and then it came to my mind that if the treasure was really fraught with evil, this coarse dark-haired man, who could not look one straight, was to become a minister of ruin to bring the curse home to us.

But if I was weak and timid Elzevir had no misgivings. He had taken the coil of twine off his arm and was undoing it. 'We will let an end of this down the well,' he said, 'and I have made a knot in it at eighty feet. This lad thinks the treasure is in the well wall, eighty feet below us, so when the knot is on well lip we shall know we have the right depth.' I tried again to see what look the turnkey wore when he heard where the treasure was, but could not, and so fell to examining the well.

A spindle ran from the axle of the wheel across the well, and on the spindle was a drum to take the rope. There was some clutch or fastening which could be fixed or loosed at will to make the drum turn with the tread-wheel, or let it run free, and a footbreak to lower the bucket fast or slow, or stop it altogether.

'I will get into the bucket,' Elzevir said, turning to me, 'and this good man will lower me gently by the break until I reach the string-end down below. Then I will shout, and so fix you the wheel and give me time to search.'

This was not what I looked for, having thought that it was I should go; and though I liked going down the well little enough, yet somehow now I felt I would rather do that than have Master Elzevir down the hole, and me left locked alone with this villainous fellow up above.

So I said, 'No, master, that cannot be; 'tis my place to go, being smaller and a lighter weight than thou; and thou shalt stop here and help this gentleman to lower me down.'

Elzevir spoke a few words to try to change my purpose, but soon gave in, knowing it was certainly the better plan, and having only thought to go himself because he doubted if I had the heart to do it. But the turnkey showed much ill-humour at the change, and strove to let the plan stand as it was, and for Elzevir to go down the well. Things that were settled, he said, should remain settled; he was not one for changes; it was a man's task this and no child's play; a boy would not have his senses about him, and might overlook the place. I fixed my eyes on Elzevir to let him know what I thought, and Master Turnkey's words fell lightly on his ears as water on a duck's back. Then this ill-eyed man tried to work upon my fears; saying that the well is deep and the bucket small, I shall get giddy and be overbalanced. I do not say that these forebodings were without effect on me, but I had made up my mind that, bad as it might be to go down, it was yet worse to have Master Elzevir prisoned in the well, and I remain above. Thus the turnkey perceived at last that he was speaking to deaf ears, and turned to the business.

Yet there was one fear that still held me, for thinking of what I had heard of the quarry shafts in Purbeck, how men had gone down to explore, and there been taken with a sudden giddiness, and never lived to tell what they had seen; and so I said to Master Elzevir, 'Art sure the well is clean, and that no deadly gases lurk below?'

'Thou mayst be sure I knew the well was sweet before I let thee talk of going down,' he answered. 'For yesterday we lowered a candle to the water, and the flame burned bright and steady; and where the candle lives, there man lives too. But thou art right: these gases change from day to day, and we will try the thing again. So bring the candle, Master Jailer.'

The jailer brought a candle fixed on a wooden triangle, which he was wont to show strangers who came to see the well, and lowered it on a string. It was not till then I knew what a task I had before me, for looking over the parapet, and taking care not to lose my balance, because the parapet was low, and the floor round it green and slippery with water-splashings, I watched the candle sink into that cavernous depth, and from a bright flame turn into a little twinkling star, and then to a mere point of light. At last it rested on the water, and there was a shimmer where the wood frame had set ripples moving.

We watched it twinkle for a little while, and the jailer raised the candle from the water, and dropped down a stone from some he kept there for that purpose. This stone struck the wall half-way down, and went from side to side, crashing and whirring till it met the water with a booming plunge; and there rose a groan and moan from the eddies, like those dreadful sounds of the surge that I heard on lonely nights in the sea-caverns underneath our hiding-place in Purbeck. The jailer looked at me then for the first time, and his eyes had an ugly meaning, as if he said, 'There—that is how you will sound when you fall from your perch.' But it was no use to frighten, for I had made up my mind.

They pulled the candle up forthwith and put it in my hand, and I flung the plasterer's hammer into the bucket, where it hung above the well, and then got in myself. The turnkey stood at the break-wheel, and Elzevir leant over the parapet to steady the rope. 'Art sure that thou canst do it, lad?' he said, speaking low, and put his hand kindly on my shoulder. 'Are head and heart sure? Thou art my diamond, and I would rather lose all other diamonds in the world than aught should come to thee. So, if thou doubtest, let me go, or let not any go at all.'

'Never doubt, master,' I said, touched by tenderness, and wrung his hand. 'My head is sure; I have no broken leg to turn it silly now'—for I guessed he was thinking of Hoar Head and how I had gone giddy on the Zigzag.

CHAPTER 15: THE WELL

The grave doth gape and doting death is near—Shakespeare

The bucket was large, for all that the turnkey had tried to frighten me into think it small, and I could crouch in it low enough to feel safe of not falling out. Moreover, such a venture was not entirely new to me, for I had once been over Gad Cliff in a basket, to get two peregrines' eggs; yet none the less I felt ill at ease and fearful, when the bucket began to sink into that dreadful depth, and the air to grow chilly as I went down. They lowered me gently enough, so that I was able to take stock of the way the wall was made, and found that for the most part it was cut through solid chalk; but here and there, where the chalk failed or was broken away, they had lined the walls with brick, patching them now on this side, now on that, and now all round. By degrees the light, which was dim even overground that rainy day, died out in the well, till all was black as night but for my candle, and far overhead I could see the well-mouth, white and round like a lustreless full-moon.

I kept an eye all the time on Elzevir's cord that hung down the well-side, and when I saw it was coming to a finish, shouted to them to stop, and they brought the bucket up near level with the end of it, so I knew I was about eighty feet deep. Then I raised myself, standing up in the bucket and holding by the rope, and began to look round, knowing not all the while what I looked for, but thinking to see a hole in the wall, or perhaps the diamond itself shining out of a cranny. But I could perceive nothing; and what made it more difficult was, that the walls here were lined completely with small flat bricks, and looked much the same all round. I examined these bricks as closely as I might, and took course by course, looking first at the north side where the plumb-line hung, and afterwards turning round in the bucket till I was afraid of getting giddy; but to little purpose. They could see my candle moving round and round from the well-top, and knew no doubt what I was at, but Master Turnkey grew impatient, and shouted down, 'What are you doing? have you found nothing? can you see no treasure?'

'No,' I called back, 'I can see nothing,' and then, 'Are you sure, Master Block, that you have measured the plummet true to eighty feet?'

I heard them talking together, but could not make out what they said, for the *bim-bom* and echo in the well, till Elzevir shouted again, 'They say this floor has been raised; you must try lower.'

Then the bucket began to move lower, slowly, and I crouched down in it again, not wishing to look too much into the unfathomable, dark abyss below. And all the while there rose groanings and moanings from eddies in the bottom of the well, as if the spirits that kept watch over me jewel were yammering together that one should be so near it; and clear above them all I heard Grace's voice, sweet and grave, 'Have a care, have a care how you touch the treasure; it was evilly come by, and will bring a curse with it.'

But I had set foot on this way now, and must go through with it, so when the bucket stopped some six feet lower down, I fell again to diligently examining the walls. They were still built of the shallow bricks, and scanning them course by course as before, I could at first see nothing, but as I moved my eyes downward they were brought up by a mark scratched on a brick, close to the hanging plummet-line.

Now, however lightly a man may glance through a book, yet if his own name, or even only one nice it, should be printed on the page, his eyes will instantly be stopped by it; so too, if his name be mentioned by others in their speech, though it should be whispered never so low, his ears will catch it. Thus it was with this mark, for though it was very slight, so that I think not one in a thousand would ever have noticed it at all, yet it stopped my eyes and brought up my thoughts suddenly, because I knew by instinct that it had something to do with me and what I sought.

The sides of this well are not moist, green, or clammy, like the sides of some others where damp and noxious exhalations abound, but dry and clean; for it is said that there are below hidden entrances and exits for the water, which keep it always moving. So these bricks were also dry and clean, and this mark as sharp as if made yesterday, though the issue showed that 'twas put there a very long time ago. Now the mark was not deeply or regularly graven, but roughly scratched, as I have known boys score their names, or alphabet letters, or a date, on the alabaster figures that lie in Moonfleet Church. And here, too, was scored a letter of the alphabet, a plain 'Y', and would have passed for nothing more perhaps to any not born in Moonfleet; but to me it was the *cross-pall*, or black 'Y' of the Mohunes, under whose shadow we were all brought up. So as soon as I saw that, I knew I was near what I sought, and that Colonel John Mohune had put this sign there a century ago, either by his own hands or by those of a servant; and then I thought of Mr. Glennie's story, that the Colonel's conscience was always unquiet, because of a servant whom he had put away, and now I seemed to understand something more of it.

My heart throbbed fiercely, as many another's heart has throbbed when he has come near the fulfilment of a great desire, whether lawful or guilty, and I tried to get at the brick. But though by holding on to the rope with my left hand, I could reach over far enough to touch the brick with my right 'twas as much as I could do, and so I shouted up the well that they must bring me nearer in to the side. They understood what I would be at, and slipped a noose over the well-rope and so drew it in to the side, and made it fast till I should give the word to loose again. Thus I was brought close to the well-wall, and the marked brick near about the level of my face when I stood up in the bucket. There was nothing to show that this brick had been tampered with, nor did it sound hollow when tapped, though when I came to look closely at the joints, it seemed as though there was more cement than usual about the edges. But I never doubted that what we sought was to be found behind it, and so got to work at once, fixing the wooden frame of the candle in the fastening of the chain, and chipping out the mortar setting with the plasterer's hammer.

When they saw above that first I was to be pulled in to the side, and afterwards fell to work on the wall of the well, they guessed, no doubt, how matters were, and I had scarce begun chipping when I heard the turnkey's voice again, sharp and greedy, 'What are you doing? have you found nothing?' It chafed me that this grasping fellow should be always shouting to me while Elzevir was content to stay quiet, so I cried back that I had found nothing, and that he should know what I was doing in good time.

Soon I had the mortar out of the joints, and the brick loose enough to prise it forward, by putting the edge of the hammer in the crack. I lifted it clean out and put it in the bucket, to see later on, in case of need, if there was a hollow for anything to be hidden in; but never had occasion to look at it again, for there, behind the brick, was a little hole in the wall, and in the hole what I sought. I had my fingers in the wall too quick for words, and brought out a little parchment bag, for all the world like those dried fish-eggs cast up on the beach that children call shepherds' purses. Now, shepherds' purses are crisp, and crackle to the touch, and sometimes I have known a pebble get inside one and rattle like a pea in a drum; and this little bag that I pulled out was dry too, and crackling, and had something of the size of a small pebble that rattled in the inside of it.

Only I knew well that this was no pebble, and set to work to get it out. But though the little bag was parched and dry, 'twas not so easily torn, and at last I struck off the corner of it with the sharp edge of my hammer against the bucket. Then I shook it carefully, and out into my hand there dropped a pure crystal as big as a walnut. I had never in my life seen a diamond, either large or small—yet even if I had not known that Blackbeard had buried a diamond, and if we had not come hither of set purpose to find it, I should not have doubted that what I had in my hand was a diamond, and this of matchless size and brilliance. It was cut into many facets, and though there was little or no light in the well save my candle, there seemed to be in this stone the light of a thousand fires that flashed out, sparkling red and blue and green, as I turned it between my fingers.

At first I could think of nothing else, neither how it got there, nor how I had come to find it, but only of it, the diamond, and that with such a prize Elzevir and I could live happily ever afterwards, and that I should be a rich man and able to go back to Moonfleet. So I crouched down in the bottom of the bucket, being filled entirely with such thoughts, and turned it over and over again, wondering continually more and more to see the fiery light fly out of it. I was, as it were, dazed by its brilliance, and by the possibilities of wealth that it contained, and had, perhaps, a desire to keep it to myself as long as might be; so that I thought nothing of the two who were waiting for me at the well-mouth, till I was suddenly called back by the harsh voice of the turnkey, crying as before—

'What are you doing? have you found nothing?'

'Yes,' I shouted back, 'I have found the treasure; you can pull me up.' The words were scarcely out of my mouth before the bucket began to move, and I went up a great deal faster than I had gone down. Yet in that short journey other thoughts came to my mind, and I heard Grace's voice again, sweet and grave, 'Have a care, have a care how you touch the treasure; it was evilly come by, and will bring a curse with it.' At the same time I remembered how I had been led to the discovery of this jewel—first, by Mr. Glennie's stories, second, by my finding the locket, and third, by Ratsey giving me the hint that the writing was a cipher, and so had come to the hiding-place without a swerve or stumble; and it seemed to me that I could not have reached it so straight without a leading hand, but whether good or evil, who should say?

As I neared the top I heard the turnkey urging the donkey to trot faster in the wheel, so that the bucket might rise the quicker, but just before my head was level with the ground he set the break on and fixed me where I was. I was glad to see the light again, and Elzevir's face looking kindly on me, but vexed to be brought up thus suddenly just when I was expecting to set foot on *terra firma*.

The turnkey had stopped me through his covetous eagerness, so that he might get sooner at the jewel, and now he craned over the low parapet and reached out his hand to me, crying—'Where is the treasure? where is the treasure? give me the treasure!'

I held the diamond between finger and thumb of my right hand, and waved it for Elzevir to see. By stretching out my arm I could have placed it in the turnkey's hand, and was just going to do so, when I caught his eyes for the second time that day, and something in them made me stop. There was a look in his face that brought back to me the memory of an autumn evening, when I sat in my aunt's parlour reading the book called the *Arabian Nights*; and how, in the story of the *Wonderful Lamp*, Aladdin's wicked uncle stands at the top of the stairs when the boy is coming up out of the underground cavern, and will not let him out, unless he first gives up the treasure. But Aladdin refused to give up his lamp until he should stand safe on the ground again, because he guessed that if he did, his uncle would shut him up in the cavern and leave him to die there; and the look in the turnkey's eyes made me refuse to hand him the jewel till I was safe out of the well, for a horrible fear seized me that, as soon as he had taken it from me, he meant to let me fall down and drown below.

So when he reached down his hand and said, 'Give me the treasure,' I answered, 'Pull me up then; I cannot show it you in the bucket.'

'Nay, lad,' he said, cozening me, ''tis safer to give it me now, and have both hands free to help you getting out; these stones are wet and greasy, and you may chance to slip, and having no hand to save you, fall back in the well.'

But I was not to be cheated, and said again sturdily, 'No, you must pull me up first.'

Then he took to scowling, and cried in an angry tone, 'Give me the treasure, I say, or it will be the worse for you'; but Elzevir would not let him speak to me that way, and broke in roughly, 'Let the boy up, he is sure-footed and will not slip. 'Tis his treasure, and he shall do with it as he likes: only that thou shalt have a third of it when we have sold it.'

Then he: "Tis not his treasure—no, nor yours either, but mine, for it is in my well, and I have let you get it. Yet I will give you a half-share in it; but as for this boy, what has he to do with it? We will give him a golden guinea, and he will be richly paid for his pains.'

'Tush,' cries Elzevir, 'let us have no more fooling; this boy shall have his share, or I will know the reason why.'

'Ay, you shall know the reason, fair enough,' answers the turnkey, 'and 'tis because your name is Block, and there is a price of 50 upon your head, and 20 upon this boy's. You thought to outwit me, and are yourself outwitted; and here I have you in a trap, and neither leaves this room, except with hands tied, and bound for the gallows, unless I first have the jewel safe in my purse.'

On that I whipped the diamond back quick into the little parchment bag, and thrust both down snug into my breeches-pocket, meaning to have a fight for it, anyway, before I let it go. And looking up again, I saw the turnkey's hand on the butt of his pistol, and cried, 'Beware, beware! he draws on you.' But before the words were out of my mouth, the turn-key had his weapon up and levelled full at Elzevir. 'Surrender,' he cries, 'or I shoot you dead, and the 50 is mine,' and never giving time for answer, fires. Elzevir stood on the other side of the well-mouth, and it seemed the other could not miss him at such a distance; but as I blinked my eyes at the flash, I felt the bullet strike the iron chain to which I was holding, and saw that Elzevir was safe.

The turnkey saw it too, and flinging away his pistol, sprang round the well and was at Elzevir's throat before he knew whether he was hit or not. I have said that the turnkey was a tall, strong man, and twenty years the younger of the two; so doubtless when he made for Elzevir, he thought he would easily have him broken down and handcuffed, and then turn to me. But he reckoned without his host, for though Elzevir was the shorter and older man, he was wonderfully strong, and seasoned as a salted thong. Then they hugged one another and began a terrible struggle: for Elzevir knew that he was wrestling for life, and I daresay the turnkey guessed that the stakes were much the same for him too.

As soon as I saw what they were at, and that the bucket was safe fixed, I laid hold of the well-chain, and climbing up by it swung myself on to the top of the parapet, being eager to help Elzevir, and get the turnkey gagged and bound while we made our escape. But before I was well on the firm ground again, I saw that little help of mine was needed, for the turnkey was flagging, and there was a look of anguish and desperate surprise upon his face, to find that the man he had thought to master so lightly was strong as a giant. They were swaying to and fro, and the jailer's grip was slackening, for his muscles were overwrought and tired; but Elzevir held him firm as a vice, and I saw from his eyes and the bearing of his body that he was gathering himself up to give his enemy a fall.

Now I guessed that the fall he would use would be the Compton Toss, for though I had never seen him give it, yet he was well known for a wrestler in his younger days, and the Compton Toss for his most certain fall. I shall not explain the method of it, but those who have seen it used will know that 'tis a deadly fall, and he who lets himself get thrown that way even upon grass, is seldom fit to wrestle another bout the same day. Still 'tis a difficult fall to use, and perhaps Elzevir would never have been able to give it, had not the other at that moment taken one hand off the waist, and tried to make a clutch with it at the throat. But the only way of avoiding that fall, and indeed most others, is to keep both hands firm between hip and shoulder-blade, and the moment Elzevir felt one hand off his back, he had the jailer off his feet and gave him Compton's Toss.

I do not know whether Elzevir had been so taxed by the fierce struggle that he could not put his fullest force into the throw, or whether the other, being a very strong and heavy man, needed more to fling him; but so it was, that instead of the turnkey going down straight as he should, with the back of his head on the floor (for that is the real damage of the toss), he must needs stagger backwards a pace or two, trying to regain his footing before he went over.

It was those few staggering paces that ruined him, for with the last he came upon the stones close to the well-mouth, that had been made wet and slippery by continual spilling there of water. Then up flew his heels, and he fell backwards with all his weight.

As soon as I saw how near the well-mouth he was got, I shouted out and ran to save him; but Elzevir saw it quicker than I, and springing forward seized him by the belt just when he turned over. The parapet wall was very low, and caught the turnkey behind the knee as he staggered, tripping him over into the well-mouth. He gave a bitter cry, and there was a wrench on his face when he knew where he was come, and 'twas then Elzevir caught him by the belt. For a moment I thought he was saved, seeing Elzevir setting his body low back with heels pressed firm against the parapet wall to stand the strain. Then the belt gave way at the fastening, and Elzevir fell sprawling on the floor. But the other went backwards down the well.

I got to the parapet just as he fell head first into that black abyss. There was a second of silence, then a dreadful noise like a coconut being broken on a pavement—for we once had coconuts in plenty at Moonfleet, when the *Bataviaman* came on the beach, then a deep echoing blow, where he rebounded and struck the wall again, and last of all, the thud and thundering splash, when he reached the water at the bottom. I held my breath for sheer horror, and listened to see if he would cry, though I knew at heart he would never cry again, after that first sickening smash; but there was no sound or voice, except the moaning voices of the water eddies that I had heard before.

Elzevir slung himself into the bucket. 'You can handle the break,' he said to me; 'let me down quick into the well.' I took the break-lever, lowering him as quickly as I durst, till I heard the bucket touch water at the bottom, and then stood by and listened. All was still, and yet I started once, and could not help looking round over my shoulder, for it seemed as if I was not alone in the well-house; and though I could see no one, yet I had a fancy of a tall black-bearded man, with coppery face, chasing another round and round the well-mouth. Both vanished from my fancy just as the pursuer had his hand on the pursued; but Mr. Glennie's story came back again to my mind, how that Colonel Mohune's conscience was always unquiet because of a servant he had put away, and I guessed now that the turnkey was not the first man these walls had seen go headlong down the well.

Elzevir had been in the well so long that I began to fear something had happened to him, when he shouted to me to bring him up. So I fixed the clutch, and set the donkey going in the tread-wheel; and the patient drudge started on his round, recking nothing whether it was a bucket of water he brought up, or a live man, or a dead man, while I looked over the parapet, and waited with a cramping suspense to see whether Elzevir would be alone, or have something with him. But when the bucket came in sight there was only Elzevir in it, so I knew the turnkey had never come to the top of the water again, and, indeed, there was but little chance he should after that first knock. Elzevir said nothing to me, till I spoke: 'Let us fling the jewel down the well after him, Master Block; it was evilly come by, and will bring a curse with it.'

He hesitated for a moment while I half-hoped yet half-feared he was going to do as I asked, but then said:

'No, no; thou art not fit to keep so precious a thing. Give it me. It is thy treasure, and I will never touch penny of it; but fling it down the well thou shalt not; for this man has lost his life for it, and we have risked ours for it—ay, and may lose them for it too, perhaps.'

So I gave him the jewel.

CHAPTER 16: THE JEWEL

All that glisters is not gold—Shakespeare

There was the turnkey's belt lying on the floor, with the keys and manacles fixed to it, just as it had failed and come off him at the fatal moment. Elzevir picked it up, tried the keys till he found the right one, and unlocked the door of the well-house.

'There are other locks to open before we get out,' I said.

'Ay,' he answered, 'but it is more than our life is worth to be seen with these keys, so send them down the well, after their master.'

I took them back and flung them, belt and keys and handcuffs, clanking down against the sides into the blackness and the hidden water at the bottom. Then we took pail and hammer, brush and ropes, and turned our backs upon that hateful place. There was the little court to cross before we came to the doors of the banquet-hall. They were locked, but we knocked until a guard opened them. He knew us for the plasterer-men, who had passed an hour before, and only asked, 'Where is Ephraim?' meaning the turnkey. 'He is stopping behind in the well-house,' Elzevir said, and so we passed on through the hall, where the prisoners were making what breakfast they might of odds and ends, with a savoury smell of cooking and a great patter of French.

At the outer gate was another guard to be passed, but they opened for us without question, cursing Ephraim under their breath, that he did not take the pains to let his own men out. Then the wicket of the great gates swung-to behind us, and we went into the open again. As soon as we were out of sight we quickened our pace, and the weather having much bettered, and a fresh breeze springing up, we came back to the Bugle about ten in the forenoon.

I believe that neither of us spoke a word during that walk, and though Elzevir had not yet seen the diamond, he never even took the pains to draw it out of the little parchment bag, in which it still lay hid in his pocket. Yet if I did not speak I thought, and my thoughts were sad enough. For here were we a second time, flying for our lives, and if we had not the full guilt of blood upon our hands, yet blood was surely there. So this flight was very bitter to me, because the scene of death of which I had been witness this morning seemed to take me farther still away from all my old happy life, and to stand like another dreadful obstacle between Grace and me. In the Family Bible lying on the table in my aunt's best parlour was a picture of Cain, which I had often looked at with fear on wet Sunday afternoons. It showed Cain striding along in the midst of a boundless desert, with his sons and their wives striding behind him, and their little children carried slung on poles.

There was a quick, swinging motion in the bodies of all, as though they must needs always stride as fast as they might, and never rest, and their faces were set hard, and thin with eternal wandering and disquiet. But the thinnest and most restless-looking and hardest face was Cain's, and on the middle of his forehead there was a dark spot, which God had set to show that none might touch him, because he was the first murderer, and cursed for ever. This had always been to me a dreadful picture, though I could not choose but look at it, and was sorry indeed for Cain, for all he was so wicked, because it seemed so hard to have to wander up and down the world all his life long, and never be able to come to moorings. And yet this very thing had come upon me now, for here we were, with the blood of two men on our hands, wanderers on the face of the earth, who durst never go home; and if the mark of Cain was not on my forehead already, I felt it might come out there at any minute.

When we reached the Bugle I went upstairs and flung myself upon the bed to try to rest a little and think, but Elzevir shut himself in with the landlord, and I could hear them talking earnestly in the room under me. After a while he came up and said that he had considered with the landlord how we could best get away, telling him that we must be off at once, but letting him suppose that we were eager to leave the place because some of the Excise had got wind of our whereabouts. He had said nothing to our host about the turnkey, wishing as few persons as possible to know of that matter, but doubted not that we should by all means hasten our departure from the island, for that as soon as the turnkey was missed inquiry would certainly be made for the plasterers with whom he was last seen.

Yet in this thing at least Fortune favoured us, for there was now lying at Cowes, and ready to sail that night, a Dutch couper that had run a cargo of Hollands on the other side of the island, and was going back to Scheveningen freighted with wool. Our landlord knew the Dutch captain well, having often done business for him, and so could give us letters of recommendation which would ensure us a passage to the Low Countries. Thus in the afternoon we were on the road, making our way from Newport to Cowes in a new disguise, for we had changed our clothes again, and now wore the common sailor dress of blue.

The clouds had returned after the rain, and the afternoon was wet, and worse than the morning, so I shall not say anything of another weary and silent walk. We arrived on Cowes quay by eight in the evening, and found the couper ready to make sail, and waiting only for the tide to set out. Her name was the *Gouden Droom*, and she was a little larger than the *Bonaventure*, but had a smaller crew, and was not near so well found. Elzevir exchanged a few words with the captain, and gave him the landlord's letter, and after that they let us come on board, but said nothing to us. We judged that we were best out of the way, so went below; and finding her laden deep, and even the cabin full of bales of wool, flung ourselves on them to rest. I was so tired and heavy with sleep that my eyes closed almost before I was lain down, and never opened till the next morning was well advanced.

I shall not say anything about our voyage, nor how we came safe to Scheveningen, because it has little to do with this story. Elzevir had settled that we should go to Holland, not only because the couper was waiting to sail thither for we might doubtless have found other boats before long to take us elsewhere—but also because he had learned at Newport that the Hague was the first market in the world for diamonds. This he told me after we were safe housed in a little tavern in the town, which was frequented by seamen, but those of the better class, such as mates and skippers of small vessels.

Here we lay for several days while Elzevir made such inquiry as he could without waking suspicion as to who were the best dealers in precious stones, and the most able to pay a good price for a valuable jewel. It was lucky, too, for us that Elzevir could speak the Dutch language—not well indeed, but enough to make himself understood, and to understand others. When I asked where he had learned it, he told me that he came of Dutch blood on his mother's side, and so got his name of Elzevir; and that he could once speak in Dutch as readily as in English, only that his mother dying when he was yet a boy he lost something of the facility.

As the days passed, the memory of that dreadful morning at Caris-brooke became dimmer to me, and my mind more cheerful or composed. I got the diamond back from Elzevir, and had it out many times, both by day and by night, and every time it seemed more brilliant and wonderful than the last. Often of nights, after all the house was gone to rest, I would lock the door of the room, and sit with a candle burning on the table, and turn the diamond over in my hands. It was, as I have said, as big as a pigeon's egg or walnut, delicately cut and faceted all over, perfect and flawless, without speck or stain, and yet, for all it was so clear and colourless, there flew out from the depth of it such flashes and sparkles of red, blue, and green, as made one wonder whence these tints could come. Thus while I sat and watched it I would tell Elzevir stories from the *Arabian Nights*, of wondrous jewels, though I believe there never was a stone that the eagles brought up from the Valley of Diamonds, no, nor any in the Caliph's crown itself, that could excel this gem of ours.

You may be sure that at such times we talked much of the value that was to be put upon the stone, and what was likely to be got for it, but never could settle, not having any experience of such things. Only, I was sure that it must be worth thousands of pounds, and so sat and rubbed my hands, saying that though life was like a game of hazard, and our throws had hitherto been bad enough, yet we had made something of this last. But all the while a strange change was coming over us both, and our parts seemed turned about. For whereas a few days before it was I who wished to fling the diamond away, feeling overwrought and heavy-hearted in that awful well-house, and Elzevir who held me from it; now it was he that seemed to set little store by it, and I to whom it was all in all. He seldom cared to look much at the jewel, and one night when I was praising it to him, spoke out:

'Set not thy heart too much upon this stone. It is thine, and thine to deal with. Never a penny will I touch that we may get for it. Yet, were I thou, and reached great wealth with it, and so came back one day to Moonfleet, I would not spend it all on my own ends, but put aside a part to build the poor-houses again, as men say Blackbeard meant to do with it'

I did not know what made him speak like this, and was not willing, even in fancy, to agree to what he counselled; for with that gem before me, lustrous, and all the brighter for lying on a rough deal table, I could only think of the wealth it was to bring to us, and how I would most certainly go back one day to Moonfleet and marry Grace. So I never answered Elzevir, but took the diamond and slipped it back in the silver locket, which still hung round my neck, for that was the safest place for it that we could think of.

We spent some days in wandering round the town making inquiries, and learnt that most of the diamond-buyers lived near one another in a certain little street, whose name I have forgotten, but that the richest and best known of them was one Krispijn Aldobrand. He was a Jew by birth, but had lived all his life in the Hague, and besides having bought and sold some of the finest stones, was said to ask few questions, and to trouble little whence stones came, so they were but good. Thus, after much thought and many changes of purpose, we chose this Aldobrand, and settled we would put the matter to the touch with him.

We took an evening in late summer for our venture, and came to Aldobrand's house about an hour before sundown. I remember the place well, though I have not seen it for so long, and am certainly never like to see it again. It was a low house of two stories standing back a little from the street, with some wooden palings and a grass plot before it, and a stone-flagged path leading up to the door. The front of it was whitewashed, with green shutters, and had a shiny-leaved magnolia trained round about the windows. These jewellers had no shops, though sometimes they set a single necklace or bracelet in a bottom window, but put up notices proclaiming their trade. Thus there was over Aldobrand's door a board stuck out to say that he bought and sold jewels, and would lend money on diamonds or other valuables.

A sturdy serving-man opened the door, and when he heard our business was to sell a jewel, left us in a stone-floored hall or lobby, while he went upstairs to ask whether his master would see us. A few minutes later the stairs creaked, and Aldobrand himself came down. He was a little wizened man with yellow skin and deep wrinkles, not less than seventy years old; and I saw he wore shoes of polished leather, silver-buckled, and tilted-heeled to add to his stature. He began speaking to us from the landing, not coming down into the hall, but leaning over the handrail:

'Well, my sons, what would you with me? I hear you have a jewel to sell, but you must know I do not purchase sailors' flotsam. So if 'tis a moonstone or catseye, or some pin-head diamonds, keep them to make brooches for your sweethearts, for Aldobrand buys no toys like

139

that.'

He had a thin and squeaky voice, and spoke to us in our own tongue, guessing no doubt that we were English from our faces. 'Twas true he handled the language badly enough, yet I was glad he used it, for so I could follow all that was said.

'No toys like that,' he said again, repeating his last words, and Elzevir answered: 'May it please your worship, we are sailors from over sea, and this boy has a diamond that he would sell.'

I had the gem in my hand all ready, and when the old man squeaked peevishly, 'Out with it then, let's see, let's see,' I reached it out to him. He stretched down over the banisters, and took it; holding out his palm hollowed, as if 'twas some little paltry stone that might otherwise fall and be lost. It nettled me to have him thus underrate our treasure, even though he had never seen it, and so I plumped it down into his hand as if it were as big as a pumpkin. Now the hall was a dim place, being lit only by a half-circle of glass over the door, and so I could not see very well; yet in reaching down he brought his head near mine, and I could swear his face changed when he felt the size of the stone in his hand, and turned from impatience and contempt to wonder and delight. He took the jewel quickly from his palm, and held it up between finger and thumb, and when he spoke again, his voice was changed as well as his face, and had lost most of the sharp impatience.

'There is not light enough to see in this dark place—follow me,' and he turned back and went upstairs rapidly, holding the stone in his hand; and we close at his heels, being anxious not to lose sight of him now that he had our diamond, for all he was so rich and well known a man.

Thus we came to another landing, and there he flung open the door of a room which looked out west, and had the light of the setting sun streaming in full flood through the window. The change from the dimness of the stairs to this level red blaze was so quick that for a minute I could make out nothing, but turning my back to the window saw presently that the room was panelled all through with painted wood, with a bed let into the wall on one side, and shelves round the others, on which were many small coffers and strong-boxes of iron. The jeweller was sitting at a table with his face to the sun, holding the diamond up against the light, and gazing into it closely, so that I could see every working of his face. The hard and cunning look had come back to it, and he turned suddenly upon me and asked quite sharply, 'What is your name, boy? Whence do you come?'

Now I was not used to walk under false names, and he took me unawares, so I must needs blurt out, 'My name is John Trenchard, sir, and I come from Moonfleet, in Dorset.'

A second later I could have bitten off my tongue for having said as much, and saw Elzevir frowning at me to make me hold my peace. But 'twas too late then, for the merchant was writing down my answer in a parchment ledger. And though it would seem to most but a little thing that he should thus take down my name and birthplace, and only vexed us at the time, because we would not have it known at all whence we came; yet in the overrulings of Providence it was ordered that this note in Mr. Aldobrand's book should hereafter change the issue of my life.

'From Moonfleet, in Dorset,' he repeated to himself, as he finished writing my answer. 'And how did John Trenchard come by this?' and he tapped the diamond as it lay on the table before him.

Then Elzevir broke in quickly, fearing no doubt lest I should be betrayed into saying more: 'Nay, sir, we are not come to play at questions and answers, but to know whether your worship will buy this diamond, and at what price. We have no time to tell long histories, and so must only say that we are English sailors, and that the stone is fairly come by.' And he let his fingers play with the diamond on the table, as if he feared it might slip away from him.

'Softly, softly,' said the old man; 'all stones are fairly come by; but had you told me whence you got this, I might have spared myself some tedious tests, which now I must crave pardon for making.'

He opened a cupboard in the panelling, and took out from it a little pair of scales, some crystals, a blackstone, and a bottle full of a green liquid. Then he sat down again, drew the diamond gently from Elzevir's fingers, which were loath to part with it, and began using his scales; balancing the diamond carefully, now against a crystal, now against some small brass weights. I stood with my back to the sunset, watching the red light fall upon this old man as he weighed the diamond, rubbed it on the black-stone, or let fall on it a drop of the liquor, and so could see the wonder and emotion fade away from his face, and only hard craftiness left in it.

I watched him meddling till I could bear to watch no longer, feeling a fierce feverish suspense as to what he might say, and my pulse beating so quick that I could scarce stand still. For was not the decisive moment very nigh when we should know, from these parched-up lips, the value of the jewel, and whether it was worth risking life for, whether the fabric of our hopes was built on sure foundation or on slippery sand? So I turned my back on the diamond merchant, and looked out of the window, waiting all the while to catch the slightest word that might come from his lips.

I have found then and at other times that in such moments, though the mind be occupied entirely by one overwhelming thought, yet the eyes take in, as it were unwittingly, all that lies before them, so that we can afterwards recall a face or landscape of which at the time we took no note. Thus it was with me that night, for though I was thinking of nothing but the jewel, yet I noted everything that could be seen through the window, and the recollection was of use to me later on. The window was made in the French style, reaching down to the floor, and opening like a door with two leaves. It led on to a little balcony, and now stood open (for the day was still very hot), and on the wall below was trained a pear-tree, which half-embowered the balcony with its green leaves.

The window could be well protected in case of need, having lat-ticed wooden blinds inside, and heavy shutters shod with iron on the outer wall, and there were besides strong bolts and sockets from which ran certain wires whose use I did not know. Below the balcony was a square garden-plot, shut in with a brick wall, and kept very neat and trim. There were hollyhocks round the walls, and many-coloured poppies, with many other shrubs and flowers. My eyes fell on one especially, a tall red-blossomed rushy kind of flower, that I had never seen before; and that seemed indeed to be something out of the common, for it stood in the middle of a little earth-plot, and had the whole bed nearly to itself.

I was looking at this flower, not thinking of it, but wondering all the while whether Mr. Aldobrand would say the diamond was worth ten thousand pounds, or fifty, or a hundred thousand, when I heard him speaking, and turned round quick. 'My sons, and you especially, son John,' he said, and turned to me: 'this stone that you have brought me is no stone at all, but glass—or rather paste, for so we call it. Not but what it is good paste, and perhaps the best that I have seen, and so I had to try it to make sure. But against high chymic tests no sham can stand; and first it is too light in weight, and second, when rubbed on this Basanus or Black-stone, traces no line of white, as any diamond must. But, third and last, I have tried it with the hermeneutic proof, and dipped it in this most costly lembic; and the liquor remains pure green and clear, not turbid orange, a diamond leaves it.'

As he spoke the room spun round, and I felt the sickness and heart-sinking that comes with the sudden destruction of long-cherished hope. So it was all a sham, a bit of glass, for which we had risked our lives. Blackbeard had only mocked us even in his death, and from rich men we were become the poorest outcasts. And all the other bright fancies that had been built on this worthless thing fell down at once, like a house of cards. There was no money now with which to go back rich to Moonfleet, no money to cloak past offences, no money to marry Grace; and with that I gave a sigh, and my knees failing should have fallen had not Elzevir held me.

'Nay, son John,' squeaked the old man, seeing I was so put about, 'take it not hardly, for though this is but paste, I say not it is worthless. It is as fine work as ever I have seen, and I will offer you ten silver crowns for it; which is a goodly sum for a sailor-lad to have in hand, and more than all the other buyers in this town would bid you for it.'

'Tush, tush,' cried Elzevir, and I could hear the bitterness and dis-appointment in his voice, however much he tried to hide it; 'we are not come to beg for silver crowns, so keep them in your purse. And the devil take this shining sham; we are well quit of it; there is a curse upon the thing!' And with that he caught up the stone and flung it away out of the window in his anger.

This brought the diamond-buyer to his feet in a moment. 'You fool, you cursed fool!' he shrieked, 'are you come here to beard me? and when I say the thing is worth ten silver crowns do you fling it to the winds?'

I had sprung forward with a half thought of catching Elzevir's arm; but it was too late—the stone flew up in the air, caught the low rays of the setting sun for a moment, and then fell among the flowers. I could not see it as it fell, yet followed with my eyes the line in which it should have fallen, and thought I saw a glimmer where it touched the earth. It was only a flash or sparkle for an instant, just at the stem of that same rushy red-flowered plant, and then nothing more to be seen; but as I faced round I saw the little man's eyes turned that way too, and perhaps he saw the flash as well as I.

'There's for your ten crowns!' said Elzevir. 'Let us be going, lad.' And he took me by the arm and marched me out of the room and down the stairs.

'Go, and a blight on you!' says Mr. Aldobrand, his voice being not so high as when he cried out last, but in his usual squeak; and then he repeated, 'a blight on you,' just for a parting shot as we went through the door.

We passed two more waiting-men on the stairs, but they said nothing to us, and so we came to the street.

We walked along together for some time without a word, and then Elzevir said, 'Cheer up, lad, cheer up. Thou saidst thyself thou fearedst there was a curse on the thing, so now it is gone, maybe we are well quit of it.'

Yet I could not say anything, being too much disappointed to find the diamond was a sham, and bitterly cast down at the loss of all our hopes. It was all very well to think there was a curse upon the stone so long as we had it, and to feign that we were ready to part with it; but now it was gone I knew that at heart I never wished to part with it at all, and would have risked any curse to have it back again. There was supper waiting for us when we got back, but I had no stomach for victuals and sat moodily while Elzevir ate, and he not much. But when I sat and brooded over what had happened, a new thought came to my mind and I jumped up and cried, 'Elzevir, we are fools! The stone is no sham; 'tis a real diamond!'

He put down his knife and fork, and looked at me, not saying anything, but waiting for me to say more, and yet did not show so much surprise as I expected. Then I reminded him how the old merchant's face was full of wonder and delight when first he saw the stone, which showed he thought it was real then, and how afterwards, though he schooled his voice to bring out long words to deceive us, he was ready enough to spring to his feet and shriek out loud when Elzevir threw the stone into the garden. I spoke fast, and in talking to him convinced myself, so when I stopped for want of breath I was quite sure that the stone was indeed a diamond, and that Aldobrand had duped us.

Still Elzevir showed little eagerness, and only said—

''Tis like enough that what you say is true, but what would you have us do? The stone is flung away.'

'Yes,' I answered; 'but I saw where it fell, and know the very place; let us go back now at once and get it.'

'Do you not think that Aldobrand saw the place too?' asked Elzevir; and then I remembered how, when I turned back to the room after seeing the stone fall, I caught the eyes of the old merchant looking the same way; and how he spoke more quietly after that, and not with the bitter cry he used when Elzevir tossed the jewel out of the window.

'I do not know,' I said doubtfully; 'let us go back and see. It fell just by the stem of a red flower that I marked well. What!' I added, seeing him still hesitate and draw back, 'do you doubt? Shall we not go and get it?'

Still he did not answer for a minute, and then spoke slowly, as if weighing his words. 'I cannot tell. I think that all you say is true, and that this stone is real. Nay, I was half of that mind when I threw it away, and yet I would not say we are not best without it. 'Twas you who first spoke of a curse upon the jewel, and I laughed at that as being a childish tale. But now I cannot tell; for ever since we first scented this treasure luck has run against us, John; yes, run against us very strong; and here we are, flying from home, called outlaws, and with blood upon our hands. Not that blood frightens me, for I have stood face to face with men in fair fight, and never felt a death-blow given so weigh on my soul; but these two men came to a tricksy kind of end, and yet I could not help it. 'Tis true that all my life I've served the Contraband, but no man ever knew me do a foul action; and now I do not like that men should call me felon, and like it less that they should call thee felon too. Perhaps there may be after all some curse that hangs about this stone, and leads to ruin those that handle it. I cannot say, for I am not a Parson Glennie in these things; but Blackbeard in an evil mood may have tied the treasure up to be a curse to any that use it for themselves. What do we want with this thing at all? I have got money to be touched at need; we may lie quiet this side the Channel, where thou shalt learn an honest trade, and when the mischief has blown over we will go back to Moonfleet. So let the jewel be, John; shall we not let the jewel be?'

He spoke earnestly, and most earnestly at the end, taking me by the hand and looking me full in the face. But I could not look him back again, and turned my eyes away, for I was wilful, and would not bring myself to let the diamond go. Yet all the while I thought that what he said was true, and I remembered that sermon that Mr. Glennie preached, saying that life was like a 'Y', and that to each comes a time when two ways part, and where he must choose whether he will take the broad and sloping road or the steep and narrow path. So now I guessed that long ago I had chosen the broad road, and now was but walking farther down it in seeking after this evil treasure, and still I could not bear to give all up, and persuaded myself that it was a child's folly to madly fling away so fine a stone. So instead of listening to good advice from one so much older than me, I set to work to talk him over, and persuaded him that if we got the diamond again, and ever could sell it, we would give the money to build up the Mohune almshouses, knowing well in my heart that I never meant to do any such thing. Thus at the last Elzevir, who was the stubbornest of men, and never yielded, was overborne by his great love to me, and yielded here.

It was ten o'clock before we set out together, to go again to Aldobrand's, meaning to climb the garden wall and get the stone. I walked quickly enough, and talked all the time to silence my own misgivings, but Elzevir hung back a little and said nothing, for it was sorely against his judgement that he came at all. But as we neared the place I ceased my chatter, and so we went on in silence, each busy with his own thoughts, We did not come in front of Aldobrand's house, but turned out of the main street down a side lane which we guessed would skirt the garden wall. There were few people moving even in the streets, and in this little lane there was not a soul to meet as we crept along in the shadow of the high walls. We were not mistaken, for soon we came to what we judged was the outside of Aldobrand's garden.

Here we paused for a minute, and I believe Elzevir was for making a last remonstrance, but I gave him no chance, for I had found a place where some bricks were loosened in the wall-face, and set myself to climb. It was easy enough to scale for us, and in a minute we both dropped down in a bed of soft mould on the other side. We pushed through some gooseberry-bushes that caught the clothes, and distinguishing the outline of the house, made that way, till in a few steps we stood on the *pelouse* or turf, which I had seen from the balcony three hours before. I knew the twirl of the walks, and the pattern of the beds; the rank of hollyhocks that stood up all along the wall, and the poppies breathing out a faint sickly odour in the night.

An utter silence held all the garden, and, the night being very clear, there was still enough light to show the colours of the flowers when one looked close at them, though the green of the leaves was turned to grey. We kept in the shadow of the wall, and looked expectantly at the house. But no murmur came from it, it might have been a house of the dead for any noise the living made there; nor was there light in any window, except in one behind the balcony, to which our eyes were turned first. In that room there was someone not yet gone to rest, for we could see a lattice of light where a lamp shone through the open work of the wooden blinds.

'He is up still,' I whispered, 'and the outside shutters are not closed.'

Elzevir nodded, and then I made straight for the bed where the red flower grew. I had no need of any light to see the bells of that great rushy thing, for it was different from any of the rest, and besides that was planted by itself.

I pointed it out to Elzevir. 'The stone lies by the stalk of that flower,' I said, 'on the side nearest to the house'; and then I stayed him with my hand upon his arm, that he should stand where he was at the bed's edge, while I stepped on and got the stone.

My feet sank in the soft earth as I passed through the fringe of poppies circling the outside of the bed, and so I stood beside the tall rushy flower. The scarlet of its bells was almost black, but there was no mistaking it, and I stooped to pick the diamond up. Was it possible? was there nothing for my outstretched hand to finger, except the soft rich loam, and on the darkness of the ground no guiding sparkle? I knelt down to make more sure, and looked all round the plant, and still found nothing, though it was light enough to see a pebble, much more to catch the gleam and flash of the great diamond I knew so well.

It was not there, and yet I knew that I had seen it fall beyond all room for doubt. 'It is gone, Elzevir; it is gone!' I cried out in my anguish, but only heard a 'Hush!' from him to bid me not to speak so loud. Then I fell on my knees again, and sifted the mould through my fingers, to make sure the stone had not sunk in and been overlooked.

But it was all to no purpose, and at last I stepped back to where Elzevir was, and begged him to light a piece of match in the shelter of the hollyhocks; and I would screen it with my hands, so that the light should fall upon the ground, and not be seen from the house, and so search round the flower. He did as I asked, not because he thought that I should find anything, but rather to humour me; and, as he put the lighted match into my hands, said, speaking low, 'Let the stone be, lad, let it be; for either thou didst fail to mark the place right, or others have been here before thee. 'Tis ruled we should not touch the stone again, and so 'tis best; let be, let be; let us get home.'

He put his hand upon my shoulder gently, and spoke with such an earnestness and pleading in his voice that one would have thought it was a woman rather than a great rough giant; and yet I would not hear, and broke away, sheltering the match in my hollowed hands, and making back to the red flower. But this time, just as I stepped upon the mould, coming to the bed from the house side, the light fell on the ground, and there I saw something that brought me up short.

It was but a dint or impress on the soft brown loam, and yet, before my eyes were well upon it, I knew it for the print of a sharp heel—a sharp deep heel, having just in front of it the outline of a little foot. There is a story every boy was given to read when I was young, of Crusoe wrecked upon a desert isle, who, walking one day on the shore, was staggered by a single footprint in the sand, because he learnt thus that there were savages in that sad place, where he thought he stood alone. Yet I believe even that footprint in the sand was never greater blow to him than was this impress in the garden mould to me, for I remembered well the little shoes of polished leather, with their silver buckles and high-tilted heels.

He *had* been here before us. I found another footprint, and another leading towards the middle of the bed; and then I flung the match away, trampling the fire out in the soil. It was no use searching farther now, for I knew well there was no diamond here for us.

I stepped back to the lawn, and caught Elzevir by the arm. 'Aldobrand has been here before us, and stole away the jewel,' I whispered sharp; and looking wildly round in the still night, saw the lattice of lamplight shining through the wooden blinds of the balcony window.

'Well, there's an end of it!' said he, 'and we are saved further question. 'Tis gone, so let us cry good riddance to it and be off.' So he turned to go back, and there was one more chance for me to choose the better way and go with him; but still I could not give the jewel up, and must go farther on the other path which led to ruin for us both. For I had my eyes fixed on the light coming through the blinds of that window, and saw how thick and strong the boughs of the pear-tree were trained against the wall about the balcony.

'Elzevir,' I said, swallowing the bitter disappointment which rose in my throat, 'I cannot go till I have seen what is doing in that room above. I will climb to the balcony and look in through the chinks'. Perhaps he is not there, perhaps he has left our diamond there and we may get it back again.' So I went straight to the house, not giving him time to raise a word to stop me, for there was something in me driving me on, and I was not to be stopped by anyone from that purpose.

There was no need to fear any seeing us, for all the windows except that one, were tight shuttered, and though our footsteps on the soft lawn woke no sound, I knew that Elzevir was following me. It was no easy task to climb the pear-tree, for all that the boughs looked so strong, for they lay close against the wall, and gave little hold for hand or foot. Twice, or more, an unripe pear was broken off, and fell rustling down through the leaves to earth, and I paused and waited to hear if anyone was disturbed in the room above; but all was deathly still, and at last I got my hand upon the parapet, and so came safe to the balcony.

I was panting from the hard climb, yet did not wait to get my breath, but made straight for the window to see what was going on inside. The outer shutters were still flung back, as they had been in the afternoon, and there was no difficulty in looking in, for I found an opening in the lattice-blind just level with my eyes, and could see all the room inside. It was well lit, as for a marriage feast, and I think there were a score of candles or more burning in holders on the table, or in sconces on the wall. At the table, on the farther side of it from me, and facing the window, sat Aldobrand, just as he sat when he told us the stone was a sham. His face was turned towards the window, and as I looked full at him it seemed impossible but that he should know that I was there.

In front of him, on the table, lay the diamond—our diamond, my diamond; for I knew it was a diamond now, and not false. It was not alone, but had a dozen more cut gems laid beside it on the table, each a little apart from the other; yet there was no mistaking mine, which was thrice as big as any of the rest. And if it surpassed them in size, how much more did it excel in fierceness and sparkle! All the candles in the room were mirrored in it, and as the splendour flashed from every line and facet that I knew so well, it seemed to call to me, 'Am I not queen of all diamonds of the world? am I not your diamond? will you not take me to yourself again? will you save me from this sorry trickster?'

I had my eyes fixed, but still knew that Elzevir was beside me. He would not let me risk myself in any hazard alone without he stood by me himself to help in case of need; and yet his faithfulness but galled me now, and I asked myself with a sneer, Am I never to stir hand or foot without this man to dog me? The merchant sat still for a minute as though thinking, and then he took one of the diamonds that lay on the table, and then another, and set them close beside the great stone, pitting them, as it were, with it. Yet how could any match with that?—for it outshone them all as the sun outshines the stars in heaven.

Then the old man took the stone and weighed it in the scales which stood on the table before him, balancing it carefully, and a dozen times, against some little weights of brass; and then he wrote with pen and ink in a sheepskin book, and afterwards on a sheet of paper as though casting up numbers. What would I not have given to see the figures that he wrote? for was he not casting up the value of the jewel, and summing out the profits he would make? After that he took the stone between finger and thumb, holding it up before his eyes, and placing it now this way, now that, so that the light might best fall on it. I could have cursed him for the wondering love of that fair jewel that overspread his face; and cursed him ten times more for the smile upon his lips, because I guessed he laughed to think how he had duped two simple sailors that very afternoon.

There was the diamond in his hands—our diamond, my diamond—in his hands, and I but two yards from my own; only a flimsy veil of wood and glass to keep me from the treasure he had basely stolen from us. Then I felt Elzevir's hand upon my shoulder. 'Let us be going,' he said; 'a minute more and he may come to put these shutters to, and find us here. Let us be going. Diamonds are not for simple folk like us; this is an evil stone, and brings a curse with it. Let us be going, John.'

But I shook off the kind hand roughly, forgetting how he had saved my life, and nursed me for many weary weeks and stood by me through bad and worse; for just now the man at the table rose and took out a little iron box from a cupboard at the back of the room. I knew that he was going to lock my treasure into it, and that I should see it no more. But the great jewel lying lonely on the table flashed and sparkled in the light of twenty candles, and called to me, 'Am I not queen of all diamonds of the world? am I not your diamond? save me from the hands of this scurvy robber.'

Then I hurled myself forward with all my weight full on the joining of the window frames, and in a second crashed through the glass, and through the wooden blind into the room behind.

The noise of splintered wood and glass had not died away before there was a sound as of bells ringing all over the house, and the wires I had seen in the afternoon dangled loose in front of my face. But I cared neither for bells nor wires, for there lay the great jewel flashing before me. The merchant had turned sharp round at the crash, and darted for the diamond, crying 'Thieves! thieves! thieves!' He was nearer to it than I, and as I dashed forward our hands met across the table, with his underneath upon the stone. But I gripped him by the wrist, and though he struggled, he was but a weak old man, and in a few seconds I had it twisted from his grasp. In a few seconds—but before they were past the diamond was well in my hand—the door burst open, and in rushed six sturdy serving-men with staves and bludgeons.

Elzevir had given a little groan when he saw me force the window, but followed me into the room and was now at my side. 'Thieves! thieves! thieves!' screamed the merchant, falling back exhausted in his chair and pointing to us, and then the knaves fell on too quick for us to make for the window. Two set on me and four on Elzevir; and one man, even a giant, cannot fight with four—above all when they carry staves.

Never had I seen Master Block overborne or worsted by any odds; and Fortune was kind to me, at least in this, that she let me not see the issue then, for a staff caught me so round a knock on the head as made the diamond drop out of my hand, and laid me swooning on the floor.

CHAPTER 17: AT YMEGUEN

As if a thief should steal a tainted vest,
Some dead man's spoil, and sicken of his pest—Hood

'Tis bitterer to me than wormwood the memory of what followed, and I shall tell the story in the fewest words I may. We were cast into prison, and lay there for months in a stone cell with little light, and only foul straw to lie on. At first we were cut and bruised from that tussle and cudgelling in Aldobrand's house, and it was long before we were recovered of our wounds, for we had nothing but bread and water to live on, and that so bad as barely to hold body and soul together. Afterwards the heavy fetters that were put about our ankles set up sores and galled us so that we scarce could move for pain. And if the iron galled my flesh, my spirit chafed ten times more within those damp and dismal walls; yet all that time Elzevir never breathed a word of reproach, though it was my wilfulness had led us into so terrible a strait.

At last came our jailer, one morning, and said that we must be brought up that day before the *Geregt*, which is their Court of Assize, to be tried for our crime. So we were marched off to the court-house, in spite of sores and heavy irons, and were glad enough to see the daylight once more, and drink the open air, even though it should be to our death that we were walking; for the jailer said they were like to hang us for what we had done. In the court-house our business was soon over, because there were many to speak against us, but none to plead our cause; and all being done in the Dutch language I understood nothing of it, except what Elzevir told me afterwards.

There was Mr. Aldobrand in his black gown and buckled shoes with tip-tilted heels, standing at a table and giving evidence: How that one afternoon in August came two evil-looking English sailors to his house under pretence of selling a diamond, which turned out to be but a lump of glass: and that having taken observation of all his dwelling, and more particularly the approaches to his business-room, they went their ways. But later in the same day, or rather night, as he sat matching together certain diamonds for a coronet ordered by the most illustrious the Holy Roman Emperor, these same ill-favoured English sailors burst suddenly through shutters and window, and made forcible entry into his business-room. There they furiously attacked him, wrenched the diamond from his hand, and beat him within an ace of his life. But by the good Providence of God, and his own fore-sight, the window was fitted with a certain alarm, which rang bells in other parts of the house. Thus his trusty servants were summoned, and after being themselves attacked and nearly overborne, succeeded at last in mastering these scurvy ruffians and handing them over to the law, from which Mr. Aldobrand claimed sovereign justice.

Thus much Elzevir explained to me afterwards, but at that time when that pretender spoke of the diamond as being his own, Elzevir cut in and said in open court that 'twas a lie, and that this precious stone was none other than the one that we had offered in the after-noon, when Aldobrand had said 'twas glass. Then the diamond mer-chant laughed, and took from his purse our great diamond, which seemed to fill the place with light and dazzled half the court. He turned it over in his hand, poising it in his palm like a great flourishing lamp of light, and asked if 'twas likely that two common sailor-men should hawk a stone like that.

Nay more, that the court might know what daring rogues they had to deal with, he pulled out from his pocket the quittance given him by Shalamof the Jew of Petersburg, for this same jewel, and showed it to the judge. Whether 'twas a forged quittance or one for some other stone we knew not, but Elzevir spoke again, saying that the stone was ours and we had found it in England. When Mr. Aldobrand laughed again, and held the jewel up once more: were such pebbles, he asked, found on the shore by every squalid fisherman? And the great dia-mond flashed as he put it back into his purse, and cried to me, 'Am I not queen of all the diamonds of the world? Must I house with this base rascal?' but I was powerless now to help.

After Aldobrand, the serving-men gave witness, telling how they had trapped us in the act, red-handed: and as for this jewel, they had seen their master handle it any time in these six months past.

But Elzevir was galled to the quick with all their falsehoods, and burst out again, that they were liars and the jewel ours; till a jailer who stood by struck him on the mouth and cut his lip, to silence him.

The process was soon finished, and the judge in his red robes stood up and sentenced us to the galleys for life; bidding us admire the mercy of the law to Outlanders, for had we been but Dutchmen, we should sure have hanged.

Then they took and marched us out of court, as well as we could walk for fetters, and Elzevir with a bleeding mouth. But as we passed the place where Aldobrand sat, he bows to me and says in English, 'Your servant, Mr. Trenchard. I wish you a good day, Sir John Trenchard—of Moonfleet, in Dorset.' The jailer paused a moment, hearing Aldobrand speak to us though not understanding what he said, so I had time to answer him:

'Good day, Sir Aldobrand, Liar, and Thief; and may the diamond bring you evil in this present life, and damnation in that which is to come.'

So we parted from him, and at that same time departed from our liberty and from all joys of life.

We were fettered together with other prisoners in droves of six, our wrists manacled to a long bar, but I was put into a different gang from Elzevir. Thus we marched a ten days' journey into the country to a place called Ymeguen, where a royal fortress was building. That was a weary march for me, for 'twas January, with wet and miry roads, and I had little enough clothes upon my back to keep off rain and cold. On either side rode guards on horseback, with loaded flint-locks across the saddlebow, and long whips in their hands with which they let fly at any laggard; though 'twas hard enough for men to walk where the mud was over the horses' fetlocks. I had no chance to speak to Elzevir all the journey, and indeed spoke nothing at all, for those to whom I was chained were brute beasts rather than men, and spoke only in Dutch to boot.

There was but little of the building of the fortress begun when we reached Ymeguen, and the task that we were set to was the digging of the trenches and other earthworks. I believe that there were five hundred men employed in this way, and all of them condemned like us to galley-work for life. We were divided into squads of twenty-five, but

Elzevir was drafted to another squad and a different part of the workings, so I saw him no more except at odd times, now and again, when our gangs met, and we could exchange a word or two in passing.

Thus I had no solace of any company but my own, and was driven to thinking, and to occupy my mind with the recollection of the past. And at first the life of my boyhood, now lost for ever, was constantly present even in my dreams, and I would wake up thinking that I was at school again under Mr. Glennie, or talking in the summer-house with Grace, or climbing Weatherbeech Hill with the salt Channel breeze singing through the trees. But alas! these things faded when I opened my eyes, and knew the foul-smelling wood-hut and floor of fetid straw where fifty of us lay in fetters every night; I say I dreamt these things at first, but by degrees remembrance grew blunted and the images less clear, and even these sweet, sad visions of the night came to me less often. Thus life became a weary round, in which month followed month, season followed season, year followed year, and brought always the same eternal profitless-work. And yet the work was merciful, for it dulled the biting edge of thought, and the unchanging evenness of life gave wings to time.

In all the years the locusts ate for me at Ymeguen, there is but one thing I need speak of here. I had been there a week when I was loosed one morning from my irons, and taken from work into a little hut apart, where there stood a half-dozen of the guard, and in the midst a stout wooden chair with clamps and bands. A fire burned on the floor, and there was a fume and smoke that filled the air with a smell of burned meat. My heart misgave me when I saw that chair and fire, and smelt that sickly smell, for I guessed this was a torture room, and these the torturers waiting. They forced me into the chair and bound me there with lashings and a cramp about the head; and then one took a red-iron from the fire upon the floor, and tried it a little way from his hand to prove the heat. I had screwed up my heart to bear the pain as best I might, but when I saw that iron sighed for sheer relief, because I knew it for only a branding tool, and not the torture.

And so they branded me on the left cheek, setting the iron between the nose and cheek-bone, where 'twas plainest to be seen. I took the pain and scorching light enough, seeing that I had looked for much worse, and should not have made mention of the thing here at all, were it not for the branding mark they used. Now this mark was a 'Y', being the first letter of Ymeguen, and set on all the prisoners that worked there, as I found afterwards; but to me 'twas much more than a mere letter, and nothing less than the black 'Y' itself, or *cross-pall* of the Mohunes. Thus as a sheep is marked, with his owner's keel and can be claimed wherever he may be, so here was I branded with the keel of the Mohunes and marked for theirs in life or death, whithersoever I should wander. 'Twas three months after that, and the mark healed and well set, that I saw Elzevir again; and as we passed each other in the trench and called a greeting, I saw that he too bore the *cross-pall* full on his left cheek.

Thus years went on and I was grown from boy to man, and that no weak one either: for though they gave us but scant food and bad, the air was fresh and strong, because Ymeguen was meant for palace as well as fortress, and they chose a healthful site. And by degrees the moats were dug, and ramparts built, and stone by stone the castle rose till 'twas near the finish, and so our labour was not wanted. Every day squads of our fellow-prisoners marched away, and my gang was left till nearly last, being engaged in making good a culvert that heavy rains had broken down.

It was in the tenth year of our captivity, and in the twenty-sixth of my age, that one morning instead of the guard marching us to work, they handed us over to a party of mounted soldiers, from whose matchlocks and long whips I knew that we were going to leave Ymeguen. Before we left, another gang joined us, and how my heart went out when I saw Elzevir among them! It was two years or more since we had met even to pass a greeting, for I worked outside the fortress and he on the great tower inside, and I took note his hair was whiter and a sadder look upon his face. And as for the *cross-pall* on his cheek, I never thought of it at all, for we were all so well used to the mark, that if one bore it not stamped upon his face we should have stared at him as on a man born with but one eye.

But though his look was sad, yet Elzevir had a kind smile and hearty greeting for me as he passed, and on the march, when they served out our food, we got a chance to speak a word or two together. Yet how could we find room for much gladness, for even the pleasure of meeting was marred because we were forced thus to take note, as it were, of each other's misery, and to know that the one had nothing for his old age but to break in prison, and the other nothing but the prison to eat away the strength of his prime.

Before long, all knew whither we were bound, for it leaked out we were to march to the Hague and thence to Scheveningen, to take ship to the settlements of Java, where they use transported felons on the sugar farms. Was this the end of young hopes and lofty aims—to live and die a slave in the Dutch plantations? Hopes of Grace, hopes of seeing Moonfleet again, were dead long long ago; and now was there to be no hope of liberty, or even wholesome air, this side the grave, but only burning sun and steaming swamps, and the crack of the slave-driver's whip till the end came? Could it be so? Could it be so? And yet what help was there, or what release? Had I not watched ten years for any gleam or loophole of relief, and never found it? If we were shut in cells or dungeons in the deepest rock we might have schemed escape, but here in the open, fettered up in-droves, what could we do?

They were bitter thoughts enough that filled my heart as I trudged along the rough roads, fettered by my wrist to the long bar; and seeing Elzevir's white hair and bowed shoulders trudging in front of me, remembered when that head had scarce a grizzle on it, and the back was straight as the massive stubborn pillars in old Moonfleet church. What was it had brought us to this pitch? And then I called to mind a July evening, years ago, the twilight summer-house and a sweet grave voice that said, 'Have a care how you touch the treasure: it was evilly come by and will bring a curse with it.' Ay, 'twas the diamond had done it all, and brought a blight upon my life, since that first night I spent in Moonfleet vault; and I cursed the stone, and Blackbeard and his lost Mohunes, and trudged on bearing their cognizance branded on my face.

We marched back to the Hague, and through that very street where Aldobrand dwelt, only the house was shut, and the board that bore his name taken away; so it seemed that he had left the place or else was dead. Thus we reached the quays at last, and though I knew that I was leaving Europe and leaving all hope behind, yet 'twas a delight to smell the sea again, and fill my nostrils with the keen salt air.

CHAPTER 18: IN THE BAY

Let broad leagues dissever Him from yonder foam,
O God! to think man ever Comes too near his home—Hood

The ship that was to carry us swung at the buoy a quarter of a mile offshore, and there were row-boats waiting to take us to her. She was a brig of some 120 tons burthen, and as we came under the stern I saw her name was the *Aurungzebe*.

'Twas with regret unspeakable I took my last look at Europe; and casting my eyes round saw the smoke of the town dark against the darkening sky; yet knew that neither smoke nor sky was half as black as was the prospect of my life.

They sent us down to the orlop or lowest deck, a foul place where was no air nor light, and shut the hatches down on top of us. There were thirty of us all told, hustled and driven like pigs into this deck, which was to be our pigsty for six months or more. Here was just light enough, when they had the hatches off, to show us what sort of place it was, namely, as foul as it smelt, with never table, seat, nor anything, but roughest planks and balks; and there they changed our bonds, taking away the bar, and putting a tight bracelet round one wrist, with a padlocked chain running through a loop on it. Thus we were still ironed, six together, but had a greater freedom and more scope to move.

And more than this, the man who shifted the chains, whether through caprice, or perhaps because he really wished to show us what pity he might, padlocked me on to the same chain with Elzevir, saying, we were English swine and might sink or swim together. Then the hatches were put on, and there they left us in the dark to think or sleep or curse the time away. The weariness of Ymeguen was bad indeed, and yet it was a heaven to this night of hell, where all we had to look for was twice a day the moving of the hatches, and half an hour's glimmer of a ship's lantern, while they served us out the broken victuals that the Dutch crew would not eat.

I shall say nothing of the foulness of this place, because 'twas too foul to be written on paper; and if 'twas foul at starting, 'twas ten times worse when we reached open sea, for of all the prisoners only Elzevir and I were sailors, and the rest took the motion unkindly.

From the first we made bad weather of it, for though we were below and could see nothing, yet 'twas easy enough to tell there was a heavy head-sea running, almost as soon as we were well out of harbour. Although Elzevir and I had not had any chance of talking freely for so long, and were now able to speak as we liked, being linked so close together, we said but little. And this, not because we did not value very greatly one another's company, but because we had nothing to talk of except memories of the past, and those were too bitter, and came too readily to our minds, to need any to summon them. There was, too, the banishment from Europe, from all and everything we loved, and the awful certainty of slavery that lay continuously on us like a weight of lead. Thus we said little.

We had been out a week, I think—for time is difficult enough to measure where there is neither clock nor sun nor stars—when the weather, which had moderated a little, began to grow much worse. The ship plunged and laboured heavily, and this added much to our discomfort; because there was nothing to hold on by, and unless we lay flat on the filthy deck, we ran a risk of being flung to the side whenever there came a more violent lurch or roll. Though we were so deep down, yet the roaring of wind and wave was loud enough to reach us, and there was such a noise when the ship went about, such grinding of ropes, with creaking and groaning of timbers, as would make a landsman fear the brig was going to pieces.

And this some of our fellow-prisoners feared indeed, and fell to crying, or kneeling chained together as they were upon the sloping deck, while they tried to remember long-forgotten prayers. For my own part, I wondered why these poor wretches should pray to be delivered from the sea, when all that was before them was lifelong slavery; but I was perhaps able to look more calmly on the matter myself as having been at sea, and not thinking that the vessel was going to founder because of the noise. Yet the storm rose till 'twas very plain that we were in a raging sea, and the streams which began to trickle through the joinings of the hatch showed that water had got below.

'I have known better ships go under for less than this,' Elzevir said to me; 'and if our skipper hath not a tight craft, and stout hands to work her, there will soon be two score slaves the less to cut the canes in Java. I cannot guess where we are now—may be off Ushant, may be not so far, for this sea is too short for the Bay; but the saints send us sea-room, for we have been wearing these three hours.'

'Twas true enough that we had gone to wearing, as one might tell from the heavier roll or wallowing when we went round, instead of the plunging of a tack; but there was no chance of getting at our whereabouts. The only thing we had to reckon time withal, was the taking off of the hatch twice a day for food; and even this poor clock kept not the hour too well, for often there were such gaps and intervals as made our bellies pine, and at this present we had waited so long that I craved even that filthy broken meat they fed us with.

So we were glad enough to hear a noise at the hatch just as Elzevir had done speaking, and the cover was flung off, letting in a splash of salt water and a little dim and dusky light. But instead of the guard with their muskets and lanterns and the tubs of broken victuals, there was only one man, and that the jailer who had padlocked us into gangs at the beginning of the voyage.

He bent down for a moment over the hatch, holding on to the combing to steady himself in the sea-way, and flung a key on a chain down into the orlop, right among us. 'Take it,' he shouted in Dutch, 'and make the most of it. God helps the brave, and the devil takes the hindmost.'

That said, he stayed not one moment, but turned about quick and was gone. For an instant none knew what this play portended, and there was the key lying on the deck, and the hatch left open. Then Elzevir saw what it all meant, and seized the key. 'John,' cries he, speaking to me in English, 'the ship is foundering, and they are giving us a chance to save our lives, and not drown like rats in a trap.' With that he tried the key on the padlock which held our chain, and it fitted so well that in a trice our gang was free. Off fell the chain clanking on the floor, and nothing left of our bonds but an iron bracelet clamped round the left wrist. You may be sure the others were quick enough to make use of the key when they knew what 'twas, but we waited not to see more, but made for the ladder.

Now Elzevir and I, being used to the sea, were first through the hatchway above, and oh, the strength and sweet coolness of the sea air, instead of the warm, fetid reek of the orlop below! There was a good deal of water sousing about on the main deck, but nothing to show the ship was sinking, yet none of the crew was to be seen. We stayed there not a second, but moved to the companion as fast as we could for the heavy pitching of the ship, and so came on deck.

The dusk of a winter's evening was setting in, yet with ample light to see near at hand, and the first thing I perceived was that the deck was empty. There was not a living soul but us upon it. The brig was broached to, with her bows against the heaviest sea I ever saw, and the waves swept her fore and aft; so we made for the tail of the deck-house, and there took stock. But before we got there I knew why 'twas the crew were gone, and why they let us loose, for Elzevir pointed to something whither we were drifting, and shouted in my ear so that I heard it above all the raging of the tempest—'We are on a lee shore.'

We were lying head to sea, and never a bit of canvas left except one storm-staysail. There were tattered ribands fluttering on the yards to show where the sails had been blown away, and every now and then the staysail would flap like a gun going off, to show it wanted to follow them. But for all we lay head to sea, we were moving backwards, and each great wave as it passed carried us on stern first with a leap and swirling lift. 'Twas over the stern that Elzevir pointed, in the course that we were going, and there was such a mist, what with the wind and rain and spindrift, that one could see but a little way.

And yet I saw too far, for in the mist to which we were making a sternboard, I saw a white line like a fringe or valance to the sea; and then I looked to starboard, and there was the same white fringe, and then to larboard, and the white fringe was there too. Only those who know the sea know how terrible were Elzevir's words uttered in such a place. A moment before I was exalted with, the keen salt wind, and with a hope and freedom that had been strangers for long; but now 'twas all dashed, and death, that is so far off to the young, had moved nearer by fifty years—was moving a year nearer every minute.

'We are on a lee shore,' Elzevir shouted; and I looked and knew what the white fringe was, and that we should be in the breakers in half an hour. What a whirl of wind and wave and sea, what a whirl of thought and wild conjecture! What was that land to which we were drifting? Was it cliff, with deep water and iron face, where a good ship is shattered at a blow, and death comes like a thunder-clap? Or was it shelving sand, where there is stranding, and the pound, pound, pound of the waves for howls, before she goes to pieces and all is over?

We were in a bay, for there was the long white crescent of surf reaching far away on either side, till it was lost in the dusk, and the brig helpless in the midst of it. Elzevir had hold of my arm, and gripped it hard as he looked to larboard. I followed his eyes, and where one horn of the white crescent faded into the mist, caught a dark shadow in the air, and knew it was high land looming behind. And then the murk and driving rain lifted ever so little, and as it were only for that purpose; and we saw a misty bluff slope down into the sea, like the long head of a basking alligator poised upon the water, and stared into each other's eyes, and cried together, 'The Snout!'

It had vanished almost before it was seen, and yet we knew there was no mistake; it was the Snout that was there looming behind the moving rack, and we were in Moonfleet Bay. Oh, what a rush of thought then came, dazing me with its sweet bitterness, to think that after all these weary years of prison and exile we had come back to Moonfleet! We were so near to all we loved, so near—only a mile of broken water—and yet so far, for death lay between, and we had come back to Moonfleet to die. There was a change came over Elzevir's features when he saw the Snout; his face had lost its sadness and wore a look of sober happiness. He put his mouth close to my ear and said: 'There is some strange leading hand has brought us home at last, and

I had rather drown on Moonfleet Beach than live in prison any more, and drown we must within an hour. Yet we will play the man, and make a fight for life.' And then, as if gathering together all his force: 'We have weathered bad times together, and who knows but we shall weather this?'

The other prisoners were on deck now, and had found their way aft. They were wild with fear, being landsmen and never having seen an angry sea, and indeed that sea might have frighted sailors too. So they stumbled along drenched with the waves, and clustered round Elzevir, for they looked on him as a leader, because he knew the ways of the sea and was the only one left calm in this dreadful strait.

It was plain that when the Dutch crew found they were embayed, and that the ship must drift into the breakers, they had taken to the boats, for gig and jolly-boat were gone and only the pinnace left amidships. 'Twas too heavy a boat perhaps for them to have got out in such a fearful sea; but there it lay, and it was to that the prisoners turned their eyes. Some had hold of Elzevir's arms, some fell upon the deck and caught him by the knees, beseeching him to show them how to get the pinnace out.

Then he spoke out, shouting to make them hear: 'Friends, any man that takes to boat is lost. I know this bay and know this beach, and was indeed born hereabouts, but never knew a boat come to land in such a sea, save bottom uppermost. So if you want my counsel, there you have it, namely, to stick by the ship. In half an hour we shall be in the breakers; and I will put the helm up and try to head the brig bows on to the beach; so every man will have a chance to fight for his own life, and God have mercy on those that drown.'

I knew what he said was the truth, and there was nothing for it but to stick to the ship, though that was small chance enough; but those poor, fear-demented souls would have nothing of his advice now 'twas given, and must needs go for the boat. Then some came up from below who had been in the spirit-room and were full of drink and drink-courage, and heartened on the rest, saying they would have the pinnace out, and every soul should be saved. Indeed, Fate seemed to point them that road, for a heavier sea than any came on board, and cleared away a great piece of larboard bulwarks that had been working loose, and made, as it were, a clear launching-way for the boat.

Again did Elzevir try to prevail with them to stand by the ship, but they turned away and all made for the pinnace. It lay amidships and was a heavy boat enough, but with so many hands to help they got it to the broken bulwarks. Then Elzevir, seeing they would have it out at any price, showed them how to take advantage of the sea, and shifted the helm a little till the *Aurungzebe* fell off to larboard, and put the gap in the bulwarks on the lee. So in a few minutes there it lay at a rope's-end on the sheltered side, deep laden with thirty men, who were ill found with oars, and much worse found with skill to use them. There were one or two, before they left, shouted to Elzevir and me to try to make us follow them; partly, I think, because they really liked Elzevir, and partly that they might have a sailor in the boat to direct them; but the others cast off and left us with a curse, saying that we might go and drown for obstinate Englishmen.

So we two were left alone on the brig, which kept drifting backwards slowly; but the pinnace was soon lost to sight, though we saw that they were rowing wild as soon as she passed out of the shelter of the ship, and that they had much ado to keep her head to the sea.

Then Elzevir went to the kicking-wheel, and beckoned me to help him, and between us we put the helm hard up. I saw then that he had given up all hope of the wind shifting, and was trying to run her dead for the beach.

She was broached-to with her bows in the wind, but gradually paid off as the staysail filled, and so she headed straight for shore. The November night had fallen, and it was very dark, only the white fringe of the breakers could be seen, and grew plainer as we drew closer to it. The wind was blowing fiercer than ever, and the waves broke more fiercely nearer the shore. They had lost their dirty yellow colour when the light died, and were rolling after us like great black mountains, with a combing white top that seemed as if they must overwhelm us every minute. Twice they pooped us, and we were up to our waists in icy water, but still held to the wheel for our lives.

The white line was nearer to us now, and above all the rage of wind and sea I could hear the awful roar of the under-tow sucking back the pebbles on the beach. The last time I could remember hearing that roar was when I lay, as a boy, one summer's night 'twixt sleep and waking, in the little whitewashed bedroom at my aunt's; and I wondered now if any sat before their inland hearths this night, and hearing that far distant roar, would throw another log on the fire, and thank God they were not fighting for their lives in Moonfleet Bay. I could picture all that was going on this night on the beach—how Ratsey and the landers would have sighted the *Aurungzebe*, perhaps at noon, perhaps before, and knew she was embayed, and nothing could save her but the wind drawing to east.

But the wind would hold pinned in the south, and they would see sail after sail blown off her, and watch her wear and wear, and every time come nearer in; and the talk would run through the street that there was a ship could not weather the Snout, and must come ashore by sundown. Then half the village would be gathered on the beach, with the men ready to risk their lives for ours, and in no wise wishing for the ship to be wrecked; yet anxious not to lose their chance of booty, if Providence should rule that wrecked she must be. And I knew Ratsey would be there, and Damen, Tewkesbury, and Laver, and like enough Parson Glennie, and perhaps—and at that perhaps, my thoughts came back to where we were, for I heard Elzevir speaking to me:

'Look,' he said, 'there's a light!'

'Twas but the faintest twinkle, or not even that; only something that told there was a light behind drift and darkness. It grew clearer as we looked at it, and again was lost in the mirk, and then Elzevir said, 'Maskew's Match!'

It was a long-forgotten name that came to me from so far off, down such long alleys of the memory, that I had, as it were, to grope and grapple with it to know what it should mean. Then it all came back, and I was a boy again on the trawler, creeping shorewards in the light breeze of an August night, and watching that friendly twinkle from the Manor woods above the village. Had she not promised she would keep that lamp alight to guide all sailors every night till I came back again; was she not waiting still for me, was I not coming back to her now? But what a coming back! No more a boy, not on an August night, but broken, branded convict in the November gale! 'Twas well, indeed, there was between us that white fringe of death, that she might never see what I had fallen to.

'Twas likely Elzevir had something of the same thoughts, for he spoke again, forgetting perhaps that I was man now, and no longer boy, and using a name he had not used for years. 'Johnnie,' he said, 'I am cold and sore downhearted. In ten minutes we shall be in the surf. Go down to the spirit locker, drink thyself, and bring me up a bottle here. We shall both need a young man's strength, and I have not got it any more.'

I did as he bid me, and found the locker though the cabin was all awash, and having drunk myself, took him the bottle back. 'Twas good Hollands enough, being from the captain's own store, but nothing to the old Ararat milk of the Why Not? Elzevir took a pull at it, and then flung the bottle away. 'Tis sound liquor,' he laughed, '"and good for autumn chills", as Ratsey would have said.'

We were very near the white fringe now, and the waves followed us higher and more curling. Then there was a sickly wan glow that spread itself through the watery air in front of us, and I knew that they were burning a blue light on the beach. They would all be there wait-ing for us, though we could not see them, and they did not know that there were only two men that they were signalling to, and those two Moonfleet born. They burn that light in Moonfleet Bay just where a little streak of clay crops out beneath the pebbles, and if a vessel can make that spot she gets a softer bottom. So we put the wheel over a bit, and set her straight for the flare.

There was a deafening noise as we came near the shore, the shriek-ing of the wind in the rigging, the crash of the combing seas, and over all the awful grinding roar of the under-tow sucking down the pebbles.

'It is coming now,' Elzevir said; and I could see dim figures moving in the misty glare from the blue light; and then, just as the *Aurungzebe* was making fair for the signal, a monstrous combing sea pooped her and washed us both from the wheel, forward in a swirling flood. We grasped at anything we could, and so brought up bruised and half-drowned in the fore-chains; but as the wheel ran free, another sea struck her and slewed her round. There was a second while the water seemed over, under, and on every side, and then the *Aurungzebe* went broadside on Moonfleet beach, with a noise like thunder and a blow that stunned us.

I have seen ships come ashore in that same place before and since, and bump on and off with every wave, till the stout balks could stand the pounding no more and parted. But 'twas not so with our poor brig, for after that first fearful shock she never moved again, being flung so firm upon the beach by one great swamping wave that never another had power to uproot her. Only she careened over beachwards, turning herself away from the seas, as a child bows his head to escape a cruel master's ferule, and then her masts broke off, first the fore and then the main, with a splitting crash that made itself heard above all.

We were on the lee side underneath the shelter of the deckhouse clinging to the shrouds, now up to our knees in water as the wave came on, now left high and dry when it went back. The blue light was still burning, but the ship was beached a little to the right of it, and the

164

dim group of fishermen had moved up along the beach till they were opposite us. Thus we were but a hundred feet distant from them, but 'twas the interval of death and life, for between us and the shore was a maddened race of seething water, white foaming waves that leapt up from all sides against our broken bulwarks, or sucked back the pebbles with a grinding roar till they left the beach nearly dry.

We stood there for a minute hanging on, and waiting for resolution to come back to us after the shock of grounding. On the weather side the seas struck and curled over the brig with a noise like thunder, and the force of countless tons. They came over the top of the deck-house in a cataract of solid water, and there was a crash, crash, crash of rending wood, as plank after plank gave way before that stern assault. We could feel the deck-house itself quiver, and shake again as we stood with our backs against it, and at last it moved so much that we knew it must soon be washed over on us.

The moment had come. 'We must go after the next big wave runs back,' Elzevir shouted. 'Jump when I give the word, and get as far up the pebbles as you can before the next comes in: they will throw us a rope's-end to catch; so now goodbye, John, and God save us both!'

I wrung his hand, and took off my convict clothes, keeping my boots on to meet the pebbles, and was so cold that I almost longed for the surf. Then we stood waiting side by side till a great wave came in, turning the space 'twixt ship and shore into a boiling caldron: a minute later 'twas all sucked back again with a roar, and we jumped.

I fell on hands and feet where the water was a yard deep under the ship, but got my footing and floundered through the slop, in a desperate struggle to climb as high as might be on the beach before the next wave came in. I saw the string of men lashed together and reaching down as far as man might, to save any that came through the surf, and heard them shout to cheer us, and marked a coil of rope flung out. Elzevir was by my side and saw it too, and we both kept our feet and plunged forward through the quivering slack water; but then there came an awful thunder behind, the crash of the sea over the wreck, and we knew that another mountain wave was on our heels. It came in with a swishing roar, a rush and rise of furious water that swept us like corks up the beach, till we were within touch of the rope's-end, and the men shouted again to hearten us as they flung it out. Elzevir seized it with his left hand and reached out his right to me.

Our fingers touched, and in that very moment the wave fell instantly, with an awful suck, and I was swept down the beach again. Yet the under-tow took me not back to sea, for amid the floating wreckage floated the shattered maintop, and in the truck of that great spar I caught, and so was left with it upon the beach thirty paces from the men and Elzevir. Then he left his own assured salvation, namely the rope, and strode down again into the very jaws of death to catch me by the hand and set me on my feet. Sight and breath were failing me; I was numb with cold and half-dead from the buffeting of the sea; yet his giant strength was powerful to save me then, as it had saved me before. So when we heard once more the warning crash and thunder of the returning wave we were but a fathom distant from the rope. 'Take heart, lad,' he cried; ''tis now or never,' and as the water reached our breasts gave me a fierce shove forward with his hands. There was a roar of water in my ears, with a great shouting of the men upon the beach, and then I caught the rope.

CHAPTER 19: ON THE BEACH

Toll for the brave,
The grave that are no more;
All sunk beneath the wave
Fast by their native shore—Cowper

The night was cold, and I had nothing on me save breeches and boots, and those drenched with the sea, and had been wrestling with the surf so long that there was little left in me. Yet once I clutched the rope I clung to it for very life, and in a minute found myself in the midst of the beachmen. I heard them shout again, and felt strong hands seize me, but could not see their faces for a mist that swam before my eyes, and could not speak because my throat and tongue were cracked with the salt water, and the voice would not come. There was a crowd about me of men and some women, and I spread out my hands, blindly, to catch hold of them, but my knees failed and let me down upon the beach. And after that I remember only having coats flung over me, and being carried off out of the wind, and laid in warmest blankets before a fire. I was numb with the cold, my hair was matted with the salt, and my flesh white and shrivelled, but they forced liquor into my mouth, and so I lay in drowsy content till utter weariness bound me in sleep.

It was a deep and dreamless sleep for hours, and when it left me, gently and as it were inch by inch, I found I was still lying wrapped in blankets by the fire. Oh, what a vast and infinite peace was that, to lie there half-asleep, yet wake enough to know that I had slipped my prison and the pains of death, and was a free man here in my native place! At last I shifted myself a little, growing more awake; and opening my eyes saw I was not alone, for two men sat at a table by me with glasses and a bottle before them.

'He is coming-to,' said one, 'and may live yet to tell us who he is, and from what port his craft sailed.'

'There has been many a craft,' the other said, 'has sailed for many a port, and made this beach her last; and many an honest man has landed on it, and never one alive in such a sea. Nor would this one be living either, if it had not been for that other brave heart to stand by and save him. Brave heart, brave heart,' he said over to himself. 'Here, pass me the bottle or I shall get the vapours. 'Tis good against these early chills, and I have not been in this place for ten years past, since poor Elzevir was cut adrift.'

I could not see the speaker's face from where I lay upon the floor, yet seemed to know his voice; and so was fumbling in my weakened mind to put a name to it, when he spoke of Elzevir, and sent my thoughts flying elsewhere.

'Elzevir,' I said, 'where is Elzevir?' and sat up to look round, expecting to see him lying near me, and remembering the wreck more clearly now, and how he had saved me with that last shove forward on the beach. But he was not to be seen, and so I guessed that his great strength had brought him round quicker than had my youth, and that he was gone back to the beach.

'Hush,' said one of the men at the table, 'lie down and get to sleep again'; and then he added, speaking to his comrade: 'His brain is wandering yet: do you see how he has caught up my words about Elzevir?'

'No,' I struck in, 'my head is clear enough; I am speaking of Elzevir Block. I pray you tell me where he is. Is, he well again?' They got up and stared at one another and at me, when I named Elzevir Block, and then I knew the one that spoke for Master Ratsey only greyer than he was.

'Who are you?' he cried, 'who talk of Elzevir Block.'

'Do you not know me, Master Ratsey?' and I looked full in his face. 'I am John Trenchard, who left you so long ago. I pray you tell me where is Master Block?'

Master Ratsey looked as if he had seen a ghost, and was struck dumb at first: but then ran up and shook me by the hand so warmly that I fell back again on my pillow, while he poured out questions in a flood. How had I fared, where had I been, whence had I come? until I stopped him, saying: 'Softly, kind friend, and I will answer; only tell me first, where is Master Elzevir?'

'Nay, that I cannot say,' he answered, 'for never a soul has set eyes on Elzevir since that summer morning we put thee and him ashore at Newport.'

'Oh, fool me not!' I cried out, chafing at his excuses; 'I am not wandering now. 'Twas Elzevir that saved me in the surf last night. 'Twas he that landed with me.'

There was a look of sad amaze that came on Ratsey's face when I said that; a look that woke in me an awful surmise. 'What!' cried he, 'was that Master Elzevir that dragged thee through the surf?'

'Ay, 'twas he landed with me, 'twas he landed with me,' I said; trying, as it were, to make true by repeating that which I feared was not the truth. There was a minute's silence, and then Ratsey spoke very softly: 'There was none landed with you; there was no soul saved from that ship alive save you.'

His words fell, one by one, upon my ear as if they were drops of molten lead. 'It is not true,' I cried; 'he pulled me up the beach himself, and it was he that pushed me forward to the rope.'

'Ay, he saved thee, and then the under-tow got hold of him and swept him down under the curl. I could not see his face, but might have known there never was a man, save Elzevir, could fight the surf on Moonfleet beach like that. Yet had we known 'twas he, we could have done no more, for many risked their lives last night to save you both. We could have done no more.' Then I gave a great groan for utter anguish, to think that he had given up the safety he had won for himself, and laid down his life, there on the beach, for me; to think that he had died on the threshold of his home; that I should never get a kind look from him again, nor ever hear his kindly voice.

It is wearisome to others to talk of deep grief, and beside that no words, even of the wisest man, can ever set it forth, nor even if we were able could our memory bear to tell it. So I shall not speak more of that terrible blow, only to say that sorrow, so far from casting my body down, as one might have expected, gave it strength, and I rose up from the mattress where I had been lying. They tried to stop me, and even to hold me back, but for all I was so weak, I pushed them aside and must needs fling a blanket round me and away back to the beach.

The morning was breaking as I left the Why Not?, for 'twas in no other place but that I lay, and the wind, though still high, had abated. There were light clouds crossing the heaven very swiftly, and between them patches of clear sky where the stars were growing paler before the dawn. The stars were growing paler; but there was another star, that shone out from the Manor woods above the village, although I could not see the house, and told me Grace, like the wise virgins, kept her lamp alight all night. Yet even that light shone without lustre for me then, for my heart was too full to think of anything but of him who had laid down his life for mine, and of the strong kind heart that was stilled for ever.

'Twas well I knew the way, so sure of old, from Why Not? to beach; for I took no heed to path or feet, but plunged along in the morning dusk, blind with sorrow and weariness of spirit. There was a fire of driftwood burning at the back of the beach, and round it crouched a group of men in reefing jackets and sou'westers waiting for morning to save what they might from the wreck; but I gave them a wide berth and so passed in the darkness without a word, and came to the top of the beach. There was light enough to make out what was doing. The sea was running very high, but with the falling wind the waves came in more leisurely and with less of broken water, curling over in a tawny sweep and regular thunderous beat all along the bay for miles. There was no sign left of the hull of the *Aurungzebe*, but the beach was strewn with so much wreckage as one would have thought could never come from so small a ship.

There were barrels and kegs, gratings and hatch-covers, booms and pieces of masts and trucks; and beside all that, the heaving water in-shore was covered with a floating mask of broken match-wood, and the waves, as they curled over, carried up and dashed down on the pebble planks and beams beyond number. There were a dozen or more of men on the seaward side of the beach, with oilskins to keep the wet out, prowling up and down the pebbles to see what they could lay their hands on; and now and then they would run down al-most into the white fringe, risking their lives to save a keg as they had risked them to save their fellows last night—as they had risked their lives to save ours, as Elzevir had risked his life to save mine, and lost it there in the white fringe.

I sat down at the top of the beach, with elbows on knees, head be-tween hands, and face set out to sea, not knowing well why I was there or what I sought, but only thinking that Elzevir was floating some-where in that floating skin of wreck-wood, and that I must be at hand to meet him when he came ashore. He would surely come in time, for I had seen others come ashore that way. For when the *Bataviaman* went on the beach, I stood as near her as our rescuers had stood to us last night, and there were some aboard who took the fatal leap from off her bows and tried to battle through the surf. I was so near them I could mark their features and read the wild hope in their faces at the first, and then the under-tow took hold of them, and never one that saved his life that day. And yet all came to beach at last, and I knew them by their dead faces for the men I had seen hoping against hope 'twixt ship and shore; some naked and some clothed, some bruised and sorely beaten by the pebbles and the sea, and some sound and untouched—all came to beach at last.

So I sat and waited for him to come; and none of the beach-walkers said anything to me, the Moonfleet men thinking I came from Ringstave, and the Langton men that I belonged to Moonfleet; and both that I had marked some cask at sea for my own and was waiting till it should come in. Only after a while Master Ratsey joined me, and sitting down by me, begged me to eat bread and meat that he had brought. Now I had little heart to eat, but took what he gave me to save myself from his importunities, and having once tasted was led by nature to eat all, and was much benefited thereby. Yet I could not talk with Ratsey, nor answer any of his questions, though another time I should have put a thousand to him myself; and he seeing 'twas no good sat by me in silence, using a spy-glass now and again to make out the things floating at sea. As the day grew the men left the fire at the back of the beach, and came down to the sea-front where the waves were continually casting up fresh spoil. And there all worked with a will, not each one for his own hand, but all to make a common hoard which should be divided afterwards.

Among the flotsam moving outside the breakers I could see more than one dark ball, like black buoys, bobbing up and down, and lifting as the wave came by: and knew them for the heads of drowned men. Yet though I took Ratsey's glass and scanned all carefully enough, I could make nothing of them, but saw the pinnace floating bottom up, and farther out another boat deserted and down to her gunwale in the water. 'Twas midday before the first body was cast up, when the sky was breaking a little, and a thin and watery sun trying to get through, and afterwards three other bodies followed. They were part of the pinnace's crew, for all had the iron ring on the left wrist, as Ratsey told me, who went down to see them, though he said nothing of the branded 'Y', and they were taken up and put under some sheeting at the back of the beach, there to lie till a grave should be made ready for them.

Then I felt something that told me he was coming and saw a body rolled over in the surf, and knew it for the one I sought. 'Twas nearest me he was flung up, and I ran down the beach, caring nothing for the white foam, nor for the under-tow, and laid hold of him: for had he not left the rescue-line last night, and run down into the surf to save my worthless life? Ratsey was at my side, and so between us we drew him up out of the running foam, and then I wrung the water from his hair, and wiped his face and, kneeling down there, kissed him.

When they saw that we had got a body, others of the men came up, and stared to see me handle him so tenderly. But when they knew, at last, I was a stranger and had the iron ring upon my wrist, and a 'Y' burned upon my cheek, they stared the more; until the tale went round that I was he who had come through the surf last night alive, and this poor body was my friend who had laid down his life for me. Then I saw Ratsey speak with one and another of the group, and knew that he was telling them our names; and some that I had known came up and shook me by the hand, not saying anything because they saw my heart was full; and some bent down and looked in Elzevir's face, and touched his hands as if to greet him.

Sea and stones had been merciful with him, and he showed neither bruise nor wound, but his face wore a look of great peace, and his eyes and mouth were shut. Even I, who knew where 'twas, could scarcely see the 'Y' mark on his cheek, for the paleness of death had taken out the colour of the scar, and left his face as smooth and mellow-white as the alabaster figures in Moonfleet church. His body was naked from the waist up, as he had stripped for jumping from the brig, and we could see the great broad chest and swelling muscles that had pulled him out of many a desperate pass, and only failed him, for the first and last time so few hours ago.

They stood for a little while looking in silence at the old lander who had run his last cargo on Moonfleet beach, and then they laid his arms down by his side, and slung him in a sail, and carried him away. I walked beside, and as we came down across the sea-meadows, the sun broke out and we met little groups of schoolchildren making their way down to the beach to see what was doing with the wreck. They stood aside to let us go by, the boys pulling their caps and the girls dropping a curtsy, when they knew that it was a poor drowned body passing; and as I saw the children I thought I saw myself among them, and I was no more a man, but just come out from Mr. Glennie's teaching in the old almshouse hall.

Thus we came to the Why Not? and there set him down. The inn had not been let, as I learned afterwards, since Maskew died; and they had put a fire in it last night for the first time, knowing that the brig would be wrecked, and thinking that some might come off with their lives and require tending. The door stood open, and they carried him into the parlour, where the fire was still burning, and laid him down on the trestle-table, covering his face and body with the sail. This done they all stood round a little while, awkwardly enough, as not knowing what to do; and then slipped away one by one, because grief is a thing that only women know how to handle, and they wanted to be back on the beach to get what might be from the wreck. Last of all went Master Ratsey, saying, he saw that I would as lief be alone, and that he would come back before dark.

So I was left alone with my dead friend, and with a host of bitterest thoughts. The room had not been cleaned; there were spider-webs on the beams, and the dust stood so thick on the window-panes as to shut out half the light. The dust was on everything: on chairs and tables, save on the trestle-table where he lay. 'Twas on this very trestle they had laid out David's body; 'twas in this very room that this still form, who would never more know either joy or sorrow, had bowed down and wept over his son. The room was just as we had left it an April evening years ago, and on the dresser lay the great backgammon board, so dusty that one could not read the lettering on it; 'Life is like a game of hazard; the skilful player will make something of the worst of throws'; but what unskilful players we had been, how bad our throws, how little we had made of them!

'Twas with thoughts like this that I was busy while the short afternoon was spent, and the story went up and down the village, how that Elzevir Block and John Trenchard, who left so long ago, were come back to Moonfleet, and that the old lander was drowned saving the young man's life. The dusk was creeping up as I turned back the sail from off his face and took another look at my lost friend, my only friend; for who was there now to care a jot for me? I might go and drown myself on Moonfleet beach, for anyone that would grieve over me. What did it profit me to have broken bonds and to be free again? what use was freedom to me now? where was I to go, what was I to do? My friend was gone.

So I went back and sat with my head in my hands looking into the fire, when I heard someone step into the room, but did not turn, thinking it was Master Ratsey come back and treading lightly so as not to disturb me. Then I felt a light touch on my shoulder, and looking up saw standing by me a tall and stately woman, girl no longer, but woman in the full strength and beauty of youth. I knew her in a moment, for she had altered little, except her oval face had something more of dignity, and the tawny hair that used to fly about her back was now gathered up. She was looking down at me, and let her hand rest on my shoulder. 'John,' she said, 'have you forgotten me? May I not share your sorrow? Did you not think to tell me you were come? Did you not see the light, did you not know there was a friend that waited for you?'

I said nothing, not being able to speak, but marvelling how she had come just in the point of time to prove me wrong to think I had no friend; and she went on:

'Is it well for you to be here? Grieve not too sadly, for none could have died nobler than he died; and in these years that you have been away, I have thought much of him and found him good at heart, and if he did aught wrong 'twas because others wronged him more.'

And while she spoke I thought how Elzevir had gone to shoot her father, and only failed of it by a hair's-breadth, and yet she spoke so well I thought he never really meant to shoot at all, but only to scare the magistrate. And what a whirligig of time was here, that I should have saved Elzevir from having that blot on his conscience, and then that he should save my life, and now that Maskew's daughter should be the one to praise Elzevir when he lay dead! And still I could not speak.

And again she said: 'John, have you no word for me? have you forgotten? do you not love me still? Have I no part in your sorrow?'

Then I took her hand in mine and raised it to my lips, and said, 'Dear Mistress Grace, I have forgotten nothing, and honour you above all others: but of love I may not speak more to you—nor you to me, for we are no more boy and girl as in times past, but you a noble lady and I a broken wretch'; and with that I told how I had been ten years a prisoner, and why, and showed her the iron ring upon my wrist, and the brand upon my cheek.

At the brand she stared, and said, 'Speak not of wealth; 'tis not wealth makes men, and if you have come back no richer than you went, you are come back no poorer, nor poorer, John, in honour. And

I am rich and have more wealth than I can rightly use, so speak not of these things; but be glad that you are poor, and were not let to profit by that evil treasure. But for this brand, it is no prison name to me, but the Mohunes' badge, to show that you are theirs and must do their bidding. Said I not to you, Have a care how you touch the treasure, it was evilly come by and will bring a curse with it? But now, I pray you, with a greater earnestness, seeing you bear this mark upon you, touch no penny of that treasure if it should some day come back to you, but put it to such uses as Colonel Mohune thought would help his sinful soul.'

With that she took her hand from mine and bade me 'goodnight', leaving me in the darkening room with the glow from the fire lighting up the sail and the outline of the body that lay under it. After she was gone I pondered long over what she had said, and what that should mean when she spoke of the treasure one day coming back to me: but wondered much the most to find how constant is the love of woman, and how she could still find a place in her heart for so poor a thing as I. But as to what she said, I was to learn her meaning this very night.

Master Ratsey had come in and gone again, not stopping with me very long, because there was much doing on the beach; but bidding me be of good cheer, and have no fear of the law; for that the ban against me and the head-price had been dead for many a year. 'Twas Grace had made her lawyers move for this, refusing herself to sign the hue and cry, and saying that the fatal shot was fired by misadventure. And so a dread which was just waking was laid to rest for ever; and when Ratsey went I made up the fire, and lay down in the blankets in front of it, for I was dog-tired and longed for sleep. I was already dozing, but not asleep, when there was a knock at the door, and in walked Mr. Glennie. He was aged, and stooped a little, as I could see by the firelight, but for all that I knew him at once, and sitting up offered him what welcome I could.

He looked at me curiously at first, as taking note of the bearded man that had grown out of the boy he remembered, but gave me very kindly greeting, and sat down beside me on a bench. First, he lifted the sail from the dead body, and looked at the sleeping face. Then he took out a Common Prayer reading the *Commendamus* over the dead, and giving me spiritual comfort, and lastly, he fell to talking about the past. From him I learnt something of what had happened while I was away, though for that matter nothing had happened at all, except a few deaths, for that is the only sort of change for which we look in

Moonfleet. And among those who had passed away was Miss Arnold, my aunt, so that I was another friend the less, if indeed I should count her a friend: for though she meant me well, she showed her care with too much strictness to let me love her, and so in my great sorrow for Elzevir I found no room to grieve for her.

Whether from the spiritual solace Mr. Glennie offered me, or whether from his pointing out how much cause for thankfulness I had in being loosed out of prison and saved from imminent death, certain it was I felt some assuagement of grief, and took pleasure in his talk.

'And though I may by some be reprehended,' he said, 'for presuming to refer to profane authors after citing Holy Scripture, yet I cannot refrain from saying that even the great poet Homer counsels moderation in mourning, "for quickly," says he, "cometh satiety of chilly grief".'

After this I thought he was going, but he cleared his throat in such a way that I guessed he had something important to say, and he drew a long folded blue paper from his pocket. 'My son,' he said, opening it leisurely and smoothing it out upon his knee, 'we should never revile Fortune, and in speaking of Fortune I only use that appellation in our poor human sense, and do not imply that there is any Chance at all but what is subject to an over-ruling Providence; we should never, I say, revile Fortune, for just at that moment when she appears to have deserted us, she may be only gone away to seek some richest treasure to bring back with her. And that this is so let what I am about to read to you prove; so light a candle and set it by me, for my eyes cannot follow the writing in this dancing firelight.'

I took an end of candle which stood on the mantelpiece and did as he bid me, and he went on: 'I shall read you this letter which I received near eight years ago, and of the weightiness of it you shall yourself judge.'

I shall not here set down that letter in full, although I have it by me, but will put it shortly, because it was from a lawyer, tricked with long-winded phrases and spun out as such letters are to afford cover afterwards for a heavier charge. It was addressed to the Reverend Horace Glennie, Perpetual Curate of Moonfleet, in the County of Dorset, England, and written in English by Heer Roosten, Attorney and Signariat of the Hague in the Kingdom of Holland. It set forth that one Krispijn Aldobrand, jeweller and dealer in precious stones, at the Hague, had sent for Heer Roosten to draw a will for him. And that the said Krispijn Aldobrand, being near his end, had deposed to the said Heer Roosten, that he, Aldobrand, was desirous to leave all his goods to one John Trenchard, of Moonfleet, Dorset, in the Kingdom of England.

And that he was moved to do this, first, by the consideration that he, Aldobrand, had no children to whom to leave aught, and second, because he desired to make full and fitting restitution to John Trenchard, for that he had once obtained from the said John a diamond without paying the proper price for it. Which stone he, Aldobrand, had sold and converted into money, and having so done, found afterwards both his fortune and his health decline; so that, although he had great riches before he became possessed of the diamond, these had forthwith melted through unfortunate ventures and speculations, till he had little remaining to him but the money that this same diamond had brought.

He therefore left to John Trenchard everything of which he should die possessed, and being near death begged his forgiveness if he had wronged him in aught. These were the instructions which Heer Roosten received from Mr. Aldobrand, whose health sensibly declined, until three months later he died. It was well, Heer Roosten added, that the will had been drawn in good time, for as Mr. Aldobrand grew weaker, he became a prey to delusions, saying that John Trenchard had laid a curse upon the diamond, and professing even to relate the words of it, namely, that it should 'bring evil in this life, and damnation in that which is to come.' Nor was this all, for he could get no sleep, but woke up with a horrid dream, in which, so he informed Heer Roosten, he saw continually a tall man with a coppery face and black beard draw the bed-curtains and mock him.

Thus he came at length to his end, and after his death Heer Roosten endeavoured to give effect to the provision of the will, by writing to John Trenchard, at Moonfleet, Dorset, to apprise him that he was left sole heir. That address, indeed, was all the indication that Aldobrand had given, though he constantly promised his attorney to let him have closer information as to Trenchard's whereabouts, in good time. This information was, however, always postponed, perhaps because Aldobrand hoped he might get better and so repent of his repentance. So all Heer Roosten had to do was to write to Trenchard at Moonfleet, and in due course the letter was returned to him, with the information that Trenchard had fled that place to escape the law, and was then nowhere to be found. After that Heer Roosten was advised to write to the minister of the parish, and so addressed these lines to

Mr. Glennie.

This was the gist of the letter which Mr. Glennie read, and you may easily guess how such news moved me, and how we sat far into the night talking and considering what steps it was best to take, for we feared lest so long an interval as eight years having elapsed, the lawyers might have made some other disposition of the money. It was midnight when Mr. Glennie left. The candle had long burnt out, but the fire was bright, and he knelt a moment by the trestle-table before he went out.

'He made a good end, John,' he said, rising from his knees, 'and I pray that our end may be in as good cause when it comes. For with the best of us the hour of death is an awful hour, and we may well pray, as every Sunday, to be delivered in it. But there is another time which those who wrote this Litany thought no less perilous, and bade us pray to be delivered in all time of our wealth. So I pray that if, after all, this wealth comes to your hand you may be led to use it well; for though I do not hold with foolish tales, or think a curse hangs on riches themselves, yet if riches have been set apart for a good purpose, even by evil men, as Colonel John Mohune set apart this treasure, it cannot be but that we shall do grievous wrong in putting them to other use. So fare you well, and remember that there are other treasures besides this, and that a good woman's love is worth far more than all the gold and jewels of the world—as I once knew.' And with that he left me.

I guessed that he had spoken with Grace that day, and as I lay dozing in front of the fire, alone in this old room I knew so well, alone with that silent friend who had died to save me, I mourned him none the less, but yet sorrowed not as one without hope.

★★★★★★

What need to tell this tale at any more length, since you may know, by my telling it, that all went well? for what man would sit down to write a history that ended in his own discomfiture? All that great wealth came to my hands, and if I do not say how great it was, 'tis that I may not wake envy, for it was far more than ever I could have thought. And of that money I never touched penny piece, having learnt a bitter lesson in the past, but laid it out in good works, with Mr. Glennie and Grace to help me. First, we rebuilt and enlarged the almshouses beyond all that Colonel John Mohune could ever think of, and so established them as to be a haven for ever for all worn-out sailors of that coast. Next, we sought the guidance of the Brethren of the Trinity, and built a lighthouse on the Snout, to be a Channel beacon for sea-going ships, as Maskew's match had been a light for our fishing-boats in the past.

Lastly, we beautified the church, turning out the cumbrous seats of oak, and neatly pewing it with deal and baize, that made it most commodious to sit in of the Sabbath. There was also much old glass which we removed, and reglazed all the windows tight against the wind, so that what with a high pulpit, reading-desk, and seat for Master Clerk and new Commandment boards each side of the Holy Table, there was not a church could vie with ours in the countryside. But that great vault below it, with its memories, was set in order, and then safely walled up, and after that nothing was more ever heard of Blackbeard and his lost Mohunes. And as for the landers, I cannot say where they went; and if a cargo is still run of a dark night upon the beach, I know nothing of it, being both Lord of the Manor and Justice of the Peace.

The village, too, renewed itself with the new almshouses and church. There were old houses rebuilt and fresh ones reared, and all are ours, except the Why Not? which still remains the Duchy Inn. And that was let again, and men left the Choughs at Ringstave and came back to their old haunt, and any shipwrecked or travel-worn sailor found board and welcome within its doors.

And of the Mohune Hospital—for that was what the alms-houses were now called—Master Glennie was first warden, with fair rooms and a full library, and Master Ratsey head of the Bedesmen. There they spent happier days, till they were gathered in the fullness of their years; and sleep on the sunny side of the church, within sound of the sea, by that great buttress where I once found Master Ratsey listening with his ear to ground. And close beside them lies Elzevir Block, most faithful and most loved by me, with a text on his tombstone: 'Greater love hath no man than this, that a man lay down his life for his friend,' and some of Mr. Glennie's verses.

And of ourselves let me speak last. The Manor House is a stately home again, with trim lawns and terraced balustrades, where we can sit and see the thin blue smoke hang above the village on summer evenings. And in the Manor woods my wife and I have seen a little Grace and a little John and little Elzevir, our firstborn, play; and now our daughter is grown up, fair to us as the polished corners of the Temple, and our sons are gone out to serve King George on sea and land. But as for us, for Grace and me, we never leave this our happy Moonfleet, being well content to see the dawn tipping the long cliff-line with gold, and the night walking in dew across the meadows; to watch the spring clothe the beech boughs with green, or the figs ripen on the southern wall: while behind all, is spread as a curtain the eternal sea, ever the same and ever changing.

Yet I love to see it best when it is lashed to madness in the autumn gale, and to hear the grinding roar and churn of the pebbles like a great organ playing all the night. 'Tis then I turn in bed and thank God, more from the heart, perhaps, than, any other living man, that I am not fighting for my life on Moonfleet Beach. And more than once I have stood rope in hand in that same awful place, and tried to save a struggling wretch; but never saw one come through the surf alive, in such a night as he saved me.

The Lost Stradivarius

Contents

LETTER FROM MISS SOPHIA MALTRAVERS TO HER NEPHEW, SIR
EDWARD MALTRAVERS, THEN A STUDENT AT CHRIST CHURCH,
OXFORD

13 Pauncefort Buildings, Bath,
Oct. 21, 1867.

My Dear Edward,
It was your late father's dying request that certain events which
occurred in his last years should be communicated to you on
your coming of age. I have reduced them to writing, partly
from my own recollection, which is, alas! still too vivid, and
partly with the aid of notes taken at the time of my brother's
death. As you are now of full age, I submit the narrative to you.
Much of it has necessarily been exceedingly painful to me to
write, but at the same time I feel it is better that you should
hear the truth from me than garbled stories from others who
did not love your father as I did.

                    Your loving Aunt,

                              Sophia Maltravers
To Sir Edward Maltravers, Bart.

A tale out of season is as music in mourning.
                              —*Ecclesiasticus* xxii. 6.

Miss Sophia Maltravers' Story

CHAPTER 1

Your father, John Maltravers, was born in 1820 at Worth, and succeeded his father and mine, who died when we were still young children. John was sent to Eton in due course, and in 1839, when he was nineteen years of age, it was determined that he should go to Oxford. It was intended at first to enter him at Christ Church; but Dr. Sarsdell, who visited us at Worth in the summer of 1839, persuaded Mr. Thoresby, our guardian, to send him instead to Magdalen Hall. Dr. Sarsdell was himself Principal of that institution, and represented that John, who then exhibited some symptoms of delicacy, would meet with more personal attention under his care than he could hope to do in so large a college as Christ Church. Mr. Thoresby, ever solicitous for his ward's welfare, readily waived other considerations in favour of an arrangement which he considered conducive to John's health, and he was accordingly matriculated at Magdalen Hall in the autumn of 1839.

Dr. Sarsdell had not been unmindful of his promise to look after my brother, and had secured him an excellent first-floor sitting-room, with a bedroom adjoining, having an aspect towards New College Lane.

I shall pass over the first two years of my brother's residence at Oxford, because they have nothing to do with the present story. They were spent, no doubt, in the ordinary routine of work and recreation common in Oxford at that period.

From his earliest boyhood he had been passionately devoted to music, and had attained a considerable proficiency on the violin. In the autumn term of 1841 he made the acquaintance of Mr. William Gaskell, a very talented student at New College, and also a more than tolerable musician. The practice of music was then very much less common at Oxford than it has since become, and there were none of those societies existing which now do so much to promote its study among undergraduates. It was therefore a cause of much gratification to the two young men, and it afterwards became a strong bond of friendship, to discover that one was as devoted to the pianoforte as was the other to the violin. Mr. Gaskell, though in easy circumstances, had not a pianoforte in his rooms, and was pleased to use a fine instrument by D'Almaine that John had that term received as a birthday present from his guardian.

From that time the two students were thrown much together, and in the autumn term of 1841 and Easter term of 1842 practised a variety of music in John's rooms, he taking the violin part and Mr. Gaskell that for the pianoforte.

It was, I think, in March 1842 that John purchased for his rooms a piece of furniture which was destined afterwards to play no unimportant part in the story I am narrating. This was a very large and low wicker chair of a form then coming into fashion in Oxford, and since, I am told, become a familiar object of most college rooms. It was cushioned with a gaudy pattern of chintz, and bought for new of an upholsterer at the bottom of the High Street.

Mr. Gaskell was taken by his uncle to spend Easter in Rome, and obtaining special leave from his college to prolong his travels; did not return to Oxford till three weeks of the summer term were passed and May was well advanced. So impatient was he to see his friend that he would not let even the first evening of his return pass without coming round to John's rooms. The two young men sat without lights until the night was late; and Mr. Gaskell had much to narrate of his travels, and spoke specially of the beautiful music which he had heard at Easter in the Roman churches. He had also had lessons on the piano from a celebrated professor of the Italian style, but seemed to have been particularly delighted with the music of the seventeenth-century composers, of whose works he had brought back some specimens set for piano and violin.

It was past eleven o'clock when Mr. Gaskell left to return to New College; but the night was unusually warm, with a moon near the full, and John sat for some time in a cushioned window-seat before the open sash thinking over what he had heard about the music of Italy. Feeling still disinclined for sleep, he lit a single candle and began to turn over some of the musical works which Mr. Gaskell had left on the table. His attention was especially attracted to an oblong book, bound in soiled vellum, with a coat of arms stamped in gilt upon the side. It was a manuscript copy of some early suites by Graziani for violin and harpsichord, and was apparently written at Naples in the year 1744, many years after the death of that composer. Though the ink was yellow and faded, the transcript had been accurately made, and could be read with tolerable comfort by an advanced musician in spite of the antiquated notation.

Perhaps by accident, or perhaps by some mysterious direction which our minds are incapable of appreciating, his eye was arrested by a suite of four movements with a *basso continuo*, or figured bass, for the harpsichord. The other suites in the book were only distinguished by numbers, but this one the composer had dignified with the name of *"l'Areopagita."* Almost mechanically John put the book on his music-stand, took his violin from its case, and after a moment's tuning stood up and played the first movement, a lively *Coranto*. The light of the single candle burning on the table was scarcely sufficient to illumine the page; the shadows hung in the creases of the leaves, which had grown into those wavy folds sometimes observable in books made of thick paper and remaining long shut; and it was with difficulty that he could read what he was playing.

But he felt the strange impulse of the old-world music urging him forward, and did not even pause to light the candles which stood ready in their sconces on either side of the desk. The *Coranto* was followed by a *Sarabanda*, and the *Sarabanda* by a *Gagliarda*. My brother stood play-ing, with his face turned to the window, with the room and the large wicker chair of which I have spoken behind him. The *Gagliarda* began with a bold and lively air, and as he played the opening bars, he heard behind him a creaking of the wicker chair. The sound was a perfectly familiar one—as of some person placing a hand on either arm of the chair preparatory to lowering himself into it, followed by another as of the same person being leisurely seated. But for the tones of the violin, all was silent, and the creaking of the chair was strangely distinct.

The illusion was so complete that my brother stopped playing sud-denly, and turned round expecting that some late friend of his had slipped in unawares, being attracted by the sound of the violin, or that Mr. Gaskell himself had returned. With the cessation of the music an absolute stillness fell upon all; the light of the single candle scarcely reached the darker corners of the room, but fell directly on the wicker chair and showed it to be perfectly empty. Half amused, half vexed with himself at having without reason interrupted his music, my brother returned to the *Gagliarda*; but some impulse induced him to light the candles in the sconces, which gave an illumination more adequate to the occasion. The *Gagliarda* and the last movement, a *Minuetto*, were finished, and John closed the book, intending, as it was now late, to seek his bed. As he shut the pages a creaking of the wicker chair again attracted his attention, and he heard distinctly sounds such as would be made by a person raising himself from a sitting posture.

This time, being less surprised, he could more aptly consider the probable causes of such a circumstance, and easily arrived at the conclusion that there must be in the wicker chair osiers responsive to certain notes of the violin, as panes of glass in church windows are observed to vibrate in sympathy with certain tones of the organ. But while this argument approved itself to his reason, his imagination was but half convinced; and he could not but be impressed with the fact that the second creaking of the chair had been coincident with his shutting the music-book; and, unconsciously, pictured to himself some strange visitor waiting until the termination of the music, and then taking his departure.

His conjectures did not, however, either rob him of sleep or even disturb it with dreams, and he woke the next morning with a cooler mind and one less inclined to fantastic imagination. If the strange episode of the previous evening had not entirely vanished from his mind, it seemed at least fully accounted for by the acoustic explanation to which I have alluded above. Although he saw Mr. Gaskell in the course of the morning, he did not think it necessary to mention to him so trivial a circumstance, but made with him an appointment to sup together in his own rooms that evening, and to amuse themselves afterwards by essaying some of the Italian music.

It was shortly after nine that night when, supper being finished, Mr. Gaskell seated himself at the piano and John tuned his violin. The evening was closing in; there had been heavy thunder-rain in the afternoon, and the moist air hung now heavy and steaming, while across it there throbbed the distant vibrations of the tenor bell at Christ Church. It was tolling the customary 101 strokes, which are rung every night in term-time as a signal for closing the college gates. The two young men enjoyed themselves for some while, playing first a suite by Cesti, and then two early *sonatas* by Buononcini. Both of them were sufficiently expert musicians to make reading at sight a pleasure rather than an effort; and Mr. Gaskell especially was well versed in the theory of music, and in the correct rendering of the *basso continuo*.

After the Buononcini Mr. Gaskell took up the oblong copy of *Graziani*, and turning over its leaves, proposed that they should play the same suite which John had performed by himself the previous evening. His selection was apparently perfectly fortuitous, as my brother had purposely refrained from directing his attention in any way to that piece of music. They played the *Coranto* and the *Sarabanda*, and in the singular fascination of the music John had entirely forgotten the episode of the previous evening, when, as the bold air of the *Gagliarda* commenced, he suddenly became aware of the same strange creaking of the wicker chair that he had noticed on the first occasion. The sound was identical, and so exact was its resemblance to that of a person sitting down that he stared at the chair, almost wondering that it still appeared empty. Beyond turning his head sharply for a moment to look round, Mr. Gaskell took no notice of the sound; and my brother, ashamed to betray any foolish interest or excitement, continued the *Gagliarda*, with its repeat.

At its conclusion Mr. Gaskell stopped before proceeding to the minuet, and turning the stool on which he was sitting round towards the room, observed, "How very strange, Johnnie,"—for these young men were on terms of sufficient intimacy to address each other in a familiar style,—"How very strange! I thought I heard some one sit down in that chair when we began the *Gagliarda*. I looked round quite expecting to see some one had come in. Did you hear nothing?"

"It was only the chair creaking," my brother answered, feigning an indifference which he scarcely felt. "Certain parts of the wicker-work seem to be in accord with musical notes and respond to them; let us continue with the *Minuetto*."

Thus they finished the suite, Mr. Gaskell demanding a repetition of the *Gagliarda*, with the air of which he was much pleased. As the clocks had already struck eleven, they determined not to play more that night; and Mr. Gaskell rose, blew out the sconces, shut the piano, and put the music aside. My brother has often assured me that he was quite prepared for what followed, and had been almost expecting it; for as the books were put away, a creaking of the wicker chair was audible, exactly similar to that which he had heard when he stopped playing on the previous night. There was a moment's silence; the young men looked involuntarily at one another, and then Mr. Gaskell said, "I cannot understand the creaking of that chair; it has never done so before, with all the music we have played. I am perhaps imaginative and excited with the fine airs we have heard tonight, but I have an impression that I cannot dispel that something has been sitting listening to us all this time, and that now when the concert is ended it has got up and gone." There was a spirit of raillery in his words, but his tone was not so light as it would ordinarily have been, and he was evidently ill at ease.

"Let us try the *Gagliarda* again," said my brother; "it is the vibration of the opening notes which affects the wicker-work, and we shall see if the noise is repeated." But Mr. Gaskell excused himself from trying the experiment, and after some desultory conversation, to which it was evident that neither was giving any serious attention, he took his leave and returned to New College.

CHAPTER 2

I shall not weary you, my dear Edward, by recounting similar experiences which occurred on nearly every occasion that the young men met in the evenings for music. The repetition of the phenomenon had accustomed them to expect it. Both professed to be quite satisfied that it was to be attributed to acoustical affinities of vibration between the wicker-work and certain of the piano wires, and indeed this seemed the only explanation possible. But, at the same time, the resemblance of the noises to those caused by a person sitting down in or rising from a chair was so marked, that even their frequent recurrence never failed to make a strange impression on them. They felt a reluctance to mention the matter to their friends, partly from a fear of being themselves laughed at, and partly to spare from ridicule a circumstance to which each perhaps, in spite of himself, attached some degree of importance.

Experience soon convinced them that the first noise as of one sitting down never occurred unless the *Gagliarda* of the *Areopagita* was played, and that this noise being once heard, the second only followed it when they ceased playing for the evening. They met every night, sitting later with the lengthening summer evenings, and every night, as by some tacit understanding, played the *Areopagita* suite before parting. At the opening bars of the *Gagliarda* the creaking of the chair occurred spontaneously with the utmost regularity. They seldom spoke even to one another of the subject; but one night, when John was putting away his violin after a long evening's music without having played the *Areopagita*, Mr. Gaskell, who had risen from the pianoforte, sat down again as by a sudden impulse and said—

"Johnnie, do not put away your violin yet. It is near twelve o'clock and I shall get shut out, but I cannot stop tonight without playing the *Gagliarda*. Suppose that all our theories of vibration and affinity are wrong, suppose that there really comes here night by night some strange visitant to hear us, some poor creature whose heart is bound up in that tune; would it not be unkind to send him away without the hearing of that piece which he seems most to relish? Let us not be ill-mannered, but humour his whim; let us play the *Gagliarda.*"

They played it with more vigour and precision than usual, and the now customary sound of one taking his seat at once ensued. It was that night that my brother, looking steadfastly at the chair, saw, or thought he saw, there some slight obscuration, some penumbra, mist, or subtle vapour which, as he gazed, seemed to struggle to take human form. He ceased playing for a moment and rubbed his eyes, but as he did so all dimness vanished and he saw the chair perfectly empty. The pianist stopped also at the cessation of the violin, and asked what ailed him.

"It is only that my eyes were dim," he answered.

"We have had enough for tonight," said Mr. Gaskell; "let us stop. I shall be locked out." He shut the piano, and as he did so the clock in New College tower struck twelve. He left the room running, but was late enough at his college door to be reported, admonished with a fine against such late hours, and confined for a week to college; for being out after midnight was considered, at that time at least, a somewhat serious offence.

Thus for some days the musical practice was compulsorily intermitted, but resumed on the first evening after Mr. Gaskell's term of confinement was expired. After they had performed several suites of Graziani, and finished as usual with the *Areopagita*, Mr. Gaskell sat for a time silent at the instrument, as though thinking with himself, and then said—

"I cannot say how deeply this old-fashioned music affects me. Some would try to persuade us that these suites, of which the airs bear the names of different dances, were always written rather as a musical essay and for purposes of performance than for persons to dance to, as their names would more naturally imply. But I think these critics are wrong at least in some instances. It is to me impossible to believe that such a melody, for instance, as the *Giga* of Corelli which we have played, was not written for actual purposes of dancing. One can almost hear the beat of feet upon the floor, and I imagine that in the time of Corelli the practice of dancing, while not a whit inferior in grace, had more of the tripudistic or beating character than is now esteemed consistent with a correct ball-room performance. The *Gagliarda* too, which we play now so constantly, possesses a singular power of assisting the imagination to picture or reproduce such scenes as those which it no doubt formerly enlivened. I know not why, but it is constantly identified in my mind with some revel which I have perhaps seen in a picture, where several couples are dancing a licentious measure in a long room lit by a number of silver sconces of the debased model common at the end of the seventeenth century. It is probably a reminiscence of my late excursion that gives to these dancers in my fancy the olive skin, dark hair, and bright eyes of the Italian type; and they wear dresses of exceedingly rich fabric and elaborate design.

"Imagination is whimsical enough to paint for me the character of the room itself, as having an arcade of arches running down one side alone, of the fantastic and paganised Gothic of the Renaissance. At the end is a gallery or balcony for the musicians, which on its coved front has a florid coat of arms of foreign heraldry. The shield bears, on a field *or*, a cherub's head blowing on three lilies—a blazon I have no doubt seen somewhere in my travels, though I cannot recollect where. This scene, I say, is so nearly connected in my brain with the *Gagliarda*, that scarcely are its first notes sounded ere it presents itself to my eyes with a vividness which increases every day. The couples advance, set, and recede, using free and licentious gestures which my imagination should be ashamed to recall.

"Amongst so many foreigners, fancy pictures, I know not in the least why, the presence of a young man of an English type of face, whose features, however, always elude my mind's attempt to fix them. I think that the opening subject of this *Gagliarda* is a superior composition to the rest of it, for it is only during the first sixteen bars that the vision of bygone revelry presents itself to me. With the last note of the sixteenth bar a veil is drawn suddenly across the scene, and with a sense almost of some catastrophe it vanishes. This I attribute to the fact that the second subject must be inferior in conception to the first, and by some sense of incongruity destroys the fabric which the fascination of the preceding one built up."

My brother, though he had listened with interest to what Mr. Gaskell had said, did not reply, and the subject was allowed to drop.

CHAPTER 3

It was in the same summer of 1842, and near the middle of June, that my brother John wrote inviting me to come to Oxford for the Commemoration festivities. I had been spending some weeks with Mrs. Temple, a distant cousin of ours, at their house of Royston in Derbyshire, and John was desirous that Mrs. Temple should come up to Oxford and chaperone her daughter Constance and myself at the balls and various other entertainments which take place at the close of the summer term.

Owing to Royston being some two hundred miles from Worth Maltravers, our families had hitherto seen little of one another, but during my present visit I had learned to love Mrs. Temple, a lady of singular sweetness of disposition, and had contracted a devoted attachment to her daughter Constance. Constance Temple was then eighteen years of age, and to great beauty united such mental graces and excellent traits of character as must ever appear to reasoning persons more enduringly valuable than even the highest personal attractions. She was well read and witty, and had been trained in those principles of true religion which she afterwards followed with devoted consistency in the self-sacrifice and resigned piety of her too short life. In person, I may remind you, my dear Edward, since death removed her ere you were of years to appreciate either her appearance or her qualities, she was tall, with a somewhat long and oval face, with brown hair and eyes.

Mrs. Temple readily accepted Sir John Maltravers' invitation. She had never seen Oxford herself, and was pleased to afford us the pleasure of so delightful an excursion. John had secured convenient rooms for us above the shop of a well-known printseller in High Street, and we arrived in Oxford on Friday evening, June 18, 1842. I shall not dilate to you on the various Commemoration festivities, which have probably altered little since those days, and with which you are familiar. Suffice it to say that my brother had secured us admission to every entertainment, and that we enjoyed our visit as only youth with its keen sensibilities and uncloyed pleasures can. I could not help observing that John was very much struck by the attractions of Miss Constance Temple, and that she for her part, while exhibiting no unbecoming forwardness, certainly betrayed no aversion to him.

I was greatly pleased both with my own powers of observation which had enabled me to discover so important a fact, and also with the circumstance itself. To a romantic girl of nineteen it appeared high time that a brother of twenty-two should be at least preparing some matrimonial project; and my friend was so good and beautiful that it seemed impossible that I should ever obtain a more lovable sister or my brother a better wife. Mrs. Temple could not refuse her sanction to such a scheme; for while their mental qualities seemed eminently compatible, John was in his own right master of Worth Maltravers, and her daughter sole heiress of the Royston estates.

The Commemoration festivities terminated on Wednesday night with a grand ball at the Music-Room in Holywell Street. This was given by a Lodge of University Freemasons, and John was there with Mr. Gaskell—whose acquaintance we had made with much gratification—both wearing blue silk scarves and small white aprons. They introduced us to many other of their friends similarly adorned, and these important and mysterious insignia sat not amiss with their youthful figures and boyish faces. After a long and pleasurable programme, it was decided that we should prolong our visit till the next evening, leaving Oxford at half-past ten o'clock at night and driving to Didcot, there to join the mail for the west. We rose late the next morning and spent the day rambling among the old colleges and gardens of the most beautiful of English cities. At seven o'clock we dined together for the last time at our lodgings in High Street, and my brother proposed that before parting we should enjoy the fine evening in the gardens of St. John's College.

This was at once agreed to, and we proceeded thither, John walking on in front with Constance and Mrs. Temple, and I following with Mr. Gaskell. My companion explained that these gardens were esteemed the most beautiful in the university, but that under ordinary circumstances it was not permitted to strangers to walk there of an evening. Here he quoted some Latin about "*aurum per medios ire satellites,*" which I smilingly made as if I understood, and did indeed gather from it that John had bribed the porter to admit us. It was a warm and very still night, without a moon, but with enough of fading light to show the outlines of the garden front. This long low line of buildings built in Charles I's reign looked so exquisitely beautiful that I shall never forget it, though I have not since seen its oriel windows and creeper-covered walls. There was a very heavy dew on the broad lawn, and we walked at first only on the paths.

No one spoke, for we were oppressed by the very beauty of the scene, and by the sadness which an imminent parting from friends and from so sweet a place combined to cause. John had been silent and depressed the whole day, nor did Mr. Gaskell himself seem inclined to conversation. Constance and my brother fell a little way behind, and Mr. Gaskell asked me to cross the lawn if I was not afraid of the dew, that I might see the garden front to better advantage from the corner. Mrs. Temple waited for us on the path, not wishing to wet her feet. Mr. Gaskell pointed out the beauties of the perspective as seen from his vantage-point, and we were fortunate in hearing the sweet descant of nightingales for which this garden has ever been famous. As we stood silent and listening, a candle was lit in a small oriel at the end, and the light showing the tracery of the window added to the picturesqueness of the scene.

Within an hour we were in a landau driving through the still warm lanes to Didcot. I had seen that Constance's parting with my brother had been tender, and I am not sure that she was not in tears during some part at least of our drive; but I did not observe her closely, having my thoughts elsewhere.

Though we were thus being carried every moment further from the sleeping city, where I believe that both our hearts were busy, I feel as if I had been a personal witness of the incidents I am about to narrate, so often have I heard them from my brother's lips. The two young men, after parting with us in the High Street, returned to their respective colleges. John reached his rooms shortly before eleven o'clock. He was at once sad and happy—sad at our departure, but happy in a new-found world of delight which his admiration for Constance Temple opened to him. He was, in fact, deeply in love with her, and the full flood of a hitherto unknown passion filled him with an emotion so overwhelming that his ordinary life seemed transfigured. He moved, as it were, in an ether superior to our mortal atmosphere, and a new region of high resolves and noble possibilities spread itself before his eyes. He slammed his heavy outside door (called an "oak") to prevent anyone entering and flung himself into the window-seat.

Here he sat for a long time, the sash thrown up and his head outside, for he was excited and feverish. His mental exaltation was so great and his thoughts of so absorbing an interest that he took no notice of time, and only remembered afterwards that the scent of a syringa-bush was borne up to him from a little garden-patch opposite, and that a bat had circled slowly up and down the lane, until he heard the clocks striking three. At the same time the faint light of dawn made itself felt almost imperceptibly; the classic statues on the roof of the schools began to stand out against the white sky, and a faint glimmer to penetrate the darkened room. It glistened on the varnished top of his violin-case lying on the table, and on a jug of toast-and-water placed there by his college servant or scout every night before he left. He drank a glass of this mixture, and was moving towards his bedroom door when a sudden thought struck him. He turned back, took the violin from its case, tuned it, and began to play the *Areopagita* suite. He was conscious of that mental clearness and vigour which not unfrequently comes with the dawn to those who have sat watching or reading through the night: and his thoughts were exalted by the effect which the first consciousness of a deep passion causes in imaginative minds.

He had never played the suite with more power; and the airs, even without the piano part, seemed fraught with a meaning hitherto unrealised. As he began the *Gagliarda* he heard the wicker chair creak; but he had his back towards it, and the sound was now too familiar to him to cause him even to look round. It was not till he was playing the repeat that he became aware of a new and overpowering sensation. At first it was a vague feeling, so often experienced by us all, of not being alone. He did not stop playing, and in a few seconds the impression of a presence in the room other than his own became so strong that he was actually afraid to look round. But in another moment he felt that at all hazards he must see what or who this presence was. Without stopping he partly turned and partly looked over his shoulder. The silver light of early morning was filling the room, making the various objects appear of less bright colour than usual, and giving to everything a pearl-grey neutral tint. In this cold but clear light he saw seated in the wicker chair the figure of a man.

In the first violent shock of so terrifying a discovery, he could not appreciate such details as those of features, dress, or appearance. He was merely conscious that with him, in a locked room of which he knew himself to be the only human inmate, there sat something which bore a human form. He looked at it for a moment with a hope, which he felt to be vain, that it might vanish and prove a phantom of his excited imagination, but still it sat there. Then my brother put down his violin, and he used to assure me that a horror overwhelmed him of an intensity which he had previously believed impossible. Whether the image which he saw was subjective or objective, I cannot pretend to say: you will be in a position to judge for yourself when you have finished this narrative. Our limited experience would lead us to believe that it was a phantom conjured up by some unusual condition of his own brain; but we are fain to confess that there certainly do exist in nature phenomena such as baffle human reason; and it is possible that, for some hidden purposes of Providence, permission may occasionally be granted to those who have passed from this life to assume again for a time the form of their earthly tabernacle.

We must, I say, be content to suspend our judgment on such matters; but in this instance the subsequent course of events is very difficult to explain, except on the supposition that there was then presented to my brother's view the actual bodily form of one long deceased. The dread which took possession of him was due, he has more than once told me when analysing his feelings long afterwards, to two predominant causes. Firstly, he felt that mental dislocation which accompanies the sudden subversion of preconceived theories, the sudden alteration of long habit, or even the occurrence of any circumstance beyond the walk of our daily experience. This I have observed myself in the perturbing effect which a sudden death, a grievous accident, or in recent years the declaration of war, has exercised upon all except the most lethargic or the most determined minds. Secondly, he experienced the profound self-abasement or mental annihilation caused by the near conception of a being of a superior order. In the presence of an existence wearing, indeed, the human form, but of attributes widely different from and superior to his own, he felt the combined reverence and revulsion which even the noblest wild animals exhibit when brought for the first time face to face with man. The shock was so great that I feel persuaded it exerted an effect on him from which he never wholly recovered.

After an interval which seemed to him interminable, though it was only of a second's duration, he turned his eyes again to the occupant of the wicker chair. His faculties had so far recovered from the first shock as to enable him to see that the figure was that of a man perhaps thirty-five years of age and still youthful in appearance. The face was long and oval, the hair brown, and brushed straight off an exceptionally high forehead. His complexion was very pale or bloodless. He was clean shaven, and his finely cut mouth, with compressed lips, wore something of a sneering smile. His general expression was unpleasing, and from the first my brother felt as by intuition that there was present some malign and wicked influence. His eyes were not visible, as he kept them cast down, resting his head on his hand in the attitude of one listening. His face and even his dress were impressed so vividly upon John's mind, that he never had any difficulty in recalling them to his imagination; and he and I had afterwards an opportunity of verifying them in a remarkable manner.

He wore a long cut-away coat of green cloth with an edge of gold embroidery, and a white satin waistcoat figured with rose-sprigs, a full cravat of rich lace, knee-breeches of buff silk, and stockings of the same. His shoes were of polished black leather with heavy silver buckles, and his costume in general recalled that worn a century ago. As my brother gazed at him, he got up, putting his hands on the arms of the chair to raise himself, and causing the creaking so often heard before. The hands forced themselves on my brother's notice: they were very white, with the long delicate fingers of a musician. He showed a considerable height; and still keeping his eyes on the floor, walked with an ordinary gait towards the end of the bookcase at the side of the room farthest from the window. He reached the bookcase, and then John suddenly lost sight of him. The figure did not fade gradually, but went out, as it were, like the flame of a suddenly extinguished candle.

The room was now filled with the clear light of the summer morning: the whole vision had lasted but a few seconds, but my brother knew that there was no possibility of his having been mistaken, that the mystery of the creaking chair was solved, that he had seen the man who had come evening by evening for a month past to listen to the rhythm of the *Gagliarda*. Terribly disturbed, he sat for some time half dreading and half expecting a return of the figure; but all remained unchanged: he saw nothing, nor did he dare to challenge its reappearance by playing again the *Gagliarda*, which seemed to have so strange an attraction for it. At last, in the full sunlight of a late June morning at Oxford, he heard the steps of early pedestrians on the pavement below his windows, the cry of a milkman, and other sounds which showed the world was awake. It was after six o'clock, and going to his bedroom he flung himself on the outside of the bed for an hour's troubled slumber.

CHAPTER 4

When his servant called him about eight o'clock my brother sent a note to Mr. Gaskell at New College, begging him to come round to Magdalen Hall as soon as might be in the course of the morning. His summons was at once obeyed, and Mr. Gaskell was with him before he had finished breakfast. My brother was still much agitated, and at once told him what had happened the night before, detailing the various circumstances with minuteness, and not even concealing from him the sentiments which he entertained towards Miss Constance Temple. In narrating the appearance which he had seen in the chair, his agitation was still so excessive that he had difficulty in controlling his voice.

Mr. Gaskell heard him with much attention, and did not at once reply when John had finished his narration. At length he said, "I suppose many friends would think it right to affect, even if they did not feel, an incredulity as to what you have just told me. They might consider it more prudent to attempt to allay your distress by persuading you that what you have seen has no objective reality, but is merely the phantasm of an excited imagination; that if you had not been in love, had not sat up all night, and had not thus overtaxed your physical powers, you would have seen no vision. I shall not argue thus, for I am as certainly convinced as of the fact that we sit here, that on all the nights when we have played this suite called the *Areopagita*, there has been someone listening to us, and that you have at length been fortunate or unfortunate enough to see him."

"Do not say fortunate," said my brother; "for I feel as though I shall never recover from last night's shock."

"That is likely enough," Mr. Gaskell answered, coolly; "for as in the history of the race or individual, increased culture and a finer mental susceptibility necessarily impair the brute courage and powers of endurance which we note in savages, so any supernatural vision such as you have seen must be purchased at the cost of physical reaction. From the first evening that we played this music, and heard the noises mimicking so closely the sitting down and rising up of some person, I have felt convinced that causes other than those which we usually call natural were at work, and that we were very near the manifestation of some extraordinary phenomenon."

"I do not quite apprehend your meaning."

"I mean this," he continued, "that this man or spirit of a man has been sitting here night after night, and that we have not been able to see him, because our minds are dull and obtuse. Last night the elevating force of a strong passion, such as that which you have confided to me, combined with the power of fine music, so exalted your mind that you became endowed, as it were, with a sixth sense, and suddenly were enabled to see that which had previously been invisible. To this sixth sense music gives, I believe, the key. We are at present only on the threshold of such a knowledge of that art as will enable us to use it eventually as the greatest of all humanising and educational agents. Music will prove a ladder to the loftier regions of thought; indeed I have long found for myself that I cannot attain to the highest range of my intellectual power except when hearing good music.

"All poets, and most writers of prose, will say that their thought is never so exalted, their sense of beauty and proportion never so just, as when they are listening either to the artificial music made by man, or to some of the grander tones of nature, such as the roar of a western ocean, or the sighing of wind in a clump of firs. Though I have often felt on such occasions on the very verge of some high mental discovery, and though a hand has been stretched forward as it were to rend the veil, yet it has never been vouchsafed me to see behind it. This you no doubt were allowed in a measure to do last night. You probably played the music with a deeper intuition than usual, and this, combined with the excitement under which you were already labouring, raised you for a moment to the required pitch of mental exaltation."

"It is true," John said, "that I never felt the melody so deeply as when I played it last night."

"Just so," answered his friend; "and there is probably some link between this air and the history of the man whom you saw last night; some fatal power in it which enables it to exert an attraction on him even after death. For we must remember that the influence of music, though always powerful, is not always for good. We can scarcely doubt that as certain forms of music tend to raise us above the sensuality of the animal, or the more degrading passion of material gain, and to transport us into the ether of higher thought, so other forms are directly calculated to awaken in us luxurious emotions, and to whet those sensual appetites which it is the business of a philosopher not indeed to annihilate or to be ashamed of, but to keep rigidly in check. This possibility of music to effect evil as well as good I have seen recognised, and very aptly expressed in some beautiful verses by Mr. Keble which I have just read:—

> Cease, stranger, cease those witching notes,
> The art of syren choirs;
> Hush the seductive voice that floats
> Across the trembling wires.
>
> Music's ethereal power was given
> Not to dissolve our clay,
> But draw Promethean beams from heaven
> To purge the dross away.

"They are fine lines," said my brother, "but I do not see how you apply your argument to the present instance."

"I mean," Mr. Gaskell answered, "that I have little doubt that the melody of this *Gagliarda* has been connected in some manner with the life of the man you saw last night. It is not unlikely, either, that it was a favourite air of his whilst in the flesh, or even that it was played by himself or others at the moment of some crisis in his history. It is possible that such connection may be due merely to the innocent pleasure the melody gave him in life; but the nature of the music itself, and a peculiar effect it has upon my own thoughts, induce me to believe that it was associated with some occasion when he either fell into great sin or when some evil fate, perhaps even death itself, overtook him. You will remember I have told you that this air calls up to my mind a certain scene of Italian revelry in which an Englishman takes part.

"It is true that I have never been able to fix his features in my mind, nor even to say exactly how he was dressed. Yet now some instinct tells me that it is this very man whom you saw last night. It is not for us to attempt to pierce the mystery which veils from our eyes the secrets of an after-death existence; but I can scarcely suppose that a spirit entirely at rest would feel so deeply the power of a certain melody as to be called back by it to his old haunts like a dog by his master's whistle. It is more probable that there is some evil history connected with the matter, and this, I think, we ought to consider if it be possible to unravel."

My brother assenting, he continued, "When this man left you, Johnnie, did he walk to the door?"

"No; he made for the side wall, and when he reached the end of the bookcase I lost sight of him."

Mr. Gaskell went to the bookcase and looked for a moment at the titles of the books, as though expecting to see something in them to assist his inquiries; but finding apparently no clue, he said—

"This is the last time we shall meet for three months or more; let us play the *Gagliarda* and see if there be any response."

My brother at first would not hear of this, showing a lively dread of challenging any reappearance of the figure he had seen: indeed he felt that such an event would probably fling him into a state of serious physical disorder. Mr. Gaskell, however, continued to press him, assuring him that the fact of his now being no longer alone should largely allay any fear on his part, and urging that this would be the last opportunity they would have of playing together for some months.

At last, being overborne, my brother took his violin, and Mr.

Gaskell seated himself at the pianoforte. John was very agitated, and as he commenced the *Gagliarda* his hands trembled so that he could scarcely play the air. Mr. Gaskell also exhibited some nervousness, not performing with his customary correctness. But for the first time the charm failed: no noise accompanied the music, nor did anything of an unusual character occur. They repeated the whole suite, but with a similar result.

Both were surprised, but neither, had any explanation to offer. My brother, who at first dreaded intensely a repetition of the vision, was now almost disappointed that nothing had occurred; so quickly does the mood of man change.

After some further conversation the young men parted for the Long Vacation—John returning to Worth Maltravers and Mr. Gaskell going to London, where he was to pass a few days before he proceeded to his home in Westmorland.

CHAPTER 5

John spent nearly the whole of this summer vacation at Worth Maltravers. He had been anxious to pay a visit to Royston; but the continued and serious illness of Mrs. Temple's sister had called her and Constance to Scotland, where they remained until the death of their relative allowed them to return to Derbyshire in the late autumn. John and I had been brought up together from childhood. When he was at Eton we had always spent the holidays at Worth, and after my dear mother's death, when we were left quite alone, the bonds of our love were naturally drawn still closer. Even after my brother went to Oxford, at a time when most young men are anxious to enjoy a new-found liberty, and to travel or to visit friends in their vacation, John's ardent affection for me and for Worth Maltravers kept him at home; and he was pleased on most occasions to make me the partner of his thoughts and of his pleasures. This long vacation of 1842 was, I think, the happiest of our lives. In my case I know it was so, and I think it was happy also for him; for none could guess that the small cloud seen in the distance like a man's hand was afterwards to rise and darken all his later days.

It was a summer of brilliant and continued sunshine; many of the old people said that they could never recollect so fine a season, and both fruit and crops were alike abundant. John hired a small cutter-yacht, the *Palestine*, which he kept in our little harbour of Encombe, and in which he and I made many excursions, visiting Weymouth,

Lyme Regis, and other places of interest on the south coast.

In this summer my brother confided to me two secrets,—his love for Constance Temple, which indeed was after all no secret, and the history of the apparition which he had seen. This last filled me with inexpressible dread and distress. It seemed cruel and unnatural that any influence so dark and mysterious should thus intrude on our bright life, and from the first I had an impression which I could not entirely shake off, that any such appearance or converse of a disembodied spirit must portend misfortune, if not worse, to him who saw or heard it. It never occurred to me to combat or to doubt the reality of the vision; he believed that he had seen it, and his conviction was enough to convince me. He had meant, he said, to tell no one, and had given a promise to Mr. Gaskell to that effect; but I think that he could not bear to keep such a matter in his own breast, and within the first week of his return he made me his confidant. I remember, my dear Edward, the look everything wore on that sad night when he first told me what afterwards proved so terrible a secret. We had dined quite alone, and he had been moody and depressed all the evening.

It was a chilly night, with some fret blowing up from the sea. The moon showed that blunted and deformed appearance which she assumes a day or two past the full, and the moisture in the air encircled her with a stormy-looking halo. We had stepped out of the dining-room windows on to the little terrace looking down towards Smedmore and Encombe. The glaucous shrubs that grow in between the balusters were wet and dripping with the salt breath of the sea, and we could hear the waves coming into the cove from the west. After standing a minute I felt chill, and proposed that we should go back to the billiard-room, where a fire was lit on all except the warmest nights. "No," John said, "I want to tell you something, Sophy," and then we walked on to the old boat summer-house. There he told me everything. I cannot describe to you my feelings of anguish and horror when he told me of the appearance of the man. The interest of the tale was so absorbing to me that I took no note of time, nor of the cold night air, and it was only when it was all finished that I felt how deadly chill it had become.

"Let us go in, John," I said; "I am cold and feel benumbed."

But youth is hopeful and strong, and in another week the impression had faded from our minds, and we were enjoying the full glory of midsummer weather, which I think only those know who have watched the blue sea come rippling in at the foot of the white chalk cliffs of Dorset.

I had felt a reluctance even so much as to hear the air of the *Gagliarda*, and though he had spoken to me of the subject on more than one occasion, my brother had never offered to play it to me. I knew that he had the copy of Graziani's suites with him at Worth Maltravers, because he had told me that he had brought it from Oxford; but I had never seen the book, and fancied that he kept it intentionally locked up. He did not, however, neglect the violin, and during the summer mornings, as I sat reading or working on the terrace, I often heard him playing to himself in the library. Though he had never even given me any description of the melody of the *Gagliarda*, yet I felt certain that he not infrequently played it. I cannot say how it was; but from the moment that I heard him one morning in the library performing an air set in a curiously low key, it forced itself upon my attention, and I knew, as it were by instinct, that it must be the *Gagliarda* of the *Areopagita*. He was using a *sordino* and playing it very softly; but I was not mistaken.

One wet afternoon in October, only a week before the time of his leaving us to return to Oxford for the autumn term, he walked into the drawing-room where I was sitting, and proposed that we should play some music together. To this I readily agreed. Though but a mediocre performer, I have always taken much pleasure in the use of the pianoforte, and esteemed it an honour whenever he asked me to play with him, since my powers as a musician were so very much inferior to his. After we had played several pieces, he took up an oblong music-book bound in white vellum, placed it upon the desk of the pianoforte, and proposed that we should play a suite by Graziani. I knew that he meant the *Areopagita*, and begged him at once not to ask me to play it. He rallied me lightly on my fears, and said it would much please him to play it, as he had not heard the pianoforte part since he had left Oxford three months ago. I saw that he was eager to perform it, and being loath to disoblige so kind a brother during the last week of his stay at home, I at length overcame my scruples and set out to play it.

But I was so alarmed at the possibility of any evil consequences ensuing, that when we commenced the *Gagliarda* I could scarcely find my notes. Nothing in any way unusual, however, occurred; and being reassured by this, and feeling an irresistible charm in the music, I finished the suite with more appearance of ease. My brother, however, was, I fear, not satisfied with my performance, and compared it, very

206

possibly, with that of Mr. Gaskell, to which it was necessarily much inferior, both through weakness of execution and from my insufficient knowledge of the principles of the *basso continuo*. We stopped playing, and John stood looking out of the window across the sea, where the sky was clearing low down under the clouds. The sun went down behind Portland in a fiery glow which cheered us after a long day's rain. I had taken the copy of Graziani's suites off the desk, and was holding it on my lap turning over the old foxed and yellow pages.

As I closed it a streak of evening sunlight fell across the room and lighted up a coat of arms stamped in gilt on the cover. It was much faded and would ordinarily have been hard to make out; but the ray of strong light illumined it, and in an instant I recognised the same shield which Mr. Gaskell had pictured to himself as hanging on the musicians' gallery of his phantasmal dancing-room. My brother had often recounted to me this effort of his friend's imagination, and here I saw before me the same florid foreign blazon, a cherub's head blowing on three lilies on a gold field. This discovery was not only of interest, but afforded me much actual relief; for it accounted rationally for at least one item of the strange story. Mr. Gaskell had no doubt noticed at some time this shield stamped on the outside of the book, and bearing the impression of it unconsciously in his mind, had reproduced it in his imagined revels. I said as much to my brother, and he was greatly interested, and after examining the shield agreed that this was certainly a probable solution of that part of the mystery. On the 12th of October John returned to Oxford.

Chapter 6

My brother told me afterwards that more than once during the summer vacation he had seriously considered with himself the propriety of changing his rooms at Magdalen Hall. He had thought that it might thus be possible for him to get rid at once of the memory of the apparition, and of the fear of any reappearance of it. He could either have moved into another set of rooms in the Hall itself, or else gone into lodgings in the town—a usual proceeding, I am told, for gentlemen near the end of their course at Oxford. Would to God that he had indeed done so! but with the supineness which has, I fear, my dear Edward, been too frequently a characteristic of our family, he shrank from the trouble such a course would involve, and the opening of the autumn term found him still in his old rooms. You will forgive me for entering here on a very brief description of your father's sitting-room.

It is, I think, necessary for the proper understanding of the incidents that follow. It was not a large room, though probably the finest in the small buildings of Magdalen Hall, and panelled from floor to ceiling with oak which successive generations had obscured by numerous coats of paint. On one side were two windows having an aspect on to New College Lane, and fitted with deep cushioned seats in the recesses. Outside these windows there were boxes of flowers, the brightness of which formed in the summer term a pretty contrast to the grey and crumbling stone, and afforded pleasure at once to the inmate and to passers-by. Along nearly the whole length of the wall opposite to the windows, some tenant in years long past had had mahogany book-shelves placed, reaching to a height of perhaps five feet from the floor. They were handsomely made in the style of the eighteenth century and pleased my brother's taste. He had always exhibited a partiality for books, and the fine library at Worth Maltravers had no doubt contributed to foster his tastes in that direction. At the time of which I write he had formed a small collection for himself at Oxford, paying particular attention to the bindings, and acquiring many excellent specimens of that art, principally I think, from Messrs. Payne & Foss, the celebrated London booksellers.

Towards the end of the autumn term, having occasion one cold day to take down a volume of Plato from its shelf, he found to his surprise that the book was quite warm. A closer examination easily explained to him the reason—namely, that the flue of a chimney, passing behind one end of the bookcase, sensibly heated not only the wall itself, but also the books in the shelves. Although he had been in his rooms now near three years, he had never before observed this fact; partly, no doubt, because the books in these shelves were seldom handled, being more for show as specimens of bindings than for practical use. He was somewhat annoyed at this discovery, fearing lest such a heat, which in moderation is beneficial to books, might through its excess warp the leather or otherwise injure the bindings. Mr. Gaskell was sitting with him at the time of the discovery, and indeed it was for his use that my brother had taken down the volume of Plato. He strongly advised that the bookcase should be moved, and suggested that it would be better to place it across that end of the room where the pianoforte then stood.

They examined it and found that it would easily admit of removal, being, in fact, only the frame of a bookcase, and showing at the back the painted panelling of the wall. Mr. Gaskell noted it as curious that all the shelves were fixed and immovable except one at the end, which had been fitted with the ordinary arrangement allowing its position to be altered at will. My brother thought that the change would improve the appearance of his rooms, besides being advantageous for the books, and gave instructions to the college upholsterer to have the necessary work carried out at once.

The two young men had resumed their musical studies, and had often played the *Areopagita* and other music of Graziani since their return to Oxford in the Autumn. They remarked, however, that the chair no longer creaked during the *Gagliarda*—and, in fact, that no unusual occurrence whatever attended its performance. At times they were almost tempted to doubt the accuracy of their own remembrances, and to consider as entirely mythical the mystery which had so much disturbed them in the summer term. My brother had also pointed out to Mr. Gaskell my discovery that the coat of arms on the outside of the music-book was identical with that which his fancy portrayed on the musicians' gallery.

He readily admitted that he must at some time have noticed and afterwards forgotten the blazon on the book, and that an unconscious reminiscence of it had no doubt inspired his imagination in this instance. He rebuked my brother for having agitated me unnecessarily by telling me at all of so idle a tale; and was pleased to write a few lines to me at Worth Maltravers, felicitating me on my shrewdness of perception, but speaking banteringly of the whole matter.

On the evening of the 14th of November my brother and his friend were sitting talking in the former's room. The position of the bookcase had been changed on the morning of that day, and Mr. Gaskell had come round to see how the books looked when placed at the end instead of at the side of the room. He had applauded the new arrangement, and the young men sat long over the fire, with a bottle of college port and a dish of medlars which I had sent my brother from our famous tree in the Upper Croft at Worth Maltravers. Later on they fell to music, and played a variety of pieces, performing also the *Areopagita* suite.

Mr. Gaskell before he left complimented John on the improvement which the alteration in the place of the bookcase had made in his room, saying, "Not only do the books in their present place very much enhance the general appearance of the room, but the change seems to me to have affected also a marked acoustical improvement.

The oak panelling now exposed on the side of the room has given a resonant property to the wall which is peculiarly responsive to the tones of your violin. While you were playing the *Gagliarda* tonight, I could almost have imagined that someone in an adjacent room was playing the same air with a *sordino*, so distinct was the echo."

Shortly after this he left.

My brother partly undressed himself in his bedroom, which adjoined, and then returning to his sitting-room, pulled the large wicker chair in front of the fire, and sat there looking at the glowing coals, and thinking perhaps of Miss Constance Temple. The night promised to be very cold, and the wind whistled down the chimney, increasing the comfortable sensation of the clear fire. He sat watching the ruddy reflection of the firelight dancing on the panelled wall, when he noticed that a picture placed where the end of the bookcase formerly stood was not truly hung, and needed adjustment. A picture hung askew was particularly offensive to his eyes, and he got up at once to alter it. He remembered as he went up to it that at this precise spot four months ago he had lost sight of the man's figure which he saw rise from the wicker chair, and at the memory felt an involuntary shudder. This reminiscence probably influenced his fancy also in another direction; for it seemed to him that very faintly, as though played far off, and with the *sordino*, he could hear the air of the *Gagliarda*.

He put one hand behind the picture to steady it, and as he did so his finger struck a very slight projection in the wall. He pulled the picture a little to one side, and saw that what he had touched was the back of a small hinge sunk in the wall, and almost obliterated with many coats of paint. His curiosity was excited, and he took a candle from the table and examined the wall carefully. Inspection soon showed him another hinge a little further up, and by degrees he perceived that one of the panels had been made at some time in the past to open, and serve probably as the door of a cupboard. At this point he assured me that a feverish anxiety to re-open this cupboard door took possession of him, and that the intense excitement filled his mind which we experience on the eve of a discovery which we fancy may produce important results. He loosened the paint in the cracks with a penknife, and attempted to press open the door; but his instrument was not adequate to such a purpose, and all his efforts remained ineffective.

His excitement had now reached an overmastering pitch; for he anticipated, though he knew not why, some strange discovery to be made in this sealed cupboard. He looked round the room for some weapon with which to force the door, and at length with his penknife cut away sufficient wood at the joint to enable him to insert the end of the poker in the hole. The clock in the New College Tower struck one at the exact moment when with a sharp effort he thus forced open the door. It appeared never to have had a fastening, but merely to have been stuck fast by the accumulation of paint.

As he bent it slowly back upon the rusted hinges his heart beat so fast that he could scarcely catch his breath, though he was conscious all the while of a ludicrous aspect of his position, knowing that it was most probable that the cavity within would be found empty. The cupboard was small but very deep, and in the obscure light seemed at first to contain nothing except a small heap of dust and cobwebs. His sense of disappointment was keen as he thrust his hand into it, but changed again in a moment to breathless interest on feeling something solid in what he had imagined to be only an accumulation of mould and dirt. He snatched up a candle, and holding this in one hand, with the other pulled out an object from the cupboard and put it on the table, covered as it was with the curious drapery of black and clinging cobwebs which I have seen adhering to bottles of old wine. It lay there between the dish of medlars and the decanter, veiled indeed with thick dust as with a mantle, but revealing beneath it the shape and contour of a violin.

Chapter 7

John was excited at his discovery, and felt his thoughts confused in a manner that I have often experienced myself on the unexpected receipt of news interesting me deeply, whether for pleasure or pain. Yet at the same time he was half amused at his own excitement, feeling that it was childish to be moved over an event so simple as the finding of a violin in an old cupboard. He soon collected himself and took up the instrument, using great care, as he feared lest age should have rendered the wood brittle or rotten. With some vigorous puffs of breath and a little dusting with a handkerchief he removed the heavy outer coating of cobwebs, and began to see more clearly the delicate curves of the body and of the scroll. A few minutes' more gentle handling left the instrument sufficiently clean to enable him to appreciate its chief points. Its seclusion from the outer world, which the heavy accumulation of dust proved to have been for many years, did not seem to have damaged it in the least; and the fact of a chimney-flue passing through

211

the wall at no great distance had no doubt conduced to maintain the air in the cupboard at an equable temperature. So far as he was able to judge, the wood was as sound as when it left the maker's hands; but the strings were of course broken, and curled up in little tangled knots. The body was of a light-red colour, with a varnish of peculiar lustre and softness. The neck seemed rather longer than ordinary, and the scroll was remarkably bold and free.

The violin which my brother was in the habit of using was a fine *Pressenda*, given to him on his fifteenth birthday by Mr. Thoresby, his guardian. It was of that maker's later and best period, and a copy of the Stradivarius model. John took this from its case and laid it side by side with his new discovery, meaning to compare them for size and form. He perceived at once that while the model of both was identical, the superiority of the older violin in every detail was so marked as to convince him that it was undoubtedly an instrument of exceptional value. The extreme beauty of its varnish impressed him vividly, and though he had never seen a genuine Stradivarius, he felt a conviction gradually gaining on him that he stood in the presence of a masterpiece of that great maker.

On looking into the interior he found that surprisingly little dust had penetrated into it, and by blowing through the sound-holes he soon cleared it sufficiently to enable him to discern a label. He put the candle close to him, and held the violin up so that a little patch of light fell through the sound-hole on to the label. His heart leapt with a violent pulsation as he read the characters, "*Antonius Stradiuarius Cremonensis faciebat*, 1704." Under ordinary circumstances it would naturally be concluded that such a label was a forgery, but the conditions were entirely altered in the case of a violin found in a forgotten cupboard, with proof so evident of its having remained there for a very long period.

He was not at that time as familiar with the history of the fiddles of the great maker as he, and indeed I also, afterwards became. Thus he was unable to decide how far the exact year of its manufacture would determine its value as compared with other specimens of Stradivarius. But although the Pressenda he had been used to play on was always considered a very fine instrument both in make and varnish, his new discovery so far excelled it in both points as to assure him that it must be one of the Cremonese master's greatest productions.

He examined the violin minutely, scrutinising each separate feature, and finding each in turn to be of the utmost perfection, so far as his knowledge of the instrument would enable him to judge. He lit more candles that he might be able better to see it, and holding it on his knees, sat still admiring it until the dying fire and increasing cold warned him that the night was now far advanced. At last, carrying it to his bedroom, he locked it carefully into a drawer and retired for the night.

He woke next morning with that pleasurable consciousness of there being some reason for gladness, which we feel on waking in seasons of happiness, even before our reason, locating it, reminds us what the actual source of our joy may be. He was at first afraid lest his excitement, working on the imagination, should have led him on the previous night to overestimate the fineness of the instrument, and he took it from the drawer half expecting to be disappointed with its daylight appearance. But a glance sufficed to convince him of the unfounded nature of his suspicions. The various beauties which he had before observed were enhanced a hundredfold by the light of day, and he realised more fully than ever that the instrument was one of altogether exceptional value.

And now, my dear Edward, I shall ask your forgiveness if in the history I have to relate any observation of mine should seem to reflect on the character of your late father, Sir John Maltravers. And I beg you to consider that your father was also my dear and only brother, and that it is inexpressibly painful to me to recount any actions of his which may not seem becoming to a noble gentleman, as he surely was. I only now proceed because, when very near his end, he most strictly enjoined me to narrate these circumstances to you fully when you should come of age. We must humbly remember that to God alone belongs judgment, and that it is not for poor mortals to decide what is right or wrong in certain instances for their fellows, but that each should strive most earnestly to do his own duty.

Your father entirely concealed from me the discovery he had made. It was not till long afterwards that I had it narrated to me, and I only obtained a knowledge of this and many other of the facts which I am now telling you at a date much subsequent to their actual occurrence.

He explained to his servant that he had discovered and opened an old cupboard in the panelling, without mentioning the fact of his having found anything in it, but merely asking him to give instructions for the paint to be mended and the cupboard put into a usable state. Before he had finished a very late breakfast Mr. Gaskell was with him, and it has been a source of lasting regret to me that my brother concealed also from his most intimate and trusted friend the discovery of the previous night. He did, indeed, tell him that he had found and opened an old cupboard in the panelling, but made no mention of there having been anything within. I cannot say what prompted him to this action; for the two young men had for long been on such intimate terms that the one shared almost as a matter of course with the other any pleasure or pain which might fall to his lot.

Mr. Gaskell looked at the cupboard with some interest, saying afterwards, "I know now, Johnnie, why the one shelf of the bookcase which stood there was made movable when all the others were fixed. Some former occupant used the cupboard, no doubt, as a secret receptacle for his treasures, and masked it with the book-shelves in front. Who knows what he kept in here, or who he was! I should not be surprised if he were that very man who used to come here so often to hear us play the *Areopagita*, and whom you saw that night last June. He had the one shelf made, you see, to move so as to give him access to this cavity on occasion: then when he left Oxford, or perhaps died, the mystery was forgotten, and with a few times of painting the cracks closed up."

Mr. Gaskell shortly afterwards took his leave as he had a lecture to attend, and my brother was left alone to the contemplation of his new-found treasure. After some consideration he determined that he would take the instrument to London, and obtain the opinion of an expert as to its authenticity and value. He was well acquainted with the late Mr. George Smart, the celebrated London dealer, from whom his guardian, Mr. Thoresby, had purchased the Pressenda violin which John commonly used. Besides being a dealer in valuable instruments, Mr. Smart was a famous collector of Stradivarius fiddles, esteemed one of the first authorities in Europe in that domain of art, and author of a valuable work of reference in connection with it. It was to him, therefore, that my brother decided to submit the violin, and he wrote a letter to Mr. Smart saying that he should give himself the pleasure of waiting on him the next day on a matter of business. He then called on his tutor, and with some excuse obtained leave to journey to London the next morning. He spent the rest of the day in very carefully cleaning the violin, and noon of the next saw him with it, securely packed, in Mr. Smart's establishment in Bond Street.

Mr. Smart received Sir John Maltravers with deference, demanded in what way he could serve him; and on hearing that his opinion was required on the authenticity of a violin, smiled somewhat dubiously and led the way into a back parlour.

"My dear Sir John," he said, "I hope you have not been led into buying any instrument by a faith in its antiquity. So many good copies of instruments by famous makers and bearing their labels are now afloat, that the chances of obtaining a genuine fiddle from an unrecognised source are quite remote; of hundreds of violins submitted to me for opinion, I find that scarce one in fifty is actually that which it represents itself to be. In fact the only safe rule," he added as a professional commentary, "is never to buy a violin unless you obtain it from a dealer with a reputation to lose, and are prepared to pay a reasonable price for it."

My brother had meanwhile unpacked the violin and laid it on the table. As he took from it the last leaf of silver paper he saw Mr. Smart's smile of condescension fade, and assuming a look of interest and excitement, he stepped forward, took the violin in his hands, and scrutinised it minutely. He turned it over in silence for some moments, looking narrowly at each feature, and even applying the test of a magnifying-glass. At last he said with an altered tone, "Sir John, I have had in my hands nearly all the finest productions of Stradivarius, and thought myself acquainted with every instrument of note that ever left his workshop; but I confess myself mistaken, and apologise to you for the doubt which I expressed as to the instrument you had brought me. This violin is of the great master's golden period, is incontestably genuine, and finer in some respects than any Stradivarius that I have ever seen, not even excepting the famous *Dolphin* itself. You need be under no apprehension as to its authenticity: no connoisseur could hold it in his hand for a second and entertain a doubt on the point."

My brother was greatly pleased at so favourable a verdict, and Mr. Smart continued—

"The varnish is of that rich red which Stradivarius used in his best period after he had abandoned the yellow tint copied by him at first from his master Amati. I have never seen a varnish thicker or more lustrous, and it shows on the back that peculiar shading to imitate wear which we term 'breaking up.' The purfling also is of an unsurpassable excellence. Its execution is so fine that I should recommend you to use a magnifying-glass for its examination."

So he ran on, finding from moment to moment some new beauties to admire.

My brother was at first anxious lest Mr. Smart should ask him whence so extraordinary an instrument came, but he saw that the expert had already jumped to a conclusion in the matter. He knew that John had recently come of age, and evidently supposed that he had found the violin among the heirlooms of Worth Maltravers. John allowed Mr. Smart to continue in this misconception, merely saying that he had discovered the instrument in an old cupboard, where he had reason to think it had remained hidden for many years.

"Are there no records attached to so splendid an instrument?" asked Mr. Smart. "I suppose it has been with your family a number of years. Do you not know how it came into their possession?"

I believe this was the first occasion on which it had occurred to John to consider what right he had to the possession of the instrument. He had been so excited by its discovery that the question of ownership had never hitherto crossed his mind. The unwelcome suggestion that it was not his after all, that the College might rightfully prefer a claim to it, presented itself to him for a moment; but he set it instantly aside, quieting his conscience with the reflection that this at least was not the moment to make such a disclosure.

He fenced with Mr. Smart's inquiry as best he could, saying that he was ignorant of the history of the instrument, but not contradicting the assumption that it had been a long time in his family's possession.

"It is indeed singular," Mr. Smart continued, "that so magnificent an instrument should have lain buried so long; that even those best acquainted with such matters should be in perfect ignorance of its existence. I shall have to revise the list of famous instruments in the next edition of my *History of the Violin*, and to write," he added smiling, "a special paragraph on the *Worth Maltravers Stradivarius*."

After much more, which I need not narrate, Mr. Smart suggested that the violin should be left with him that he might examine it more at leisure, and that my brother should return in a week's time, when he would have the instrument opened, an operation which would be in any case advisable. "The interior," he added, "appears to be in a strictly original state, and this I shall be able to ascertain when opened. The label is perfect, but if I am not mistaken I can see something higher up on the back which appears like a second label. This excites my interest, as I know of no instance of an instrument bearing two labels."

To this proposal my brother readily assented, being anxious to enjoy alone the pleasure of so gratifying a discovery as that of the undoubted authenticity of the instrument.

As he thought over the matter more at leisure, he grew anxious as to what might be the import of the second label in the violin of which Mr. Smart had spoken. I blush to say that he feared lest it might bear some owner's name or other inscription proving that the instrument had not been so long in the Maltravers family as he had allowed Mr. Smart to suppose. So within so short a time it was possible that Sir John Maltravers of Worth should dread being detected, if not in an absolute falsehood, at least in having by his silence assented to one.

During the ensuing week John remained in an excited and anxious condition. He did little work, and neglected his friends, having his thoughts continually occupied with the strange discovery he had made. I know also that his sense of honour troubled him, and that he was not satisfied with the course he was pursuing. The evening of his return from London he went to Mr. Gaskell's rooms at New College, and spent an hour conversing with him on indifferent subjects. In the course of their talk he proposed to his friend as a moral problem the question of the course of action to be taken were one to find some article of value concealed in his room.

Mr. Gaskell answered unhesitatingly that he should feel bound to disclose it to the authorities. He saw that my brother was ill at ease, and with a clearness of judgment which he always exhibited, guessed that he had actually made some discovery of this sort in the old cupboard in his rooms. He could not divine, of course, the exact nature of the object found, and thought it might probably relate to a hoard of gold; but insisted with much urgency on the obligation to at once disclose anything of this kind. My brother, however, misled, I fear, by that feeling of inalienable right which the treasure-hunter experiences over the treasure, paid no more attention to the advice of his friend than to the promptings of his own conscience, and went his way.

From that day, my dear Edward, he began to exhibit a spirit of secretiveness and reserve entirely alien to his own open and honourable disposition, and also saw less of Mr. Gaskell. His friend tried, indeed, to win his confidence and affection in every way in his power; but in spite of this the rift between them widened insensibly, and my brother lost the fellowship and counsel of a true friend at a time when he could ill afford to be without them.

He returned to London the ensuing week, and met Mr. George Smart by appointment in Bond Street. If the expert had been enthusiastic on a former occasion, he was ten times more so on this. He spoke in terms almost of rapture about the violin. He had compared it with two magnificent instruments in the collection of the late Mr. James Loding, then the finest in Europe; and it was admittedly superior to either, both in the delicate markings of its wood and singularly fine varnish. "Of its tone," he said, "we cannot, of course, yet pronounce with certainty, but I am very sure that its voice will not belie its splendid exterior. It has been carefully opened, and is in a strangely perfect condition. Several persons eminently qualified to judge unite with me in considering that it has been exceedingly little played upon, and admit that never has so intact an interior been seen. The scroll is exceptionally bold and original. Although undoubtedly from the hand of the great master, this is of a pattern entirely different and distinct from any that have ever come under my observation."

He then pointed out to my brother that the side lines of the scroll were unusually deeply cut, and that the front of it projected far more than is common with such instruments.

"The most remarkable feature," he concluded, "is that the instrument bears a double label. Besides the label which you have already seen bearing '*Antonius Stradiuarius Cremonensis faciebat*,' with the date of his most splendid period, 1704, so clearly that the ink seems scarcely dry, there is another smaller one higher up on the back which I will show you."

He took the violin apart and showed him a small label with characters written in faded ink. "That is the writing of Antonio Stradivarius himself, and is easily recognisable, though it is much firmer than a specimen which I once saw, written in extreme old age, and giving his name and the date 1736. He was then ninety-two, and died in the following year. But this, as you will see, does not give his name, but merely the two words '*Porphyrius philosophus*.' What this may refer to I cannot say: it is beyond my experience. My friend Mr. Calvert has suggested that Stradivarius may have dedicated this violin to the pagan philosopher, or named it after him; but this seems improbable. I have, indeed, heard of two famous violins being called 'Peter' and 'Paul,' but the instances of such naming are very rare; and I believe it to be altogether without precedent to find a name attached thus on a label.

"In any case, I must leave this matter to your ingenuity to decipher. Neither the sound-post nor the bass-bar have ever been moved, and you see here a Stradivarius violin wearing exactly the same appearance as it once wore in the great master's workshop, and in exactly the same condition; yet I think the belly is sufficiently strong to stand modern stringing. I should advise you to leave the instrument with me for some little while, that I may give it due care and attention and ensure its being properly strung."

My brother thanked him and left the violin with him, saying that he would instruct him later by letter to what address he wished it sent.

CHAPTER 8

Within a few days after this the autumn term came to an end, and in the second week of December John returned to Worth Maltravers for the Christmas vacation. His advent was always a very great pleasure to me, and on this occasion I had looked forward to his company with anticipation keener than usual, as I had been disappointed of the visit of a friend and had spent the last month alone. After the joy of our first meeting had somewhat sobered, it was not long before I remarked a change in his manner, which puzzled me. It was not that he was less kind to me, for I think he was even more tenderly forbearing and gentle than I had ever known him, but I had an uneasy feeling that some shadow had crept in between us. It was the small cloud rising in the distance that afterwards darkened his horizon and mine. I missed the old candour and open-hearted frankness that he had always shown; and there seemed to be always something in the background which he was trying to keep from me.

It was obvious that his thoughts were constantly elsewhere, so much so that on more than one occasion he returned vague and incoherent answers to my questions. At times I was content to believe that he was in love, and that his thoughts were with Miss Constance Temple; but even so, I could not persuade myself that his altered manner was to be thus entirely accounted for. At other times a dazed air, entirely foreign to his bright disposition, which I observed particularly in the morning, raised in my mind the terrible suspicion that he was in the habit of taking some secret narcotic or other deleterious drug.

We had never spent a Christmas away from Worth Maltravers, and it had always been a season of quiet joy for both of us. But under these altered circumstances it was a great relief and cause of thankfulness to me to receive a letter from Mrs. Temple inviting us both to spend Christmas and New Year at Royston. This invitation had upon my brother precisely the effect that I had hoped for. It roused him from his moody condition, and he professed much pleasure in accepting it, especially as he had never hitherto been in Derbyshire.

There was a small but very agreeable party at Royston, and we passed a most enjoyable fortnight. My brother seemed thoroughly to have shaken off his indisposition; and I saw my fondest hopes realised in the warm attachment which was evidently springing up between him and Miss Constance Temple.

Our visit drew near its close, and it was within a week of John's return to Oxford. Mrs. Temple celebrated the termination of the Christmas festivities by giving a ball on Twelfth-night, at which a large party were present, including most of the county families. Royston was admirably adapted for such entertainments, from the number and great size of its reception-rooms. Though Elizabethan in date and external appearance, succeeding generations had much modified and enlarged the house; and an ancestor in the middle of the last century had built at the back an enormous hall after the classic model, and covered it with a dome or cupola. In this room the dancing went forward. Supper was served in the older hall in the front, and it was while this was in progress that a thunderstorm began.

The rarity of such a phenomenon in the depth of winter formed the subject of general remark; but though the lightning was extremely brilliant, being seen distinctly through the curtained windows, the storm appeared to be at some distance, and, except for one peal, the thunder was not loud. After supper dancing was resumed, and I was taking part in a polka (called, I remember, the "*King Pippin*"), when my partner pointed out that one of the footmen wished to speak with me. I begged him to lead me to one side, and the servant then informed me that my brother was ill. Sir John, he said, had been seized with a fainting fit, but had been got to bed, and was being attended by Dr. Empson, a physician who chanced to be present among the visitors.

I at once left the hall and hurried to my brother's room. On the way I met Mrs. Temple and Constance, the latter much agitated and in tears. Mrs. Temple assured me that Dr. Empson reported favourably of my brother's condition, attributing his faintness to over-exertion in the dancing-room. The medical man had got him to bed with the assistance of Sir John's valet, had given him a quieting draught, and ordered that he should not be disturbed for the present. It was better that I should not enter the room; she begged that I would kindly comfort and reassure Constance, who was much upset, while she herself returned to her guests.

I led Constance to my bedroom, where there was a bright fire burning, and calmed her as best I could. Her interest in my brother was evidently very real and unaffected, and while not admitting her partiality for him in words, she made no effort to conceal her sentiments from me. I kissed her tenderly, and bade her narrate the circumstances of John's attack.

It seemed that after supper they had gone upstairs into the music-room, and he had himself proposed that they should walk thence into the picture-gallery, where they would better he able to see the lightning, which was then particularly vivid. The picture-gallery at Royston is a very long, narrow, and rather low room, running the whole length of the south wing, and terminating in a large Tudor oriel or flat bay window looking east. In this oriel they had sat for some time watching the flashes, and the wintry landscape revealed for an instant and then plunged into outer blackness. The gallery itself was not illuminated, and the effect of the lightning was very fine.

There had been an unusually bright flash accompanied by that single reverberating peal of thunder which I had previously noticed. Constance had spoken to my brother, but he had not replied, and in a moment she saw that he had swooned. She summoned aid without delay, but it was some short time before consciousness had been restored to him.

She had concluded this narrative, and sat holding my hand in hers. We were speculating on the cause of my brother's illness, thinking it might be due to over-exertion, or to sitting in a chilly atmosphere as the picture-gallery was not warmed, when Mrs. Temple knocked at the door and said that John was now more composed and desired earnestly to see me.

On entering my brother's bedroom I found him sitting up in bed wearing a dressing-gown. Parnham, his valet, who was arranging the fire, left the room as I came in. A chair stood at the head of the bed and I sat down by him. He took my hand in his and without a word burst into tears. "Sophy," he said, "I am so unhappy, and I have sent for you to tell you of my trouble, because I know you will be forbearing to me. An hour ago all seemed so bright. I was sitting in the picture-gallery with Constance, whom I love dearly. We had been watching the lightning, till the thunder had grown fainter and the storm seemed past. I was just about to ask her to become my wife when a brighter flash than all the rest burst on us, and I saw—I saw, Sophy, standing in the gallery as close to me as you are now—I saw—that man I told you about at Oxford; and then this faintness came on me."

"Whom do you mean?" I said, not understanding what he spoke

of, and thinking for a moment he referred to someone else. "Did you see Mr. Gaskell?"

"No, it was not he; but that dead man whom I saw rising from my wicker chair the night you went away from Oxford."

You will perhaps smile at my weakness, my dear Edward, and indeed I had at that time no justification for it; but I assure you that I have not yet forgotten, and never shall forget, the impression of overwhelming horror which his words produced upon me. It seemed as though a fear which had hitherto stood vague and shadowy in the background, began now to advance towards me, gathering more distinctness as it approached. There was to me something morbidly terrible about the apparition of this man at such a momentous crisis in my brother's life, and I at once recognised that unknown form as being the shadow which was gradually stealing between John and myself. Though I feigned incredulity as best I might, and employed those arguments or platitudes which will always be used on such occasions, urging that such a phantom could only exist in a mind disordered by physical weakness, my brother was not deceived by my words, and perceived in a moment that I did not even believe in them myself.

"Dearest Sophy," he said, with a much calmer air, "let us put aside all dissimulation. I *know* that what I have tonight seen, and that what I saw last summer at Oxford, are *not* phantoms of my brain; and I believe that you too in your inmost soul are convinced of this truth. Do not, therefore, endeavour to persuade me to the contrary. If I am not to believe the evidence of my senses, it were better at once to admit my madness—and I know that I am not mad. Let us rather consider what such an appearance can portend, and who the man is who is thus presented. I cannot explain to you why this appearance inspires me with so great a revulsion. I can only say that in its presence I seem to be brought face to face with some abysmal and repellent wickedness. It is not that the form he wears is hideous. Last night I saw him exactly as I saw him at Oxford—his face waxen pale, with a sneering mouth, the same lofty forehead, and hair brushed straight up so as almost to appear standing on end. He wore the same long coat of green cloth and white waistcoat. He seemed as if he had been standing listening to what we said, though we had not seen him till this bright flash of lightning made him manifest. You will remember that when I saw him at Oxford his eyes were always cast down, so that I never knew their colour. This time they were wide open; indeed he was looking full at us, and they were a light brown and very brilliant."

222

I saw that my brother was exciting himself, and was still weak from his recent swoon. I knew, too, that any ordinary person of strong mind would say at once that his brain wandered, and yet I had a dreadful conviction all the while that what he told me was the truth. All I could do was to beg him to calm himself, and to reflect how vain such fancies must be. "We must trust, dear John," I said, "in God. I am sure that so long as we are not living in conscious sin, we shall never be given over to any evil power; and I know my brother too well to think that he is doing anything he knows to be evil. If there be evil spirits, as we are taught there are, we are taught also that there are good spirits stronger than they, who will protect us."

So I spoke with him a little while, until he grew calmer; and then we talked of Constance and of his love for her. He was deeply pleased to hear from me how she had shown such obvious, signs of interest in his illness, and sincere affection for him. In any case, he made me promise that I would never mention to her either what he had seen this night or last summer at Oxford.

It had grown late, and the undulating beat of the dances, which had been distinctly sensible in his room—even though we could not hear any definite noise—had now ceased. Mrs. Temple knocked at the door as she went to bed and inquired how he did, giving him at the same time a kind message of sympathy from Constance, which afforded him much gratification. After she had left I prepared also to retire; but before going he begged me to take a prayer-book lying on the table, and to read aloud a collect which he pointed out. It was that for the second Sunday in Lent, and evidently well known to him. As I read it the words seemed to bear a new and deeper significance, and my heart repeated with fervour the petition for protection from those "evil thoughts which may assault and hurt the soul." I bade him good night and went away very sorrowful. Parnham, at John's request, had arranged to sleep on a sofa in his master's bedroom.

I rose betimes the next morning and inquired at my brother's room how he was. Parnham reported that he had passed a restless night, and on entering a little later I found him in a high fever, slightly delirious, and evidently not so well as when I saw him last. Mrs. Temple, with much kindness and forethought, had begged Dr. Empson to remain at Royston for the night, and he was soon in attendance on his patient. His verdict was sufficiently grave: John was suffering from a sharp access of brain-fever; his condition afforded cause for alarm; he could not answer for any turn his sickness might take. You will easily imagine how much this intelligence affected me; and Mrs. Temple and Constance shared my anxiety and solicitude. Constance and I talked much with one another that morning. Unaffected anxiety had largely removed her reserve, and she spoke openly of her feelings towards my brother, not concealing her partiality for him. I on my part let her understand how welcome to me would be any union between her and John, and how sincerely I should value her as a sister.

It was a wild winter's morning, with some snow falling and a high wind. The house was in the disordered condition which is generally observable on the day following a ball or other important festivity. I roamed restlessly about, and at last found my way to the picture-gallery, which had formed the scene of John's adventure on the previous night. I had never been in this part of the house before, as it contained no facilities for heating, and so often remained shut in the winter months. I found a listless pleasure in admiring the pictures which lined the walls, most of them being portraits of former members of the family, including the famous picture of Sir Ralph Temple and his family, attributed to Holbein. I had reached the end of the gallery and sat down in the oriel watching the snowflakes falling sparsely, and the evergreens below me waving wildly in the sudden rushes of the wind. My thoughts were busy with the events of the previous evening,— with John's illness, with the ball,—and I found myself humming the air of a waltz that had caught my fancy. At last I turned away from the garden scene towards the gallery, and as I did so my eyes fell on a remarkable picture just opposite to me.

It was a full-length portrait of a young man, life-size, and I had barely time to appreciate even its main features when I knew that I had before me the painted counterfeit of my brother's vision. The discovery caused me a violent shock, and it was with an infinite repulsion that I recognised at once the features and dress of the man whom John had seen rising from the chair at Oxford. So accurately had my brother's imagination described him to me, that it seemed as if I had myself seen him often before. I noted each feature, comparing them with my brother's description, and finding them all familiar and corresponding exactly. He was a man still in the prime of life. His features were regular and beautifully modelled; yet there was something in his face that inspired me with a deep aversion, though his brown eyes were open and brilliant. His mouth was sharply cut, with a slight sneer on the lips, and his complexion of that extreme pallor which had impressed itself deeply on my brother's imagination and my own.

After the first intense surprise had somewhat subsided, I experienced a feeling of great relief, for here was an extraordinary explanation of my brother's vision of last night. It was certain that the flash of lightning had lit up this ill-starred picture, and that to his predisposed fancy the painted figure had stood forth as an actual embodiment. That such an incident, however startling, should have been able to fling John into a brain-fever, showed that he must already have been in a very low and reduced state, on which excitement would act much more powerfully than on a more robust condition of health. A similar state of weakness, perturbed by the excitement of his passion for Constance Temple, might surely also have conjured up the vision which he thought he saw the night of our leaving Oxford in the summer. These thoughts, my dear Edward, gave me great relief; for it seemed a comparatively trivial matter that my brother should be ill, even seriously ill, if only his physical indisposition could explain away the supernatural dread which had haunted us for the past six months.

The clouds were breaking up. It was evident that John had been seriously unwell for some months; his physical weakness had acted on his brain; and I had lent colour to his wandering fancies by being alarmed by them, instead of rejecting them at once or gently laughing them away as I should have done. But these glad thoughts took me too far, and I was suddenly brought up by a reflection that did not admit of so simple an explanation. If the man's form my brother saw at Oxford were merely an effort of disordered imagination, how was it that he had been able to describe it exactly like that represented in this picture? He had never in his life been to Royston, therefore he could have no image of the picture impressed unconsciously on or hidden away in his mind. Yet his description had never varied. It had been so close as to enable me to produce in my fancy a vivid representation of the man he had seen; and here I had before me the features and dress exactly reproduced. In the presence of a coincidence so extraordinary reason stood confounded, and I knew not what to think. I walked nearer to the picture and scrutinised it closely.

The dress corresponded in every detail with that which my brother had described the figure as wearing at Oxford: a long cut-away coat of green cloth with an edge of gold embroidery, a white satin waistcoat with sprigs of embroidered roses, gold-lace at the pocket-holes, buff silk knee-breeches, and low down on the finely modelled neck a full cravat of rich lace. The figure was posed negligently against a fluted stone pedestal or short column on which the left elbow leant, and the right foot was crossed lightly over the left. His shoes were of polished black leather with heavy silver buckles, and the whole costume was very old-fashioned, and such as I had only seen worn at fancy dress balls. On the foot of the pedestal was the painter's name, "*Battoni pinxit, Romæ*, 1750." On the top of the pedestal, and under his left elbow, was a long roll apparently of music, of which one end, unfolded, hung over the edge.

For some minutes I stood still gazing at this portrait which so much astonished me, but turned on hearing footsteps in the gallery, and saw Constance, who had come to seek for me.

"Constance," I said, "whose portrait is this? It is a very striking picture, is it not?"

"Yes, it is a splendid painting, though of a very bad man. His name was Adrian Temple, and he once owned Royston. I do not know much about him, but I believe he was very wicked and very clever. My mother would be able to tell you more. It is a picture we none of us like, although so finely painted; and perhaps because he was always pointed out to me from childhood as a bad man, I have myself an aversion to it. It is singular that when the very bright flash of lightning came last night while your brother John and I were sitting here, it lit this picture with a dazzling glare that made the figure stand out so strangely as to seem almost alive. It was just after that I found that John had fainted."

The memory was not a pleasant one for either of us and we changed the subject. "Come," I said, "let us leave the gallery, it is very cold here."

Though I said nothing more at the time, her words had made a great impression on me. It was so strange that, even with the little she knew of this Adrian Temple, she should speak at once of his notoriously evil life, and of her personal dislike to the picture. Remembering what my brother had said on the previous night, that in the presence of this man he felt himself brought face to face with some indescribable wickedness, I could not but be surprised at the coincidence. The whole story seemed to me now to resemble one of those puzzle pictures or maps which I have played with as a child, where each bit fits into some other until the outline is complete. It was as if I were finding the pieces one by one of a bygone history, and fitting them to one another until some terrible whole should be gradually built up and stand out in its complete deformity.

Dr. Empson spoke gravely of John's illness, and entertained without reluctance the proposal of Mrs. Temple, that Dr. Dobie, a celebrated physician in Derby, should be summoned to a consultation. Dr. Dobie came more than once, and was at last able to report an amendment in John's condition, though both the doctors absolutely forbade anyone to visit him, and said that under the most favourable circumstances a period of some weeks must elapse before he could be moved.

Mrs. Temple invited me to remain at Royston until my brother should be sufficiently convalescent to be moved; and both she and Constance, while regretting the cause, were good enough to express themselves pleased that accident should detain me so long with them.

As the reports of the doctors became gradually more favourable, and our minds were in consequence more free to turn to other subjects, I spoke to Mrs. Temple one day about the picture, saying that it interested me, and asking for some particulars as to the life of Adrian Temple.

"My dear child," she said, "I had rather that you should not exhibit any curiosity as to this man, whom I wish that we had not to call an ancestor. I know little of him myself, and indeed his life was of such a nature as no woman, much less a young girl, would desire to be well acquainted with. He was, I believe, a man of remarkable talent, and spent most of his time between Oxford and Italy, though he visited Royston occasionally, and built the large hall here, which we use as a dancing-room. Before he was twenty wild stories were prevalent as to his licentious life, and by thirty his name was a by-word among sober and upright people. He had constantly with him at Oxford and on his travels a boon companion called Jocelyn, who aided him in his wickednesses, until on one of their Italian tours Jocelyn left him suddenly and became a Trappist monk. It was currently reported that some wild deed of Adrian Temple had shocked even him, and so outraged his surviving instincts of common humanity that he was snatched as a brand from the burning and enabled to turn back even in the full tide of his wickedness.

"However that may be, Adrian went on in his evil course without him, and about four years after disappeared. He was last heard of in Naples, and it is believed that he succumbed during a violent outbreak of the plague which took place in Italy in the autumn of 1752. That is all I shall tell you of him, and indeed I know little more myself. The only good trait that has been handed down concerning him is that he was a masterly musician, performing admirably upon the violin, which he had studied under the illustrious Tartini himself. Yet even his art of music, if tradition speaks the truth, was put by him to the basest of uses."

I apologised for my indiscretion in asking her about an unpleasant subject, and at the same time thanked her for what she had seen fit to tell me, professing myself much interested, as indeed I really was.

"Was he a handsome man?"

"That is a girl's question," she answered, smiling. "He is said to have been very handsome; and indeed his picture, painted after his first youth was past, would still lead one to suppose so. But his complexion was spoiled, it is said, and turned to deadly white by certain experiments, which it is neither possible nor seemly for us to understand. His face is of that long oval shape of which all the Temples are proud, and he had brown eyes: we sometimes tease Constance, saying she is like Adrian."

It was indeed true, as I remembered after Mrs. Temple had pointed it out, that Constance had a peculiarly long and oval face. It gave her, I think, an air of staid and placid beauty, which formed in my eyes, and perhaps in John's also, one of her greatest attractions.

"I do not like even his picture," Mrs. Temple continued, "and strange tales have been narrated of it by idle servants which are not worth repeating. I have sometimes thought of destroying it; but my late husband, being a Temple, would never hear of this, or even of removing it from its present place in the gallery; and I should be loath to do anything now contrary to his wishes, once so strongly expressed. It is, besides, very perfect from an artistic point of view, being painted by Battoni, and in his happiest manner."

I could never glean more from Mrs. Temple; but what she told me interested me deeply. It seemed another link in the chain, though I could scarcely tell why, that Adrian Temple should be so great a musician and violinist. I had, I fancy, a dim idea of that malign and outlawed spirit sitting alone in darkness for a hundred years, until he was called back by the sweet tones of the Italian music, and the lilt of the *Areopagita* that he had loved so long ago.

CHAPTER 9

John's recovery, though continuous and satisfactory, was but slow; and it was not until Easter, which fell early, that his health was pronounced to be entirely re-established. The last few weeks of his convalescence had proved to all of us a time of thankful and tranquil enjoyment. If I may judge from my own experience, there are few epochs in our life more favourable to the growth of sentiments of affection and piety, or more full of pleasurable content, than is the period of gradual recovery from serious illness. The chastening effect of our recent sickness has not yet passed away, and we are at once grateful to our Creator for preserving us, and to our friends for the countless acts of watchful kindness which it is the peculiar property of illness to evoke.

No mother ever nursed a son more tenderly than did Mrs. Temple nurse my brother, and before his restoration to health was complete the attachment between him and Constance had ripened into a formal betrothal. Such an alliance was, as I have before explained, particularly suitable, and its prospect afforded the most lively pleasure to all those concerned. The month of March had been unusually mild, and Royston being situated in a valley, as is the case with most houses of that date, was well sheltered from cold winds. It had, moreover, a south aspect, and as my brother gradually gathered strength, Constance and he and I would often sit out of doors in the soft spring mornings. We put an easy-chair with many cushions for him on the gravel by the front door, where the warmth of the sun was reflected from the red brick walls, and he would at times read aloud to us while we were engaged with our crochet-work.

Mr. Tennyson had just published anonymously a first volume of poems, and the sober dignity of his verse well suited our frame of mind at that time. The memory of those pleasant spring mornings, my dear Edward, has not yet passed away, and I can still smell the sweet moist scent of the violets, and see the bright colours of the crocus-flowers in the parterres in front of us.

John's mind seemed to be gathering strength with his body. He had apparently flung off the cloud which had overshadowed him before his illness, and avoided entirely any reference to those unpleasant events which had been previously so constantly in his thoughts. I had, indeed, taken an early opportunity of telling him of my discovery of the picture of Adrian Temple, as I thought it would tend to show him that at least the last appearance of this ghostly form admitted of a rational explanation. He seemed glad to hear of this, but did not exhibit the same interest in the matter that I had expected, and allowed it at once to drop. Whether through lack of interest, or from a lingering dislike to revisit the spot where he was seized with illness, he did not, I believe, once enter the picture-gallery before he left Royston.

I cannot say as much for myself. The picture of Adrian Temple exerted a curious fascination over me, and I constantly took an opportunity of studying it. It was, indeed, a beautiful work; and perhaps because John's recovery gave a more cheerful tone to my thoughts, or perhaps from the power of custom to dull even the keenest antipathies, I gradually got to lose much of the feeling of aversion which it had at first inspired. In time the unpleasant look grew less unpleasing, and I noticed more the beautiful oval of the face, the brown eyes, and the fine chiselling of the features. Sometimes, too, I felt a deep pity for so clever a gentleman who had died young, and whose life, were it ever so wicked, must often have been also lonely and bitter. More than once I had been discovered by Mrs. Temple or Constance sitting looking at the picture, and they had gently laughed at me, saying that I had fallen in love with Adrian Temple.

One morning in early April, when the sun was streaming brightly through the oriel, and the picture received a fuller light than usual, it occurred to me to examine closely the scroll of music painted as hanging over the top of the pedestal on which the figure leant. I had hitherto thought that the signs depicted on it were merely such as painters might conventionally use to represent a piece of musical notation. This has generally been the case, I think, in such pictures as I have ever seen in which a piece of music has been introduced. I mean that while the painting gives a general representation of the musical staves, no attempt is ever made to paint any definite notes such as would enable an actual piece to be identified. Though, as I write this, I do remember that on the monument to Handel in Westminster Abbey there is represented a musical scroll similar to that in Adrian Temple's picture, but actually sculptured with the opening phrase of the majestic melody, "I know that my Redeemer liveth."

On this morning, then, at Royston I thought I perceived that there were painted on the scroll actual musical staves, bars, and notes; and my interest being excited, I stood upon a chair so as better to examine them. Though time had somewhat obscured this portion of the picture as with a veil or film, yet I made out that the painter had intended to depict some definite piece of music. In another moment I saw that the air represented consisted of the opening bars of the *Gagliarda* in the suite by Graziani with which my brother and I were so well acquainted. Though I believe that I had not seen the volume of music in which that piece was contained more than twice, yet the melody was very familiar to me, and I had no difficulty whatever in making myself sure that I had here before me the air of the *Gagliarda* and none other. It was true that it was only roughly painted, but to one who knew the tune there was no room left for doubt.

Here was a new cause, I will not say for surprise, but for reflection. It might, of course, have been merely a coincidence that the artist should have chosen to paint in this picture this particular piece of music; but it seemed more probable that it had actually been a favourite air of Adrian Temple, and that he had chosen deliberately to have it represented with him. This discovery I kept entirely to myself, not thinking it wise to communicate it to my brother, lest by doing so I might reawaken his interest in a subject which I hoped he had finally dismissed from his thoughts.

In the second week of April the happy party at Royston was dispersed, John returning to Oxford for the summer term, Mrs. Temple making a short visit to Scotland, and Constance coming to Worth Maltravers to keep me company for a time.

It was John's last term at Oxford. He expected to take his degree in June, and his marriage with Constance Temple had been provisionally arranged for the September following. He returned to Magdalen Hall in the best of spirits, and found his rooms looking cheerful with well-filled flower-boxes in the windows. I shall not detain you with any long narration of the events of the term, as they have no relation to the present history. I will only say that I believe my brother applied himself diligently to his studies, and took his amusement mostly on horseback, riding two horses which he had had sent to him from Worth Maltravers.

About the second week after his return he received a letter from Mr. George Smart to the effect that the Stradivarius violin was now in complete order. Subsequent examination, Mr. Smart wrote, and the unanimous verdict of connoisseurs whom he had consulted, had merely confirmed the views he had at first expressed—namely, that the violin was of the finest quality, and that my brother had in his possession a unique and intact example of Stradivarius's best period. He had had it properly strung; and as the bass-bar had never been moved, and was of a stronger nature than that usual at the period of its manufacture, he had considered it unnecessary to replace it. If any signs should become visible of its being inadequate to support the tension of modern stringing, another could be easily substituted for it at a later date. He had allowed a young German *virtuoso* to play on it, and though this gentleman was one of the first living performers, and had had an opportunity of handling many splendid instruments, he assured Mr. Smart that he had never performed on one that could in any way compare with this. My brother wrote in reply thanking him, and begging that the violin might be sent to Magdalen Hall.

The pleasant musical evenings, however, which John had formerly been used to spend in the company of Mr. Gaskell were now entirely pretermitted. For though there was no cause for any diminution of friendship between them, and though on Mr. Gaskell's part there was an ardent desire to maintain their former intimacy, yet the two young men saw less and less of one another, until their intercourse was confined to an accidental greeting in the street. I believe that during all this time my brother played very frequently on the Stradivarius violin, but always alone. Its very possession seemed to have engendered from the first in his mind a secretive tendency which, as I have already observed, was entirely alien to his real disposition. As he had concealed its discovery from his sister, so he had also from his friend, and Mr. Gaskell remained in complete ignorance of the existence of such an instrument.

On the evening of its arrival from London, John seems to have carefully unpacked the violin and tried it with a new bow of Tourte's make which he had purchased of Mr. Smart. He had shut the heavy outside door of his room before beginning to play, so that no one might enter unawares; and he told me afterwards that though he had naturally expected from the instrument a very fine tone, yet its actual merits so far exceeded his anticipations as entirely to overwhelm him. The sound issued from it in a volume of such depth and purity as to give an impression of the passages being chorded, or even of another violin being played at the same time. He had had, of course, no opportunity of practising during his illness, and so expected to find his skill with the bow somewhat diminished; but he perceived, on the contrary, that his performance was greatly improved, and that he was playing with a mastery and feeling of which he had never before been conscious.

While attributing this improvement very largely to the beauty of the instrument on which he was performing, yet he could not but believe that by his illness, or in some other unexplained way, he had actually acquired a greater freedom of wrist and fluency of expression, with which reflection he was not a little elated. He had had a lock fixed on the cupboard in which he had originally found the violin, and here he carefully deposited it on each occasion after playing, before he opened the outer door of his room.

So the summer term passed away. The examinations had come in their due time, and were now over. Both the young men had submitted themselves to the ordeal, and while neither would of course have admitted as much to anyone else, both felt secretly that they had no reason to be dissatisfied with their performance. The results would not be published for some weeks to come. The last night of the term had arrived, the last night too of John's Oxford career. It was near nine o'clock, but still quite light, and the rich orange glow of sunset had not yet left the sky. The air was warm and sultry, as on that eventful evening when just a year ago he had for the first time seen the figure or the illusion of the figure of Adrian Temple. Since that time he had played the *Areopagita* many, many times; but there had never been any reappearance of that form, nor even had the once familiar creaking of the wicker chair ever made itself heard.

As he sat alone in his room, thinking with a natural melancholy that he had seen the sun set for the last time on his student life, and reflecting on the possibilities of the future and perhaps on opportunities wasted in the past, the memory of that evening last June recurred strongly to his imagination, and he felt an irresistible impulse to play once more the *Areopagita*. He unlocked the now familiar cupboard and took out the violin, and never had the exquisite gradations of colour in its varnish appeared to greater advantage than in the soft mellow light of the fading day. As he began the *Gagliarda* he looked at the wicker chair, half expecting to see a form he well knew seated in it; but nothing of the kind ensued, and he concluded the *Areopagita* without the occurrence of any unusual phenomenon.

It was just at its close that he heard some one knocking at the outer door. He hurriedly locked away the violin and opened the "oak." It was Mr. Gaskell. He came in rather awkwardly, as though not sure whether he would be welcomed.

"Johnnie," he began, and stopped.

The force of ancient habit sometimes, dear nephew, leads us unwittingly to accost those who were once our friends by a familiar or nickname long "after the intimacy that formerly justified it has vanished. But sometimes we intentionally revert to the use of such a name, not wishing to proclaim openly, as it were, by a more formal address that we are no longer the friends we once were. I think this latter was the case with Mr. Gaskell as he repeated the familiar name.

"Johnnie, I was passing down New College Lane, and heard the violin from your open windows. You were playing the 'Areopagita,' and it all sounded so familiar to me that I thought I must come up. I am not interrupting you, am I?"

"No, not at all," John answered.

"It is the last night of our undergraduate life, the last night we shall meet in Oxford as students. Tomorrow we make our bow to youth and become men. We have not seen much of each other this term at any rate, and I daresay that is my fault. But at least let us part as friends. Surely our friends are not so many that we can afford to fling them lightly away."

He held out his hand frankly, and his voice trembled a little as he spoke—partly perhaps from real emotion, but more probably from the feeling of reluctance which I have noticed men always exhibit to discovering any sentiment deeper than those usually deemed conventional in correct society. My brother was moved by his obvious wish to renew their former friendship, and grasped the proffered hand.

There was a minute's pause, and then the conversation was resumed, a little stiffly at first, but more freely afterwards. They spoke on many indifferent subjects, and Mr. Gaskell congratulated John on the prospect of his marriage, of which he had heard. As he at length rose up to take his departure, he said, "You must have practised the violin diligently of late, for I never knew anyone make so rapid progress with it as you have done. As I came along I was spellbound by your music. I never before heard you bring from the instrument so exquisite a tone: the chorded passages were so powerful that I believed there had been another person playing with you. Your Pressenda is certainly a finer instrument than I ever imagined."

My brother was pleased with Mr. Gaskell's compliment, and the latter continued, "Let me enjoy the pleasure of playing with you once more in Oxford; let us play the *Areopagita*."

And so saying he opened the pianoforte and sat down.

John was turning to take out the Stradivarius when he remembered that he had never even revealed its existence to Mr. Gaskell, and that if he now produced it an explanation must follow. In a moment his mood changed, and with less geniality he excused himself, somewhat awkwardly, from complying with the request, saying that he was fatigued.

Mr. Gaskell was evidently hurt at his friend's altered manner, and without renewing his petition rose at once from the pianoforte, and after a little forced conversation took his departure. On leaving he shook my brother by the hand, wished him all prosperity in his marriage and after-life, and said, "Do not entirely forget your old comrade, and remember that if at any time you should stand in need of a true friend, you know where to find him!"

John heard his footsteps echoing down the passage and made a half-involuntary motion towards the door as if to call him back, but did not do so, though he thought over his last words then and on a subsequent occasion.

Chapter 10

The summer was spent by us in the company of Mrs. Temple and Constance, partly at Royston and partly at Worth Maltravers. John had again hired the cutter-yacht *Palestine*, and the whole party made several expeditions in her. Constance was entirely devoted to her lover; her life seemed wrapped up in his; she appeared to have no existence except in his presence.

I can scarcely enumerate the reasons which prompted such thoughts, but during these months I sometimes found myself wondering if John still returned her affection as ardently as I knew had once been the case. I can certainly call to mind no single circumstance which could justify me in such a suspicion. He performed punctiliously all those thousand little acts of devotion which are expected of an accepted lover; he seemed to take pleasure in perfecting any scheme of enjoyment to amuse her; and yet the impression grew in my mind that he no longer felt the same heart-whole love to her that she bore him, and that he had himself shown six months earlier. I cannot say, my dear Edward, how lively was the grief that even the suspicion of such a fact caused me, and I continually rebuked myself for entertaining for a moment a thought so unworthy, and dismissed it from my mind with reprobation.

Alas! ere long it was sure again to make itself felt. We had all seen the Stradivarius violin; indeed it was impossible for my brother longer to conceal it from us, as he now played continually on it. He did not recount to us the story of its discovery, contenting himself with saying that he had become possessed of it at Oxford. We imagined naturally that he had purchased it; and for this I was sorry, as I feared Mr. Thoresby, his guardian, who had given him some years previously an excellent violin by Pressenda, might feel hurt at seeing his present so unceremoniously laid aside. None of us were at all intimately acquainted with the fancies of fiddle-collectors, and were consequently quite ignorant of the enormous value that fashion attached to so splendid an instrument. Even had we known, I do not think that we should have been surprised at John purchasing it; for he had recently come of age, and was in possession of so large a fortune as would amply justify him in such an indulgence had he wished to gratify it.

No one, however, could remain unaware of the wonderful musical qualities of the instrument. Its rich and melodious tones would commend themselves even to the most unmusical ear, and formed a subject of constant remark. I noticed also that my brother's knowledge of the violin had improved in a very perceptible manner, for it was impossible to attribute the great beauty and power of his present performance entirely to the excellence of the instrument he was using. He appeared more than ever devoted to the art, and would shut himself up in his room alone for two or more hours together for the purpose of playing the violin—a habit which was a source of sorrow to Constance, for he would never allow her to sit with him on such occasions, as she naturally wished to do.

So the summer fled. I should have mentioned that in July, after going up to complete the *viva-voce* part of their examination, both Mr. Gaskell and John received information that they had obtained "first-classes." The young men had, it appears, done excellently well, and both had secured a place in that envied division of the first-class which was called "above the line." John's success proved a source of much pleasure to us all, and mutual congratulations were freely exchanged. We were pleased also at Mr. Gaskell's high place, remembering the kindness which he had shown us at Oxford in the previous year. I desired to send him my compliments and felicitations when he should next be writing to him. I did not doubt that my brother would return Mr. Gaskell's congratulations, which he had already received: he said, however, that his friend had given no address to which he could write, and so the matter dropped.

On the 1st of September John and Constance Temple were married. The wedding took place at Royston, and by John's special desire (with which Constance fully agreed) the ceremony was of a strictly private and unpretentious nature. The newly married pair had determined to spend their honeymoon in Italy, and left for the Continent in the forenoon.

Mrs. Temple invited me to remain with her for the present at Royston, which I was very glad to do, feeling deeply the loss of a favourite brother, and looking forward with dismay to six weeks of loneliness which must elapse before I should again see him and my dearest Constance.

We received news of our travellers about a fortnight afterwards, and then heard from them at frequent intervals. Constance wrote in the best of spirits, and with the keenest appreciation. She had never travelled in Switzerland or Italy before and all was enchantingly novel to her. They had journeyed through Basle to Lucerne, spending a few days in that delightful spot, and thence proceeding by the Simplon Pass to Lugano and the Italian lakes. Then we heard that they had gone further south than had been at first contemplated; they had reached Rome, and were intending to go on to Naples.

After the first few weeks we neither of us received any more letters from John. It was always Constance who wrote, and even her letters grew very much less frequent than had at first been the case. This was perhaps natural, as the business of travel no doubt engrossed their thoughts. But ere long we both perceived that the letters of our dear girl were more constrained and formal than before. It was as if she was writing now rather to comply with a sense of duty than to give vent to the light-hearted gaiety and naïve enjoyment which breathed in every line of her earlier communications. So at least it seemed to us, and again the old suspicion presented itself to my mind, and I feared that all was not as it should be.

Naples was to be the turning-point of their travels, and we expected them to return to England by the end of October. November had arrived, however, and we still had no intimation that their return journey had commenced or was even decided on. From John there was no word, and Constance wrote less often than ever. John, she said, was enraptured with Naples and its surroundings; he devoted himself much to the violin, and though she did not say so, this meant, I knew, that she was often left alone. For her own part, she did not think that a continued residence in Italy would suit her health; the sudden changes of temperature tried her, and people said that the airs rising in the evening from the bay were unwholesome.

Then we received a letter from her which much alarmed us. It was written from Naples and dated October 25. John, she said, had been ailing of late with nervousness and insomnia. On Wednesday, two days before the date of her letter, he had suffered all day from a strange restlessness, which increased after they had retired for the evening. He could not sleep and had dressed again, telling her he would walk a little in the night air to compose himself. He had not returned till near six in the morning, and then was so deadly pale and seemed so exhausted that she insisted on his keeping to his bed till she could get medical advice. The doctors feared that he had been attacked by some strange form of malarial fever, and said he needed much care. Our anxiety was, however, at least temporarily relieved by the receipt of later tidings which spoke of John's recovery; but November drew to a close without any definite mention of their return having reached us.

That month is always, I think, a dreary one in the country. It has neither the brilliant tints of October, nor the cosy jollity of mid-winter with its Christmas joys to alleviate it. This year it was more gloomy than usual. Incessant rain had marked its close, and the Roy, a little brook which skirted the gardens not far from the house, had swollen to unusual proportions. At last one wild night the flood rose so high as to completely cover the garden terraces, working havoc in the parterres, and covering the lawns with a thick coat of mud. Perhaps this gloominess of nature's outer face impressed itself in a sense of apprehension on our spirits, and it was with a feeling of more than ordinary pleasure and relief that early in December we received a letter dated from Laon, saying that our travellers were already well advanced on their return journey, and expected to be in England a week after the receipt by us of this advice. It was, as usual, Constance who wrote. John begged, she said, that Christmas might be spent at Worth Maltravers, and that we would at once proceed thither to see that all was in order against their return. They reached Worth about the middle of the month, and were, I need not say, received with the utmost affection by Mrs. Temple and myself.

In reply to our inquiries John professed that his health was com-pletely restored; but though we could indeed discern no other signs of any special weakness, we were much shocked by his changed ap-pearance. He had completely lost his old healthy and sunburnt com-plexion, and his face, though not thin or sunken, was strangely pale. Constance assured us that though in other respects he had apparently recovered, he had never regained his old colour from the night of his attack of fever at Naples.

I soon perceived that her own spirits were not so bright as was ordinarily the case with her; and she exhibited none of the eagerness to narrate to others the incidents of travel which is generally observ-able in those who have recently returned from a journey. The cause of this depression was, alas! not difficult to discover, for John's former abstraction and moodiness seemed to have returned with an increased force. It was a source of infinite pain to Mrs. Temple, and perhaps even more so to me, to observe this sad state of things. Constance never complained, and her affection towards her husband seemed only to increase in the face of difficulties. Yet the matter was one which could not be hid from the anxious eyes of loving kinswomen, and I believe that it was the consciousness that these altered circumstances could not but force themselves upon our notice that added poignancy to my poor sister's grief.

While not markedly neglecting her, my brother had evidently ceased to take that pleasure in her company which might reasonably have been expected in any case under the circumstances of a recent marriage, and a thousand times more so when his wife was so loving and beautiful a creature as Constance Temple. He appeared little except at meals, and not even always at lunch, shutting himself up for the most part in his morning-room or study and playing continually on the violin. It was in vain that we attempted even by means of his music to win him back to a sweeter mood. Again and again I begged him to allow me to accompany him on the pianoforte, but he would never do so, always putting me off with some excuse. Even when he sat with us in the evening, he spoke little, devoting himself for the most part to reading. His books were almost always Greek or Latin, so that I am ignorant of the subjects of his study; but he was content that either Constance or I should play on the pianoforte, saying that the melody, so far from distracting his attention, helped him rather to appreciate what he was reading. Constance always begged me to allow her to take her place at the instrument on these occasions, and would play to him sometimes for hours without receiving a word of thanks, being eager even in this unreciprocated manner to testify her love and devotion to him.

Christmas Day, usually so happy a season, brought no alleviation of our gloom. My brother's reserve continually increased, and even his longest-established habits appeared changed. He had been always most observant of his religious duties, attending divine service with the utmost regularity whatever the weather might be, and saying that it was a duty a landed proprietor owed as much to his tenantry as himself to set a good example in such matters. Ever since our earliest years he and I had gone morning and afternoon on Sundays to the little church of Worth, and there sat together in the Maltravers chapel where so many of our name had sat before us. Here their monuments and achievements stood about us on every side, and it had always seemed to me that with their name and property we had inherited also the obligation to continue those acts of piety, in the practice of which so many of them had lived and died. It was, therefore, a source of surprise and great grief to me when on the Sunday after his return my brother omitted all religious observances, and did not once attend the parish church. He was not present with us at breakfast, ordering coffee and a roll to be taken to his private sitting-room.

At the hour at which we usually set out for church I went to his room to tell him that we were all dressed and waiting for him. I tapped at the door, but on trying to enter found it locked. In reply to my message he did not open the door, but merely begged us to go on to church, saying he would possibly follow us later. We went alone, and I sat anxiously in our seat with my eyes fixed on the door, hoping against hope that each late comer might be John, but he never came. Perhaps this will appear to you, Edward, a comparatively trivial circumstance (though I hope it may not), but I assure you that it brought tears to my eyes. When I sat in the Maltravers chapel and thought that for the first time my dear brother had preferred in an open way his convenience or his whim to his duty, and had of set purpose neglected to come to the house of God, I felt a bitter grief that seemed to rise up in my throat and choke me. I could not think of the meaning of the prayers nor join in the singing: and all the time that Mr. Butler, our clergyman, was preaching, a verse of a little piece of poetry which I learnt as a girl was running in my head:—

How easy are the paths of ill;
How steep and hard the upward ways;
A child can roll the stone down hill
That breaks a giant's arm to raise.

It seemed to me that our loved one had set his foot upon the downward slope, and that not all the efforts of those who would have given their lives to save him could now hold him back.

It was even worse on Christmas Day. Ever since we had been confirmed John and I had always taken the Sacrament on that happy morning, and after service he had distributed the Maltravers dole in our chapel. There are given, as you know, on that day to each of twelve old men £5 and a green coat, and a like sum of money with a blue cloth dress to as many old women. These articles of dress are placed on the altar-tomb of Sir Esmoun de Maltravers, and have been thence distributed from days immemorial by the head of our house. Ever since he was twelve years old it had been my pride to watch my handsome brother doing this deed of noble charity, and to hear the kindly words he added with each gift.

Alas! alas! it was all different this Christmas. Even on this holy day my brother did not approach either the altar or the house of God. Till then Christmas had always seemed to me to be a day given us from above, that we might see even while on earth a faint glimpse of that serenity and peaceful love which will hereafter gild all days in heaven. Then covetous men lay aside their greed and enemies their rancour, then warm hearts grow warmer, and Christians feel their common brotherhood. I can scarcely imagine any man so lost or guilty as not to experience on that day some desire to turn back to the good once more, as not to recognise some far-off possibility of better things. It was thoughts free and happy such as these that had previously come into my heart in the service of Christmas Day, and been particularly associated with the familiar words that we all love so much. But that morning the harmonies were all jangled: it seemed as though some evil spirit was pouring wicked thoughts into my ear; and even while children sang "Hark the herald angels," I thought I could hear through it all a melody which I had learnt to loathe, the *Gagliarda* of the *Areopagita*.

Poor Constance! Though her veil was down, I could see her tears, and knew her thoughts must be sadder even than mine: I drew her hand towards me, and held it as I would a child's. After the service was over a new trial awaited us. John had made no arrangement for the distribution of the dole. The coats and dresses were all piled ready on Sir Esmoun's tomb, and there lay the little leather pouches of money, but there was no one to give them away. Mr. Butler looked puzzled, and approaching us, said he feared Sir John was ill—had he made no provision for the distribution? Pride kept back the tears which were rising fast, and I said my brother was indeed unwell, that it would be better for Mr. Butler to give away the dole, and that Sir John would himself visit the recipients during the week. Then we hurried away, not daring to watch the distribution of the dole, lest we should no longer be able to master our feelings, and should openly betray our agitation.

From one another we no longer attempted to conceal our grief. It seemed as though we had all at once resolved to abandon the farce of pretending not to notice John's estrangement from his wife, or of explaining away his neglectful and unaccountable treatment of her.

I do not think that three poor women were ever so sad on Christmas Day before as were we on our return from church that morning. None of us had seen my brother, but about five in the afternoon Constance went to his room, and through the locked door begged piteously to see him. After a few minutes he complied with her request and opened the door. The exact circumstances of that interview she never revealed to me, but I knew from her manner when she returned that something she had seen or heard had both grieved and frightened her. She told me only that she had flung herself in an agony of tears at his feet, and kneeling there, weary and broken-hearted, had begged him to tell her if she had done aught amiss, had prayed him to give her back his love. To all this he answered little, but her entreaties had at least such an effect as to induce him to take his dinner with us that evening. At that meal we tried to put aside our gloom, and with feigned smiles and cheerful voices, from which the tears were hardly banished, sustained a weary show of conversation and tried to wile away his evil mood. But he spoke little; and when Foster, my father's butler, put on the table the three-handled Maltravers' loving-cup that he had brought up Christmas by Christmas for thirty years, my brother merely passed it by without a taste. I saw by Foster's face that the master's malady was no longer a secret even from the servants.

I shall not harass my own feelings nor yours, my dear Edward, by entering into further details of your father's illness, for such it was obvious his indisposition had become. It was the only consolation, and that was a sorry one, that we could use with Constance, to persuade her that John's estrangement from her was merely the result or manifestation of some physical infirmity. He obviously grew worse from week to week, and his treatment of his wife became colder and more callous. We had used all efforts to persuade him to take a change of air—to go to Royston for a month, and place himself under the care of Dr. Dobie. Mrs. Temple had even gone so far as to write privately to this physician, telling him as much of the ease as was prudent, and asking his advice. Not being aware of the darker sides of my brother's ailment, Dr. Dobie replied in a less serious strain than seemed to us convenient, but recommended in any case a complete change of air and scene.

It was, therefore, with no ordinary pleasure and relief that we heard my brother announce quite unexpectedly one morning in March that he had made up his mind to seek change, and was going to leave almost immediately for the Continent. He took his valet Parnham with him, and quitted Worth one morning before lunch, bidding us an unceremonious *adieu*, though he kissed Constance with some apparent tenderness. It was the first time for three months, she confessed to me afterwards, that he had shown her even so ordinary a mark of affection; and her wounded heart treasured up what she hoped would prove a token of returning love. He had not proposed to take her with him, and even had he done so, we should have been reluctant to assent, as signs were not wanting that it might have been imprudent for her to undertake foreign travel at that period.

For nearly a month we had no word of him. Then he wrote a short note to Constance from Naples, giving no news, and indeed, scarce speaking of himself at all, but mentioning as an address to which she might write if she wished, the Villa de Angelis at Posilipo. Though his letter was cold and empty, yet Constance was delighted to get it, and wrote henceforth herself nearly every day, pouring out her heart to him, and retailing such news as she thought would cheer him.

CHAPTER 11

A month later Mrs. Temple wrote to John warning him of the state in which Constance now found herself, and begging him to return at least for a few weeks in order that he might be present at the time of her confinement. Though it would have been in the last degree unkind, or even inhuman, that a request of this sort should have been refused, yet I will confess to you that my brother's recent strangeness had prepared me for behaviour on his part however wild; and it was with a feeling of extreme relief that I heard from Mrs. Temple a little later that she had received a short note from John to say that he was already on his return journey. I believe Mrs. Temple herself felt as I did in the matter, though she said nothing.

When he returned we were all at Royston, whither Mrs. Temple had taken Constance to be under Dr. Dobie's care. We found John's physical appearance changed for the worse. His pallor was as remarkable as before, but he was visibly thinner; and his strange mental abstraction and moodiness seemed little if any abated. At first, indeed, he greeted Constance kindly or even affectionately. She had been in a terrible state of anxiety as to the attitude he would assume towards her, and this mental strain affected prejudicially her very delicate bodily condition. His kindness, of an ordinary enough nature indeed, seemed to her yearning heart a miracle of condescending love, and she was transported with the idea that his affection to her, once so sincere, was indeed returning. But I grieve to say that his manner thawed only for a very short time, and ere long he relapsed into an attitude of complete indifference.

It was as if his real, true, honest, and loving character had made one more vigorous effort to assert itself,—as though it had for a moment broken through the hard and selfish crust that was forming around him; but the blighting influence which was at work proved seemingly too strong for him to struggle against, and riveted its chains again upon him with a weight heavier than before. That there was some malefic influence, mental or physical, thus working on him, no one who had known him before could for a moment doubt. But while Mrs. Temple and I readily admitted this much, we were entirely unable even to form a conjecture as to its nature. It is true that Mrs. Temple's fancy suggested that Constance had some rival in his affections; but we rejected such a theory almost before it was proposed, feeling that it was inherently improbable, and that, had it been true, we could not have remained entirely unaware of the circumstances which had conduced to such a state of things.

It was this inexplicable nature of my brother's affliction that added immeasurably to our grief. If we could only have ascertained its cause we might have combated it; but as it was, we were fighting in the dark, as against some enemy who was assaulting us from an obscurity so thick that we could not see his form. Of any mental trouble we thus knew nothing, nor could we say that my brother was suffering from any definite physical ailment, except that he was certainly growing thinner.

Your birth, my dear Edward, followed very shortly. Your poor mother rallied in an unusually short time, and was filled with rapture at the new treasure which was thus given as a solace to her afflictions. Your father exhibited little interest at the event, though he sat nearly half an hour with her one evening, and allowed her even to stroke his hair and caress him as in time long past. Although it was now the height of summer he seldom left the house, sitting much and sleeping in his own room, where he had a field-bed provided for him, and continually devoting himself to the violin.

One evening near the end of July we were sitting after dinner in the drawing-room at Royston, having the French windows looking on to the lawn open, as the air was still oppressively warm. Though things were proceeding as indifferently as before, we were perhaps less cast down than usual, for John had taken his dinner with us that evening. This was a circumstance now, alas! sufficiently uncommon, for he had nearly all his meals served for him in his own rooms. Constance, who was once more downstairs, sat playing at the pianoforte, performing chiefly melodies by Scarlatti or Bach, of which old-fashioned music she knew her husband to be most fond. A later fashion, as you know, has revived the cultivation of these composers, but at the time of which I write their works were much less commonly known. Though she was more than a passable musician, he would not allow her to accompany him; indeed he never now performed at all on the violin before us, reserving his practice entirely for his own chamber.

There was a pause in the music while coffee was served. My brother had been sitting in an easy-chair apart reading some classical work during his wife's performance, and taking little notice of us. But after a while he put down his book and said, "Constance, if you will accompany me, I will get my violin and play a little while." I cannot say how much his words astonished us. It was so simple a matter for him to say, and yet it filled us all with an unspeakable joy. We concealed our emotion till he had left the room to get his instrument, then Constance showed how deeply she was gratified by kissing first her mother and then me, squeezing my hand but saying nothing. In a minute he returned, bringing his violin and a music-book.

By the soiled vellum cover and the shape I perceived instantly that it was the book containing the *Areopagita*. I had not seen it for near two years, and was not even aware that it was in the house, but I knew at once that he intended to play that suite. I entertained an unreasoning but profound aversion to its melodies, but at that moment I would have welcomed warmly that or any other music, so that he would only choose once more to show some thought for his neglected wife. He put the book open at the *Areopagita* on the desk of the pianoforte, and asked her to play it with him. She had never seen the music before, though I believe she was not unacquainted with the melody, as she had heard him playing it by himself, and once heard, it was not easily forgotten.

They began the *Areopagita* suite, and at first all went well. The tone of the violin, and also, I may say with no undue partiality, my brother's performance, were so marvellously fine that though our thoughts were elsewhere when, the music commenced, in a few seconds they were wholly engrossed in the melody, and we sat spellbound. It was as if the violin had become suddenly endowed with life, and was sing-

245

ing to us in a mystical language more deep and awful than any human words. Constance was comparatively unused to the figuring of the *basso continuo*, and found some trouble in reading it accurately, especially in manuscript; but she was able to mask any difficulty she may have had until she came to the *Gagliarda*. Here she confessed to me her thoughts seemed against her will to wander, and her attention became too deeply riveted on her husband's performance to allow her to watch her own. She made first one slight fault, and then growing nervous, another, and another. Suddenly John stopped and said brusquely, "Let Sophy play, I cannot keep time with you."

Poor Constance! The tears came swiftly to my own eyes when I heard him speak so thoughtlessly to her, and I was almost provoked to rebuke him openly. She was still weak from her recent illness; her nerves were excited by the unusual pleasure she felt in playing once more with her husband, and this sudden shattering of her hopes of a renewed tenderness proved more than she could bear: she put her head between her hands upon the keyboard and broke into a paroxysm of tears.

We both ran to her; but while we were attempting to assuage her grief, John shut his violin into its case, took the music-book under his arm, and left the room without saying a word to any of us, not even to the weeping girl, whose sobs seemed as though they would break her heart.

We got her put to bed at once, but it was some hours before her convulsive sobbing ceased. Mrs. Temple had administered to her a soothing draught of proved efficacy, and after sitting with her till after one o'clock, I left her at last dozing off to sleep, and myself sought repose. I was quite wearied out with the weight of my anxiety, and with the crushing bitterness of seeing my dearest Constance's feelings so wounded. Yet in spite, or rather perhaps on account of my trouble, my head had scarcely touched my pillow ere I fell into a deep sleep.

A room in the south wing had been converted for the nonce into a nursery, and for the convenience of being near her infant Constance now slept in a room adjoining. As this portion of the house was somewhat isolated, Mrs. Temple had suggested that I should keep her daughter company, and occupy a room in the same passage, only removed a few doors, and this I had accordingly done. I was aroused from my sleep that night by some one knocking gently on the door of my bedroom; but it was some seconds before my thoughts became sufficiently awake to allow me to remember where I was. There was some moonlight, but I lighted a candle, and looking at my watch saw that it was two o'clock. I concluded that either Constance or her baby was unwell, and that the nurse needed my assistance. So I left my bed, and moving to the door, asked softly who was there. It was, to my surprise, the voice of Constance that replied, "O Sophy, let me in."

In a second I had opened the door, and found my poor sister wearing only her nightdress, and standing in the moonlight before me.

She looked frightened and unusually pale in her white dress and with the cold gleam of the moon upon her. At first I thought she was walking in her sleep, and perhaps rehearsing again in her dreams the troubles which dogged her waking footsteps. I took her gently by the arm, saying, "Dearest Constance, come back at once to bed; you will take cold."

She was not asleep, however, but made a motion of silence, and said in a terrified whisper, "Hush; do you hear nothing?" There was something so vague and yet so mysterious in the question and in her evident perturbation that I was infected too by her alarm. I felt myself shiver, as I strained my ear to catch if possible the slightest sound. But a complete silence pervaded everything: I could hear nothing.

"Can you hear it?" she said again. All sorts of images of ill presented themselves to my imagination: I thought the baby must be ill with croup, and that she was listening for some *stertorous* breath of anguish; and then the dread came over me that perhaps her sorrows had been too much for her, and that reason had left her seat. At that thought the marrow froze in my bones.

"Hush," she said again; and just at that moment, as I strained my ears, I thought I caught upon the sleeping air a distant and very faint murmur.

"Oh, what is it, Constance?" I said. "You will drive me mad;" and while I spoke the murmur seemed to resolve itself into the vibration, felt almost rather than heard, of some distant musical instrument. I stepped past her into the passage. All was deadly still, but I could perceive that music was being played somewhere far away; and almost at the same minute my ears recognised faintly but unmistakably the *Gagliarda* of the *Areopagita*.

I have already mentioned that for some reason which I can scarcely explain, this melody was very repugnant to me. It seemed associated in some strange and intimate way with my brother's indisposition and moral decline. Almost at the moment that I had heard it first two years ago, peace seemed to have risen up and left our house, gathering her skirts about her, as we read that the angels left the Temple at the siege of Jerusalem. And now it was even more detestable to my ears, recalling as it did too vividly the cruel events of the preceding evening.

"John must be sitting up playing," I said.

"Yes," she answered; "but why is he in this part of the house, and why does he always play *that* tune?"

It was if some irresistible attraction drew us towards the music. Constance took my hand in hers and we moved together slowly down the passage. The wind had risen, and though there was a bright moon, her beams were constantly eclipsed by driving clouds. Still there was light enough to guide us, and I extinguished the candle. As we reached the end of the passage the air of the *Gagliarda* grew more and more distinct.

Our passage opened on to a broad landing with a balustrade, and from one side of it ran out the picture-gallery which you know.

I looked at Constance significantly. It was evident that John was playing in this gallery. We crossed the landing, treading carefully and making no noise with our naked feet, for both of us had been too excited even to think of putting on shoes.

We could now see the whole length of the gallery. My poor brother sat in the oriel window of which I have before spoken. He was sitting so as to face the picture of Adrian Temple, and the great windows of the oriel flung a strong light on him. At times a cloud hid the moon, and all was plunged in darkness; but in a moment the cold light fell full on him, and we could trace every feature as in a picture. He had evidently not been to bed, for he was fully dressed, exactly as he had left us in the drawing-room five hours earlier when Constance was weeping over his thoughtless words. He was playing the violin, playing with a passion and reckless energy which I had never seen, and hope never to see again.

Perhaps he remembered that this spot was far removed from the rest of the house, or perhaps he was careless whether any were awake and listening to him or not; but it seemed to me that he was playing with a sonorous strength greater than I had thought possible for a single violin. There came from his instrument such a volume and torrent of melody as to fill the gallery so full, as it were, of sound that it throbbed and vibrated again. He kept his eyes fixed on something at the opposite side of the gallery; we could not indeed see on what, but I have no doubt at all that it was the portrait of Adrian Temple. His gaze was eager and expectant, as though he were waiting for something to occur which did not.

I knew that he had been growing thin of late, but this was the first time I had realised how sunk were the hollows of his eyes and how haggard his features had become. It may have been some effect of moonlight which I do not well understand, but his fine-cut face, once so handsome, looked on this night worn and thin like that of an old man. He never for a moment ceased playing. It was always one same dreadful melody, the *Gagliarda* of the *Areopagita*, and he repeated it time after time with the perseverance and apparent aimlessness of an automaton.

He did not see us, and we made no sign, standing afar off in silent horror at that nocturnal sight. Constance clutched me by the arm: she was so pale that I perceived it even in the moonlight. "Sophy," she said, "he is sitting in the same place as on the first night when he told me how he loved me." I could answer nothing, my voice was frozen in me. I could only stare at my brother's poor withered face, realising then for the first time that he must be mad, and that it was the haunting of the *Gagliarda* that had made him so.

We stood there I believe for half an hour without speech or motion, and all the time that sad figure at the end of the gallery continued its performance. Suddenly he stopped, and an expression of frantic despair came over his face as he laid down the violin and buried his head in his hands. I could bear it no longer. "Constance," I said, "come back to bed. We can do nothing," So we turned and crept away silently as we had come. Only as we crossed the landing Constance stopped, and looked back for a minute with a heart-broken yearning at the man she loved. He had taken his hands from his head, and she saw the profile of his face clear cut and hard in the white moonlight.

It was the last time her eyes ever looked upon it.

She made for a moment as if she would turn back and go to him, but her courage failed her, and we went on. Before we reached her room we heard in the distance, faintly but distinctly, the burden of the *Gagliarda*.

CHAPTER 12

The next morning, my maid brought me a hurried note written in pencil by my brother. It contained only a few lines, saying that he found that his continued sojourn at Royston was not beneficial to his health, and had determined to return to Italy. If we wished to write, letters would reach him at the Villa de Angelis: his valet Parnham was to follow him thither with his baggage as soon as it could be got together. This was all; there was no word of *adieu* even to his wife.

We found that he had never gone to bed that night. But in the early morning he had himself saddled his horse *Sentinel* and ridden in to Derby, taking the early mail thence to London. His resolve to leave Royston had apparently been arrived at very suddenly, for so far as we could discover, he had carried no luggage of any kind. I could not help looking somewhat carefully round his room to see if he had taken the Stradivarius violin. No trace of it or even of its case was to be seen, though it was difficult to imagine how he could have carried it with him on horseback. There was, indeed, a locked travelling-trunk which Parnham was to bring with him later, and the instrument might, of course, have been in that; but I felt convinced that he had actually taken it with him in some way or other, and this proved afterwards to have been the case.

I shall draw a veil, my dear Edward, over the events which immediately followed your father's departure. Even at this distance of time the memory is too inexpressibly bitter to allow me to do more than briefly allude to them.

A fortnight after John's departure, we left Royston and removed to Worth, wishing to get some sea-air, and to enjoy the late summer of the south coast. Your mother seemed entirely to have recovered from her confinement, and to be enjoying as good health as could be reasonably expected under the circumstances of her husband's indisposition. But suddenly one of those insidious maladies which are incidental to women in her condition seized upon her. We had hoped and believed that all such period of danger was already happily past; but, alas! it was not so, and within a few hours of her first seizure all realised how serious was her case. Everything that human skill can do under such conditions was done, but without avail. Symptoms of blood-poisoning showed themselves, accompanied with high fever, and within a week she was in her coffin.

Though her delirium was terrible to watch, yet I thank God to this day, that if she was to die, it pleased Him to take her while in an unconscious condition. For two days before her death she recognised no one, and was thus spared at least the sadness of passing from life without one word of kindness or even of reconciliation from her unhappy husband.

The communication with a place so distant as Naples was not then to be made under fifteen or twenty days, and all was over before we could hope that the intelligence even of his wife's illness had reached John. Both Mrs. Temple and I remained at Worth in a state of complete prostration, awaiting his return. When more than a month had passed without his arrival, or even a letter to say that he was on his way, our anxiety took a new turn, as we feared that some accident had befallen him, or that the news of his wife's death, which would then be in his hands, had so seriously affected him as to render him incapable of taking any action.

To repeated subsequent communications we received no answer; but at last, to a letter which I wrote to Parnham, the servant replied, stating that his master was still at the Villa de Angelis, and in a condition of health little differing from that in which he left Royston, except that he was now slightly paler if possible and thinner. It was not till the end of November that any word came from him, and then he wrote only one page of a sheet of note-paper to me in pencil, making no reference whatever to his wife's death, but saying that he should not return for Christmas, and instructing me to draw on his bankers for any moneys that I might require for household purposes at Worth.

I need not tell you the effect that such conduct produced on Mrs. Temple and myself; you can easily imagine what would have been your own feelings in such a case. Nor will I relate any other circumstances which occurred at this period, as they would have no direct bearing upon my narrative. Though I still wrote to my brother at frequent intervals, as not wishing to neglect a duty, no word from him ever came in reply.

About the end of March, indeed, Parnham returned to Worth Maltravers, saying that his master had paid him a half-year's wages in advance, and then dispensed with his services. He had always been an excellent servant, and attached to the family, and I was glad to be able to offer him a suitable position with us at Worth until his master should return. He brought disquieting reports of John's health, saying that he was growing visibly weaker. Though I was sorely tempted to ask him many questions as to his master's habits and way of life, my pride forbade me to do so. But I heard incidentally from my maid that Parnham had told her Sir John was spending money freely in alterations at the Villa de Angelis, and had engaged Italians to attend him, with which his English valet was naturally much dissatisfied.

So the spring passed and the summer was well advanced.

On the last morning of July I found waiting for me on the breakfast-table an envelope addressed in my brother's hand. I opened it hastily. It only contained a few words, which I have before me as I write now. The ink is a little faded and yellow, but the impression it made is yet vivid as on that summer morning.

It began,—

My Dearest Sophy, come to me here at once, if possible, or it may be too late. I want to see you. They say that I am ill, and too weak to travel to England.

Your loving brother,

John.

There was a great change in the style, from the cold and conventional notes that he had hitherto sent at such long intervals; from the stiff "Dear Sophia" and "Sincerely yours" to which, I grieve to say, I had grown accustomed. Even the writing itself was altered. It was more the bold boyish hand he wrote when first he went to Oxford, than the smaller cramped and classic character of his later years. Though it was a little matter enough, God knows, in comparison with his grievous conduct, yet it touched me much that he should use again the once familiar "Dearest Sophy," and sign himself "my loving brother." I felt my heart go out towards him; and so strong is woman's affection for her own kin, that I had already forgotten any resentment and reprobation in my great pity for the poor wanderer, lying sick perhaps unto death and alone in a foreign land.

I took his note at once to Mrs. Temple. She read it twice or thrice, trying to take in the meaning of it. Then she drew me to her and, kissing me, said, "Go to him at once, Sophy. Bring him back to Worth; try to bring him back to the right way."

I ordered my things to be packed, determining to drive to Southampton and take train thence to London; and at the same time Mrs. Temple gave instructions that all should be prepared for her own return to Royston within a few days. I knew she did not dare to see John after her daughter's death.

I took my maid with me, and Parnham to act as courier. At London we hired a carriage for the whole journey, and from Calais posted direct to Naples. We took the short route by Marseilles and Genoa, and travelled for seventeen days without intermission, as my brother's note made me desirous of losing no time on the way. I had never been in Italy before; but my anxiety was such that my mind was unable to appreciate either the beauty of the scenery or the incidents of travel.

I can, in fact, remember nothing of our journey now, except the wearisome and interminable jolting over bad roads and the insufferable heat. It was the middle of August in an exceptionally warm summer, and after passing Genoa the heat became almost tropical. There was no relief even at night, for the warm air hung stagnant and suffocating, and the inside of my travelling coach was often like a furnace.

We were at last approaching the conclusion of our journey, and had left Rome behind us. The day that we set out from Aversa was the hottest that I have ever felt, the sun beating down with an astonishing power even in the early hours, and the road being thick with a white and blinding dust. It was soon after midnight that our carriage began rattling over the great stone blocks with which the streets of Naples are paved. The suburbs that we at first passed through were, I remember, in darkness and perfect quiet; but after traversing the heart of the city and reaching the western side, we suddenly found ourselves in the midst of an enormous and very dense crowd. There were lanterns everywhere, and interminable lanes of booths, whose proprietors were praising their wares with loud shouts; and here acrobats, jugglers, minstrels, black-vested priests, and blue-coated soldiers mingled with a vast crowd whose numbers at once arrested the progress of the carriage.

Though it was so late of a Sunday night, all seemed here awake and busy as at noonday. Oil-lamps with reeking fumes of black smoke flung a glare over the scene, and the discordant cries and chattering conversation united in so deafening a noise as to make me turn faint and giddy, wearied as I already was with long travelling. Though I felt that intense eagerness and expectation which the approaching termination of a tedious journey inspires, and was desirous of pushing forward with all imaginable despatch, yet here our course was sadly delayed. The horses could only proceed at the slowest of foot-paces, and we were constantly brought to a complete stop for some minutes before the post-boy could force a passage through the unwilling crowd. This produced a feeling of irritation, and despair of ever reaching my destination; and the mirth and careless hilarity of the people round us chafed with bitter contrast on my depressed spirits.

I inquired from the post-boy what was the origin of so great a commotion, and understood him to say in reply that it was a religious festival held annually in honour of "Our Lady of the Grotto." I cannot, however, conceive of any truly religious person countenancing such a gathering, which seemed to me rather like the unclean orgies of a heathen deity than an act of faith of Christian people. This disturbance occasioned us so serious a delay, that as we were climbing the steep slope leading up to Posilipo it was already three in the morning and the dawn was at hand.

After mounting steadily for a long time we began to rapidly descend, and just as the sun came up over the sea we arrived at the Villa de Angelis. I sprang from the carriage, and passing through a trellis of vines, reached the house. A man-servant was in waiting, and held the door open for me; but he was an Italian, and did not understand me when I asked in English where Sir John Maltravers was. He had evidently, however, received instructions to take me at once to my brother, and led the way to an inner part of the house. As we proceeded I heard the sound of a rich alto voice singing very sweetly to a *mandoline* some soothing or religious melody. The servant pulled aside a heavy curtain and I found myself in my brother's room. An Italian youth sat on a stool near the door, and it was he who had been singing. At a few words from John, addressed to him in his own language, he set down his *mandoline* and left the room, pulling to the curtain and shutting a door behind it.

The room looked directly on to the sea: the villa was, in fact, built upon rocks at the foot of which the waves lapped. Through two folding windows which opened on to a balcony the early light of the summer morning streamed in with a rosy flush. My brother sat on a low couch or sofa, propped up against a heap of pillows, with a rug of brilliant colours flung across his feet and legs. He held out his arms to me, and I ran to him; but even in so brief an interval I had perceived that he was terribly weak and wasted.

All my memories of his past faults had vanished and were dead in that sad aspect of his worn features, and in the conviction which I felt, even from the first moment, that he had but little time longer to remain with us. I knelt by him on the floor, and with my arms round his neck, embraced him tenderly, not finding any place for words, but only sobbing in great anguish. Neither of us spoke, and my weariness from long travel and the strangeness of the situation caused me to feel that paralysing sensation of doubt as to the reality of the scene, and even of my own existence, which all, I believe, have experienced at times of severe mental tension.

That I, a plain English girl, should be kneeling here beside my brother in the Italian dawn; that I should read, as I believed, on his young face the unmistakable image and superscription of death; and reflect that within so few months he had married, had wrecked his home, that my poor Constance was no more;—these things seemed so unrealisable that for a minute I felt that it must all be a nightmare, that I should immediately wake with the fresh salt air of the Channel blowing through my bedroom window at Worth, and find I had been dreaming. But it was not so; the light of day grew stronger and brighter, and even in my sorrow the panorama of the most beautiful spot on earth, the Bay of Naples, with Vesuvius lying on the far side, as seen then from these windows, stamped itself for ever on my mind. It was unreal as a scene in some brilliant dramatic spectacle, but, alas! no unreality was here. The flames of the candles in their silver sconces waxed paler and paler, the lines and shadows on my brother's face grew darker, and the pallor of his wasted features showed more striking in the bright rays of the morning sun.

CHAPTER 13

I had spent near a week at the Villa de Angelis. John's manner to me was most tender and affectionate; but he showed no wish to refer to the tragedy of his wife's death and the sad events which had preceded it, or to attempt to explain in any way his own conduct in the past. Nor did I ever lead the conversation to these topics; for I felt that even if there were no other reason, his great weakness rendered it inadvisable to introduce such subjects at present, or even to lead him to speak at all more than was actually necessary. I was content to minister to him in quiet, and infinitely happy in his restored affection. He seemed desirous of banishing from his mind all thoughts of the last few months, but spoke much of the years before he had gone to Oxford, and of happy days which we had spent together in our childhood at Worth Maltravers. His weakness was extreme, but he complained of no particular malady except a short cough which troubled him at night.

I had spoken to him of his health, for I could see that his state was such as to inspire anxiety, and begged that he would allow me to see if there was an English doctor at Naples who could visit him. This he would not assent to, saying that he was quite content with the care of an Italian doctor who visited him almost daily, and that he hoped to be able, under my escort, to return within a very short time to England.

"I shall never be much better, dear Sophy," he said one day. "The doctor tells me that I am suffering from some sort of consumption, and that I must not expect to live long. Yet I yearn to see Worth once more, and to feel again the west winds blowing in the evening across from Portland, and smell the thyme on the Dorset downs. In a few days I hope perhaps to be a little stronger, and I then wish to show you a discovery which I have made in Naples. After that you may order them to harness the horses, and carry me back to Worth Maltravers."

I endeavoured to ascertain from Signor Baravelli, the doctor, something as to the actual state of his patient; but my knowledge of Italian was so slight that I could neither make him understand what I would be at, nor comprehend in turn what he replied, so that this attempt was relinquished. From my brother himself I gathered that he had begun to feel his health much impaired as far back as the early spring, but though his strength had since then gradually failed him, he had not been confined to the house until a month past. He spent the day and often the night reclining on his sofa and speaking little. He had apparently lost the taste for the violin which had once absorbed so much of his attention; indeed I think the bodily strength necessary for its performance had probably now failed him.

The Stradivarius instrument lay near his couch in its case; but I only saw the latter open on one occasion, I think, and was deeply thankful that John no longer took the same delight as heretofore in the practice of this art,—not only because the mere sound of his violin was now fraught to me with such bitter memories, but also because I felt sure that its performance had in some way which I could not explain a deleterious effect upon himself. He exhibited that absence of vitality which is so often noticeable in those who have not long to live, and on some days lay in a state of semi-lethargy from which it was difficult to rouse him. But at other times he suffered from a distressing restlessness which forbade him to sit still even for a few minutes, and which was more painful to watch than his lethargic stupor.

The Italian boy, of whom I have already spoken, exhibited an untiring devotion to his master which won my heart. His name was Raffaelle Carotenuto, and he often sang to us in the evening, accompanying himself on the *mandoline*. At nights, too, when John could not sleep, Raffaelle would read for hours till at last his master dozed off. He was well educated, and though I could not understand the subject he read, I often sat by and listened, being charmed with his evident attachment to my brother and with the melodious intonation of a sweet voice.

My brother was nervous apparently in some respects, and would never be left alone even for a few minutes; but in the intervals while Raffaelle was with him I had ample opportunity to examine and appreciate the beauties of the Villa de Angelis. It was built, as I have said, on some rocks jutting into the sea, just before coming to the Capo di Posilipo as you proceed from Naples. The earlier foundations were, I believe, originally Roman, and upon them a modern villa had been constructed in the eighteenth century, and to this again John had made important additions in the past two years.

Looking down upon the sea from the windows of the villa, one could on calm days easily discern the remains of Roman piers and moles lying below the surface of the transparent water; and the tufa-rock on which the house was built was burrowed with those unintelligible excavations of a classic date so common in the neighbourhood. These subterranean rooms and passages, while they aroused my curiosity, seemed at the same time so gloomy and repellent that I never explored them. But on one sunny morning, as I walked at the foot of the rocks by the sea, I ventured into one of the larger of these chambers, and saw that it had at the far end an opening leading apparently to an inner room. I had walking with me an old Italian female servant who took a motherly interest in my proceedings, and who, relying principally upon a very slight knowledge of English, had constituted herself my bodyguard. Encouraged by her presence, I penetrated this inner room and found that it again opened in turn into another, and so on until we had passed through no less than four chambers.

They were all lighted after a fashion through vent-holes which somewhere or other reached the outer air, but the fourth room opened into a fifth which was unlighted. My companion, who had been showing signs of alarm and an evident reluctance to proceed further, now stopped abruptly and begged me to return. It may have been that her fear communicated itself to me also, for on attempting to cross the threshold and explore the darkness of the fifth cell, I was seized by an unreasoning panic and by the feeling of undefined horror experienced in a nightmare. I hesitated for an instant, but my fear became suddenly more intense, and springing back, I followed my companion, who had set out to run back to the outer air. We never paused until we stood panting in the full sunlight by the sea.

As soon as the maid had found her breath, she begged me never to go there again, explaining in broken English that the caves were known in the neighbourhood as the "Cells of Isis," and were reputed to be haunted by demons. This episode, trifling as it may appear, had so great an effect upon me that I never again ventured on to the lower walk which ran at the foot of the rocks by the sea.

In the house above, my brother had built a large hall after the ancient Roman style, and this, with a dining-room and many other chambers, were decorated in the fashion of those discovered at Pompeii. They had been furnished with the utmost luxury, and the beauty of the paintings, furniture, carpets, and hangings was enhanced by statues in bronze and marble. The villa, indeed, and its fittings were of a kind to which I was little used, and at the same time of such beauty that I never ceased to regard all as a creation of an enchanter's wand, or as the drop-scene to some drama which might suddenly be raised and disappear from my sight. The house, in short, together with its furniture, was, I believe, intended to be a reproduction of an ancient Roman villa, and had something about it repellent to my rustic and insular ideas. In the contemplation of its perfection I experienced a curious mental sensation, which I can only compare to the physical oppression produced on some persons by the heavy and cloying perfume of a bouquet of gardenias or other too highly scented exotics.

In my brother's room was a medieval reproduction in mellow alabaster of a classic group of a dolphin encircling a Cupid. It was, I think, the fairest work of art I ever saw, but it jarred upon my sense of propriety that close by it should hang an ivory crucifix. I would rather, I think, have seen all things material and pagan entirely, with every view of the future life shut out, than have found a medley of things sacred and profane, where the emblems of our highest hopes and aspirations were placed in insulting indifference side by side with the embodied forms of sensuality. Here, in this scene of magical beauty, it seemed to me for a moment that the years had rolled back, that Christianity had still to fight with a *living* Paganism, and that the battle was not yet won. It was the same all through the house; and there were many other matters which filled me with regret, mingled with vague and apprehensive surmises which I shall not here repeat.

At one end of the house was a small library, but it contained few works except Latin and Greek classics. I had gone thither one day to look for a book that John had asked for, when in turning out some drawers I found a number of letters written from Worth by my lost Constance to her husband. The shock of being brought suddenly face to face with a handwriting that evoked memories at once so dear and sad was in itself a sharp one; but its bitterness was immeasurably increased by the discovery that not one of these envelopes had ever been opened. While that dear heart, now at rest, was pouring forth her love and sorrow to the ears that should have been above all others ready to receive them, her letters, as they arrived, were flung uncared for, unread, even unopened, into any haphazard receptacle.

The days passed one by one at the Villa de Angelis with but little incident, nor did my brother's health either visibly improve or decline. Though the weather was still more than usually warm, a grateful breeze came morning and evening from the sea and tempered the heat so much as to render it always supportable. John would sometimes in the evening sit propped up with cushions on the trellised balcony looking towards Baia, and watch the fishermen setting their nets. We could hear the melody of their deep-voiced songs carried up on the night air. "It was here, Sophy," my brother said, as we sat one evening looking on a scene like this,—"It was here that the great epicure Pollio built himself a famous house, and called it by two Greek words meaning a 'truce to care,' from which our name of Posilipo is derived. It was his *sans-souci*, and here he cast aside his vexations; but they were lighter than mine. Posilipo has brought no cessation of care to me. I do not think I shall find any truce this side the grave; and beyond, who knows?"

This was the first time John had spoken in this strain, and he seemed stirred to an unusual activity, as though his own words had suddenly reminded him how frail was his state. He called Raffaelle to him and despatched him on an errand to Naples. The next morning he sent for me earlier than usual, and begged that a carriage might be ready by six in the evening, as he desired to drive into the city. I tried at first to dissuade him from his project, urging him to consider his weak state of health. He replied that he felt somewhat stronger, and had something that he particularly wished me to see in Naples. This done, it would be better to return at once to England: he could, he thought, bear the journey if we travelled by very short stages.

CHAPTER 14

Shortly after six o'clock in the evening we left the Villa de Angelis. The day had been as usual cloudlessly serene; but a gentle sea-breeze, of which I have spoken, rose in the afternoon and brought with it a refreshing coolness. We had arranged a sort of couch in the landau with many cushions for my brother, and he mounted into the carriage with more ease than I had expected. I sat beside him, with Raffaelle facing me on the opposite seat. We drove down the hill of Posilipo through the ilex-trees and tamarisk-bushes that then skirted the sea, and so into the town. John spoke little except to remark that the carriage was an easy one. As we were passing through one of the principal streets he bent over to me and said, "You must not be alarmed if I show you to-day a strange sight. Some women might perhaps be frightened at what We are going to see; but my poor sister has known already so much of trouble that a light thing like this will not affect her." In spite of his encomiums upon my supposed courage, I felt alarmed and agitated by his words. There was a vagueness in them which frightened me, and bred that indefinite apprehension which is often infinitely more terrifying than the actual object which inspires it.

To my inquiries he would give no further response than to say that he had whilst at Posilipo made some investigations in Naples leading to a strange discovery, which he was anxious to communicate to me. After traversing a considerable distance, we had penetrated apparently into the heart of the town. The streets grew narrower and more densely thronged; the houses were more dirty and tumbledown, and the appearance of the people themselves suggested that we had reached some of the lower quarters of the city. Here we passed through a further network of small streets of the name of which I took no note, and found ourselves at last in a very dark and narrow lane called the *Via del Giardino*. Although my brother had, so far as I had observed, given no orders to the coachman, the latter seemed to have no difficulty in finding his Way, driving rapidly in the Neapolitan fashion, and proceeding direct as to a place with which he was already familiar.

In the Via del Giardino the houses were of great height, and overhung the street so as nearly to touch one another. It seemed that this quarter had been formerly inhabited, if not by the aristocracy, at least by a class very much superior to that which now lived there; and many of the houses were large and dignified, though long since parcelled out into smaller tenements. It was before such a house that we at last brought up. Here must have been at one time a house or palace of some person of distinction, having a long and fine *façade* adorned with delicate pilasters, and much florid ornamentation of the Renaissance period. The ground-floor was divided into a series of small shops, and its upper storeys were evidently peopled by sordid families of the lowest class

Before one of these little shops, now closed and having its windows carefully blocked with boards, our carriage stopped. Raffaelle alighted, and taking a key from his pocket unlocked the door, and assisted John to leave the carriage. I followed, and directly we had crossed the threshold, the boy locked the door behind us, and I heard the carriage drive away.

We found ourselves in a narrow and dark passage, and as soon as my eyes grew accustomed to the gloom I perceived there was at the end of it a low staircase leading to some upper room, and on the right a door which opened into the closed shop. My brother moved slowly along the passage, and began to ascend the stairs. He leant with one hand on Raffaelle's arm, taking hold of the balusters with the other. But I could see that to mount the stairs cost him considerable effort, and he paused frequently to cough and get his breath again. So we reached a landing at the top, and found ourselves in a small chamber or magazine directly over the shop. It was quite empty except for a few broken chairs, and appeared to be a small loft formed by dividing what had once been a high room into two storeys, of which the shop formed the lower.

A long window, which had no doubt once formed one of several in the walls of this large room, was now divided across its width by the flooring, and with its upper part served to light the loft, while its lower panes opened into the shop. The ceiling was, in consequence of these alterations, comparatively low, but though much mutilated, retained evident traces of having been at one time richly decorated, with the raised mouldings and pendants common in the sixteenth century. At one end of the loft was a species of coved and elaborately carved dado, of which the former use was not obvious; but the large original room had without doubt been divided in length as Well as in height, as the lath-and-plaster walls at either end of the loft had evidently been no part of the ancient structure.

My brother sat down in one of the old chairs, and seemed to be collecting his strength before speaking. My anxiety was momentarily increasing, and it was a great relief when he began, talking in a low voice as one that had much to say and wished to husband his strength.

"I do not know whether you will recollect my having told you of something Mr. Gaskell once said about the music of Graziani's *Areopagita* suite. It had always, he used to say, a curious effect upon his imagination, and the melody of the *Gagliarda* especially called up to his thoughts in some strange way a picture of a certain hall where people were dancing. He even went so far as to describe the general appearance of the room itself, and of the persons who were dancing there."

"Yes," I answered, "I remember your telling me of this;" and indeed my memory had in times past so often rehearsed Mr. Gaskell's description that, although I had not recently thought of it, its chief features immediately returned to my mind.

"He described it," my brother continued, "as a long hall with an arcade of arches running down one side, of the fantastic Gothic of the Renaissance. At the end was a gallery or balcony for the musicians, which on its front carried a coat of arms."

I remembered this perfectly and told John so, adding that the shield bore a cherub's head fanning three lilies on a golden field.

"It is strange," John went on, "that the description of a scene which our friend thought a mere effort of his own imagination has impressed itself so deeply on both our minds. But the picture which he drew was more than a fancy, for we are at this minute in the very hall of his dream."

I could not gather what my brother meant, and thought his reason was failing him; but he continued, "This miserable floor on which we stand has of course been afterwards built in; but you see above you the old ceiling, and here at the end was the musicians' gallery with the shield upon its front."

He pointed to the carved and whitewashed dado which had hitherto so puzzled me. I stepped up to it, and although the lath-and-plaster partition wall was now built around it, it was clear that its curved outline might very easily, as John said, have formed part of the front of a coved gallery. I looked closet at the relief-work which had adorned it. Though the edges were all rubbed off, and the mouldings in some cases entirely removed, I could trace without difficulty a shield in the midst; and a more narrow inspection revealed underneath the whitewash, which had partly peeled away, enough remnants of colour to show that it had certainly been once painted gold and borne a cherub's head with three lilies.

"That is the shield of the old Neapolitan house of Doma-Cavalli," my brother continued; "they bore a cherub's head fanning three lilies on a shield or. It was in the balcony behind this shield, long since blocked up as you see, that the musicians sat on that ball night of which Gaskell dreamt. From it they looked down on the hall below where dancing was going forward, and I will now take you downstairs that you may see if the description tallies."

So saying, he raised himself, and descending the stairs with much less difficulty than he had shown in mounting them, flung open the door which I had seen in the passage and ushered us into the shop on the ground-floor. The evening light had now faded so much that we could scarcely see even in the passage, and the shop having its windows barricaded with shutters, was in complete darkness. Raffaelle, however, struck a match and lit three half-burnt candles in a tarnished sconce upon the wall.

The shop had evidently been lately in the occupation of a wine-seller, and there were still several empty wooden wine-butts, and some broken flasks on shelves. In one corner I noticed that the earth which formed the floor had been turned up with spades. There was a small heap of mould, and a large flat stone was thus exposed below the surface. This stone had an iron ring attached to it, and seemed to cover the aperture of a well, or perhaps a vault. At the back of the shop, and furthest from the street, were two lofty arches separated by a column in the middle, from which the outside casing had been stripped.

To these arches John pointed and said, "That is a part of the arcade which once ran down the whole length of the hall. Only these two arches are now left, and the fine marbles which doubtless coated the outside of this dividing pillar have been stripped off. On a summer's night about one hundred years ago dancing was going on in this hall. There were a dozen couples dancing a wild step such as is never seen now. The tune that the musicians were playing in the gallery above was taken from the *Areopagita* suite of Graziani. Gaskell has often told me that when he played it the music brought with it to his mind a sense of some impending catastrophe, which culminated at the end of the first movement of the *Gagliarda*. It was just at that moment, Sophy, that an Englishman who was dancing here was stabbed in the back and foully murdered."

I had scarcely heard all that John had said, and had certainly not been able to take in its import; but without waiting to hear if I should say anything, he moved across to the uncovered stone with the ring in it. Exerting a strength which I should have believed entirely impossible in his weak condition, he applied to the stone a lever which lay ready at hand. Raffaelle at the same time seized the ring, and so they were able between them to move the covering to one side sufficiently to allow access to a small staircase which thus appeared to view. The stair was a winding one, and once led no doubt to some vaults below the ground-floor. Raffaelle descended first, taking in his hand the sconce of three candles, which he held above his head so as to fling a light down the steps. John went next, and then I followed, trying to support my brother if possible with my hand.

The stairs were very dry, and on the walls there was none of the damp or mould which fancy usually associates with a subterraneous vault. I do not know what it was I expected to see, but I had an uneasy feeling that I was on the brink of some evil and distressing discovery. After we had descended about twenty steps we could see the entry to some vault or underground room, and it was just at the foot of the stairs that I saw something lying, as the light from the candles fell on it from above. At first I thought it was a heap of dust or refuse, but on looking closer it seemed rather a bundle of rags. As my eyes penetrated the gloom, I saw there was about it some tattered cloth of a faded green tint, and almost at the same minute I seemed to trace under the clothes the lines or dimensions of a human figure. For a moment I imagined it was some poor man lying face downwards and bent up against the wall.

The idea of a man or of a dead body being there shocked me violently, and I cried to my brother, "Tell me, what is it?" At that instant the light from. Raffaelle's candles fell in a somewhat different direction. It lighted up the white bowl of a human skull, and I saw that what I had taken for a man's form was instead that of a clothed skeleton. I turned faint and sick for an instant, and should have fallen had it not been for John, who put his arm about me and sustained me with an unexpected strength.

"God help us!" I exclaimed, "let us go. I cannot bear this; there are foul vapours here; let us get back to the outer air."

He took me by the arm, and pointing at the huddled heap, said, "Do you know whose bones those are? That is Adrian Temple. After it was all over, they flung his body down the steps, dressed in the clothes he wore."

At that name, uttered in so ill-omened a place, I felt a fresh access of terror. It seemed as though the soul of that wicked man must be still hovering over his unburied remains, and boding evil to us all. A chill crept over me, the light, the walls, my brother, and Raffaelle all swam round, and I sank swooning on the stairs.

When I returned fully to my senses we were in the landau again making our way back to the Villa de Angelis.

CHAPTER 14

The next morning my health and strength were entirely restored to me, but my brother, on the contrary, seemed weak and exhausted from his efforts of the previous night. Our return journey to the Villa de Angelis had passed in complete silence. I had been too much perturbed to question him on the many points relating to the strange events as to which I was still completely in the dark, and he on his side had shown no desire to afford me any further information. When I saw him the next morning he exhibited signs of great weakness, and in response to an effort on my part to obtain some explanation of the discovery of Adrian Temple's body, avoided an immediate reply, promising to tell me all he knew after our return to Worth Maltravers.

I pondered over the last terrifying episode very frequently in my own mind, and as I thought more deeply of it all, it seemed to me that the outlines of some evil history were piece by piece developing themselves, that I had almost within my grasp the clue that would make all plain, and that had eluded me so long. In that dim story Adrian Temple, the music of the *Gagliarda*, my brother's fatal passion for the violin, all seemed to have some mysterious connection, and to have conspired in working John's mental and physical ruin. Even the Stradivarius violin bore a part in the tragedy, becoming, as it were, an actively malignant spirit, though I could not explain how, and was yet entirely unaware of the manner in which it had come into my brother's possession.

I found that John was still resolved on an immediate return to England. His weakness, it is true, led me to entertain doubts as to how he would support so long a journey; but at the same time I did not feel justified in using any strong efforts to dissuade him from his purpose. I reflected that the more wholesome air and associations of England would certainly re-invigorate both body and mind, and that any extra strain brought about by the journey would soon be repaired by the comforts and watchful care with which we could surround him at Worth Maltravers.

So the first week in October saw us once more with our faces set towards England. A very comfortable swinging-bed or hammock had been arranged for John in the travelling carriage, and we determined to avoid fatigue as much as possible by dividing our journey into very short stages. My brother seemed to have no intention of giving up the Villa de Angelis. It was left complete with its luxurious furniture, and with all his servants, under the care of an Italian *maggior-duomo*. I felt that as John's state of health forbade his entertaining any hope of an immediate return thither, it would have been much better to close entirely his Italian house. But his great weakness made it impossible for him to undertake the effort such a course would involve, and even if my own ignorance of the Italian tongue had not stood in the way, I was far too eager to get my invalid back to Worth to feel inclined to import any further delay, while I should myself adjust matters which were after all comparatively trifling.

As Parnham was now ready to discharge his usual duties of valet, and as my brother seemed quite content that he should do so, Raffaelle was of course to be left behind. The boy had quite won my heart by his sweet manners, combined with his evident affection to his master, and in making him understand that he was now to leave us, I offered him a present of a few pounds as a token of my esteem. He refused, however, to touch this money, and shed tears when he learnt that he was to be left in Italy, and begged with many protestations of devotion that he might be allowed to accompany us to England. My heart was not proof against his entreaties, supported by so many signs of attachment, and it was agreed, therefore, that he should at least attend us as far as Worth Maltravers. John showed no surprise at the boy being with us; indeed I never thought it necessary to explain that I had originally purposed to leave him behind.

Our journey, though necessarily prolonged by the shortness of its stages, was safely accomplished. John bore it as well as I could have hoped, and though his body showed no signs of increased vigour, his mind, I think, improved in tone, at any rate for a time. From the evening on which he had shown me the terrible discovery in the Via del Giardino he seemed to have laid aside something of his care and depression. He now exhibited little trace of the moroseness and selfishness which had of late so marred his character; and though he naturally felt severely at times the fatigue of travel, yet we had no longer to dread any relapse into that state of lethargy or stupor which had so often baffled every effort to counteract it at Posilipo.

Some feeling of superstitious aversion had prompted me to give orders that the Stradivarius violin should be left behind at Posilipo. But before parting my brother asked for it, and insisted that it should be brought with him, though I had never heard him play a note on it for many weeks. He took an interest in all the petty episodes of travel, and certainly appeared to derive more entertainment from the journey than was to have been anticipated in his feeble state of health.

To the incidents of the evening spent in the Via del Giardino he made no allusion of any kind, nor did I for my part wish to renew memories of so unpleasant a nature. His only reference occurred one

Sunday evening as we were passing a small graveyard near Genoa. The scene apparently turned his thoughts to that subject, and he told me that he had taken measures before leaving Naples to ensure that the remains of Adrian Temple should be decently interred in the cemetery of Santa Bibiana. His words set me thinking again, and unsatisfied curiosity prompted me strongly to inquire of him how he had convinced himself that the skeleton at the foot of the stairs was indeed that of Adrian Temple. But I restrained myself, partly from a reliance on his promise that he would one day explain the whole story to me, and partly being very reluctant to mar the enjoyment of the peaceful scenes through which we were passing, by the introduction of any subjects so jarring and painful as those to which I have alluded.

We reached London at last, and here we stopped a few days to make some necessary arrangements before going down to Worth Maltravers. I had urged upon John during the journey that immediately on his arrival in London he should obtain the best English medical advice as to his own health. Though he at first demurred, saying that nothing more was to be done, and that he was perfectly satisfied with the medicine given him by Dr. Baravelli, which he continued to take, yet by constant entreaty I prevailed upon him to accede to so reasonable a request. Dr. Frobisher, considered at that time the first living authority on diseases of the brain and nerves, saw him on the morning after our arrival. He was good enough to speak with me at some length after seeing my brother, and to give me many hints and recipes whereby I might be better enabled to nurse the invalid.

Sir John's condition, he said, was such as to excite serious anxiety. There was, indeed, no brain mischief of any kind to be discovered, but his lungs were in a state of advanced disease, and there were signs of grave heart affection. Yet he did not bid me to despair, but said that with careful nursing life might certainly be prolonged, and even some measure of health in time restored. He asked me more than once if I knew of any trouble or worry that preyed upon Sir John's mind. Were there financial difficulties; had he been subjected to any mental shock; had he received any severe fright? To all this I could only reply in the negative.

At the same time I told Dr. Frobisher as much of John's history as I considered pertinent to the question. He shook his head gravely, and recommended that Sir John should remain for the present in London, under his own constant supervision. To this course my brother would by no means consent. He was eager to proceed at once to his own house, saying that if necessary we could return again to London for Christmas. It was therefore agreed that we should go down to Worth Maltravers at the end of the week.

Parnham had already left us for Worth in order that he might have everything ready against his master's return, and when we arrived we found all in perfect order for our reception. A small morning-room next to the library, with a pleasant south aspect and opening on to the terrace, had been prepared for my brother's use, so that he might avoid the fatigue of mounting stairs, which Dr. Frobisher considered very prejudicial in his present condition. We had also purchased in London a chair fitted with wheels, which enabled him to be moved, or, if he were feeling equal to the exertion, to move himself, without difficulty, from room to room.

His health, I think, improved; very gradually, it is true, but still sufficiently to inspire me with hope that he might yet be spared to us. Of the state of his mind or thoughts I knew little, but I could see that he was at times a prey to nervous anxiety. This showed itself in the harassed look which his pale face often wore, and in his marked dislike to being left alone. He derived, I think, a certain pleasure from the quietude and monotony of his life at Worth, and perhaps also from the consciousness that he had about him loving and devoted hearts. I say hearts, for every servant at Worth was attached to him, remembering the great consideration and courtesy of his earlier years, and grieving to see his youthful and once vigorous frame reduced to so sad a strait. Books he never read himself, and even the charm of Raffaelle's reading seemed to have lost its power; though he never tired of hearing the boy sing, and liked to have him sit by his chair even when his eyes were shut and he was apparently asleep. His general health seemed to me to change but little either for better or worse.

Dr. Frobisher had led me to expect some such a sequel. I had not concealed from him that I had at times entertained suspicions as to my brother's sanity; but he had assured me that they were totally unfounded, that Sir John's brain was as clear as his own. At the same time he confessed that he could not account for the exhausted vitality of his patient,—a condition which he would under ordinary circumstances have attributed to excessive study or severe trouble. He had urged upon me the pressing necessity for complete rest, and for much sleep. My brother never even incidentally referred to his wife, his child, or to Mrs. Temple, who constantly wrote to me from Royston, sending kind messages to John, and asking how he did. These messages I never dared to give him, fearing to agitate him, or retard his recovery by diverting his thoughts into channels which must necessarily be of a painful character. That he should never even mention her name, or that of Lady Maltravers, led me to wonder sometimes if one of those curious freaks of memory which occasionally accompany a severe illness had not entirely blotted out from his mind the recollection of his marriage and of his wife's death. He was unable to consider any affairs of business, and the management of the estate remained as it had done for the last two years in the hands of our excellent agent, Mr. Baker.

But one evening in the early part of December he sent Raffaelle about nine o'clock, saying he wished to speak to me. I went to his room, and without any warning he began at once, "You never show me my boy now, Sophy; he must be grown a big child, and I should like to see him." Much startled by so unexpected a remark, I replied that the child was at Royston under the care of Mrs. Temple, but that I knew that if it pleased him to see Edward she would be glad to bring him down to Worth. He seemed gratified with this idea, and begged me to ask her to do so, desiring that his respects should be at the same time conveyed to her. I almost ventured at that moment to recall his lost wife to his thoughts, by saying that his child resembled her strongly; for your likeness at that time, and even now, my dear Edward, to your poor mother was very marked.

But my courage failed me, and his talk soon reverted to an earlier period, comparing the mildness of the month to that of the first winter which he spent at Eton. His thoughts, however, must, I fancy, have returned for a moment to the days when he first met your mother, for he suddenly asked, "Where is Gaskell? Why does he never come to see me?" This brought quite a new idea to my mind. I fancied it might do my brother much good to have by him so sensible and true a friend as I knew Mr. Gaskell to be. The latter's address had fortunately not slipped from my memory, and I put all scruples aside and wrote by the next mail to him, setting forth my brother's sad condition, saying that I had heard John mention his name, and begging him on my own account to be so good as to help us if possible and come to us in this hour of trial. Though he was so far off as Westmorland, Mr. Gaskell's generosity brought him at once to our aid, and within a week he was installed at Worth Maltravers, sleeping, in the library, where we had arranged a bed at his own desire, so that he might be near his sick friend.

His presence was of the utmost assistance to us all. He treated John at once with the tenderness of a woman and the firmness of a clever and strong man. They sat constantly together in the mornings, and Mr. Gaskell told me John had not shown with him the same reluctance to talk freely of his married life as he had discovered with me. The tenor of his communications I cannot guess, nor did I ever ask; but I knew that Mr. Gaskell was much affected by them.

John even amused himself now at times by having Mr. Baker into his rooms of a morning, that the management of the estate might be discussed with his friend; and he also expressed his wish to see the family solicitor, as he desired to draw his will. Thinking that any diversion of this nature could not but be beneficial to him, we sent to Dorchester for our solicitor, Mr. Jeffreys, who together with his clerk spent three nights at Worth, and drew up a testament for my brother.

So time went on, and the year was drawing to a close.

It was Christmas Eve, and I had gone to bed shortly after twelve o'clock, having an hour earlier bid good night to John and Mr. Gaskell. The long habit of watching with, or being in charge of an invalid at night, had made my ears extraordinarily quick to apprehend even the slightest murmur. It must have been, I think, near three in the morning when I found myself awake and conscious of some unusual sound. It was low and far off, but I knew instantly what it was, and felt a choking sensation of fear and horror, as if an icy hand had gripped my throat, on recognising the air of the *Gagliarda*. It was being played on the violin, and a long way off, but I knew that tune too well to permit of my having any doubt on the subject.

Any trouble or fear becomes, as you will some day learn, my dear nephew, immensely intensified and exaggerated at night. It is so, I suppose, because our nerves are in an excited condition, and our brain not sufficiently awake to give a due account of our foolish imaginations. I have myself many times lain awake wrestling in thought with difficulties which in the hours of darkness seemed insurmountable, but with the dawn resolved themselves into merely trivial inconveniences. So on this night, as I sat up in bed looking into the dark, with the sound of that melody in my ears, it seemed as if something too terrible for words had happened; as though the evil spirit, which we had hoped was exorcised, had returned with others sevenfold more wicked than himself, and taken up his abode again with my lost brother.

The memory of another night rushed to my mind when Constance had called me from my bed at Royston, and we had stolen together down the moonlit passages with the lilt of that wicked music vibrating on the still summer air. Poor Constance! She was in her grave now; yet *her* troubles at least were over, but here, as by some bitter irony, instead of carol or sweet symphony, it was the *Gagliarda* that woke me from my sleep on Christmas morning.

I flung my dressing-gown about me, and hurried through the corridor and down the stairs which led to the lower storey and my brother's room. As I opened my bedroom door the violin ceased suddenly in the middle of a bar. Its last sound was not a musical note, but rather a horrible scream, such as I pray I may never hear again. It was a sound such as a wounded beast might utter. There is a picture I have seen of Blake's, showing the soul of a strong wicked man leaving his body at death. The spirit is flying out through the window with awful staring eyes, aghast at the desolation into which it is going. If in the agony of dissolution such a lost soul could utter a cry, it would, I think, sound like the wail which I heard from the violin that night.

Instantly all was in absolute stillness. The passages were silent and ghostly in the faint light of my candle; but as I reached the bottom of the stairs I heard the sound of other footsteps, and Mr. Gaskell met me. He was fully dressed, and had evidently not been to bed. He took me kindly by the hand and said, "I feared you might be alarmed by the sound of music. John has been walking in his sleep; he had taken out his violin and was playing on it in a trance. Just as I reached him something in it gave way, and the discord caused by the slackened strings roused him at once. He is awake now and has returned to bed. Control your alarm for his sake and your own. It is better that he should not know you have been awakened."

He pressed my hand and spoke a few more reassuring words, and I went back to my room still much agitated, and yet feeling half ashamed for having shown so much anxiety with so little reason.

That Christmas morning was one of the most beautiful that I ever remember. It seemed as though summer was so loath to leave our sunny Dorset coast that she came back on this day to bid us *adieu* before her final departure. I had risen early and had partaken of the Sacrament at our little church. Dr. Butler had recently introduced this early service, and though any alteration of time-honoured customs in such matters might not otherwise have met with my approval, I was glad to avail myself of the privilege on this occasion, as I wished in any case to spend the later morning with my brother.

The singular beauty of the early hours, and the tranquillising effect of the solemn service brought back serenity to my mind, and effectually banished from it all memories of the preceding night. Mr. Gaskell met me in the hall on my return, and after greeting me kindly with the established compliments of the day, inquired after my health, and hoped that the disturbance of my slumber on the previous night had not affected me injuriously. He had good news for me: John seemed decidedly better, was already dressed, and desired, as it was Christmas morning, that we would take our breakfast with him in his room.

To this, as you may imagine, I readily assented. Our breakfast party passed off with much content, and even with some quiet humour, John sitting in his easy-chair at the head of the table and wishing us the compliments of the season. I found laid in my place a letter from Mrs. Temple greeting us all (for she knew Mr. Gaskell was at Worth), and saying that she hoped to bring little Edward to us at the New Year. My brother seemed much pleased at the prospect of seeing his son, and though perhaps it was only imagination, I fancied he was particularly gratified that Mrs. Temple herself was to pay us a visit. She had not been to Worth since the death of Lady Maltravers.

Before we had finished breakfast the sun beat on the panes with an unusual strength and brightness. His rays cheered us all, and it was so warm that John first opened the windows, and then wheeled his chair on to the walk outside. Mr. Gaskell brought him a hat and mufflers, and we sat with him on the terrace basking in the sun. The sea was still and glassy as a mirror, and the Channel lay stretched before us like a floor of moving gold. A rose or two still hung against the house, and the sun's rays reflected from the red sandstone gave us a December morning more mild and genial than many June days that I have known in the north. We sat for some minutes without speaking, immersed in our own reflections and in the exquisite beauty of the scene.

The stillness was broken by the bells of the parish church ringing for the morning service. There were two of them, and their sound, familiar to us from childhood, seemed like the voices of old friends. John looked at me and said with a sigh, "I should like to go to church. It is long since I was there. You and I have always been on Christmas mornings, Sophy, and Constance would have wished it had she been with us."

His words, so unexpected and tender, filled my eyes with tears; not tears of grief, but of deep thankfulness to see my loved one turning once more to the old ways. It was the first time I had heard him speak of Constance, and that sweet name, with the infinite pathos of her death, and of the spectacle of my brother's weakness, so overcame me that I could not speak. I only pressed his hand and nodded. Mr. Gaskell, who had turned away for a minute, said he thought John would take no harm in attending the morning service provided the church were warm. On this point I could reassure him, having found it properly heated even in the early morning.

Mr. Gaskell was to push John's chair, and I ran off to put on my cloak, with my heart full of profound thankfulness for the signs of returning grace so mercifully vouchsafed to our dear sufferer on this happy day. I was ready dressed and had just entered the library when Mr. Gaskell stepped hurriedly through the window from the terrace. "John has fainted!" he said. "Run for some smelling salts and call Parnham!"

There was a scene of hurried alarm, giving place ere long to terrified despair. Parnham mounted a horse and set off at a wild gallop to Swanage to fetch Dr. Bruton; but an hour before he returned we knew the worst. My brother was beyond the aid of the physician: his wrecked life had reached a sudden term!

★★★★★★

I have now, dear Edward, completed the brief narrative of some of the facts attending the latter years of your father's life. The motive which has induced me to commit them to writing has been a double one. I am anxious to give effect as far as may be to the desire expressed most strongly to Mr. Gaskell by your father, that you should be put in possession of these facts on your coming of age. And for my own part I think it better that you should thus hear the plain truth from me, lest you should be at the mercy of haphazard reports, which might at any time reach you from ignorant or interested sources. Some of the circumstances were so remarkable that it is scarcely possible to suppose that they were not known, and most probably frequently discussed, in so large an establishment as that of Worth Maltravers. I even have reason to believe that exaggerated and absurd stories were current at the time of Sir John's death, and I should be grieved to think that such foolish tales might by any chance reach your ear without your having any sure means of discovering where the truth lay.

God knows how grievous it has been to me to set down on paper some of the facts that I have here narrated. You as a dutiful son will reverence the name even of a father whom you never knew; but you must remember that his sister did more; she loved him with a single-hearted devotion, and it still grieves her to the quick to write anything which may seem to detract from his memory. Only, above all things, let us speak the truth. Much of what I have told you needs, I feel, further explanation, but this I cannot give, for I do not understand the circumstances. Mr. Gaskell, your guardian, will, I believe, add to this account a few notes of his own, which may tend to elucidate some points, as he is in possession of certain facts of which I am still ignorant.

Mr. Gaskell's Note

I have read what Miss Maltravers has written, and have but little to add to it. I can give no explanation that will tally with all the facts or meet all the difficulties involved in her narrative. The most obvious solution of some points would be, of course, to suppose that Sir John Maltravers was insane. But to anyone who knew him as intimately as I did, such an hypothesis is untenable; nor, if admitted, would it explain some of the strangest incidents. Moreover, it was strongly negatived by Dr. Frobisher, from whose verdict in such matters there was at the time no appeal, by Dr. Dobie, and by Dr. Bruton, who had known Sir John from his infancy. It is possible that towards the close of his life he suffered occasionally from hallucination, though I could not positively affirm even so much; but this was only when his health had been completely undermined by causes which are very difficult to analyse.

When I first knew him at Oxford he was a strong man physically as well as mentally; open-hearted, and of a merry and genial temperament. At the same time he was, like most cultured persons—and especially musicians,—highly strung and excitable. But at a certain point in his career his very nature seemed to change; he became reserved, secretive, and saturnine. On this moral metamorphosis followed an equally startling physical change. His robust health began to fail him, and although there was no definite malady which doctors could combat, he went gradually from bad to worse until the end came.

The commencement of this extraordinary change coincided, I believe, almost exactly with his discovery of the Stradivarius violin; and whether this was, after all, a mere coincidence or something more it is not easy to say. Until a very short time before his death neither Miss Maltravers nor I had any idea how that instrument had come into his possession, or I think something might perhaps have been done to save him.

Though towards the end of his life he spoke freely to his sister of the finding of the violin, he only told her half the story, for he concealed from her entirely that there was anything else in the hidden cupboard at Oxford. But as a matter of fact, he had found there also two manuscript books containing an elaborate diary of some years of a man's life. That man was Adrian Temple, and I believe that in the perusal of this diary must be sought the origin of John Maltravers's ruin. The manuscript was beautifully written in a clear but cramped eighteenth century hand, and gave the idea of a man writing with deliberation, and wishing to transcribe his impressions with accuracy for further reference. The style was excellent, and the minute details given were often of high antiquarian interest; but the record throughout was marred by gross licence. Adrian Temple's life had undoubtedly so definite an influence on Sir John's that a brief outline of it, as gathered from his diaries, is necessary for the understanding of what followed.

Temple went up to Oxford in 1737. He was seventeen years old, without parents, brothers, or sisters; and he possessed the Royston estates in Derbyshire, which were then, as now, a most valuable property. With the year 1738 his diaries begin, and though then little more than a boy, he had tasted every illicit pleasure that Oxford had to offer. His temptations were no doubt great; for besides being wealthy he was handsome, and had probably never known any proper control, as both his parents had died when he was still very young. But in spite of other failings, he was a brilliant scholar, and on taking his degree, was made at once a fellow of St. John's.

He took up his abode in that College in a fine set of rooms looking on to the gardens, and from this period seems to have used Royston but little, living always either at Oxford or on the Continent. He formed at this time the acquaintance of one Jocelyn, whom he engaged as companion and amanuensis. Jocelyn was a man of talent, but of irregular life, and was no doubt an accomplice in many of Temple's excesses. In 1743 they both undertook the so-called "grand tour," and though it was not his first visit, it was then probably that Temple first felt the fascination of pagan Italy,—a fascination which increased with every year of his after-life.

On his return from foreign travel he found himself among the stirring events of 1745. He was an ardent supporter of the Pretender, and made no attempt to conceal his views. Jacobite tendencies were indeed generally prevalent in the College at the time, and had this been the sum of his offending, it is probable that little notice would have been taken by the College authorities. But his notoriously wild life told against the young man, and certain dark suspicions were not easily passed over. After the *fiasco* of the Rebellion Dr. Holmes, then President of the College, seems to have made a scapegoat of Temple. He was deprived of his fellowship, and though not formally expelled, such pressure was put upon him as resulted in his leaving St. John's and removing to Magdalen Hall. There his great wealth evidently secured him consideration, and he was given the best rooms in the Hall, that very set looking on to New College Lane which Sir John Maltravers afterwards occupied.

In the first half of the eighteenth century the romance of the middle ages, though dying, was not dead, and the occult sciences still found followers among the Oxford towers. From his early years Temple's mind seems to have been set strongly towards mysticism of all kinds, and he and Jocelyn were versed in the jargon of the alchemist and astrologer, and practised according to the ancient rules. It was his reputation as a necromancer, and the stories current of illicit rites performed in the garden-rooms at St. John's, that contributed largely to his being dismissed from that College. He had also become acquainted with Francis Dashwood, the notorious Lord le Despencer, and many a winter's night saw him riding through the misty Thames meadows to the door of the sham Franciscan abbey. In his diaries were more notices than one of the "Franciscans" and the nameless orgies of Medmenham.

He was devoted to music. It was a rare enough accomplishment then, and a rarer thing still to find a wealthy landowner performing on the violin. Yet so he did, though he kept his passion very much to himself, as fiddling was thought lightly of in those days. His musical skill was altogether exceptional, and he was the first possessor of the Stradivarius violin which afterwards fell so unfortunately into Sir John's hands. This violin Temple bought in the autumn of 1738, on the occasion of a first visit to Italy. In that year died the nonagenarian Antonius Stradivarius, the greatest violin-maker the world has ever seen. After Stradivarius's death the stock of fiddles in his shop was sold by auction. Temple happened to be travelling in Cremona at the time with a tutor, and at the auction he bought that very instrument which we afterwards had cause to know so well. A note in his diary gave its cost at four *louis*, and said that a curious history attached to it.

Though it was of his golden period, and probably the finest instrument he ever made, Stradivarius would never sell it, and it had hung for more than thirty years in his shop. It was said that from some whim as he lay dying he had given orders that it should be burnt; but if that were so, the instructions were neglected, and after his death it came under the hammer. Adrian Temple from the first recognised the great value of the instrument. His notes show that he only used it on certain special occasions, and it was no doubt for its better protection that he devised the; hidden cupboard where Sir John eventually found it.

The later years of Temple's life were spent for the most part in Italy. On the Scoglio di Venere, near Naples, he built the Villa de Angelis, and there henceforth passed all except the hottest months of the year. Shortly after the completion of the villa Jocelyn left him suddenly, and became a Carthusian monk. A caustic note in his diary hinted that even this foul parasite was shocked into the austerest form of religion by something he had seen going forward.

At Naples Temple's dark life became still darker. He dallied, it is true, with Neo-Platonism, and boasts that he, like Plotinus, had twice passed the circle of the *nous* and enjoyed the fruition of the deity; but the ideals of even that easy doctrine grew in his evil life still more miserably debased. More than once in the manuscript he made mention by name of the *Gagliarda* of Graziani as having been played at pagan mysteries which these enthusiasts revived at Naples, and the air had evidently impressed itself deeply on his memory. The last entry in his diary is made on the 16th of December, 1752. He was then in Oxford for a few days, but shortly afterwards returned to Naples. The accident of his having just completed a second volume, induced him, no doubt, to leave it behind him in the secret cupboard. It is probable that he commenced a third, but if so it was never found.

In reading the manuscript I was struck with the author's clear and easy style, and found the interest of the narrative increase rather than diminish. At the same time its study was inexpressibly painful to me. Nothing could have supported me in my determination to thoroughly master it but the conviction that if I was to be of any real assistance to my poor friend Maltravers, I must know as far as possible every circumstance connected with his malady. As it was, I felt myself breathing an atmosphere of moral contagion during the perusal of the manuscript, and certain passages have since returned at times to haunt me in spite of all efforts to dislodge them from my memory. When I came to Worth at Miss Maltravers's urgent invitation, I found my friend Sir John terribly altered. It was not only that he was ill and physically weak, but he had entirely lost the manner of youth, which, though indefinable, is yet so appreciable, and draws so sharp a distinction between the first period of life and middle age.

But the most striking feature of his illness was the extraordinary pallor of his complexion, which made his face resemble a subtle counterfeit of white wax rather than that of a living man. He welcomed me undemonstratively, but with evident sincerity; and there was an entire absence of the constraint which often accompanies the meeting again of friends whose cordial relations have suffered interruption. From the time of my arrival at Worth until his death we were constantly together; indeed I was much struck by the almost childish dislike which he showed to be left alone even for a few moments. As night approached this feeling became intensified. Parnham slept always in his master's room; but if anything called the servant away even for a minute, he would send for Carotenuto or myself to be with him until his return. His nerves were weak; he started violently at any unexpected noise, and above all, he dreaded being in the dark. When night fell he had additional lamps brought into his room, and even when he composed himself to sleep, insisted on a strong light being kept by his bedside.

I had often read in books of people wearing a "hunted" expression, and had laughed at the phrase as conventional and unmeaning. But when I came to Worth I knew its truth; for if any face ever wore a hunted—I had almost written a haunted—look, it was the white face of Sir John Maltravers. His air seemed that of a man who was constantly expecting the arrival of some evil tidings, and at times reminded me painfully of the guilty expectation of a felon who knows that a warrant is issued for his arrest.

During my visit he spoke to me frequently about his past life, and instead of showing any reluctance to discuss the subject, seemed glad of the opportunity of disburdening his mind. I gathered from him that the reading of Adrian Temple's memoirs had made a deep impression on his mind, which was no doubt intensified by the vision which he thought he saw in his rooms at Oxford, and by the discovery of the portrait at Royston. Of those singular phenomena I have no explanation to offer.

The romantic element in his disposition rendered him peculiarly susceptible to the fascination of that mysticism which breathed through Temple's narrative. He told me that almost from the first time he read it he was filled with a longing to visit the places and to revive the strange life of which it spoke. This inclination he kept at first in check, but by degrees it gathered strength enough to master him.

There is no doubt in my mind that the music of the *Gagliarda* of Graziani helped materially in this process of mental degradation. It is curious that Michael Prætorius in the *Syntagma musicum* should speak of the Galliard generally as an "invention of the devil, full of shameful and licentious gestures and immodest movements," and the singular melody of the *Gagliarda* in the *Areopagita* suite certainly exercised from the first a strange influence over me. I shall not do more than touch on the question here, because I see Miss Maltravers has spoken of it at length, and will only say, that though since the day of Sir John's death I have never heard a note of it, the air is still fresh in my mind, and has at times presented itself to me unexpectedly, and always with an unwholesome effect. This I have found happen generally in times of physical depression, and the same air no doubt exerted a similar influence on Sir John, which his impressionable nature rendered from the first more deleterious to him.

I say this advisedly, because I am sure that if some music is good for man and elevates him, other melodies are equally bad and enervating. An experience far wider than any we yet possess is necessary to enable us to say how far this influence is capable of extension. How far, that is, the mind may be directed on the one hand to ascetic abnegation by the systematic use of certain music, or on the other to illicit and dangerous pleasures by melodies of an opposite tendency. But this much is, I think, certain, that after a comparatively advanced standard of culture has once been attained, music is the readiest if not the only key which admits to the yet narrower circle of the highest imaginative thought.

On the occasion for travel afforded him by his honeymoon, an impulse which he could not at the time explain, but which after-events have convinced me was the haunting suggestion of the *Gagliarda*, drove him to visit the scenes mentioned so often in Temple's diary. He had always been an excellent scholar, and a classic of more than ordinary ability. Rome and Southern Italy filled him with a strange delight. His education enabled him to appreciate to the full what he saw; he peopled the stage with the figures of the original actors, and tried to assimilate his thought to theirs. He began reading classical literature widely, no longer from the scholarly but the literary standpoint. In Rome he spent much time in the librarians' shops, and there met with copies of the numerous authors of the later empire and of those Alexandrine philosophers which are rarely seen in England. In these he found a new delight and fresh food for his mysticism.

Such study, if carried to any extent, is probably dangerous to the English character, and certainly was to a man of Maltravers's romantic sympathies. This reading produced in time so real an effect upon his mind that if he did not definitely abandon Christianity, as I fear he did, he at least adulterated it with other doctrines till it became to him Neo-Platonism. That most seductive of philosophies, which has enthralled so many minds from Proclus and Julian to Augustine and the Renaissancists, found an easy convert in John Maltravers. Its passionate longing for the vague and undefined good, its tolerance of æsthetic impressions, the pleasant superstitions of its dynamic pantheism, all touched responsive chords in his nature. His mind, he told me, became filled with a measureless yearning for the old culture of pagan philosophy, and as the past became clearer and more real, so the present grew dimmer, and his thoughts were gradually weaned entirely from all the natural objects of affection and interest which should otherwise have occupied them.

To what a terrible extent this process went on, Miss Maltravers's narrative shows. Soon after reaching Naples he visited the Villa de Angelis, which Temple had built on the ruins of a sea-house of Pomponius. The later building had in its turn become dismantled and ruinous, and Sir John found no difficulty in buying the site outright. He afterwards rebuilt it on an elaborate scale, endeavouring to reproduce in its equipment the luxury of the later empire. I had occasion to visit the house more than once in my capacity of executor, and found it full of priceless works of art, which, though neither so difficult to procure at that time nor so costly as they would be now, were yet sufficiently valuable to have necessitated an unjustifiable outlay.

The situation of the building fostered his infatuation for the past. It lay between the Bay of Naples and the Bay of Baia, and from its windows commanded the same exquisite view which had charmed Cicero and Lucullus, Severus and the Antonines. Hard by stood Baia, the princely seaside resort of the empire. That most luxurious and wanton of all cities of antiquity survived the cataclysms of ages, and only lost its civic continuity and became the ruined village of today in the sack of the fifteenth century. But a continuity of wickedness is not so easily broken, and those who know the spot best say that it is still instinct with memories of a shameful past.

For miles along that haunted coast the foot cannot be put down except on the ruins of some splendid villa, and over all there broods a spirit of corruption and debasement actually sensible and oppressive.

Of the dawns and sunsets, of the noonday sun tempered by the sea-breeze and the shade of scented groves, those who have been there know the charm, and to those who have not no words can describe it. But there are malefic vapours rising from the corpse of a past not altogether buried, and most cultivated Englishmen who tarry there long feel their influence as did John Maltravers. Like so many *decepti deceptores* of the Neo-Platonic school, he did not practise the abnegation enjoined by the very cult he professed to follow. Though his nature was far too refined, I believe, ever to sink into the sensualism revealed in Temple's diaries, yet it was through the gratification of corporeal tastes that he endeavoured to achieve the divine *extasis*; and there were constantly lavish and sumptuous entertainments at the villa, at which strange guests were present.

In such a nightmare of a life it was not to be expected that any mind would find repose, and Maltravers certainly found none. All those cares which usually occupy men's minds, all thoughts of wife, child, and home were, it is true, abandoned; but a wild unrest had hold of him, and never suffered him to be at ease. Though he never told me as much, yet I believe he was under the impression that the form which he had seen at Oxford and Royston had reappeared to him on more than one subsequent occasion. It must have been, I fancy, with a vague hope of "laying" this spectre that he now set himself with eagerness to discover where or how Temple had died. He remembered that Royston tradition said he had succumbed at Naples in the plague of 1752, but an idea seized him that this was not the case; indeed I half suspect his fancy unconsciously pictured that evil man as still alive.

The methods by which he eventually discovered the skeleton, or learnt the episodes which preceded Temple's death, I do not know. He promised to tell me some day at length, but a sudden death prevented his ever doing so. The facts as he narrated them, and as I have little doubt they actually occurred, were these: Adrian Temple, after Jocelyn's departure, had made a confidant of one Palamede Domacavalli, a scion of a splendid Parthenopean family of that name. Palamede had a palace in the heart of Naples, and was Temple's equal in age and also in his great wealth. The two men became boon companions, associated in all kinds of wickedness and excess. At length Palamede married a beautiful girl named Olimpia Aldobrandini, who was also of the noblest lineage; but the intimacy between him and Temple was not interrupted. About a year subsequent to this marriage dancing was going on after a splendid banquet in the great hall of the Palazzo

Domacavalli. Adrian, who was a favoured guest, called to the musicians in the gallery to play the "Areopagita" suite, and danced it with Olimpia, the wife of his host. The *Gagliarda* was reached but never finished, for near the end of the second movement Palamede from behind drove a stiletto into his friend's heart. He had found out that day that Adrian had not spared even Olimpia's honour.

I have endeavoured to condense into a connected story the facts learnt piecemeal from Sir John in conversation. To a certain extent they supplied, if not an explanation, at least an account of the change that had come over my friend. But only to a certain extent; there the explanation broke down and I was left baffled. I could imagine that a life of unwholesome surroundings and disordered studies might in time produce such a loss of mental tone as would lead in turn to moral *acolasia*, sensual excess, and physical ruin. But in Sir John's case the cause was not adequate; he had, so far as I know, never wholly given the reins to sensuality, and the change was too abrupt and the breakdown of body and mind too complete to be accounted for by such events as those of which he had spoken.

I had, too, an uneasy feeling, which grew upon me the more I saw of him, that while he spoke freely enough on certain topics, and obviously meant to give a complete history of his past life, there was in reality something in the background which he always kept from my view. He was, it seemed, like a young man asked by an indulgent father to disclose his debts in order that they may be discharged, who, although he knows his parent's leniency, and that any debt not now disclosed will be afterwards but a weight upon his own neck, yet hesitates for very shame to tell the full amount, and keeps some items back. So poor Sir John kept something back from me his friend, whose only aim was to afford him consolation and relief, and whose compassion would have made me listen without rebuke to the narration of the blackest crimes.

I cannot say how much this conviction grieved me. I would most willingly have given my all, my very life, to save my friend and Miss Maltravers's brother; but my efforts were paralysed by the feeling that I did not know what I had to combat, that some evil influence was at work on him which continually evaded my grasp. Once or twice it seemed as though he were within an ace of telling me all; once or twice, I believe, he had definitely made up his mind to do so; but then the mood changed, or more probably his courage failed him.

It was on one of these occasions that he asked me, somewhat suddenly, whether I thought that a man could by any conscious act committed in the flesh take away from himself all possibility of repentance and ultimate salvation. Though, I trust, a sincere Christian, I am nothing of a theologian, and the question touching on a topic which had not occurred to my mind since childhood, and which seemed to savour rather of medieval romance than of practical religion, took me for a moment aback. I hesitated for an instant, and then replied that the means of salvation offered man were undoubtedly so sufficient as to remove from one truly penitent the guilt of any crime however dark. My hesitation had been but momentary; but Sir John seemed to have noticed it, and sealed his lips to any confession, if he had indeed intended to make any, by changing the subject abruptly. This question naturally gave me food for serious reflection and anxiety. It was the first occasion on which he appeared to me to be undoubtedly suffering from definite hallucination, and I was aware that any illusions connected with religion are generally most difficult to remove. At the same time, anything of this sort was the more remarkable in Sir John's case, as he had, so far as I knew, for a considerable time entirely abandoned the Christian belief.

Unable to elicit any further information from him, and being thus thrown entirely upon my own resources, I determined that I would read through again the whole of Temple's diaries. The task was a very distasteful one, as I have already explained, but I hoped that a second reading might perhaps throw some light on the dark misgiving that was troubling Sir John. I read the manuscript again with the closest attention. Nothing, however, of any importance seemed to have escaped me on the former occasions, and I had reached nearly the end of the second volume when a comparatively slight matter arrested my attention. I have said that the pages were all carefully numbered, and the events of each day recorded separately; even where Temple had found nothing of moment to notice on a given day, he had still inserted the date with the word *nil* written against it.

But as I sat one evening in the library at Worth after Sir John had gone to bed, and was finally glancing through the days of the months in Temple's diary to make sure that all were complete, I found one day was missing. It was towards the end of the second volume, and the day was the 23rd of October in the year 1752. A glance at the numbering of the pages revealed the fact that three leaves had been entirely removed, and that the pages numbered 349 to 354 were not to be found. Again I ran through the diaries to see whether there were any leaves removed in other places, but found no other single page missing. All was complete except at this one place, the manuscript beautifully written, with scarcely an error or erasure throughout. A closer examination showed that these leaves had been cut out close to the back, and the cut edges of the paper appeared too fresh to admit of this being done a century ago. A very short reflection convinced me, in fact, that the excision was not likely to have been Temple's, and that it must have been made by Sir John.

My first intention was to ask him at once what the lost pages had contained, and why they had been cut out. The matter might be a mere triviality which he could explain in a moment. But on softly opening his bedroom door I found him sleeping, and Parnham (whom the strong light always burnt in the room rendered more wakeful) informed me that his master had been in a deep sleep for more than an hour. I knew how sorely his wasted energies needed such repose, and stepped back to the library without awaking him. A few minutes before, I had been feeling sleepy at the conclusion of my task, but now all wish for sleep was suddenly banished and a painful wakefulness took its place. I was under a species of mental excitement which reminded me of my feelings some years before at Oxford on the first occasion of our ever playing the *Gagliarda* together, and an idea struck me with the force of intuition that in these three lost leaves lay the secret of my friend's ruin.

I turned to the context to see whether there was anything in the entries preceding or following the lacuna that would afford a clue to the missing passage. The record of the few days immediately preceding the 23rd of October was short and contained nothing of any moment whatever. Adrian and Jocelyn were alone together at the Villa de Angelis. The entry on the 22nd was very unimportant and apparently quite complete, ending at the bottom of page 348. Of the 23rd there was, as I have said, no record at all, and the entry for the 24th began at the top of page 355. This last memorandum was also brief, and written when the author was annoyed by Jocelyn leaving him.

The defection of his companion had been apparently entirely unexpected. There was at least no previous hint of any such intention. Temple wrote that Jocelyn had left the Villa de Angelis that day and taken up his abode with the Carthusians of San Martino. No reason for such an extraordinary change was given; but there was a hint that Jocelyn had professed himself shocked at something that had happened. The entry concluded with a few bitter remarks:

So farewell to my holy anchoret; and if I cannot speed him with a leprosie as one Elisha did his servant, yet at least he went out from my presence with a face as white as snow.

I had read this sentence more than once before without its attracting other than a passing attention. The curious expression, that Jocelyn had gone out from his presence with a face as white as snow, had hitherto seemed to me to mean nothing more than that the two men had parted in violent anger, and that Temple had abused or bullied his companion. But as I sat alone that night in the library the words seemed to assume an entirely new force, and a strange suspicion began to creep over me.

I have said that one of the most remarkable features of Sir John's illness was his deadly pallor. Though I had now spent some time at Worth, and had been daily struck by this lack of colour, I had never before remembered in this connection that a strange paleness had also been an attribute of Adrian Temple, and was indeed very clearly marked in the picture painted of him by Battoni. In Sir John's account, moreover, of the vision which he thought he had seen in his rooms at Oxford, he had always spoken of the white and waxen face of his spectral visitant. The family tradition of Royston said that Temple had lost his colour in some deadly magical experiment, and a conviction now flashed upon me that Jocelyn's face "as white as snow" could refer only to this same unnatural pallor, and that he too had been smitten with it as with the mark of the beast.

In a drawer of my despatch-box, I kept by me all the letters which the late Lady Maltravers had written home during her ill-fated honeymoon. Miss Maltravers had placed them in my hands in order that I might be acquainted with every fact that could at all elucidate the progress of Sir John's malady. I remembered that in one of these letters mention was made of a sharp attack of fever in Naples, and of her noticing in him for the first time this singular pallor. I found the letter again without difficulty and read it with a new light. Every line breathed of surprise and alarm. Lady Maltravers feared that her husband was very seriously ill.

On the Wednesday, two days before she wrote, he had suffered all day from a strange restlessness, which had increased after they had retired in the evening. He could not sleep and had dressed again, saying he would walk a little in the night air to compose himself. He had not returned till near six in the morning, and then seemed so exhausted that he had since been confined to his bed. He was terribly pale, and the doctors feared he had been attacked by some strange fever.

The date of the letter was the 25th of October, fixing the night of the 23rd as the time of Sir John's first attack. The coincidence of the date with that of the day missing in Temple's diary was significant, but it was not needed now to convince me that Sir John's ruin was due to something that occurred on that fatal night at Naples.

The question that Dr. Frobisher had asked Miss Maltravers when he was first called to see her brother in London returned to my memory with an overwhelming force. "Had Sir John been subjected to any mental shock; had he received any severe fright?" I knew now that the question should have been answered in the affirmative, for I felt as certain as if Sir John had told me himself that he *had* received a violent shock, probably some terrible fright, on the night of the 23d of October. What the nature of that shock could have been my imagination was powerless to conceive, only I knew that whatever Sir John had done or seen, Adrian Temple and Jocelyn had done or seen also a century before and at the same place. That horror which had blanched the face of all three men for life had fallen perhaps with a less overwhelming force on Temple's seasoned wickedness, but had driven the worthless Jocelyn to the cloister, and was driving Sir John to the grave.

These thoughts as they passed through my mind filled me with a vague alarm. The lateness of the hour, the stillness and the subdued light, made the library in which I sat seem so vast and lonely that I began to feel the same dread of being alone that I had observed so often in my friend. Though only a door separated me from his bedroom, and I could hear his deep and regular breathing, I felt as though I must go in and waken him or Parnham to keep me company and save me from my own reflections. By a strong effort I restrained myself, and sat down to think the matter over and endeavour to frame some hypothesis that might explain the mystery. But it was all to no purpose. I merely wearied myself without being able to arrive at even a plausible conjecture, except that it seemed as though the strange coincidence of date might point to some ghastly charm or incantation which could only be carried out on one certain night of the year.

It must have been near morning when, quite exhausted, I fell into an uneasy slumber in the armchair where I sat. My sleep, however brief, was peopled with a succession of fantastic visions, in which I continually saw Sir John, not ill and wasted as now, but vigorous and handsome as I had known him at Oxford, standing beside a glowing brazier and reciting words I could not understand, while another man with a sneering white face sat in a corner playing the air of the *Gagliarda* on a violin. Parnham woke me in my chair at seven o'clock; his master, he said, was still sleeping easily.

I had made up my mind that as soon as he awoke I would inquire of Sir John as to the pages missing from the diary; but though my expectation and excitement were at a high pitch, I was forced to restrain my curiosity, for Sir John's slumber continued late into the day. Dr. Bruton called in the morning, and said that this sleep was what the patient's condition most required, and was a distinctly favourable symptom; he was on no account to be disturbed. Sir John did not leave his bed, but continued dozing all day till the evening. When at last he shook off his drowsiness, the hour was already so late that, in spite of my anxiety, I hesitated to talk with him about the diaries, lest I should unduly excite him before the night.

As the evening advanced he became very uneasy, and rose more than once from his bed. This restlessness, following on the repose of the day, ought perhaps to have made me anxious, for I have since observed that when death is very near an apprehensive unrest often sets in both with men and animals. It seems as if they dreaded to resign themselves to sleep, lest as they slumber the last enemy should seize them unawares. They try to fling off the bedclothes, they sometimes must leave their beds and walk. So it was with poor John Maltravers on his last Christmas Eve. I had sat with him grieving for his disquiet until he seemed to grow more tranquil, and at length fell asleep. I was sleeping that night in his room instead of Parnham, and tired with sitting up through the previous night, I flung myself, dressed as I was, upon the bed. I had scarcely dozed off, I think, before the sound of his violin awoke me. I found he had risen from his bed, had taken his favourite instrument, and was playing in his sleep.

The air was the *Gagliarda* of the *Areopagita* suite, which I had not heard since we had played it last together at Oxford, and it brought back with it a crowd of far-off memories and infinite regrets. I cursed the sleepiness which had overcome me at my watchman's post, and allowed Sir John to play once more that melody which had always been fraught with such evil for him; and I was about to wake him gently when he was startled from sleep by a strange accident. As I walked towards him the violin seemed entirely to collapse in his hands, and, as a matter of fact, the belly then gave way and broke under the strain of

288

the strings. As the strings slackened, the last note became an unearthly discord. If I were superstitious I should say that some evil spirit then went out of the violin, and broke in his parting throes the wooden tabernacle which had so long sheltered him. It was the last time the instrument was ever used, and that hideous chord was the last that Maltravers ever played.

I had feared that the shock of waking thus suddenly from sleep would have a very prejudicial effect upon the sleep-walker, but this seemed not to be the case. I persuaded him to go back at once to bed, and in a few minutes he fell asleep again. In the morning he seemed for the first time distinctly better; there was indeed something of his old self in his manner. It seemed as though the breaking of the violin had been an actual relief to him; and I believe that on that Christmas morning his better instincts woke, and that his old religious training and the associations of his boyhood then made their last appeal. I was pleased at such a change, however temporary it might prove. He wished to go to church, and I determined that again I would subdue my curiosity and defer the questions I was burning to put till after our return from the morning service. Miss Maltravers had gone indoors to make some preparation, Sir John was in his wheelchair on the terrace, and I was sitting by him in the sun. For a few moments he appeared immersed in silent thought, and then bent over towards me till his head was close to mine, and said, "Dear William, there is something I must tell you. I feel I cannot even go to church till I have told you all."

His manner shocked me beyond expression. I knew that he was going to tell me the secret of the lost pages, but instead of wishing any longer to have my curiosity satisfied, I felt a horrible dread of what he might say next. He took my hand in his and held it tightly, as a man who was about to undergo severe physical pain and sought the consolation of a friend's support. Then he went on—"You will be shocked at what I am going to tell you; but listen, and do not give me up: You must stand by me and comfort me and help me to turn again." He paused for a moment and continued—"It was one night in October, when Constance and I were at Naples. I took that violin and went by myself to the ruined villa on the Scoglio di Venere." He had been speaking with difficulty. His hand clutched mine convulsively, but still I felt it trembling, and I could see the moisture standing thick on his forehead. At this point the effort seemed too much for him and he broke off. "I cannot go on, I cannot tell you, but you can read it for yourself. In that diary which I gave you there are some pages missing."

The suspense was becoming intolerable to me, and I broke in, "Yes, yes, I know; you cut them out. Tell me where they are," He went on— "Yes, I cut them out lest they should possibly fall into anyone's hands unaware. But before you read them you must swear, as you hope for salvation, that you will never try to do what is written in them. Swear this to me now, or I never can let you see them." My eagerness was too great to stop now to discuss trifles, and to humour him I swore as desired. He had been speaking with a continual increasing effort; he cast a hurried and fearful glance round as though he expected to see someone listening, and it was almost in a whisper that he went on, "You will find them in—"

His agitation had become most painful to watch, and as he spoke the last words a convulsion passed over his face, and speech failing him, he sank back on his pillow. A strange fear took hold of me. For a moment I thought there were others on the terrace beside myself, and turned round expecting to see Miss Maltravers returned; but we were still alone. I even fancied that just as Sir John spoke his last words I felt something brush swiftly by me. He put up his hands, beating the air with a most painful gesture, as though he were trying to keep off an antagonist who had gripped him by the throat, and made a final struggle to speak. But the spasm was too strong for him; a dreadful stillness followed, and he was gone.

There is little more to add; for Sir John's guilty secret, perished with him. Though I was sure from his manner that the missing leaves were concealed somewhere at Worth, and though as executor I caused the most diligent search to be made, no trace of them was afterwards found; nor did any circumstance ever transpire to fling further light upon the matter. I must confess that I should have felt the discovery of these pages as a relief; for though I dreaded what I might have had to read, yet I was more anxious lest, being found at a later period and falling into other hands, they should cause a recrudescence of that plague which had blighted Sir John's life.

Of the nature of the events which took place on that night at Naples I can form no conjecture. But as certain physical sights have ere now proved so revolting as to unhinge the intellect, so I can imagine that the mind may in a state of extreme tension conjure up to itself some form of moral evil so hideous as metaphysically to sear it: and this, I believe, happened in the case both of Adrian Temple and of Sir

John Maltravers.

It is difficult to imagine the accessories used to produce the mental excitation in which alone such a presentment of evil could become imaginable. Fancy and legend, which have combined to represent as possible appearances of the supernatural, agree also in considering them as more likely to occur at certain times and places than at others; and it is possible that the missing pages of the diary contained an account of the time, place, and other conditions chosen by Temple for some deadly experiment. Sir John most probably re-enacted the scene under precisely similar conditions, and the effect on his overwrought imagination was so vivid as to upset the balance of his mind. The time chosen was no doubt the night of the 23rd of October, and I cannot help thinking that the place was one of those evil-looking and ruinous sea-rooms which had so terrifying an effect on Miss Maltravers. Temple may have used on that night one of the medieval incantations, or possibly the more ancient invocation of the Isiac rite with which a man of his knowledge and proclivities would certainly be familiar. The accessories of either are sufficiently hideous to weaken the mind by terror, and so prepare it for a belief in some frightful apparition. But whatever was done, I feel sure that the music of the *Gagliarda* formed part of the ceremonial.

Medieval philosophers and theologians held that evil is in its essence so horrible that the human mind, if it could realise it, must perish at its contemplation. Such realisation was by mercy ordinarily withheld, but its possibility was hinted in the legend of the *Visio malefica*. The *Visio Beatifica* was, as is well known, that vision of the Deity or realisation of the perfect Good which was to form the happiness of heaven, and the reward of the sanctified in the next world. Tradition says that this vision was accorded also to some specially elect spirits even in this life, as to Enoch, Elijah, Stephen, and Jerome. But there was a converse to the Beatific Vision in the *Visio malefica*, or presentation of absolute Evil, which was to be the chief torture of the damned, and which, like the Beatific Vision, had been made visible in life to certain desperate men. It visited Esau, as was said, when he found no place for repentance, and Judas, whom it drove to suicide.

Cain saw it when he murdered his brother, and legend relates that in his case, and in that of others, it left a physical brand to be borne by the body to the grave. It was supposed that the Malefic Vision, besides being thus spontaneously presented to typically abandoned men, had actually been purposely called up by some few great adepts, and used

291

by them to blast their enemies. But to do so was considered equivalent to a conscious surrender to the powers of evil, as the vision once seen took away all hope of final salvation.

Adrian Temple would undoubtedly be cognisant of this legend, and the lost experiment may have been an attempt to call up the Malefic Vision. It is but a vague conjecture at the best, for the tree of the knowledge of Evil bears many sorts of poisonous fruit, and no one can give full account of the extravagances of a wayward fancy.

Conjointly with Miss Sophia, Sir John appointed me his executor and guardian of his only son. Two months later we had lit a great fire in the library at Worth. In it, after the servants were gone to bed, we burnt the book containing the *Areopagita* of Graziani, and the Stradivarius fiddle. The diaries of Temple I had already destroyed, and wish that I could as easily blot out their foul and debasing memories from my mind. I shall probably be blamed by those who would exalt art at the expense of everything else, for burning a unique violin. This reproach I am content to bear. Though I am not unreasonably superstitious, and have no sympathy for that potential pantheism to which Sir John Maltravers surrendered his intellect, yet I felt so great an aversion to this violin that I would neither suffer it to remain at Worth, nor pass into other hands.

Miss Sophia was entirely at one with me on this point. It was the same feeling which restrains any except fools or braggarts from wishing to sleep in "haunted" rooms, or to live in houses polluted with the memory of a revolting crime. No sane mind believes in foolish apparitions, but fancy may at times bewitch the best of us. So the Stradivarius was burnt. It was, after all, perhaps not so serious a matter, for, as I have said, the bass-bar had given way. There had always been a question whether it was strong enough to resist the strain of modern stringing. Experience showed at last that it was not. With the failure of the bass-bar the belly collapsed, and the wood broke across the grain in so extraordinary a manner as to put the fiddle beyond repair, except as a curiosity. Its loss, therefore, is not to be so much regretted. Sir Edward has been brought up to think more of a cricket-bat than of a violin-bow; but if he wishes at any time to buy a Stradivarius, the fortunes of Worth and Royston, nursed through two long minorities, will certainly justify his doing so.

Miss Sophia and I stood by and watched the holocaust. My heart misgave me for a moment when I saw the mellow red varnish blistering off the back, but I put my regret resolutely aside. As the bright flames jumped up and lapped it round, they flung a red glow on the scroll. It was wonderfully wrought, and differed, as I think Miss Maltravers has already said, from any known example of Stradivarius. As we watched it, the scroll took form, and we saw what we had never seen before, that it was cut so that the deep lines in a certain light showed as the profile of a man. It was a wizened little paganish face, with sharp-cut features and a bald head. As I looked at it I knew at once (and a cameo has since confirmed the fact) that it was a head of Porphyry. Thus the second label found in the violin was explained and Sir John's view confirmed, that Stradivarius had made the instrument for some Neo-Platonist enthusiast who had dedicated it to his master Porphyrius.

★★★★★★

A year after Sir John's death I went with Miss Maltravers to Worth church to see a plain slab of slate which we had placed over her brother's grave. We stood in bright sunlight in the Maltravers chapel, with the monuments of that splendid family about us. Among them were the altar-tomb of Sir Esmoun, and the effigies of more than one Crusader. As I looked on their knightly forms, with their heads resting on their tilting helms, their faces set firm, and their hands joined in prayer, I could not help envying them that full and unwavering faith for which they had fought and died. It seemed to stand out in such sharp contrast with our latter-day sciolism and half-believed creeds, and to be flung into higher relief by the dark shadow of John Maltravers's ruined life.

At our feet was the great brass of one Sir Roger de Maltravers. I pointed out the end of the inscription to my companion—"*Cvjvs Animæ, Atqve Animabvs Omnivm Fidelivm Defvnctorvm, Atqve Nostris Animabvs Qvvm Ex Hac Lvce Transiverimvs, Propitietvr Devs.*" Though no Catholic, I could not refuse to add a sincere Amen. Miss Sophia, who is not ignorant of Latin, read the inscription after me. "*Ex hac luce,*" she said, as though speaking to herself, "*out of this light; alas! alas! for some the light is darkness.*"

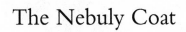
The Nebuly Coat

Contents

Sir George Farquhar, Baronet, builder of railway-stations, and institutes, and churches, author, antiquarian, and senior partner of Farquhar and Farquhar, leant back in his office chair and turned it sideways to give more point to his remarks. Before him stood an understudy, whom he was sending to superintend the restoration work at Cullerne Minster.

"Well, goodbye, Westray; keep your eyes open, and don't forget that you have an important job before you. The church is too big to hide its light under a bushel, and this Society-for-the-Conservation-of-National-Inheritances has made up its mind to advertise itself at our expense. Ignoramuses who don't know an aumbry from an abacus, charlatans, amateur faddists, they *will* abuse our work. Good, bad, or indifferent, it's all one to them; they are pledged to abuse it."

His voice rang with a fine professional contempt, but he sobered himself and came back to business.

"The south transept roof and the choir vaulting will want careful watching. There is some old trouble, too, in the central tower; and I should like later on to underpin the main crossing piers, but there is no money. For the moment I have said nothing about the tower; it is no use raising doubts that one can't set at rest; and I don't know how we are going to make ends meet, even with the little that it is proposed to do now. If funds come in, we must tackle the tower; but transept and choir-vaults are more pressing, and there is no risk from the bells, because the cage is so rotten that they haven't been rung for years.

"You must do your best. It isn't a very profitable stewardship, so try to give as good an account of it as you can. We shan't make a penny out of it, but the church is too well known to play fast-and-loose with. I have written to the parson—a foolish old fellow, who is no more fit than a lady's-maid to be trusted with such a church as Cullerne—to say you are coming tomorrow, and will put in an appearance at the church in the afternoon, in case he wishes to see you. The man is an ass, but he is legal guardian of the place, and has not done badly in collecting money for the restoration; so we must bear with him."

CHAPTER ONE

Cullerne Wharf of the Ordnance maps, or plain Cullerne as known to the countryside, lies two miles from the coast today; but it was once much nearer, and figures in history as a seaport of repute, having sent six ships to fight the *Armada*, and four to withstand the Dutch a century later. But in fullness of time the estuary of the Cull silted up, and a bar formed at the harbour mouth; so that sea-borne commerce was driven to seek other havens. Then the Cull narrowed its channel, and instead of spreading itself out prodigally as heretofore on this side or on that, shrunk to the limits of a well-ordered stream, and this none of the greatest. The *burghers*, seeing that their livelihood in the port was gone, reflected that they might yet save something by reclaiming the salt-marshes, and built a stone dyke to keep the sea from getting in, with a sluice in the midst of it to let the Cull out.

Thus were formed the low-lying meadows called Cullerne Flat, where the Freemen have a right to pasture sheep, and where as good-tasting mutton is bred as on any *pré-salé* on the other side of the Channel. But the sea has not given up its rights without a struggle, for with a south-east wind and spring-tide the waves beat sometimes over the top of the dyke; and sometimes the Cull forgets its good behaviour, and after heavy rainfalls inland breaks all bonds, as in the days of yore. Then anyone looking out from upper windows in Cullerne town would think the little place had moved back once more to the seaboard; for the meadows are under water, and the line of the dyke is scarcely broad enough to make a division in the view, between the inland lake and the open sea beyond.

The main line of the Great Southern Railway passes seven miles to the north of this derelict port, and converse with the outer world was kept up for many years by carriers' carts, which journeyed to and fro between the town and the wayside station of Cullerne Road. But by-and-by deputations of the Corporation of Cullerne, properly introduced by Sir Joseph Carew, the talented and widely-respected member for that ancient borough, persuaded the railway company that better communication was needed, and a branch-line was made, on which the service was scarcely less primitive than that of the carriers in the past.

The novelty of the railway had not altogether worn off at the time when the restorations of the church were entrusted to Messrs. Farquhar and Farquhar; and the arrival of the trains was still attended by Cullerne loungers as a daily ceremonial. But the afternoon on which Westray came, was so very wet that there were no spectators. He had taken a third-class ticket from London to Cullerne Road to spare his pocket, and a first-class ticket from the junction to Cullerne to support the dignity of his firm. But this forethought was wasted, for, except certain broken-down railway officials, who were drafted to Cullerne as to an asylum, there were no witnesses of his advent.

He was glad to learn that the enterprise of the Blandamer Arms led that family and commercial hotel to send an omnibus to meet all trains, and he availed himself the more willingly of this conveyance because he found that it would set him down at the very door of the church itself. So he put himself and his modest luggage inside—and there was ample room to do this, for he was the only passenger— plunged his feet into the straw which covered the floor, and endured for ten minutes such a shaking and rattling as only an omnibus moving over cobble-stones can produce.

With the plans of Cullerne Minster Mr Westray was thoroughly familiar, but the reality was as yet unknown to him; and when the omnibus lumbered into the market-place, he could not suppress an exclamation as he first caught sight of the great church of Saint Sepulchre shutting in the whole south side of the square. The drenching rain had cleared the streets of passengers, and save for some peeping-Toms who looked over the low green blinds as the omnibus passed, the place might indeed have been waiting for Lady Godiva's progress, all was so deserted.

The heavy sheets of rain in the air, the misty water-dust raised by the drops as they struck the roofs, and the vapour steaming from the earth, drew over everything a veil invisible yet visible, which softened outlines like the gauze curtain in a theatre. Through it loomed the minster, larger and far more mysteriously impressive than Westray had in any moods imagined. A moment later the omnibus drew up before an iron gate, from which a flagged pathway led through the churchyard to the north porch.

The conductor opened the carriage-door.

"This is the church, sir," he said, somewhat superfluously. "If you get out here, I will drive your bag to the hotel."

Westray fixed his hat firmly on his head, turned up the collar of his coat, and made a dash through the rain for the door. Deep puddles had formed in the worn places of the gravestones that paved the alley, and he splashed himself in his hurry before he reached the shelter of the porch. He pulled aside the hanging leather mattress that covered a wicket in the great door, and found himself inside the church.

It was not yet four o'clock, but the day was so overcast that dusk was already falling in the building. A little group of men who had been talking in the choir turned round at the sound of the opening door, and made towards the architect. The protagonist was a clergyman past middle age, who wore a stock, and stepped forward to greet the young architect.

"Sir George Farquhar's assistant, I presume. One of Sir George Farquhar's assistants I should perhaps say, for no doubt Sir George has more than one assistant in carrying out his many and varied professional duties."

Westray made a motion of assent, and the clergyman went on: "Let me introduce myself as Canon Parkyn. You will no doubt have heard of me from Sir George, with whom I, as rector of this church, have had exceptional opportunities of associating. On one occasion, indeed, Sir George spent the night under my own roof, and I must say that I think any young man should be proud of studying under an architect of such distinguished ability. I shall be able to explain to you very briefly the main views which Sir George has conceived with regard to the restoration; but in the meantime let me make you known to my worthy parishioners—and friends," he added in a tone which implied some doubt as to whether condescension was not being stretched too far, in qualifying as friends persons so manifestly inferior.

"This is Mr Sharnall, the organist, who under my direction presides over the musical portion of our services; and this is Dr Ennefer, our excellent local practitioner; and this is Mr Joliffe, who, though engaged in trade, finds time as churchwarden to assist me in the supervision of the sacred edifice."

The doctor and the organist gave effect to the presentation by a nod, and something like a shrug of the shoulders, which deprecated the rector's conceited pomposity, and implied that if such an exceedingly unlikely contingency as their making friends with Mr Westray should ever happen, it would certainly not be due to any introduction of Canon Parkyn. Mr Joliffe, on the other hand, seemed fully to recognise the dignity to which he was called by being numbered among the rector's friends, and with a gracious bow, and a polite "Your servant, sir," made it plain that he understood how to condescend in his turn, and was prepared to extend his full protection to a young and struggling architect.

Beside these leading actors, there were present the clerk, and a handful of walking-gentlemen in the shape of idlers who had strolled in from the street, and who were glad enough to find shelter from the rain, and an afternoon's entertainment gratuitously provided.

"I thought you would like to meet me here," said the rector, "so that I might point out to you at once the more salient features of the building. Sir George Farquhar, on the occasion of his last visit, was pleased to compliment me on the lucidity of the explanations which I ventured to offer."

There seemed to be no immediate way of escape, so Westray resigned himself to the inevitable, and the little group moved up the nave, enveloped in an atmosphere of its own, of which wet overcoats and umbrellas were resolvable constituents. The air in the church was raw and cold, and a smell of sodden matting drew Westray's attention to the fact that the roofs were not water-tight, and that there were pools of rain-water on the floor in many places.

"The nave is the oldest part," said the cicerone, "built about 1135 by Walter Le Bec."

"I am very much afraid our friend is too young and inexperienced for the work here. What do *you* think?" he put in as a rapid aside to the doctor.

"Oh, I dare say if you take him in hand and coach him a little he will do all right," replied the doctor, raising his eyebrows for the organist's delectation.

"Yes, this is all Le Bec's work," the rector went on, turning back to Westray. "So sublime the simplicity of the Norman style, is it not? The nave arcades will repay your close attention; and look at these wonderful arches in the crossing. Norman, of course, but how light; and yet strong as a rock to bear the enormous weight of the tower which later builders reared on them. Wonderful, wonderful!"

Westray recalled his chief's doubts about the tower, and looking up into the lantern saw on the north side a seam of old brick filling; and on the south a thin jagged fissure, that ran down from the sill of the lantern-window like the impress of a lightning-flash. There came into his head an old architectural saw, "*The arch never sleeps*"; and as he looked up at the four wide and finely-drawn semicircles they seemed to say:

"The arch never sleeps, never sleeps. They have bound on us a burden too heavy to be borne. We are shifting it. The arch never sleeps."

"Wonderful, wonderful!" the rector still murmured. "Daring fellows, these Norman builders."

"Yes, yes," Westray was constrained to say; "but they never reckoned that the present tower would be piled upon their arches."

"What, *you* think them a little shaky?" put in the organist. "Well, I have fancied so, many a time, myself."

"Oh, I don't know. I dare say they will last our time," Westray answered in a nonchalant and reassuring tone; for he remembered that, as regards the tower, he had been specially cautioned to *let sleeping dogs lie*, but he thought of the Ossa heaped on Pelion above their heads, and conceived a mistrust of the wide crossing-arches which he never was able entirely to shake off.

"No, no, my young friend," said the rector with a smile of forbearance for so mistaken an idea, "do not alarm yourself about these arches. 'Mr Rector,' said Sir George to me the very first time we were here together, 'you have been at Cullerne forty years; have you ever observed any signs of movement in the tower?' 'Sir George,' I said, 'will you wait for your fees until my tower tumbles down?' Ha, ha, ha! He saw the joke, and we never heard anything more about the tower. Sir George has, no doubt, given you all proper instructions; but as I had the privilege of personally showing him the church, you must forgive me if I ask you to step into the south transept for a moment, while I point out to you what Sir George considered the most pressing matter."

They moved into the transept, but the doctor managed to buttonhole Westray for a moment *en route*.

"You will be bored to death," he said, "with this man's ignorance and conceit. Don't pay the least attention to him, but there *is* one thing I want to take the first opportunity of pressing on you. Whatever is done or not done, however limited the funds may be, let us at least have a sanitary floor. You must have all these stones up, and put a foot or two of concrete under them. Can anything be more monstrous than that the dead should be allowed to poison the living? There must be hundreds of burials close under the floor, and look at the pools of water standing about. Can anything, I say, be more insanitary?"

They were in the south transept, and the rector had duly pointed out the dilapidations of the roof, which, in truth, wanted but little showing.

"Some call this the Blandamer aisle," he said, "from a noble family of that name who have for many years been buried here."

"*Their* vaults are, no doubt, in a most insanitary condition," interpolated the doctor.

"These Blandamers ought to restore the whole place," the organist said bitterly. "They would, if they had any sense of decency. They are as rich as Croesus, and would miss pounds less than most people would miss pennies. Not that I believe in any of this sanitary talk—things have gone on well enough as they are; and if you go digging up the floors you will only dig up pestilences. Keep the fabric together, make the roofs water-tight, and spend a hundred or two on the organ. That is all we want, and these Blandamers would do it, if they weren't curmudgeons and skinflints."

"You will forgive me, Mr Sharnall," said the rector, "if I remark that an hereditary peerage is so important an institution, that we should be very careful how we criticise any members of it. At the same time," he went on, turning apologetically to Westray, "there is perhaps a modicum of reason in our friend's remarks. I had hoped that Lord Blandamer would have contributed handsomely to the restoration fund, but he has not hitherto done so, though I dare say that his continued absence abroad accounts for some delay. He only succeeded his grandfather last year, and the late lord never showed much interest in this place, and was indeed in many ways a very strange character. But it's no use raking up these stories; the old man is gone, and we must hope for better things from the young one."

"I don't know why you call him young," said the doctor. "He's young, maybe, compared to his grandfather, who died at eighty-five; but he must be forty, if he's a day."

"Oh, impossible; and yet I don't know. It was in my first year at Cullerne that his father and mother were drowned. You remember that, Mr Sharnall—when the *Corisand* upset in Pallion Bay?"

"Ay, I mind that well enough," struck in the clerk; "and I mind their being married, becos' we wor ringing of the bells, when old Mason Parmiter run into the church, and says: 'Do'ant-'ee, boys—do'ant-'ee ring 'em any more. These yere old tower'll never stand it. I see him rock,' he says, 'and the dust a-running out of the cracks like rain.' So out we come, and glad enough to stop it, too, because there wos a feast down in the meadows by the London Road, and drinks and dancing, and we wanted to be there. That were two-and-forty years ago come Lady Day, and there was some shook their heads, and said we never ought to have stopped the ring, for a broken peal broke life or happiness. But what was we to do?"

"Did they strengthen the tower afterwards?" Westray asked. "Do you find any excessive motion when the peal is rung now?"

"Lor' bless you, sir; them bells was never rung for thirty years afore that, and wouldn't a been rung then, only Tom Leech, he says: 'The ropes is there, boys; let's have a ring out of these yere tower. He ain't been rung for thirty year. None on us don't recollect the last time he *was* rung, and if 'er were weak then, 'ers had plenty of time to get strong again, and there'll be half a crown a man for ringing of a peal.' So up we got to it, till old Parmiter come in to stop us. And you take my word for it, they never have been rung since. There's only that rope there"—and he pointed to a bell-rope that came down from the lantern far above, and was fastened back against the wall—"wot we tolls the bell with for service, and that ain't the big bell neither."

"Did Sir George Farquhar know all this?" Westray asked the rector.

"No, sir; Sir George did not know it," said the rector, with some tartness in his voice, "because it was not material that he should know it; and Sir George's time, when he was here, was taken up with more pressing matters. I never heard this old wife's tale myself till the present moment, and although it is true that we do not ring the bells, this is on account of the supposed weakness of the cage in which they swing, and has nothing whatever to do with the tower itself. You may take my word for that. 'Sir George,' I said, when Sir George asked me—'Sir George, I have been here forty years, and if you will agree not to ask for your fees till my tower tumbles down, why, I shall be very glad.' Ha, ha, ha! how Sir George enjoyed that joke! Ha, ha, ha!"

Westray turned away with a firm resolve to report to headquarters the story of the interrupted peal, and to make an early examination of the tower on his own behalf.

The clerk was nettled that the rector should treat his story with such scant respect, but he saw that the others were listening with interest, and he went on:

"Well, 'taint for I to say the old tower's a-going to fall, and I hope Sir Jarge won't ever live to larf the wrong side o' his mouth; but stopping of a ring never brought luck with it yet, and it brought no luck to my lord. First he lost his dear son and his son's wife in Cullerne Bay, and I remember as if 'twas yesterday how we grappled for 'em all night, and found their bodies lying close together on the sand in three fathoms, when the tide set inshore in the morning. And then he fell out wi' my lady, and she never spoke to him again—no, not to the day of her death. They lived at Fording—that's the great hall over there," he said to Westray, jerking his thumb towards the east—"for twenty years in separate wings, like you mi'd say each in a house to themselves. And then he fell out wi' Mr Fynes, his grandson, and turned him out of house and lands, though he couldn't leave them anywhere else when he died. 'Tis Mr Fynes as is the young lord now, and half his life he's bin a wanderer in foreign parts, and isn't come home yet. Maybe he never will come back. It's like enough he's got killed out there, or he'd be tied to answer parson's letters. Wouldn't he, Mr Sharnall?" he said, turning abruptly to the organist with a wink, which was meant to retaliate for the slight that the rector had put on his stories.

"Come, come; we've had enough of these tales," said the rector. "Your listeners are getting tired."

"The man's in love with his own voice," he added in a lower tone, as he took Westray by the arm; "when he's once set off there's no stopping him. There are still a good many points which Sir George and I discussed, and on which I shall hope to give you our conclusions; but we shall have to finish our inspection tomorrow, for this talkative fellow has sadly interrupted us. It is a great pity the light is failing so fast just now; there is some good painted glass in this end window of the transept."

Westray looked up and saw the great window at the end of the transept shimmering with a dull lustre; light only in comparison with the shadows that were falling inside the church. It was an insertion of Perpendicular date, reaching from wall to wall, and almost from floor to roof. Its vast breadth, parcelled out into eleven lights, and the infinite division of the stonework in the head, impressed the imagination; while mullions and tracery stood out in such inky contrast against the daylight yet lingering outside, that the architect read the scheme of subarcuation and the tracery as easily as if he had been studying a plan. Sundown had brought no gleam to lift the pall of the dying day, but the monotonous grey of the sky was still sufficiently light to enable a practised eye to make out that the head of the window was filled with a broken medley of ancient glass, where translucent blues and yellows and reds mingled like the harmony of an old patchwork quilt. Of the lower divisions of the window, those at the sides had no colour to clothe their nakedness, and remained in ghostly whiteness; but the three middle lights were filled with strong browns and purples of the seventeenth century.

Here and there in the rich colour were introduced medallions, representing apparently scriptural scenes, and at the top of each light, under the cusping, was a coat of arms. The head of the middle division formed the centre of the whole scheme, and seemed to represent a shield of silver-white crossed by waving sea-green bars. Westray's attention was attracted by the unusual colouring, and by the transparency of the glass, which shone as with some innate radiance where all was dim. He turned almost unconsciously to ask whose arms were thus represented, but the rector had left him for a minute, and he heard an irritating "Ha, ha, ha!" at some distance down the nave, that convinced him that the story of Sir George Farquhar and the postponed fees was being retold in the dusk to a new victim.

Someone, however, had evidently read the architect's thoughts, for a sharp voice said:

"That is the coat of the Blandamers—barry nebuly of six, argent and vert." It was the organist who stood near him in the deepening shadows. "I forgot that such jargon probably conveys no meaning to you, and, indeed, I know no heraldry myself excepting only this one coat of arms, and sometimes wish," he said with a sigh, "that I knew nothing of that either. There have been queer tales told of that shield, and maybe there are queerer yet to be told. It has been stamped for good or evil on this church, and on this town, for centuries, and every tavern loafer will talk to you about the 'nebuly coat' as if it was a thing he wore. You will be familiar enough with it before you have been a week at Cullerne."

There was in the voice something of melancholy, and an earnestness that the occasion scarcely warranted. It produced a curious effect on Westray, and led him to look closely at the organist; but it was too dark to read any emotion in his companion's face, and at this moment the rector rejoined them.

"Eh, what? Ah, yes; the nebuly coat. Nebuly, you know, from the Latin *nebulum, nebulus* I should say, a cloud, referring to the wavy outline of the bars, which are supposed to represent *cumulus* clouds. Well, well, it is too dark to pursue our studies further this evening, but tomorrow I can accompany you the whole day, and shall be able to tell you much that will interest you."

Westray was not sorry that the darkness had put a stop to further investigations. The air in the church grew every moment more clammy and chill, and he was tired, hungry, and very cold. He was anxious, if possible, to find lodgings at once, and so avoid the expense of an hotel, for his salary was modest, and Farquhar and Farquhar were not more liberal than other firms in the travelling allowances which they granted their subordinates.

He asked if anyone could tell him of suitable rooms.

"I am sorry," the rector said, "not to be able to offer you the hospitality of my own house, but the indisposition of my wife unfortunately makes that impossible. I have naturally but a very slight acquaintance with lodging-houses or lodging-house keepers; but Mr Sharnall, I dare say, may be able to give you some advice. Perhaps there may be a spare room in the house where Mr Sharnall lodges. I think your landlady is a relation of our worthy friend Joliffe, is she not, Mr Sharnall? And no doubt herself a most worthy woman."

"Pardon, Mr Rector," said the churchwarden, in as offended a tone as he dared to employ in addressing so superior a dignitary—"pardon, no relation at all, I assure you. A namesake, or, at the nearest, a very distant connection of whom—I speak with all Christian forbearance—my branch of the family have no cause to be proud."

The organist had scowled when the rector was proposing Westray as a fellow-lodger, but Joliffe's disclaimer of the landlady seemed to pique him.

"If no branch of your family brings you more discredit than my landlady, you may hold your head high enough. And if all the pork you sell is as good as her lodgings, your business will thrive. Come along," he said, taking Westray by the arm; "I have no wife to be indisposed, so I can offer you the hospitality of my house; and we will stop at Mr Joliffe's shop on our way, and buy a pound of sausages for tea."

CHAPTER TWO

There was a rush of outer air into the building as they opened the door. The rain still fell heavily, but the wind was rising, and had in it a clean salt smell, that contrasted with the close and mouldering atmosphere of the church.

The organist drew a deep breath.

"Ah," he said, "what a blessed thing to be in the open air again—to be quit of all their niggling and naggling, to be quit of that pompous old fool the rector, and of that hypocrite Joliffe, and of that pedant of a doctor! Why does he want to waste money on cementing the vaults? It's only digging up pestilences; and they won't spend a farthing on the organ. Not a penny on the *Father Smith*, clear and sweet-voiced as a mountain brook. Oh," he cried, "it's too bad! The naturals are worn down to the quick, you can see the wood in the gutters of the keys, and the pedal-board's too short and all to pieces. Ah well! the organ's like me—old, neglected, worn-out. I wish I was dead." He had been talking half to himself, but he turned to Westray and said: "Forgive me for being peevish; you'll be peevish, too, when you come to my age— at least, if you're as poor then as I am, and as lonely, and have nothing to look forward to. Come along."

They stepped out into the dark—for night had fallen—and plashed along the flagged path which glimmered like a white streamlet between the dark turves.

"I will take you a short-cut, if you don't mind some badly-lighted lanes," said the organist, as they left the churchyard; "it's quicker, and we shall get more shelter." He turned sharply to the left, and plunged into an alley so narrow and dark that Westray could not keep up with him, and fumbled anxiously in the obscurity. The little man reached up, and took him by the arm. "Let me pilot you," he said; "I know the way. You can walk straight on; there are no steps."

There was no sign of life, nor any light in the houses, but it was not till they reached a corner where an isolated lamp cast a wan and uncertain light that Westray saw that there was no glass in the windows, and that the houses were deserted.

"It's the old part of the town," said the organist; "there isn't one house in ten with anyone in it now. All we fashionables have moved further up. Airs from the river are damp, you know, and wharves so very vulgar."

They left the narrow street, and came on to what Westray made out to be a long wharf skirting the river. On the right stood abandoned warehouses, square-fronted, and huddled together like a row of gigantic packing-cases; on the left they could hear the gurgle of the current among the mooring-posts, and the flapping of the water against the quay wall, where the east wind drove the wavelets up the river. The lines of what had once been a horse-tramway still ran along the quay, and the pair had some ado to thread their way without tripping, till a low building on the right broke the line of lofty warehouses. It seemed to be a church or chapel, having mullioned windows with stone tracery, and a bell-turret at the west end; but its most marked feature was a row of heavy buttresses which shored up the side facing the road. They were built of brick, and formed triangles with the ground and the wall which they supported. The shadows hung heavy under the building, but where all else was black the recesses between the buttresses were blackest. Westray felt his companion's hand tighten on his arm.

"You will think me as great a coward as I am," said the organist, "if I tell you that I never come this way after dark, and should not have come here tonight if I had not had you with me. I was always frightened as a boy at the very darkness in the spaces between the buttresses, and I have never got over it. I used to think that devils and hobgoblins lurked in those cavernous depths, and now I fancy evil men may be hiding in the blackness, all ready to spring out and strangle one. It is a lonely place, this old wharf, and after nightfall—" He broke off, and clutched Westray's arm. "Look," he said; "do you see nothing in the last recess?"

His abruptness made Westray shiver involuntarily, and for a moment the architect fancied that he discerned the figure of a man standing in the shadow of the end buttress. But, as he took a few steps nearer, he saw that he had been deceived by a shadow, and that the space was empty.

"Your nerves are sadly overstrung," he said to the organist. "There is no one there; it is only some trick of light and shade. What is the building?"

"It was once a chantry of the Grey Friars," Mr Sharnall answered, "and afterwards was used for excise purposes when Cullerne was a real port. It is still called the Bonding-House, but it has been shut up as long as I remember it. Do you believe in certain things or places being bound up with certain men's destinies? because I have a presentiment that this broken-down old chapel will be connected somehow or other with a crisis of my life."

Westray remembered the organist's manner in the church, and began to suspect that his mind was turned. The other read his thoughts, and said rather reproachfully:

"Oh no, I am not mad—only weak and foolish and very cowardly."

They had reached the end of the wharf, and were evidently returning to civilisation, for a sound of music reached them. It came from a little beer-house, and as they passed they heard a woman singing inside. It was a rich *contralto*, and the organist stopped for a moment to listen.

"She has a fine voice," he said, "and would sing well if she had been taught. I wonder how she comes here."

The blind was pulled down, but did not quite reach the bottom of the window, and they looked in. The rain blurred the pains on the outside, and the moisture had condensed within, so that it was not easy to see clearly; but they made out that a Creole woman was singing to a group of topers who sat by the fire in a corner of the room. She was middle-aged, but sang sweetly, and was accompanied on the harp by an old man:

"Oh, take me back to those I love! Or bring them here to me! I have no heart to rove, to rove Across the rolling sea."

"Poor thing!" said the organist; "she has fallen on bad days to have so scurvy a company to sing to. Let us move on."

They turned to the right, and came in a few minutes to the highroad. Facing them stood a house which had once been of some pretensions, for it had a porch carried on pillars, under which a semicircular flight of steps led up to the double door. A street-lamp which stood before it had been washed so clean in the rain that the light was shed with unusual brilliance, and showed even at night that the house was fallen from its high estate. It was not ruinous, but *Ichabod* was written on the paintless window-frames and on the rough-cast front, from which the plaster had fallen away in more than one place. The pillars of the porch had been painted to imitate marble, but they were marked with scabrous patches, where the brick core showed through the broken stucco.

The organist opened the door, and they found themselves in a stone-floored hall, out of which dingy doors opened on both sides. A broad stone staircase, with shallow steps and iron balustrades, led from the hall to the next story, and there was a little pathway of worn matting that threaded its way across the flags, and finally ascended the stairs.

"Here is my town house," said Mr Sharnall. "It used to be a coaching inn called The Hand of God, but you must never breathe a word of that, because it is now a private mansion, and Miss Joliffe has christened it Bellevue Lodge."

A door opened while he was speaking, and a girl stepped into the hall. She was about nineteen, and had a tall and graceful figure. Her warm brown hair was parted in the middle, and its profusion was gathered loosely up behind in the half-formal, half-natural style of a preceding generation. Her face had lost neither the rounded outline nor the delicate bloom of girlhood, but there was something in it that negatived any impression of inexperience, and suggested that her life had not been free from trouble. She wore a close-fitting dress of black, and had a string of pale corals round her neck.

"Good-evening, Mr Sharnall," she said. "I hope you are not very wet"—and gave a quick glance of inquiry at Westray.

The organist did not appear pleased at seeing her. He grunted testily, and, saying "Where is your aunt? Tell her I want to speak to her," led Westray into one of the rooms opening out of the hall.

It was a large room, with an upright piano in one corner, and a great litter of books and manuscript music. A table in the middle was set for tea; a bright fire was burning in the grate, and on either side of it stood a rush-bottomed armchair.

"Sit down," he said to Westray; "this is my reception-room, and we will see in a minute what Miss Joliffe can do for *you*." He glanced at his companion, and added, "That was her niece we met in the passage," in so unconcerned a tone as to produce an effect opposite to that intended, and to lead Westray to wonder whether there was any reason for his wishing to keep the girl in the background.

In a few moments the landlady appeared. She was a woman of sixty, tall and spare, with a sweet and even distinguished face. She, too, was dressed in black, well-worn and shabby, but her appearance suggested that her thinness might be attributed to privation or self-denial, rather than to natural habit.

Preliminaries were easily arranged; indeed, the only point of discussion was raised by Westray, who was disturbed by scruples lest the terms which Miss Joliffe offered were too low to be fair to herself. He said so openly, and suggested a slight increase, which, after some demur, was gratefully accepted.

"You are too poor to have so fine a conscience," said the organist snappishly. "If you are so scrupulous now, you will be quite unbearable when you get rich with battening and fattening on this restoration." But he was evidently pleased with Westray's consideration for Miss Joliffe, and added with more cordiality: "You had better come down and share my meal; your rooms will be like an ice-house such a night as this. Don't be long, or the turtle will be cold, and the ortolans baked to a cinder. I will excuse evening dress, unless you happen to have your court suit with you."

Westray accepted the invitation with some willingness, and an hour later he and the organist were sitting in the rush-bottomed armchairs at either side of the fireplace. Miss Joliffe had herself cleared the table, and brought two tumblers, wine-glasses, sugar, and a jug of water, as if they were natural properties of the organist's sitting-room.

"I did Churchwarden Joliffe an injustice," said Mr Sharnall, with the reflective mood that succeeds a hearty meal; "his sausages are good. Put on some more coal, Mr Westray; it is a sinful luxury, a fire in September, and coal at twenty-five shillings a ton; but we must have *some* festivity to inaugurate the restoration and your advent. Fill a pipe yourself, and then pass me the tobacco."

"Thank you, I do not smoke," Westray said; and, indeed, he did not look like a smoker. He had something of the thin, unsympathetic traits of the professional water-drinker in his face, and spoke as if he regarded smoking as a crime for himself, and an offence for those of less lofty principles than his own.

The organist lighted his pipe, and went on:

"This is an airy house—sanitary enough to suit our friend the doctor; every window carefully ventilated on the crack-and-crevice principle. It was an old inn once, when there were more people hereabouts; and if the rain beats on the front, you can still read the name through the colouring—the Hand of God. There used to be a market held outside, and a century or more ago an apple-woman sold some pippins to a customer just before this very door. He said he had paid for them, and she said he had not; they came to wrangling, and she called Heaven to justify her. 'God strike me dead if I have ever touched your money!' She was taken at her word, and fell dead on the cobbles. They found clenched in her hand the two coppers for which she had lost her soul, and it was recognised at once that nothing less than an inn could properly commemorate such an exhibition of Divine justice. So the Hand of God was built, and flourished while Cullerne flourished, and fell when Cullerne fell.

"It stood empty ever since I can remember it, till Miss Joliffe took it fifteen years ago. She elevated it into Bellevue Lodge, a select boarding-house, and spent what little money that niggardly landlord old Blandamer would give for repairs, in painting out the Hand of God on the front. It was to be a house of resort for Americans who came to Cullerne. They say in our guide-book that Americans come to see Cullerne Church because some of the Pilgrim Fathers' fathers are buried in it; but I've never seen any Americans about. They never come to me; I have been here boy and man for sixty years, and never knew an American do a pennyworth of good to Cullerne Church; and they never did a pennyworth of good for Miss Joliffe, for none of them ever came to Bellevue Lodge, and the select boarding-house is so select that you and I are the only boarders."

He paused for a minute and went on: "Americans—no, I don't think much of Americans; they're too hard for me—spend a lot of money on their own pleasure, and sometimes cut a dash with a big donation, where they think it will be properly trumpeted. But they haven't got warm hearts. I don't care for Americans. Still, if you know any about, you can say I am quite venal; and if any one of them restores my organ, I am prepared to admire the whole lot. Only they must give a little water-engine for blowing it into the bargain. Shutter, the organist of Carisbury Cathedral, has just had a water-engine put in, and, now we've got our own new waterworks at Cullerne, we could manage it very well here too."

The subject did not interest Westray, and he flung back:

"Is Miss Joliffe very badly off?" he asked; "she looks like one of those people who have seen better days."

"She is worse than badly off—I believe she is half starved. I don't know how she lives at all. I wish I could help her, but I haven't a copper myself to jingle on a tombstone, and she is too proud to take it if I had."

He went to a cupboard in a recess at the back of the room, and took out a squat black bottle.

"Poverty's a chilly theme," he said; "let's take something to warm us before we go on with the variations."

He pushed the bottle towards his friend, but, though Westray felt inclined to give way, the principles of severe moderation which he had recently adopted restrained him, and he courteously waved away the temptation.

"You're hopeless," said the organist. "What are we to do for you, who neither smoke nor drink, and yet want to talk about poverty? This is some *eau-de-vie* old Martelet the solicitor gave me for playing the Wedding March at his daughter's marriage. 'The Wedding March was magnificently rendered by the organist, Mr John Sharnall,' you know, as if it was the Fourth Organ-Sonata. I misdoubt this ever having paid duty; he's not the man to give away six bottles of anything he'd paid the excise upon."

He poured out a portion of spirit far larger than Westray had expected, and then, becoming intuitively aware of his companion's surprise, said rather sharply: "If you despise good stuff, I must do duty for us both. Up to the top of the church windows is a good maxim." And he poured in yet more, till the spirit rose to the top of the cuts, which ran higher than halfway up the sides of the tumbler. There was silence for a few minutes, while the organist puffed testily at his pipe; but a copious draught from the tumbler melted his chagrin, and he spoke again:

"I've had a precious hard life, but Miss Joliffe's had a harder; and I've got myself to thank for my bad luck, while hers is due to other people. First, her father died. He had a farm at Wydcombe, and people thought he was well off; but when they came to reckon up, he only left just enough to go round among his creditors; so Miss Euphemia gave up the house, and came into Cullerne. She took this rambling great place because it was cheap at twenty pounds a year, and lived, or half lived, from hand to mouth, giving her niece (the girl you saw) all the grains, and keeping the husks for herself. Then a year ago turned up her brother Martin, penniless and broken, with paralysis upon him. He was a harum-scarum ne'er-do-well. Don't stare at me with that Saul-among-the-prophets look; *he* never drank; he would have been a better man if he had." And the organist made a further call on the squat bottle. "He would have given her less bother if he had drunk, but he was always getting into debt and trouble, and then used to come back to his sister, as to a refuge, because he knew she loved him.

"He was clever enough—brilliant they call it now—but unstable as water, with no lasting power. I don't believe he meant to sponge on his sister; I don't think he knew he did sponge, only he sponged. He would go off on his travels, no one knew where, though they knew well what he was seeking. Sometimes he was away two months, and sometimes he was away two years; and then, when Miss Joliffe had kept Anastasia—I mean her niece—all the time, and perhaps got a summer lodger, and seemed to be turning the corner, back would come Martin again to beg money for debts, and eat them out of house and home. I've seen that many a time, and many a time my heart has ached for them; but what could I do to help? I haven't a farthing. Last he came back a year ago, with death written on his face. I was glad enough to read it there, and think he was come for the last time to worry them; but it was paralysis, and he a strong man, so that it took that fool Ennefer a long time to kill him. He only died two months ago; here's better luck to him where he's gone."

The organist drank as deeply as the occasion warranted.

"Don't look so glum, man," he said; "I'm not always as bad as this, because I haven't always the means. Old Martelet doesn't give me brandy every day."

Westray smoothed away the deprecating expression with which

he had felt constrained to discountenance such excesses, and set Mr Sharnall's tongue going again with a question:

"What did you say Joliffe used to go away for?"

"Oh, it's a long story; it's the nebuly coat again. I spoke of it in the church—the silver and sea-green that turned his head. He would have it he wasn't a Joliffe at all, but a Blandamer, and rightful heir to Fording. As a boy, he went to Cullerne Grammar School, and did well, and got a scholarship at Oxford. He did still better there, and just when he seemed starting strong in the race of life, this nebuly coat craze seized him and crept over his mind, like the paralysis that crept over his body later on."

"I don't quite follow you," Westray said. "Why did he think he was a Blandamer? Did he not know who his father was?"

"He was brought up as a son of old Michael Joliffe, a yeoman who died fifteen years ago. But Michael married a woman who called herself a widow, and brought a three-year-old son ready-made to his wedding; and that son was Martin. Old Michael made the boy his own, was proud of his cleverness, would have him go to college, and left him all he had. There was no talk of Martin being anything but a Joliffe till Oxford puffed him up, and then he got this crank, and spent the rest of his life trying to find out who his father was. It was a forty-years' wandering in the wilderness; he found this clue and that, and thought at last he had climbed Pisgah and could see the promised land. But he had to be content with the sight, or mirage I suppose it was, and died before he tasted the milk and honey."

"What was his connection with the nebuly coat? What made him think he was a Blandamer?"

"Oh, I can't go into that now," the organist said; "I have told you too much, perhaps, already. You won't let Miss Joliffe guess I have said anything, will you? She is Michael Joliffe's own child—his only child—but she loved her half-brother dearly, and doesn't like his cranks being talked about. Of course, the Cullerne wags had many a tale to tell of him, and when he came back, greyer each time and wilder-looking, from his wanderings, they called him 'Old Nebuly,' and the boys would make their bow in the streets, and say 'Good-morning, Lord Blandamer.' You'll hear stories enough about him, and it was a bitter thing for his poor sister to bear, to see her brother a butt and laughing-stock, all the time that he was frittering away her savings. But it's all over now, and Martin's gone where they don't wear nebuly coats."

"There was nothing in his fancies, I suppose?" Westray asked.

"You must put that to wiser folk than me," said the organist lightly; "ask the rector, or the doctor, or some really clever man."

He had fallen back into his sneering tone, but there was something in his words that recalled a previous doubt, and led Westray to wonder whether Mr Sharnall had not lived so long with the Joliffes as to have become himself infected with Martin's delusions.

His companion was pouring out more brandy, and the architect wished him good-night.

Mr Westray's apartment was on the floor above, and he went at once to his bedroom; for he was very tired with his journey, and with standing so long in the church during the afternoon. He was pleased to find that his portmanteau had been unpacked, and that his clothes were carefully arranged in the drawers. This was a luxury to which he was little accustomed; there was, moreover, a fire to fling cheerful flickerings on spotlessly white curtains and bedlinen.

Miss Joliffe and Anastasia had between them carried the portmanteau up the great well-staircase of stone, which ran from top to bottom of the house. It was a task of some difficulty, and there were frequent pauses to take breath, and settings-down of the portmanteau to rest aching arms. But they got it up at last, and when the straps were undone Miss Euphemia dismissed her niece.

"No, my dear," she said; "let *me* set the things in order. It is not seemly that a young girl should arrange men's clothes. There was a time when I should not have liked to do so myself, but now I am so old it does not very much matter."

She gave a glance at the mirror as she spoke, adjusted a little bit of grizzled hair which had strayed from under her cap, and tried to arrange the bow of ribbon round her neck so that the frayed part should be as far as possible concealed. Anastasia Joliffe thought, as she left the room, that there were fewer wrinkles and a sweeter look than usual in the old face, and wondered that her aunt had never married. Youth looking at an old maid traces spinsterhood to man's neglect. It is so hard to read in sixty's plainness the beauty of sixteen—to think that underneath the placidity of advancing years may lie buried, yet unforgotten, the memory of suits urged ardently, and quenched long ago in tears.

Miss Euphemia put everything carefully away. The architect's wardrobe was of the most modest proportions, but to her it seemed well furnished, and even costly. She noted, however, with the eye of a sportsman marking down a covey, sundry holes, rents, and missing buttons, and resolved to devote her first leisure to their rectification. Such mending, in anticipation and accomplishment, forms, indeed, a well-defined and important pleasure of all properly constituted women above a certain age.

"Poor young man!" she said to herself. "I am afraid he has had no one to look after his clothes for a long time." And in her pity she rushed into the extravagance of lighting the bedroom fire.

After things were arranged upstairs, she went down to see that all was in order in Mr Westray's sitting-room, and, as she moved about there, she heard the organist talking to the architect in the room below. His voice was so deep and raucous that it seemed to jar the soles of her feet. She dusted lightly a certain structure which, resting in tiers above the chimney-piece, served to surround a looking-glass with meaningless little shelves and niches. Miss Joliffe had purchased this piece-of-resistance when Mrs Cazel, the widow of the ironmonger, had sold her household effects preparatory to leaving Cullerne.

"It is an overmantel, my dear," she had said to dubious Anastasia, when it was brought home. "I did not really mean to buy it, but I had not bought anything the whole morning, and the auctioneer looked so fiercely at me that I felt I must make a bid. Then no one else said anything, so here it is; but I dare say it will serve to smarten the room a little, and perhaps attract lodgers."

Since then it had been brightened with a coat of blue enamel paint, and a strip of Brusa silk which Martin had brought back from one of his wanderings was festooned at the side, so as to hide a patch where the quicksilver showed signs of peeling off. Miss Joliffe pulled the festoon a little forward, and adjusted in one of the side niches a present-for-a-good-girl cup and saucer which had been bought for herself at Beacon Hill Fair half a century ago. She wiped the glass dome that covered the basket of artificial fruit, she screwed up the "banner-screen" that projected from the mantelpiece, she straightened out the bead mat on which the stereoscope stood, and at last surveyed the room with an expression of complete satisfaction on her kindly face.

An hour later Westray was asleep, and Miss Joliffe was saying her prayers. She added a special thanksgiving for the providential direction to her house of so suitable and gentlemanly a lodger, and a special request that he might be happy whilst he should be under her roof. But her devotions were disturbed by the sound of Mr Sharnall's piano.

"He plays most beautifully," she said to her niece, as she put out the candle; "but I wish he would not play so late. I am afraid I have not thought so earnestly as I should at my prayers."

Anastasia Joliffe said nothing. She was grieved because the organist was thumping out old waltzes, and she knew by his playing that he had been drinking.

CHAPTER THREE

The Hand of God stood on the highest point in all the borough, and Mr Westray's apartments were in the third story. From the window of his sitting-room he could look out over the houses on to Cullerne Flat, the great tract of salt-meadows that separated the town from the sea. In the foreground was a broad expanse of red-tiled roofs; in the middle distance Saint Sepulchre's Church, with its tower and soaring ridges, stood out so enormous that it seemed as if every house in the place could have been packed within its walls; in the background was the blue sea.

In summer the purple haze hangs over the mouth of the estuary, and through the shimmer of the heat off the marsh, can be seen the silver windings of the Cull as it makes its way out to sea, and snow-white flocks of geese, and here and there the gleaming sail of a pleasure-boat. But in autumn, as Westray saw it for the first time, the rank grass is of a deeper green, and the face of the salt-meadows is seamed with irregular clay-brown channels, which at high-tide show out like crows'-feet on an ancient countenance, but at the ebb dwindle to little gullies with greasy-looking banks and a dribble of iridescent water in the bottom. It is in the autumn that the moles heap up meanders of miniature barrows, built of the softest brown loam; and in the turbaries the turf-cutters pile larger and darker stacks of peat.

Once upon a time there was another feature in the view, for there could have been seen the masts and yards of many stately ships, of timber vessels in the Baltic trade, of tea-clippers, and Indiamen, and emigrant ships, and now and then the raking spars of a privateer owned by Cullerne adventurers. All these had long since sailed for their last port, and of ships nothing more imposing met the eye than the mast of Dr Ennefer's centre-board laid up for the winter in a backwater. Yet the scene was striking enough, and those who knew best said that nowhere in the town was there so fine an outlook as from the upper windows of the Hand of God.

Many had looked out from those windows upon that scene: the

skipper's wife as her eyes followed her husband's barque warping down the river for the voyage from which he never came back; honeymoon couples who broke the posting journey from the West at Cullerne, and sat hand in hand in summer twilight, gazing seaward till the white mists rose over the meadows and Venus hung brightening in the violet sky; old Captain Frobisher, who raised the Cullerne Yeomanry, and watched with his spy-glass for the French vanguard to appear; and, lastly, Martin Joliffe, as he sat dying day by day in his easy-chair, and scheming how he would spend the money when he should come into the inheritance of all the Blandamers.

Westray had finished breakfast, and stood for a time at the open window. The morning was soft and fine, and there was that brilliant clearness in the air that so often follows heavy autumn rain. His full enjoyment of the scene was, however, marred by an obstruction which impeded free access to the window. It was a case of ferns, which seemed to be formed of an aquarium turned upside down, and supported by a plain wooden table.

Westray took a dislike to the dank-looking plants, and to the moisture beaded on the glass inside, and made up his mind that the ferns must be banished. He would ask Miss Joliffe if she could take them away, and this determination prompted him to consider whether there were any other articles of furniture with which it would be advisable to dispense.

He made a mental inventory of his surroundings. There were several pieces of good mahogany furniture, including some open-backed chairs, and a glass-fronted book-case, which were survivals from the yeoman's equipment at Wydcombe Farm. They had been put up for auction with the rest of Michael Joliffe's effects, but Cullerne taste considered them old-fashioned, and no bidders were found for them. Many things, on the other hand, such as bead mats, and wool-work mats, and fluff mats, a case of wax fruit, a basket of shell flowers, chairs with worsted-work backs, sofa-cushions with worsted-work fronts, two cheap vases full of pampas-grass, and two candlesticks with dangling prisms, grated sadly on Westray's taste, which he had long since been convinced was of all tastes the most impeccable.

There were a few pictures on the walls—a coloured representation of young Martin Joliffe in Black Forest costume, a faded photograph of a boating crew, and another of a group in front of some ruins, which was taken when the Carisbury Field Club made an expedition to Wydcombe Abbey. Besides these, there were conventional copies in oils of a shipwreck, and an avalanche, and a painting of still-life representing a bowl full of flowers.

This last picture weighed on Westray's mind by reason of its size, its faulty drawing, and vulgar, flashy colours. It hung full in front of him while he sat at breakfast, and though its details amused him for the time, he felt it would become an eyesore if he should continue to occupy the room. In it was represented the polished top of a mahogany table on which stood a blue and white china bowl filled with impossible flowers. The bowl occupied one side of the picture, and the other side was given up to a meaningless expanse of table-top. The artist had perceived, but apparently too late, the bad balance of the composition, and had endeavoured to redress this by a few more flowers thrown loose upon the table. Towards these flowers a bulbous green caterpillar was wriggling, at the very edge of the table, and of the picture.

The result of Westray's meditations was that the fern-case and the flower-picture stood entirely condemned. He would approach Miss Joliffe at the earliest opportunity about their removal. He anticipated little trouble in modifying by degrees many other smaller details, but previous experience in lodgings had taught him that the removal of pictures is sometimes a difficult and delicate problem.

He opened his rolls of plans, and selecting those which he required, prepared to start for the church, where he had to arrange with the builder for the erection of scaffolding. He wished to order dinner before he left, and pulled a broad worsted-work bell-pull to summon his landlady. For some little time he had been aware of the sound of a fiddle, and as he listened, waiting for the bell to be answered, the intermittance and reiteration of the music convinced him that the organist was giving a violin lesson. His first summons remained unanswered, and when a second attempt met with no better success, he gave several testy pulls in quick succession. This time he heard the music cease, and made no doubt that his indignant ringing had attracted the notice of the musicians, and that the organist had gone to tell Miss Joliffe that she was wanted.

He was ruffled by such want of attention, and when there came at last a knock at his door, was quite prepared to expostulate with his landlady on her remissness. As she entered the room, he began, without turning from his drawings:

"Never knock, please, when you answer the bell; but I do wish you—"

Here he broke off, for on looking up he found he was speaking, not to the elder Miss Joliffe, but to her niece Anastasia. The girl was graceful, as he had seen the evening before, and again he noticed the peculiar fineness of her waving brown hair. His annoyance had instantaneously vanished, and he experienced to the full the embarrassment natural to a sensitive mind on finding a servant's role played by a lady, for that Anastasia Joliffe was a lady he had no doubt at all. Instead of blaming her, he seemed to be himself in fault for having somehow brought about an anomalous position.

She stood with downcast eyes, but his chiding tone had brought a slight flush to her cheeks, and this flush began a discomfiture for Westray, that was turned into a rout when she spoke.

"I am very sorry, I am afraid I have kept you waiting. I did not hear your bell at first, because I was busy in another part of the house, and then I thought my aunt had answered it. I did not know she was out."

It was a low, sweet voice, with more of weariness in it than of humility. If he chose to blame her, she was ready to take the blame; but it was Westray who now stammered some incoherent apologies. Would she kindly tell Miss Joliffe that he would be in for dinner at one o'clock, and that he was quite indifferent as to what was provided for him. The girl showed some relief at his blundering courtesy, and it was not till she had left the room that Westray recollected that he had heard that Cullerne was celebrated for its red mullet; he had meant to order red mullet for dinner. Now that he was mortifying the flesh by drinking only water, he was proportionately particular to please his appetite in eating. Yet he was not sorry that he had forgotten the fish; it would surely have been a bathos to discuss the properties and application of red mullet with a young lady who found herself in so tragically lowly a position.

After Westray had set out for the church, Anastasia Joliffe went back to Mr Sharnall's room, for it was she who had been playing the violin. The organist sat at the piano, drumming chords in an impatient and irritated way.

"Well," he said, without looking at her as she came in—"well, what does my lord want with my lady? What has he made you run up to the top of the house for now? I wish I could wring his neck for him. Here we are out of breath, as usual, and our hands shaking; we shan't be able to play even as well as we did before, and that isn't saying much. Why," he cried, as he looked at her, "you're as red as a turkey-cock. I believe he's been making love to you."

"Mr Sharnall," she retorted quickly, "if you say those things I will never come to your room again. I hate you when you speak like that, and fancy you are not yourself."

She took her violin, and putting it under her arm, plucked arpeggio sharply.

"There," he said, "don't take all I say so seriously; it is only because I am out of health and out of temper. Forgive me, child; I know well enough that there'll be no lovemaking with you till the right man comes, and I hope he never will come, Anastasia—I hope he never will."

She did not accept or refuse his excuses, but tuned a string that had gone down.

"Good heavens!" he said, as she walked to the music-stand to play; "can't you hear the A's as flat as a pancake?"

She tightened the string again without speaking, and began the movement in which they had been interrupted. But her thoughts were not with the music, and mistake followed mistake.

"What *are* you doing?" said the organist. "You're worse than you were when we began five years ago. It's mere waste of time for you to go on, and for me, too."

Then he saw that she was crying in the bitterness of vexation, and swung round on his music-stool without getting up.

"Anstice, I didn't mean it, dear. I didn't mean to be such a brute. You are getting on well—well; and as for wasting my time, why, I haven't got anything to do, nor anyone to teach except you, and you know I would slave all day and all night, too, if I could give you any pleasure by it. Don't cry. Why are you crying?"

She laid the violin on the table, and sitting down in that rush-bottomed chair in which Westray had sat the night before, put her head between her hands and burst into tears.

"Oh," she said between her sobs in a strange and uncontrolled voice—"oh, I am so miserable—*everything* is so miserable. There are father's debts not paid, not even the undertaker's bill paid for his funeral, and no money for anything, and poor Aunt Euphemia working herself to death. And now she says she will have to sell the little things we have in the house, and then when there is a chance of a decent lodger, a quiet, gentlemanly man, you go and abuse him, and say these rude things to me, because he rings the bell. How does he know aunt is out? how does he know she won't let me answer the bell when she's in? Of course, he thinks we have a servant, and then *you* make me so sad. I couldn't sleep last night, because I knew you were drinking. I heard you when we went to bed playing trashy things that you hate except when you are not yourself. It makes me ill to think that you have been with us all these years, and been so kind to me, and now are come to this. Oh, do not do it! Surely we all are wretched enough, without your adding this to our wretchedness."

He got up from the stool and took her hand.

"Don't, Anstice—don't! I broke myself of it before, and I will break myself again. It was a woman drove me to it then, and sent me down the hill, and now I didn't know there was a living soul would care whether old Sharnall drank himself to death or not. If I could only think there was someone who cared; if I could only think you cared."

"Of course I care"—and as she felt his hand tighten she drew her own lightly away—"of course we care—poor aunt and I—or she would care, if she knew, only she is so good she doesn't guess. I hate to see those horrid glasses taken in after your supper. It used to be so different, and I loved to hear the 'Pastoral' and '*Les Adieux*' going when the house was still."

It is sad when man's unhappiness veils from him the smiling face of nature. The promise of the early morning was maintained. The sky was of a translucent blue, broken with islands and continents of clouds, dazzling white like cotton-wool. A soft, warm breeze blew from the west, the birds sang merrily in every garden bush, and Cullerne was a town of gardens, where men could sit each under his own vine and fig-tree. The bees issued forth from their hives, and hummed with cheery droning chorus in the ivy-berries that covered the wall-tops with deep purple. The old vanes on the corner pinnacles of Saint Sepulchre's tower shone as if they had been regilt. Great flocks of plovers flew wheeling over Cullerne marsh, and flashed with a blinking silver gleam as they changed their course suddenly. Even through the open window of the organist's room fell a shaft of golden sunlight that lit up the peonies of the faded, threadbare carpet.

But inside beat two poor human hearts, one unhappy and one hopeless, and saw nothing of the gold vanes, or the purple ivy-berries, or the plovers, or the sunlight, and heard nothing of the birds or the bees.

"Yes, I will give it up," said the organist, though not quite so enthusiastically as before; and as he moved closer to Anastasia Joliffe, she got up and left the room, laughing as she went out.

"I must get the potatoes peeled, or you will have none for dinner."

Mr Westray, being afflicted neither with poverty nor age, but having a good digestion and entire confidence both in himself and in his prospects, could fully enjoy the beauty of the day. He walked this morning as a child of the light, forsaking the devious back-ways through which the organist had led him on the previous night, and choosing the main streets on his road to the church. He received this time a different impression of the town. The heavy rain had washed the pavements and roadway, and as he entered the Market Square he was struck with the cheerfulness of the prospect, and with the air of quiet prosperity which pervaded the place.

On two sides of the square the houses overhung the pavement, and formed an arcade supported on squat pillars of wood. Here were situated some of the best "establishments," as their owners delighted to call them. Custance, the grocer; Rose and Storey, the drapers, who occupied the fronts of no less than three houses, and had besides a "department" round the corner "exclusively devoted to tailoring"; Lucy, the bookseller, who printed the *Cullerne Examiner*, and had published several of Canon Parkyn's sermons, as well as a tractate by Dr Ennefer on the means adopted in Cullerne for the suppression of cholera during the recent outbreak; Calvin, the saddler; Miss Adcutt, of the toyshop; and Prior, the chemist, who was also postmaster.

In the middle of the third side stood the Blandamer Arms, with a long front of buff, low green blinds, and window-sashes grained to imitate oak. At the edge of the pavement before the inn were some stone mounting steps, and by them stood a tall white pole, on which swung the green and silver of the nebuly coat itself. On either side of the Blandamer Arms clustered a few more modern shops, which, possessing no arcade, had to be content with awnings of brown stuff with red stripes. One of these places of business was occupied by Mr Joliffe, the pork-butcher. He greeted Westray through the open window.

"Good-morning. About your work betimes, I see," pointing to the roll of drawings which the architect carried under his arm. "It is a great privilege, this restoration to which you are called," and here he shifted a chop into a more attractive position on the show-board—"and I trust blessing will attend your efforts. I often manage to snatch a few minutes from the whirl of business about mid-day myself, and seek a little quiet meditation in the church. If you are there then, I shall be glad to give you any help in my power. Meanwhile, we must both be busy with our own duties."

He began to turn the handle of a sausage-machine, and Westray was glad to be quit of his pious words, and still more of his insufferable patronage.

CHAPTER FOUR

The north side of Cullerne Church, which faced the square, was still in shadow, but, as Westray stepped inside, he found the sunshine pouring through the south windows, and the whole building bathed in a flood of most mellow light. There are in England many churches larger than that of Saint Sepulchre, and fault has been found with its proportions, because the roof is lower than in some other conventual buildings of its size. Yet, for all this, it is doubtful whether architecture has ever produced a composition more truly dignified and imposing.

The nave was begun by Walter Le Bec in 1135, and has on either side an arcade of low, round-headed arches. These arches are divided from one another by cylindrical pillars, which have no incised ornamentation, as at Durham or Waltham or Lindisfarne, nor are masked with Perpendicular work, as in the nave of Winchester or in the choir of Gloucester, but rely for effect on severe plainness and great diameter. Above them is seen the dark and cavernous depth of the triforium, and higher yet the clerestory with minute and infrequent openings. Over all broods a stone vault, divided across and diagonally by the chevron-mouldings of heavy vaulting-ribs.

Westray sat down near the door, and was so engrossed in the study of the building and in the strange play of the shafts of sunlight across the massive stonework, that half an hour passed before he rose to walk up the church.

A solid stone screen separates the choir from the nave, making, as it were, two churches out of one; but as Westray opened the doors between them, he heard four voices calling to him, and, looking up, saw above his head the four tower arches. "The arch never sleeps," cried one. "They have bound on us a burden too heavy to be borne," answered another. "We never sleep," said the third; and the fourth returned to the old refrain, "The arch never sleeps, never sleeps."

As he considered them in the daylight, he wondered still more at their breadth and slenderness, and was still more surprised that his chief had made so light of the settlement and of the ominous crack in the south wall.

The choir is a hundred and forty years later than the nave, ornate

Early English, with a multiplication of lancet-windows which rich hood-mouldings group into twos and threes, and at the east end into seven. Here are innumerable shafts of dark-grey purbeck marble, elaborate capitals, deeply undercut foliage, and broad-winged angels bearing up the vaulting shafts on which rests the sharply-pointed roof.

The spiritual needs of Cullerne were amply served by this portion of the church alone, and, except at confirmations or on Militia Sunday, the congregation never overflowed into the nave. All who came to the minster found there full accommodation, and could indeed worship in much comfort; for in front of the canopied stalls erected by Abbot Vinnicomb in 1530 were ranged long rows of pews, in which green baize and brass nails, cushions and hassocks, and Prayer-Book boxes ministered to the devotion of the occupants. Anybody who aspired to social status in Cullerne rented one of these pews, but for as many as could not afford such luxury in their religion there were provided other seats of deal, which had, indeed, no baize or hassocks, nor any numbers on the doors, but were, for all that, exceedingly appropriate and commodious.

The clerk was dusting the stalls as the architect entered the choir, and made for him at once as the hawk swoops on its quarry. Westray did not attempt to escape his fate, and hoped, indeed, that from the old man's garrulity he might glean some facts of interest about the building, which was to be the scene of his work for many months to come. But the clerk preferred to talk of people rather than of things, and the conversation drifted by easy stages to the family with whom Westray had taken up his abode.

The doubt as to the Joliffe ancestry, in the discussion of which Mr Sharnall had shown such commendable reticence, was not so sacred to the clerk. He rushed in where the organist had feared to tread, nor did Westray feel constrained to check him, but rather led the talk to Martin Joliffe and his imaginary claims.

"Lor' bless you!" said the clerk, "I was a little boy myself when Martin's mother runned away with the soldier, yet mind well how it was in everybody's mouth. But folks in Cullerne like novelties; it's all old-world talk now, and there ain't one perhaps, beside me and rector, could tell you *that* tale. Sophia Flannery her name was when Farmer Joliffe married her, and where he found her no one knew. He lived up at Wydcombe Farm, did Michael Joliffe, where his father lived afore him, and a gay one he was, and dressed in yellow breeches and a blue waistcoat all his time. Well, one day he gave out he was to be married, and came into Cullerne, and there was Sophia waiting for him at the Blandamer Arms, and they were married in this very church. She had a three-year-old boy with her then, and put about she was a widow, though there were many who thought she couldn't show her marriage lines if she'd been asked for them. But p'raps Farmer Joliffe never asked to see 'em, or p'raps he knew all about it.

"A fine upstanding woman she was, with a word and a laugh for everyone, as my father told me many a time; and she had a bit of money beside. Every quarter, up she'd go to London town to collect her rents, so she said, and every time she'd come back with terrible grand new clothes. She dressed that fine, and had such a way with her, the people called her Queen of Wydcombe. Wherever she come from, she had a boarding-school education, and could play and sing beautiful. Many a time of a summer evening we lads would walk up to Wydcombe, and sit on the fence near the farm, to hear Sophy a-singing through the open window. She'd a pianoforty, too, and would sing powerful long songs about captains and moustachers and broken hearts, till people was nearly fit to cry over it. And when she wasn't singing she was painting. My old missis had a picture of flowers what she painted, and there was a lot more sold when they had to give up the farm. But Miss Joliffe wouldn't part with the biggest of 'em, though there was many would ha' liked to buy it. No, she kep' that one, and has it by her to this day—a picture so big as a signboard, all covered with flowers most beautiful."

"Yes, I've seen that," Westray put in; "it's in my room at Miss Joliffe's."

He said nothing about its ugliness, or that he meant to banish it, not wishing to wound the narrator's artistic susceptibilities, or to interrupt a story which began to interest him in spite of himself.

"Well, to be sure!" said the clerk, "it used to hang in the best parlour at Wydcombe over the sideboard; I seed'n there when I was a boy, and my mother was helping spring-clean up at the farm. 'Look, Tom,' my mother said to me, 'did 'ee ever see such flowers? and such a pritty caterpillar a-going to eat them!' You mind, a green caterpillar down in the corner."

Westray nodded, and the clerk went on:

"'Well, Mrs Joliffe,' says my mother to Sophia, 'I never want for to see a more beautiful picture than that.' And Sophia laughed, and said my mother know'd a good picture when she saw one. Some folks 'ud stand her out, she said, that 'tweren't worth much, but she knew she could get fifty or a hundred pound or more for't any day she liked to sell, if she took it to the right people. *Then* she'd soon have the laugh of those that said it were only a daub; and with that she laughed herself, for she were always laughing and always jolly.

"Michael were well pleased with his strapping wife, and used to like to see the people stare when he drove her into Cullerne Market in the high cart, and hear her crack jokes with the farmers what they passed on the way. Very proud he was of her, and prouder still when one Saturday he stood all comers glasses round at the Blandamer, and bid 'em drink to a pritty little lass what his wife had given him. Now he'd got a brace of 'em, he said; for he'd kep' that other little boy what Sophia brought when she married him, and treated the child for all the world as if he was his very son.

"So 'twas for a year or two, till the practice-camp was put up on Wydcombe Down. I mind that summer well, for 'twere a fearful hot one, and Joey Garland and me taught ourselves to swim in the sheep-wash down in Mayo's Meads. And there was the white tents all up the hillside, and the brass band a-playing in the evenings before the officers' dinner-tent. And sometimes they would play Sunday afternoons too; and parson were terrible put about, and wrote to the colonel to say as how the music took the folk away from church, and likened it to the worship of the golden calf, when 'the people sat down to eat and drink, and rose up again to play.' But colonel never took no notice of it, and when 'twas a fine evening there was a mort of people trapesing over the Downs, and some poor lasses wished afterwards they'd never heard no music sweeter than the clar'net and bassoon up in the gallery of Wydcombe Church.

"Sophia was there, too, a good few times, walking round first on her husband's arm, and afterwards on other people's; and some of the boys said they had seen her sitting with a redcoat up among the juniper-bushes. 'Twas Michaelmas Eve before they moved the camp, and 'twas a sorry goose was eat that Michaelmas Day at Wydcombe Farm; for when the soldiers went, Sophia went too, and left Michael and the farm and the children, and never said goodbye to anyone, not even to the baby in the cot. 'Twas said she ran off with a sergeant, but no one rightly knew; and if Farmer Joliffe made any search and found out, he never told a soul; and she never come back to Wydcombe.

"She never come back to Wydcombe," he said under his breath, with something that sounded like a sigh. Perhaps the long-forgotten break-up of Farmer Joliffe's home had touched him, but perhaps he was only thinking of his own loss, for he went on: "Ay, many's the time she would give a poor fellow an ounce of baccy, and many's the pound of tea she sent to a labourer's cottage. If she bought herself fine clothes, she'd give away the old ones; my missis has a fur tippet yet that her mother got from Sophy Joliffe. She was free with her money, whatever else she mid have been. There wasn't a labourer on the farm but what had a good word for her; there wasn't one was glad to see her back turned.

"Poor Michael took on dreadful at the first, though he wasn't the man to say much. He wore his yellow breeches and blue waistcoat just the same, but lost heart for business, and didn't go to market so reg'lar as he should. Only he seemed to stick closer by the children—by Martin that never know'd his father, and little Phemie that never know'd her mother. Sophy never come back to visit 'em by what I could learn; but once I seed her myself twenty years later, when I took the hosses over to sell at Beacon Hill Fair.

"That was a black day, too, for 'twas the first time Michael had to raise the wind by selling aught of his'n. He'd got powerful thin then, had poor master, and couldn't fill the blue waistcoat and yellow breeches like he used to, and *they* weren't nothing so gay by then themselves neither.

"'Tom,' he said—that's me, you know—'take these here hosses over to Beacon Hill, and sell 'em for as much as 'ee can get, for I want the money.'

"'What, sell the best team, dad!' says Miss Phemie—for she was standing by—'you'll never sell the best team with White-face and old Strike-a-light!' And the hosses looked up, for they know'd their names very well when she said 'em.

"'Don't 'ee take on, lass,' he said; 'we'll buy 'em back again come Lady Day.'

"And so I took 'em over, and knew very well why he wanted the money; for Mr Martin had come back from Oxford, wi' a nice bit of debt about his neck, and couldn't turn his hand to the farm, but went about saying he was a Blandamer, and Fording and all the lands belonged to he by right. 'Quiries he was making, he said, and gadded about here and there, spending a mort of time and money in making 'quiries that never came to nothing. 'Twas a black day, that day, and a thick rain falling at Beacon Hill, and all the turf cut up terrible. The poor beasts was wet through, too, and couldn't look their best, because they knowed they was going to be sold; and so the afternoon came, and never a bid for one of 'em. 'Poor old master!' says I to the horses, 'what'll 'ee say when we get back again?' And yet I was glad-like to think me and they weren't going to part.

"Well, there we was a-standing in the rain, and the farmers and the dealers just give us a glimpse, and passed by without a word, till I see someone come along, and that was Sophia Joliffe. She didn't look a year older nor when I met her last, and her face was the only cheerful thing we saw that afternoon, as fresh and jolly as ever. She wore a yellow mackintosh with big buttons, and everybody turned to measure her up as she passed. There was a horse-dealer walking with her, and when the people stared, he looked at her just so proud as Michael used to look when he drove her in to Cullerne Market. She didn't take any heed of the hosses, but she looked hard at me, and when she was passed turned her head to have another look, and then she come back.

"'Bain't you Tom Janaway,' says she, 'what used to work up to Wydcombe Farm?'

"'Ay, that I be,' says I, but stiff-like, for it galled me to think what she'd a-done for master, and yet could look so jolly with it all.

"She took no note that I were glum, but 'Whose hosses is these?' she asked.

"'Your husband's, mum,' I made bold to say, thinking to take her down a peg. But, lor'! she didn't care a rush for that, but 'Which o' my husbands?' says she, and laughed fit to bust, and poked the horse-dealer in the side. He looked as if he'd like to throttle her, but she didn't mind that neither. 'What for does Michael want to sell his hosses?'

"And then I lost my pluck, and didn't think to humble her any more, but just told her how things was, and how I'd stood the blessed day, and never got a bid. She never asked no questions, but I see her eyes twinkle when I spoke of Master Martin and Miss Phemie; and then she turned sharp to the horse-dealer and said:

"'John, these is fine horses; you buy these cheap-like, and we can sell 'em again tomorrow.'

"Then he cursed and swore, and said the hosses was old scraws, and he'd be damned afore he'd buy such hounds'-meat.

"'John,' says she, quite quiet, ''tain't polite to swear afore ladies. These here is good hosses, and I want you to buy 'em.'

"Then he swore again, but she'd got his measure, and there was a mighty firm look in her face, for all she laughed so; and by degrees he quieted down and let her talk.

"'How much do you want for the four of 'em, young man?' she says; and I had a mind to say eighty pounds, thinking maybe she'd rise to that for old times' sake, but didn't like to say so much for fear of spoiling the bargain. 'Come,' she says, 'how much? Art thou dumb? Well, if thou won't fix the price, I'll do it for 'ee. Here, John, you bid a hundred for this lot.'

"He stared stupid-like, but didn't speak.

"Then she look at him hard.

"'You've got to do it,' she says, speaking low, but very firm; and out he comes with, 'Here, I'll give 'ee a hundred.' But before I had time to say 'Done,' she went on: 'No—this young man says no; I can see it in his face; he don't think 'tis enough; you try him with a hundred and twenty.'

"'Twas as if he were overlooked, for he says quite mild, 'Well, I'll give 'ee a hundred and twenty.'

"'Ay, that's better,' says she; 'he says that's better.' And she takes out a little leather wallet from her bosom, holding it under the flap of her waterproof so that the rain shouldn't get in, and counts out two dozen clean banknotes, and puts 'em into my hand. There was many more where they come from, for I could see the book was full of 'em; and when she saw my eyes on them, she takes out another, and gives it me, with, 'There's one for thee, and good luck to 'ee; take that, and buy a fairing for thy sweetheart, Tom Janaway, and never say Sophy Flannery forgot an old friend.'

"'Thank 'ee kindly, mum,' says I; 'thank 'ee kindly, and may you never miss it! I hope your rents do still come in reg'lar, mum.'

"She laughed out loud, and said there was no fear of that; and then she called a lad, and he led off White-face and Strike-a-light and Jenny and the Cutler, and they was all gone, and the horse-dealer and Sophia, afore I had time to say goodnight. She never come into these parts again—at least, I never seed her; but I heard tell she lived a score of years more after that, and died of a broken blood-vessel at Beriton Races."

He moved a little further down the choir, and went on with his dusting; but Westray followed, and started him again.

"What happened when you got back? You haven't told me what Farmer Joliffe said, nor how you came to leave farming and turn clerk."

The old man wiped his forehead.

"I wasn't going to tell 'ee that," he said, "for it do fair make I sweat still to think o' it; but you can have it if you like. Well, when they was gone, I was nigh dazed with such a stroke o' luck, and said the Lord's Prayer to see I wasn't dreaming. But 'twas no such thing, and so I cut a slit in the lining of my waistcoat, and dropped the notes in, all except the one she give me for myself, and that I put in my fob-pocket. 'Twas getting dark, and I felt numb with cold and wet, what with standing so long in the rain and not having bite nor sup all day.

"'Tis a bleak place, Beacon Hill, and 'twas so soft underfoot that day the water'd got inside my boots, till they fair bubbled if I took a step. The rain was falling steady, and sputtered in the naphtha-lamps that they was beginning to light up outside the booths. There was one powerful flare outside a long tent, and from inside there come a smell of fried onions that made my belly cry 'Please, master, please!'

"'Yes, my lad,' I said to un, 'I'm darned if I don't humour 'ee; thou shan't go back to Wydcombe empty.' So in I step, and found the tent mighty warm and well lit, with men smoking and women laughing, and a great smell of cooking. There were long tables set on trestles down the tent, and long benches beside 'em, and folks eating and drinking, and a counter cross the head of the room, and great tin dishes simmering a-top of it—trotters and sausages and tripe, bacon and beef and colliflowers, cabbage and onions, blood-puddings and plum-duff. It seemed like a chance to change my banknote, and see whether 'twere good and not elf-money that folks have found turn to leaves in their pocket. So up I walks, and bids 'em gie me a plate of beef and jack-pudding, and holds out my note for't. The maid—for 'twas a maid behind the counter—took it, and then she looks at it and then at me, for I were very wet and muddy; and then she carries it to the gaffer, and he shows it to his wife, who holds it up to the light, and then they all fall to talking, and showed it to a 'cise-man what was there marking down the casks.

"The people sitting nigh saw what was up, and fell to staring at me till I felt hot enough, and lief to leave my note where 'twas, and get out and back to Wydcombe. But the 'cise-man must have said 'twere all right, for the gaffer comes back with four gold sovereigns and nineteen shillings, and makes a bow and says:

"'Your servant, sir; can I give you summat to drink?'

"I looked round to see what liquor there was, being main glad all the while to find the note were good; and he says:

"'Rum and milk is very helping, sir; try the rum and milk hot.'

"So I took a pint of rum and milk, and sat down at the nighest table, and the people as were waiting to see me took up, made room now, and stared as if I'd been a lord. I had another plate o' beef, and another rum-and-milk, and then smoked a pipe, knowing they wouldn't make no bother of my being late that night at Wydcombe, when I brought back two dozen banknotes.

"The meat and drink heartened me, and the pipe and the warmth of the tent seemed to dry my clothes and take away the damp, and I didn't feel the water any longer in my boots. The company was pleasant, too, and some very genteel dealers sitting near.

"'My respec's to you, sir,' says one, holding up his glass to me—'best respec's. These pore folk isn't used to the flimsies, and was a bit surprised at your paper-money; but directly I see you, I says to my friends, "Mates, that gentleman's one of us; that's a monied man, if ever I see one." I knew you for a gentleman the minute you come in.'

"So I was flattered like, and thought if they made so much o' one banknote, what'd they say to know I'd got a pocket full of them? But didn't speak nothing, only chuckled a bit to think I could buy up half the tent if I had a mind to. After that I stood 'em drinks, and they stood me, and we passed a very pleasant evening—the more so because when we got confidential, and I knew they were men of honour, I proved that I was worthy to mix with such by showing 'em I had a packet of banknotes handy. They drank more respec's, and one of them said as how the liquor we were swallowing weren't fit for such a gentleman as me; so he took a flask out o' his pocket, and filled me a glass of his own tap, what his father 'ud bought in the same year as Waterloo. 'Twas powerful strong stuff that, and made me blink to get it down; but I took it with a good face, not liking to show I didn't know old liquor when it come my way.

"So we sat till the tent was very close, and them hissing naphtha-lamps burnt dim with tobacco-smoke. 'Twas still raining outside, for you could hear the patter heavy on the roof; and where there was a belly in the canvas, the water began to come through and drip inside. There was some rough talking and wrangling among folk who had been drinking; and I knew I'd had as much as I could carry myself, 'cause my voice sounded like someone's else, and I had to think a good bit before I could get out the words. 'Twas then a bell rang, and the 'size-man called out, 'Closing time,' and the gaffer behind the counter said, 'Now, my lads, goodnight to 'ee; hope the fleas won't bite 'ee. God save the Queen, and give us a merry meeting tomorrow.' So all got up, and pulled their coats over their ears to go out, except half a dozen what was too heavy, and was let lie for the night on the grass under the trestles.

"I couldn't walk very firm myself, but my friends took me one under each arm; and very kind of them it was, for when we got into the open air, I turned sleepy and giddy-like. I told 'em where I lived to, and they said never fear, they'd see me home, and knew a cut through the fields what'd take us to Wydcombe much shorter. We started off, and went a bit into the dark; and then the very next thing I know'd was something blowing in my face, and woke up and found a white heifer snuffing at me. 'Twas broad daylight, and me lying under a hedge in among the cuckoo-pints. I was wet through, and muddy (for 'twas a loamy ditch), and a bit dazed still, and sore ashamed; but when I thought of the bargain I'd made for master, and of the money I'd got in my waistcoat, I took heart, and reached in my hand to take out the notes, and see they weren't wasted with the wet.

"But there was no notes there—no, not a bit of paper, for all I turned my waistcoat inside out, and ripped up the lining. 'Twas only half a mile from Beacon Hill that I was lying, and I soon made my way back to the fair-ground, but couldn't find my friends of the evening before, and the gaffer in the drinking-tent said he couldn't remember as he'd ever seen any such. I spent the livelong day searching here and there, till the folks laughed at me, because I looked so wild with drinking the night before, and with sleeping out, and with having nothing to eat; for every penny was took from me. I told the constable, and he took it all down, but I see him looking at me the while, and at the torn lining hanging out under my waistcoat, and knew he thought 'twas only a light tale, and that I had the drink still in me. 'Twas dark afore I give it up, and turned to go back.

"'Tis seven mile good by the nigh way from Beacon Hill to Wydcombe; and I was dog-tired, and hungry, and that shamed I stopped a half-hour on the bridge over Proud's mill-head, wishing to throw myself in and ha' done with it, but couldn't bring my mind to that, and so went on, and got to Wydcombe just as they was going to bed. They stared at me, Farmer Michael, and Master Martin, and Miss Phemie, as if I was a spirit, while I told my tale; but I never said as how 'twas Sophia Joliffe as had bought the horses. Old Michael, he said nothing, but had a very blank look on his face, and Miss Phemie was crying; but Master Martin broke out saying 'twas all make-up, and I'd stole the money, and they must send for a constable.

"''Tis lies,' he said. 'This fellow's a rogue, and too great a fool even to make up a tale that'll hang together. Who's going to believe a woman 'ud buy the team, and give a hundred and twenty pounds in notes for hosses that 'ud be dear at seventy pounds? Who was the woman? Did 'ee know her? There must be many in the fair 'ud know such a woman. They ain't so common as go about with their pockets full of banknotes, and pay double price for hosses what they buy.'

"I knew well enough who'd bought 'em, but didn't want to give her name for fear of grieving Farmer Joliffe more nor he was grieved already, so said nothing, but held my peace.

"Then the farmer says: 'Tom, I believe 'ee; I've know'd 'ee thirty year, and never know'd 'ee tell a lie, and I believe 'ee now. But if thou knows her name, tell it us, and if thou doesn't know, tell us what she looked like, and maybe some of us 'll guess her.'

"But still I didn't say aught till Master Martin goes on:

"'Out with her name. He must know her name right enough, if there ever was a woman as did buy the hosses; and don't you be so soft, father, as to trust such fool's tales. We'll get a constable for 'ee. Out with her name, I say.'

"Then I was nettled like, at his speaking so rough, when the man that suffered had forgiven me, and said:

"'Yes, I know her name right enough, if 'ee will have it. 'Twas the missis.'

"'Missis?' he says; 'what missis?'

"'Your mother,' says I. 'She was with a man, but he weren't the man she runned away from here with, and she made he buy the team.'

"Master Martin didn't say any more, and Miss Phemie went on crying; but there was a blanker look come on old master's face, and he said very quiet:

"'There, that'll do, lad. I believe 'ee, and forgive thee. Don't matter much to I now if I have lost a hundred pound. 'Tis only my luck, and if 'tweren't lost there, 'twould just as like be lost somewhere else. Go in and wash thyself, and get summat to eat; and if I forgive 'ee this time, don't 'ee ever touch the drink again.'

"'Master,' I says, 'I thank 'ee, and if I ever get a bit o' money I'll pay thee back what I can; and there's my sacred word I'll never touch the drink again.'

"I held him out my hand, and he took it, for all 'twas so dirty.

"'That's right, lad; and tomorrow we'll put the p'leece on to trace them fellows down.'

"I kep' my promise, Mr—Mr—Mr—"

"Westray," the architect suggested.

"I didn't know your name, you see, because rector never introduced *me* yesterday. I kep' my promise, Mr Westray, and bin teetotal ever since; but he never put the p'leece on the track, for he was took with a stroke next morning early, and died a fortnight later. They laid him up to Wydcombe nigh his father and his grandfather, what have green rails round their graves; and give his yellow breeches and blue waistcoat to Timothy Foord the shepherd, and he wore them o' Sundays for many a year after that. I left farming the same day as old master was put underground, and come into Cullerne, and took odd jobs till the sexton fell sick, and then I helped dig graves; and when he died they made I sexton, and that were forty years ago come Whitsun."

"Did Martin Joliffe keep on the farm after his father's death?" Westray asked, after an interval of silence.

They had wandered along the length of the stalls as they talked, and were passing through the stone screen which divides the minster into two parts. The floor of the choir at Cullerne is higher by some feet than that of the rest of the church, and when they stood on the steps which led down into the nave, the great length of the transepts opened before them on either side. The end of the north transept, on the outside of which once stood the chapter-house and dormitories of the monastery, has only three small lancet-windows high up in the wall, but at the south end of the cross-piece there is no wall at all, for the whole space is occupied by Abbot Vinnicomb's window, with its double transoms and infinite subdivisions of tracery. Thus is produced a curious contrast, for, while the light in the rest of the church is subdued to sadness by the smallness of the windows, and while the north transept is the most sombre part of all the building, the south transept, or Blandamer aisle, is constantly in clear daylight.

Moreover, while the nave is of the Norman style, and the transepts and choir of the Early English, this window is of the latest Perpendicular, complicated in its scheme, and meretricious in the elaboration of its detail. The difference is so great as to force itself upon the attention even of those entirely unacquainted with architecture, and it has naturally more significance for the professional eye. Westray stood a moment on the steps as he repeated his question:

"Did Martin keep on the farm?"

"Ay, he kep' it on, but he never had his heart in it. Miss Phemie did the work, and would have been a better farmer than her father, if Martin had let her be; but he spent a penny for every ha'penny she made, till all came to the hammer. Oxford puffed him up, and there was no one to check him; so he must needs be a gentleman, and give himself all kinds of airs, till people called him 'Gentleman Joliffe,' and later on 'Old Neb'ly' when his mind was weaker. 'Twas that turned his brain," said the sexton, pointing to the great window; "'twas the silver and green what done it."

Westray looked up, and in the head of the centre light saw the nebuly coat shining among the darker painted glass with a luminosity which was even more striking in daylight than in the dusk of the previous evening.

CHAPTER FIVE

After a week's trial, Westray made up his mind that Miss Joliffe's lodgings would suit him. It was true that the Hand of God was somewhat distant from the church, but, then, it stood higher than the rest of the town, and the architect's fads were not confined to matters of eating and drinking, but attached exaggerated importance to bracing air and the avoidance of low-lying situations. He was pleased also by the scrupulous cleanliness pervading the place, and by Miss Joliffe's cooking, which a long experience had brought to some perfection, so far as plain dishes were concerned.

He found that no servant was kept, and that Miss Joliffe never allowed her niece to wait at table, so long as she herself was in the house. This occasioned him some little inconvenience, for his naturally considerate disposition made him careful of overtaxing a landlady no longer young. He rang his bell with reluctance, and when he did so, often went out on to the landing and shouted directions down the well-staircase, in the hopes of sparing any unnecessary climbing of the great nights of stone steps. This consideration was not lost upon Miss Joliffe, and Westray was flattered by an evident anxiety which she displayed to retain him as a lodger.

It was, then, with a proper appreciation of the favour which he was conferring, that he summoned her one evening near teatime, to communicate to her his intention of remaining at Bellevue Lodge. As an outward and visible sign of more permanent tenure, he decided to ask for the removal of some of those articles which did not meet his taste, and especially of the great flower-picture that hung over the sideboard.

Miss Joliffe was sitting in what she called her study. It was a little apartment at the back of the house (once the still-room of the old inn), to which she retreated when any financial problem had to be grappled. Such problems had presented themselves with unpleasant frequency for many years past, and now her brother's long illness and death brought about something like a crisis in the weary struggle to make two and two into five. She had spared him no luxury that illness is supposed to justify, nor was Martin himself a man to be over-scrupulous in such matters. Bedroom fires, beef-tea, champagne, the thousand and one little matters which scarcely come within the cognisance of the rich, but tax so heavily the devotion of the poor, had all left their mark on the score. That such items should figure in her domestic accounts, seemed to Miss Joliffe so great a violation of the rules which govern prudent housekeeping, that all the urgency of the situation was needed to free her conscience from the guilt of extravagance—from that *luxuria* or wantonness, which leads the van among the seven deadly sins.

Philpotts the butcher had half smiled, half sighed to see sweetbreads entered in Miss Joliffe's book, and had, indeed, forgotten to keep record of many a similar purchase; using that kindly, quiet charity which the recipient is none the less aware of, and values the more from its very unostentation. So, too, did Custance the grocer tremble in executing champagne orders for the thin and wayworn old lady, and gave her full measure pressed down and running over in teas and sugars, to make up for the price which he was compelled to charge for such refinements in the way of wine. Yet the total had mounted up in spite of all forbearance, and Miss Joliffe was at this moment reminded of its gravity by the gold-foil necks of three bottles of the universally-appreciated Duc de Bentivoglio brand, which still projected from a shelf above her head. Of Dr Ennefer's account she scarcely dared even to think; and there was perhaps less need of her doing so, for he never sent it in, knowing very well that she would pay it as she could, and being quite prepared to remit it entirely if she could never pay it at all.

She appreciated his consideration, and overlooked with rare tolerance a peculiarly irritating breach of propriety of which he was constantly guilty. This was nothing less than addressing medicines to her house as if it were still an inn. Before Miss Joliffe moved into the Hand of God, she had spent much of the little allowed her for repairs, in covering up the name of the inn painted on the front. But after heavy rains the great black letters stared perversely through their veil, and the organist made small jokes about it being a difficult thing to thwart the Hand of God. Silly and indecorous, Miss Joliffe termed such witticisms, and had Bellevue House painted in gold upon the fanlight over the door. But the Cullerne painter wrote Bellevue too small, and had to fill up the space by writing House too large; and the organist sneered again at the disproportion, saying it should have been the other way, for everyone knew it was a house, but none knew it was Bellevue.

And then Dr Ennefer addressed his medicine to "Mr Joliffe, The Hand"—not even to The Hand of God, but simply The Hand; and Miss Joliffe eyed the bottles askance as they lay on the table in the dreary hall, and tore the wrappers off them quickly, holding her breath the while that no exclamation of impatience might escape her. Thus, the kindly doctor, in the hurry of his workaday life, vexed, without knowing it, the heart of the kindly lady, till she was constrained to retire to her study, and read the precepts about turning the other cheek to the smiters, before she could quite recover her serenity.

Miss Joliffe sat in her study considering how Martin's accounts were to be met. Her brother, throughout his disorderly and unbusinesslike life, had prided himself on orderly and business habits. It was true that these were only manifested in the neat and methodical arrangement of his bills, but there he certainly excelled. He never paid a bill; it was believed it never occurred to him to pay one; but he folded each account to exactly the same breadth, using the cover of an old glove-box as a gauge, wrote very neatly on the outside the date, the name of the creditor, and the amount of the debt, and with an indiarubber band enrolled it in a company of its fellows. Miss Joliffe found drawers full of such disheartening packets after his death, for Martin had a talent for distributing his favours, and of planting small debts far and wide, which by-and-by grew up into a very upas forest.

Miss Joliffe's difficulties were increased a thousandfold by a letter which had reached her some days before, and which raised a case of conscience. It lay open on the little table before her:

139, New Bond Street.

Madam,

We are entrusted with a commission to purchase several pictures of still-life, and believe that you have a large painting of flowers for the acquiring of which we should be glad to treat. The picture to which we refer was formerly in the possession of the late Michael Joliffe, Esquire, and consists of a basket of flowers on a mahogany table, with a caterpillar in the left-hand corner. We are so sure of our client's taste and of the excellence of the painting that we are prepared to offer for it a sum of fifty pounds, and to dispense with any previous inspection.

We shall be glad to receive a reply at your early convenience, and in the meantime

> We remain, madam,
>> Your most obedient servants,
>>> Baunton and Lutterworth.

Miss Joliffe read this letter for the hundredth time, and dwelt with unabated complacency on the "formerly in the possession of the late Michael Joliffe, Esquire." There was about the phrase something of ancestral dignity and importance that gratified her, and dulled the sordid bitterness of her surroundings. "The late Michael Joliffe, Esquire"—it read like a banker's will; and she was once more Euphemia Joliffe, a romantic girl sitting in Wydcombe church of a summer Sunday morning, proud of a new sprigged muslin, and proud of many tablets to older Joliffes on the walls about her; for yeomen in Southavonshire have pedigrees as well as dukes.

At first sight it seemed as if Providence had offered her in this letter a special solution of her difficulties, but afterwards scruples had arisen that barred the way of escape. "A large painting of flowers"— her father had been proud of it—proud of his worthless wife's work; and when she herself was a little child, had often held her up in his arms to see the shining table-top and touch the caterpillar. The wound his wife had given him must still have been raw, for that was only a year after Sophia had left him and the children; yet he was proud of her cleverness, and perhaps not without hope of her coming back. And when he died he left to poor Euphemia, then half-way through the dark gorge of middle age, an old writing-desk full of little tokens of her mother—the pair of gloves she wore at her wedding, a flashy brooch, a pair of flashy earrings, and many other unconsidered trifles that he had cherished. He left her, too, Sophia's long wood paint-box, with its little bottles of coloured powders for mixing oil-paints, and this same "basket of flowers on a mahogany table, with a caterpillar in the left-hand corner."

There had always been a tradition as to the value of this picture. Her father had spoken little of his wife to the children, and it was only piecemeal, as she grew into womanhood, that Miss Euphemia learnt from hints and half-told truths the story of her mother's shame. But Michael Joliffe was known to have considered this painting his wife's masterpiece, and old Mrs Janaway reported that Sophia had told her many a time it would fetch a hundred pounds. Miss Euphemia herself never had any doubt as to its worth, and so the offer in this letter occasioned her no surprise. She thought, in fact, that the sum named was considerably less than its market value, but sell it she could not. It was a sacred trust, and the last link (except the silver spoons marked "J.") that bound the squalid present to the comfortable past. It was an heirloom, and she could never bring herself to part with it.

Then the bell rang, and she slipped the letter into her pocket, smoothed the front of her dress, and climbed the stone stairs to see what Mr Westray wanted. The architect told her that he hoped to remain as her lodger during his stay in Cullerne, and he was pleased at his own magnanimity when he saw what pleasure the announcement gave Miss Joliffe. She felt it as a great relief, and consented readily enough to take away the ferns, and the mats, and the shell flowers, and the wax fruit, and to make sundry small alterations of the furniture which he desired. It seemed to her, indeed, that, considering he was an architect, Mr Westray's taste was strangely at fault; but she extended to him all possible forbearance, in view of his kindly manner and of his intention to remain with her.

Then the architect approached the removal of the flower-painting. He hinted delicately that it was perhaps rather too large for the room, and that he should be glad of the space to hang a plan of Cullerne Church, to which he would have constantly to refer. The rays of the setting sun fell full on the picture at the time, and, lighting up its vulgar showiness, strengthened him in his resolution to be free of it at any cost. But the courage of his attack flagged a little, as he saw the look of dismay which overspread Miss Joliffe's face.

"I think, you know, it is a little too bright and distracting for this room, which will really be my workshop."

Miss Joliffe was now convinced that her lodger was devoid of all appreciation, and she could not altogether conceal her surprise and sadness in replying:

"I am sure I want to oblige you in every way, sir, and to make you comfortable, for I always hope to have gentlefolk for my lodgers, and could never bring myself to letting the rooms down by taking anyone who was not a gentleman; but I hope you will not ask me to move the picture. It has hung here ever since I took the house, and my brother, 'the late Martin Joliffe'"—she was unconsciously influenced by the letter which she had in her pocket, and almost said "the late Martin Joliffe, Esquire"—"thought very highly of it, and used to sit here for hours in his last illness studying it. I hope you will not ask me to move the picture. You may not be aware, perhaps, that, besides being painted by my mother, it is in itself a very valuable work of art."

There was a suggestion, however faint, in her words, of condescension for her lodger's bad taste, and a desire to enlighten his ignorance which nettled Westray; and he contrived in his turn to throw a tone of superciliousness into his reply.

"Oh, of course, if you wish it to remain from sentimental reasons, I have nothing more to say, and I must not criticise your mother's work; but—" And he broke off, seeing that the old lady took the matter so much to heart, and being sorry that he had been ruffled at a trifle.

Miss Joliffe gulped down her chagrin. It was the first time she had heard the picture openly disparaged, though she had thought that on more than one occasion it had not been appreciated so much as it deserved. But she carried a guarantee of its value in her pocket, and could afford to be magnanimous.

"It has always been considered very valuable," she went on, "though I daresay I do not myself understand all its beauties, because I have not been sufficiently trained in art. But I am quite sure that it could be sold for a great deal of money, if I could only bring myself to part with it."

Westray was irritated by the hint that he knew little of art, and his sympathy for his landlady in her family attachment to the picture was much discounted by what he knew must be wilful exaggeration as to its selling value.

Miss Joliffe read his thoughts, and took a piece of paper from her pocket.

"I have here," she said, "an offer of fifty pounds for the picture from some gentlemen in London. Please read it, that you may see it is not I who am mistaken."

She held him out the dealers' letter, and Westray took it to humour her. He read it carefully, and wondered more and more as he went on. What could be the explanation? Could the offer refer to some other picture? for he knew Baunton and Lutterworth as being most reputable among London picture-dealers; and the idea of the letter being a hoax was precluded by the headed paper and general style of the communication. He glanced at the picture. The sunlight was still on it, and it stood out more hideous than ever; but his tone was altered as he spoke again to Miss Joliffe.

"Do you think," he said, "that this is the picture mentioned? Have you no other pictures?"

"No, nothing of this sort. It is certainly this one; you see, they speak of the caterpillar in the corner." And she pointed to the bulbous green animal that wriggled on the table-top.

"So they do," he said; "but how did they know anything about it?"—quite forgetting the question of its removal in the new problem that was presented.

"Oh, I fancy that most really good paintings are well-known to dealers. This is not the first inquiry we have had, for the very day of my dear brother's death a gentleman called here about it. None of us were at home except my brother, so I did not see him; but I believe he wanted to buy it, only my dear brother would never have consented to its being sold."

"It seems to me a handsome offer," Westray said; "I should think very seriously before I refused it."

"Yes, it is very serious to me in my position," answered Miss Joliffe; "for I am not rich; but I could not sell this picture. You see, I have known it ever since I was a little girl, and my father set such store by it. I hope, Mr Westray, you will not want it moved. I think, if you let it stop a little, you will get to like it very much yourself."

Westray did not press the matter further; he saw it was a sore point with his landlady, and reflected that he might hang a plan in front of the painting, if need be, as a temporary measure. So a concordat was established, and Miss Joliffe put Baunton and Lutterworth's letter back into her pocket, and returned to her accounts with equanimity at least partially restored.

After she had left the room, Westray examined the picture once more, and more than ever was he convinced of its worthlessness. It had all the crude colouring and hard outlines of the worst amateur work, and gave the impression of being painted with no other object than to cover a given space. This view was, moreover, supported by the fact that the gilt frame was exceptionally elaborate and well made, and he came to the conclusion that Sophia must somehow have come into possession of the frame, and had painted the flower-piece to fill it.

The sun was a red ball on the horizon as he flung up the window and looked out over the roofs towards the sea. The evening was very still, and the town lay steeped in deep repose. The smoke hung blue above it in long, level *strata*, and there was perceptible in the air a faint smell of burning weeds. The belfry story of the centre tower glowed with a pink flush in the sunset, and a cloud of jackdaws wheeled round the golden vanes, chattering and fluttering before they went to bed.

"It is a striking scene, is it not?" said a voice at his elbow; "there is a curious aromatic scent in this autumn air that makes one catch one's breath." It was the organist who had slipped in unawares. "I feel down on my luck," he said. "Take your supper in my room tonight, and let us have a talk."

Westray had not seen much of him for the last few days, and agreed gladly enough that they should spend the evening together; only the venue was changed, and supper taken in the architect's room. They talked over many things that night, and Westray let his companion ramble on to his heart's content about Cullerne men and manners; for he was of a receptive mind, and anxious to learn what he could about those among whom he had taken up his abode.

He told Mr Sharnall of his conversation with Miss Joliffe, and of the unsuccessful attempt to get the picture removed. The organist knew all about Baunton and Lutterworth's letter.

"The poor thing has made the question a matter of conscience for the last fortnight," he said, "and worried herself into many a sleepless night over that picture. 'Shall I sell it, or shall I not?' 'Yes,' says poverty—'sell it, and show a brave front to your creditors.' 'Yes,' say Martin's debts, clamouring about her with open mouths, like a nest of young starlings, 'sell it, and satisfy us.' 'No,' says pride, 'don't sell it; it is a patent of respectability to have an oil-painting in the house.' 'No,' says family affection, and the queer little piping voice of her own childhood—'don't sell it. Don't you remember how fond poor daddy was of it, and how dear Martin treasured it?' 'Dear Martin'—psh! Martin never did her anything but evil turns all his threescore years, but women canonise their own folk when they die.

"Haven't you seen what they call a religious woman damn the whole world for evil-doers? and then her husband or her brother dies, and may have lived as ill a life as any other upon earth, but she don't damn him. Love bids her penal code halt; she makes a way of escape for her own, and speaks of dear Dick and dear Tom for all the world as if they had been double Baxter-saints. No, blood is thicker than water; damnation doesn't hold good for her own. Love is stronger than hell-fire, and works a miracle for Dick and Tom; only *she* has to make up the balance by giving other folks an extra dose of brimstone.

"Lastly, worldly wisdom, or what Miss Joliffe thinks wisdom, says, 'No, don't sell it; you should get more than fifty pounds for such a gem.' So she is tossed about, and if she'd lived when there were monks in Cullerne Church, she would have asked her father confessor, and he would have taken down his 'Summa Angelica,' and looked it out under V.—'*Vendetur? utrum vendetur an non?*'—and set her mind at rest. You didn't know I could chaffer Latin with the best of 'em, did you? Ah, but I can, even with the rector, for all the *nebulus* and *nebulum*; only I don't trot it out too often. I'll show you a copy of the *Summa* when you come down to my room; but there aren't any confessors now, and dear Protestant Parkyn couldn't read the *Summa* if he had it; so there is no one to settle the case for her."

The little man had worked himself into a state of exaltation, and his eyes twinkled as he spoke of his scholastic attainments. "Latin," he said—"damn it! I can talk Latin against anyone—yes, with Beza himself—and could tell you tales in it which would make you stop your ears. Ah, well, more fool I—more fool I. '*Contentus esto, Paule mi, lasciva, Paule, pagina*,'" he muttered to himself, and drummed nervously with his fingers on the table.

Westray was apprehensive of these fits of excitement, and led the conversation back to the old theme.

"It baffles me to understand how *anyone* with eyes at all could think a daub like this was valuable—that is strange enough; but how come these London people to have made an offer for it? I know the firm quite well; they are first-rate dealers."

"There are some people," said the organist, "who can't tell 'Pop goes the weasel' from the 'Hallelujah Chorus,' and others are as bad with pictures. I'm very much that way myself. No doubt all you say is right, and this picture an eyesore to any respectable person, but I've been used to it so long I've got to like it, and should be sorry to see her sell it. And as for these London buyers, I suppose some other ignoramus has taken a fancy to it, and wants to buy. You see, there *have* been chance visitors staying in this room a night or two between whiles—perhaps even Americans, for all I said about them—and you can never reckon what *they'll* do. The very day Martin Joliffe died there was a story of someone coming to buy the picture of him. I was at church in the afternoon, and Miss Joliffe at the Dorcas meeting, and Anastasia gone out to the chemist.

"When I got back, I came up to see Martin in this same room, and found him full of a tale that he had heard the bell ring, and after

347

that someone walking in the house, and last his door opened, and in walked a stranger. Martin was sitting in the chair I'm using now, and was too weak then to move out of it; so he was forced to sit until this man came in. The stranger talked kindly to him, so he said, and wanted to buy the picture of the flowers, bidding as high as twenty pounds for it; but Martin wouldn't hear him, and said he wouldn't let him have it for ten times that, and then the man went away. That was the story, and I thought at the time 'twas all a cock-and-bull tale, and that Martin's mind was wandering; for he was very weak, and seemed flushed too, like one just waken from a dream. But he had a cunning look in his eye when he told me, and said if he lived another week he would be Lord Blandamer himself, and wouldn't want then to sell any pictures. He spoke of it again when his sister came back, but couldn't say what the man was like, except that his hair reminded him of Anastasia's.

"But Martin's time was come; he died that very night, and Miss Joliffe was terribly cast down, because she feared she had given him an overdose of sleeping-draught; for Ennefer told her he had taken too much, and she didn't see where he had got it from unless she gave it him by mistake. Ennefer wrote the death certificate, and so there was no inquest; but that put the stranger out of our thoughts until it was too late to find him, if, indeed, he ever was anything more than the phantom of a sick man's brain. No one beside had seen him, and all we had to ask for was a man with wavy hair, because he reminded Martin of Anastasia. But if 'twas true, then there was someone else who had a fancy for the painting, and poor old Michael must have thought a lot of it to frame it in such handsome style."

"I don't know," Westray said; "it looks to me as if the picture was painted to fill the frame."

"Perhaps so, perhaps so," answered the organist dryly. "What made Martin Joliffe think he was so near success?"

"Ah, that I can't tell you. He was always thinking he had squared the circle, or found the missing bit to fit into the puzzle; but he kept his schemes very dark. He left boxes full of papers behind him when he died, and Miss Joliffe handed them to me to look over, instead of burning them. I shall go through them some day; but no doubt the whole thing is moonshine, and if he ever had a clue it died with him."

There was a little pause; the chimes of Saint Sepulchre's played "Mount Ephraim," and the great bell tolled out midnight over Cullerne Flat.

"It's time to be turning in. You haven't a drop of whisky, I suppose?" he said, with a glance at the kettle which stood on a trivet in front of the fire; "I have talked myself thirsty."

There was a pathos in his appeal that would have melted many a stony heart, but Westray's principles were unassailable, and he remained obdurate.

"No, I am afraid I have not," he said; "you see, I never take spirits myself. Will you not join me in a cup of cocoa? The kettle boils."

Mr Sharnall's face fell.

"You ought to have been an old woman," he said; "only old women drink cocoa. Well, I don't mind if I do; any port in a storm."

The organist went to bed that night in a state of exemplary sobriety, for when he got down to his own room he could find no spirit in the cupboard, and remembered that he had finished the last bottle of old Martelet's *eau-de-vie* at his tea, and that he had no money to buy another.

Chapter Six

A month later the restoration work at Saint Sepulchre's was fairly begun, and in the south transept a wooden platform had been raised on scaffold-poles to such a height as allowed the masons to work at the vault from the inside. This roof was no doubt the portion of the fabric that called most urgently for repair, but Westray could not disguise from himself that delay might prove dangerous in other directions, and he drew Sir George Farquhar's attention to more than one weak spot which had escaped the great architect's cursory inspection.

But behind all Westray's anxieties lurked that dark misgiving as to the tower arches, and in his fancy the enormous weight of the central tower brooded like the incubus over the whole building. Sir George Farquhar paid sufficient attention to his deputy's representations to visit Cullerne with a special view to examining the tower. He spent an autumn day in making measurements and calculations, he listened to the story of the interrupted peal, and probed the cracks in the walls, but saw no reason to reconsider his former verdict or to impugn the stability of the tower. He gently rallied Westray on his nervousness, and, whilst he agreed that in other places repair was certainly needed, he pointed out that lack of funds must unfortunately limit for the present both the scope of operations and the rate of progress.

Cullerne Abbey was dissolved with the larger religious houses in 1539, when Nicholas Vinnicomb, the last abbot, being recalcitrant, and refusing to surrender his house, was hanged as a traitor in front of the great West Gate-house. The general revenues were impropriated by the King's Court of Augmentations, and the abbey lands in the immediate vicinity were given to Shearman, the King's Physician. Spellman, in his book on sacrilege, cites Cullerne as an instance where church lands brought ruin to their new owner's family; for Shearman had a spendthrift son who squandered his patrimony, and then, caballing with Spanish *intriguants*, came to the block in Queen Elizabeth's days.

For evil hands have abbey lands,
Such evil fate in store;
Such is the heritage that waits
Church-robbers evermore.

Thus, in the next generation the name of Shearman was clean put away; but Sir John Fynes, purchasing the property, founded the Grammar School and almshouses as a sin-offering for the misdoings of his predecessors. This measure of atonement succeeded admirably, for Horatio Fynes was ennobled by James the First, and his family, with the title of Blandamer, endures to this present.

On the day before the formal dissolution of their house the monks sung the last service in the abbey church. It was held late in the evening, partly because this time seemed to befit such a farewell, and partly that less public attention might be attracted; for there was a doubt whether the king's servants would permit any further ceremonies. Six tall candles burnt upon the altar, and the usual sconces lit the service-books that lay before the brothers in the choir-stalls. It was a sad service, as every good and amiable thing is sad when done for the last time. There were agonising hearts among the brothers, especially among the older monks, who knew not whither to go on the morrow; and the voice of the sub-prior was broken with grief, and failed him as he read the lesson.

The nave was in darkness except for the warming-braziers, which here and there cast a ruddy glow on the vast Norman pillars. In the obscurity were gathered little groups of townsmen. The nave had always been open for their devotions in happier days, and at the altars of its various chapels they were accustomed to seek the means of grace. That night they met for the last time—some few as curious spectators, but most in bitterness of heart and profound sorrow, that the great church with its splendid services was lost to them for ever. They clustered between the pillars of the arcades; and, the doors that separated the nave from the choir being open, they could look through the stone screen, and see the *serges* twinking far away on the high altar.

Among all the sad hearts in the abbey church, there was none sadder than that of Richard Vinnicomb, merchant and wool-stapler. He was the abbot's elder brother, and to all the bitterness naturally incident to the occasion was added in his case the grief that his brother was a prisoner in London, and would certainly be tried for his life.

He stood in the deep shadow of the pier that supported the northwest corner of the tower, weighed down with sorrow for the abbot and for the fall of the abbey, and uncertain whether his brother's condemnation would not involve his own ruin. It was December 6, Saint Nicholas' Day, the day of the abbot's patron saint. He was near enough to the choir to hear the collect being read on the other side of the screen:

Deus qui beatum Nicolaum pontificem innumeris decorasti miraculis: tribue quaesumus ut ejus mentis, et precibus, a gehennae incendiis liberemur, per Dominum nostrum Jesum Christum. Amen.

"Amen," he said in the shadow of his pillar. "Blessed Nicholas, save me; blessed Nicholas, save us all; blessed Nicholas, save my brother, and, if he must lose this temporal life, pray to our Lord Christ that He will shortly accomplish the number of His elect, and reunite us in His eternal Paradise."

He clenched his hands in his distress, and, as a flicker from the brazier fell upon him, those standing near saw the tears run down his cheeks.

"*Nicholas qui omnem terram doctrina replevisti, intercede pro peccatis nostris,*" said the *officiant*; and the monks gave the antiphon:

Iste est qui contempsit vitam mundi et pervenit ad coelestia regna.

One by one a server put out the altar-lights, and as the last was extinguished the monks rose in their places, and walked out in procession, while the organ played a dirge as sad as the wind in a ruined window.

The abbot was hanged before his abbey gate, but Richard Vinnicomb's goods escaped confiscation; and when the great church was sold, as it stood, for building material, he bought it for three hundred pounds, and gave it to the parish. One part of his prayer was granted, for within a year death reunited him to his brother; and in his pious will he bequeathed his "sowle to Allmyhtie God his Maker and Redemer, to have the fruition of the Deitie with Our Blessed Ladie and all Saints and the Abbey Churche of Saint Sepulchre with the implements thereof, to the Paryshe of Cullerne, so that the said Parishioners shall not sell, alter, or alienate the said Churche, or Implements or anye part or parcell thereof for ever." Thus it was that the church which Westray had to restore was preserved at a critical period of its history.

Richard Vinnicomb's generosity extended beyond the mere purchase of the building, for he left in addition a sum to support the dignity of a daily service, with a complement of three chaplains, an organist, ten singing-men, and sixteen choristers. But the negligence of trustees and the zeal of more religious-minded men than poor superstitious Richard had sadly diminished these funds. Successive rectors of Cullerne became convinced that the spiritual interests of the town would be better served by placing a larger income at their own disposal for good works, and by devoting less to the mere lip-service of much daily singing. Thus, the stipend of the rector was gradually augmented, and Canon Parkyn found an opportunity soon after his installation to increase the income of the living to a round two thousand by curtailing extravagance in the payment of an organist, and by reducing the emoluments of that office from two hundred to eighty pounds a year.

It was true that this scheme of economy included the abolition of the weekday morning-service, but at three o'clock in the afternoon evensong was still rehearsed in Cullerne Church. It was the thin and vanishing shadow of a cathedral service, and Canon Parkyn hoped that it might gradually dwindle away until it was dispersed to nought. Such formalism must certainly throttle any real devotion, and it was regrettable that many of the prayers in which his own fine voice and personal magnetism must have had a moving effect upon his hearers should be constantly obscured by vain intonations.

It was only by doing violence to his own high principles that he constrained himself to accept the emoluments which poor Richard Vinnicomb had provided for a singing foundation, and he was scrupulous in showing his disapproval of such vanities by punctilious absence from the week-day service. This ceremony was therefore entrusted to white-haired Mr Noot, whose zeal in his Master's cause had left him so little opportunity for pushing his own interests that at sixty he was stranded as an underpaid curate in the backwater of Cullerne.

At four o'clock, therefore, on a week-day afternoon, anyone who happened to be in Saint Sepulchre's Church might see a little surpliced procession issue from the vestries in the south transept, and wind its way towards the choir. It was headed by clerk Janaway, who carried a silver-headed mace; then followed eight choristers (for the number fixed by Richard Vinnicomb had been diminished by half); then five singing-men, of whom the youngest was fifty, and the rear was brought up by Mr Noot. The procession having once entered the choir, the clerk shut the doors of the screen behind it, that the minds of the officiants might be properly removed from contemplation of the outer world, and that devotion might not be interrupted by any intrusion of profane persons from the nave.

These outside Profane existed rather in theory than fact, for, except in the height of summer, visitors were rarely seen in the nave or any other part of the building. Cullerne lay remote from large centres, and archaeologic interest was at this time in so languishing a condition that few, except professed antiquaries, were aware of the grandeur of the abbey church. If strangers troubled little about Cullerne, the interest of the inhabitants in the week-day service was still more lukewarm, and the pews in front of the canopied stalls remained constantly empty.

Thus, Mr Noot read, and Mr Sharnall the organist played, and the choir-men and choristers sang, day by day, entirely for clerk Janaway's benefit, because there was no one else to listen to them. Yet, if a stranger given to music ever entered the church at such times, he was struck with the service; for, like the Homeric housewife who did the best with what she had by her, Mr Sharnall made the most of his defective organ and inadequate choir. He was a man if much taste and resource, and, as the echoes of the singing rolled round the vaulted roofs, a generous critic thought little of cracked voices and leaky bellows and rattling trackers, but took away with him an harmonious memory of sunlight and coloured glass and eighteenth-century music; and perhaps of some clear treble voice, for Mr Sharnall was famed for training boys and discovering the gift of song.

Saint Luke's little summer, in the October that followed the commencement of the restoration, amply justified its name. In the middle of the month there were several days of such unusual beauty as to recall the real summer, and the air was so still and the sunshine so warm that anyone looking at the soft haze on Cullerne Flat might well have thought that August had returned.

Cullerne Minster was, as a rule, refreshingly cool in the warmth of summer, but something of the heat and oppressiveness of the outside air seemed to have filtered into the church on these unseasonably warm autumn days. On a certain Saturday a more than usual drowsiness marked the afternoon service. The choir plumped down into their places when the Psalms were finished, and abandoned themselves to slumber with little attempt at concealment, as Mr Noot began the first lesson. There were, indeed, honourable exceptions to the general somnolence. On the *cantoris* side the worn-out alto held an animated conversation with the cracked tenor. They were comparing some specially fine onions under the desk, for both were gardeners and the autumn leek-show was near at hand. On the *decani* side Patrick Ovens, a red-haired little treble, was kept awake by the necessity for altering *Magnificat* into *Magnified Cat* in his copy of Aldrich in G.

The lesson was a long one. Mr Noot, mildest and most beneficent of men, believed that he was at his best in denunciatory passages of Scripture. The Prayer-Book, it was true, had appointed a portion of the Book of Wisdom for the afternoon lesson, but Mr Noot made light of authorities, and read instead a chapter from Isaiah. If he had been questioned as to this proceeding, he would have excused himself by saying that he disapproved of the Apocrypha, even for instruction of manners (and there was no one at Cullerne at all likely to question this right of private judgment), but his real, though perhaps unconscious, motive was to find a suitable passage for declamation. He thundered forth judgments in a manner which combined, he believed, the terrors of supreme justice with an infinite commiseration for the blindness of errant, but long-forgotten peoples. He had, in fact, that "Bible voice" which seeks to communicate additional solemnity to the Scriptures by reciting them in a tone never employed in ordinary life, as the fledgling curate adds gravity to the Litany by whispering "the hour of death and Day of Judgment."

Mr Noot, being short-sighted, did not see how lightly the punishments of these ancient races passed over the heads of his dozing audience, and was bringing the long lesson to a properly dramatic close when the unexpected happened: the screen-door opened and a stranger entered. As the blowing of a horn by the paladin broke the repose of a century, and called back to life the spellbound princess and her court, so these slumbering churchmen were startled from their dreams by the intruder. The choir-boys fell to giggling, the choir-men stared, clerk Janaway grasped his mace as if he would brain so rash an adventurer, and the general movement made Mr Sharnall glance nervously at his stops; for he thought that he had overslept himself, and that the choir had stood up for the *Magnificat*.

The stranger seemed unconscious of the attention which his appearance provoked. He was no doubt some casual sightseer, and had possibly been unaware that any service was in progress until he opened the screen-door. But once there, he made up his mind to join in the devotions, and was walking to the steps which led up to the stalls when clerk Janaway popped out of his place and accosted him, quoting the official regulations in something louder than a stage whisper:

"Ye cannot enter the choir during the hours of Divine service. Ye cannot come in."

The stranger was amused at the old man's officiousness.

"I am in," he whispered back, "and, being in, will take a seat, if you please, until the service is over."

The clerk looked at him doubtfully for a moment, but if there was amusement to be read in the other's countenance, there was also a decision that did not encourage opposition. So he thought better of the matter, and opened the door of one of the pews that run below the stalls in Cullerne Church.

But the stranger did not appear to notice that a place was being shown him, and walked past the pew and up the little steps that led to the stalls on the *cantoris* side. Directly behind the singing-men were five stalls, which had canopies richer and more elaborate than those of the others, with heraldic escutcheons painted on the backs. From these seats the vulgar herd was excluded by a faded crimson cord, but the stranger lifted the cord from its hook, and sat down in the first reserved seat, as if the place belonged to him.

Clerk Janaway was outraged, and bustled up the steps after him like an angry turkey-cock.

"Come, come!" he said, touching the intruder on the shoulder; "you cannot sit here; these are the Fording seats, and kep' for Lord Blandamer's family."

"I will make room if Lord Blandamer brings his family," the stranger said; and, seeing that the old man was returning to the attack, added, "Hush! that is enough."

The clerk looked at him again, and then turned back to his own place, routed.

"*And in that day they shall roar against thee like the roaring of the sea, and if one look unto the land behold darkness and sorrow, and the light is darkened in the heavens thereof,*" said Mr Noot, and shut the book, with a glance of general fulmination through his great round spectacles.

The choir, who had been interested spectators of this conflict of lawlessness as personified in the intruder, and authority as in the clerk, rose to their feet as the organ began the *Magnificat*.

The singing-men exchanged glances of amusement, for they were not altogether averse to seeing the clerk worsted. He was an autocrat in his own church, and ruffled them now and again with what they called his bumptiousness. Perhaps he did assume a little as he led the procession, for he forgot at times that he was a peaceable servant of the sanctuary, and fancied, as he marched mace in hand to the music of the organ, that he was a daring officer leading a forlorn hope. That very afternoon he had had a heated discussion in the vestry with Mr Milligan, the bass, on a question of gardening, and the singer, who still smarted under the clerk's overbearing tongue, was glad to emphasise his adversary's defeat by paying attention to the intruder.

The tenor on the *cantoris* side was taking holiday that day, and Mr Milligan availed himself of the opportunity to offer the absentee's copy of the service to the intruder, who was sitting immediately behind him. He turned round, and placed the book, open at the *Magnificat*, before the stranger with much deference, casting as he faced round again a look of misprision at Janaway, of which the latter was quick to appreciate, the meaning.

This by-play was lost upon the stranger, who nodded his acknowledgment of the civility, and turned to the study of the score which had been offered him.

Mr Sharnall's resources in the way of men's voices were so limited that he was by no means unused to finding himself short of a voice-part on the one side or the other. He had done his best to remedy the deficiency in the Psalms by supplying the missing part with his left hand, but as he began the *Magnificat* he was amazed to hear a mellow and fairly strong tenor taking part in the service with feeling and precision. It was the stranger who stood in the gap, and when the first surprise was past, the choir welcomed him as being versed in their own arts, and Clerk Janaway forgot the presumption of his entrance and even the rebellious conduct of Mr Milligan. The men and boys sang with new life; they wished, in fact, that so knowledgeable a person should be favourably impressed, and the service was rendered in a more creditable way than Cullerne Church had known for many a long day. Only the stranger was perfectly unmoved. He sang as if he had been a lay-vicar all his life, and when the *Magnificat* was ended, and Mr Sharnall could look through the curtains of the organ-loft, the organist saw him with a Bible devoutly following Mr Noot in the second lesson.

He was a man of forty, rather above the middle height, with dark eyebrows and dark hair, that was beginning to turn grey. His hair, indeed, at once attracted the observer's attention by its thick profusion and natural wavy curl. He was clean-shaven, his features were sharply cut without being thin, and there was something contemptuous about the firm mouth. His nose was straight, and a powerful face gave the impression of a man who was accustomed to be obeyed. To anyone looking at him from the other side of the choir, he presented a remarkable picture, for which the black oak of Abbot Vinnicomb's stalls supplied a frame. Above his head the canopy went soaring up into crockets and finials, and on the woodwork at the back was painted a shield which nearer inspection would have shown to be the Blandamer cognisance, with its nebuly bars of green and silver. It was, perhaps, so commanding an appearance that made red-haired Patrick Ovens take out an Australian postage-stamp which he had acquired that very day, and point out to the boy next to him the effigy of Queen Victoria sitting crowned in a gothic chair.

The stranger seemed to enter thoroughly into the spirit of the performance; he bore his part in the service bravely, and, being furnished with another book, lent effective aid with the anthem. He stood up decorously as the choir filed out after the Grace, and then sat down again in his seat to listen to the voluntary. Mr Sharnall determined to play something of quality as a tribute to the unknown tenor, and gave as good a rendering of the Saint Anne's fugue as the state of the organ would permit. It was true that the trackers rattled terribly, and that a cipher marred the effect of the second subject; but when he got to the bottom of the little winding stairs that led down from the loft, he found the stranger waiting with a compliment.

"Thank you very much," he said; "it is very kind of you to give us so fine a fugue. It is many years since I was last in this church, and I am fortunate to have chosen so sunny an afternoon, and to have been in time for your service."

"Not at all, not at all," said the organist; "it is we who are fortunate in having you to help us. You read well, and have a useful voice, though I caught you tripping a little in the lead of the *Nunc Dimittis* Gloria." And he sung it over by way of reminder. "You understand church music, and have sung many a service before, I am sure, though you don't look much given that way," he added, scanning him up and down.

The stranger was amused rather than offended at these blunt criticisms, and the catechising went on.

"Are you stopping in Cullerne?"

"No," the other replied courteously; "I am only here for the day, but I hope I may find other occasions to visit the place and to hear your service. You will have your full complement of voices next time I come, no doubt, and I shall be able to listen more at my ease than today?"

"Oh no, you won't. It's ten to one you will find us still worse off. We are a poverty-stricken lot, and no one to come over into Macedonia to help us. These cursed priests eat up our substance like cankerworms, and grow sleek on the money that was left to keep the music going. I don't mean the old woman that read this afternoon; he's got *his* nose on the grindstone like the rest of us—poor Noot! He has to put brown paper in his boots because he can't afford to have them resoled. No, it's the Barabbas in the rectory-house, that buys his stocks and shares, and starves the service."

This tirade fell lightly on the stranger's ears. He looked as if his thoughts were a thousand miles away, and the organist broke off:

"Do you play the organ? Do you understand an organ?" he asked quickly.

"Alas! I do not play," the stranger said, bringing his mind back with a jerk for the answer, "and understand little about the instrument."

"Well, next time you are here come up into the loft, and I will show you what a chest of rattletraps I have to work with. We are lucky to get through a service without a breakdown; the pedal-board is too short and past its work, and now the bellows are worn-out."

"Surely you can get that altered," the stranger said; "the bellows shouldn't cost so much to mend."

"They are patched already past mending. Those who would like to pay for new ones haven't got the money, and those who have the money won't pay. Why, that very stall you sat in belongs to a man who could give us new bellows, and a new organ, and a new church, if we wanted it. Blandamer, that's his name—Lord Blandamer. If you had looked, you could have seen his great coat of arms on the back of the seat; and he won't spend a halfpenny to keep the roofs from falling on our heads."

"Ah," said the stranger, "it seems a very sad case." They had reached the north door, and, as they stepped out, he repeated meditatively: "It seems a very sad case; you must tell me more about it next time we meet."

The organist took the hint, and wished his companion good-afternoon, turning down towards the wharves for a constitutional on the riverside. The stranger raised his hat with something of foreign courtesy, and walked back into the town.

Chapter Seven

Miss Euphemia Joliffe devoted Saturday afternoons to Saint Sepulchre's Dorcas Society. The meetings were held in a class-room of the Girls' National School, and there a band of devoted females gathered week by week to make garments for the poor. If there was in Cullerne some threadbare gentility, and a great deal of middle-class struggling, there was happily little actual poverty, as it is understood in great towns. Thus the poor, to whom the clothes made by the Dorcas Society were ultimately distributed, could sometimes afford to look the gift-horse in the mouth, and to lament that good material had been marred in the making. "They wept," the organist said, "when they showed the coats and garments that Dorcas made, because they were so badly cut;" but this was a libel, for there were many excellent needlewomen in the society, and among the very best was Miss Euphemia Joliffe.

She was a staunch supporter of the church, and, had her circumstances permitted, would have been a Scripture-reader or at least a district visitor. But the world was so much with her, in the shape of domestic necessities at Bellevue Lodge, as to render parish work impossible, and so the Dorcas meeting was the only systematic philanthropy in which she could venture to indulge. But in the discharge of this duty she was regularity personified; neither wind nor rain, snow nor heat, sickness nor amusement, stopped her, and she was to be found each and every Saturday afternoon, from three to five, in the National School.

If the Dorcas Society was a duty for the little old lady, it was also a pleasure—one of her few pleasures, and perhaps the greatest. She liked the meetings, because on such occasions she felt herself to be the equal of her more prosperous neighbours. It is the same feeling that makes the half-witted attend funerals and church services. At such times they feel themselves to be for once on an equal footing with their fellow-men: all are reduced to the same level; there are no speeches to be made, no accounts to be added up, no counsels to be given, no decisions to be taken; all are as fools in the sight of God.

At the Dorcas meeting Miss Joliffe wore her "best things" with the exception only of head-gear, for the wearing of her best bonnet was a crowning grace reserved exclusively for the Sabbath. Her wardrobe was too straightened to allow her "best" to follow the shifting seasons closely. If it was bought as best for winter, it might have to play the same role also in summer, and thus it fell sometimes to her lot to wear alpaca in December, or, as on this day, to be adorned with a fur necklet when the weather asked for muslin. Yet "in her best" she always felt "fit to be seen"; and when it came to cutting out, or sewing, there were none that excelled her.

Most of the members greeted her with a kind word, for even in a place where envy, hatred and malice walked the streets arm in arm from sunrise to sunset, Miss Euphemia had few enemies. Lying and slandering, and speaking evil of their fellows, formed a staple occupation of the ladies of Cullerne, as of many another small town; and to Miss Joliffe, who was foolish and old-fashioned enough to think evil of no one, it had seemed at first the only drawback of these delightful meetings that a great deal of such highly-spiced talk was to be heard at them. But even this fly was afterwards removed from the amber; for Mrs Bulteel—the brewer's lady—who wore London dresses, and was much the most fashionable person in Cullerne, proposed that some edifying book should be read aloud on Dorcas afternoons to the assembled workers.

It was true that Mrs Flint said she only did so because she thought she had a fine voice; but however that might be, she proposed it, and no one cared to run counter to her. So Mrs Bulteel read properly religious stories, of so touching a nature that an afternoon seldom passed without her being herself dissolved in tears, and evoking sympathetic sniffs and sobs from such as wished to stand in her good books. If Miss Joliffe was not herself so easily moved by imaginary sorrow, she set it down to some lack of loving-kindness in her own disposition, and mentally congratulated the others on their superior sensitiveness.

Miss Joliffe was at the Dorcas meeting, Mr Sharnall was walking by the riverside, Mr Westray was with the masons on the roof of the transept; only Anastasia Joliffe was at Bellevue Lodge when the front-doorbell rang. When her aunt was at home, Anastasia was not allowed to "wait on the gentlemen," nor to answer the bell; but her aunt being absent, and there being no one else in the house, she duly opened one leaf of the great front-door, and found a gentleman standing on the semicircular flight of steps outside. That he was a gentleman she knew at a glance, for she had a *flair* for such useless distinctions, though the genus was not sufficiently common at Cullerne to allow her much practice in its identification near home.

It was, in fact, the stranger of the *tenor* voice, and such is the quickness of woman's wit, that she learnt in a moment as much concerning his outward appearance as the organist and the choir-men and the clerk had learnt in an hour; and more besides, for she saw that he was well dressed. There was about him a complete absence of personal adornment. He wore no rings and no scarf-pin, even his watch-chain was only of leather. His clothes were of so dark a grey as to be almost black, but Miss Anastasia Joliffe knew that the cloth was good, and the cut of the best. She had thrust a pencil into the pages of *Northanger Abbey* to keep the place while she answered the bell, and as the stranger stood before her, it seemed to her he might be a Henry Tilney, and she was prepared, like a Catherine Morland, for some momentous announcement when he opened his lips. Yet there came nothing very weighty from them; he did not even inquire for lodgings, as she half hoped that he would.

"Does the architect in charge of the works at the church lodge here? Is Mr Westray at home?" was all he said.

"He does live here," she answered, "but is out just now, and we do not expect him back till six. I think you will probably find him at the church if you desire to see him."

"I have just come from the minster, but could see nothing of him there."

It served the stranger right that he should have missed the architect, and been put to the trouble of walking as far as Bellevue Lodge, for his inquiries must have been very perfunctory. If he had taken the trouble to ask either organist or clerk, he would have learnt at once where Mr Westray was.

"I wonder if you would allow me to write a note. If you could give me a sheet of paper I should be glad to leave a message for him."

Anastasia gave him a glance from head to foot, rapid as an instantaneous exposure. "Tramps" were a permanent bugbear to the ladies of Cullerne, and a proper dread of such miscreants had been instilled into Anastasia Joliffe by her aunt. It was, moreover, a standing rule of the house that no strange men were to be admitted on any pretence, unless there was some man-lodger at home, to grapple with them if occasion arose. But the glance was sufficient to confirm her first verdict—he *was* a gentleman; there surely could not be such things as gentlemen-tramps. So she answered "Oh, certainly," and showed him into Mr Sharnall's room, because that was on the ground-floor.

The visitor gave a quick look round the room. If he had ever been in the house before, Anastasia would have thought he was trying to identify something that he remembered; but there was little to be seen except an open piano, and the usual litter of music-books and manuscript paper.

"Thank you," he said; "can I write here? Is this Mr Westray's room?"

"No, another gentleman lodges here, but you can use this room to write in. He is out, and would not mind in any case; he is a friend of Mr Westray."

"I had rather write in Mr Westray's room if I may. You see I have nothing to do with this other gentleman, and it might be awkward if he came in and found me in his apartment."

It seemed to Anastasia that the information that the room in which they stood was not Mr Westray's had in some way or other removed an anxiety from the stranger's mind. There was a faint and indefinable indication of relief in his manner, however much he professed to be embarrassed at the discovery. It might have been, she thought, that he was a great friend of Mr Westray, and had been sorry to think that his room should be littered and untidy as Mr Sharnall's certainly was, and so was glad when he found out his mistake.

"Mr Westray's room is at the top of the house," she said deprecatingly.

"It is no trouble to me, I assure you, to go up," he answered.

Anastasia hesitated again for an instant. If there were no gentlemen-tramps, perhaps there were gentlemen-burglars, and she hastily made a mental inventory of Mr Westray's belongings, but could think of nothing among them likely to act as an incentive to crime. Still she would not venture to show a strange man to the top of the house, when there was no one at home but herself. The stranger ought not to have asked her. He could not be a gentleman after all, or he would have seen how irregular was such a request, unless he had indeed some particular motive for wishing to see Mr Westray's room.

The stranger perceived her hesitation, and read her thoughts easily enough.

"I beg your pardon," he said. "I ought, of course, to have explained who it is who has the honour of speaking to you. I am Lord Blandamer, and wish to write a few words to Mr Westray on questions connected with the restoration of the church. Here is my card."

There was probably no lady in the town that would have received this information with as great composure as did Anastasia Joliffe. Since the death of his grandfather, the new Lord Blandamer had been a constant theme of local gossip and surmise. He was a territorial magnate, he owned the whole of the town, and the whole of the surrounding country. His stately house of Fording could be seen on a clear day from the minster tower. He was reputed to be a man of great talents and distinguished appearance; he was not more than forty, and he was unmarried. Yet no one had seen him since he came to man's estate; it was said he had not been in Cullerne for twenty years.

There was a tale of some mysterious quarrel with his grandfather, which had banished the young man from his home, and there had been no one to take his part, for both his father and mother were drowned when he was a baby. For a quarter of a century he had been a wanderer abroad: in France and Germany, in Russia and Greece, in Italy and Spain. He was believed to have visited the East, to have fought in Egypt, to have run blockades in South America, to have found priceless diamonds in South Africa.

He had suffered the awful penances of the *fakirs*, he had fasted with the monks of Mount Athos; he had endured the silence of La Trappe; men said that the Sheik-ul-Islam had himself bound the green turban round Lord Blandamer's head. He could shoot, he could hunt, he could fish, he could fight, he could sing, he could play all instruments; he could speak all languages as fluently as his own; he was the very wisest and the very handsomest, and—some hinted—the very wickedest man that ever lived, yet no one had ever seen him. Here was indeed a conjunction of romance for Anastasia, to find so mysterious and distinguished a stranger face to face with her alone under the same roof; yet she showed none of those hesitations, tremblings, or faintings that the situation certainly demanded.

Martin Joliffe, her father, had been a handsome man all his life, and had known it. In youth he prided himself on his good looks, and in old age he was careful of his personal appearance. Even when his circumstances were at their worst he had managed to obtain well-cut clothes. They were not always of the newest, but they sat well on his tall and upright figure; "Gentleman Joliffe" people called him, and laughed, though perhaps something less ill-naturedly than was often the case in Cullerne, and wondered whence a farmer's son had gotten such manners. To Martin himself an aristocratic bearing was less an affectation than a duty; his position demanded it, for he was in his own eyes a Blandamer kept out of his rights.

It was his good appearance, even at five-and-forty, which induced Miss Hunter of the Grove to run away with him, though Colonel Hunter had promised to disown her if she ever married so far beneath her. She did not, it is true, live long to endure her father's displeasure, but died in giving birth to her first child. Even this sad result had failed to melt the colonel's heart. Contrary to all precedents of fiction, he would have nothing to do with his little granddaughter, and sought refuge from so untenable a position in removing from Cullerne. Nor was Martin himself a man to feel a parent's obligations too acutely; so the child was left to be brought up by Miss Joliffe, and to become an addition to her cares, but much more to her joys. Martin Joliffe considered that he had amply fulfilled his responsibilities in christening his daughter Anastasia, a name which Debrett shows to have been borne for generations by ladies of the Blandamer family; and, having given so striking a proof of affection, he started off on one of those periodic wanderings which were connected with his genealogical researches, and was not seen again in Cullerne for a lustre.

For many years afterwards Martin showed but little interest in the child. He came back to Cullerne at intervals; but was always absorbed in his efforts to establish a right to the nebuly coat, and content to leave the education and support of Anastasia entirely to his sister. It was not till his daughter was fifteen that he exercised any paternal authority; but, on his return from a long absence about that period, he pointed out to Miss Joliffe, senior, that she had shamefully neglected her niece's education, and that so lamentable a state of affairs must be remedied at once. Miss Joliffe most sorrowfully admitted her shortcomings, and asked Martin's forgiveness for her remissness.

Nor did it ever occur to her to plead in excuse that the duties of a lodging-house, and the necessity of providing sustenance for herself and Anastasia, made serious inroads on the time that ought, no doubt, to have been devoted to education; or that the lack of means prevented her from engaging teachers to supplement her own too limited instruction. She had, in fact, been able to impart to Anastasia little except reading, writing and arithmetic, some geography, a slight knowledge of Miss Magnall's questions, a wonderful proficiency with the needle, an unquenchable love of poetry and fiction, a charity for her neighbours which was rare enough in Cullerne, and a fear of God which was sadly inconsistent with the best Blandamer traditions.

The girl was not being brought up as became a Blandamer, Martin had said; how was she to fill her position when she became the Honourable Anastasia? She must learn French, not such rudiments as Miss Joliffe had taught her, and he travestied his sister's "Doo, dellah, derlapostrof, day" with a laugh that flushed her withered cheeks with crimson, and made Anastasia cry as she held her aunt's hand under the table; not *that* kind of French, but something that would really pass muster in society. And music, she *must* study that; and Miss Joliffe blushed again as she thought very humbly of some elementary duets in which she had played a bass for Anastasia till household work and gout conspired to rob her knotty fingers of all pliancy. It had been a great pleasure to her, the playing of these duets with her niece; but they must, of course, be very poor things, and quite out of date now, for she had played them when she was a child herself, and on the very same piano in the parlour at Wydcombe.

So she listened with attention while Martin revealed his scheme of reform, and this was nothing less than the sending of Anastasia to Mrs Howard's boarding-school at the county town of Carisbury. The project took away his sister's breath, for Mrs Howard's was a finishing school of repute, to which only Mrs Bulteel among Cullerne ladies could afford to send her daughters. But Martin's high-minded generosity knew no limits. "It was no use making two bites at a cherry; what had to be done had better be done quickly." And he clinched the argument by taking a canvas bag from his pocket, and pouring out a little heap of sovereigns on to the table.

Miss Joliffe's wonder as to how her brother had become possessed of such wealth was lost in admiration of his magnanimity, and if for an instant she thought wistfully of the relief that a small portion of these riches would bring to the poverty-stricken *ménage* at Bellevue Lodge, she silenced such murmurings in a burst of gratitude for the means of improvement that Providence had vouchsafed to Anastasia. Martin counted out the sovereigns on the table; it was better to pay in advance, and so make an impression in Anastasia's favour, and to this Miss Joliffe agreed with much relief, for she had feared that before the end of the term Martin would be off on his travels again, and that she herself would be left to pay.

So Anastasia went to Carisbury, and Miss Joliffe broke her own rules, and herself incurred a number of small debts because she could not bear to think of her niece going to school with so meagre an equipment as she then possessed, and yet had no ready money to buy better. Anastasia remained for two half-years at Carisbury. She made such progress with her music that after much wearisome and lifeless practising she could stumble through Thalberg's variations on the air of "Home, Sweet Home"; but in French she never acquired the true Parisian accent, and would revert at times to the "Doo, dellah, derla-postrof, day," of her earlier teaching, though there is no record that these shortcomings were ever a serious drawback to her in after-life. Besides such opportunities of improvement, she enjoyed the privilege of association with thirty girls of the upper middle-classes, and ate of the tree of knowledge of good and evil, the fruits of which had hith-erto escaped her notice. At the end of her second term, however, she was forced to forego these advantages, for Martin had left Cullerne without making any permanent provision for his daughter's school-ing; and there was in Mrs Howard's prospectus a law, inexorable as that of gravity, that no pupil shall be permitted to return to the academy whose account for the previous term remains unsettled.

Thus Anastasia's schooling came to an end. There was some excuse put forward that the air of Carisbury did not agree with her; and she never knew the real reason till nearly two years later, by which time Miss Joliffe's industry and self-denial had discharged the greater part of Martin's obligation to Mrs Howard. The girl was glad to remain at Cullerne, for she was deeply attached to Miss Joliffe; but she came back much older in experience; her horizon had widened, and she was beginning to take a more perspective view of life. These enlarged ideas bore fruit both pleasant and unpleasant, for she was led to form a juster estimate of her father's character, and when he next returned she found it difficult to tolerate his selfishness and abuse of his sister's devotion.

That this should be so was a cause of great grief to Miss Joliffe. Though she herself felt for her niece a love which had in it something of adoration, she was at the same time conscientious enough to re-member that a child's first duty should be towards its parents. Thus she forced herself to lament that Anastasia should be more closely attached to her than to Martin, and if there were times when she could not feel properly dissatisfied that she possessed the first place in her niece's af-fections, she tried to atone for this frailty by sacrificing opportunities of being with the girl herself, and using every opportunity of bring-ing her into her father's company. It was a fruitless endeavour, as every endeavour to cultivate affection where no real basis for it exists, must eternally remain fruitless.

Martin was wearied by his daughter's society, for he preferred to be alone, and set no store by her except as a cooking, house-cleaning, and clothes-mending machine; and Anastasia resented this attitude, and could find, moreover, no interest in the torn peerage which was her father's Bible, or in the genealogical research and jargon about the nebuly coat which formed the staple of his conversation. Later on, when he came back for the last time, her sense of duty enabled her to tend and nurse him with exemplary patience, and to fulfil all those offices of affection which even the most tender filial devotion could have suggested. She tried to believe that his death brought her sorrow and not relief, and succeeded so well that her aunt had no doubts at all upon the subject.

Martin Joliffe's illness and death had added to Anastasia's experience of life by bringing her into contact with doctors and clergymen; and it was no doubt this training, and the association with the superior classes afforded by Mrs Howard's academy, that enabled her to stand the shock of Lord Blandamer's announcement without giving any more perceptible token of embarrassment than a very slight blush.

"Oh, of course there is no objection," she said, "to your writing in Mr Westray's room. I will show you the way to it."

She accompanied him to the room, and having provided writing materials, left him comfortably ensconced in Mr Westray's chair. As she pulled the door to behind her in going out, something prompted her to look round—perhaps it was merely a girl's light fancy, perhaps it was that indefinite fascination which the consciousness that we are being looked at sometimes exercises over us; but as she looked back her eyes met those of Lord Blandamer, and she shut the door sharply, being annoyed at her own foolishness.

She went back to the kitchen, for the kitchen of the Hand of God was so large that Miss Joliffe and Anastasia used part of it for their sitting-room, took the pencil out of *Northanger Abbey*, and tried to transport herself to Bath. Five minutes ago she had been in the Grand Pump Room herself, and knew exactly where Mrs Allen and Isabella Thorpe and Edward Morland were sitting; where Catherine was standing, and what John Thorpe was saying to her when Tilney walked up. But alas! Anastasia found no re-admission; the lights were put out, the Pump Room was in darkness. A sad change to have happened in five minutes; but no doubt the charmed circle had dispersed in a huff on finding that they no longer occupied the first place in

Miss Anastasia Joliffe's interest. And, indeed, she missed them the less because she had discovered that she herself possessed a wonderful talent for romance, and had already begun the first chapter of a thrilling story.

Nearly half an hour passed before her aunt returned, and in the interval Miss Austen's knights and dames had retired still farther into the background, and Miss Anastasia's hero had entirely monopolised the stage. It was twenty minutes past five when Miss Joliffe, senior, returned from the Dorcas meeting; "precisely twenty minutes past five," as she remarked many times subsequently, with that factitious importance which the ordinary mind attaches to the exact moment of any epoch-making event.

"Is the water boiling, my dear?" she asked, sitting down at the kitchen table. "I should like to have tea today before the gentlemen come in, if you do not mind. The weather is quite oppressive, and the schoolroom was very close because we only had one window open. Poor Mrs Bulteel is so subject to take cold from draughts, and I very nearly fell asleep while she was reading."

"I will get tea at once," Anastasia said; and then added, in a tone of fine unconcern: "There is a gentleman waiting upstairs to see Mr Westray."

"My dear," Miss Joliffe exclaimed deprecatingly, "how could you let anyone in when I was not at home? It is exceedingly dangerous with so many doubtful characters about. There is Mr Westray's presentation inkstand, and the flower-picture for which I have been offered so much money. Valuable paintings are often cut out of their frames; one never has an idea what thieves may do."

There was the faintest trace of a smile about Anastasia's lips.

"I do not think we need trouble about that, dear Aunt Phemie, because I am sure he is a gentleman. Here is his card. Look!" She handed Miss Joliffe the insignificant little piece of white cardboard that held so momentous a secret, and watched her aunt put on her spectacles to read it.

Miss Joliffe focussed the card. There were only two words printed on it, only "Lord Blandamer" in the most unpretending and simple characters, but their effect was magical. Doubt and suspicion melted suddenly away, and a look of radiant surprise overspread her countenance, such as would have become a Constantine at the vision of the Labarum. She was a thoroughly unworldly woman, thinking little of the things of this life in general, and keeping her affections on that which is to come, with the constancy and realisation that is so often denied to those possessed of larger temporal means.

Her views as to right and wrong were defined and inflexible; she would have gone to the stake most cheerfully rather than violate them, and unconsciously lamented perhaps that civilisation has robbed the faithful of the luxury of burning. Yet with all this were inextricably bound up certain little weaknesses among which figured a fondness for great names, and a somewhat exaggerated consideration for the lofty ones of this earth. Had she been privileged to be within the same four walls as a peer at a bazaar or missionary meeting, she would have revelled in a great opportunity; but to find Lord Blandamer under her own roof was a grace so wondrous and surprising as almost to overwhelm her.

"Lord Blandamer!" she faltered, as soon as she had collected herself a little. "I hope Mr Westray's room was tidy. I dusted it thoroughly this morning, but I wish he had given some notice of his intention to call. I should be so vexed if he found anything dusty. What is he doing, Anastasia? Did he say he would wait till Mr Westray came back?"

"He said he would write a note for Mr Westray. I found him writing things."

"I hope you gave his lordship Mr Westray's presentation inkstand."

"No, I did not think of that; but there was the little black inkstand, and plenty of ink in it."

"Dear me, dear me!" Miss Joliffe said, ruminating on so extraordinary a position, "to think that Lord Blandamer, whom no one has ever seen, should have come to Cullerne at last, and is now in this very house. I will just change this bonnet for my Sunday one," she added, looking at herself in the glass, "and then tell his lordship how very welcome he is, and ask him if I can get anything for him. He will see at once, from my bonnet, that I have only just returned, otherwise it would appear to him very remiss of me not to have paid him my respects before. Yes, I think it is undoubtedly more fitting to appear in a bonnet."

Anastasia was a little perturbed at the idea of her aunt's interview with Lord Blandamer. She pictured to herself Miss Joliffe's excess of zeal, the compliments which she would think it necessary to shower upon him the marked attention and homage which he might interpret as servility, though it was only intended as a proper deference to exalted rank. Anastasia was quite unaccountably anxious that the family should appear to the distinguished visitor in as favourable a light as possible, and thought for a moment of trying to persuade Miss Joliffe that there was no need for her to see Lord Blandamer at all, unless he summoned her.

But she was of a philosophic temperament, and in a moment had rebuked her own folly. What could any impression of Lord Blandamer's matter to her? she would probably never see him again unless she opened the door when he went out. Why should he think anything at all about a commonplace lodging-house, and its inmates? And if such trivial matters did ever enter his thoughts, a man so clever as he would make allowance for those of a different station to himself, and would see what a good woman her aunt was in spite of any little mannerisms.

So she made no remonstrance, but sat heroically quiet in her chair, and re-opened *Northanger Abbey* with a determination to entirely forget Lord Blandamer, and the foolish excitement which his visit had created.

CHAPTER EIGHT

Miss Joliffe must have had a protracted conversation with Lord Blandamer. To Anastasia, waiting in the kitchen, it seemed as if her aunt would never come down. She devoted herself to *Northanger Abbey* with fierce resolution, but though her eyes followed the lines of type, she had no idea what she was reading, and found herself at last turning the pages so frequently and with so much rustling as to disturb her own reverie. Then she shut the book with a bang, got up from her chair, and paced the kitchen till her aunt came back.

Miss Joliffe was full of the visitor's affability.

"It is *always* the way with these really great people, my dear," she said with effusion. "I have *always* noticed that the nobility are condescending; they adapt themselves so entirely to their surroundings." Miss Joliffe fell into a common hyperbole in qualifying an isolated action as a habit. She had never before been brought face to face with a peer, yet she represented her first impression of Lord Blandamer's manner as if it were a mature judgment based upon long experience of those of his rank and position.

"I insisted on his using the presentation inkstand, and took away that shabby little black thing; and I could see at once that the silver one was far more like what he had been accustomed to use. He seemed to know something about us, and even asked if the young lady who had shown him in was my niece. That was you; he meant you, Anastasia; he asked if it was *you*. I think he must have met dear Martin somewhere, but I really was so agitated by such a very unexpected visit that I scarcely took in all he said. Yet he was so careful all the time to put me at my ease that at last I ventured to ask him if he would take some light refreshment. 'My lord,' I said, 'may I be so bold as to offer your lordship a cup of tea? It would be a great honour if you would partake of our humble hospitality.' And what *do* you think he answered, my dear? 'Miss Joliffe'—and he had such a winning look—'there is nothing I should like better. I am very tired with walking about in the church, and have still some little time to wait, for I am going to London by the evening train.' Poor young man! (for Lord Blandamer was still young in Cullerne, which had only known his octogenarian predecessor) he is no doubt called to London on some public business—the House of Lords, or the Court, or something like that. I wish he would take as much care of himself as he seems to take for others. He looks so very tired, and a sad face too, Anastasia, and yet is most considerate. 'I should like a cup of tea very much'—those were his exact words—'but you must not trouble to come all the way upstairs again to bring it to me. Let me come down and take it with you.'

"'Forgive me, my lord,' was my answer, 'but I could not permit that. Our establishment is much too homely, and I shall feel it a privilege to wait on you, if you will kindly excuse my walking-clothes, as I have just come back from an afternoon meeting. My niece often wishes to relieve me, but I tell her my old legs are more active than her young ones even still.'"

Anastasia's cheeks were red, but she said nothing, and her aunt went on: "So I will take him some tea at once. You can make it, my dear, if you like, but put a great deal more in than we use ourselves. The upper classes have no call to practise economy in such matters, and he is no doubt used to take his tea very strong. I think Mr Sharnall's teapot is the best, and I will get out the silver sugar-tongs and one of the spoons with the 'J' on them."

As Miss Joliffe was taking up the tea, she met Westray in the hall. He had just come back from the church, and was not a little concerned at his landlady's greeting. She put down her tray, and, with a fateful gesture and an "Oh, Mr Westray, what do you think?" beckoned him aside into Mr Sharnall's room. His first impression was that some grave accident had happened, that the organist was dead, or that Anastasia Joliffe had sprained an ankle; and he was relieved to hear the true state of affairs. He waited a few minutes while Miss Joliffe took the visitor his tea, and then went upstairs himself.

Lord Blandamer rose.

"I must apologise," he said, "for making myself at home in your room; but I hope your landlady may have explained who I am, and how I come to take so great a liberty. I am naturally interested in Cullerne and all that concerns it, and hope ere long to get better acquainted with the place—and the people," he added as an after-thought. "At present I know disgracefully little about it, but that is due to my having been abroad for many years; I only came back a few months ago. But I need not bother you with all this; what I really wanted was to ask you if you would give me some idea of the scheme of restoration which it is proposed to undertake at the minster. Until last week I had not heard that anything of the kind was in contemplation."

His tone was measured, and a clear, deep, voice gave weight and sincerity to his words. His clean-shaven face and olive complexion, his regular features and dark eyebrows, suggested a Spaniard to Westray as he spoke, and the impression was strengthened by the decorous and grave courtesy of his manner.

"I shall be delighted to explain anything I can," said the architect, and took down a bundle of plans and papers from a shelf.

"I fear I shall not be able to do much this evening," Lord Blandamer said; "for I have to catch the train to London in a short time; but, if you will allow me, I will take an early opportunity of coming over again. We might then, perhaps, go to the church together. The building has a great fascination for me, not only on account of its own magnificence, but also from old associations. When I was a boy, and sometimes a very unhappy boy, I used often to come over from Fording, and spend hours rambling about the minster. Its winding staircases, its dark wall-passages, its mysterious screens and stalls, brought me romantic dreams, from which I think I have never entirely wakened. I am told the building stands in need of extensive restoration, though to the outsider it looks much the same as ever. It always had a dilapidated air."

Westray gave a short outline of what it was considered should ultimately be done, and of what it was proposed to attack for the present.

"You see, we have our work cut out for us," he said. "The transept roof is undoubtedly the most urgent matter, but there are lots of other things that cannot be left to themselves for long. I have grave doubts about the stability of the tower, though my chief doesn't share them to anything like the same extent: and perhaps that is just as well, for we are hampered on every side by lack of funds. They are going to have a bazaar next week to try to give the thing a lift, but a hundred bazaars would not produce half that is wanted."

"I gathered that there were difficulties of this kind," the visitor said reflectively. "As I came out of the church after service today I met the organist. He had no idea who I was, but gave his views very strongly as to Lord Blandamer's responsibilities for things in general, and for the organ in particular. We are, I suppose, under some sort of moral obligation for the north transept, from having annexed it as a burying-place. It used to be called, I fancy, the Blandamer Aisle."

"Yes, it is called so still," Westray answered. He was glad to see the turn the conversation had taken, and hoped that a *deus ex machina* had appeared. Lord Blandamer's next question was still more encouraging.

"At what do you estimate the cost of the transept repairs?"

Westray ran through his papers till he found a printed leaflet with a view of Cullerne Minster on the outside.

"Here are Sir George Farquhar's figures," he said. "This was a circular that was sent everywhere to invite subscriptions, but it scarcely paid the cost of printing. No one will give a penny to these things nowadays. Here it is, you see—seven thousand eight hundred pounds for the north transept."

There was a little pause. Westray did not look up, being awkwardly conscious that the sum was larger than Lord Blandamer had anticipated, and fearing that such an abrupt disclosure might have damped the generosity of an intended contributor.

Lord Blandamer changed the subject.

"Who is the organist? I rather liked his manner, for all he took me so sharply, if impersonally, to task. He seems a clever musician, but his instrument is in a shocking state."

"He *is* a very clever organist," Westray answered. It was evident that Lord Blandamer was in a subscribing frame of mind, and if his generosity did not extend to undertaking the cost of the transept, he might at least give something towards the organ. The architect tried to do his friend Mr Sharnall a service. "He is a very clever organist," he repeated; "his name is Sharnall, and he lodges in this house. Shall I call him? Would you like to ask him about the organ?"

"Oh no, not now; I have so little time; another day we can have a chat. Surely a very little money—comparatively little money, I mean—

would put the organ in proper repair. Did they never approach my grandfather, the late Lord Blandamer, on the question of funds for these restorations?"

Westray's hopes of a contribution were again dashed, and he felt a little contemptuous at such evasions. They came with an ill grace after Lord Blandamer's needlessly affectionate panegyric of the church.

"Yes," he said; "Canon Parkyn, the rector here, wrote to the late Lord Blandamer begging for a subscription to the restoration fund for the church, but never got any answer."

Westray flung something like a sneer into his tone, and was already sorry for his ungracious words before he had finished speaking. But the other seemed to take no offence, where some would have been offended.

"Ah," he said, "my grandfather was no doubt a very sad old man indeed. I must go now, or I shall miss my train. You shall introduce me to Mr Sharnall the next time I come to Cullerne; I have your promise, remember, to take me over the church. Is it not so?"

"Yes—oh yes, certainly," Westray said, though with less cordiality perhaps than he had used on the previous occasion. He was disappointed that Lord Blandamer had promised no subscription, and accompanied him to the foot of the stairs with much the same feelings as a shop-assistant entertains for the lady who, having turned over goods for half an hour, retreats with the promise that she will consider the matter and call again.

Miss Joliffe had been waiting on the kitchen stairs, and so was able to meet Lord Blandamer in the hall quite accidentally. She showed him out of the front-door with renewed professions of respect, for she knew nothing of his niggardly evasions of a subscription, and in her eyes a lord was still a lord. He added the comble to all his graces and courtesies by shaking her hand as he left the house, and expressing a hope that she would be so kind as to give him another cup of tea, the very next time he was in Cullerne.

The light was failing as Lord Blandamer descended the flight of steps outside the door of Bellevue Lodge. The evening must have closed in earlier than usual, for very soon after the visitor had gone upstairs Anastasia found it too dark to read in the kitchen; so she took her book, and sat in the window-seat of Mr Sharnall's room.

It was a favourite resort of hers, both when Mr Sharnall was out, and also when he was at home; for he had known her from childhood, and liked to watch the graceful girlish form as she read quietly while he worked at his music. The deep window-seat was panelled in painted deal, and along the side of it hung a faded cushion, which could be turned over on to the sill when the sash was thrown up, so as to form a rest for the arms of anyone who desired to look out on a summer evening.

The window was still open, though it was dusk; but Anastasia's head, which just appeared above the sill, was screened from observation by a low blind. This blind was formed of a number of little green wooden slats, faded and blistered by the suns of many summers, and so arranged that, by the turning of a brass, urn-shaped knob, they could be made to open and afford a prospect of the outer world to anyone sitting inside.

It had been for some time too dark for Anastasia to read, but she still sat in the window-seat; and as she heard Lord Blandamer come down the stairs, she turned the brass urn so as to command a view of the street. She felt herself blushing in the dusk, at the reiterated and voluminous compliments which her aunt was paying in the hall. She blushed because Westray's tone was too off-handed and easy towards so important a personage to please her critical mood; and then she blushed again at her own folly in blushing. The front-door shut at last, and the gaslight fell on Lord Blandamer's active figure and straight, square shoulders as he went down the steps. Three thousand years before, another maiden had looked between the doorpost and the door, at the straight broad back of another great stranger as he left her father's palace; but Anastasia was more fortunate than Nausicaa, for there is no record that Ulysses cast any backward glance as he walked down to the Phaeacian ship, and Lord Blandamer did turn and look back.

He turned and looked back; he seemed to Anastasia to look between the little blistered slats into her very eyes. Of course, he could not have guessed that a very foolish girl, the niece of a very foolish landlady in a very commonplace lodging-house, in a very commonplace country town, was watching him behind a shutter; but he turned and looked, and Anastasia stayed for half an hour after he had gone, thinking of the hard and clean-cut face that she had seen for an instant in the flickering gaslight.

It was a hard face, and as she sat in the dark with closed eyes, and saw that face again and again in her mind, she knew that it was hard. It was hard—it was almost cruel. No, it was not cruel, but only recklessly resolved, with a resolution that would not swerve from cruelty, if cruelty were needed to accomplish its purpose. Thus she reasoned in the approved manner of fiction. She knew that such reasonings were demanded of heroines. A heroine must be sadly unworthy of her lofty role if she could not with a glance unmask even the most enigmatic countenance, and trace the passions writ in it, clearly as a page of *Reading without Tears*. And was she, Anastasia, to fall short in such a simple craft? No, she had measured the man's face in a moment; it was resolved, even to cruelty. It was hard, but ah! how handsome! and she remembered how the grey eyes had met hers and blinded them with power, when she first saw him on the doorstep. Wondrous musings, wondrous thought-reading, by a countrified young lady in her teens; but is it not out of the mouths of babes and sucklings that strength has been eternally ordained?

She was awakened from her reverie by the door being flung open, and she leapt from her perch as Mr Sharnall entered the room.

"Heyday! heyday!" he said, "what have we here? Fire out, and window open; missy dreaming of Sir Arthur Bedevere, and catching a cold—a very poetic cold in the head."

His words jarred on her mood like the sharpening of a slate-pencil. She said nothing, but brushed by him, shut the door behind her, and left him muttering in the dark.

The excitement of Lord Blandamer's visit had overtaxed Miss Joliffe. She took the gentlemen their supper—and Mr Westray was supping in Mr Sharnall's room that evening—and assured Anastasia that she was not in the least tired. But ere long she was forced to give up this pretence, and to take refuge in a certain high-backed chair with ears, which stood in a corner of the kitchen, and was only brought into use in illness or other emergency. The bell rang for supper to be taken away, but Miss Joliffe was fast asleep, and did not hear it. Anastasia was not allowed to "wait" under ordinary circumstances, but her aunt must not be disturbed when she was so tired, and she took the tray herself and went upstairs.

"He is a striking-looking man enough," Westray was saying as she entered the room; "but I must say he did not impress me favourably in other respects. He spoke too enthusiastically about the church. It would have sat on him with a very good grace if he had afterwards come down with five hundred pounds, but ecstasies are out of place when a man won't give a halfpenny to turn them into reality."

"He is a chip of the old block," said the organist.

Leap year's February twenty-nine days,

And on the thirtieth Blandamer pays.

"That's a saw about here. Well, I rubbed it into him this afternoon, and all the harder because I hadn't the least idea who he was."

There was a fierce colour in Anastasia's cheeks as she packed the dirty plates and supper debris into the tray, and a fiercer feeling in her heart. She tried hard to conceal her confusion, and grew more confused in the effort. The organist watched her closely, without ever turning his eyes in her direction. He was a cunning little man, and before the table was cleared had guessed who was the hero of those dreams, from which he had roused her an hour earlier.

Westray waved away with his hand a puff of smoke which drifted into his face from Mr Sharnall's pipe.

"He asked me whether anyone had ever approached the old lord about the restoration, and I said the rector had written, and never got an answer."

"It wasn't to the *old* lord he wrote," Mr Sharnall cut in; "it was to this very man. Didn't you know it was to this very man? No one ever thought it worth ink and paper to write to *old* Blandamer. I was the only one, fool enough to do that. I had an appeal for the organ printed once upon a time, and sent him a copy, and asked him to head the list. After a bit he sent me a cheque for ten shillings and sixpence; and then I wrote and thanked him, and said it would do very nicely to put a new leg on the organ-stool if one should ever break. But he had the last word, for when I went to the bank to cash the cheque, I found it stopped."

Westray laughed with a thin and tinkling merriment that irritated Anastasia more than an honest guffaw.

"When he stuck at seven thousand eight hundred pounds for the church, I tried to give *you* a helping hand with the organ. I told him you lived in the house; would he not like to see you? 'Oh no, not *now*,' he said; 'some other day.'"

"He is a chip of the old block," the organist said again bitterly. "Gather figs of thistles, if you will, but don't expect money from Blandamers."

Anastasia's thumb went into the curry as she lifted the dish, but she did not notice it. She was only eager to get away, to place herself outside the reach of these slanderous tongues, to hide herself where she could unburden her heart of its bitterness. Mr Sharnall fired one more shaft at her as she left the room.

377

"He takes after his grandfather in other ways besides close-fistedness. The old man had a bad enough name with women, and this man has a worse. They are a poor lot—lock, stock, and barrel."

Lord Blandamer had certainly been unhappy in the impression which he created at Bellevue Lodge; a young lady had diagnosed his countenance as hard and cruel, an architect had detected niggardliness in his disposition, and an organist was resolved to regard him at all hazards as a personal foe. It was fortunate indeed for his peace of mind that he was completely unaware of this, but, then, he might not perhaps have troubled much even if he had known all about it. The only person who had a good word for him was Miss Euphemia Joliffe. She woke up flushed, but refreshed, after her nap, and found the supper-things washed and put away in their places.

"My dear, my dear," she said deprecatingly, "I am afraid I have been asleep, and left all the work to you. You should not have done this, Anastasia. You ought to have awakened me." The flesh was weak, and she was forced to hold her hand before her mouth for a moment to conceal a yawn; but her mind reverted instinctively to the great doings of the day, and she said with serene reflection: "A very remarkable man, so dignified and yet so affable, and *very* handsome too, my dear."

CHAPTER NINE.

Among the letters which the postman brought to Bellevue Lodge on the morning following these remarkable events was an envelope which possessed a dreadful fascination. It bore a little coronet stamped in black upon the flap, and "Edward Westray, Esquire, Bellevue Lodge, Cullerne," written on the front in a bold and clear hand. But this was not all, for low in the left corner was the inscription "Blandamer." A single word, yet fraught with so mystical an import that it set Anastasia's heart beating fast as she gave it to her aunt, to be taken upstairs with the architect's breakfast.

"There is a letter for you, sir, from Lord Blandamer," Miss Joliffe said, as she put down the tray on the table.

But the architect only grunted, and went on with ruler and compass at the plan with which he was busy. Miss Joliffe would have been more than woman had she not felt a burning curiosity to know the contents of so important a missive; and to leave a nobleman's letter neglected on the table seemed to her little short of sacrilege.

Never had breakfast taken longer to lay, and still there was the letter lying by the tin cover, which (so near is grandeur to our dust) concealed a simple bloater. Poor Miss Joliffe made a last effort ere she left the room to bring Westray to a proper appreciation of the situation.

"There is a letter for you, sir; I think it is from Lord Blandamer."

"Yes, yes," the architect said sharply; "I will attend to it presently."

And so she retired, routed.

Westray's nonchalance had been in part assumed. He was anxious to show that he, at any rate, could rise superior to artificial distinctions of rank, and was no more to be impressed by peers than peasants. He kept up this philosophic indifference even after Miss Joliffe left the room; for he took life very seriously, and felt his duty towards himself to be at least as important as that towards his neighbours. Resolution lasted till the second cup of tea, and then he opened the letter.

Dear Sir

I understood from you yesterday that the repairs to the north transept of Cullerne Minster are estimated to cost 7,800 pounds. This charge I should like to bear myself, and thus release for other purposes of restoration the sum already collected. I am also prepared to undertake whatever additional outlay is required to put the whole building in a state of substantial repair. Will you kindly inform Sir George Farquhar of this, and ask him to review the scheme of restoration as modified by these considerations? I shall be in Cullerne on Saturday next, and hope I may find you at home if I call about five in the afternoon, and that you may then have time to show me the church.

I am, dear sir,

Very truly yours,

Blandamer.

Westray had scanned the letter so rapidly that he knew its contents by intuition rather than by the more prosaic method of reading. Nor did he re-read it several times, as is generally postulated by important communications in fiction; he simply held it in his hand, and crumpled it unconsciously, while he thought. He was surprised, and he was pleased—pleased at the wider *vista* of activity that Lord Blandamer's offer opened, and pleased that he should be chosen as the channel through which an announcement of such gravity was to be made. He felt, in short, that pleasurable and confused excitement, that mental inebriation, which unexpected good fortune is apt to produce in any except the strongest minds, and went down to Mr Sharnall's room still crumpling the letter in his hand. The bloater was left to waste its sweetness on the morning air.

"I have just received some extraordinary news," he said, as he opened the door.

Mr Sharnall was not altogether unprepared, for Miss Joliffe had already informed him that a letter from Lord Blandamer had arrived for Mr Westray; so he only said "Ah!" in a tone that implied compassion for the lack of mental balance which allowed Westray to be so easily astonished, and added "Ah, yes?" as a manifesto that no sublunary catastrophe could possibly astonish him, Mr Sharnall. But Westray's excitement was cold-waterproof, and he read the letter aloud with much jubilation.

"Well," said the organist, "I don't see much in it; seven thousand pounds is nothing to him. When we have done all that we ought to do, we are unprofitable servants."

"It isn't only seven thousand pounds; don't you see he gives carte-blanche for repairs in general? Why, it may be thirty or forty thousand, or even more."

"Don't you wish you may get it?" the organist said, raising his eyebrows and shutting his eyelids.

Westray was nettled.

"Oh, I think it's mean to sneer at everything the man does. We abused him yesterday as a niggard; let us have the grace today to say we were mistaken." He was afflicted with the over-scrupulosity of a refined, but strictly limited mind, and his conscience smote him. "I, at any rate, was quite mistaken," he went on; "I quite misinterpreted his hesitation when I mentioned the cost of the transept repairs."

"Your chivalrous sentiments do you the greatest credit," the organist said, "and I congratulate you on being able to change your ideas so quickly. As for me, I prefer to stick to my first opinion. It is all humbug; either he doesn't mean to pay, or else he has some plan of his own to push. *I* wouldn't touch his money with a barge-pole."

"Oh no, of course not," Westray said, with the exaggerated sarcasm of a schoolboy in his tone. "If he was to offer a thousand pounds to restore the organ, you wouldn't take a penny of it."

"He hasn't offered a thousand yet," rejoined the organist; "and when he does, I'll send him away with a flea in his ear."

"That's a very encouraging announcement for would-be contributors," Westray sneered; "they ought to come forward very strongly after that."

"Well, I must get on with some copying," the organist said dryly;

and Westray went back to the bloater.

If Mr Sharnall was thus pitiably wanting in appreciation of a munificent offer, the rest of Cullerne made no pretence of imitating his example. Westray was too elated to keep the good news to himself, nor did there appear, indeed, to be any reason for making a secret of it. So he told the foreman-mason, and Mr Janaway the clerk, and Mr Noot the curate, and lastly Canon Parkyn the rector, whom he certainly ought to have told the first of all. Thus, before the carillon of Saint Sepulchre's played "New Sabbath," at three o'clock that afternoon, the whole town was aware that the new Lord Blandamer had been among them, and had promised to bear the cost of restoring the great minster of which they were all so proud—so very much more proud when their pride entailed no sordid considerations of personal subscription.

Canon Parkyn was ruffled. Mrs Parkyn perceived it when he came in to dinner at one o'clock, but, being a prudent woman, she did not allude directly to his ill-humour, though she tried to dispel it by leading the conversation to topics which experience had shown her were soothing to him. Among such the historic visit of Sir George Farquhar, and the deference which he had paid to the rector's suggestions, occupied a leading position: but the mention of the great architect's name, was a signal for a fresh exhibition of vexation on her husband's part.

"I wish," he said, "that Sir George would pay a little more personal attention to the work at the minster. His representative, this Mr—er—er—this Mr Westray, besides being, I fear, very inexperienced and deficient in architectural knowledge, is a most conceited young man, and constantly putting himself forward in an unbecoming way. He came to me this morning with an exceedingly strange communication—a letter from Lord Blandamer."

Mrs Parkyn laid down her knife and fork.

"A letter from Lord Blandamer?" she said in unconcealed amazement—"a letter from Lord Blandamer to Mr Westray!"

"Yes," the rector went on, losing some of his annoyance in the pleasurable consciousness that his words created a profound sensation—"a letter in which his lordship offers to bear in the first place the cost of the repairs of the north transept, and afterwards to make good any deficiency in the funds required for the restoration of the rest of the fabric. Of course, I am very loath to question any action taken by a member of the Upper House, but at the same time I am compelled to characterise the proceeding as most irregular. That such a communication should be made to a mere clerk of the works, instead of to the rector and duly appointed guardian of the sacred edifice, is so grave a breach of propriety that I am tempted to veto the matter entirely, and to refuse to accept this offer."

His face wore a look of sublime dignity, and he addressed his wife as if she were a public meeting. *Ruat coelum*, Canon Parkyn was not to be moved a hair's-breadth from the line traced by propriety and rectitude. He knew in his inmost heart that under no possible circumstances would he have refused any gift that was offered him, yet his own words had about them so heroic a ring that for a moment he saw himself dashing Lord Blandamer's money on the floor, as early Christians had flung to the wind that pinch of incense that would have saved them from the lions.

"I think I *must* refuse this offer," he repeated.

Mrs Parkyn knew her husband intimately—more intimately, perhaps, than he knew himself—and had an additional guarantee that the discussion was merely academic in the certainty that, even were he really purposed to refuse the offer, she would not *allow* him to do so. Yet she played the game, and feigned to take him seriously.

"I quite appreciate your scruples, my dear; they are just what anyone who knew you would expect. It is a positive affront that you should be told of such a proposal by this impertinent young man; and Lord Blandamer has so strange a reputation himself that one scarcely knows how far it is right to accept anything from him for sacred purposes. I honour your reluctance. Perhaps it *would* be right for you to decline this proposal, or, at any rate, to take time for consideration."

The rector looked furtively at his wife. He was a little alarmed at her taking him so readily at his word. He had hoped that she would be dismayed—that she could have brought proper arguments to bear to shake his high resolve.

"Ah, your words have unwittingly reminded me of my chief difficulty in refusing. It is the sacred purpose which makes me doubt my own judgment. It would be a painful reflection to think that the temple should suffer by my refusing this gift. Maybe I should be yielding to my own petulance or personal motives if I were to decline. I must not let my pride stand in the way of higher obligations."

He concluded in his best pulpit manner, and the farce was soon at an end. It was agreed that the gift must be accepted, that proper measures should be taken to rebuke Mr Westray's presumption, as *he* had no doubt induced Lord Blandamer to select so improper a channel of communication, and that the rector should himself write direct to thank the noble donor. So, after dinner, Canon Parkyn retired to his "study," and composed a properly fulsome letter, in which he attributed all the noblest possible motives and qualities to Lord Blandamer, and invoked all the most unctuously conceived blessings upon his head. And at teatime the letter was perused and revised by Mrs Parkyn, who added some finishing touches of her own, especially a preamble which stated that Canon Parkyn had been informed by the clerk of the works that Lord Blandamer had expressed a desire to write to Canon Parkyn to make a certain offer, but had asked the clerk of the works to find out first whether such an offer would be acceptable to Canon Parkyn, and a peroration which hoped that Lord Blandamer would accept the hospitality of the rectory on the occasion of his next visit to Cullerne.

The letter reached Lord Blandamer at Fording the next morning as he sat over a late breakfast, with a Virgil open on the table by his coffee-cup. He read the rector's stilted periods without a smile, and made a mental note that he would at once send a specially civil acknowledgment. Then he put it carefully into his pocket, and turned back to the *Di patrii indigetes et Romule Vestaque Mater* of the First Georgic, which he was committing to memory, and banished the invitation so completely from his mind that he never thought of it again till he was in Cullerne a week later.

Lord Blandamer's visit, and the offer which he had made for the restoration of the church, formed the staple of Cullerne conversation for a week. All those who had been fortunate enough to see or to speak to him discussed him with one another, and compared notes. Scarcely a detail of his personal appearance, of his voice or manner escaped them; and so infectious was this interest that some who had never seen him at all were misled by their excitement into narrating how he had stopped them in the street to ask the way to the architect's lodgings, and how he had made so many striking and authentic remarks that it was wonderful that he had ever reached Bellevue Lodge at all that night. Clerk Janaway, who was sorely chagrined to think that he should have missed an opportunity of distinguished converse, declared that he had felt the stranger's grey eyes go through and through him like a knife, and had only made believe to stop him entering the choir, in order to convince himself by the other's masterful insistence that his own intuition was correct. He had known all the time, he said, that he was speaking to none other than Lord Blandamer.

Westray thought the matter important enough to justify him in going to London to consult Sir George Farquhar, as to the changes in the scheme of restoration which Lord Blandamer's munificence made possible; but Mr Sharnall, at any rate, was left to listen to Miss Joliffe's recollections, surmises, and panegyrics.

In spite of all the indifference which the organist had affected when he first heard the news, he showed a surprising readiness to discuss the affair with all comers, and exhibited no trace of his usual impatience with Miss Joliffe, so long as she was talking of Lord Blandamer. To Anastasia it seemed as if he could talk of nothing else, and the more she tried to check him by her silence or by change of subject, the more bitterly did he return to the attack.

The only person to exhibit no interest in this unhappy nobleman, who had outraged propriety by offering to contribute to the restoration of the minster, was Anastasia herself; and even tolerant Miss Joliffe was moved to chide her niece's apathy in this particular.

"I do not think it becomes us, love, young or old, to take so little notice of great and good deeds. Mr Sharnall is, I fear, discontented with the station of life to which it has pleased Providence to call him, and I am less surprised at *his* not always giving praise where praise should be given; but with the young it is different. I am sure if anyone had offered to restore Wydcombe Church when I was a girl—and specially a nobleman—I should have been as delighted, or nearly as delighted, as if he—as if I had been given a new frock."

She altered the "as if he had given me" which was upon her tongue because the proposition, even for purposes of illustration, that a nobleman could ever have offered her a new frock seemed to have in itself something of the scandalous and unfitting.

"I should have been delighted, but, dear me! in those days people were so blind as never to think of restorations. We used to sit in quite *comfortable* seats every Sunday, with cushions and hassocks, and the aisles were paved with flagstones—simple worn flagstones, and none of the caustic tiles which look so much more handsome; though I am always afraid I am going to slip, and glad to be off them, they are so hard and shiny. Church matters were very behindhand then. All round the walls were tablets that people had put up to their relations, white caskets on black marble slates, and urns and cherubs' heads, and just opposite where I used to sit a poor lady, whose name I have forgotten, weeping under a willow-tree. No doubt they were very much out of place in the sanctuary, as the young gentleman said in his lecture on 'How to make our Churches Beautiful' in the Town Hall last winter.

"He called them 'mural blisters,' my dear, but there was no talk of removing them in my young days, and that was, I dare say, because there was no one to give the money for it. But now, here is this good young nobleman, Lord Blandamer, come forward so handsomely, and I have no doubt at Cullerne all will be much improved ere long. We are not meant to *loll* at our devotions, as the lecturer told us. That was his word, to '*loll*'; and they will be sure to take away the baize and hassocks, though I do hope there will be a little strip of *something* on the seats; the bare wood is apt to make one ache sometimes. I should not say it to anyone else in the world but you, but it *does* make me ache a little sometimes; and when the caustic is put down in the aisle, I shall take your arm, my dear, to save me from slipping. Here is Lord Blandamer going to do all this for us, and you do not show yourself in the least grateful. It is not becoming in a young girl."

"Dear aunt, what would you have me do? I cannot go and thank him publicly in the name of the town. That would be still more unbecoming; and I am sure I hope they will not do all the dreadful things in the church that you speak of. I love the old monuments, and like *lolling* much better than bare forms."

So she would laugh the matter off; but if she could not be induced to talk of Lord Blandamer, she thought of him the more, and rehearsed again and again in day-dreams and in night-dreams every incident of that momentous Saturday afternoon, from the first bars of the overture, when he had revealed in so easy and simple a way that he was none other than Lord Blandamer, to the ringing down of the curtain, when he turned to look back—to that glance when his eyes had seemed to meet hers, although she was hidden behind a blind, and he could not have guessed that she was there.

Westray came back from London with the scheme of restoration reconsidered and amplified in the light of altered circumstances, and with a letter for Lord Blandamer in which Sir George Farquhar hoped that the munificent donor would fix a day on which Sir George might come down to Cullerne to offer his respects, and to discuss the matter in person. Westray had looked forward all the week to the appointment which he had with Lord Blandamer for five o'clock on the Saturday afternoon, and had carefully thought out the route which he would pursue in taking him round the church. He returned to Bellevue Lodge at a quarter to five, and found his visitor already awaiting him. Miss Joliffe was, as usual, at her Saturday meeting, but Anastasia told Westray that Lord Blandamer had been waiting more than half an hour.

"I must apologise, my lord, for keeping you waiting," Westray said, as he went in. "I feared I had made some mistake in the time of our meeting, but I see it *was* five that your note named." And he held out the open letter which he had taken from his pocket.

"The mistake is entirely mine," Lord Blandamer admitted with a smile, as he glanced at his own instructions; "I fancied I had said four o'clock; but I have been very glad of a few minutes to write one or two letters."

"We can post them on our way to the church; they will just catch the mail."

"Ah, then I must wait till tomorrow; there are some enclosures which I have not ready at this moment."

They set out together for the minster, and Lord Blandamer looked back as they crossed the street.

"The house has a good deal of character," he said, "and might be made comfortable enough with a little repair. I must ask my agent to see what can be arranged; it does not do me much credit as landlord in its present state."

"Yes, it has a good many interesting features," Westray answered; "you know its history, of course—I mean that it was an old inn."

He had turned round as his companion turned, and for an instant thought he saw something moving behind the blind in Mr Sharnall's room. But he must have been mistaken; only Anastasia was in the house, and she was in the kitchen, for he had called to her as they went out to say that he might be late for tea.

Westray thoroughly enjoyed the hour and a half which the light allowed him for showing and explaining the church. Lord Blandamer exhibited what is called, so often by euphemism, an intelligent interest in all that he saw, and was at no pains either to conceal or display a very adequate architectural knowledge. Westray wondered where he had acquired it, though he asked no questions; but before the inspection was ended he found himself unconsciously talking to his companion of technical points, as to a professional equal and not to an amateur. They stopped for a moment under the central tower.

"I feel especially grateful," Westray said, "for your generosity in giving us a free hand for all fabric work, because we shall now be able to tackle the tower. Nothing will ever induce me to believe that all is right up there. The arches are extraordinarily wide and thin for their date. You will laugh when I tell you that I sometimes think I hear them crying for repair, and especially that one on the south with the jagged crack in the wall above it. Now and then, when I am alone in the church or the tower, I seem to catch their very words. '*The arch never sleeps,*' they say; '*we never sleep.*'"

"It is a romantic idea," Lord Blandamer said. "Architecture is poetry turned into stone, according to the old aphorism, and you, no doubt, have something of the poet in you."

He glanced at the thin and rather bloodless face, and at the high cheekbones of the water-drinker as he spoke. Lord Blandamer never made jokes, and very seldom was known to laugh, yet if anyone but Westray had been with him, they might have fancied that there was a whimsical tone in his words, and a trace of amusement in the corners of his eyes. But the architect did not see it, and coloured slightly as he went on:

"Well, perhaps you are right; I suppose architecture does inspire one. The first verses I ever wrote, or the first, at least, that I ever had printed, were on the Apse of Tewkesbury Abbey. They came out in the *Gloucester Herald*, and I dare say I shall scribble something about these arches some day."

"Do," said Lord Blandamer, "and send me a copy. This place ought to have its poet, and it is much safer to write verses to arches than to arched eyebrows."

Westray coloured again, and put his hand in his breast-pocket. Could he have been so foolish as to leave those half-finished lines on his desk for Lord Blandamer or anyone else to see? No, they were quite safe; he could feel the sharp edge of the paper folded lengthways, which differentiated them from ordinary letters.

"We shall just have time to go up to the roof-space, if you care to do so," he suggested, changing the subject. "I should like to show you the top of the transept groining, and explain what we are busy with at present. It is always more or less dark up there, but we shall find lanterns."

"Certainly, with much pleasure." And they climbed the newel staircase that was carried in the north-east pier.

Clerk Janaway had been hovering within a safe distance of them as they went their round. He was nominally busy in "putting things straight" for the Sunday, before the church was shut up; and had kept as much out of sight as was possible, remembering how he had withstood Lord Blandamer to the face a week before. Yet he was anxious to meet him, as it were, by accident, and explain that he had acted in ignorance of the real state of affairs; but no favourable opportunity for such an explanation presented itself. The pair had gone up to the roof, and the clerk was preparing to lock up—for Westray had a key of his own—when he heard someone coming up the nave.

It was Mr Sharnall, who carried a pile of music-books under his arm.

"Hallo!" he said to the clerk, "what makes *you* so late? I expected to have to let myself in. I thought you would have been off an hour ago."

"Well, things took a bit longer tonight than usual to put away." He broke off, for there was a little noise somewhere above them in the scaffolding, and went on in what was meant for a whisper: "Mr Westray's taking his lordship round; they're up in the roof now. D'ye hear 'em?"

"Lordship! What lordship? D'you mean that fellow Blandamer?"

"Yes, that's just who I do mean. But I don't know as how he's a fellow, and he *is* a lordship; so that's why I call him a lordship and not a fellow. And might I ask what he's been doing to set *your* back up? Why don't you wait here for him, and talk to him about the organ? Maybe, now he's in the giving mood, he'd set it right for 'ee, or anyways give 'ee that little blowin'-engine you talk so much about. Why do 'ee always go about showin' your teeth?—metaforally, I mean, for you haven't that many real ones left to make much show—why ain't you like other folk sometimes? Shall I tell 'ee? 'Cause you wants to be young when you be old, and rich when you be poor. That's why. That makes 'ee miserable, and then you drinks to drown it. Take my advice, and act like other folk. I'm nigh a score of years older than you, and take a vast more pleasure in my life than when I was twenty. The neighbours and their ways tickle me now, and my pipe's sweeter; and there's many a foolish thing a young man does that age don't give an old one the chanst to. You've spoke straight to me, and now I've spoke straight to you, 'cause I'm a straight-speaking man, and have no call to be afraid of anyone—lord or fellow or organist. So take an old man's word: cheer up, and wait on my lord, and get him to give 'ee a new organ."

"Bah!" said Mr Sharnall, who was far too used to Janaway's manner to take umbrage or pay attention to it. "Bah! I hate all Blandamers. I wish they were as dead and buried as dodos; and I'm not at all sure they aren't. I'm not at all sure, mind you, that this strutting peacock has any more right to the name of Blandamer than you or I have. I'm sick of all this wealth. No one's thought anything of today, who can't build a church or a museum or a hospital. 'So long as thou doest well unto *thyself*, men will speak good of thee.' If you've got the money, you're everything that's wonderful, and if you haven't, you may go rot. I wish all Blandamers were in their graves," he said, raising his thin and strident voice till it rang again in the vault above, "and wrapped up in their nebuly coat for a shroud. I should like to fling a stone through their damned badge." And he pointed to the sea-green and silver shield high up in the transept window. "Sunlight and moonlight, it is always there. I used to like to come down and play here to the bats of a full moon, till I saw *that* would always look into the loft and haunt me."

He thumped his pile of books down on a seat, and flung out of the church. He had evidently been drinking, and the clerk made his escape at the same time, being anxious not to be identified with senti-ments which had been so loudly enunciated that he feared those in the roof might have overheard them.

Lord Blandamer wished Westray goodnight at the church-door, excusing himself from an invitation to tea on the ground of business which necessitated his return to Fording.

"We must spend another afternoon in the minster," he said. "I hope you will allow me to write to make an appointment. I am afraid that it may possibly be for a Saturday again, for I am much occupied at present during the week."

✶✶✶✶✶✶

Clerk Janaway lived not far from the church, in Governor's Lane. No one knew whence its name was derived, though Dr Ennefer thought that the Military Governour might have had his quarters thereabouts when Cullerne was held for the Parliament. Serving as a means of communication between two quiet back-streets, it was itself more quiet than either, and yet; for all this, had about it a certain air of comfort and well-being. The passage of vehicles was barred at either end by old cannon. Their breeches were buried in the ground, and their muzzles stood up as sturdy iron posts, while the brown cobbles of the roadway sloped to a shallow stone gutter which ran down the middle of the lane. Custom ordained that the houses should be col-oured with a pink wash; and the shutters, which were a feature of the place, shone in such bright colours as to recall a Dutch town.

Shutter-painting was indeed an event of some importance in Governour's Lane. Not a few of its inhabitants had followed the sea as fishermen or smack-owners, and when fortune so smiled on them that they could retire, and there were no more boats to be painted, shutters and doors and window-frames came in to fill the gap. So, on a fine morning, when the turpentine oozing from cracks, and the warm smell of blistering varnish brought to Governour's Lane the first tokens of returning summer, might have been seen sexagenarians and septuagenarians, and some so strong that they had come to fourscore years, standing paint-pot and paint-brush in hand, while they gave a new coat to the woodwork of their homes.

They were a kindly folk, open of face, and fresh-complexioned, broad in the beam, and vested as to their bodies in dark blue, brass-buttoned pilot coats. Insuperable smokers, inexhaustible yarn-spinners, they had long welcomed Janaway as a kindred spirit—the more so that in their view a clerk and grave-digger was in some measure an expert in things unseen, who might *anon* assist in piloting them on that last cruise for which some had already the *Blue Peter* at the fore.

A myrtle-bush which grew out of a hole in the cobbles was carefully trained against the front of a cottage in the middle of the row, and a brass plate on the door informed the wayfarer and ignorant man that "T. Janaway, Sexton," dwelt within. About eight o'clock on the Saturday evening, some two hours after Lord Blandamer and Westray had parted, the door of the myrtle-fronted cottage was open, and the clerk stood on the threshold smoking his pipe, while from within came a cheerful, ruddy light and a well-defined smell of cooking; for Mrs Janaway was preparing supper.

"Tom," she called, "shut the door, and come to thy victuals."

"Ay," he answered, "I'll be with 'ee directly; but gi'e me a minute. I want to see who this is coming up the lane."

Someone that the clerk knew at once for a stranger had entered the little street at the bottom. There was half a moon, and light enough to see that he was in search of some particular house; for he crossed from one side of the lane to the other, and peered at the numbers on the doors. As he came nearer, the clerk saw that he was of spare build, and wore a loose overcoat or cape, which fluttered in the breeze that blew at evening from the sea. A moment later Janaway knew that the stranger was Lord Blandamer, and stepped back instinctively to let him pass. But the open door had caught the attention of the passer-by; he stopped, and greeted the householder cheerily.

"A beautiful night, but with a cold touch in the air that makes your warm room look very cheerful." He recognised the clerk's face as he spoke, and went on: "Ah, ha! we are old friends already; we met in the minster a week ago, did we not?"

Mr Janaway was a little disconcerted at the unexpectedness of the meeting, and returned the salutation in a confused way. The attempt which he had made to prevent Lord Blandamer from entering the choir was fresh in his memory, and he stammered some unready excuses.

Lord Blandamer smiled with much courtesy.

"You were quite right to stop me; you would have been neglecting your duty if you had not done so. I had no idea that service was going on, or I should not have come in; you may make your mind quite easy on that score. I hope you will have many more opportunities of finding a place for me in Cullerne Church."

"No need to find any place for *you*, my Lord. You have your own seat appointed and fixed, as sure as Canon Parkyn, and your own arms painted up clear on the back of it. Don't you trouble for that. It is all laid down in the statutes, and I shall make the very same obeisance for your lordship when you take your seat as for my Lord Bishop. 'Two inclinations of the body, the mace being held in the right hand, and supported on the left arm.' I cannot say more fair than that, for only royalties have three inclinations, and none of them has ever been to church in my time—no, nor yet a Lord Blandamer neither, since the day that your dear father and mother, what you never knew, was buried."

Mrs Janaway drummed with her knuckles on the supper-table, in amazement that her husband should dare to stand chattering at the door when she had told him that the meal was ready. But, as the conversation revealed by degrees the stranger's identity, curiosity to see the man whose name was in all Cullerne mouths got the better of her, and she came curtseying to the door.

Lord Blandamer flung the flapping cape of his overcoat over the left shoulder in a way that made the clerk think of foreigners, and of woodcuts of Italian opera in a bound volume of the *Illustrated London News* which he studied on Sunday evenings.

"I must be moving on," said the visitor, with a shiver. "I must not keep you standing here; there is a very chill air this evening."

Then Mrs Janaway was seized with a sudden temerity.

"Will your lordship not step in and warm yourself for a moment?"

she interposed. "We have a clear fire burning, if you will overlook the smell of cooking."

The clerk trembled for a moment at his wife's boldness, but Lord Blandamer accepted the invitation with alacrity.

"Thank you very much," said he; "I should be very glad to rest a few minutes before my train leaves. Pray make no apology for the smell of cookery; it is very appetising, especially at supper-time."

He spoke as if he took supper every evening, and had never heard of a late dinner in his life; and five minutes later he sat at table with Mr and Mrs Janaway. The cloth was of roughest homespun, but clean; the knives and forks handled in old green horn, and the piece-of-resistance tripe; but the guest made an excellent meal.

"Some folk think highly of squash tripe or ribband tripe," the clerk said meditatively, looking at the empty dish; "but they don't compare, according to my taste, with cushion tripe." He was emboldened to make these culinary remarks by that moral elevation which comes to every properly-constituted host, when a guest has eaten heartily of the viands set before him.

"No," Lord Blandamer said, "there can be no doubt that cushion tripe is the best."

"Quite as much depends upon the cooking as upon the tripe itself," remarked Mrs Janaway, bridling at the thought that her art had been left out of the reckoning; "a bad cook will spoil the best tripe. There are many ways of doing it, but a little milk and a leek is the best for me."

"You cannot beat it," Lord Blandamer assented—"you cannot beat it"—and then went on suggestively: "Have you ever tried a sprig of mace with it?"

No, Mrs Janaway had never heard of that; nor, indeed, had Lord Blandamer either, if the point had been pushed; but she promised to use it the very next time, and hoped that the august visitor would honour them again when it was to be tasted.

"'Tis only Saturday nights that we can get the cushion," she went on; "and it's well it don't come oftener, for we couldn't afford it. No woman ever had a call to have a better husband nor Thomas, who spends little enough on hisself. He don't touch nothing but tea, sir, but Saturday nights we treat ourselves to a little tripe, which is all the more convenient in that it is very strengthening, and my husband's duties on Sunday being that urgent-like. So, if your lordship is fond of tripe, and passing another Saturday night, and will do us the honour, you will always find something ready."

"Thank you very much for your kind invitation," Lord Blandamer said; "I shall certainly take you at your word, the more so that Saturday is the day on which I am oftenest in Cullerne, or, I should say, have happened to be lately."

"There's poor and poor," said the clerk reflectively; "and *we're* poor, but we're happy; but there's Mr Sharnall poor and unhappy. 'Mr Sharnall,' says I to him, 'many a time have I heard my father say over a pot of tenpenny, "Here's to poverty in a plug-hole, and a man with a wooden leg to trample it down;" but you never puts your poverty in a plug-hole, much less tramples it down. You always has it out and airs it, and makes yourself sad with thinking of it. 'Tisn't because you're poor that you're sad; 'tis because you *think* you're poor, and talk so much about it. You're not so poor as we, only you have so many grievances.'"

"Ah, you are speaking of the organist?" Lord Blandamer asked. "I fancy it was he who was talking with you in the minster this afternoon, was it not?"

The clerk felt embarrassed once more, for he remembered Mr Sharnall's violent talk, and how his anathema of all Blandamers had rang out in the church.

"Yes," he said; "poor organist was talking a little wild; he gets took that way sometimes, what with his grievances, and a little drop of the swanky what he takes to drown them. Then he talks loud; but I hope your lordship didn't hear all his foolishness."

"Oh dear no; I was engaged at the time with the architect," Lord Blandamer said; but his tone made Janaway think that Mr Sharnall's voice had carried further than was convenient. "I did not hear what he said, but he seemed to be much put out. I chatted with him in the church some days ago; he did not know who I was, but I gathered that he bore no very good will to my family."

Mrs Janaway saw it was a moment for prudent words. "Don't pay no manner of attention to him, if I may make so bold as to advise your lordship," she said; "he talks against my husband just as well. He is crazy about his organ, and thinks he ought to have a new one, or, at least, a waterworks to blow it, like what they have at Carisbury. Don't pay no attention to him; no one minds what Sharnall says in Cullerne."

The clerk was astonished at his wife's wisdom, yet apprehensive as to how it might be taken. But Lord Blandamer bowed his head graciously by way of thanks for sage counsel, and went on:

"Was there not some queer man at Cullerne who thought he was kept out of his rights, and should be in my place—who thought, I mean, he ought to be Lord Blandamer?"

The question was full of indifference, and there was a little smile of pity on his face; but the clerk remembered how Mr Sharnall had said something about a strutting peacock, and that there were no real Blandamers left, and was particularly ill at ease.

"Oh yes," he answered after a moment's pause, "there was a poor doited body who, saving your presence, had some cranks of that kind; and, more by token, Mr Sharnall lived in the same house with him, and so I dare say he has got touched with the same craze."

Lord Blandamer took out a cigar instinctively, and then, remembering that there was a lady present, put it back into his case and went on:

"Oh, he lived in the same house with Mr Sharnall, did he? I should like to hear more of this story; it naturally interests me. What was his name?"

"His name was Martin Joliffe," said the clerk quickly, being surprised into eagerness by the chance of telling a story; and then the whole tale of Martin, and Martin's father and mother and daughter, as he had told it to Westray, was repeated for Lord Blandamer.

The night was far advanced before the history came to an end, and the local policeman walked several times up and down Governour's Lane, and made pauses before Mr Janaway's house, being surprised to see a window lighted so late. Lord Blandamer must have changed his intention of going by train, for the gates of Cullerne station had been locked for hours, and the boiler of the decrepit branch-line engine was cooling in its shed.

"It is an interesting tale, and you tell tales well," he said, as he got up and put on his coat. "All good things must have an end, but I hope to see you again ere long." He shook hands with hostess and host, drained the pot of beer that had been fetched from a public-house, with a "Here's to poverty in a plug-hole, and a man with a wooden leg to trample it down," and was gone.

A minute later the policeman, coming back for yet another inspection of the lighted window, passed a man of middle height, who wore a loose overcoat, with the cape tossed lightly over the left shoulder. The stranger walked briskly, and hummed an air as he went, turning his face up to the stars and the wind-swept sky, as if entirely oblivious of all sublunary things. A midnight stranger in Governour's Lane was even more surprising than a lighted window, and the policeman had it in his mind to stop him and ask his business. But before he could decide on so vigorous a course of action, the moment was past, and the footsteps were dying away in the distance.

The clerk was pleased with himself, and proud of his success as a story-teller.

"That's a clever, understanding sort of chap," he said to his wife, as they went to bed; "he knows a good tale when he hears one."

"Don't you be too proud of yourself, my man," answered she; "there's more in that tale than your telling, I warrant you, for my lord to think about."

CHAPTER TEN

The extension of the scheme of restoration which Lord Blandamer's liberality involved, made it necessary that Westray should more than once consult Sir George Farquhar in London. On coming back to Cullerne from one of these visits on a Saturday night, he found his meal laid in Mr Sharnall's room.

"I thought you would not mind our having supper together," Mr Sharnall said. "I don't know how it is, I always feel gloomy just when the winter begins, and the dark sets in so soon. It is all right later on; I rather enjoy the long evenings and a good fire, when I can afford a good one, but at first it is a little gloomy. So come and have supper with me. There *is* a good fire tonight, and a bit of driftwood that I got specially for your benefit."

They talked of indifferent subjects during the meal, though once or twice it seemed to Westray that the organist gave inconsequential replies, as though he were thinking of something else. This was no doubt the case, for, after they had settled before the fire, and the lambent blue flames of the driftwood had been properly admired, Mr Sharnall began with a hesitating cough:

"A rather curious thing happened this afternoon. When I got back here after evening-service, who should I find waiting in my room but that Blandamer fellow. There was no light and no fire, for I had thought if we lit the fire late we could afford a better one. He was sitting at one end of the window-seat, damn him!"—(the expletive was caused by Mr Sharnall remembering that this was Anastasia's favourite seat, and his desire to reprobate the use of it by anyone else)—"but got up, of course, as I came in, and made a vast lot of soft speeches. He must really apologise for such an intrusion. He had come to see

Mr Westray, but found that Mr Westray had unfortunately been called away. He had taken the liberty of waiting a few minutes in Mr Sharnall's room. He was anxious to have a few moments' conversation with Mr Sharnall, and so on, and so on. You know how I hate palaver, and how I disliked—how I dislike" (he corrected himself)—"the man; but he took me at a disadvantage, you see, for here he was actually in my room, and one cannot be so rude in one's own room as one can in other people's. I felt responsible, too, to some extent for his having had to wait without fire or light, though why he shouldn't have lit the gas himself I'm sure I don't know.

"So I talked more civilly than I meant to, and then, just at the moment that I was hoping to get rid of him, Anastasia, who it seems was the only person at home, must needs come in to ask if I was ready for my tea. You may imagine my disgust, but there was nothing for it but to ask him if he would like a cup of tea. I never dreamt of his taking it, but he did; and so, behold! there we were hobnobbing over the tea-table as if we were cronies."

Westray was astonished. Mr Sharnall had rebuked him so short a time before for not having repulsed Lord Blandamer's advances that he could scarcely understand such a serious falling away from all the higher principles of hatred and malice as were implied in this tea-drinking. His experience of life had been as yet too limited to convince him that most enmities and antipathies, being theoretical rather than actual, are apt to become mitigated, or to disappear altogether on personal contact—that it is, in fact, exceedingly hard to keep hatred at concert-pitch, or to be consistently rude to a person face to face who has a pleasant manner and a desire to conciliate.

Perhaps Mr Sharnall read Westray's surprise in his face, for he went on with a still more apologetic manner:

"That is not the worst of it; he has put me in a most awkward position. I must admit that I found his conversation amusing enough. We spoke a good deal of music, and he showed a surprising knowledge of the subject, and a correct taste; I do not know where he has got it from."

"I found exactly the same thing with his architecture," Westray said. "We started to go round the minster as master and pupil, but before we finished I had an uncomfortable impression that he knew more about it than I did—at least, from the archaeologic point of view."

"Ah!" said the organist, with that indifference with which a person who wishes to recount his own experiences listens to those of someone else, however thrilling they may be. "Well, his taste was singularly refined. He showed a good acquaintance with the contrapuntists of the last century, and knew several of my own works. A very curious thing this. He said he had been in some cathedral—I forget which—heard the service, and been so struck with it that he went afterwards to look it up on the bill, and found it was Sharnall in D flat. He hadn't the least idea that it was mine till we began to talk. I haven't had that service by me for years; I wrote it at Oxford for the Gibbons' prize; it has a fugal movement in the *Gloria*, ending with a tonic pedal-point that you would like. I must look it up."

"Yes, I should like to hear it," Westray said, more to fill the interval while the speaker took breath than from any great interest in the matter.

"So you shall—so you shall," went on the organist; "you will find the pedal-point adds immensely to the effect. Well, by degrees we came to talking of the organ. It so happens that we had spoken of it the very first day I met him in the church, though you know I *never* talk about my instrument, do I? At that time it didn't strike me that he was so well up in the matter, but now he seemed to know all about it, and so I gave him my ideas as to what ought to be done. Then, before I knew where I was, he cut in with, 'Mr Sharnall, what you say interests me immensely; you put things in such a lucid way that even an outsider like myself can understand them. It would be a thousand pities if neglect were permanently to injure this sweet-toned instrument that Father Smith made so long ago.

"It is no use restoring the church without the organ, so you must draw up a specification of the repairs and additions required, and understand that anything you suggest shall be done. In the meantime pray order at once the water-engine and new pedal-board of which you speak, and inform me as to the cost.' He took me quite aback, and was gone before I had time to say anything. It puts me in a very equivocal position; I have such an antipathy to the man. I shall refuse his offer point-blank. I will not put myself under any obligation to such a man. You would refuse in my position? You would write a strong letter of refusal at once, would you not?"

Westray was of a guileless disposition, and apt to assume that people meant what they said. It seemed to him a matter for much regret that Mr Sharnall's independence, however lofty, should stand in the way of so handsome a benefaction, and he was at pains to elaborate and press home all the arguments that he could muster to shake the organist's resolve. The offer was kindly-meant; he was sure that Mr Sharnall took a wrong view of Lord Blandamer's character—that Mr Sharnall was wrong in imputing motives to Lord Blandamer. What motives could he have except the best? and however much Mr Sharnall might personally refuse, how was a man to be stopped eventually from repairing an organ which stood so manifestly in need of repair?

Westray spoke earnestly, and was gratified to see the effect which his eloquence produced on Mr Sharnall. It is so rarely that argument prevails to change opinion that the young man was flattered to see that the considerations which he was able to marshal were strong enough, at any rate, to influence Mr Sharnall's determination.

Well, perhaps there was something in what Mr Westray said. Mr Sharnall would think it over. He would not write the letter of refusal that night; he could write to refuse the next day quite as well. In the meantime he *would* see to the new pedal-board, and order the water-engine. Ever since he had seen the water-engine at Carisbury, he had been convinced that sooner or later they must have one at Cullerne. It *must* be ordered; they could decide later on whether it should be paid for by Lord Blandamer, or should be charged to the general restoration fund.

This conclusion, however inconclusive, was certainly a triumph for Westray's persuasive oratory, but his satisfaction was chastened by some doubts as to how far he was justified in assailing the scrupulous independence which had originally prompted Mr Sharnall to refuse to have anything to do with Lord Blandamer's offer. If Mr Sharnall had scruples in the matter, ought not he, Westray, to have respected those scruples? Was it not tampering with rectitude to have overcome them by a too persuasive rhetoric?

His doubts were not allayed by the observation that Mr Sharnall himself had severely felt the strain of this mental quandary, for the organist said that he was upset by so difficult a question, and filled himself a bumper of whisky to steady his nerves. At the same time he took down from a shelf two or three notebooks and a mass of loose papers, which he spread open upon the table before him. Westray looked at them with a glance of unconscious inquiry.

"I must really get to work at these things again," said the organist; "I have been dreadfully negligent of late. They are a lot of papers and notes that Martin Joliffe left behind him. Poor Miss Euphemia never had the heart to go through them. She was going to burn them just as they were, but I said, 'Oh, you mustn't do that; turn them over to me. I will look into them, and see whether there is anything worth keeping.' So I took them, but haven't done nearly as much as I ought, what with one interruption and another. It's always sad going through a dead man's papers, but sadder when they're all that's left of a life's labour—lost labour, so far as Martin was concerned, for he was taken away just when he began to see daylight. 'We brought nothing into this world, and it is certain that we shall carry nothing out.' When that comes into my mind, I think rather of the *little* things than of gold or lands. Intimate letters that a man treasured more than money; little tokens of which the clue has died with him; the unfinished work to which he was coming back, and never came; even the unpaid bills that worried him; for death transfigures all, and makes the commonplace pathetic."

He stopped for a moment. Westray said nothing, being surprised at this momentary softening of the other's mood.

"Yes, it's sad enough," the organist resumed; "all these papers are nebuly coat—the sea-green and silver."

"He was quite mad, I suppose?" Westray said.

"Everyone except me will tell you so," replied the organist; "but I'm not so very sure after all that there wasn't a good deal more in it than madness. That's all that I can say just now, but those of us who live will see. There is a queer tradition hereabout. I don't know how long ago it started, but people say that there *is* some mystery about the Blandamer descent, and that those in possession have no right to what they hold. But there is something else. Many have tried to solve the riddle, and some, you may depend, have been very hot on the track. But just as they come to the touch, something takes them off; that's what happened to Martin. I saw him the very day he died. 'Sharnall,' he said to me, 'if I can last out forty-eight hours more, you may take off your hat to me, and say "My lord."'

"But the nebuly coat was too much for him; he had to die. So don't you be surprised if I pop off the hooks some of these fine days; if I don't, I'm going to get to the bottom, and you will see some changes here before so very long."

He sat down at the table, and made a show for a minute of looking at the papers.

"Poor Martin!" he said, and got up again, opened the cupboard, and took out the bottle. "You'll have a drop," he asked Westray, "won't you?"

"No, thanks, not I," Westray said, with something as near contempt as his thin voice was capable of expressing.

"Just a drop—do! I must have just a drop myself; I find it a great strain working at these papers; there may be more at stake in the reading than I care to think of."

He poured out half a tumbler of spirit. Westray hesitated for a moment, and then his conscience and an early puritan training forced him to speak.

"Sharnall," he said, "put it away. That bottle is your evil angel. Play the man, and put it away. You force me to speak. I cannot sit by with hands folded and see you going down the hill."

The organist gave him a quick glance; then he filled up the tumbler to the brim with neat spirit.

"Look you," he said: "I was going to drink half a glass; now I'm going to drink a whole one. That much for your advice! Going down the hill indeed! Go to the devil with your impertinence! If you can't keep a civil tongue in your head, you had better get your supper in someone else's room."

A momentary irritation dragged Westray down from the high podium of judicial reproof into the arena of retort.

"Don't worry yourself," he said sharply; "you may rely on my not troubling you with my company again." And he got up and opened the door. As he turned to go out, Anastasia Joliffe passed through the passage on her way to bed.

The glimpse of her as she went by seemed still further to aggravate Mr Sharnall. He signed to Westray to stay where he was, and to shut the door again.

"Damn you!" he said; "that's what I called you back to say. Damn you! Damn Blandamer! Damn everybody! Damn poverty! Damn wealth! I will not touch a farthing of his money for the organ. Now you can go."

Westray had been cleanly bred. He had been used neither to the vulgarity of ill-temper nor to the coarser insolence of personal abuse. He shrank by natural habit even from gross adjectives, from the "beastly" and the "filthy" which modern manners too often condone, and still more from the abomination of swearing. So Mr Sharnall's obloquy wounded him to the quick. He went to bed in a flutter of agitation, and lay awake half the night mourning over a friendship so irreparably broken, bitter with the resentment of an unjustified attack, yet reproaching himself lest through his unwittingness he might have brought it all upon himself.

The morning found him unrefreshed and dejected, but, whilst he sat at breakfast, the sun came out brightly, and he began to take a less despondent view of the situation. It was possible that Mr Sharnall's friendship might not after all be lost beyond repair; he would be sorry if it were, for he had grown fond of the old man, in spite of all his faults of life and manner. It was he, Westray, who had been entirely to blame. In another man's room he had lectured the other man. He, a young man, had lectured the other, who was an old man. It was true that he had done so with the best motives; he had only spoken from a painful sense of duty. But he had shown no tact, he had spoken much too strongly; he had imperilled his own good cause by the injudicious manner in which he had put it forward. At the risk of all rebuffs, he would express his regret; he would go down and apologise to Mr Sharnall, and offer, if need be, the other cheek to the smiter.

Good resolves, if formed with the earnest intention of carrying them into effect, seldom fail to restore a measure of peace to the troubled mind. It is only when a regular and ghastly see-saw of wrong-doing and repentance has been established, and when the mind can no longer deceive even itself as to the possibility of permanent upright-ness of life, that good resolves cease to tranquillise. Such a see-saw must gradually lose its regularity; the set towards evil grows more and more preponderant; the return to virtue rarer and more brief. Despair of any continuity of godliness follows, and then it is that good resolves, becoming a mere reflex action of the mind, fail in their gracious in-fluence, and cease to bring quiet. These conditions can scarcely occur before middle age, and Westray, being young and eminently conscien-tious, was feeling the full peacefulness of his high-minded intention steal over him, when the door opened, and the organist entered.

An outbreak of temper and a night of hard drinking had left their tokens on Mr Sharnall's face. He looked haggard, and the rings that a weak heart had drawn under his eyes were darker and more puffed. He came in awkwardly, and walked quickly to the architect, holding out his hand.

"Forgive me, Westray," he said; "I behaved last night like a fool and a cad. You were quite right to speak to me as you did; I honour you for it. I wish to God there had been someone to speak to me like that years ago."

His outstretched hand was not so white as it should have been, the nails were not so well trimmed as a more fastidious mood might have demanded; but Westray did not notice these things. He took the

401

shaky old hand, and gripped it warmly, not saying anything, because he could not speak.

"We *must* be friends," the organist went on, after a moment's pause; "we must be friends, because I can't afford to lose you. I haven't known you long, but you are the only friend I have in the world. Is it not an awful thing to confess?" he said, with a tremulous little laugh. "I have no other friend in the world. Say those things you said last night whenever you like; the oftener you say them the better."

He sat down, and, the situation being too strained to remain longer at so high a pitch, the conversation drifted, however awkwardly, to less personal topics.

"There is a thing I wanted to speak about last night," the organist said. "Poor old Miss Joliffe is very hard up. She hasn't said a word to me about it—she never would to anyone—but I happen to know it for a fact: she *is* hard up. She is in a chronic state of hard-up-ishness always, and that we all are; but this is an acute attack—she has her back against the wall. It is the fag-end of Martin's debts that bother her; these blood-sucking tradesmen are dunning her, and she hasn't the pluck to tell them go hang, though they know well enough she isn't responsible for a farthing. She has got it into her head that she hasn't a right to keep that flower-and-caterpillar picture so long as Martin's debts are unpaid, because she could raise money on it. You remember those people, Baunton and Lutterworth, offered her fifty pounds for it."

"Yes, I remember," Westray said; "more fools they."

"More fools, by all means," rejoined the organist; "but still they offer it, and I believe our poor old landlady will come to selling it. 'All the better for her,' you will say, and anyone with an ounce of common-sense would have sold it long ago for fifty pounds or fifty pence. But, then, she has no common-sense, and I do believe it would break her pride and worry her into a fever to part with it. Well, I have been at the pains to find out what sum of money would pull her through, and I fancy something like twenty pounds would tide over the crisis."

He paused a moment, as if he half expected Westray to speak; but the architect making no suggestion, he went on.

"I didn't know," he said timidly; "I wasn't quite sure whether you had been here long enough to take much interest in the matter. I had an idea of buying the picture myself, so that we could still keep it here. It would be no good offering Miss Euphemia money as a *gift*; she wouldn't accept it on any condition. I know her quite well enough to be sure of that. But if I was to offer her twenty pounds for it, and tell her it must always stop here, and that she could buy it back from me when she was able, I think she would feel such an offer to be a godsend, and accept it readily."

"Yes,"Westray said dubitatively;"I suppose it couldn't be construed into attempting to outwit her, could it? It seems rather funny at first sight to get her to sell a picture for twenty pounds for which others have offered fifty pounds."

"No, I don't think so," replied the organist. "It wouldn't be a real sale at all, you know, but only just a colour for helping her."

"Well, as you have been kind enough to ask my advice, I see no further objection, and think it very good of you to show such thoughtfulness for poor Miss Joliffe."

"Thank you," said the organist hesitatingly—"thank you; I had hoped you would take that view of the matter. There is a further little difficulty: I am as poor as a church mouse. I live like an old screw, and never spend a penny, but, then, I haven't got a penny to spend, and so can't save."

Westray had already wondered how Mr Sharnall could command so large a sum as twenty pounds, but thought it more prudent to make no comments.

Then the organist took the bull by the horns.

"I didn't know," he said, "whether you would feel inclined to join me in the purchase. I have got ten pounds in the savings' bank; if you could find the other ten pounds, we could go shares in the picture; and, after all, that wouldn't much matter, for Miss Euphemia is quite sure to buy it back from us before very long."

He stopped and looked at Westray. The architect was taken aback. He was of a cautious and calculating disposition, and a natural inclination to save had been reinforced by the conviction that any unnecessary expenditure was in itself to be severely reprobated. As the Bible was to him the foundation of the world to come, so the keeping of meticulous accounts and the putting by of however trifling sums, were the foundation of the world that is. He had so carefully governed his life as to have been already able, out of a scanty salary, to invest more than a hundred pounds in Railway Debentures. He set much store by the half-yearly receipt of an exiguous interest cheque, and derived a certain dignity and feeling of commercial stability from envelopes headed the "Great Southern Railway," which brought him from time to time a proxy form or a notice of shareholders' meetings. A recent examination of his bankbook had filled him with the hope of being able ere long to invest a second hundred pounds, and he had been turning over in his mind for some days the question of the stocks to be selected; it seemed financially unsound to put so large a sum in any single security.

This suddenly presented proposal that he should make a serious inroad on his capital filled him with dismay; it was equivalent to granting a loan of ten pounds without any tangible security. No one in their senses could regard this miserable picture as a security; and the bulbous green caterpillar seemed to give a wriggle of derision as he looked at it across the breakfast-table. He had it on his tongue to refuse Mr Sharnall's request, with the sympathetic but judicial firmness with which all high-minded persons refuse to lend. There is a tone of sad resolution particularly applicable to such occasions, which should convey to the borrower that only motives of great moral altitude constrain us for the moment to override an earnest desire to part with our money. If it had not been for considerations of the public weal, we would most readily have given him ten times as much as was asked.

Westray was about to express sentiments of this nature when he glanced at the organist's face, and saw written in its folds and wrinkles so paramount and pathetic an anxiety that his resolution was shaken. He remembered the quarrel of the night before, and how Mr Sharnall, in coming to beg his pardon that morning, had humbled himself before a younger man. He remembered how they had made up their differences; surely an hour ago he would willingly have paid ten pounds to know that their differences could be made up. Perhaps, after all, he might agree to make this loan as a thank-offering for friendship restored. Perhaps, after all, the picture *was* a security: someone *had* offered fifty pounds for it.

The organist had not followed the change of Westray's mind; he retained only the first impression of reluctance, and was very anxious— curiously anxious, it might have seemed, if his only motive in the acquiring of the picture was to do a kindness to Miss Euphemia.

"It *is* a large sum, I know," he said in a low voice. "I am very sorry to ask you to do this. It is not for myself; I never asked a penny for myself in my life, and never will, till I go to the workhouse. Don't answer at once, if you don't see your way. Think it over. Take time to think it over; but do try, Westray, to help in the matter, if you can. It would be a sad pity to let the picture go out of the house just now."

The eagerness with which he spoke surprised Westray. Could it be that Mr Sharnall had motives other than mere kindness? Could it be that the picture *was* valuable after all? He walked across the room to look closer at the tawdry flowers and the caterpillar. No, it could not be that; the painting was absolutely worthless. Mr Sharnall had followed him, and they stood side by side looking out of the window. Westray was passing through a very brief interval of indecision. His emotional and perhaps better feelings told him that he ought to accede to Mr Sharnall's request; caution and the hoarding instinct reminded him that ten pounds was a large proportion of his whole available capital.

Bright sunshine had succeeded the rain. The puddles flashed on the pavements; the long rows of raindrops glistened on the ledges which overhung the shop-windows, and a warm steam rose from the sandy roadway as it dried in the sun. The front-door of Bellevue Lodge closed below them, and Anastasia, in a broad straw hat and a pink print dress, went lightly down the steps. On that bright morning she looked the brightest thing of all, as she walked briskly to the market with a basket on her arm, unconscious that two men were watching her from an upper window.

It was at that minute that thrift was finally elbowed by sentiment out of Westray's mind.

"Yes," he said, "by all means let us buy the picture. You negotiate the matter with Miss Joliffe, and I will give you two five-pound notes this evening."

"Thank you—thank you," said the organist, with much relief. "I will tell Miss Euphemia that she can buy it back from us whenever it suits her to do so; and if she should not buy it back before one of us dies, then it shall remain the sole property of the survivor."

So that very day the purchase of a rare work of art was concluded by private treaty between Miss Euphemia Joliffe of the one part, and Messrs. Nicholas Sharnall and Edward Westray of the other. The hammer never fell upon the showy flowers with the green caterpillar wriggling in the corner; and Messrs. Baunton and Lutterworth received a polite note from Miss Joliffe to say that the painting late in the possession of Martin Joliffe, Esquire, deceased, was not for sale.

CHAPTER ELEVEN

The old Bishop of Carisbury was dead, and a new Bishop of Carisbury reigned in his stead. The appointment had caused some chagrin in Low-Church circles, for Dr Willis, the new bishop, was a High Churchman of pronounced views. But he had a reputation for deep personal piety, and a very short experience sufficed to show that he was full of Christian tolerance and tactful loving-kindness.

One day, as Mr Sharnall was playing a voluntary after the Sunday morning-service, a chorister stole up the little winding steps, and appeared in the organ-loft just as his master had pulled out a handful of stops and dashed into the *stretto*. The organist had not heard the boy on the stairs, and gave a violent start as he suddenly caught sight of the white surplice. Hands and feet for an instant lost their place, and the music came perilously near breaking down. It was only for an instant; he pulled himself together, and played the fugue to its logical conclusion.

Then the boy began, "Canon Parkyn's compliments," but broke off; for the organist greeted him with a sound cuff and a "How many times have I told you, sir, not to come creeping up those stairs when I am in the middle of a voluntary? You startle me out of my senses, coming round the corner like a ghost."

"I'm very sorry, sir," the boy said, whimpering. "I'm sure I never meant—I never thought—"

"You never *do* think," Mr Sharnall said. "Well, well, don't go on whining. Old heads don't grow on young shoulders; don't do it again, and there's a sixpence for you. And now let's hear what you have to say."

Sixpences were rare things among Cullerne boys, and the gift consoled more speedily than any balm in Gilead.

"Canon Parkyn's compliments to you, sir, and he would be glad to have a word with you in the clergy-vestry."

"All in good time. Tell him I'll be down as soon as I've put my books away."

Mr Sharnall did not hurry. There were the Psalter and the chant-book to be put open on the desk for the afternoon; there were the morning-service and anthem-book to be put away, and the evening-service and anthem-book to be got out.

The establishment had once been able to afford good music-books, and in the attenuated list of subscribers to the first-edition Boyce you may see to this day, "The rector and Foundation of Cullerne Minster (6 copies)." Mr Sharnall loved the great Boyce, with its parchment paper and largest of large margins. He loved the crisp sound of the leaves as he turned them, and he loved the old-world clefs that he could read nine staves at a time as easily as a short score. He looked at the weekly list to check his memory—"Awake up my Glory" (*Wise*). No, it was in Volume 3 instead of 2; he had taken down the wrong volume—a stupid mistake for one who knew the copy so well. How the rough calf backs were crumbling away! The rusty red-leather dust had come off on his coat-sleeves; he really was not fit to be seen, and he took some minutes more to brush it all off. So it was that Canon Parkyn chafed at being kept waiting in the clergy-vestry, and greeted Mr Sharnall on his appearance with a certain tartness:

"I wish you could be a little quicker when you are sent for. I am particularly busy just now, and you have kept me waiting a quarter of an hour at least."

As this was precisely what Mr Sharnall had intended to do, he took no umbrage at the rector's remarks, but merely said:

"Pardon me; scarcely so long as a quarter of an hour, I think."

"Well, do not let us waste words. What I wanted to tell you was that it has been arranged for the Lord Bishop of Carisbury to hold a confirmation in the minster on the eighteenth of next month, at three o'clock in the afternoon. We must have a full musical service, and I shall be glad if you will submit a sketch of what you propose for my approval. There is one point to which I must call your attention particularly. As his lordship walks up the nave, we must have a becoming march on the organ—not any of this old-fashioned stuff of which I have had so often to complain, but something really dignified and with tune in it."

"Oh yes, we can easily arrange that," Mr Sharnall said obsequiously—"'See the Conquering Hero comes,' by Handel, would be very appropriate; or there is an air out of one of Offenbach's Operas that I think I could adapt to the purpose. It is a very sweet thing if rendered with proper feeling; or I could play a '*Danse Macabre*' slowly on the full organ."

"Ah, that is from the 'Judas Maccabaeus,' I conclude," said the rector, a little mollified at this unexpected acquiescence in his views. "Well, I see that you understand my wishes, so I hope I may leave that matter in your hands. By the way," he said, turning back as he left the vestry, "what *was* the piece which you played after the service just now?"

"Oh, only a fugal movement—just a fugue of Kirnberger's."

"I *wish* you would not give us so much of this fugal style. No doubt it is all very fine from a scholastic point of view, but to most it seems merely confused. So far from assisting me and the choir to go out with dignity, it really fetters our movements. We want something with pathos and dignity, such as befits the end of a solemn service, yet with a marked rhythm, so that it may time our footsteps as we leave the choir. Forgive these suggestions; the *practical* utility of the organ is so much overlooked in these days. When Mr Noot is taking the service it does not so much matter, but when I am here myself I beg that there may be no more fugue."

The visit of the Bishop of Carisbury to Cullerne was an important matter, and necessitated some forethought and arrangement.

"The bishop must, of course, lunch with us," Mrs Parkyn said to her husband; "you will ask him, of course, to lunch, my dear."

"Oh yes, certainly," replied the Canon; "I wrote yesterday to ask him to lunch."

He assumed an unconcerned air, but with only indifferent success, for his heart misgave him that he had been guilty of an unpardonable breach of etiquette in writing on so important a subject without reference to his wife.

"Really, my dear!" she rejoined—"really! I hope at least that your note was couched in proper terms."

"Psha!" he said, a little nettled in his turn, "do you suppose I have never written to a bishop before?"

"That is not the point; *any* invitation of this kind should always be given by me. The bishop, if he has any *breeding*, will be very much astonished to receive an invitation to lunch that is not given by the lady of the house. This, at least, is the usage that prevails among persons of *breeding*." There was just enough emphasis in the repetition of the last formidable word to have afforded a *casus belli*, if the rector had been minded for the fray; but he was a man of peace.

"You are quite right, my dear," was the soft answer; "it was a slip of mine, which we must hope the bishop will overlook. I wrote in a hurry yesterday afternoon, as soon as I received the official information of his coming. You were out calling, if you recollect, and I had to catch the post. One never knows what tuft-hunting may not lead people to do; and if I had not caught the post, some pushing person or other might quite possibly have asked him sooner. I meant, of course, to have reported the matter to you, but it slipped my memory."

"Really," she said, with fine deprecation, being only half pacified, "I do not see who there *could* be to ask the bishop except ourselves. Where should the Bishop of Carisbury lunch in Cullerne except at the rectory?" In this unanswerable conundrum she quenched the smouldering embers of her wrath. "I have no doubt, dear, that you did it all for the best, and I hate these vulgar pushing nobodies, who try to get hold of everyone of the least position quite as much as you do. So let us consider whom we *ought* to ask to meet him. A small party, I think it should be; he would take it as a greater compliment if the party were small."

She had that shallow and ungenerous mind which shrinks instinctively from admitting any beauty or intellect in others, and which grudges any participation in benefits, however amply sufficient they may be for all. Thus, few must be asked to meet the Bishop, that it might the better appear that few indeed, beside the rector and Mrs Parkyn, were fit to associate with so distinguished a man.

"I quite agree with you," said the rector, considerably relieved to find that his own temerity in asking the bishop might now be considered as condoned. "Our party must above all things be select; indeed, I do not know how we could make it anything but very small; there are so few people whom we *could* ask to meet the bishop."

"Let me see," his wife said, making a show of reckoning Cullerne respectability with the fingers of one hand on the fingers of the other. "There is—" She broke off as a sudden idea seized her. "Why, of course, we must ask Lord Blandamer. He has shown such marked interest in ecclesiastical matters that he is sure to wish to meet the bishop."

"A most fortunate suggestion—admirable in every way. It may strengthen his interest in the church; and it must certainly be beneficial to him to associate with correct society after his wandering and Bohemian life. I hear all kinds of strange tales of his hobnobbing with this Mr Westray, the clerk of the works, and with other persons entirely out of his own rank. Mrs Flint, who happened to be visiting a poor woman in a back lane, assures me that she has every reason to believe that he spent an hour or more in the clerk's house, and even ate there. They say he positively ate tripe."

"Well, it will certainly do him good to meet the bishop," the lady said. "That would make four with ourselves; and we can ask Mrs Bulteel. We need not ask her husband; he is painfully rough, and the bishop might not like to meet a brewer. It will not be at all strange to ask her alone; there is always the excuse of not liking to take a businessman away from his work in the middle of the day."

"That would be five; we ought to make it up to six. I suppose it would not do to ask this architect-fellow or Mr Sharnall."

"My dear! what can you be thinking of? On no account whatever. Such guests would be *most* inappropriate."

The rector looked so properly humble and cast down at this reproof that his wife relented a little.

"Not that there is any *harm* in asking them, but they would be so very ill at ease themselves, I fear, in such surroundings. If you think the number should be even, we might perhaps ask old Noot. He *is* a gentleman, and would pass as your chaplain, and say grace."

Thus the party was made up, and Lord Blandamer accepted, and Mrs Bulteel accepted; and there was no need to trouble about the curate's acceptance—he was merely ordered to come to lunch. But, after all had gone so well up to this point, the unexpected happened—the Bishop could not come. He regretted that he could not accept the hospitality so kindly offered him by Canon Parkyn; he had an engagement which would occupy him for any spare time that he would have in Cullerne; he had made other arrangements for lunch; he would call at the rectory half an hour before the service.

The rector and his wife sat in the "study," a dark room on the north side of the rectory-house, made sinister from without by dank laurestinus, and from within by glass cases of badly-stuffed birds. A Bradshaw lay on the table before them.

"He cannot be *driving* from Carisbury," Mrs Parkyn said. "Dr Willis does not keep at all the same sort of stables that his predecessor kept. Mrs Flint, when she was attending the annual Christian Endeavour meeting at Carisbury, was told that Dr Willis thinks it wrong that a bishop should do more in the way of keeping carriages than is absolutely necessary for church purposes. She said she had passed the bishop's carriage herself, and that the coachman was a most unkempt creature, and the horses two wretched screws."

"I heard much the same thing," assented the rector. "They say he would not have his own coat of arms painted on the carriage, for what was there already was quite good enough for him. He cannot possibly be driving here from Carisbury; it is a good twenty miles."

"Well, if he does not drive, he must come by the 12:15 train; that would give him two hours and a quarter before the service. What business can he have in Cullerne? Where can he be lunching? What can he be doing with himself for two mortal hours and a quarter?"

Here was another conundrum to which probably only one person in Cullerne town could have supplied an answer, and that was Mr

Sharnall. A letter had come for the organist that very day:

The Palace,
Carisbury.

My Dear Sharnall,

I had almost written 'My dear Nick'; forty years have made my pen a little stiff, but you must give me your official permission to write 'My dear Nick' the very next time. You may have forgotten my hand, but you will not have forgotten me. Do you know, it is I, Willis, who am your new bishop? It is only a fortnight since I learnt that you were so near me—

Quam dulce amicitias,
Redintegrare nitidas

—and the very first point of it is that I am going to sponge on you, and ask myself to lunch. I am coming to Cullerne at 12:45 today fortnight for the Confirmation, and have to be at the rectory at 2:30, but till then an old friend, Nicholas Sharnall, will give me food and shelter, will he not? Make no excuses, for I shall not accept them; but send me word to say that in this you will not fail of your duty, and believe me always to be

Yours,

John Carum.

There was something that moved strangely inside Mr Sharnall's battered body as he read the letter—an upheaval of emotion; the child's heart within the man's; his young hopeful self calling to his old hopeless self. He sat back in his armchair, and shut his eyes, and the organ-loft in a little college chapel came back to him, and long, long practisings, and Willis content to stand by and listen as long as he should play. How it pleased Willis to stand by, and pull the stops, and fancy he knew something of music! No, Willis never knew any music, and yet he had a good taste, and loved a fugue.

There came to him country rambles and country churches and Willis with an *A.B.C. of Gothic Architecture*, trying to tell an Early English from a Decorated moulding. There came to him inimitably long summer evenings, with the sky clearest yellow in the north, hours after sunset; dusty white roads, with broad galloping-paths at the side, drenched with heavy dew; the dark, mysterious boskage of Stow Wood; the scent of the syringa in the lane at Beckley; the white mist sheeting the Cherwell vale. And supper when they got home—for memory is so powerful an alchemist as to transmute suppers as well as sunsets. What suppers! Cider-cup with borage floating in it, cold lamb and mint sauce, watercress, and a triangular commons of Stilton. Why, he had not tasted Stilton for forty years!

No, Willis never knew any music, but he loved a fugue. Ah, the fugues they had! And then a voice crossed Mr Sharnall's memory, saying, "When I am here myself, I beg that there may be no more fugue." "No more fugue"—there was a finality in the phrase uncompromising as the "no more sea" of the Apocalyptic vision. It made Mr Sharnall smile bitterly; he woke from his daydream, and was back in the present.

Oh yes, he knew very well that it was his old friend when he first saw on whom the choice had fallen for the Bishopric. He was glad Willis was coming to see him. Willis knew all about the row, and how it was that Sharnall had to leave Oxford. Ay, but the Bishop was too generous and broad-minded to remember that now. Willis must know very well that he was only a poor, out-at-elbows old fellow, and yet he was coming to lunch with him; but did Willis know that he still—He did not follow the thought further, but glanced in a mirror, adjusted his tie, fastened the top button of his coat, and with his uncertain hands brushed the hair back on either side of his head. No, Willis did not know that; he never should know; it was *never* too late to mend.

He went to the cupboard, and took out a bottle and a tumbler. Only very little spirit was left, and he poured it all into the glass. There was a moment's hesitation, a moment while enfeebled will-power was nerving itself for the effort. He was apparently engaged in making sure that not one minim of this most costly liquor was wasted. He held the bottle carefully inverted, and watched the very last and smallest drop detach itself and fall into the glass. No, his will-power was not yet altogether paralysed—not yet; and he dashed the contents of the glass into the fire. There was a great blaze of light-blue flame, and a puff in the air that made the window-panes rattle; but the heroic deed was done, and he heard a mental blast of trumpets, and the acclaiming voice of the *Victor Sui*. Willis should never know that he still—because he never would again.

He rang the bell, and when Miss Euphemia answered it she found him walking briskly, almost tripping, to and fro in the room. He stopped as she entered, drew his heels together, and made her a profound bow.

"Hail, most fair *chastelaine!* Bid the varlets lower the draw-bridge and raise the portcullis. Order pasties and souse-fish and a butt of malmsey; see the great hall is properly decored for my Lord Bishop of Carisbury, who will take his *ambigue* and bait his steeds at this castle."

Miss Joliffe stared; she saw a bottle and an empty tumbler on the table, and smelt a strong smell of whisky; and the mirth faded from Mr Sharnall's face as he read her thoughts.

"No, wrong," he said—"wrong this once; I am as sober as a judge, but excited. A bishop is coming to lunch with me. *You* are excited when Lord Blandamer takes tea with you—a mere trashy temporal peer; am I not to be excited when a real spiritual lord pays me a visit? Hear, O woman! The Bishop of Carisbury has written to ask, not me to lunch with him, but him to lunch with me. You will have a bishop lunching at Bellevue Lodge."

"Oh, Mr Sharnall! pray, sir, speak plainly. I am so old and stupid, I can never tell whether you are joking or in earnest."

So he put off his exaltation, and told her the actual facts.

"I am sure I don't know, sir, what you will give him for lunch," Miss Joliffe said. She was always careful to put in a proper number of "sirs," for, though she was proud of her descent, and considered that so far as birth went she need not fear comparison with other Cullerne dames, she thought it a Christian duty to accept fully the position of landlady to which circumstances had led her. "I am sure I don't know what you will give him for lunch; it is always so difficult to arrange meals for the clergy. If one provides *too* much of the good things of this world, it seems as if one was not considering sufficiently their sacred calling; it seems like Martha, too cumbered with much serving, too careful and troubled, to gain all the spiritual advantage that must come from clergymen's society. But, of course, even the most spiritually-minded must nourish their *bodies*, or they would not be able to do so much good.

"But when less provision has been made, I have sometimes seen clergymen eat it all up, and become quite wearied, poor things! for want of food. It was so, I remember, when Mrs Sharp invited the parishioners to meet the deputation after the Church Missionary Meeting. All the patties were eaten before the deputation came, and he was so tired, poor man! with his long speech that when he found there was nothing to eat he got quite annoyed. It was only for a moment, of course, but I heard him say to someone, whose name I forget, that he had much better have trusted to a ham-sandwich in the station refreshment-room.

"And if it is difficult with the food, it is worse still with what they

413

are to drink. Some clergymen do so dislike wine, and others feel they need it before the exertion of speaking. Only last year, when Mrs Bulteel gave a drawing-room meeting, and champagne with biscuits was served before it, Dr Stimey said quite openly that though he did not consider all who drank to be *reprobate*, yet he must regard alcohol as the Mark of the Beast, and that people did not come to drawing-room meetings to drink themselves sleepy before the speaking. With Bishops it must be much worse; so I don't know what we shall give him."

"Don't distress yourself too much," the organist said, having at last spied a gap in the serried ranks of words; "I have found out what bishops eat; it is all in a little book. We must give him cold lamb—cold ribs of lamb—and mint sauce, boiled potatoes, and after that Stilton cheese."

"Stilton?" Miss Joliffe asked with some trepidation. "I am afraid it will be very expensive."

As a drowning man in one moment passes in review the events of a lifetime, so her mind took an instantaneous conspectus of all cheeses that had ever stood in the cheese-cradle in the palmy days of Wydcombe, when hams and plum-puddings hung in bags from the rafters, when there was cream in the dairy and beer in the cellar. Blue Vinny, little Gloucesters, double Besants, even sometimes a cream-cheese with rushes on the bottom, but Stilton never!

"I am afraid it is a *very* expensive cheese; I do not think anyone in Cullerne keeps it."

"It is a pity," Mr Sharnall said; "but we cannot help ourselves, for bishops *must* have Stilton for lunch; the book says so. You must ask Mr Custance to get you a piece, and I will tell you later how it is to be cut, for there are rules about that too."

He laughed to himself with a queer little chuckle. Cold lamb and mint sauce, with a piece of Stilton afterwards—they would have an Oxford lunch; they would be young again, and undefiled.

The stimulus that the bishop's letter had brought Mr Sharnall soon wore off. He was a man of moods, and in his nervous temperament depression walked close at the heels of exaltation. Westray felt sure in those days that followed that his friend was drinking to excess, and feared something more serious than a mere nervous breakdown, from the agitation and strangeness that he could not fail to observe in the organist's manner.

The door of the architect's room opened one night, as he sat late over his work, and Mr Sharnall entered. His face was pale, and there was a startled, wide-open look in his eyes that Westray did not like.

"I wish you would come down to my room for a minute," the organist said; "I want to change the place of my piano, and can't move it by myself."

"Isn't it rather late tonight?" Westray said, pulling at his watch, while the deep and slow melodious chimes of Saint Sepulchre told the dreaming town and the silent sea-marshes that it lacked but a quarter of an hour to midnight. "Wouldn't it be better to do it tomorrow morning?"

"Couldn't you come down tonight?" the organist asked; "it wouldn't take you a minute."

Westray caught the disappointment in the tone.

"Very well," he said, putting his drawing-board aside. "I've worked at this quite long enough; let us shift your piano."

They went down to the ground-floor.

"I want to turn the piano right-about-face," the organist said, "with its back to the room and the keyboard to the wall—the keyboard quite close to the wall, with just room for me to sit."

"It seems a curious arrangement," Westray criticised; "is it better acoustically?"

"Oh, I don't know; but, if I want to rest a bit, I can put my back against the wall, you see."

The change was soon accomplished, and they sat down for a moment before the fire.

"You keep a good fire," Westray said, "considering it is bedtime." And, indeed, the coals were piled high, and burning fiercely.

The organist gave them a poke, and looked round as if to make sure that they were alone.

"You'll think me a fool," he said; "and I am. You'll think I've been drinking, and I have. You'll think I'm drunk, but I'm not. Listen to me: I'm not drunk; I'm only a coward. Do you remember the very first night you and I walked home to this house together? Do you remember the darkness and the driving rain, and how scared I was when we passed the Old Bonding-house? Well, it was beginning then, but it's much worse now. I had a horrible idea even then that there was something always following me—following me close. I didn't know what it was—I only knew there was *something* close behind me."

His manner and appearance alarmed Westray. The organist's face was very pale, and a curious raising of the eyelids, which showed the whites of the eyes above the pupils, gave him the staring appearance of one confronted suddenly with some ghastly spectacle. Westray remembered that the hallucination of pursuant enemies is one of the most common symptoms of incipient madness, and put his hand gently on the organist's arm.

"Don't excite yourself," he said; "this is all nonsense. Don't get excited so late at night."

Mr Sharnall brushed the hand aside.

"I only used to have that feeling when I was out of doors, but now I have it often indoors—even in this very room. Before I never knew what it was following me—I only knew it was something. But now I know what it is: it is a man—a man with a hammer. Don't laugh. You don't *want* to laugh; you only laugh because you think it will quiet me, but it won't. I think it is a man with a hammer. I have never seen his face yet, but I shall some day. Only I know it is an evil face—not hideous, like pictures of devils or anything of that kind, but worse—a dreadful, disguised face, looking all right, but wearing a mask. He walks constantly behind me, and I feel every moment that the hammer may brain me."

"Come, come!" Westray said in what is commonly supposed to be a soothing tone, "let us change this subject, or go to bed. I wonder how you will find the new position of your piano answer."

The organist smiled.

"Do you know why I really put it like that?" he said. "It is because I am such a coward. I like to have my back against the wall, and then I know there can be no one behind me. There are many nights, when it gets late, that it is only with a great effort I can sit here. I grow so nervous that I should go to bed at once, only I say to myself, 'Nick'— that's what they used to call me at home, you know, when I was a boy—'Nick, you're not going to be beat; you're not going to be scared out of your own room by ghosts, surely.' And then I sit tight, and play on, but very often don't think much of what I'm playing. It is a sad state for a man to get into, is it not?" And Westray could not traverse the statement.

"Even in the church," Mr Sharnall went on, "I don't care to practise much in the evening by myself. It used to be all right when Cutlow was there to blow for me. He is a daft fellow, but still was some sort of company; but now the water-engine is put in, I feel lonely there, and don't care to go as often as I used. Something made me tell Lord Blandamer how his water-engine contrived to make me frightened, and he said he should have to come up to the loft himself sometimes to keep me company."

"Well, let me know the first evening you want to practise," Westray said, "and I will come, too, and sit in the loft. Take care of yourself, and you will soon grow out of all these fancies, and laugh at them as much as I do." And he feigned a smile. But it was late at night; he was high-strung and nervous himself, and the fact that Mr Sharnall should have been brought to such a pitiable state of mental instability depressed him.

The report that the bishop was going to lunch with Mr Sharnall on the day of the Confirmation soon spread in Cullerne. Miss Joliffe had told Mr Joliffe the pork-butcher, as her cousin, and Mr Joliffe, as churchwarden, had told Canon Parkyn. It was the second time within a few weeks that a piece of important news had reached the rector at second-hand. But on this occasion he experienced little of the chagrin that had possessed him when Lord Blandamer made the great offer to the restoration fund through Westray. He did not feel resentment against Mr Sharnall; the affair was of too solemn an importance for any such personal and petty sentiments to find a place. Any act of any Bishop was vicariously an act of God, and to chafe at this dispensation would have been as out of place as to be incensed at a shipwreck or an earthquake. The fact of being selected as the entertainer of the Bishop of Carisbury invested Mr Sharnall in the rector's eyes with a distinction which could not have been possibly attained by mere intellect or technical skill or devoted drudgery. The organist became *ipso facto* a person to be taken into account.

The rectory had divined and discussed, and discussed and divined, how it was, could, would, should, have been that the bishop could be lunching with Mr Sharnall. Could it be that the bishop had thought that Mr Sharnall kept an eating-house, or that the bishop took some special diet which only Mr Sharnall knew how to prepare? Could it be that the Bishop had some idea of making Mr Sharnall organist in his private chapel, for there was no vacancy in the cathedral? Conjecture charged the blank wall of mystery full tilt, and retired broken from the assault. After talking of nothing else for many hours, Mrs Parkyn declared that the matter had no interest at all for her.

"For my part, I cannot profess to understand such goings-on," she said in that convincing and convicting tone which implies that the speaker knows far more than he cares to state, and that the solution of the mystery must in any case be discreditable to all concerned.

"I wonder, my dear," the rector said to his wife, "whether Mr Sharnall has the means to entertain the bishop properly."

"Properly!" said Mrs Parkyn—"properly! I think the whole proceeding entirely improper. Do you mean has Mr Sharnall money enough to purchase a proper repast? I should say certainly not. Or has he proper plates or forks or spoons, or a proper room in which to eat? Of course he has not. Or do you mean can he get things properly cooked? Who is to do it? There is only feckless old Miss Joliffe and her stuck-up niece."

The Canon was much perturbed by the vision of discomfort which his wife had called up.

"The bishop ought to be spared as much as *possible*," he said; "we ought to do all we *can* to save him annoyance. What do you think? Should we not put up with a little inconvenience, and ask Sharnall to bring the bishop here, and lunch himself? He must know perfectly well that entertaining a bishop in a lodging-house is an unheard-of thing, and he would do to make up the sixth instead of old Noot. We could easily tell Noot he was not wanted."

"Sharnall is such a disreputable creature," Mrs Parkyn answered; "he is quite as likely as not to come tipsy; and, if he does not, he has no *breeding* or education, and would scarcely understand polite conversation."

"You forget, my dear, that the bishop is already pledged to lunch with Mr Sharnall, so that we should not be held responsible for introducing him. And Sharnall has managed to pick up some sort of an education—I can't imagine where; but I found on one occasion that he could understand a little Latin. It was the Blandamer motto, '*Aut Fynes, aut finis.*' He may have been told what it meant, but he certainly seemed to know. Of course, no real knowledge of Latin can be obtained without a *University* education"—and the rector pulled up his tie and collar—"but still chemists and persons of that sort do manage to get a smattering of it."

"Well, well, I don't suppose we are going to talk Latin all through lunch," interrupted his wife. "You can do precisely as you please about asking him."

The rector contented himself with the permission, however ungraciously accorded, and found himself a little later in Mr Sharnall's room.

"Mrs Parkyn was hoping that she might have prevailed on you to lunch with us on the day of the Confirmation. She was only waiting for the bishop's acceptance to send you an invitation; but we hear now," he said in a dubitative and tentative way—"we hear now that it is possible that the bishop may be lunching with you."

There was a twitch about the corners of Canon Parkyn's mouth. The position that a bishop should be lunching with Mr Sharnall in a common lodging-house was so exquisitely funny that he could only restrain his laughter with difficulty.

Mr Sharnall gave an assenting nod.

"Mrs Parkyn was not quite sure whether you might have in your lodgings exactly everything that might be necessary for entertaining his lordship."

"Oh dear, yes," Mr Sharnall said. "It looks a little dowdy just this minute, because the chairs are at the upholsterers to have the gilt touched up; we are putting up new curtains, of *course*, and the house-keeper has already begun to polish the best silver."

"It occurred to Mrs Parkyn," the rector continued, being too bent on saying what he had to say to pay much attention to the organist's remarks—"it occurred to Mrs Parkyn that it might perhaps be more convenient to you to bring the bishop to lunch at the rectory. It would spare you all trouble in preparation, and you would of course lunch with us yourself. It would be putting us to no inconvenience; Mrs Parkyn would be glad that you should lunch with us yourself."

Mr Sharnall nodded, this time deprecatingly.

"You are very kind. Mrs Parkyn is very considerate, but the Bishop has signified his intention of lunching in *this* house; I could scarcely venture to contravene his lordship's wishes."

"The bishop is a friend of yours?" the rector asked.

"You can scarcely say that; I do not think I have set eyes on the man for forty years."

The rector was puzzled.

"Perhaps the bishop is under some misconception; perhaps he thinks that this house is still an inn—the Hand of God, you know."

"Perhaps," said the organist; and there was a little pause.

"I hope you will consider the matter. May I not tell Mrs Parkyn that you will urge the bishop to lunch at the rectory—that you both"—and he brought out the word bravely, though it cost him a pang to yoke the bishop with so unworthy a mate, and to fling the door of select hospitality open to Mr Sharnall—"that you both will lunch with us?"

"I fear not," the organist said; "I fear I must say no. I shall be very busy preparing for the extra service, and if I am to play 'See the Conquering Hero' as the bishop enters the church, I shall need time for practice. A piece like that takes some playing, you know."

"I hope you will endeavour to render it in the very best manner," the rector said, and withdrew his forces *re infecta*.

The story of Mr Sharnall's mental illusions, and particularly of the hallucination as to someone following him, had left an unpleasant impression on Westray's mind. He was anxious about his fellow-lodger, and endeavoured to keep a kindly supervision over him, as he felt it to be possible that a person in such a state might do himself a mischief. On most evenings he either went down to Mr Sharnall's room, or asked the organist to come upstairs to his, considering that the solitude incident to bachelor life in advancing years was doubtless to blame to a large extent for these wandering fancies. Mr Sharnall occupied himself at night in sorting and reading the documents which had once belonged to Martin Joliffe. There was a vast number of them, representing the accumulation of a lifetime, and consisting of loose memoranda, of extracts from registers, of manuscript-books full of pedigrees and similar material.

When he had first begun to examine them, with a view to their classification or destruction, he showed that the task was distinctly uncongenial to him; he was glad enough to make any excuse for interruption or for invoking Westray's aid. The architect, on the other hand, was by nature inclined to archaeologic and genealogic studies, and would not have been displeased if Mr Sharnall had handed over to him the perusal of these papers entirely. He was curious to trace the origin of that chimera which had wasted a whole life—to discover what had led Martin originally to believe that he had a claim to the Blandamer peerage. He found, perhaps, an additional incentive in an interest which he was beginning unconsciously to take in Anastasia Joliffe, whose fortunes might be supposed to be affected by these investigations.

But in a little while Westray noticed a change in the organist's attitude as touching the papers. Mr Sharnall evinced a dislike to the architect examining them further; he began himself to devote a good deal more time and attention to their study, and he kept them jealously under lock and key. Westray's nature led him to resent anything that suggested suspicion; he at once ceased to concern himself with the matter, and took care to show Mr Sharnall that he had no wish whatever to see more of the documents.

As for Anastasia, she laughed at the idea of there being any foundation underlying these fancies; she laughed at Mr Sharnall, and rallied Westray, saying she believed that they both were going to embark on the quest of the nebuly coat. To Miss Euphemia it was no laughing matter.

"I think, my dear," she said to her niece, "that all these searchings after wealth and fortune are not of God. I believe that trying to discover things"—and she used "things" with the majestic comprehensiveness of the female mind—"is generally bad for man. If it is good for us to be noblemen and rich, then Providence will bring us to that station; but to try to prove one's self a nobleman is like star-gazing and fortune-telling. Idolatry is as the sin of witchcraft. There can be no *blessing* on it, and I reproach myself for ever having given dear Martin's papers to Mr Sharnall at all. I only did so because I could not bear to go through them myself, and thought perhaps that there might be cheques or something valuable among them. I wish I had burnt everything at first, and now Mr Sharnall says he will not have the papers destroyed till he has been through them. I am sure they were no blessing at all to dear Martin. I hope they may not bewitch these two gentlemen as well."

CHAPTER TWELVE

The scheme of restoration had been duly revised in the light of Lord Blandamer's generosity, and the work had now entered on such a methodical progress that Westray was able on occasion to relax something of that close personal supervision which had been at first so exacting. Mr Sharnall often played for half an hour or more after the evening-service, and on such occasions Westray found time, now and then, to make his way to the organ-loft. The organist liked to have him there; he was grateful for the token of interest, however slight, that was implied in such visits; and Westray, though without technical knowledge, found much to interest him in the unfamiliar surroundings of the loft.

It was a curious little kingdom of itself, situate over the great stone screen, which at Cullerne divides the choir from the nave, but as remote and cut off from the outside world as a desert island. Access was gained to it by a narrow, round, stone staircase, which led up from the nave at the south end of the screen. After the bottom door of this windowless staircase was opened and shut, anyone ascending was left for a moment in bewildering darkness. He had to grope the way by his feet feeling the stairs, and by his hand laid on the central stone shaft which had been polished to the smoothness of marble by countless other hands of past times.

But, after half a dozen steps, the darkness resolved; there was first the dusk of dawn, and soon a burst of mellow light, when he reached the stairhead and stepped out into the loft. Then there were two things which he noticed before any other—the bow of that vast Norman arch which spanned the opening into the south transept, with its lofty and over-delicate roll and cavetto mouldings; and behind it the head of the Blandamer window, where in the centre of the infinite multiplication of the tracery shone the sea-green and silver of the nebuly coat. Afterwards he might remark the long-drawn roof of the nave, and the chevroned ribs of the Norman vault, delimiting bay and bay with a saltire as they crossed; or his eyes might be led up to the lantern of the central tower, and follow the lighter ascending lines of Abbot Vinnicomb's Perpendicular panelling, till they vanished in the windows far above.

Inside the loft there was room and to spare. It was formed on ample lines, and had space for a stool or two beside the performer's seat, while at the sides ran low bookcases which held the music library. In these shelves rested the great folios of Boyce, and Croft, and Arnold, Page and Greene, Battishill and Crotch—all those splendid and ungrudging tomes for which the "rectors and Foundation of Cullerne" had subscribed in older and richer days. Yet these were but the children of a later birth. Round about them stood elder brethren, for Cullerne Minster was still left in possession of its seventeenth-century music-books.

A famous set they were, a hundred or more bound in their old black polished calf, with a great gold medallion, and "*Tenor. Decani*," or "*Contra-tenor: Cantoris*", "*Basso*," or "*Sopra*," stamped in the middle of every cover. And inside was parchment with red-ruled margins, and on the parchment were inscribed services and "verse-anthems" and "ffull-anthems," all in engrossing hand and the most uncompromising of black ink. Therein was a generous table of contents— Mr Batten and Mr Gibbons, Mr Mundy and Mr Tomkins, Doctor Bull and Doctor Giles, all neatly filed and paged; and Mr Bird would incite singers long since turned to churchyard mould to "bring forthe ye timbrell, ye pleasant harp and ye violl," and reinsist with six parts, and a red capital letter, "ye pleasant harp and ye violl."

It was a great place for dust, the organ-loft—dust that fell, and dust that rose; dust of wormy wood, dust of crumbling leather, dust of tattered mothy curtains that were dropping to pieces, dust of primeval green baize; but Mr Sharnall had breathed the dust for forty years, and felt more at home in that place than anywhere else. If it was Crusoe's island, he was Crusoe, monarch of all he surveyed.

"Here, you can take this key," he said one day to Westray; "it unlocks the staircase-door; but either tell me when to expect you, or make a noise as you come up the steps. I don't like being startled. Be sure you push the door to after you; it fastens itself. I am always particular about keeping the door locked, otherwise one doesn't know what stranger may take it into his head to walk up. I can't bear being startled." And he glanced behind him with a strange look in his eyes.

A few days before the bishop's visit Westray was with Mr Sharnall in the organ-loft. He had been there through most of the service, and, as he sat on his stool in the corner, had watched the curious diamond pattern of light and dark that the clerestory windows made with the vaulting-ribs. Anyone outside would have seen islands of white cloud drifting across the blue sky, and each cloud as it passed threw the heavy chevroned diagonals inside into bold relief, and picked out that rebus of a carding-comb encircled by a wreath of vine-leaves which Nicholas Vinnicomb had inserted for a vaulting-boss.

The architect had learned to regard the beetling roof with an almost superstitious awe, and was this day so fascinated with the strange effect as to be scarcely aware that the service was over till Mr Sharnall spoke.

"You said you would like to hear my service in D flat—'Sharnall in D flat,' did you not? I will play it through to you now, if you care to listen. Of course, I can only give you the general effect, without voices, though, after all, I don't know that you won't get quite as good an idea of it as you could with any voices that we have here."

Westray woke up from his dreams and put himself into an attitude of proper attention, while Mr Sharnall played the service from a faded manuscript.

"Now," he said, as he came towards the end—"now listen. This is the best part of it—a fugal *Gloria*, ending with a pedal-point. Here you are, you see—a tonic pedal-point, this D flat, the very last raised note in my new pedal-board, held down right through." And he set his left foot on the pedal. "What do you think of *that* for a *Magnificat*?" he said, when it was finished; and Westray was ready with all the conventional expressions of admiration. "It is not bad, is it?" Mr Sharnall asked; "but the gem of it is the *Gloria*—not real fugue, but fugal, with a pedal-point. Did you catch the effect of that point? I will keep the note down by itself for a second, so that you may get thoroughly hold of it, and then play the *Gloria* again."

He held down the D flat, and the open pipe went booming and throbbing through the long nave arcades, and in the dark recesses of the *triforium*, and under the beetling vaulting, and quavered away high up in the lantern, till it seemed like the death-groan of a giant.

"Take it up," Westray said; "I can't bear the throbbing."

"Very well; now listen while I give you the *Gloria*. No, I really think I had better go through the whole service again; you see, it leads up more naturally to the *finale*."

He began the service again, and played it with all the conscientious attention and sympathy that the creative artist must necessarily give to his own work. He enjoyed, too, that pleasurable surprise which awaits the discovery that a composition laid aside for many years and half forgotten is better and stronger than had been imagined, even as a disused dress brought out of the wardrobe sometimes astonishes us with its freshness and value.

Westray stood on a foot-pace at the end of the loft which allowed him to look over the curtain into the church. His eyes roamed through the building as he listened, but he did not appreciate the music the less. Nay, rather, he appreciated it the more, as some writers find literary perception and power of expression quickened at the influence of music itself. The great church was empty. Janaway had left for his tea; the doors were locked, no strangers could intrude; there was no sound, no murmur, no voice, save only the voices of the organ-pipes. So Westray listened. Stay, were there no other voices? was there nothing he heard—nothing that spoke within him?

At first he was only conscious of *something*—something that drew his attention away from the music, and then the disturbing influence was resolved into another voice, small, but rising very clear even above "Sharnall in D flat." "The arch never sleeps," said that still and ominous voice. "The arch never sleeps; they have bound on us a burden too heavy to be borne. We are shifting it; we never sleep." And his eyes turned to the cross arches under the tower. There, above the bow of the south transept, showed the great crack, black and writhen as a lightning-flash, just as it had showed any time for a century—just the same to the ordinary observer, but not to the architect. He looked at it fixedly for a moment, and then, forgetting Mr Sharnall and the music, left the loft, and made his way to the wooden platform that the masons had built up under the roof.

Mr Sharnall did not even perceive that he had gone down, and dashed *con furore* into the *Gloria*. "Give me the full great," he called to the architect, who he thought was behind him; "give me the full great, all but the reed," and snatched the stops out himself when there was no response. "It went better that time—distinctly better," he said, as the last note ceased to sound, and then turned round for Westray's comment; but the loft was empty—he was alone.

"Curse the fellow!" he said; "he might at least have let me know that he was going away. Ah, well, it's all poor stuff, no doubt." And he shut up the manuscript with a lingering and affectionate touch, that contrasted with so severe a criticism. "It's poor stuff; why should I expect anyone to listen to it?"

It was full two hours later that Westray came quickly into the organist's room at Bellevue Lodge.

"I beg your pardon, Sharnall," he said, "for leaving you so cavalierly. You must have thought me rude and inappreciative; but the fact is I was so startled that I forgot to tell you why I went. While you were playing I happened to look up at that great crack over the south transept arch, and saw something very like recent movement. I went up at once to the scaffolding, and have been there ever since. I don't like it at all; it seems to me that the crack is opening, and extending. It may mean very serious mischief, and I have made up my mind to go up to London by the last train tonight. I must get Sir George Farquhar's opinion at once."

The organist grunted. The wound inflicted on his susceptibility had rankled deeply, and indignation had been tenderly nursed. A piece of his mind was to have been given to Westray, and he regretted the very reasonableness of the explanation that robbed him of his opportunity.

"Pray don't apologise," he said; "I never noticed that you had gone. I really quite forgot that you had been there."

Westray was too full of his discovery to take note of the other's annoyance. He was one of those excitable persons who mistake hurry for decision of action.

"Yes," he said, "I must be off to London in half an hour. The matter is far too serious to play fast-and-loose with. It is quite possible that we shall have to stop the organ, or even to forbid the use of the church altogether, till we can shore and strut the arch. I must go and put my things together."

So, with heroic promptness and determination, he flung himself into the last train, and spent the greater part of the night in stopping at every wayside station, when his purpose would have been equally served by a letter or by taking the express at Cullerne Road the next morning.

Chapter Thirteen

The organ was not silenced, nor was the service suspended. Sir George came down to Cullerne, inspected the arch, and rallied his subordinate for an anxiety which was considered to be unjustifiable. Yes, the wall above the arch *had* moved a little, but not more than was to be expected from the repairs which were being undertaken with the vaulting. It was only the old wall coming to its proper bearings— he would have been surprised, in fact, if no movement had taken place; it was much safer as it was.

Canon Parkyn was in high good-humour. He rejoiced in seeing the pert and officious young clerk of the works put in his proper place; and Sir George had lunched at the rectory. There was a repetition of the facetious proposal that Sir George should wait for payment of his fees until the tower should fall, which acquired fresh point from the circumstance that all payments were now provided for by Lord Blandamer. The ha-ha-ing which accompanied this witticism palled at length even upon the robust Sir George, and he winced under a dig in the ribs, which an extra glass of port had emboldened the canon to administer.

"Well, well, Mr Rector," he said, "we cannot put old heads on young shoulders. Mr Westray was quite justified in referring the matter to me. It *has* an ugly look; one needs experience to be able to see through things like this." And he pulled up his collar, and adjusted his tie.

Westray was content to accept his chief's decision as a matter of faith, though not of conviction. The black lightning-flash was impressed on his mental retina, the restless cry of the arches was continually in his ear; he seldom passed the transept-crossing without hearing it. But he bore his rebuke with exemplary resignation—the more so that he was much interested in some visits which Lord Blandamer paid him at this period. Lord Blandamer called more than once at Bellevue Lodge in the evenings, even as late as nine o'clock, and would sit with Westray for two hours together, turning over plans and discussing the restoration. The architect learnt to appreciate the charm of his manner, and was continually astonished at the architectural knowledge and critical power which he displayed. Mr Sharnall would sometimes join them for a few minutes, but Lord Blandamer never appeared quite at his ease when the organist was present; and Westray could not help thinking that Mr Sharnall was sometimes tactless, and even rude, considering that he was beholden to Lord Blandamer for new pedals and new bellows and a water-engine *in esse,* and for the entire repair of the organ *in posse.*

"I can't help being 'beholden to him,' as you genteelly put it," Mr Sharnall said one evening, when Lord Blandamer had gone. "I can't *stop* his giving new bellows or a new pedal-board. And we do want the new board and the additional pipes. As it is, I can't play German music, can't touch a good deal of Bach's organ work. Who is to say this man nay, if he chooses to alter the organ? But I'm not going to truckle to anyone, and least of all to him. Do you want me to fall flat on my face because he is a lord? Pooh! we could all be lords like him. Give me another week with Martin's papers, and I'll open your eyes. Ay, you may stare and sniff if you please, but you'll open your eyes then. *Ex oriente lux*—that's where the light's coming from, out of Martin's papers. Once this Confirmation over, and you'll see. I can't settle to the papers till that's done with. What do people want to confirm these boys and girls for? It only makes hypocrites of wholesome children. I hate the whole business. If people want to make their views public, let them do it at five-and-twenty; then we should believe that they knew something of what they were about."

The day of the Bishop's visit had arrived; the bishop had arrived himself; he had entered the door of Bellevue Lodge; he had been received by Miss Euphemia Joliffe as one who receives an angel awares; he had lunched in Mr Sharnall's room, and had partaken of the cold lamb, and the Stilton, and even of the cider-cup, to just such an extent as became a healthy and good-hearted and host-considering bishop.

"You have given me a regular Oxford lunch," he said. "Your landlady has been brought up in the good tradition." And he smiled, never doubting that he was partaking of the ordinary provision of the house, and that Mr Sharnall fared thus sumptuously every day. He knew not that the meal was as much a set piece as a dinner on the stage, and that cold lamb and Stilton and cider-cup were more often represented by the bottom of a tin of potted meat and—a gill of cheap whisky.

"A regular Oxford lunch." And then they fell to talking of old days, and the bishop called Mr Sharnall "Nick," and Mr Sharnall called the Bishop of Carum "John"; and they walked round the room looking at pictures of college groups and college eights, and the Bishop examined very tenderly the little water-colour sketch that Mr Sharnall had once made of the inner quad; and they identified in it their own old rooms, and the rooms of several other men of their acquaintance.

The talk did Mr Sharnall good; he felt the better for it every moment. He had meant to be very proud and reserved with the bishop—to be most dignified and coldly courteous. He had meant to show that, though John Willis might wear the gaiters, Nicholas Sharnall could retain his sturdy independence, and was not going to fawn or to admit himself to be the mental inferior of any man. He had meant to *give* a tirade against Confirmation, against the neglect of music, against rectors, with perhaps a back-thrust at the Bench of Bishops itself. But he had done none of these things, because neither pride nor reserve nor assertiveness were possible in John Willis's company. He had merely eaten a good lunch, and talked with a kindly, broad-minded gentleman, long enough to warm his withered heart, and make him feel that there were still possibilities in life.

There is a bell that rings for a few strokes three-quarters of an hour before every service at Cullerne. It is called the Burgess Bell—some say because it was meant to warn such burgesses as dwelt at a distance that it was time to start for church; whilst others will have it that Burgess is but a broken-down form of *expergiscere*—"Awake! awake!"— that those who dozed might rise for prayer. The still air of the afternoon was yet vibrating with the Burgess Bell, and the bishop rose to take his leave.

If it was the organist of Cullerne who had been ill at ease when their interview began, it was the Bishop of Carisbury who was embarrassed at the end of it. He had asked himself to lunch with Mr Sharnall with a definite object, and towards the attainment of that object nothing had been done. He had learnt that his old friend had fallen upon evil times, and, worse, had fallen into evil courses—that the failing which had ruined his Oxford career had broken out again with a fresh fire in advancing age, that Nicholas Sharnall was in danger of a drunkard's judgment.

There had been lucid intervals in the organist's life; the plague would lie dormant for years, and then break out, to cancel all the progress that had been made. It was like a "race-game" where the little leaden horse is moved steadily forward, till at last the die falls on the fatal number, and the racer must lose a turn, or go back six, or, even in the worst issue, begin his whole course again.

It was in the forlorn hope of doing something, however little, to arrest a man on the downward slope that the bishop had come to Bellevue Lodge; he hoped to speak the word in season that should avail. Yet nothing had been said. He felt like a clerk who has sought an interview with his principal to ask for an increase of salary, and then, fearing to broach the subject, pretends to have come on other business. He felt like a son longing to ask his father's counsel in some grievous scrape, or like an extravagant wife waiting her opportunity to confess some heavy debt.

"A quarter past two," the bishop said; "I must be going. It has been a great pleasure to recall the old times. I hope we shall meet again soon; but remember it is your turn now to come and see me. Carisbury is not so very far off, so do come. There is always a bed ready for you. Will you walk up the street with me now? I have to go to the rectory, and I suppose you will be going to the church, will you not?"

"Yes," said Mr Sharnall; "I'll come with you if you wait one minute. I think I'll take just a drop of something before I go, if you'll excuse me. I feel rather run down, and the service is a long one. You won't join me, of course?" And he went to the cupboard.

The bishop's opportunity was come.

"Don't, Sharnall. Don't, Nick," he said; "don't take that stuff. Forgive me for speaking openly, the time is so short. I am not speaking professionally or from the religious standpoint, but only just as one man of the world to another, just as one friend to another, because I cannot bear to see you going on like this without trying to stop you. Don't take offence, Nick," he added, as he saw the change of the other's countenance; "our old friendship gives me a right to speak; the story you are writing on your own face gives me a right to speak. Give it up. There is time yet to turn; give it up. Let me help you; is there nothing I can do to help?"

The angry look that crossed Mr Sharnall's face had given way to sadness.

"It is all very easy for you," he said; "you've done everything in life, and have a long row of milestones behind you to show how you've moved on. I have done nothing, only gone back, and have all the milestones in front to show how I've failed. It's easy to twit me when you've got everything you want—position, reputation, fortune, a living faith to keep you up to it. I am nobody, miserably poor, have no

429

friends, and don't believe half we say in church. What am I to do? No one cares a fig about me; what have I got to live for? To drink is the only chance I have of feeling a little pleasure in life; of losing for a few moments the dreadful consciousness of being an outcast; of losing for a moment the remembrance of happy days long ago: that's the greatest torment of all, Willis. Don't blame me if I drink; it's the *elixir vitae* for me just as much as for Paracelsus." And he turned the handle of the cupboard.

"Don't," the bishop said again, putting his hand on the organist's arm; "don't do it; don't touch it. Don't make success any criterion of life; don't talk about 'getting on.' We shan't be judged by how we have got on. Come along with me; show you've got your old resolution, your old will-power."

"I *haven't* got the power," Mr Sharnall said; "I can't help it." But he took his hand from the cupboard-door.

"Then let me help it for you," said the bishop; and he opened the cupboard, found a half-used bottle of whisky, drove the cork firmly into it, and put it under his arm inside the lappet of his coat. "Come along."

So the Bishop of Carisbury walked up the High Street of Cullerne with a bottle of whisky under his left arm. But no one could see that, because it was hid under his coat; they only saw that he had his right arm inside Mr Sharnall's. Some thought this an act of Christian condescension, but others praised the times that were past; bishops were losing caste, they said, and it was a sad day for the Church when they were found associating openly with persons so manifestly their inferiors.

"We must see more of each other," the bishop said, as they walked under the arcade in front of the shops. "You must get out of this quag somehow. You can't expect to do it all at once, but we must make a beginning. I have taken away your temptation under my coat, and you must make a start from this minute; you must make me a promise *now*. I have to be in Cullerne again in six days' time, and will come and see you. You must promise me not to touch anything for these six days, and you must drive back with me to Carisbury when I go back then, and spend a few days with me. Promise me this, Nick; the time is pressing, and I must leave you, but you must promise me this first."

The organist hesitated for a moment, but the bishop gripped his arm.

"Promise me this; I will not go till you promise."

"Yes, I promise."

And lying-and-mischief-making Mrs Flint, who was passing, told afterwards how she had overheard the Bishop discussing with Mr Sharnall the best means for introducing ritualism into the minster, and how the organist had promised to do his very best to help him so far as the musical part of the *sendee* was concerned.

The Confirmation was concluded without any contretemps, save that two of the Grammar School boys incurred an open and well-merited rebuke from the master for appearing in gloves of a much lighter slate colour than was in any way decorous, and that this circumstance reduced the youngest Miss Bulteel to such a state of hysteric giggling that her mother was forced to remove her from the church, and thus deprive her of spiritual privileges for another year.

Mr Sharnall bore his probation bravely. Three days had passed, and he had not broken his vow—no, not in one jot or tittle. They had been days of fine weather, brilliantly clear autumn days of blue sky and exhilarating air. They had been bright days for Mr Sharnall; he was himself exhilarated; he felt a new life coursing in his veins. The bishop's talk had done him good; from his heart he thanked the bishop for it. Giving up drinking had done him no harm; he felt all the better for his abstinence. It had not depressed him at all; on the contrary, he was more cheerful than he had been for years. Scales had fallen from his eyes since that talk; he had regained his true bearings; he began to see the verities of life. How he had wasted his time! Why *had* he been so sour? why *had* he indulged his spleen? why *had* he taken such a jaundiced view of life?

He would put aside all jealousies; he would have no enmities; he would be broader-minded—oh, so much broader-minded; he would embrace all mankind—yes, even Canon Parkyn. Above all, he would recognise that he was well advanced in life; he would be more sober-thinking, would leave childish things, would resolutely renounce his absurd infatuation for Anastasia. What a ridiculous idea—a crabbed old sexagenarian harbouring affection for a young girl! Henceforth she should be nothing to him—absolutely nothing. No, that would be foolish; it would not be fair to her to cut her off from all friendship; he could feel for her a fatherly affection—it should be paternal and nothing more. He would bid *adieu* to all that folly, and his life should not be a whit the emptier for the loss. He would fill it with interests—all kinds of interests, and his music should be the first. He would take up again, and carry out to the end, that *oratorio* which he had turned over in his mind for years—the "Absalom." He had several numbers at his fingers' ends; he would work out the bass solo, "Oh, Absalom, my son, my son!" and the double chorus that followed it, "Make ready, ye mighty; up and bare your swords!"

So he discoursed joyfully with his own heart, and felt above measure elated at the great and sudden change that was wrought in him, not recognising that the clouds return after the rain, and that the leopard may change his spots as easily as man may change his habits. To change a habit at fifty-five or forty-five or thirty-five; to ordain that rivers shall flow uphill; to divert the relentless sequence of cause and effect—how often dare we say this happens? *Nemo repente*—no man ever suddenly became good. A moment's spiritual agony may blunt our instincts and paralyse the evil in us—for a while, even as chloroform may dull our bodily sense; but for permanence there is no sudden turning of the mind; sudden repentances in life or death are equally impossible.

Three halcyon days were followed by one of those dark and lowering mornings when the blank life seems blanker, and when the gloom of nature is too accurately reflected in the nervous temperament of man. On healthy youth climatic influences have no effect, and robust middle age, if it perceive them, goes on its way steadfast or stolid, with a *cela passera, tout passera*. But on the feeble and the failing such times fall with a weight of fretful despondency; and so they fell on Mr Sharnall.

He was very restless about the time of the mid-day meal. There came up a thick, dark fog from the sea, which went rolling in great masses over Cullerne Flat, till its fringe caught the outskirts of the town. After that, it settled in the streets, and took up its special abode in Bellevue Lodge; till Miss Euphemia coughed so that she had to take two *ipecacuanha* lozenges, and Mr Sharnall was forced to ring for a lamp to see his victuals. He went up to Westray's room to ask if he might eat his dinner upstairs, but he found that the architect had gone to London, and would not be back till the evening train; so he was thrown upon his own resources.

He ate little, and by the end of the meal depression had so far got the better of him, that he found himself standing before a well-known cupboard. Perhaps the abstemiousness of the last three days had told upon him, and drove him for refuge to his usual comforter. It was by instinct that he went to the cupboard; he was not even conscious of doing so till he had the open door in his hand. Then resolution returned to him, aided, it may be, by the reflection that the cupboard was bare (for the bishop had taken away the whisky), and he shut the door sharply. Was it possible that he had so soon forgotten his promise—had come so perilously near falling back into the mire, after the bright prospects of the last days, after so lucid an interval? He went to his bureau and buried himself in Martin Joliffe's papers, till the Burgess Bell gave warning of the afternoon service.

The gloom and fog made way by degrees for a drizzling rain, which resolved itself into a steady downpour as the afternoon wore on. It was so heavy that Mr Sharnall could hear the indistinct murmur of millions of raindrops on the long lead roofs, and their more noisy splash and spatter as they struck the windows in the lantern and north transept. He was in a bad humour as he came down from the loft. The boys had sung sleepily and flat; Jaques had murdered the tenor solo with his strained and raucous voice; and old Janaway remembered afterwards that Mr Sharnall had never vouchsafed a good-afternoon as he strode angrily down the aisle.

Things were no better when he reached Bellevue Lodge. He was wet and chilled, and there was no fire in the grate, because it was too early in the year for such luxuries to be afforded. He would go to the kitchen, and take his tea there. It was Saturday afternoon. Miss Joliffe would be at the Dorcas meeting, but Anastasia would be in; and this reflection came to him as a ray of sunlight in a dark and lowering time. Anastasia would be in, and alone; he would sit by the fire and drink a cup of hot tea, while Anastasia should talk to him and gladden his heart. He tapped lightly at the kitchen-door, and as he opened it a gusty buffet of damp air smote him on the face; the room was empty. Through a half-open sash the wet had driven in, and darkened the top of the deal table which stood against the window; the fire was but a smouldering ash. He shut the window instinctively while he reflected. Where could Anastasia be? She must have left the kitchen some time, otherwise the fire would not be so low, and she would have seen that the rain was beating in. She must be upstairs; she had no doubt taken advantage of Westray's absence to set his room in order. He would go up to her; perhaps there was a fire in Westray's room.

He went up the circular stone staircase, that ran like a wide well from top to bottom of the old Hand of God. The stone steps and the stone floor of the hall, the stuccoed walls, and the coved stucco roof which held the skylight at the top, made a whispering-gallery of that gaunt staircase; and before Mr Sharnall had climbed half-way up he heard voices.

They were voices in conversation; Anastasia had company. And then he heard that one was a man's voice. What right had any man to be in Westray's room? What man had any right to be talking to Anastasia? A wild suspicion passed through his mind—no, that was quite impossible. He would not play the eavesdropper or creep near them to listen; but, as he reflected, he had mounted a step or two higher, and the voices were now more distinct. Anastasia had finished speaking, and the man began again. There was one second of uncertainty in Mr Sharnall's mind, while the hope that it was not, balanced the fear that it was; and then doubt vanished, and he knew the voice to be Lord Blandamer's.

The organist sprang up two or three steps very quickly. He would go straight to them—straight into Westray's room; he would—And then he paused; he would do, what? What right had he to go there at all? What had he to do with them? What was there for anyone to do? He paused, then turned and went downstairs again, telling himself that he was a fool—that he was making mountains of molehills, that there did not exist, in fact, even a molehill; yet having all the while a sickening feeling within him, as if some gripping hand had got hold of his poor physical and material heart, and was squeezing it. His room looked more gloomy than ever when he got back to it, but it did not matter now, because he was not going to remain there. He only stopped for a minute to sweep back into the bureau all those loose papers of Martin Joliffe's that were lying in a tumble on the open desk-flap. He smiled grimly as he put them back and locked them in. *Le jour viendra qui tout paiera.* These papers held a vengeance that would atone for all wrongs.

He took down his heavy and wet-sodden overcoat from the peg in the hall, and reflected with some satisfaction that the bad weather could not seriously damage it, for it had turned green with wear, and must be replaced as soon as he got his next quarter's salary. The rain still fell heavily, but he *must* go out. Four walls were too narrow to hold his chafing mood, and the sadness of outward nature accorded well with a gloomy spirit. So he shut the street-door noiselessly, and went down the semicircular flight of stone steps in front of the Hand of God, just as Lord Blandamer had gone down them on that historic evening when Anastasia first saw him. He turned back to look at the house, just as Lord Blandamer had turned back then; but was not so fortunate as his illustrious predecessor, for Westray's window was tight shut, and there was no one to be seen.

"I wish I may never look upon the place again," he said to himself, half in earnest, and half with that cynicism which men affect because they know Fate seldom takes them at their word.

For an hour or more he wandered aimlessly, and found himself, as night fell, on the western outskirts of the town, where a small tannery carries on the last pretence of commercial activity in Cullerne. It is here that the Cull, which has run for miles under willow and alder, through deep pastures golden with marsh marigolds or scented with meadow-sweet, past cuckoo-flower and pitcher-plant and iris and nodding bulrush, forsakes better traditions, and becomes a common town-sluice before it deepens at the wharves, and meets the sandy churn of the tideway. Mr Sharnall had become aware that he was tired, and he stood and leant over the iron paling that divides the roadway from the stream. He did not know how tired he was till he stopped walking, nor how the rain had wetted him till he bent his head a little forward, and a cascade of water fell from the brim of his worn-out hat.

It was a forlorn and dismal stream at which he looked. The low tannery buildings of wood projected in part over the water, and were supported on iron props, to which were attached water-whitened skins and repulsive portions of entrails, that swung slowly from side to side as the river took them. The water here is little more than three feet deep, and beneath its soiled current can be seen a sandy bottom on which grow patches of coarse duck-weed. To Mr Sharnall these patches of a green so dark and drain-soiled as to be almost black in the failing light, seemed tresses of drowned hair, and he weaved stories about them for himself as the stream now swayed them to and fro, and now carried them out at length.

He observed things with that vacant observation which the body at times insists on maintaining, when the mind is busy with some overmastering preoccupation. He observed the most trivial details; he made an inventory of the things which he could see lying on the dirty bed of the river underneath the dirty water. There was a tin bucket with a hole in the bottom; there was a brown teapot without a spout; there was an earthenware blacking-bottle too strong to be broken; there were other shattered glass bottles and shards of crockery; there was a rim of a silk hat, and more than one toeless boot. He turned away, and looked down the road towards the town. They were beginning to light the lamps, and the reflections showed a criss-cross of white lines on the muddy road, where the water stood in the wheel-tracks. There was a dark vehicle coming down the road now, making a fresh track in the mud, and leaving two shimmering lines behind it as it went. He gave a little start when it came nearer, and he saw that it was the undertaker's cart carrying out a coffin for some pauper at the Union Workhouse.

He gave a start and a shiver; the wet had come through his over-coat; he could feel it on his arms; he could feel the cold and clinging wet striking at his knees. He was stiff with standing so long, and a rheumatic pain checked him suddenly as he tried to straighten him-self. He would walk quickly to warm himself—would go home at once. Home—what *home* had he? That great, gaunt Hand of God. He detested it and all that were within its walls. That was no home. Yet he was walking briskly towards it, having no other whither to go.

He was in the mean little streets, he was within five minutes of his goal, when he heard singing. He was passing the same little inn which he had passed the first night that Westray came. The same voice was singing inside which had sung the night that Westray came. Westray had brought discomfort; Westray had brought Lord Blandamer. Things had never been the same since; he wished Westray had never come at all; he wished—oh, how he wished!—that all might be as it was before—that all might jog along quietly as it had for a generation before. She certainly had a fine voice, this woman. It really would be worth while seeing who she was; he wished he could just look inside the door. Stay, he could easily make an excuse for looking in: he would order a little hot whisky-and-water. He was so wet, it was prudent to take something to drink. It might ward off a bad chill. He would only take a very little, and only as a medicine, of course; there could be no harm in *that*—it was mere prudence.

He took off his hat, shook the rain from it, turned the handle of the door very gently, with the consideration of a musician who will do nothing to interrupt another who is making music, and went in.

He found himself in that sanded parlour which he had seen once before through the window. It was a long, low room, with heavy beams crossing the roof, and at the end was an open fireplace, where a kettle hung above a smouldering fire. In a corner sat an old man playing on a fiddle, and near him the Creole woman stood singing; there were some tables round the room, and behind them benches on which a dozen men were sitting. There was no young man among them, and most had long passed the meridian of life. Their faces were sun-tanned and mahogany-coloured; some wore earrings in their ears, and strange curls of grey hair at the side of their heads. They looked as if they might have been sitting there for years—as if they might be the crew of some long-foundered vessel to whom has been accorded a Nirvana of endless tavern-fellowship. None of them took any notice of Mr Sharnall, for music was exercising its transporting power, and their thoughts were far away. Some were with old Cullerne whalers, with the harpoon and the ice-floe; some dreamt of square-stemmed timber-brigs, of the Baltic and the white Memel-logs, of wild nights at sea and wilder nights ashore; and some, remembering violet skies and moonlight through the mango-groves, looked on the Creole woman, and tried to recall in her faded features, sweet, swart faces that had kindled youthful fires a generation since.

Then the grog, boys—the grog, boys, bring hither,

—sang the Creole.

Fill it up true to the brim.
May the mem'ry of Nelson ne'er wither
Nor the star of his glory grow dim.

There were rummers standing on the tables, and now and then a drinking-brother would break the sugar-knobs in his liquor with a glass stirrer, or take a deep draught of the brown jorum that steamed before him. No one spoke to Mr Sharnall; only the landlord, without asking what he would take, set before him a glass filled with the same hot spirit as the other guests were drinking.

The organist accepted his fate with less reluctance than he ought perhaps to have displayed, and a few minutes later was drinking and smoking with the rest. He found the liquor to his liking, and soon experienced the restoring influences of the warm room and of the spirit. He hung his coat up on a peg, and in its dripping condition, and in the wet which had penetrated to his skin, found ample justification for accepting without demur a second bumper with which the landlord replaced his empty glass. Rummer followed rummer, and still the Creole woman sang at intervals, and still the company smoked and drank.

Mr Sharnall drank too, but by-and-by saw things less clearly, as the room grew hotter and more clouded with tobacco-smoke. Then he found the Creole woman standing before him, and holding out a shell for contributions. He had in his pocket only one single coin—a half-crown that was meant to be a fortnight's pocket-money; but he was excited, and had no hesitation.

"There," he said, with an air of one who gives a kingdom—"there, take that: you deserve it; but sing me a song that I heard you sing once before, something about the rolling sea."

She nodded that she understood, and after the collection was finished, gave the money to the blind man, and bade him play for her.

It was a long ballad, with many verses and a refrain of:

Oh, take me back to those I love,
Or bring them here to me;
I have no heart to rove, to rove
Across the rolling sea.

At the end she came back, and sat down on the bench by Mr Sharnall.

"Will you not give me something to drink?" she said, speaking in very good English. "You all drink; why should not I?"

He beckoned to the landlord to bring her a glass, and she drank of it, pledging the organist.

"You sing well," he said, "and with a little training should sing very well indeed. How do you come to be here? You ought to do better than this; if I were you, I would not sing in such company."

She looked at him angrily.

"How do *I* come to be here? How do *you* come to be here? If I had a little training, I should sing better, and if I had your training, Mr Sharnall"—and she brought out his name with a sneering emphasis—"I should not be here at all, drinking myself silly in a place like this."

She got up, and went back to the old fiddler, but her words had a sobering influence on the organist, and cut him to the quick. So all his good resolutions had vanished. His promise to the Bishop was broken; the Bishop would be back again on Monday, and find him as bad as ever—would find him worse; for the devil had returned, and was making riot in the garnished house. He turned to pay his reckoning, but his half-crown had gone to the Creole; he had no money, he was forced to explain to the landlord, to humiliate himself, to tell his name and address. The man grumbled and made demur. Gentlemen who drank in good company, he said, should be prepared to pay their shot like gentlemen. Mr Sharnall had drunk enough to make it a serious thing for a poor man not to get paid. Mr Sharnall's story might be true, but it was a funny thing for an organist to come and drink at the

Merrymouth, and have no money in his pocket. It had stopped raining; he could leave his overcoat as a pledge of good faith, and come back and fetch it later. So Mr Sharnall was constrained to leave this part of his equipment, and was severed from a well-worn overcoat, which had been the companion of years. He smiled sadly to himself as he turned at the open door, and saw his coat still hang dripping on the peg. If it were put up to auction, would it ever fetch enough to pay for what he had drunk?

It was true that it had stopped raining, and though the sky was still overcast, there was a lightness diffused behind the clouds that spoke of a rising moon. What should he do? Whither should he turn? He could not go back to the Hand of God; there were some there who did not want him—whom he did not want. Westray would not be home, or, if he were, Westray would know that he had been drinking; he could not bear that they should see that he had been drinking again.

And then there came into his mind another thought: he would go to the church, the water-engine should blow for him, and he would play himself sober. Stay, *should* he go to the church—the great church of Saint Sepulchre alone? Would he be alone there? If he thought that he would be alone, he would feel more secure; but might there not be someone else there, or something else? He gave a little shiver, but the drink was in his veins; he laughed pot-valiantly, and turned up an alley towards the centre tower, that loomed dark in the wet, misty whiteness of the cloud screened moon.

Chapter Fourteen.

Westray returned to Cullerne by the evening train. It was near ten o'clock, and he was finishing his supper, when someone tapped at the door, and Miss Euphemia Joliffe came in.

"I beg your pardon for interrupting you, sir," she said; "I am a little anxious about Mr Sharnall. He was not in at teatime, and has not come back since. I thought you might know perhaps where he was. It is years since he has been out so late in the evening."

"I haven't the least idea where he is," Westray said rather testily, for he was tired with a long day's work. "I suppose he has gone out somewhere to supper."

"No one ever asks Mr Sharnall out. I do not think he can be gone out to supper."

"Oh, well, I dare say he will turn up in due course; let me hear before you go to bed if he has come back;" and he poured himself out another cup of tea, for he was one of those thin-blooded and old-womanly men who elevate the drinking of tea instead of other liquids into a special merit. "He could not understand," he said, "why everybody did not drink tea. It was so much more refreshing—one could work so much better after drinking tea."

He turned to some calculations for the section of a tie-rod, with which Sir George Farquhar had at last consented to strengthen the south side of the tower, and did not notice how time passed till there came another irritating tap, and his landlady reappeared.

"It is nearly twelve o'clock," she said, "and we have seen nothing of Mr Sharnall. I am so alarmed! I am sure I am very sorry to trouble you, Mr Westray, but my niece and I are so alarmed."

"I don't quite see what I am to do," Westray said, looking up. "Could he have gone out with Lord Blandamer? Do you think Lord Blandamer could have asked him to Fording?"

"Lord Blandamer was here this afternoon," Miss Joliffe answered, "but he never saw Mr Sharnall, because Mr Sharnall was not at home."

"Oh, Lord Blandamer was here, was he?" asked Westray. "Did he leave no message for me?"

"He asked if you were in, but he left no message for you. He drank a cup of tea with us. I think he came in merely as a friendly visitor," Miss Joliffe said with some dignity. "I think he came in to drink a cup of tea with me. I was unfortunately at the Dorcas meeting when he first arrived, but on my return he drank tea with me."

"It is curious; he seems generally to come on Saturday afternoons," said Westray. "Are you *always* at the Dorcas meeting on Saturday afternoons?"

"Yes," Miss Joliffe said, "I am always at the meeting on Saturday afternoons."

There was a minute's pause—Westray and Miss Joliffe were both thinking.

"Well, well," Westray said, "I shall be working for some time yet, and will *let* Mr Sharnall in if he comes; but I suspect that he has been invited to spend the night at Fording. Anyhow, you can go to bed with a clear conscience, Miss Joliffe; you have waited up far beyond your usual time."

So Miss Euphemia went to bed, and left Westray alone; and a few minutes later the four quarter-chimes rang, and the tenor struck twelve, and then the bells fell to playing a tune, as they did every three hours day and night. Those who dwell near Saint Sepulchre's take no note of the bells. The ear grows so accustomed to them, that quarter by quarter and hour by hour strike unperceived. If strangers come to stop under the shadow of the church the clangour disturbs their sleep for the first night, and after that they, too, hear nothing. So Westray would sit working late night by night, and could not say whether the bells had rung or not. It was only when attention was too wide awake that he heard them, but he heard them this night, and listened while they played the sober melody of "Mount Ephraim."

He got up, flung his window open, and looked out. The storm had passed; the moon, which was within a few hours of the full, rode serenely in the blue heaven with a long bank of dappled white cloud below, whose edge shone with an amber iridescence. He looked over the clustered roofs and chimneys of the town; the upward glow from the market-place showed that the lamps were still burning, though he could not see them. Then, as the glow lessened gradually and finally became extinct, he knew that the lights were being put out because midnight was past. The moonlight glittered on the roofs, which were still wet, and above all towered in gigantic sable mass the centre tower of Saint Sepulchre's.

Westray felt a curious physical tension. He was excited, he could not tell why; he knew that sleep would be impossible if he were to go to bed. It *was* an odd thing that Sharnall had not come home; Sharnall *must* have gone to Fording. He had spoken vaguely of an invitation to Fording that he had received; but if he had gone there he must have taken some things with him for the night, and he had not taken any- thing, or Miss Euphemia would have said so. Stay, he would go down to Sharnall's room and see if he could find any trace of his taking lug- gage; perhaps he had left some message to explain his absence. He lit a candle and went down, down the great well-staircase where the stone steps echoed under his feet. A patch of bright moonshine fell on the stairs from the skylight at the top, and a noise of someone moving in the attics told him that Miss Joliffe was not yet asleep. There was noth- ing in the organist's room to give any explanation of his absence. The light of the candle was reflected on the front of the piano, and Westray shuddered involuntarily as he remembered the conversation which he had a few weeks before with this friend, and Mr Sharnall's strange hallucinations as to the man that walked behind him with a hammer. He looked into the bedroom with a momentary apprehension that his friend might have been seized with illness, and be lying all this time

441

unconscious; but there was no one there—the bed was undisturbed. So he went back to his own room upstairs, but the night had turned so chill that he could no longer bear the open window. He stood with his hand upon the sash looking out for a moment before he pulled it down, and noticed how the centre tower dominated and prevailed over all the town. It was impossible, surely, that this rock-like mass could be insecure; how puny and insufficient to uphold such a tottering giant seemed the tie-rods whose section he was working out. And then he thought of the crack above the south transept arch that he had seen from the organ-loft, and remembered how "Sharnall in D flat" had been interrupted by the discovery. Why, Mr Sharnall might be in the church; perhaps he had gone down to practise and been shut in. Perhaps his key had broken, and he could not get out; he wondered that he had not thought of the church before.

In a minute he had made up his mind to go to the minster. As resident architect he possessed a master key which opened all the doors; he would walk round, and see if he could find anything of the missing organist before going to bed. He strode quickly through the deserted streets. The lamps were all put out, for Cullerne economised gas at times of full moon. There was nothing moving, his footsteps rang on the pavement, and echoed from wall to wall. He took the short-cut by the wharves, and in a few minutes came to the old Bonding-house.

The shadows hung like black velvet in the spaces between the brick buttresses that shored up the wall towards the quay. He smiled to himself as he thought of the organist's nervousness, of those strange fancies as to someone lurking in the black hiding-holes, and as to buildings being in some way connected with man's fate. Yet he knew that his smile was assumed, for he felt all the while the oppression of the loneliness, of the sadness of a half-ruined building, of the gurgling mutter of the river, and instinctively quickened his pace. He was glad when he had passed the spot, and again that night, as he looked back, he saw the strange effect of light and darkness which produced the impression of someone standing in the shadow of the last buttress space. The illusion was so perfect that he thought he could make out the figure of a man, in a long loose cape that napped in the wind.

He had passed the wrought-iron gates now—he was in the churchyard, and it was then that he first became aware of a soft, low, droning sound which seemed to fill the air all about him. He stopped for a moment to listen; what was it? Where was the noise? It grew more distinct as he passed along the flagged stone path which led to the north door. Yes, it certainly came from inside the church. What could it be? What could anyone be doing in the church at this hour of night?

He was in the north porch now, and then he knew what it was. It was a low note of the organ—a pedal-note; he was almost sure it was that very pedal-point which the organist had explained to him with such pride. The sound reassured him nothing had happened to Mr Sharnall—he was practising in the church; it was only some mad freak of his to be playing so late; he was practising that service "Sharnall in D flat."

He took out his key to unlock the wicket, and was surprised to find it already open, because he knew that it was the organist's habit to lock himself in. He passed into the great church. It was strange, there was no sound of music; there was no one playing; there was only the intolerably monotonous booming of a single pedal-note, with an occasional muffled thud when the water-engine turned spasmodically to replenish the emptying bellows.

"Sharnall!" he shouted—"Sharnall, what are you doing? Don't you know how late it is?"

He paused, and thought at first that someone was answering him— he thought that he heard people muttering in the choir; but it was only the echo of his own voice, his own voice tossed from pillar to pillar and arch to arch, till it faded into a wail of "Sharnall, Sharnall!" in the lantern.

It was the first time that he had been in the church at night, and he stood for a moment overcome with the mystery of the place, while he gazed at the columns of the nave standing white in the moonlight like a row of vast shrouded figures. He called again to Mr Sharnall, and again received no answer, and then he made his way up the nave to the little doorway that leads to the organ-loft stairs.

This door also was open, and he felt sure now that Mr Sharnall was not in the organ-loft at all, for had he been he would certainly have locked himself in. The pedal-note must be merely ciphering, or something, perhaps a book, might have fallen upon it, and was holding it down. He need not go up to the loft now; he would not go up. The throbbing of the low note had on him the same unpleasant effect as on a previous occasion. He tried to reassure himself, yet felt all the while a growing premonition that something might be wrong, something might be terribly wrong. The lateness of the hour, the isolation from all things living, the spectral moonlight which made the darkness darker—this combination of utter silence, with the distressing vibration of the pedal-note, filled him with something akin to panic. It seemed to him as if the place was full of phantoms, as if the monks of Saint Sepulchre's were risen from under their gravestones, as if there were other dire faces among them such as wait continually on deeds of evil. He checked his alarm before it mastered him. Come what might, he would go up to the organ-loft, and he plunged into the staircase that leads up out of the nave.

It is a circular stair, twisted round a central pillar, of which mention has already been made, and though short, is very dark even in bright daylight. But at night the blackness is inky and impenetrable, and Westray fumbled for an appreciable time before he had climbed sufficiently far up to perceive the glimmer of moonlight at the top. He stepped out at last into the loft, and saw that the organ seat was empty. The great window at the end of the south transept shone full in front of him; it seemed as if it must be day and not night—the light from the window was so strong in comparison with the darkness which he had left. There was a subdued shimmer in the tracery where the stained glass gleamed diaphanous—amethyst and topaz, chrysoprase and jasper, a dozen jewels as in the foundations of the city of God. And in the midst, in the head of the centre light, shone out brighter than all, with an inherent radiance of its own, the cognisance of the Blandamers, the sea-green and silver of the nebuly coat.

Westray gave a step forward into the loft, and then his foot struck against something, and he nearly fell. It was something soft and yielding that he had struck, something of which the mere touch filled him with horrible surmise. He bent down to see what it was, and a white object met his eyes. It was the white face of a man turned up towards the vaulting; he had stumbled over the body of Mr Sharnall, who lay on the floor with the back of his head on the pedal-note. Westray had bent low down, and he looked full in the eyes of the organist, but they were fixed and glazing.

The moonlight that shone on the dead face seemed to fall on it through that brighter spot in the head of the middle light; it was as if the nebuly coat had blighted the very life out of the man who lay so still upon the floor.

CHAPTER FIFTEEN

No evidence of any importance was given at the inquest except Westray's and the doctor's, and no other evidence was, in fact, required. Dr Ennefer had made an autopsy, and found that the immediate cause of death was a blow on the back of the head. But the organs showed traces of alcoholic habit, and the heart was distinctly diseased. It was probable that Mr Sharnall had been seized with a fainting fit as he left the organ-stool, and had fallen backwards with his head on the pedal-board. He must have fallen with much violence, and the pedal-note had made a bad wound, such as would be produced by a blunt instrument.

The inquest was nearly finished when, without any warning, Westray found himself, as by intuition, asking:

"The wound was such a one, you mean, as might have been produced by the blow of a hammer?"

The doctor seemed surprised, the jury and the little audience stared, but most surprised of all was Westray at his own question.

"You have no *locus standi*, sir," the coroner said severely; "such an interrogation is irregular. You are to esteem it an act of grace if I allow the medical man to reply."

"Yes," said Dr Ennefer, with a reserve in his voice that implied that he was not there to answer every irrelevant question that it might please foolish people to put to him—"yes, such a wound as might have been caused by a hammer, or by any other blunt instrument used with violence."

"Even by a heavy stick?" Westray suggested.

The doctor maintained a dignified silence, and the coroner struck in:

"I must say I think you are wasting our time, Mr Westray. I am the last person to stifle legitimate inquiry, but no inquiry is really needed here; it is quite certain that this poor man came to his end by falling heavily, and dashing his head against this wooden note in the pedals."

"*Is* it quite certain?" Westray asked. "Is Dr Ennefer quite sure that the wound *could* have been caused by a mere fall; I only want to know that Dr Ennefer is quite sure."

The coroner looked at the doctor with a deprecating glance, which implied apologies that so much unnecessary trouble should be given, and a hope that he would be graciously pleased to put an end to it by an authoritative statement.

"Oh, I am quite sure," the doctor responded. "Yes"—and he hesitated for the fraction of a second—"oh yes, there is no doubt such a wound could be caused by a fall."

"I merely wish to point out," said Westray, "that the pedal-note on

445

which he fell is to a certain extent a yielding substance; it would yield, you must remember, at the first impact."

"That is quite true," the doctor said; "I had taken that into account, and admit that one would scarcely expect so serious an injury to have been caused. But, of course, it *was* so caused, because there is no other explanation; you don't suggest, I presume, that there was any foul play. It is certainly a case of accident or foul play."

"Oh no, I don't suggest anything."

The coroner raised his eyebrows; he was tired, and could not understand such waste of time. But the doctor, curiously enough, seemed to have grown more tolerant of interruption.

"I have examined the injury very carefully," he said, "and have come to the deliberate conclusion that it must have been caused by the wooden key. We must also recollect that the effect of any blow would be intensified by a weak state of health. I don't wish to rake up anything against the poor fellow's memory, or to say any word that may cause you pain, Mr Westray, as his friend; but an examination of the body revealed traces of chronic alcoholism. We must recollect that."

"The man was, in fact, a confirmed drunkard," the coroner said. He lived at Carisbury, and, being a stranger both to Cullerne and its inhabitants, had no scruple in speaking plainly; and, besides this, he was nettled at the architect's interference. "You mean the man was a confirmed drunkard," he repeated.

"He was nothing of the kind," Westray said hotly. "I do not say that he never took more than was good for him, but he was in no sense an habitual drunkard."

"I did not ask *your* opinion," retorted the coroner; "we do not want any lay conjectures. What do you say, Mr Ennefer?"

The surgeon was vexed in his turn at not receiving the conventional title of doctor, the more so because he knew that he had no legal right to it. To be called "Mr" demeaned him, he considered, in the eyes of present or prospective patients, and he passed at once into an attitude of opposition.

"Oh no, you quite mistake me, Mr Coroner. I did not mean that our poor friend was an habitual drunkard. I never remember to have actually seen him the worse for liquor."

"Well, what do you mean? You say the body shows traces of alcoholism, but that he was not a drunkard."

"Have we any evidence as to Mr Sharnall's state on the evening of his death?" a juror asked, with a pleasant consciousness that he was taking a dispassionate view, and making a point of importance.

"Yes, we have considerable evidence," said the coroner. "Call Charles White."

There stepped forward a little man with a red face and blinking eyes. His name was Charles White; he was landlord of the Merrymouth Inn. The deceased visited his inn on the evening in question. He did not know deceased by sight, but found out afterwards who he was. It was a bad night, deceased was very wet, and took something to drink; he drank a fairish amount, but not *that* much, not more than a gentleman should drink. Deceased was not drunk when he went away.

"He was drunk enough to leave his top-coat behind him, was he not?" the coroner asked. "Did you not find this coat after he was gone?" and he pointed to a poor masterless garment, that looked greener and more outworn than ever as it hung over the back of a chair.

"Yes, deceased had certainly left his coat behind him, but he was not drunk."

"There are different standards of drunkenness, gentlemen," said the coroner, imitating as well as he might the facetious cogency of a real judge, "and I imagine that the standard of the Merrymouth may be more advanced than in some other places. I don't think"—and he looked sarcastically at Westray—"I do *not* think we need carry this inquiry farther. We have a man who drinks, not an habitual drunkard, Mr Ennefer says, but one who drinks enough to bring himself into a thoroughly diseased state. This man sits fuddling in a low public-house all the evening, and is so far overtaken by liquor when he goes away, that he leaves his overcoat behind him. He actually leaves his coat behind him, though we have it that it was a pouring wet night. He goes to the organ-loft in a tipsy state, slips as he is getting on to his stool, falls heavily with the back of his head on a piece of wood, and is found dead some hours later by an unimpeachable and careful witness"— and he gave a little sniff—"with his head still on this piece of wood. Take note of that—when he was found his head was still on this very pedal which had caused the fatal injury. Gentlemen, I do not think we need any further evidence; I think your course is pretty clear."

All was, indeed, very clear. The jury with a unanimous verdict of accidental death put the colophon to the sad history of Mr Sharnall, and ruled that the same failing which had blighted his life, had brought him at last to a drunkard's end.

Westray walked back to the Hand of God with the forlorn old top-coat over his arm. The coroner had formally handed it over to him. He was evidently a close friend of the deceased, he would perhaps take charge of his wearing apparel. The architect's thoughts were too preoccupied to allow him to resent the sneer which accompanied these remarks; he went off full of sorrow and gloomy forebodings.

Death in so strange a shape formed a topic of tavern discussion in Cullerne, second only to a murder itself. Not since Mr Leveritt, the timber-merchant, shot a barmaid at the Blandamer Arms, a generation since, had any such dramatic action taken place on Cullerne boards. The loafers swore over it in all its bearings as they spat upon the pavement at the corner of the market square. Mr Smiles, the shop-walker in Rose and Storey's general drapery mart, discussed it genteelly with the ladies who sat before the counter on the high wicker-seated chairs.

Dr Ennefer was betrayed into ill-advised conversation while being shaved, and got his chin cut. Mr Joliffe gave away a packet of moral reflections gratis with every pound of sausage, and turned up the whites of his eyes over the sin of intemperance, which had called away his poor friend in so terrible a state of unpreparedness. Quite a crowd followed the coffin to its last resting-place, and the church was unusually full on the Sunday morning which followed the catastrophe. People expected a "pulpit reference" from Canon Parkyn, and there were the additional, though subordinate, attractions of the playing of the Dead March, and the possibility of an amateur organist breaking down in the anthem.

Church-going, which sprung from such unworthy motives, was very properly disappointed. Canon Parkyn would not, he said, pander to sensationalism by any allusion in his discourse, nor could the Dead March, he conceived, be played with propriety under such very unpleasant circumstances. The new organist got through the service with provokingly colourless mediocrity, and the congregation came out of Saint Sepulchre's in a disappointed mood, as people who had been defrauded of their rights.

Then the nine days' wonder ceased, and Mr Sharnall passed into the great oblivion of middle-class dead. His successor was not immediately appointed. Canon Parkyn arranged that the second master at the National School, who had a pretty notion of music, and was a pupil of Mr Sharnall, should be spared to fill the gap. As Queen Elizabeth, of pious memory, recruited the privy purse by keeping in her own hand vacant bishoprics, so the rector farmed the post of organist at Cullerne Minster. He thus managed to effect so important a reduction in the sordid emoluments of that office, that he was five pounds in pocket before a year was ended.

But if the public had forgotten Mr Sharnall, Westray had not. The architect was a man of gregarious instinct. As there is a tradition and bonding of common interest about the Universities, and in a less degree about army, navy, public schools, and professions, which draws together and marks with its impress those who are attached to them, so there is a certain *cabala* and membership among lodgers which none can understand except those who are free of that guild.

The lodging-house life, call it squalid, mean, dreary if you will, is not without its alleviations and counterpoises. It is a life of youth for the most part, for lodgers of Mr Sharnall's age are comparatively rare; it is a life of simple needs and simple tastes, for lodgings are not artistic, nor favourable to the development of any undue refinement; it is not a rich life, for men as a rule set up their own houses as soon as they are able to do so; it is a life of work and buoyant anticipation, where men are equipping for the struggle, and laying the foundations of fortune, or digging the pit of indigence. Such conditions beget and foster good fellowship, and those who have spent time in lodgings can look back to whole-hearted and disinterested friendships, when all were equal before high heaven, hail-fellows well met, who knew no artificial distinctions of rank—when all were travelling the first stage of life's journey in happy chorus together, and had not reached that point where the high road bifurcates, and the diverging branches of success and failure lead old comrades so very far apart.

Ah, what a *camaraderie* and fellowship, knit close by the urgency of making both ends meet, strengthened by the necessity of withstanding rapacious, or negligent, or tyrannous landladies, sweetened by kindnesses and courtesies which cost the giver little, but mean much to the receiver! Did sickness of a transitory sort (for grievous illness is little known in lodgings) fall on the ground-floor tenant, then did not the first-floor come down to comfort him in the evenings? First-floor might be tired after a long day's work, and note when his frugal meal was done that 'twas a fine evening, or that a good company was billed for the local theatre; yet he would grudge not his leisure, but go down to sit with ground-floor, and tell him the news of the day, perhaps even would take him a few oranges or a tin of sardines. And ground-floor, who had chafed all the day at being shut in, and had read himself stupid for want of anything else to do, how glad he was to see first-floor, and how the chat did him more good than all the doctor's stuff!

And later on, when some ladies came to lunch with first-floor on the day of the flower-show, did not ground-floor go out and place his sitting-room completely at his fellow-lodger's disposal, so that the company might find greater convenience and change of air after meat? They were fearful joys, these feminine visits, when ladies who were kind enough to ask a young man to spend a Sunday with them, still further added to their kindness, by accepting with all possible effusion the invitation which he one day ventured to give. It was a fearful joy, and cost the host more anxious preparation than a state funeral brings to earl-marshal. As brave a face as might be must be put on everything; so many details were to be thought out, so many little insufficiencies were to be masked. But did not the result recompense all? Was not the young man conscious that, though his rooms might be small, there was about them a delicate touch which made up for much, that everything breathed of refinement from the photographs and silver toddy-spoon upon the mantelpiece to Rossetti's poems and "Marius the Epicurean," which covered negligently a stain on the green tablecloth?

And these kindly ladies came in riant mood, well knowing all his little anxieties and preparations, yet showing they knew none of them; resolved to praise his rooms, his puny treasures, even his cookery and perilous wine, and skilful to turn little contretemps into interesting novelties. Householders, yours is a noble lot, ye are the men, and wisdom shall die with you. Yet pity not too profoundly him that inhabiteth lodgings, lest he turn and rend you, pitying you in turn that have bound on your shoulders heavy burdens of which he knows nothing; saying to you that seed time is more profitable than harvest, and the wandering years than the practice of the master. Refrain from too much pity, and believe that loneliness is not always lonely.

Westray was of a gregarious temperament, and missed his fellow-lodger. The cranky little man, with all his soured outlook, must still have had some power of evoking sympathy, some attractive element in his composition. He concealed it under sharp words and moody bitterness, but it must still have been there, for Westray felt his loss more than he had thought possible. The organist and he had met twice and thrice a day for a year past. They had discussed the minster that both loved so well, within whose walls both were occupied; they had discussed the nebuly coat, and the Blandamers, and Miss Euphemia.

There was only one subject which they did not discuss—namely, Miss Anastasia Joliffe, though she was very often in the thoughts of both.

It was all over now, yet every day Westray found himself making a mental note to tell this to Mr Sharnall, to ask Mr Sharnall's advice on that, and then remembering that there is no knowledge in the grave. The gaunt Hand of God was ten times gaunter now that there was no lodger on the ground-floor. Footfalls sounded more hollow at night on the stone steps of the staircase, and Miss Joliffe and Anastasia went early to bed.

"Let us go upstairs, my dear," Miss Euphemia would say when the chimes sounded a quarter to ten. "These long evenings are so lonely, are they not? and be sure you see that the windows are properly hasped." And then they hurried through the hall, and went up the staircase together side by side, as if they were afraid to be separated by a single step. Even Westray knew something of the same feeling when he returned late at night to the cavernous great house. He tried to put his hand as quickly as he might upon the matchbox, which lay ready for him on the marble-topped sideboard in the dark hall; and sometimes when he had lit the candle would instinctively glance at the door of Mr Sharnall's room, half expecting to see it open, and the old face look out that had so often greeted him on such occasions. Miss Joliffe had made no attempt to find a new lodger. No "Apartments to Let" was put in the window, and such chattels as Mr Sharnall possessed remained exactly as he left them. Only one thing was moved—the collection of Martin Joliffe's papers, and these Westray had taken upstairs to his own room.

When they opened the dead man's bureau with the keys found in his pocket to see whether he had left any will or instructions, there was discovered in one of the drawers a note addressed to Westray. It was dated a fortnight before his death, and was very short:

If I go away and am not heard of, or if anything happens to me, get hold of Martin Joliffe's papers at once. Take them up to your own room, lock them up, and don't let them out of your hands. Tell Miss Joliffe it is my wish, and she will hand them over to you. Be very careful there isn't a fire, or lest they should be destroyed in any other way. Read them carefully, and draw your own conclusions; you will find some notes of mine in the little red pocket-book.

The architect had read these words many times. They were no

doubt the outcome of the delusions of which Mr Sharnall had more than once spoken—of that dread of some enemy pursuing him, which had darkened the organist's latter days. Yet to read these things set out in black and white, after what had happened, might well give rise to curious thoughts. The coincidence was so strange, so terribly strange. A man following with a hammer—that had been the organist's hallucination; the vision of an assailant creeping up behind, and doing him to death with an awful, stealthy blow. And the reality—an end sudden and unexpected, a blow on the back of the head, which had been caused by a heavy fall.

Was it mere coincidence, was it some inexplicable presentiment, or was it more than either? Had there, in fact, existed a reason why the organist should think that someone had a grudge against him, that he was likely to be attacked? Had some dreadful scene been really enacted in the loneliness of the great church that night? Had the organist been taken unawares, or heard some movement in the silence, and, turning round, found himself alone with his murderer? And if a murderer, whose was the face into which the victim looked? And as Westray thought he shuddered; it seemed it might have been no human face at all, but some fearful presence, some visible presentment of the evil that walketh in darkness.

Then the architect would brush such follies away like cobwebs, and, turning back, consider who could have found his interest in such a deed. Against whom did the dead man urge him to be on guard lest Martin's papers should be spirited away? Was there some other claimant of that ill-omened peerage of whom he knew nothing, or was it—And Westray resolutely quenched the thought that had risen a hundred times before his mind, and cast it aside as a malign and baseless suspicion.

If there was any clue it must lie in those same papers, and he followed the instruction given him, and took them to his own room. He did not show Miss Joliffe the note; to do so could only have shaken her further, and she had felt the shock too severely already. He only told her of Mr Sharnall's wishes for the temporary disposal of her brother's papers. She begged him not to take them.

"Dear Mr Westray," she said, "do not touch them, do not let us have anything to do with them. I wanted poor dear Mr Sharnall not to go meddling with them, and now see what has happened. Perhaps it is a judgment"—and she uttered the word under her breath, having a medieval faith in the vengeful irritability of Providence, and seeing

452

manifestations of it in any untoward event, from the overturning of an inkstand to the death of a lodger. "Perhaps it is a judgment, and he might have been alive now if he had refrained. What good would it do us if all dear Martin hoped should turn out true? He always said, poor fellow, that he would be 'my lord' some day; but now he is gone there is no one except Anastasia, and she would never wish to be 'my lady,' I am sure, poor girl. You would not, darling, wish to be 'my lady' even if you could, would you?"

Anastasia looked up from her book with a deprecating smile, which lost itself in an air of vexation, when she found that the architect's eyes were fixed steadfastly upon her, and that a responsive smile spread over his face. She flushed very slightly, and turned back abruptly to her book, feeling quite unjustifiably annoyed at the interest in her doings which the young man's gaze was meant to imply. What right had he to express concern, even with a look, in matters which affected *her*? She almost wished she *was* indeed a peeress, and could slay him with her noble birth, as did one Lady Clara of old times. It was only lately that she had become conscious of this interested, would-be interesting, look, which Westray assumed in her presence. Was it possible that *he* was falling in love with her? And at the thought there rose before her fancy the features of someone else, haughty, hard, perhaps malign, but oh, so powerful, and quite eclipsed and blotted out the lifeless amiability of this young man who hung upon her lips.

Could Mr Westray be thinking of falling in love with her? It was impossible, and yet this following her with his eyes, and the mellific manner which he adopted when speaking to her, insisted on its possibility. She ran over hastily in her mind, as she had done several times of late, the course of their relations. Was she to blame? Could anything that she had ever done be wrested into predilection or even into appreciation? Could natural kindness or courtesy have been so utterly misunderstood? She was victoriously acquitted by this commission of mental inquiry, and left the court without a stain upon her character. She certainly had never given him the very least encouragement. At the risk of rudeness she *must* check these attentions in their beginning. Short of actual discourtesy, she must show him that this warm interest in her doings, these sympathetic glances, were exceedingly distasteful. She never would look near him again, she would keep her eyes rigorously cast down whenever he was present, and as she made this prudent resolution she quite unintentionally looked up, and found his patient gaze again fixed upon her.

"Oh, you are too severe, Miss Joliffe," the architect said; "we should all be delighted to see a title come to Miss Anastasia, and," he added softly, "I am sure no one would become it better."

He longed to drop the formal prefix of Miss, and to speak of her simply as Anastasia. A few months before he would have done so naturally and without reflection, but there was something in the girl's manner which led him more recently to forego this pleasure.

Then the potential peeress got up and left the room.

"I am just going to look after the bread," she said; "I think it ought to be baked by this time."

Miss Joliffe's scruples were at last overborne, and Westray retained the papers, partly because it was represented to her that if he did not examine them it would be a flagrant neglect of the wishes of a dead man—wishes that are held sacred above all others in the circles to which Miss Joliffe belonged—and partly because possession is nine points of the law, and the architect already had them safe under lock and key in his own room. But he was not able to devote any immediate attention to them, for a crisis in his life was approaching, which tended for the present to engross his thoughts.

He had entertained for some time an attachment to Anastasia Joliffe. When he originally became aware of this feeling he battled vigorously against it, and his efforts were at first attended with some success. He was profoundly conscious that any connection with the Joliffes would be derogatory to his dignity; he feared that the discrepancy between their relative positions was sufficiently marked to attract attention, if not to provoke hostile criticism. People would certainly say that an architect was marrying strangely below him, in choosing a landlady's niece. If he were to do such a thing, he would no doubt be throwing himself away socially. His father, who was dead, had been a Wesleyan pastor; and his mother, who survived, entertained so great a respect for the high position of that ministry that she had impressed upon Westray from boyhood the privileges and responsibilities of his birth. But apart from this objection, there was the further drawback that an early marriage might unduly burden him with domestic cares, and so arrest his professional progress. Such considerations had due weight with an equally-balanced mind, and Westray was soon able to congratulate himself on having effectually extinguished any dangerous inclinations by sheer strength of reason.

This happy and philosophic state of things was not of long duration. His admiration smouldered only, and was not quenched, but it was a totally extraneous influence, rather than the constant contemplation of Anastasia's beauty and excellencies, which fanned the flame into renewed activity. This extraneous factor was the entrance of Lord Blandamer into the little circle of Bellevue Lodge. Westray had lately become doubtful as to the real object of Lord Blandamer's visits, and nursed a latent idea that he was using the church, and the restoration, and Westray himself, to gain a *pied-à-terre* at Bellevue Lodge for the prosecution of other plans. The long conversations in which the architect and the munificent donor still indulged, the examination of plans, the discussion of details, had lost something of their old savour.

Westray had done his best to convince himself that his own suspicions were groundless; he had continually pointed out to himself, and insisted to himself, that the mere fact of Lord Blandamer contributing such sums to the restoration as he either had contributed, or had promised to contribute, showed that the church was indeed his primary concern. It was impossible to conceive that any man, however wealthy, should spend many thousand pounds to obtain an entree to Bellevue Lodge; moreover, it was impossible to conceive that Lord Blandamer should ever marry Anastasia—the disparity in such a match would, Westray admitted, be still greater than in his own. Yet he was convinced that Anastasia was often in Lord Blandamer's thoughts. It was true that the Master of Fording gave no definite outward sign of any predilection when Westray was present. He never singled Anastasia out either for regard or conversation on such occasions as chance brought her into his company. At times he even made a show of turning away from her, of studiously neglecting her presence.

But Westray felt that the fact was there.

There is some subtle effluence of love which hovers about one who entertains a strong affection for another. Looks may be carefully guarded, speech may be framed to mislead, yet that pervading ambient of affection is strong to betray where perception is sharpened by jealousy.

Now and then the architect would persuade himself that he was mistaken; he would reproach himself with his own suspicious disposition, with his own lack of generosity. But then some little episode would occur, some wholly undemonstrable trifle, which swept his cooler judgment to the winds, and gave him a quite incommensurate heartburn. He would recall, for instance, the fact that for their interviews Lord Blandamer had commonly selected a Saturday afternoon. Lord Blandamer had explained this by saying that he was busy through the week; but then a lord was not like a schoolboy with a Saturday half-holiday. What business could he have to occupy him all the week, and leave him free on Saturdays? It was strange enough, and stranger from the fact that Miss Euphemia Joliffe was invariably occupied on that particular afternoon at the Dorcas meeting; stranger from the fact that there had been some unaccountable misunderstandings between Lord Blandamer and Westray as to the exact hour fixed for their interviews, and that more than once when the architect had returned at five, he had found that Lord Blandamer had taken four as the time of their meeting, and had been already waiting an hour at Bellevue Lodge.

Poor Mr Sharnall also must have noticed that something was going on, for he had hinted as much to Westray a fortnight or so before he died. Westray was uncertain as to Lord Blandamer's feelings; he gave the architect the idea of a man who had some definite object to pursue in making himself interesting to Anastasia, while his own affections were not compromised. That object could certainly not be marriage, and if it was not marriage, what was it? In ordinary cases an answer might have been easy, yet Westray hesitated to give it. It was hard to think that this grave man, of great wealth and great position, who had roamed the world, and known men and manners, should stoop to common lures. Yet Westray came to think it, and his own feelings towards Anastasia were elevated by the resolve to be her knightly champion against all base attempts.

Can man's deepest love be deepened? Then it must surely be by the knowledge that he is protector as well as lover, by the knowledge that he is rescuing innocence, and rescuing it for—himself. Thoughts such as these bring exaltation to the humblest-minded, and they quickened the slow-flowing and thin fluid that filled the architect's veins.

He came back one evening from the church weary with a long day's work, and was sitting by the fire immersed in a medley of sleepy and half-conscious consideration, now of the crack in the centre tower, now of the tragedy of the organ-loft, now of Anastasia, when the elder Miss Joliffe entered.

"Dear me, sir," she said, "I did not know you were in! I only came to see your fire was burning. Are you ready for your tea? Would you like anything special tonight? You do look so very tired. I am sure you are working too hard; all the running about on ladders and scaffolds must be very trying. I think indeed, sir, if I may make so bold, that you should take a holiday; you have not had a holiday since you came to live with us."

"It is not impossible, Miss Joliffe, that I may take your advice before very long. It is not impossible that I may before long go for a holiday."

He spoke with that preternatural gravity which people are accustomed to throw into their reply, if asked a trivial question when their own thoughts are secretly occupied with some matter that they consider of deep importance. How could this commonplace woman guess that he was thinking of death and love? He must be gentle with her and forgive her interruption. Yes, fate might, indeed, drive him to take a holiday. He had nearly made up his mind to propose to Anastasia. It was scarcely to be doubted that she would at once accept him, but there must be no half-measures, he would brook no shilly-shallying, he would not be played fast and loose with. She must either accept him fully and freely, and at once, or he would withdraw his offer, and in that case, or still more in the entirely improbable case of refusal, he would leave Bellevue Lodge forthwith.

"Yes, indeed, I may ere long have to go away for a holiday."

The conscious forbearance of replying at all gave a quiet dignity to his tone, and an involuntary sigh that accompanied his words was not lost upon Miss Joliffe. To her this speech seemed oracular and ominous; there was a sepulchral mystery in so vague an expression. He might *have* to take a holiday. What could this mean? Was this poor young man completely broken by the loss of his friend Mr Sharnall, or was he conscious of the seeds of some fell disease that others knew nothing of? He might *have to* take a holiday. Ah, it was not a mere holiday of which he spoke—he meant something more serious than that; his grave, sad manner could only mean some long absence. Perhaps he was going to leave Cullerne.

To lose him would be a very serious matter to Miss Joliffe from the material point of view; he was her sheet-anchor, the last anchor that kept Bellevue Lodge from drifting into bankruptcy. Mr Sharnall was dead, and with him had died the tiny pittance which he contributed to the upkeep of the place, and lodgers were few and far between in Cullerne. Miss Joliffe might well have remembered these things, but she did not. The only thought that crossed her mind was that if Mr Westray went away she would lose yet another friend. She did not approach the matter from the material point of view, she looked on him only as a friend; she viewed him as no money-making machine, but only as that most precious of all treasures—a last friend.

457

"I may have to leave you for awhile," he said again, with the same portentous solemnity.

"I hope not, sir," she interrupted, as though by her very eagerness she might avert threatened evil—"I hope not; we should miss you terribly, Mr Westray, with dear Mr Sharnall gone too. I do not know what we should do having no man in the house. It is so very lonely if you are away even for a night. I am an old woman now, and it does not matter much for me, but Anastasia is so nervous at night since the dreadful accident."

Westray's face brightened a little at the mention of Anastasia's name. Yes, his must certainly be a very deep affection, that the naming of her very name should bring him such pleasure. It was on *his* protection, then, that she leant; she looked on *him* as her defender. The muscles of his not gigantic arms seemed to swell and leap to bursting in his coat-sleeves. Those arms should screen his loved one from all evil. Visions of Perseus, and Sir Galahad, and Cophetua, swept before his eyes; he had almost cried to Miss Euphemia, "You need have no fear, I love your niece. I shall bow down and raise her to my throne. They that would touch her shall only do so over my dead body," when hesitating common-sense plucked him by the sleeve; he must consult his mother before taking this grave step.

It was well that reason thus restrained him, for such a declaration might have brought Miss Joliffe to a swoon. As it was, she noticed the cloud lifting on his face, and was pleased to think that her conversation cheered him. A little company was no doubt good for him, and she sought in her mind for some further topic of interest. Yes, of course, she had it.

"Lord Blandamer was here this afternoon. He came just like anyone else might have come, in such a very kind and condescending way to ask after me. He feared that dear Mr Sharnall's death might have been too severe a shock for us both, and, indeed, it has been a terrible blow. He was so considerate, and sat for nearly an hour—for forty-seven minutes I should say by the clock, and took tea with us in the kitchen as if he were one of the family. I never could have expected such condescension, and when he went away he left a most polite message for you, sir, to say that he was sorry that you were not in, but he hoped to call again before long."

The cloud had returned to Westray's face. If he had been the hero of a novel his brow would have been black as night; as it was he only looked rather sulky.

"I shall have to go to London tonight," he said stiffly, without acknowledging Miss Joliffe's remarks; "I shall not be back tomorrow, and may be away a few days. I will write to let you know when I shall be back."

Miss Joliffe started as if she had received an electric shock.

"To London tonight," she began—"this very night?"

"Yes," Westray said, with a dryness that would have suggested of itself that the interview was to be terminated, even if he had not added: "I shall be glad to be left alone now; I have several letters to write before I can get away."

So Miss Euphemia went to impart this strange matter to the maiden who was *ex hypothesi* leaning on the architect's strong arm.

"What *do* you think, Anastasia?" she said. "Mr Westray is going to London tonight, perhaps for some days."

"Is he?" was all her niece's comment; but there was a languor and indifference in the voice, that might have sent the thermometer of the architect's affection from boiling-point to below blood-heat, if he could have heard her speak.

Westray sat moodily for a few moments after his landlady had gone. For the first time in his life he wished he was a smoker. He wished he had a pipe in his mouth, and could pull in and puff out smoke as he had seen Sharnall do when *he* was moody. He wanted some work for his restless body while his restless mind was turning things over. It was the news of Lord Blandamer's visit, as on this very afternoon, that fanned smouldering thoughts into flame. This was the first time, so far as Westray knew, that Lord Blandamer had come to Bellevue Lodge without at least a formal excuse of business. With that painful effort which we use to convince ourselves of things of which we wish to be convinced in the face of all difficulties; with that blind, stumbling hope against hope with which we try to reconcile things irreconcilable, if only by so doing we can conjure away a haunting spectre, or lull to sleep a bitter suspicion; the architect had hitherto resolved to believe that if Lord Blandamer came with some frequency to Bellevue Lodge, he was only prompted to do so by a desire to keep in touch with the restoration, to follow with intelligence the expenditure of money which he was so lavishly providing.

It had been the easier for Westray to persuade himself that Lord Blandamer's motives were legitimate, because he felt that the other must find a natural attraction in the society of a talented young professional man. An occasional conversation with a clever architect on things architectural, or on other affairs of common interest (for Westray was careful to avoid harping unduly on any single topic) must undoubtedly prove a relief to Lord Blandamer from the monotony of bachelor life in the country; and in such considerations Westray found a subsidiary, and sometimes he was inclined to imagine primary, interest for these visits to Bellevue Lodge.

If various circumstances had conspired of late to impugn the sufficiency of these motives, Westray had not admitted as much in his own mind; if he had been disquieted, he had constantly assured himself that disquietude was unreasonable. But now disillusion had befallen him. Lord Blandamer had visited Bellevue Lodge as it were in his own right; he had definitely abandoned the pretence of coming to see Westray; he had been drinking tea with Miss Joliffe; he had spent an hour in the kitchen with Miss Joliffe and—Anastasia. It could only mean one thing, and Westray's resolution was taken.

An object which had seemed at best but mildly desirable, became of singular value when he believed that another was trying to possess himself of it; jealousy had quickened love, duty and conscience insisted that he should save the girl from the snare that was being set for her. The great renunciation must be made; he, Westray, must marry beneath him, but before doing so he would take his mother into his confidence, though there is no record of Perseus doing as much before he cut loose Andromeda.

Meanwhile, no time must be lost; he would start this very night. The last train for London had already left, but he would walk to Cullerne Road Station and catch the night-mail from thence. He liked walking, and need take no luggage, for there were things that he could use at his mother's house. It was seven o'clock when he came to this resolve, and an hour later he had left the last house in Cullerne behind him, and entered upon his night excursion.

The line of the Roman way which connected Carauna (Carisbury) with its port Culurnum (Cullerne) is still followed by the modern road, and runs as nearly straight as may be for the sixteen miles which separate those places. About halfway between them the Great Southern main line crosses the highway at right angles, and here is Cullerne Road Station. The first half of the way runs across a flat sandy tract called Mallory Heath, where the short greensward encroaches on the road, and where the eye roaming east or west or north can discern nothing except a limitless expanse of heather, broken here and there by patches of gorse and bracken, or by clumps of tousled and wind-thinned pines and Scotch firs. The tawny-coloured, sandy, track is difficult to follow in the dark, and there are posts set up at intervals on the skirts of the way for travellers' guidance. These posts show out white against a starless night, and dark against the snow which sometimes covers the heath with a silvery sheet.

On a clear night the traveller can see the far-off lamps of the station at Cullerne Road a mile after he has left the old seaport town. They stand out like a thin line of light in the distant darkness, a line continuous at first, but afterwards resolvable into individual units of lamps as he walks further along the straight road. Many a weary wayfarer has watched those lamps hang changeless in the distance, and chafed at their immobility. They seem to come no nearer to him for all the milestones, with the distance from Hyde Park Corner graven in old figures on their lichened faces, that he has passed. Only the increasing sound of the trains tells him that he is nearing his goal, and by degrees the dull rumble becomes a clanking roar as the expresses rush headlong by. On a crisp winter day they leave behind them a trail of whitest wool, and in the night-time a fiery serpent follows them when the open furnace-door flings on the cloud a splendid radiance. But in the dead heats of midsummer the sun dries up the steam, and they speed along, the more wonderful because there is no trace to tell what power it is that drives them.

Of all these things Westray saw nothing. A soft white fog had fallen upon everything. It drifted by in delicate whirling wreaths, that seemed to have an innate motion of their own where all had been still but a minute before. It covered his clothes with a film of the finest powdery moisture that ran at a touch into heavy drops, it hung in dripping dew on his moustache, and hair, and eyebrows, it blinded him, and made him catch his breath. It had come rolling in from the sea as on that night when Mr Sharnall was taken, and Westray could hear the distant groaning of fog-horns in the Channel; and looking backwards towards Cullerne, knew from a blurred glare, now green, now red, that a vessel in the offing was signalling for a coastwise pilot. He plodded steadily forward, stopping now and then when he found his feet on the grass sward to recover the road, and rejoicing when one of the white posts assured him that he was still keeping the right direction.

The blinding fog isolated him in a strange manner; it cut him off from Nature, for he could see nothing of her; it cut him off from man, for he could not have seen even a legion of soldiers had they surrounded him. This removal of outside influences threw him back upon himself, and delivered him to introspection; he began for the hundredth time to weigh his position, to consider whether the momentous step that he was taking was necessary to his ease of mind, was right, was prudent.

To make a proposal of marriage is a matter that may give the strongest-minded pause, and Westray's mind was not of the strongest. He was clever, imaginative, obstinate, scrupulous to a fault; but had not that broad outlook on life which comes of experience, nor the power and resolution to readily take a decision under difficult circumstances, and to abide by it once taken. So it was that reason made a shuttlecock of his present resolve, and half a dozen times he stopped in the road meaning to abandon his purpose, and turn back to Cullerne. Yet half a dozen times he went on, though with slow feet, thinking always, Was he right in what he was doing, was he right? And the fog grew thicker; it seemed almost to be stifling him; he could not see his hand if he held it at arm's length before his face. Was he right, was there any right or any wrong, was anything real, was not everything subjective—the creation of his own brain? Did he exist, was he himself, was he in the body or out of the body? And then a wild dismay, a horror of the darkness and the fog, seized hold of him. He stretched out his arms, and groped in the mist as if he hoped to lay hold of someone, or something, to reassure him as to his own identity, and at last a mind-panic got the better of him; he turned and started back to Cullerne.

It was only for a moment, and then reason began to recover her sway; he stopped, and sat down on the heather at the side of the road, careless that every spray was wet and dripping, and collected his thoughts. His heart was beating madly as in one that wakes from a nightmare, but he was now ashamed of his weakness and of the mental *debacle*, though there had been none to see it. What could have possessed him, what madness was this? After a few minutes he was able to turn round once more, and resumed his walk towards the railway with a firm, quick step, which should prove to his own satisfaction that he was master of himself.

For the rest of his journey he dismissed bewildering questions of right and wrong, of prudence and imprudence, laying it down as an axiom that his emprise was both right and prudent, and busied himself with the more material and homely considerations of ways and means. He amused himself in attempting to fix the sum for which it would be possible for him and Anastasia to keep house, and by mentally straining to the utmost the resources at his command managed to make them approach his estimate. Another man in similar circumstances might perhaps have given himself to reviewing the chances of success in his proposal, but Westray did not trouble himself with any doubts on this point. It was a foregone conclusion that if he once offered himself Anastasia would accept him; she could not be so oblivious to the advantages which such a marriage would offer, both in material considerations and in the connection with a superior family. He only regarded the matter from his own standpoint; once he was convinced that *he* cared enough for Anastasia to make her an offer, then he was sure that she would accept him.

It was true that he could not, on the spur of the moment, recollect many instances in which she had openly evinced a predilection for him, but he was conscious that she thought well of him, and she was no doubt too modest to make manifest, feelings which she could never under ordinary circumstances hope to see returned. Yet he certainly *had* received encouragement of a quiet and unobtrusive kind, quite sufficient to warrant the most favourable conclusions. He remembered how many, many times their eyes had met when they were in one another's company; she must certainly have read the tenderness which had inspired his glances, and by answering them she had given perhaps the greatest encouragement that true modesty would permit. How delicate and infinitely gracious her acknowledgment had been, how often had she looked at him as it were furtively, and then, finding his passionate gaze upon her, had at once cast her own eyes shyly to the ground!

And in his reveries he took not into reckoning, the fact that through these later weeks he had scarcely ever taken his gaze off her, so long as she was in the same room with him. It would have been strange if their eyes had not sometimes met, because she must needs now and then obey that impulse which forces us to look at those who are looking at us. Certainly, he meditated, her eyes had given him encouragement, and then she had accepted gratefully a bunch of lilies of the valley which he said lightly had been given him, but which he had really bought *ad hoc* at Carisbury. But, again, he ought perhaps to have reflected that it would have been difficult for her to refuse them. How could she have refused them? How could any girl under the circumstances do less than take with thanks a few lilies of the valley? To decline them would be affectation; by declining she might attach a false and ridiculous significance to a kindly act.

Yes, she had encouraged him in the matter of the lilies, and if she had not worn some of them in her bosom, as he had hoped she might, that, no doubt, was because she feared to show her preference too markedly. He had noticed particularly the interest she had shown when a bad cold had confined him for a few days to the house, and this very evening had he not heard that she missed him when he was absent even for a night? He smiled at this thought, invisibly in the fog; and has not a man a right to some complacence, on whose presence in the house hang a fair maiden's peace and security? Miss Joliffe had said that Anastasia felt nervous whenever he, Westray, was away; it was very possible that Anastasia had given her aunt a hint that she would like him to be told this, and he smiled again in the fog; he certainly need have no fear of any rejection of his suit.

He had been so deeply immersed in these reassuring considerations that he walked steadily on unconscious of all exterior objects and conditions until he saw the misty lights of the station, and knew that his goal was reached. His misgivings and tergiversations had so much delayed him by the way, that it was past midnight, and the train was already due. There were no other travellers on the platform, or in the little waiting-room where a paraffin-lamp with blackened chimney struggled feebly with the fog. It was not a cheery room, and he was glad to be called back from a contemplation of a roll of texts hanging on the wall, and a bottle of stale water on the table, to human things by the entry of a drowsy official who was discharging the duties of station-master, booking-clerk, and porter all at once.

"Are you waiting for the London train, sir?" he asked in a surprised tone, that showed that the night-mail found few passengers at Cullerne Road. "She will be in now in a few minutes; have you your ticket?"

They went together to the booking-office. The station-master handed him a third-class ticket, without even asking how he wished to travel.

"Ah, thank you," Westray said, "but I think I will go first-class tonight. I shall be more likely to have a compartment to myself, and shall be less disturbed by people getting in and out."

"Certainly, sir," said the station-master, with the marked increase of respect due to a first-class passenger—"certainly, sir; please give me back the other ticket. I shall have to write you one—we do not keep them ready; we are so very seldom asked for first-class at this station."

"No, I suppose not," Westray said.

"Things happen funny," the station-master remarked while he *got* his pen. "I wrote one by this same train a month ago, and before that I don't think we have ever sold one since the station was opened."

"Ah," Westray said, paying little attention, for he was engaged in a new mental disputation as to whether he was really justified in travelling first-class. He had just settled that at such a life-crisis as he had now reached, it was necessary that the body should be spared fatigue in order that the mind might be as vigorous as possible for dealing with a difficult situation, and that the extra expense was therefore justified; when the station-master went on:

"Yes, I wrote a ticket, just as I might for you, for Lord Blandamer not a month ago. Perhaps you know Lord Blandamer?" he added venturously; yet with a suggestion that even the sodality of first-class travelling was not in itself a passport to so distinguished an acquaintance. The mention of Lord Blandamer's name gave a galvanic shock to Westray's flagging attention.

"Oh yes," he said, "I know Lord Blandamer."

"Do you, indeed, sir"—and respect had risen by a skip greater than any allowed in counterpoint. "Well, I wrote a ticket for his lordship by this very train not a month ago; no, it was not a month ago, for 'twas the very night the poor organist at Cullerne was took."

"Yes," said the would-be indifferent Westray; "where did Lord Blandamer come from?"

"I do not know," the station-master replied—"I do *not* know, sir," he repeated, with the unnecessary emphasis common to the uneducated or unintelligent.

"Was he driving?"

"No, he walked up to this station just as you might yourself. Excuse me, sir," he broke off; "here she comes."

They heard the distant thunder of the approaching train, and were in time to see the gates of the level-crossing at the end of the platform swing silently open as if by ghostly hands, till their red lanterns blocked the Cullerne Road.

No one got out, and no one but Westray got in; there was some interchanging of post-office bags in the fog, and then the station-master-booking-clerk-porter waved a lamp, and the train steamed away. Westray found himself in a cavernous carriage, of which the cloth seats were cold and damp as the lining of a coffin. He turned up the collar of his coat, folded his arms in a Napoleonic attitude, and threw himself back into a corner to think. It was curious—it was very curious. He had been under the impression that Lord Blandamer had left Cullerne early on the night of poor Sharnall's accident; Lord Blandamer had told them at Bellevue Lodge that he was going away by the afternoon train when he left them. Yet here he was at Cullerne Road at midnight, and if he had not come from Cullerne, whence had he come? He could not have come from Fording, for from Fording he would certainly have taken the train at Lytchett. It was curious, and while he was so thinking he fell asleep.

Chapter Sixteen

A day or two later Miss Joliffe said to Anastasia:

"I think you had a letter from Mr Westray this morning, my dear, had you not? Did he say anything about his return? Did he say when he was coming back?"

"No, dear aunt, he said nothing about coming back. He only wrote a few lines on a matter of business."

"Oh yes, just so," Miss Joliffe said dryly, feeling a little hurt at what seemed like any lack of confidence on her niece's part.

Miss Joliffe would have said that she knew Anastasia's mind so well that no secrets were hid from her. Anastasia would have said that her aunt knew everything except a few *little* secrets, and, as a matter of fact, the one perhaps knew as much of the other as it is expedient that age should know of youth. "The mind is its own place, and in itself can make a hell of heaven, a heaven of hell." Of all earthly consolations this is the greatest, that the mind is its own place. The mind is an impregnable fortress which can be held against all comers, the mind is a sanctuary open day or night to the pursued, the mind is a flowery pleasance where shade refreshes even in summer droughts. To some trusted friend we try to give the clue of the labyrinth, but the ball of silk is too short to guide any but ourselves along all the way. There are sunny mountain-tops, there are innocent green arbours, or closes of too highly-perfumed flowers, or dank dungeons of despair, or guilty *mycethmi* black as night, where we walk alone, whither we may lead no one with us by the hand.

Miss Euphemia Joliffe would have liked to ignore altogether the matter of Westray's letter, and to have made no further remarks thereon; but curiosity is in woman a stronger influence than pride, and curiosity drove her to recur to the letter.

"Thank you, my dear, for explaining about it. I am sure you will tell me if there are any messages for me in it."

"No, there was no message at all for you, I think," said Anastasia. "I

466

will get it for you by-and-by, and you shall see all he says;" and with that she left the room as if to fetch the letter. It was only a subterfuge, for she felt Westray's correspondence burning a hole in her pocket all the while; but she was anxious that her aunt should not see the letter until an answer to it had been posted; and hoped that if she once escaped from the room, the matter would drop out of memory. Miss Joliffe fired a parting shot to try to bring her niece to her bearings as she was going out:

"I do not know, my dear, that I should encourage any correspondence from Mr Westray, if I were you. It would be more seemly, perhaps, that he should write to me on any little matter of business than to you." But Anastasia feigned not to hear her, and held on her course.

She betook herself to the room that had once been Mr Sharnall's, but was now distressingly empty and forlorn, and there finding writing materials, sat down to compose an answer to Westray's letter. She knew its contents thoroughly well, she knew its expressions almost by heart, yet she spread it out on the table before her, and read and re-read it as many times as if it were the most difficult of cryptograms.

"Dearest Anastasia," it began, and she found a grievance in the very first word, "Dearest." What right had he to call her "Dearest"? She was one of those unintelligible females who do not shower superlatives on every chance acquaintance. She must, no doubt, have been callous as judged by modern standards, or at least, singularly unimaginative, for among her few correspondents she had not one whom she addressed as "dearest." No, not even her aunt, for at such rare times of absence from home as she had occasion to write to Miss Joliffe, "My dear Aunt Euphemia" was the invocation.

It was curious that this same word "Dearest" had occasioned Westray also considerable thought and dubiety. Should he call her "Dearest Anastasia," or "Dear Miss Joliffe"? The first sounded too forward, the second too formal. He had discussed this and other details with his mother, and the die had at last fallen on "Dearest." At the worst such an address could only be criticised as proleptic, since it must be justified almost immediately by Anastasia's acceptance of his proposal.

Dearest Anastasia—for dearest you are and ever will be to me—I feel sure that your heart will go out to meet my heart in what I am saying; that your kindness will support me in the important step which has now to be taken.

Anastasia shook her head, though there was no one to see her. There was a suggestion of fate overbearing prudence in Westray's words, a suggestion that he needed sympathy in an unpleasant predicament, that jarred on her intolerably.

I have known you now a year, and know that my happiness is centred in you; you too have known me a year, and I trust that I have read aright the message that your eyes have been sending to me.

For I shall happiest be tonight,
Or saddest in the town;
Heaven send I read their message right,
Those eyes of hazel brown.

Anastasia found space in the press of her annoyance to laugh. It was more than a smile, it was a laugh, a quiet little laugh to herself, which in a man would have been called a buckle. Her eyes were not hazel brown, they were no brown at all; but then brown rhymed with town, and after all the verse might perhaps be a quotation, and must so be taken only to apply to the situation in general. She read the sentence again, "I have known you now a year; you too have known me a year." Westray had thought this poetic insistence gave a touch of romance, and balanced the sentence; but to Anastasia it seemed the reiteration of a platitude. If he had known her a year, then she had known him a year, and to a female mind the sequitur was complete.

Have I read the message right, dearest? Is your heart my own?

Message? What message did he speak of? What message did he imagine she had wished to give *him* with her eyes? He had stared at her persistently for weeks past, and if her eyes sometimes caught his, that was only because she could not help it; except when between whiles she glanced at him of set purpose, because it amused her to see how silly a man in love may look.

Say that it is; tell me that your heart is my own" (and the request seemed to her too preposterous to admit even of comment). I watch your present, dear Anastasia, with solicitude. Sometimes I think that you are even now exposed to dangers of whose very existence you know nothing; and sometimes I look forward with anxiety to the future, so undecipherable, if misfortune or death should overtake your aunt. Let me help you to decipher this riddle. Let me be your shield now, and your support in the days to come. Be my wife, and give me the right to be your protector. I am detained in London by business for some days more; but I shall await your answer here with overwhelming eagerness, yet, may I say it? not without hope.

Your most loving and devoted

Edward Westray.

She folded the letter up with much deliberation, and put it back into its envelope. If Westray had sought far and wide for means of damaging his own cause, he could scarcely have found anything better calculated for that purpose than these last paragraphs. They took away much of that desire to spare, to make unpleasantness as little unpleasant as may be, which generally accompanies a refusal. His sententiousness was unbearable. What right had he to advise before he knew whether she would listen to him? What were these dangers to which she was even now exposed, and from which Mr Westray was to shield her? She asked herself the question formally, though she knew the answer all the while. Her own heart had told her enough of late, to remove all difficulty in reading between Mr Westray's lines. A jealous man is, if possible, more contemptible than a jealous woman. Man's greater strength postulates a broader mind and wider outlook; and if he fail in these, his failure is more conspicuous than woman's. Anastasia had traced to jealousy the origin of Westray's enigmatic remarks; but if she was strong enough to hold him ridiculous for his pains, she was also weak enough to take a woman's pleasure in having excited the interest of the man she ridiculed.

She laughed again at the proposal that she should join him in deciphering any riddles, still more such as were undecipherable; and the air of patronage involved in his anxiety to provide for her future was the more distasteful in that she had great ideas of providing for it herself. She had told herself a hundred times that it was only affection for her aunt that kept her at home. Were "anything to happen" to Miss Joliffe, she would at once seek her own living. She had often reckoned up the accomplishments which would aid her in such an endeavour. She had received her education—even if it were somewhat desultory and discontinuous—at good schools. She had always been a voracious reader, and possessed an extensive knowledge of English literature, particularly of the masters of fiction; she could play the piano and the violin tolerably, though Mr Sharnall would have qualified her estimate.

She had an easy touch in oils and water-colour, which her father said she must have inherited from his mother—from that Sophia Joliffe who painted the great picture of the flowers and caterpillar, and her spirited caricatures had afforded much merriment to her schoolfellows. She made her own clothes, and was sure that she had a taste in matters of dress design and manufacture that would bring her distinction if she were only given the opportunity of employing it; she believed that she had an affection for children, and a natural talent for training them, though she never saw any at Cullerne. With gifts such as these, which must be patent to others as well as herself, there would surely be no difficulty in obtaining an excellent place as governess if she should ever determine to adopt that walk of life; and she was sometimes inclined to gird at Fate, which for the present led her to deprive the world of these benefits.

In her inmost heart, however, she doubted whether she would be really justified in devoting herself to teaching; for she was conscious that she might be called to fill a higher mission, and to instruct by the pen rather than by word of mouth. As every soldier carries in his knapsack the baton of the field marshal, so every girl in her teens knows that there lie hidden in the recesses of her *armoire*, the robes and coronet and full insignia of a first-rate novelist. She may not choose to take them out and air them, the crown may tarnish by disuse, the moth of indolence may corrupt, but there lies the panoply in which she may on any day appear fully dight, for the astonishment of an awakening world. Jane Austen and Maria Edgworth are heroines, whose aureoles shine in the painted windows of such airy castles; Charlotte Bronte wrote her masterpieces in a seclusion as deep as that of Bellevue Lodge; and Anastasia Joliffe thought many a time of that day when, afar off from her watch-tower in quiet Cullerne, she would follow the triumphant progress of an epoch-making romance.

It would be published under a *nom de plume*, of course, she would not use her own name till she had felt her feet; and the choice of the pseudonym was the only definite step towards this venture that she had yet made. The period was still uncertain. Sometimes the action was to be placed in the eighteenth century, with tall silver urns and spindled-legged tables, and breast-waisted dresses; sometimes in the struggle of the Roses, when barons swam rivers in full armour after a bloody bout; sometimes in the Civil War, when Vandyke drew the arched eyebrow and taper hand, and when the shadow of death was over all.

470

It was to the Civil War that her fancy turned oftenest, and now and again, as she sat before her looking-glass, she fancied that she had a Vandyke face herself. And so it was indeed; and if the mirror was fogged and dull and outworn, and if the dress that it reflected was not of plum or amber velvet, one still might fancy that she was a loyalist daughter whose fortunes were fallen with her master's. The Limner of the King would have rejoiced to paint the sweet, young, oval face and little mouth; he would have found the space between the eyebrow and the eyelid to his liking.

If the plot were still shadowy, her characters were always with her, in armour or sprigged prints; and, the mind being its own place, she took about a little court of her own, where dreadful tragedies were enacted, and valorous deeds done; where passionate young love suffered and wept, and where a mere girl of eighteen, by consummate resolution, daring, beauty, genius, and physical strength, always righted the situation, and brought peace at the last.

With resources such as these, the future did not present itself in dark colours to Anastasia; nor did its riddle appear to her nearly so undecipherable as Mr Westray had supposed. She would have resented, with all the confidence of inexperience, *any* attempt to furnish her with prospects; and she resented Westray's offer all the more vigorously because it seemed to carry with it a suggestion of her own forlorn position, to insist unduly on her own good fortune in receiving such a proposal, and on his condescension in making it.

There are women who put marriage in the forefront of life, whose thoughts revolve constantly about it as a centre, and with whom an advantageous match, or, failing that, a match of some sort, is the primary object. There are others who regard marriage as an eventuality, to be contemplated without either eagerness or avoidance, to be accepted or declined according as its circumstances may be favourable or unfavourable. Again, there are some who seem, even from youth, to resolutely eliminate wedlock from their thoughts, to permit themselves no mental discussion upon this subject. Though a man profess that he will never marry, experience has shown that his resolve is often subject to reconsideration.

But with unmarrying women the case is different, and unmarried for the most part they remain, for man is often so weak-kneed a creature in matters of the heart, that he refrains from pursuing where an unsympathetic attitude discourages pursuit. It may be that some of these women, also, would wish to reconsider their verdict, but find that they have reached an age when there is no place for repentance; yet, for the most part, woman's resolve upon such matters is more stable than man's, and that because the interests at stake in marriage are for her more vital than can ever be the case with man.

It was to the class of indifferentists that Anastasia belonged; she neither sought nor shunned a change of state, but regarded marriage as an accident that, in befalling her, might substantially change the outlook. It would render a life of teaching, no doubt, impossible; domestic or maternal cares might to some extent trammel even literary activity (for, married or not married, she was determined to fulfil her mission of writing), but in no case was she inclined to regard marriage as an escape from difficulties, as the solution of so trivial a problem as that of existence.

She read Westray's letter once more from beginning to end. It was duller than ever. It reflected its writer; she had always thought him unromantic, and now he seemed to her intolerably prosaic, conceited, pettifogging, utilitarian. To be his wife! She had rather slave as a nursery-governess all her life! And how could she write fiction with such a one for mentor and company? He would expect her to be methodic, to see that eggs were fresh, and beds well aired. So, by thinking, she reasoned herself into such a theoretic reprobation of this attempt upon her, that his offer became a heinous crime. If she answered him shortly, brusquely, nay rudely, it would be but what he deserved for making her ridiculous to herself by so absurd a proposal, and she opened her writing-case with much firmness and resolution.

It was a little wooden case covered in imitation leather, with *Papeterie* stamped in gold upon the top. She had no exaggerated notions as to its intrinsic worth, but it was valuable in her eyes as being a present from her father. It was, in fact, the only gift he ever had bestowed upon her; but on this he had expended at least half a crown, in a fit of unusual generosity when he sent her with a great flourish of trumpets to Mrs Howard's school at Carisbury. She remembered his very words. "Take this, child," he said; "you are now going to a first-class place of education, and it is right that you should have a proper equipment," and so gave her the *papeterie*. It had to cover a multitude of deficiencies, and poor Anastasia lamented that it had not been a new hair-brush, half a dozen pocket-handkerchiefs, or even a sound pair of shoes.

Still it had stood in good stead, for with it she had written all her letters ever since, and being the only receptacle with lock and key to which she had access, she had made it a little ark and coffer for certain girlish treasures. With such it was stuffed so full that they came crowding out as she opened it. There were several letters to which romance attached, relics of that delightful but far too short school-time at Carisbury; there was her programme, with rudely-scribbled names of partners, for the splendid dance at the term's end, to which a selection of other girls' brothers were invited; a pressed rose given her by someone which she had worn in her bosom on that historic occasion, and many other equally priceless mementoes.

Somehow these things seemed now neither so romantic nor so precious as on former occasions; she was even inclined to smile, and to make light of them, and then a little bit of paper fluttered off the table on to the floor. She stooped and picked up the flap of an envelope with the coronet and "Fording" stamped in black upon it which she had found one day when Westray's waste-paper basket was emptied. It was a simple device enough, but it must have furnished her food for thought, for it lay under her eyes on the table for at least ten minutes before she put it carefully back into the *papeterie*, and began her letter to Westray.

She found no difficulty in answering, but the interval of reflection had soothed her irritation, and blunted her animosity. Her reply was neither brusque nor rude, it leant rather to conventionalism than to originality, and she used, after all, those phrases which have been commonplaces in such circumstances, since man first asked and woman first refused. She thanked Mr Westray for the kind interest which he had taken in her, she was deeply conscious of the consideration which he had shown her. She was grieved—sincerely grieved—to tell him that things could not be as he wished. She was so afraid that her letter would seem unkind; she did not mean it to be unkind. However difficult it was to say it now, she thought it was the truest kindness not to disguise from him that things *never* could be as he wished.

She paused a little to review this last sentiment, but she allowed it to remain, for she was anxious to avoid any recrudescence of the suppliant's passion, and to show that her decision was final. She should always feel the greatest esteem for Mr Westray; she trusted that the present circumstances would not interrupt their friendship in any way. She hoped that their relations might continue as in the past, and in this hope she remained very truly his.

She gave a sigh of relief when the letter was finished, and read it through carefully, putting in commas and semicolons and colons at what she thought appropriate places. Such punctilio pleased her; it was, she considered, due from one who aspired to a literary style, and aimed at making a living by the pen. Though this was the first answer to a proposal that she had written on her own account, she was not altogether without practice in such matters, as she had composed others for her heroines who had found themselves in like position. Her manner, also, was perhaps unconsciously influenced by a perusal of *The Young Person's Compleat Correspondent, and Guide to Answers to be given in the Various Circumstances of Life,* which, in a tattered calf covering, formed an item in Miss Euphemia's library.

It was not till the missive was duly sealed up and posted that she told her aunt of what had happened. "There is Mr Westray's letter," she said, "if you would care to read it," and passed over to Miss Joliffe the piece of white paper on which a man had staked his fate.

Miss Joliffe took the letter with an attempt to assume an indifferent manner, which was unsuccessful, because an offer of marriage has about it a certain exhalation and atmosphere that betrays its importance even to the most unsuspicious. She was a slow reader, and, after wiping and adjusting her spectacles, sat down for a steady and patient consideration of the matter before her.

But the first word that she deciphered, "Dearest," startled her composure, and she pressed on through the letter with a haste that was foreign to her disposition. Her mouth grew rounder as she read, and she sighed out "Dear's" and "Dear Anastasia's" and "Dear Child's" at intervals as a relief to her feelings.

Anastasia stood by her, following the lines of writing that she knew by heart, with all the impatience of one who is reading ten times faster than another who turns the page.

Miss Joliffe's mind was filled with conflicting emotions; she was glad at the prospect of a more assured future that was opening before her niece, she was hurt at not having been taken sooner into confidence, for Anastasia must certainly have known that he was going to propose; she was chagrined at not having noticed a courtship which had been carried on under her very eyes; she was troubled at the thought that the marriage would entail the separation from one who was to her as a child.

How weary she would find it to walk alone down the long paths of old age! how hard it was to be deprived of a dear arm on whose support she had reckoned for when "the slow dark hours begin"! But she thrust this reflection away from her as selfish, and contrition for

having harboured it found expression in a hand wrinkled and rough-
ened by hard wear, which stole into Anastasia's.

"My dear," she said, "I am very glad at your good fortune; this is
a great thing that has befallen you." A general content that Anastasia
should have received a proposal silenced her misgivings.

To the recipient, an offer of marriage, be it good, bad, or indifferent, to be accepted or to be refused, brings a certain complacent satisfaction. She may pretend to make light of it, to be displeased at it, to
resent it, as did Anastasia; but in her heart of hearts there lurks the self-
appreciating reflection that she has won the completest admiration of
a man. If he be a man that she would not marry under any conditions,
if he be a fool, or a spendthrift, or an evil-liver, he is still a man, and she
has captured him. Her relations share in the same pleasurable reflections. If the offer is accepted, then a future has been provided for one
whose future, maybe, was not too certain; if it is declined, then they
congratulate themselves on the high morale or strong common-sense
of a kinswoman who refuses to be won by gold, or to link her destiny
with an unsuitable partner.

"It is a great thing, my dear, that has befallen you," Miss Joliffe repeated. "I wish you all happiness, dear Anastasia, and may all blessings
wait upon you in this engagement."

"Aunt," interrupted her niece, "please don't say that. I have refused
him, *of course*; how could you think that I should marry Mr Westray? I
never have thought of any such thing with him. I never had the least
idea of his writing like this."

"You have refused him?" said the elder lady with a startled emphasis. Again a selfish reflection crossed her mind—they were not to
be parted after all—and again she put it resolutely away. She ran over
in her mind all the possible objections that could have influenced her
niece in arriving at such a conclusion. Religion was the keynote of
Miss Joliffe's life; to religion her thought reverted as the needle to the
pole, and to it she turned for an explanation now. It must be some
religious consideration that had proved an obstacle to Anastasia.

"I do not think you need find any difficulty in his having been
brought up as a Wesleyan," she said, with a profound conviction that
she had put her finger on the matter, and with some consciousness
of her own perspicacity. "His father has been dead some time, and
though his mother is still alive, you would not have to live with her. I
do not think, dear, she would at all wish you to become a Methodist.
As for our Mr Westray, your Mr Westray, I should say now," and she

assumed that expression of archness which is considered appropriate to such occasions, "I am sure he is a sound Churchman. He goes regularly to the minster on Sundays, and I dare say, being an architect, and often in church on weekdays, he has found out that the order of the Church of England is more satisfactory than that of any other sect. Though I am sure I do not wish to say one word against Wesleyans; they are no doubt true Protestants, and a bulwark against more serious errors. I rejoice that your lover's early training will have saved him from any inclination to ritualism."

"My dear aunt," Anastasia broke in, with a stress of earnest deprecation on the "dear" that startled her aunt, "please do *not* go on like that. Do not call Mr Westray my lover; I have told you that I will have nothing to do with him."

Miss Joliffe's thoughts had moved through a wide arc. Now that this offer of marriage was about to be refused, now that this engagement was not to be, the advantages that it offered stood out in high relief. It seemed too sad that the curtain should be rung down just as the action of a drama of intense interest was beginning, that the good should slip through their fingers just as they were grasping it. She gave no thought now to that fear of a lonely old age which had troubled her a few minutes before; she only saw the provision for the future which Anastasia was wilfully sacrificing. Her hand tightened automatically, and crumpled a long piece of paper that she was holding. It was only a milkman's bill, and yet it might perhaps have unconsciously given a materialistic colour to her thoughts.

"We should not reject any good thing that is put before us," she said a little stiffly, "without being very certain that we are right to do so. I do not know what would become of you, Anastasia, if anything were to happen to me."

"That is exactly what he says, that is the very argument which he uses. Why should you take such a gloomy view of things? Why should something *happening* always mean something bad. Let us hope something good will happen, that someone else will make me a better offer." She laughed, and went on reflectively: "I wonder whether Mr Westray will come back here to lodge; I hope he won't."

Hardly were the words out of her mouth when she was sorry for uttering them, for she saw the look of sadness which overspread Miss Joliffe's face.

"Dear aunt," she cried, "I am so sorry; I didn't mean to say that. I know what a difference it would make; we cannot afford to lose our last lodger. I hope he *will* come back, and I will do everything I can to make things comfortable, short of marrying him. I will earn some money myself. I will *write*."

"How will you write? Who is there to write to?" Miss Joliffe said, and then the blank look on her face grew blanker, and she took out her handkerchief. "There is no one to help us. Anyone who ever cared for us is dead long ago; there is no one to write to now."

Chapter Seventeen

Westray played the role of rejected lover most conscientiously; he treated the episode of his refusal on strictly conventional lines. He assured himself and his mother that the light of his life was extinguished, that he was the most unhappy of mortals. It was at this time that he wrote some verses called *Autumn*, with a refrain of—

For all my hopes are cold and dead,
And fallen like the fallen leaves,

—which were published in the *Clapton Methodist*, and afterwards set to music by a young lady who wished to bind up another wounded heart. He attempted to lie awake of nights with indifferent success, and hinted in conversation at the depressing influence which insomnia exerts over its victims. For several meals in succession he refused to eat heartily of such dishes as he did not like, and his mother felt serious anxiety as to his general state of health. She inveighed intemperately against Anastasia for having refused her son, but then she would have inveighed still more intemperately had Anastasia accepted him. She wearied him with the portentous gloom which she affected in his presence, and quoted Lady Clara Vere de Vere's cruelty in turning honest hearts to gall, till even the rejected one was forced to smile bitterly at so inapposite a parallel.

Though Mrs Westray senior poured out the vials of her wrath on Anastasia for having refused to become Mrs Westray junior, she was at heart devoutly glad at the turn events had taken. At heart Westray could not have said whether he was glad or sorry. He told himself that he was deeply in love with Anastasia, and that this love was further ennobled by a chivalrous desire to shield her from evil; but he could not altogether forget that the unfortunate event had at least saved him from the unconventionality of marrying his landlady's niece. He told himself that his grief was sincere and profound, but it was possible that chagrin and wounded pride were after all his predominant feelings.

There were other reflections which he thrust aside as indecorous at this acute stage of the tragedy, but which, nevertheless, were able to exercise a mildly consoling influence in the background. He would be spared the anxieties of early and impecunious marriage, his professional career would not be weighted by family cares, the whole world was once more open before him, and the slate clean. These were considerations which could not prudently be overlooked, though it would be unseemly to emphasise them too strongly when the poignancy of regret should dominate every other feeling.

He wrote to Sir George Farquhar, and obtained ten days' leave of absence on the score of indisposition; and he wrote to Miss Euphemia Joliffe to tell her that he intended to seek other rooms. From the first he had decided that this latter step was inevitable. He could not bear the daily renewal of regret, the daily opening of the wound that would be caused by the sight of Anastasia, or by such chance intercourse with her as further residence at Bellevue Lodge must entail. There is no need to speculate whether his decision was influenced in part by a concession to humiliated pride; men do not take pleasure in revisiting the scenes of a disastrous rout, and it must be admitted that the possibility of summoning a lost love to his presence when he rang for boiling water, had in it something of the grotesque. He had no difficulty in finding other lodgings by correspondence, and he spared himself the necessity of returning at all to his former abode by writing to ask Clerk Janaway to move his belongings.

One morning, a month later, Miss Joliffe sat in that room which had been occupied by the late Mr Sharnall. She was alone, for Anastasia had gone to the office of the *Cullerne Advertiser* with an announcement in which one A.J. intimated that she was willing to take a post as nursery-governess. It was a bright morning but cold, and Miss Joliffe drew an old white knitted shawl closer about her, for there was no fire in the grate. There was no fire because she could not afford it, yet the sun pouring in through the windows made the room warmer than the kitchen, where the embers had been allowed to die out since breakfast. She and Anastasia did without fire on these bright autumn days to save coals; they ate a cold dinner, and went early to bed for the same reason, yet the stock in the cellar grew gradually less. Miss Joliffe had examined it that very morning, and found it terribly small; nor was there any money nor any credit left with which to replenish it.

On the table before her was a pile of papers, some yellow, some pink, some white, some blue, but all neatly folded. They were folded lengthways and to the same breadth, for they were Martin Joliffe's bills, and he had been scrupulously neat and orderly in his habits. It is true that there were among them some few that she had herself contracted, but then she had always been careful to follow exactly her brother's method both of folding and also of docketing them on the exterior. Yes, no doubt she was immediately responsible for some, and she knew just which they were from the outside without any need to open them. She took up one of them: "Rose and Storey, importers of French millinery, flowers, feathers, ribbons, etcetera. Mantle and jacket show-rooms."

Alas, alas! how frail is human nature! Even in the midst of her misfortunes, even in the eclipse of old age, such words stirred Miss Joliffe's interest—flowers, feathers, ribbons, mantles, and jackets; she saw the delightful show-room 19, 20, 21, and 22, Market Place, Cullerne— saw it in the dignified solitude of a summer morning when a dress was to be tried on, saw it in the crush and glorious scramble of a remnant sale. "Family and complimentary mourning, costumes, skirts, etcetera; foreign and British silks, guaranteed makes." After that the written entry seemed mere bathos: "Material and trimming one bonnet, 11 shillings and 9 pence; one hat, 13 shillings 6 pence. Total, 1 pound 5 shillings 3 pence." It really was not worth while making a fuss about, and the bunch of cherries and bit of spangled net were well worth the 1 shilling 9 pence, that Anastasia's had cost more than hers.

Hole, pharmaceutical chemist: "Drops, 1 shilling 6 pence; liniment, 1 shilling; mixture, 1 shilling 9 pence," repeated many times. "Codliver oil, 1 shilling 3 pence, and 2 shillings 6 pence, and 1 shilling 3 pence again. 2 pounds 13 shillings 2 pence, with 4 shillings 8 pence interest," for the bill was four years old. That was for Anastasia at a critical time when nothing seemed to suit her, and Dr Ennefer feared a decline; but all the medicine for poor Martin was entered in Dr Ennefer's own account.

Pilkington, the shoemaker, had his tale to tell: "Miss Joliffe: Semipold. lace boots, treble soles, 1 pound 1 shilling 0 pence. Miss A. Jol.: Semi-pold. lace boots, treble soles, 1 pound 1 shilling 0 pence. 6 pair mohair laces, 9 pence. 3 ditto, silk, 1 shilling." Yes, she was indeed a guilty woman. It was she that had "run up" *these* accounts, and she grew red to think that her own hand should have helped to build so dismal a pile.

Debt, like every other habit that runs counter to the common good, brings with it its own punishment, because society protects itself by making unpleasant the ways of such as inconvenience their neighbours. It is true that some are born with a special talent and capacity for debt—they live on it, and live merrily withal, but most debtors feel the weight of their chains, and suffer greater pangs than those which they inflict on any defrauded creditor. If the millstone grinds slowly it grinds small, and undischarged accounts bring more pain than the goods to which they relate ever brought pleasure. Among such bitternesses surely most bitter are the bills for things of which the fruition has ceased—for worn-out finery, for withered flowers, for drunk wine. Pilkington's boots, were they never so treble soled, could not endure for ever, and Miss Joliffe's eyes followed unconsciously under the table to where a vertical fissure showed the lining white at the side of either boot. Where were new boots to come from now, whence was to come clothing to wear, and bread to eat?

Nay, more, the day of passive endurance was past; action had begun. The Cullerne Water Company threatened to cut off the water, the Cullerne Gas Company threatened to cut off the gas. Eaves, the milkman, threatened a summons unless that long, long bill of his (all built up of pitiful little pints) was paid forthwith. The Thing had come to the *Triarii*, Miss Joliffe's front was routed, the last rank was wavering. What was she to do, whither was she to turn? She must sell some of the furniture, but who would buy such old stuff? And if she sold furniture, what lodger would take half-empty rooms? She looked wildly round, she thrust her hands into the pile of papers, she turned them over with a feverish action, till she seemed to be turning hay once more as a little girl in the meadows at Wydcombe.

Then she heard footsteps on the pavement outside, and thought for a moment that it was Anastasia returned before she was expected, till a heavy tread told her that a man was coming, and she saw that it was Mr Joliffe, her cousin, churchwarden and pork-butcher. His bulky and unwieldy form moved levelly past the windows; he paused and looked up at the house as if to make sure that he was not mistaken, and then he slowly mounted the semicircular flight of stone steps and rang the bell.

In person he was tall, but disproportionately stout for his height. His face was broad, and his loose double chin gave it a flabby appearance. A pallid complexion and black-grey hair, brushed straightly down where he was not bald, produced an impression of sanctimoniousness which was increased by a fawning manner of speech. Mr Sharnall was used to call him a hypocrite, but the aspersion was false, as such an aspersion commonly is.

Hypocrites, in the pure and undiluted sense, rarely exist outside the pages of fiction. Except in the lower classes, where deceit thrives under the incentive of clerical patronage, men seldom assume deliberately the garb of religion to obtain temporal advantages or to further their own ends. It is probable that in nine cases out of ten, where practice does not accord sufficiently with profession to please the censorious, the discrepancy is due to inherent weakness of purpose, to the duality of our nature, and not to any conscious deception. If a man leading the lower life should find himself in religious, or high-minded, or pure society, and speak or behave as if he were religious, or high-minded, or pure, he does so in nine cases out of ten not with any definite wish to deceive, but because he is temporarily influenced by better company. For the time he believes what he says, or has persuaded himself that he believes it. If he is froward with the froward, so he is just with the just, and the more sympathetic and susceptible his nature, the more amenable is he to temporary influences. It is this chameleon adaptability that passes for hypocrisy.

Cousin Joliffe was no hypocrite, he acted up to his light; and even if the light be a badly-trimmed, greasy, evil-smelling paraffin-lamp, the man who acts up to it is only the more to be pitied. Cousin Joliffe was one of those amateur ecclesiastics whose talk is of things religious, whom Church questions interest, and who seem to have missed their vocation in not having taken Orders. If Canon Parkyn had been a High Churchman, Cousin Joliffe would have been High Church; but the Canon being Low-Church, Cousin Joliffe was an earnest evangelical, as he delighted to describe himself. He was rector's church-warden, took a leading part in prayer-meetings, with a keen interest in school-treats, ham teas, and magic lanterns, and was particularly proud of having been asked more than once to assist in the Mission Room at Carisbury, where the Vicar of Christ Church carried on revival work among the somnolent surroundings of a great cathedral. He was without any sense of humour or any refinement of feeling—self-important, full of the dignity of his office, thrifty to meanness, but he acted up to his light, and was no hypocrite.

In that petty middle-class, narrow-minded and penuriously pretentious, which was the main factor of Cullerne life, he possessed considerable influence and authority. Among his immediate surroundings a word from Churchwarden Joliffe carried more weight than an outsider would have imagined, and long usage had credited him with the delicate position of *censor morum* to the community. Did the wife of a parishioner venture into such a place of temptation as the theatre at Carisbury, was she seen being sculled by young Bulteel in his new skiff of a summer evening, the churchwarden was charged to interview her husband, to point out to him privately the scandal that was being caused, and to show him how his duty lay in keeping his belongings in better order. Was a man trying to carry fire in his bosom by dalliance at the bar of the Blandamer Arms, then a hint was given to his spouse that she should use such influence as would ensure evenings being spent at home. Did a young man waste the Sabbath afternoon in walking with his dog on Cullerne Flat, he would receive *The Tishbite's Warning, a Discourse showing the Necessity of a Proper Observance of the Lord's Day*. Did a pig-tailed hoyden giggle at the Grammar School boys from her pew in the minster, the impropriety was reported by the churchwarden to her mother.

On such occasions he was scrupulous in assuming a frock-coat and a silk hat. Both were well-worn, and designed in the fashion of another day; but they were in his eyes insignia of office, and as he felt the tails of the coat about his knees they seemed to him as it were the skirts of Aaron's garment. Miss Joliffe was not slow to notice that he was thus equipped this morning; she knew that he had come to pay her a visit of circumstance, and swept her papers hurriedly into a drawer. She felt as if they were guilty things these bills, as if she had been engaged in a guilty action in even "going through" them, as if she had been detected in doing that which she should not do, and guiltiest of all seemed the very hurry of concealment with which she hid such compromising papers.

She tried to perform that feat of mental gymnastics called retaining one's composure, the desperate and forced composure which the coiner assumes when opening the door to the police, the composure which a woman assumes in returning to her husband with the kisses of a lover tingling on her lips. It *is* a feat to change the current of the mind, to let the burning thought that is dearest or bitterest to us go by the board, to answer coherently to the banalities of conversation, to check the throbbing pulse. The feat was beyond Miss Joliffe's powers; she was but a poor actress, and the churchwarden saw that she was ill at ease as she opened the door.

"Good-morning, cousin," he said with one of those interrogative glances which are often more irritating and more difficult to parry than a direct question; "you are not looking at all the thing this morning. I hope you are not feeling unwell; I hope I do not intrude."

"Oh no," she said, making as good an attempt at continuous speech as the quick beating of her heart allowed; "it is only that your visit is a little surprise. I am a little flurried; I am not quite so young as I was."

"Ay," he said, as she showed him into Mr Sharnall's room, "we are all of us growing older; it behoves us to walk circumspectly, for we never know when we may be taken." He looked at her so closely and compassionately that she felt very old indeed; it really seemed as if she ought to be "taken" at once, as if she was neglecting her duty in not dying away incontinently. She drew the knitted shawl more tightly round her spare and shivering body.

"I am afraid you will find this room a little cold," she said; "we are having the kitchen chimney cleaned, so I was sitting here." She gave a hurried glance at the bureau, feeling a suspicion that she might not have shut the drawer tight, or that one of the bills might have somehow got left out. No, all was safe, but her excuse had not deceived the churchwarden.

"Phemie," he said, not unkindly, though the word brought tears to her eyes, for it was the first time that anyone had called her by the old childhood name since the night that Martin died—"Phemie, you should not stint yourself in fires. It is a false economy; you must let me send you a coal ticket."

"Oh no, thank you very much; we have plenty," she cried, speaking quickly, for she would rather have starved outright, than that it should be said a member of the Dorcas Society had taken a parish coal ticket. He urged her no more, but took the chair that she offered him, feeling a little uncomfortable withal, as a well-clothed and overfed man should, in the presence of penury. It was true he had not been to see her for some time; but, then, Bellevue Lodge was so far off, and he had been so pressed with the cares of the parish and of his business. Besides that, their walks of life were so different, and there was naturally a strong objection to any kinswoman of his keeping a lodging-house. He felt sorry now that compassion had betrayed him into calling her "cousin" and "Phemie"; she certainly *was* a distant kinswoman, but *not*, he repeated to himself, a cousin; he hoped she had not noticed his familiarity. He wiped his face with a pocket-handkerchief that had seen some service, and gave an introductory cough.

"There is a little matter on which I should like to have a few words with you," he said, and Miss Joliffe's heart was in her mouth; he *had* heard, then, of these terrible debts and of the threatened summons.

"Forgive me if I go direct to business. I am a business man and a plain man, and like plain speaking."

It is wonderful to what rude remarks, and unkind remarks and untrue remarks such words as these commonly form the prelude, and how very few of these plain speakers enjoy being plainly spoken to in turn.

"We were talking just now," he went on, "of the duty of walking circumspectly, but it is our duty, Miss Joliffe, to see that those over whom we are set in authority walk circumspectly as well. I mean no reproach to you, but others beside me think it would be well that you should keep closer watch over your niece. There is a nobleman of high station that visits much too often at this house. I will *not* name any names"—and this with a tone of magnanimous forbearance—"but you will guess who I mean, because the nobility is not that frequent hereabout. I am sorry to have to speak of such things which ladies generally see quick enough for themselves, but as churchwarden I can't shut my ears to what is matter of town talk; and more by token when a namesake of my own is concerned."

The composure which Miss Joliffe had been seeking in vain, came back to her at the pork-butcher's words, partly in the relief that he had not broached the subject of debts which had been foremost in her mind, partly in the surprise and indignation occasioned by his talk of Anastasia. Her manner and very appearance changed, and none would have recognised the dispirited and broken-down old lady in the sharpness of her rejoinder.

"Mr Joliffe," she apostrophised with tart dignity, "you must forgive me for thinking that I know a good deal more about the nobleman in question than you do, and I can assure you *he* is a perfect gentleman. If he has visited this house, it has been to see Mr Westray about the restoration of the minster. I should have thought one that was churchwarden would have known better than to go bandying scandals about his betters; it is small encouragement for a nobleman to take an interest in the church if the churchwarden is to backbite him for it."

She saw that her cousin was a little taken aback, and she carried the war into the enemy's country, and gave another thrust.

"Not but what Lord Blandamer has called upon me too, apart from Mr Westray. And what have you to say to *that*? If his lordship has thought fit to honour me by drinking a cup of tea under my roof, there are many in Cullerne would have been glad to get out their best china if he had only asked himself to *their* houses. And there are some might well follow his example, and show themselves a little oftener to their friends and relations."

The churchwarden wiped his face again, and puffed a little.

"Far be it from me," he said, dwelling on the expression with all the pleasure that a man of slight education takes in a book phrase that he has got by heart—"far be it from me to set scandals afloat—'twas *you* that used the word scandal—but I have daughters of my own to consider. I have nothing to say against Anastasia, who, I believe, is a good girl enough"—and his patronising manner grated terribly on Miss Joliffe—"though I wish I could see her take more interest in the Sunday-school, but I won't hide from you that she has a way of carrying herself and mincing her words which does *not* befit her station. It makes people take notice, and 'twould be more becoming she should drop it, seeing she will have to earn her own living in service. I don't want to say anything against Lord Blandamer either—he seems to be well-intentioned to the church—but if tales are true the *old* lord was no better than he should be, and things have happened before now on your side of the family, Miss Joliffe, that make connections feel uncomfortable about Anastasia. We are told that the sins of the fathers will be visited to the third and fourth generation."

"Well," Miss Joliffe said, and made a formidable pause on this adverb, "if it is the manners of your side of the family to come and insult people in their own houses, I am glad I belong to the other side."

She was alive to the profound gravity of such a sentiment, yet was prepared to take her stand upon it, and awaited another charge from the churchwarden with a dignity and confidence that would have become the Old Guard. But no fierce passage of arms followed; there was a pause, and if a dignified ending were desired the interview should here have ended. But to ordinary mortals the sound of their own voices is so musical as to deaden any sense of anticlimax; talking is continued for talking's sake, and heroics tail off into desultory conversation. Both sides were conscious that they had overstated their sentiments, and were content to leave main issues undecided.

Miss Joliffe did not take the bills out of their drawer again after the churchwarden had left her. The current of her ideas had been changed, and for the moment she had no thought for anything except the innuendoes of her visitor. She rehearsed to herself without difficulty the occasions of Lord Blandamer's visits, and although she was fully persuaded that any suspicions as to his motives were altogether without foundation, she was forced to admit that he *had* been at Bellevue Lodge more than once when she had been absent. This was no doubt a pure coincidence, but we were enjoined to be wise as serpents as well as innocent as doves, and she would take care that no further occasion was given for idle talk.

Anastasia on her return found her aunt unusually reserved and taciturn. Miss Joliffe had determined to behave exactly as usual to Anastasia because her niece was entirely free from fault; but she was vexed at what the churchwarden had said, and her manner was so mysterious and coldly dignified as to convince Anastasia that some cause for serious annoyance had occurred. Did Anastasia remark that it was a close morning, her aunt looked frowningly abstracted and gave no reply; did Anastasia declare that she had not been able to get any 14 knitting-needles, they were quite out of them, her aunt said, "Oh!" in a tone of rebuke and resignation which implied that there were far more serious matters in the world than knitting-needles.

This dispensation lasted a full half-hour, but beyond that the kindly old heart was quite unequal to supporting a proper hauteur. The sweet warmth of her nature thawed the chilly exterior; she was ashamed of her moodiness, and tried to "make up" for it to Anastasia by manifestation of special affection. But she evaded her niece's attempts at probing the matter, and was resolved that the girl should know nothing of Cousin Joliffe's suggestions or even of the fact of his visit.

But if Anastasia knew nothing of these things, she was like to be singular in her ignorance. All Cullerne knew; it was in the air. The churchwarden had taken a few of the elders into his confidence, and asked their advice as to the propriety of his visit of remonstrance. The elders, male and female, heartily approved of his action, and had in their turn taken into confidence a few of their intimate and specially-to-be-trusted friends. Then ill-natured and tale-bearing Miss Sharp told lying and mischief-making Mrs Flint, and lying and mischief-making Mrs Flint talked the matter over at great length with the rector, who loved all kinds of gossip, especially of the highly-spiced order.

It was speedily matter of common knowledge that Lord Blandamer was at the Hand of God (so ridiculous of a lodging-house keeper christening a public-house Bellevue Lodge!) at *all* hours of the day *and* night, and that Miss Joliffe was content to look at the ceiling on such occasions; and worse, to go to meetings so as to leave the field undisturbed (what intolerable hypocrisy making an excuse of the Dorcas meetings!); that Lord Blandamer loaded—simply loaded—that pert and good-for-nothing girl with presents; that even the young architect was forced to change his lodgings by such disreputable goings-on. People wondered how Miss Joliffe and her niece had the effrontery to show themselves at church on Sundays; the younger creature, at least, must have *some* sense of shame left, for she never ventured to exhibit in *public* either the fine dresses or the jewellery that her lover gave her.

Such stories came to Westray's ears, and stirred in him the modicum of chivalry which leavens the lump of most men's being. He was still smarting under his repulse, but he would have felt himself disgraced if he had allowed the scandal to pass unchallenged, and he rebutted it with such ardour that people shrugged their shoulders, and hinted that there had been something between *him*, too, and Anastasia.

Clerk Janaway was inclined to take a distressingly opportunist and matter-of-fact view of the question. He neither reprobated nor defended. In his mind the Divine right of peers was firmly established. So long as they were rich and spent their money freely, we should not be too particular. They were to be judged by standards other than those of common men; for his part, he was glad they had got in place of an old curmudgeon a man who would take an interest in the Church, and spend money on the place and the people. If he took a fancy to a pretty face, where was the harm? 'Twas nothing to the likes of them, best let well alone; and then he would cut short the churchwarden's wailings and godly lamentations by "decanting" on the glories of Fording, and the boon it was to the countryside to have the place kept up once more.

"Clerk Janaway, your sentiments do you no credit," said the pork-butcher on one such occasion, for he was given to gossip with the sexton on terms of condescending equality. "I have seen Fording myself, having driven there with the Carisbury Field Club, and felt sure it must be a source of temptation if not guarded against. That one man should live in such a house is an impiety; he is led to go about like Nebuchadnezzar, saying: 'Is not this great Babylon that I have builded?'"

"*He* never builded it," said the clerk with some inconsequence; "'twere builded centuries ago. I've heard 'tis that old no one don't know *who* builded it. Your parents was Dissenters, Mr Joliffe, and never taught you the Catechism when you was young; but as for me, I order myself to my betters as I should, so long as they orders themselves to me. 'Taint no use to say as how we're all level; you've only got to go to Mothers' Meetings, my old missus says, to see that. 'Tis no use looking

487

for too much, nor eating salt with red herrings."

"Well, well," the other deprecated, "I'm not blaming his lordship so much as them that lead him on."

"Don't go for to blame the girl, neither, too hardly; there's faults on both sides. His grandfather didn't always toe the line, and there were some on her side didn't set too good an example, neither. I've seen many a queer thing in my time, and have got to think blood's blood, and forerunners more to blame than children. If there's drink in fathers, there'll be drink in sons and grandsons till 'tis worked out; and if there's wild love in the mothers, daughters 'll likely sell their apples too. No, no, God-amighty never made us equal, and don't expect us all to be churchwardens. Some on us comes of virtuous forerunners, and are born with wings at the back of our shoulders like you"—and he gave a whimsical look at his listener's heavy figure—"to lift us up to the vaulting; and some on us our fathers fits out with lead soles to the bottom of our boots to keep us on the floor."

Saturday afternoon was Lord Blandamer's hour, and for three Saturdays running Miss Joliffe deserted the Dorcas meeting in order to keep guard at home. It rejoiced the moral hearts of ill-natured and tale-bearing Miss Sharp and of lying and mischief-making Mrs Flint that the disreputable old woman had at least the decency not to show herself among her betters, but such defection was a sore trial to Miss Joliffe. She told herself on each occasion that she *could* not make such a sacrifice again, and yet the love of Anastasia constrained her. To her niece she offered the patent excuse of being unwell, but the girl watched her with wonder and dismay chafe feverishly through the two hours, which had been immemorially consecrated to these meetings. The recurrence of a weekly pleasure, which seems so limitless in youth and middle age, becomes less inexhaustible as life turns towards sunset. Thirty takes lightly enough the foregoing of a Saturday reunion, the uncongenial spending of a Sunday; but seventy can see the end of the series, and grudges every unit of the total that remains.

For three Saturdays Miss Joliffe watched, and for three Saturdays no suspicious visitor appeared.

"We have seen nothing of Lord Blandamer lately," she would remark at frequent intervals with as much indifference as the subject would allow.

"There is nothing to bring him here now that Mr Westray has gone. Why should he come?"

Why, indeed, and what difference would it make to her if he never came again? These were questions that Anastasia had discussed with herself, at every hour of every day of those blank three weeks. She had ample time for such foolish discussions, for such vain imaginings, for she was left much to herself, having no mind-companions either of her own age or of any other. She was one of those unfortunate persons whose education and instincts' unfit them for their position.

The diversions of youth had been denied her, the pleasures of dress or company had never been within her reach. For pastime she was turned back continually to her own thoughts, and an active imagination and much desultory reading had educated her in a school of romance, which found no counterpart in the life of Cullerne. She was proud at heart (and it is curious that those are often the proudest who in their neighbours' estimation have least cause for pride), but not conceited in manner in spite of Mr Joliffe's animadversion on the mincing of her words. Yet it was not her pride that had kept her from making friends, but merely the incompatibility of mental temperament, which builds the barrier not so much between education and ignorance, as between refinement and materialism, between romance and commonplace.

That barrier is so insurmountable that any attempt upon it must end in failure that is often pathetic from its very hopelessness; even the warmth of ardent affection has never yet succeeded in evolving a mental companionship from such discordant material. By kindly dispensation of nature the breadth of the gulf, indeed, is hidden from those who cannot cross it. They know it is there, they have some inkling of the difference of view, but they think that love may build a bridge across, or that in time they may find some other access to the further side. Sometimes they fancy that they are nearer to the goal, that they walk step and step with those they love; but this, alas! is not to be, because the mental sympathy, the touch of illumination that welds minds together, is wanting.

It was so with Miss Joliffe the elder—she longed to be near her niece, and was so very far away; she thought that they went hand in hand, when all the while a different mental outlook set them poles asunder. With all her thousand good honest qualities, she was absolutely alien to the girl; and Anastasia felt as if she was living among people of another nation, among people who did not understand her language, and she took refuge in silence.

The dullness of Cullerne had grown more oppressive to her in the last year. She longed for a life something wider, she longed for sympathy. She longed for what a tall and well-favoured maiden of her years most naturally desires, however much she may be ignorant of her desire; she longed for someone to admire her and to love her; she longed for someone about whom she could weave a romance.

The junior partner in Rose and Storey perhaps discerned her need, and tried to supply it. He paid her such odious compliments on the "hang of her things," that she would never have entered the shop again, were it not that Bellevue Lodge was bound hand and foot to Rose and Storey, for they were undertakers as well as milliners; and, besides, the little affair of the bonnets, the expenses of Martin's funeral, were still unsatisfied. There was a young dairy farmer, with a face like a red harvest moon, who stopped at her aunt's door on his way to market. He would sell Miss Joliffe eggs and butter at wholesale prices, and grinned in a most tiresome way whenever he caught sight of Anastasia. The rector patronised her insufferably; and though old Mr Noot was kind, he treated her like a small child, and sometimes patted her cheek, which she felt to be disconcerting at eighteen.

And then the Prince of Romance appeared in Lord Blandamer. The moment that she first saw him on the doorstep that windy autumn afternoon, when yellow leaves were flying, she recognised him for a prince. The moment that he spoke to her she knew that he recognised her for a lady, and for this she felt unspeakably glad and grateful. Since then the wonder had grown. It grew all the faster from the hero's restraint. He had seen Anastasia but little, he spoke but little to her, he never gave her even a glance of interest, still less such glances as Westray launched at her so lavishly. And yet the wonder grew. He was so different from other men she had seen, so different from all the other people she had ever met. She could not have told how she knew this, and yet she knew. It must have been an atmosphere which followed him wherever he went—that penumbra with which the gods wrap heroes—which told her he was different.

The gambits of the great game of love are strangely limited, and there is little variation in the after-play. If it were not for the personal share we take, such doings would lack interest by reason of their monotony, by their too close resemblance to the primeval type. This is why the game seems dull enough to onlookers; they shock us with the callousness with which they are apt to regard our ecstasies. This is why the straightforward game palls sometimes on the players themselves after a while; and why they are led to take refuge from dullness in solving problems, in the tangled irregularities of the knight's move.

Anastasia would have smiled if she had been told that she had fallen in love; it might have been a thin smile, pale as winter's sunshine, but she would have smiled. It was *impossible* for her to fall in love, because she knew that kings no longer marry beggar-maids, and she was far too well brought up to fall in love, except as a preliminary to marriage. No heroine of Miss Austen would permit herself even to feel attraction to a quarter from which no offer of marriage was possible; therefore Anastasia could not have fallen in love. She certainly was not in the least in love, but it was true Lord Blandamer interested her. He interested her so much, in fact, as to be in her thoughts at all hours of the day; it was strange that no matter with what things her mind was occupied, his image should continually present itself. She wondered why this was; perhaps it was his power—she thought it was the feeling of his power, a very insolence of power that dominated all these little folk, and yet was most powerful in its restraint. She liked to think of the compact, close-knit body, of the curling, crisp, iron-grey hair, of the grey eyes, and of the hard, clear-cut face. Yes, she liked the face because it *was* hard, because it had a resolute look in it that said he meant to go whither he wished to go.

There was no doubt she must have taken considerable interest in him, for she found herself dreading to pronounce his name even in the most ordinary conversation, because she felt it difficult to keep her voice at the dead level of indifference. She dreaded when others spoke of him, and yet there was no other subject that occupied her so much. And sometimes when they talked of him she had a curious feeling of jealousy, a feeling that no one had a right even to talk of him except herself; and she would smile to herself with a little scornful smile, because she thought that she knew more about him, could understand him better than them all. It was fortunate, perhaps, that the arbitrament of Cullerne conversation did not rest with Anastasia, or there would have been but little talking at this time; for if it seemed preposterous that others should dare to discuss Lord Blandamer, it seemed equally preposterous that they should take an interest in discussing anything else.

She certainly was *not* in love; it was only the natural interest, she told herself, that anyone—anyone with education and refinement—must take in a strange and powerful character. Every detail about him interested her. There was a fascination in his voice, there was a melody in his low, clear voice that charmed, and made even trifling remarks seem important. Did he but say it was a rainy afternoon, did he but ask if Mr Westray were at home, there was such mystery in his tone that no rabbinical cabalist ever read more between the lines than did Miss Anastasia Joliffe. Even in her devotions thought wandered far from the pew where she and her aunt sat in Cullerne Church; she found her eyes looking for the sea-green and silver, for the nebuly coat in Abbot Vinnicomb's window; and from the clear light yellow of the aureole round John Baptist's head, fancy called up a whirl of faded lemon-coloured acacia leaves, that were in the air that day the hero first appeared.

Yet, if heart wavered, head stood firm. He should never know her interest in him; no word, no changing colour should ever betray her; he should never guess that agitation sometimes scarcely left her breath to make so short a rejoinder as "Good-night."

For three Saturdays, then, Miss Joliffe the elder sat on guard at Bellevue Lodge; for three Saturday afternoons in succession, she sat and chafed as the hours of the Dorcas meeting came and went. But nothing happened; the heavens remained in their accustomed place, the minster tower stood firm, and then she knew that the churchwarden had been duped, that her own judgment had been right, that Lord Blandamer's only motive for coming to her house had been to see Mr Westray, and that now Mr Westray was gone Lord Blandamer would come no more. The fourth Saturday arrived; Miss Joliffe was brighter than her niece had seen her for a calendar month.

"I feel a good deal better, my dear, this afternoon," she said; "I think I shall be able to go to the Dorcas meeting. The room gets so close that I have avoided going of late, but I think I shall not feel it too much today. I will just change, and put on my bonnet; you will not mind staying at home while I am away, will you?" And so she went.

Anastasia sat in the window-seat of the lower room. The sash was open, for the spring days were lengthening, and a soft, sweet air was moving about sundown. She told herself that she was making a bodice; an open workbox stood beside her, and there was spread around just such a medley of patterns, linings, scissors, cotton-reels, and buttons as is required for the proper and ceremonious carrying on of "work." But she was not working. The bodice itself, the very cause and spring of all these preparations, lay on her lap, and there, too, had fallen her hands. She half sat, half lay back on the window-seat, roaming in fancy far away, while she drank in the breath of the spring, and watched a little patch of transparent yellow sky between the houses grow pinker and more golden, as the sunset went on.

492

Then a man came down the street and mounted the steps in front of Bellevue Lodge; but she did not see him, because he was walking in from the country, and so did not pass her window. It was the door-bell that first broke her dreams. She slid down from her perch, and hastened to let her aunt in, for she had no doubt that it was Miss Joliffe who had come back from the meeting. The opening of the front-door was not a thing to be hurried through, for though there was little indeed in Bellevue Lodge to attract burglars, and though if burglars came they would surely select some approach other than the main entrance, yet Miss Joliffe insisted that when she was from home the door should be secured as if to stand a siege. So Anastasia drew the top bolt, and slipped the chain, and unlocked the lock. There was a little difficulty with the bottom bolt, and she had to cry out: "I am sorry for keeping you waiting; this fastening *will* stick." But it gave at last; she swung the heavy door back, and found herself face to face with Lord Blandamer.

CHAPTER EIGHTEEN

They stood face to face, and looked at one another for a second. Anyone seeing those two figures silhouetted against the yellow sunset sky might have taken them for cousins, or even for brother and sister. They were both dressed in black, were both dark, and of nearly the same height, for though the man was not short, the girl was very tall.

The pause that Anastasia made was due to surprise. A little while ago it would have been a natural thing enough to open the door and find Lord Blandamer, but the month that had elapsed since last he came to Bellevue Lodge had changed the position. It seemed to her that she stood before him confessed, that he must know that all these weeks she had been thinking of him, had been wondering why he did not come, had been longing for him to come, that he must know the pleasure which filled her now because he was come back again. And if he knew all this, she, too, had learnt to know something, had learnt to know how great a portion of her thoughts he filled. This eating of the tree of knowledge had abashed her, for now her soul stood before her naked. Did it so stand naked before him too? She was shocked that she should feel this attraction where there could be no thought of marriage; she thought that she should die if he should ever guess that one so lowly had gazed upon the sun and been dazzled.

The pause that Lord Blandamer made was not due to surprise, for he knew quite well that it would be Anastasia who opened the door.

It was rather that pause which a man makes who has undertaken a difficult business, and hesitates for a moment when it comes to the touch. She cast her eyes down to the ground; he looked full at her, looked at her from head to foot, and knew that his resolution was strong enough to carry to a conclusion the affair on which he had come. She spoke first.

"I am sorry my aunt is not at home," and kept her right hand on the edge of the open door, feeling grateful for any support. As the words came out she was relieved to find that it was indeed she herself who was speaking, that it was her own voice, and that her voice sounded much as usual.

"I am sorry she is not in," he said, and he, too, spoke after all in just those same low, clear tones to which she was accustomed—"I am sorry she is not in, but it was you that I came to see."

She said nothing; her heart beat so fast that she could not have spoken even in monosyllables. She did not move, but kept her hand still on the edge of the door, feeling afraid lest she should fall if she let it go.

"I have something I should like to say to you; may I come in?"

She hesitated for a moment, as he knew that she would hesitate, and then let him in, as he knew that she would let him in. He shut the heavy front-door behind them, and there was no talk now of turning locks or shooting bolts; the house was left at the mercy of any burglars who might happen to be thereabout.

Anastasia led the way. She did not take him into Mr Sharnall's old room, partly because she had left half-finished clothes lying there, and partly from the more romantic reflection that it was in Westray's room that they had met before. They walked through the hall and up the stairs, she going first and he following, and she was glad of the temporary respite which the long flights secured her. They entered the room, and again he shut the door behind them. There was no fire, and the window was open, but she felt as if she were in a fiery furnace. He saw her distress, but made as if he saw nothing, and pitied her for the agitation which he caused. For the past six months Anastasia had concealed her feelings so very well that he had read them like a book. He had watched the development of the plot without pride, or pleasure of success, without sardonic amusement, without remorse; with some dislike for a role which force of circumstances imposed on him, but with an unwavering resolve to walk the way which he had set before him. He knew the exact point which the action of the play had reached, he knew that Anastasia would grant whatever he asked of her.

They were standing face to face again. To the girl it all seemed a dream; she did not know whether she was waking or sleeping; she did not know whether she was in the body or out of the body. It was all a dream, but it was a delightful dream; there was no bitterness of reflection now, no anxiety, no regard for past or future, only utter absorption in the present moment. She was with the man who had possessed her thoughts for a month past; he had come back to her. She had not to consider whether she should ever see him again; he was with her now. She had not to think whether he was there for good or evil, she had lost all volition in the will of the man who stood before her; she was the slave of his ring, rejoicing in her slavery, and ready to do his bidding as all the other slaves of that ring.

He was sorry for the feelings which he had aroused, sorry for the affection he had stirred, sorry for the very love of himself that he saw written in her face. He took her hand in his, and his touch filled her with an exquisite content; her hand lay in his neither lifelessly nor entirely passively, yet only lightly returning the light pressure of his fingers. To her the situation was the supreme moment of a life; to him it was passionless as the betrothal piece in a Flemish window.

"Anastasia," he said, "you guess what it is I have to tell you; you guess what it is that I have to ask you."

She heard him speaking, and his voice was as delightful music in her delightful dream; she knew that he was going to ask something of her, and she knew that she would give him anything and all that he asked.

"I know that you love me," he went on, with an inversion of the due order of the proposition, and an assumption that would have been intolerable in anyone else, "and you know that I love you dearly." It was a proper compliment to her perspicuity that she should know already that he loved her, but his mind smiled as he thought how insufficient sometimes are the bases of knowledge. "I love you dearly, and am come to ask you to be my wife."

She heard what he said, and understood it; she had been prepared for his asking anything save this one thing that he had asked. The surprise of it overwhelmed her, the joy of it stunned her; she could neither speak nor move. He saw that she was powerless and speechless, and drew her closer to him. There was none of the impetuous eagerness of a lover in the action; he drew her gently towards him because it seemed appropriate to the occasion that he should do so. She lay for a minute in his arms, her head bent down, and her face hidden, while he looked not so much at her as above her. His eyes wandered over the mass of her dark-brown wavy hair that Mrs Flint said was not wavy by nature, but crimped to make her look like a Blandamer, and so bolster up her father's nonsensical pretensions. His eyes took full account of that wave and the silken fineness of her dark-brown hair, and then looked vaguely out beyond till they fell on the great flower-picture that hung on the opposite wall.

The painting had devolved upon Westray on Mr Sharnall's death, but he had not yet removed it, and Lord Blandamer's eyes rested on it now so fixedly, that he seemed to be thinking more of the trashy flowers and of the wriggling caterpillar, than of the girl in his arms. His mind came back to the exigencies of the situation.

"Will you marry me, Anastasia—will you marry me, dear Anstice?" The home name seemed to add a touch of endearment, and he used it advisedly. "Anstice, will you let me make you my wife?"

She said nothing, but threw her arms about his neck, and raised her face a little for the first time. It was an assent that would have contented any man, and to Lord Blandamer it came as a matter of course; he had never for a moment doubted her acceptance of his offer. If she had raised her face to be kissed, her expectation was gratified; he kissed her indeed, but only lightly on the brow, as actor may kiss actress on the stage. If anyone had been there to see, they would have known from his eyes that his thoughts were far from his body, that they were busied with somebody or something, that seemed to him of more importance than the particular action in which he was now engaged. But Anastasia saw nothing; she only knew that he had asked her to marry him, and that she was in his arms.

He waited a moment, as if wondering how long the present position would continue, and what was the next step to take; but the girl was the first to relieve the tension. The wildest intoxication of the first surprise was passing off, and with returning capacity for reflection a doubt had arisen that flung a shadow like a cloud upon her joy. She disengaged herself from his arms that strove in orthodox manner to retain her.

"Don't," she said—"don't. We have been too rash. I know what you have asked me. I shall remember it always, and love you for it to my dying day, but it cannot be. There are things you must know before you ask me. I do not think you would ask me if you knew all."

For the first time he seemed a little more in earnest, a little more like a man living life, a little less like a man rehearsing a part that he had got by heart. This was an unexpected piece of action, an episode that was not in his acting edition, that put him for the moment at a loss; though he knew it could not in any way affect the main issues of the play. He expostulated, he tried to take her hand again.

"Tell me what it is, child, that is troubling you," he said; "there can be nothing, nothing under heaven that could make me wish to unsay what I have said, nothing that could make us wish to undo what we have done. Nothing can rob me now of the knowledge that you love me. Tell me what it is."

"I cannot tell you," she answered him. "It is something I cannot tell; don't ask me. I will write it. Leave me now—please leave me; no one shall know that you have been here, no one must know what has passed between us."

Miss Joliffe came back from the Dorcas meeting a little down-hearted and out of humour. Things had not gone so smoothly as usual. No one had inquired after her health, though she had missed three meetings in succession; people had received her little compliments and cheery small-talk with the driest of negatives or affirmatives; she had an uncomfortable feeling that she was being cold-shouldered. That high moralist, Mrs Flint, edged her chair away from the poor lady of set purpose, and Miss Joliffe found herself at last left isolated from all, except Mrs Purlin, the builder's wife, who was far too fat and lethargic to be anything but ignorantly good-natured. Then, in a fit of pained abstraction, Miss Joliffe had made such a bad calculation as entirely to spoil a flannel petticoat with a rheumatic belt and camphor pockets, which she had looked upon as something of a *chef d'oeuvre*.

But when she got back to Bellevue Lodge her vexation vanished, and was entirely absorbed in solicitude for her niece.

Anstice was unwell, Anstice was quite ill, quite flushed, and complaining of headache. If Miss Joliffe had feigned indisposition for three Saturdays as an excuse for not leaving the house, Anastasia had little need for simulation on this the fourth Saturday. She was, in effect, so dazed by the event which had happened, and so preoccupied by her own thoughts, that she could scarcely return coherent replies to her aunt's questions. Miss Joliffe had rung and received no answer, had discovered that the front-door was unlocked, and had at last found Anastasia sitting forlorn in Mr Westray's room with the window open. A chill was indicated, and Miss Joliffe put her to bed at once.

Bed is a first aid that even ambulance classes have not entirely taught us to dispense with; it is, moreover, a poor man's remedy, being exceedingly cheap, if, indeed, the poor man is rich enough to have a bed at all. Had Anastasia been Miss Bulteel, or even Mrs Parkyn, or lying and mischief-making Mrs Flint, Dr Ennefer would have been summoned forthwith; but being only Anastasia, and having the vision of debt before her eyes, she prevailed on her aunt to wait to see what the night brought forth, before sending for the doctor. Meanwhile Dr Bed, infinitely cleverest and infinitely safest of physicians, was called in, and with him was associated that excellent general practitioner Dr Wait. Hot flannels, hot bottles, hot possets, and a bedroom fire were exhibited, and when at nine o'clock Miss Joliffe kissed her niece and retired for the night, she by no means despaired of the patient's speedy recovery from so sudden and unaccountable an attack.

Anastasia was alone; what a relief to be alone again, though she felt that such a thought was treasonable and unkind to the warm old heart that had just left her, to that warm old heart which yearned so deeply to her, but with which she had not shared her story! She was alone, and she lay a little while in quiet content looking at the fire through the iron bars at the foot of her bedstead. It was the first bedroom fire she had had for two years, and she enjoyed the luxury with a pleasure proportionate to its rarity. She was not sleepy, but grew gradually more composed, and was able to reflect on the letter which she had promised to write. It would be difficult, and she assured herself with much vigour that it must raise insurmountable obstacles, that they were obstacles which one in Lord Blandamer's position must admit to be quite insurmountable. Yes, in this letter she would write the colophon of so wondrous a romance, the epilogue of so amazing a tragedy. But it was her conscience that demanded the sacrifice, and she took the more pleasure in making it, because she felt at heart that the pound of flesh might never really after all be cut.

How thoroughly do we enjoy these sacrifices to conscience, these followings of honour's code severe, when we know that none will be mean enough to take us at our word! To what easily-gained heights of morality does it raise us to protest that we never could accept the gift that will eventually be forced into our reluctant hands, to insist that we regard as the shortest of loans the money which we never shall be called upon to repay. It was something of the same sort with Anastasia. She told herself that by her letter she would give the death-blow to her love, and perhaps believed what she told, yet all the while kept hope hidden at the bottom of the box, even as in the most real perils of a dream we sometimes are supported by the sub-waking sense that we *are* dreaming.

A little later Anastasia was sitting before her bedroom fire writing. It has a magic of its own—the bedroom fire. Not such a one as night by night warms hothouse bedrooms of the rich, but that which burns but once or twice a year. How the coals glow between the bars, how the red light shimmers on the black-lead bricks, how the posset steams upon the hob! Milk or tea, cocoa or coffee, poor commonplace liquids, are they not transmuted in the alembic of a bedroom fire, till they become nepenthe for a heartache or a philtre for romance? Ah, the romance of it, when youth forestalls tomorrow's conquest, when middle life forgets that yesterday is past for ever, when even querulous old age thinks it may still have its "honour and its toil"!

An old blue cloak, which served the turn of dressing-gown, had fallen apart in the exigencies of composition, and showed underlying tracts of white nightgown. Below, the firelight fell on bare feet resting on the edge of the brass fender till the heat made her curl up her toes, and above, the firelight contoured certain generous curves. The roundness and the bloom of maidenhood was upon her, that bloom so transient, so irreplaceable, that renders any attempt to simulate it so profoundly ludicrous. The mass of dark hair, which turned lying-and-mischief-making Mrs Flint so envious, was gathered behind with a bow of black ribbon, and hung loosely over the back of her chair. She sat there writing and rewriting, erasing, blotting, tearing up, till the night was far spent, till she feared that the modest resources of the *papeterie* would be exhausted before toil came to fruition.

It was finished at last, and if it was a little formal or high-flown, or stilted, is not a certain formality postulated on momentous occasions? Who would write that he was "delighted" to accept a bishopric? Who would go to a levee in a straw hat?

The letter ran:

Dear Lord Blandamer"
I do not know how I ought to write to you, for I have little experience of life to guide me. I thank you with all my heart for what you have told me. I am glad to think of it, and I always shall be. I believe there must be many strong reasons why you should not think of marrying me, yet if there are, you must know them far better than I, and you have disregarded them.

But there is one reason that you cannot know, for it is known to very few; I hope it is known only to some of our own relations. Perhaps I ought not to write of it at all, but I have no one to advise me. I mean what is right, and if I am doing wrong you will forgive me, will you not? and burn this letter when you have read it.

I have no right to the name I am called by; my cousins in the Market Place think we should use some other, but we do not even know what our real name would be. When my grand-mother married old Mr Joliffe, she had already a son two or three years old. This son was my father, and Mr Joliffe adopted him; but my grandmother had no right to any but her maiden name. We never knew what that was, though my father tried all his life to find it out, and thought he was very near finding out when he fell into his last illness. We think his head must have been affected, for he used to say strange things about his parent-age. Perhaps the thought of this disgrace troubled him, as it has often troubled me, though I never thought it would trouble me so much as now.

I have not told my aunt about what you have said to me, and no one else shall ever know it, but it will be the sweetest memory to me of all my life.

Your very sincere friend,

Anastasia Joliffe.

It was finished at last; she had slain all her hopes, she had slain her love. He would never marry her, he would never come near her again; but she had unburdened herself of her secret, and she could not have married him with that secret untold. It was three o'clock when she crept back again to bed. The fire had gone out, she was very cold, and she was glad to get back to her bed. Then Nature came to her aid and sent her kindly sleep, and if her sleep was not dreamless, she dreamt of dresses, and horses, and carriages, of men-servants, and maid-servants, of Lady Blandamer's great house of Fording, and of Lady Blandamer's husband.

Lord Blandamer also sat up very late that night. As he read before another bedroom fire he turned the pages of his book with the utmost regularity; his cigar never once went out. There was nothing to show that his thoughts wandered, nothing to show that his mind was in any way preoccupied. He was reading Eugenid's *Aristeia* of the pagans martyred under Honorius; and weighed the pros and cons of the argument as dispassionately as if the events of the afternoon had never taken place, as if there had been no such person as Anastasia Joliffe in the world.

Anastasia's letter reached him the next day at lunch, but he finished his meal before opening it. Yet he must have known whence it came, for there was a bold "Bellevue Lodge" embossed in red on the flap of the envelope. Martin Joliffe had ordered stamped paper and envelopes years ago, because he said that people of whom he made genealogical inquiries paid more attention to stamped than to plain paper—it was a credential of respectability. In Cullerne this had been looked upon as a gross instance of his extravagance; Mrs Bulteel and Canon Parkyn alone could use headed paper with propriety, and even the rectory only printed, and did not emboss. Martin had exhausted his supply years ago, and never ordered a second batch, because the first was still unpaid for; but Anastasia kept by her half a dozen of these fateful envelopes. She had purloined them when she was a girl at school, and to her they were still a cherished remnant of gentility, that pallium under which so many of us would fain hide our rags. She had used one on this momentous occasion; it seemed a fitting cover for despatches to Fording, and might divert attention from the straw paper on which her letter was written.

Lord Blandamer had seen the Bellevue Lodge, had divined the genesis of the embossed inscription, had unravelled all Anastasia's thoughts in using it, yet let the letter lie till he had finished lunch. When he read it afterwards he criticised it as he might the composition of a stranger, as a document with which he had no very close concern. Yet he appreciated the effort which it must have cost the girl to write it, was touched by her words, and felt a certain grave compassion for her. But it was the strange juggle of circumstance, the Sophoclean irony of a position of which he alone held the key, that most impressed themselves upon his mood.

He ordered his horse, and took the road to Cullerne, but his agent met him before he had passed the first lodge, and asked some further instructions for the planting at the top of the park. So he turned and rode up to the great belt of beeches which was then being planted, and was so long engaged there that dusk forced him to abandon his journey to the town. He rode back to Fording at a foot-pace, choosing devious paths, and enjoying the sunset in the autumn woods. He would write to Anastasia, and put off his visit till the next day.

501

With him there was no such wholesale destruction of writing-paper as had attended Anastasia's efforts on the previous night. One single sheet saw his letter begun and ended, a quarter of an hour sufficed for committing his sentiments very neatly to writing; he flung off his sentences easily, as easily as Odysseus tossed his heavy stone beyond all the marks of the Phaeacians:

My dearest Child,

I need not speak now of the weary hours of suspense which I passed in waiting for your letter. They are over, and all is sunshine after the clouds. I need not tell you how my heart beat when I saw an envelope with your address, nor how eagerly my fingers tore it open, for now all is happiness. Thank you, a thousand times thank you for your letter; it is like you, all candour, all kindness, and all truth. Put aside your scruples; everything that you say is not a featherweight in the balance; do not trouble about your name in the past, for you will have a new name in the future. It is not I, but you, who overlook obstacles, for have you not overlooked all the years that lie between your age and mine? I have but a moment to scribble these lines; you must forgive their weakness, and take for said all that should be said. I shall be with you tomorrow morning, and till then am, in all love and devotion,

Yours,

Blandamer.

He did not even read it through before he sealed it up, for he was in a hurry to get back to Eugenid and to the *Aristeia* of the heathens martyred under Honorius.

Two days later, Miss Joliffe put on her Sunday mantle and bonnet in the middle of the week, and went down to the Market Place to call on her cousin the pork-butcher. Her attire at once attracted attention. The only justification for such extravagance would be some parish function or festivity, and nothing of that sort could be going on without the knowledge of the churchwarden's family. Nor was it only the things which she wore, but the manner in which she wore them, that was so remarkable. As she entered the parlour at the back of the shop, where the pork-butcher's lady and daughters were sitting, they thought that they had never seen their cousin look so well dressed. She had lost the pinched, perplexed, down-trodden air which had overcast her later years; there was in her face a serenity and content which communicated itself in some mysterious way even to her apparel.

"Cousin Euphemia looks quite respectable this morning," whispered the younger to the elder daughter; and they had to examine her closely before they convinced themselves that only a piece of mauve ribbon in her bonnet was new, and that the coat and dress were just the same as they had seen every Sunday for two years past.

With *"nods and becks and wreathed smiles"* Miss Euphemia seated herself. "I have just popped in," she began, and the very phrase had something in it so light and flippant that her listeners started—"I have just popped in for a minute to tell you some news. You have always been particular, my dears, that no one except your branch had a right to the name of Joliffe in this town. You can't deny, Maria," she said deprecatingly to the churchwarden's wife, "that you have always held out that you were the real Joliffes, and been a little sore with me and Anstice for calling ourselves by what we thought we had a right to. Well, now there will be one less outside your family to use the name of Joliffe, for Anstice is going to give it up. Somebody has offered to find another name for her."

The real Joliffes exchanged glances, and thought of the junior partner in the drapery shop, who had affirmed with an oath that Anastasia Joliffe did as much justice to his goods as any girl in Cullerne; and thought again of the young farmer who was known for certain to let Miss Euphemia have eggs at a penny cheaper than anyone else.

"Yes, Anstice is going to change her name, so that will be one grievance the less. And another thing that will make matters straighter between us, Maria: I can promise the little bit of silver shall never go out of the family. You know what I mean—the teapot and the spoons marked with 'J' that you've always claimed for yours by right. I shall leave them all back to you when my time comes; Anstice will never want such odds and ends in the station to which she's called now."

The real Joliffes looked at each other again, and thought of young Bulteel, who had helped Anastasia with the gas-standards when the minster was decorated at Christmas. Or was it possible that her affected voice and fine lady airs had after all caught Mr Westray, that rather good-looking and interesting young man, on whom both the churchwarden's daughters were not without hopes of making an impression?

Miss Joliffe enjoyed their curiosity; she was in a teasing and mischievous mood, to which she had been a stranger for thirty years.

"Yes," she said, "I am one that like to own up to it when I make a mistake, and I will state I *have* made a mistake. I suppose I must take to spectacles; it seems I cannot see things that are going on under my very eyes—no, not even when they are pointed out to me. I've come round to tell you, Maria, one and all, that I was completely mistaken when I told the churchwarden that it was not on Anstice's account that Lord Blandamer has been visiting at Bellevue Lodge. It seems it was just for that he came, and the proof of it is he's going to marry her. In three weeks' time she will be Lady Blandamer, and if you want to say goodbye to her you'd better come back and have tea with me now, for she's packed her box, and is off to London tomorrow. Mrs Howard, who keeps the school in Carisbury where Anstice went in dear Martin's lifetime, will meet her and take charge of her, and get her trousseau. Lord Blandamer has arranged it all, and he is going to marry Anstice and take her for a long tour on the Continent, and I'm sure I don't know where else."

It was all true. Lord Blandamer made no secret of the matter, and his engagement to Anastasia, only child of the late Martin Joliffe, Esquire, of Cullerne, was duly announced in the London papers. It was natural that Westray should have known vacillation and misgiving before he made up his mind to offer marriage. It is with a man whose family or position are not strong enough to bear any extra strain, that public opinion plays so large a part in such circumstances. If he marries beneath him he falls to the wife's level, because he has no margin of resource to raise her to his own. With Lord Blandamer it was different: his reliance upon himself was so great, that he seemed to enjoy rather than not, the flinging down of a gauntlet to the public in this marriage.

Bellevue Lodge became a centre of attraction. The ladies who had contemned a lodging-house keeper's daughter courted the betrothed of a peer. From themselves they did not disguise the motive for this change, they did not even attempt to find an excuse in public. They simply executed their *volte face* simultaneously and with most commendable regularity, and felt no more reluctance or shame in the process than a cat feels in following the man who carries its meat. If they were disappointed in not seeing Anastasia herself (for she left for London almost immediately after the engagement was made public), they were in some measure compensated by the extreme readiness of Miss Euphemia to discuss the matter in all its bearings. Each and every detail was conscientiously considered and enlarged upon, from the buttons on Lord Blandamer's boots to the engagement-ring on Anastasia's finger; and Miss Joliffe was never tired of explaining that this last had an emerald—"A very large emerald, my dear, surrounded by diamonds, green and white being the colours of his lordship's shield, what they call the nebuly coat, you know."

A variety of wedding gifts found their way to Bellevue Lodge. "Great events, such as marriages and deaths, certainly do call forth the sympathy of our neighbours in a wonderful way," Miss Joliffe said, with all the seriousness of an innocent belief in the general goodness of mankind. "Till Anstice was engaged, I never knew, I am sure, how many friends I had in Cullerne." She showed "the presents" to successive callers, who examined them with the more interest because they had already seen most of them in the shop-windows of Cullerne, and so were able to appreciate the exact monetary outlay with which their acquaintances thought it prudent to conciliate the Fording interest. Every form of useless ugliness was amply represented among them— vulgarity masqueraded as taste, niggardliness figured as generosity— and if Miss Joliffe was proud of them as she forwarded them from Cullerne, Anastasia was heartily ashamed of them when they reached her in London.

"We must let bygones be bygones," said Mrs Parkyn to her husband with truly Christian forbearance, "and if this young man's choice has not fallen exactly where we could have wished, we must remember, after all, that he *is* Lord Blandamer, and make the best of the lady for his sake. We must give her a present; in your position as rector you could not afford to be left out. Everyone, I hear, is giving something."

"Well, don't let it be anything extravagant," he said, laying down his paper, for his interest was aroused by any question of expense. "A too costly gift would be quite out of place under the circumstances. It should be rather an expression of goodwill to Lord Blandamer than anything of much intrinsic value."

"Of course, of course. You may trust me not to do anything foolish. I have my eye on just the thing. There is a beautiful set of four salt-cellars with their spoons at Laverick's, in a case lined with puffed satin. They only cost thirty-three shillings, and look worth at least three pounds."

CHAPTER NINETEEN

The wedding was quiet, and there being no newspapers at that time to take such matters for their province, Cullerne curiosity had to be contented with the bare announcement: "At Saint Agatha's-at-Bow, Horatio Sebastian Fynes, Lord Blandamer, to Anastasia, only child of the late Michael Joliffe, of Cullerne Wharfe." Mrs Bulteel had been heard to say that she could not allow dear Lord Blandamer to be married without her being there. Canon Parkyn and Mrs Parkyn felt that their presence also was required *ex-officio*, and Clerk Janaway averred with some redundancies of expletive that he, too, "must see 'em turned off." He hadn't been to London for twenty year. If 'twere to cost a sovereign, why, 'twas a poor heart that never made merry, and he would never live to see another Lord Blandamer married. Yet none of them went, for time and place were not revealed.

But Miss Joliffe was there, and on her return to Cullerne she held several receptions at Bellevue Lodge, at which only the wedding and the events connected with it were discussed. She was vested for these functions in a new dress of coffee-coloured silk, and what with a tea-urn hissing in Mr Sharnall's room, and muffins, toast, and sweet-cakes, there were such goings-on in the house, as had not been seen since the last coach rolled away from the old Hand of God thirty years before. The company were very gracious and even affectionate, and Miss Joliffe, in the exhilaration of the occasion, forgot all those cold-shoulderings and askance looks which had grieved her at a certain Dorcas meeting only a few weeks before.

At these reunions many important particulars transpired. The wedding had been celebrated early in the morning at the special instance of the bride; only Mrs Howard and Miss Euphemia herself were present. Anstice had worn a travelling dress of dark-green cloth, so that she might go straight from the church to the station. "And, my dears," she said, with a glance of all-embracing benevolence, "she looked a perfect young peeress."

The kind and appreciative audience, who had all been expecting and hoping for the past six weeks, that some bolt might fall from the blue to rob Anastasia of her triumph, were so astonished at the wedding having finally taken place that they could not muster a sneer among them. Only lying-and-mischief-making Mrs Flint found courage for a sniff, and muttered something to her next neighbour about there being such things as mock marriages.

The honeymoon was much extended. Lord and Lady Blandamer went first to the Italian lakes, and thence, working their way home by Munich, Nuremburg, and the Rhine, travelled by such easy stages that autumn had set in when they reached Paris. There they wintered, and there in the spring was born a son and heir to all the Blandamer estates. The news caused much rejoicing in the domain; and when it was announced that the family were returning to Cullerne, it was decided to celebrate the event by ringing a peal from the tower of Saint Sepulchre's. The proposal originated with Canon Parkyn.

"It is a graceful compliment," he said, "to the nobleman to whose munificence the restoration is so largely due. We must show him how much stronger we have made our old tower, eh, Mr Westray? We must get the Carisbury ringers over to teach Cullerne people how such things should be done. Sir George will have to stand out of his fees longer than ever, if he is to wait till the tower tumbles down now. Eh, eh?"

"Ah, I do so dote on these old customs," assented his wife. "It is so delightful, a merry peal. I do think these good old customs should always be kept up." It was the cheapness of the entertainment that particularly appealed to her. "But is it necessary, my dear," she demurred, "to bring the ringers over from Carisbury? They are a sad drunken lot. I am sure there must be plenty of young men in Cullerne, who would delight to help ring the bells on such an occasion."

But Westray would have none of it. It was true, he said, that the tie-rods were fixed, and the tower that much the stronger; but he could countenance no ringing till the great south-east pier had been properly under-pinned.

His remonstrances found little favour. Lord Blandamer would think it so ungracious. Lady Blandamer, to be sure, counted for very little; it was ridiculous, in fact, to think of ringing the minster bells for a landlady's niece, but Lord Blandamer would certainly be offended.

"I call that clerk of the works a vain young upstart," Mrs Parkyn said to her husband. "I cannot think how you keep your temper with such a popinjay. I hope you will not allow yourself to be put upon again. You are so sweet-tempered and forbearing, that *everyone* takes advantage of you."

So she stirred him up till he assured her with considerable boldness that he was *not* a man to be dictated to; the bells *should* be rung, and he would get Sir George's views to fortify his own. Then Sir George wrote one of those cheery little notes for which he was famous, with a proper admixture of indifferent puns and a classic conceit: that when Gratitude was climbing the temple steps to lay an offering on Hymen's altar, Prudence must wait silent at the base till she came down.

Sir George should have been a doctor, his friends said; his manner was always so genial and reassuring. So having turned these happy phrases, and being overwhelmed with the grinding pressure of a great practice, he dismissed the tower of Saint Sepulchre from his mind, and left rector and ringers to their own devices.

Thus on an autumn afternoon there was a sound in Cullerne that few of the inhabitants had ever heard, and the little town stopped its business to listen to the sweetest peal in all the West Country. How they swung and rung and sung together, the little bells and the great bells, from Beata Maria, the sweet, silver-voiced treble, to Taylor John, the deep-voiced tenor, that the Guild of Merchant Taylors had given three hundred years ago. There was a charm in the air like the singing of innumerable birds; people flung up their windows to listen, people stood in the shop-doors to listen, and the melody went floating away over the salt-marshes, till the fishermen taking up their lobster-pots paused in sheer wonder at a music that they had never heard before.

It seemed as if the very bells were glad to break their long repose; they sang together like the morning stars, they shouted together like the sons of God for joy. They remembered the times that were gone, and how they had rung when Abbot Harpingdon was given his red hat, and rung again when Henry defended the Faith by suppressing the Abbey, and again when Mary defended the Faith by restoring the Mass, and again when Queen Bess was given a pair of embroidered gloves as she passed through the Market Place on her way to Fording. They remembered the long counter-change of life and death that had passed under the red roofs at their feet, they remembered innumerable births and marriages and funerals of old time; they sang together like the morning stars, they shouted together like the sons of God for joy, they shouted for joy.

The Carisbury ringers came over after all; and Mrs Parkyn bore their advent with less misgiving, in the hope that directly Lord Blandamer heard of the honour that was done him, he would send a handsome donation for the ringers as he had already sent to the workhouse, and the old folk, and the schoolchildren of Cullerne. The ropes and the cage, and the pins and the wheels, had all been carefully overhauled; and when the day came, the ringers stood to their work like men, and rang a full peal of grandsire triples in two hours and fifty-nine minutes.

There was a little cask of Bulteel's brightest tenpenny that some magician's arm had conjured up through the well-hole in the belfry floor: and Clerk Janaway, for all he was teetotaler, eyed the foaming pots wistfully as he passed them round after the work was done.

"Well," he said, "there weren't no int'rupted peal this time, were there? These here old bells never had a finer set of ringing-men under them, and I lay you never had a finer set of bells above your heads, my lads; now did 'ee? I've heard the bells swung many a time in Carisbury tower, and heard 'em when the queen was set upon her throne, but, lor'! they arn't so deep-like nor yet so sweet as this here old ring. Perhaps they've grow'd the sweeter for lying by a bit, like port in the cellars of the Blandamer Arms, though I've heard Dr Ennefer say some of it was turned so like sherry, that no man living couldn't tell the difference."

Westray had bowed like loyal subaltern to the verdict of his Chief. Sir George's decision that the bells might safely be rung lifted the responsibility from the young man's shoulders, but not the anxiety from his mind. He never left the church while the peal was ringing. First he was in the bell-chamber steadying himself by the beams of the cage, while he marked the wide-mouthed bells now open heavenwards, now turn back with a rush into the darkness below. Then he crept deafened with the clangour down the stairs into the belfry, and sat on the sill of a window watching the ringers rise and fall at their work. He felt the tower sway restlessly under the stress of the swinging metal, but there was nothing unusual in the motion; there was no falling of mortar, nothing to attract any special attention. Then he went down into the church, and up again into the organ-loft, whence he could see the wide bow of that late Norman arch which spanned the south transept.

Above the arch ran up into the lantern the old fissure, zigzag like a baleful lightning-flash, that had given him so much anxiety. The day was overcast, and heavy masses of cloud drifting across the sky darkened the church. But where the shadows hung heaviest, under a stone gallery passage that ran round the inside of the lantern, could be traced one of those heavy tie-rods with which the tower had recently been strengthened. Westray was glad to think that the ties were there; he hoped that they might indeed support the strain which this bell-ringing was bringing on the tower; he hoped that Sir George was right, and that he, Westray, was wrong. Yet he had pasted a strip of paper across the crack, so that by tearing it might give warning if any serious movement were taking place.

As he leant over the screen of the organ-loft, he thought of that afternoon when he had first seen signs of the arch moving, of that afternoon when the organist was playing "Sharnall in D flat." How much had happened since then! He thought of that scene which had happened in this very loft, of Sharnall's end, of the strange accident that had terminated a sad life on that wild night. What a strange accident it was, what a strange thing that Sharnall should have been haunted by that wandering fancy of a man following him with a hammer, and then have been found in this very loft, with the desperate wound on him that the pedal-note had dealt! How much had happened—his own proposal to Anastasia, his refusal, and now that event for which the bells were ringing! How quickly the scenes changed! What a creature of an hour was he, was every man, in face of these grim walls that had stood enduring, immutable, for generation after generation, for age after age! And then he smiled as he thought that these eternal realities of stone were all created by ephemeral man; that he, ephemeral man, was even now busied with schemes for their support, with anxieties lest they should fall and grind to powder all below.

The bells sounded fainter and far off inside the church. As they reached his ears through the heavy stone roof they were more harmonious, all harshness was softened; the *sordino* of the vaulting produced the effect of a muffled peal. He could hear deep-voiced Taylor John go striding through his singing comrades in the intricacies of the Treble Bob Triples, and yet there was another voice in Westray's ears that made itself heard even above the booming of the tenor bell. It was the cry of the tower arches, the small still voice that had haunted him ever since he had been at Cullerne. "*The arch never sleeps,*" they said—"*the arch never sleeps;*" and again, "They have bound on us a burden too heavy to be borne; but we are shifting it. The arch never sleeps."

The ringers were approaching the end; they had been at their work for near three hours, the 5,040 changes were almost finished. Westray went down from the organ-loft, and as he walked through the church the very last change was rung. Before the hum and mutter had died out of the air, and while the red-faced ringers in the belfry were quaffing their tankards, the architect had made his way to the scaffolding, and stood face to face with the zigzag crack. He looked at it carefully, as a doctor might examine a wound; he thrust his hand like Thomas into the dark fissure. No, there was no change; the paper strip was unbroken, the tie-rods had done their work nobly. Sir George had been quite right after all.

And as he looked there was the very faintest noise heard—a whisper, a mutter, a noise so slight that it might have passed a hundred times unnoticed. But to the architect's ear it spoke as loudly as a thunderclap. He knew exactly what it was and whence it came; and looking at the crack, saw that the broad paper strip was torn half-way across. It was a small affair; the paper strip was not quite parted, it was only torn half-way through. Though Westray watched for an hour, no further change took place. The ringers had left the tower, the little town had resumed its business. Clerk Janaway was walking across the church, when he saw the architect leaning against a cross-pole of the scaffolding, on the platform high up under the arch of the south transept.

"I'm just a-locking up," he called out. "You've got your own key, sir, no doubt?"

Westray gave an almost imperceptible nod.

"Well, we haven't brought the tower down this time," the clerk went on. But Westray made no answer; his eyes were fixed on the little half-torn strip of paper, and he had no thought for anything else. A minute later the old man stood beside him on the platform, puffing after the ladders that he had climbed. "No int'rupted peal this time," he said; "we've fair beat the neb'ly coat at last. Lord Blandamer back, and an heir to keep the family going. Looks as if the neb'ly coat was losing a bit of his sting, don't it?" But Westray was moody, and said nothing. "Why what's the matter? You bain't took bad, be you?"

"Don't bother me now," the architect said sharply. "I wish to Heaven the peal *had* been interrupted. I wish your bells had never been rung. Look there"—and he pointed at the strip of paper.

The clerk went closer to the crack, and looked hard at the silent witness. "Lor' bless you! that ain't nothing," he said; "'tis only just the jarring of the bells done that. You don't expect a mushet of paper to stand as firm as an anvil-stone, when Taylor John's a-swinging up aloft."

"Look you," Westray said; "you were in church this morning. Do you remember the lesson about the prophet sending his servant up to the top of a hill, to look at the sea? The man went up ever so many times and saw nothing. Last he saw a little cloud like a man's hand rising out of the sea, and after that the heaven grew black, and the storm broke. I'm not sure that bit of torn paper isn't the man's hand for this tower."

"Don't bother yourself," rejoined the clerk; "the man's hand showed the rain was a-coming, and the rain was just what they wanted. I never can make out why folks twist the Scripture round and make the man's hand into something bad. 'Twas a *good* thing, so take heart and get home to your victuals; you can't mend that bit of paper for all your staring at it."

Westray paid no attention to his remarks, and the old man wished him goodnight rather stiffly. "Well," he said, as he turned down the ladder, "I'm off. I've got to be in my garden afore dark, for they're going to seal the leek leaves tonight against the leek-show next week. My grandson took first prize last year, and his old grandad had to put up with eleventh; but I've got half a dozen leeks this season as'll beat any plant that's growed in Cullerne."

By the next morning the paper strip was entirely parted. Westray wrote to Sir George, but history only repeated itself; for his chief again made light of the matter, and gave the young man a strong hint that he was making mountains of molehills, that he was unduly nervous, that his place was to diligently carry out the instructions he had received. Another strip of paper was pasted across the crack, and remained intact. It seemed as if the tower had come to rest again, but Westray's scruples were not so easily allayed this time, and he took measures for pushing forward the under-pinning of the south-east pier with all possible despatch.

Chapter Twenty

That inclination or predilection of Westray's for Anastasia, which he had been able to persuade himself was love, had passed away. His peace of mind was now completely restored, and he discounted the humiliation of refusal, by reflecting that the girl's affections must have been already engaged at the time of his proposal. He was ready to admit that Lord Blandamer would in any case have been a formidable competitor, but if they had started for the race at the same time he would have been quite prepared to back his own chances. Against his rival's position and wealth, might surely have been set his own youth, regularity of life, and professional skill; but it was a mere tilting against windmills to try to win a heart that was already another's. Thus disturbing influences were gradually composed, and he was able to devote an undivided attention to his professional work.

As the winter evenings set in, he found congenial occupation in an attempt to elucidate the heraldry of the great window at the end of the south transept. He made sketches of the various shields blazoned in it, and with the aid of a county history, and a manual which Dr Ennefer had lent him, succeeded in tracing most of the alliances represented by the various quarterings. These all related to marriages of the Blandamer family, for Van Linge had filled the window with glass to the order of the third Lord Blandamer, and the sea-green and silver of the nebuly coat was many times repeated, beside figuring in chief at the head of the window. In these studies Westray was glad to have Martin Joliffe's papers by him. There was in them a mass of information which bore on the subject of the architect's inquiries, for Martin had taken the published genealogy of the Blandamer family, and elaborated and corrected it by all kinds of investigation as to marriages and collaterals.

The story of Martin's delusion, the idea of the doited grey-beard whom the boys called "Old Nebuly," had been so firmly impressed on Westray's mind, that when he first turned over the papers he expected to find in them little more than the hallucinations of a madman. But by degrees he became aware that however disconnected many of Martin's notes might appear, they possessed a good deal of interest, and the coherence which results from a particular object being kept more or less continuously in view. Besides endless genealogies and bits of family history extracted from books, there were recorded all kinds of personal impressions and experiences, which Martin had met with in his journeyings. But in all his researches and expeditions he professed to have but one object—the discovery of his father's name; though what record he hoped to find, or where or how he hoped to find it, whether in document or register or inscription, was nowhere set out.

It was evident that the old fancy that he was the rightful owner of Fording, which had been suggested to him in his Oxford days, had taken such hold of his mind that no subsequent experience had been able to dislodge it. Of half his parentage there was no doubt. His mother was that Sophia Flannery who had married Yeoman Joliffe, had painted the famous picture of the flowers and caterpillar, and done many other things less reputable; but over his father hung a veil of obscurity which Martin had tried all his life to lift. Westray had heard those early stories from Clerk Janaway a dozen times, how that when Yeoman Joliffe took Sophia to church she brought him a four-year-old son by a former marriage. By a former *marriage* Martin had always stoutly maintained, as in duty bound, for any other theory would have dishonoured himself. With his mother's honour he had little concern, for where was the use of defending the memory of a mother who had made shipwreck of her own reputation with soldiers and horse-copers? It was this previous marriage that Martin had tried so hard to establish, tried all the harder because other folk had wagged their heads and said there was no marriage to discover, that Sophia was neither wife nor widow.

Towards the end of his notes it seemed as if he had found some clue—had found some clue, or thought that he had found it. In this game of hunt the slipper he had imagined that he was growing "hotter" and "hotter" till death balked him at the finish. Westray recollected Mr Sharnall saying more than once that Martin had been on the brink of solving the riddle when the end overtook him. And Sharnall, too, had he not almost grasped the Will-of-the-wisp when fate tripped *him* on that windy night? Many thoughts came to Westray's mind as he turned these papers, many memories of others who had turned them before him. He thought of clever, worthless Martin, who had wasted his days on their writing, who had neglected home and family for their sake; he thought of the little organist who had held them in his feverish hands, who had hoped by some dramatic discovery to illumine the dark setting of his own life.

And as Westray read, the interest grew with him too, till it absorbed the heraldry of the Blandamer window from which the whole matter had started. He began to comprehend the vision that had possessed Martin, that had so stirred the organist's feelings; he began to think that it was reserved for himself to make the long-sought discovery, and that he had in his own hand the clue to the strangest of romances.

One evening as he sat by the fire, with a plan in his hands and a litter of Martin's papers lying on a table at his side, there was a tap at the door, and Miss Joliffe entered. They were still close friends in spite of his leaving Bellevue Lodge. However sorry she had been at the time to lose her lodger, she recognised that the course he had taken was correct, and, indeed, obligatory. She was glad that he had seen his duty in this matter; it would have been quite impossible for any man of ordinary human feelings, to continue to live on in the same house under such circumstances. To have made a bid for Anstice's hand, and to have been refused, was a blow that moved her deepest pity, and she endeavoured in many ways to show her consideration for the victim.

Providence had no doubt overruled everything for the best in ordaining that Anstice should refuse Mr Westray, but Miss Joliffe had favoured his suit, and had been sorry at the time that it was not successful. So there existed between them that curious sympathy, which generally exists between a rejected lover and a woman who has done her best to further his proposal. They had since met not unfrequently, and the year which had elapsed had sufficiently blunted the edge of Westray's disappointment, to enable him to talk of the matter with equanimity. He took a sad pleasure in discussing with Miss Joliffe the motives which might have conduced to so inexplicable a refusal, and in considering whether his offer would have been accepted if it had been made a little sooner or in another manner. Nor was the subject in any way distasteful to her, for she felt a reflected glory in the fact of her niece having first refused a thoroughly eligible proposal, and having afterwards accepted one transcendently better.

"Forgive me, sir—forgive me, Mr Westray," she corrected herself, remembering that their relation was no longer one of landlady and lodger. "I am sorry to intrude on you so late, but it is difficult to find you in during the day. There is a matter that has been weighing lately on my mind. You have never taken away the picture of the flowers, which you and dear Mr Sharnall purchased of me. I have not hurried in the matter, feeling I should like to see you nicely settled in before it was moved, but now it is time all was set right, so I have brought it over tonight."

If her dress was no longer threadbare, it was still of the neatest black, and if she had taken to wearing every day the moss-agate brooch which had formerly been reserved for Sundays, she was still the very same old sweet-tempered, spontaneous, Miss Joliffe as in time past. Westray looked at her with something like affection.

"Sit down," he said, offering her a chair; "did you say you had brought the picture with you?" and he scanned her as if he expected to see it produced from her pocket.

"Yes," she said; "my maid is bringing it upstairs"—and there was just a suspicion of hesitation on the word "maid," that showed that she was still unaccustomed to the luxury of being waited on.

It was with great difficulty that she had been persuaded to accept such an allowance at Anastasia's hands, as would enable her to live on at Bellevue Lodge and keep a single servant; and if it brought her infinite relief to find that Lord Blandamer had paid all Martin's bills within a week of his engagement, such generosity filled her at the same time with a multitude of scruples. Lord Blandamer had wished her to live with them at Fording, but he was far too considerate and appreciative of the situation to insist on this proposal when he saw that such a change would be uncongenial to her. So she remained at Cullerne, and spent her time in receiving with dignity visits from the innumerable friends that she found she now possessed, and in the fullest enjoyment of church services, meetings, parish work, and other privileges.

"It is very good of you, Miss Joliffe," Westray said; "it is very kind of you to think of the picture. But," he went on, with a too vivid recollection of the painting, "I know how much you have always prized it, and I could not bear to take it away from Bellevue Lodge. You see, Mr Sharnall, who was part owner with me, is dead; I am only making you a present of half of it, so you must accept that from me as a little token of gratitude for all the kindness you have shown me. You *have* been very kind to me, you know," he said with a sigh, which was meant to recall Miss Joliffe's friendliness, and his own grief, in the affair of the proposal.

Miss Joliffe was quick to take the cue, and her voice was full of sympathy. "Dear Mr Westray, you know how glad I should have been if all could have happened as you wished. Yet we should try to recognise the ordering of Providence in these things, and bear sorrow with meekness. But about the picture, you must let me have my own way this once. There may come a time, and that before very long, when I shall be able to buy it back from you just as we arranged, and then I am sure you will let me have it. But for the present it must be with you, and if anything should happen to me I should wish you to keep it altogether."

Westray had meant to insist on her retaining the picture; he would not for a second time submit to be haunted with the gaudy flowers and the green caterpillar. But while she spoke, there fell upon him one of those gusty changes of purpose to which he was peculiarly liable. There came into his mind that strange insistence with which Sharnall had begged him at all hazards to retain possession of the picture. It seemed as if there might be some mysterious influence which had brought Miss Joliffe with it just now, and that he might be playing false to his trust with Sharnall if he sent it back again. So he did not remain obdurate, but said: "Well, if you really wish it, I will keep the picture for a time, and whenever you want it you can take it back again." While he was speaking there was a sound of stumbling on the stairs outside, and a bang as if something heavy had been let drop.

"It is that stupid girl again," Miss Joliffe said; "she is always tumbling about. I am sure she has broken more china in the six months she has been with me than was broken before in six years."

They went to the door, and as Westray opened it great red-faced and smiling Anne Janaway walked in, bearing the glorious picture of

516

the flowers and caterpillar.

"What have you been doing now?" her mistress asked sharply.

"Very sorry, mum," said the maid, mingling some indignation with her apology, "this here gurt paint tripped I up. I'm sure I hope I haven't hurt un"—and she planted the picture on the floor against the table.

Miss Joliffe scanned the picture with an eye which was trained to detect the very flakiest chip on a saucer, the very faintest scratch upon a teapot.

"Dear me, dear me!" she said, "the beautiful frame is ruined; the bottom piece is broken almost clean off."

"Oh, come," Westray said in a pacifying tone, while he lifted the picture and laid it flat on the table, "things are not so bad as all that."

He saw that the piece which formed the bottom of the frame was indeed detached at both corners and ready to fall away, but he pushed it back into position with his hand till it stuck in its place, and left little damage apparent to a casual observer.

"See," he said, "it looks nearly all right. A little glue will quite repair the mischief tomorrow I am sure I wonder how your servant managed to get it up here at all—it is such a weight and size."

As a matter of fact, Miss Joliffe herself had helped Ann to carry the picture as far as the Grands Mulets of the last landing. The final ascent she thought could be accomplished in safety by the girl alone, while it would have been derogatory to her new position of an independent lady to appear before Westray carrying the picture herself.

"Do not vex yourself," Westray begged; "look, there is a nail in the wall here under the ceiling which will do capitally for hanging it till I can find a better place; the old cord is just the right length." He climbed on a chair and adjusted the picture, standing back as if to admire it, till Miss Joliffe's complacency was fairly restored.

Westray was busied that night long after Miss Joliffe had left him, and the hands of the loud-ticking clock on the mantelpiece showed that midnight was near before he had finished his work. Then he sat a little while before the dying fire, thinking much of Mr Sharnall, whom the picture had recalled to his mind, until the blackening embers warned him that it was time to go to bed. He was rising from his chair, when he heard behind him a noise as of something falling, and looking round, saw that the bottom of the picture-frame, which he had temporarily pushed into position, had broken away again of its own weight, and was fallen on the floor. The frame was handsomely wrought with a peculiar interlacing fillet, as he had noticed many times before. It was curious that so poor a picture should have obtained a rich setting, and sometimes he thought that Sophia Flannery must have bought the frame at a sale, and had afterwards daubed the flower-piece to fill it.

The room had grown suddenly cold with the chill which dogs the heels of a dying fire on an early winter's night. An icy breath blew in under the door, and made something flutter that lay on the floor close to the broken frame. Westray stooped to pick it up, and found that he had in his hand a piece of folded paper.

He felt a curious reluctance in handling it. Those fantastic scruples to which he was so often a prey assailed him. He asked himself had he any right to examine this piece of paper? It might be a letter; he did not know whence it had come, nor whose it was, and he certainly did not wish to be guilty of opening someone else's letter. He even went so far as to put it solemnly on the table, like a skipper on whose deck the phantom whale-boat of the *Flying Dutchman* has deposited a packet of mails. After a few minutes, however, he appreciated the absurdity of the situation, and with an effort unfolded the mysterious missive.

It was a long narrow piece of paper, yellowed with years, and lined with the creases of a generation; and had on it both printed and written characters. He recognised it instantly for a certificate of marriage— those "marriage lines" on which so often hang both the law and the prophets. There it was with all the little pigeon-holes duly filled in, and set forth how that on "March 15, 1800, at the Church of Saint Medard Within, one Horatio Sebastian Fynes, bachelor, aged twenty-one, son of Horatio Sebastian Fynes, gentleman, was married to one Sophia Flannery, spinster, aged twenty-one, daughter of James Flannery, merchant," with witnesses duly attesting. And underneath an ill-formed straggling hand had added a superscription in ink that was now brown and wasted: "Martin born January 2, 1801, at ten minutes past twelve, night." He laid it on the table and folded it out flat, and knew that he had under his eyes that certificate of the first marriage (of the only true marriage) of Martin's mother, which Martin had longed all his life to see, and had not seen; that patent of legitimacy which Martin thought he had within his grasp when death overtook him, that clue which Sharnall thought that he had within his grasp when death overtook him also.

On March 15, 1800, Sophia Flannery was married by special licence to Horatio Sebastian Fynes, gentleman, and on January 2, 1801, at ten minutes past twelve, night, Martin was born. Horatio Sebastian—the names were familiar enough to Westray. Who was this Horatio Sebastian Fynes, son of Horatio Sebastian Fynes, gentleman? It was only a formal question that he asked himself, for he knew the answer very well. This document that he had before him might be no legal proof, but not all the lawyers in Christendom could change his conviction, his intuition, that the "gentleman" Sophia Flannery had married was none other than the octogenarian Lord Blandamer deceased three years ago.

There was to his eyes an air of authenticity about that yellowed strip of paper that nothing could upset, and the date of Martin's birth given in the straggling hand at the bottom coincided exactly with his own information. He sat down again in the cold with his elbows on the table and his head between his hands while he took in some of the corollaries of the position. If the old Lord Blandamer had married Sophia Flannery on March 15, 1800, then his second marriage was no marriage at all, for Sophia was living long after that, and there had been no divorce. But if his second marriage was no marriage, then his son, Lord Blandamer, who was drowned in Cullerne Bay, had been illegitimate, and his grandson, Lord Blandamer, who now sat on the throne of Fording, was illegitimate too. And Martin's dream had been true. Selfish, thriftless, idle Martin, whom the boys called "Old Nebuly," had not been mad after all, but had been Lord Blandamer.

It all hung on this strip of paper, this bolt fallen from the blue, this message that had come from no one knew where. Whence *had* it come? Could Miss Joliffe have dropped it? No, that was impossible; she would certainly have told him if she had any information of this kind, for she knew that he had been trying for months to unravel the tangle of Martin's papers. It must have been hidden behind the picture, and have fallen out when the bottom piece of the frame fell.

He went to the picture. There was the vase of flaunting, ill-drawn flowers, there was the green caterpillar wriggling on the table-top, but at the bottom was something that he had never seen before. A long narrow margin of another painting was now visible where the frame was broken away; it seemed as if the flower-piece had been painted over some other subject, as if Sophia Flannery had not even been at the pains to take the canvas out, and had only carried her daub up to the edge of the frame. There was no question that the flowers masked some better painting, some portrait, no doubt, for enough was shown at the bottom to enable him to make out a strip of a brown velvet coat, and even one mother-of-pearl button of a brown velvet waistcoat. He stared at the flowers, he held a candle close to them in the hope of being able to trace some outline, to discover something of what lay behind. But the colour had been laid on with no sparing hand, the veil was impenetrable. Even the green caterpillar seemed to mock him, for as he looked at it closely, he saw that Sophia in her wantonness had put some minute touches of colour, which gave its head two eyes and a grinning mouth.

He sat down again at the table where the certificate still lay open before him. That entry of Martin's birth must be in the handwriting of Sophia Flannery, of faithless, irresponsible Sophia Flannery, flaunting as her own flowers, mocking as the face of her own caterpillar.

There was a dead silence over all, the utter blank silence that falls upon a country town in the early morning hours. Only the loud-ticking clock on the mantelpiece kept telling of time's passage till the carillon of Saint Sepulchre's woke the silence with New Sabbath. It was three o'clock, and the room was deadly cold, but that chill was nothing to the chill that was rising to his own heart. He knew it all now, he said to himself—he knew the secret of Anastasia's marriage, and of Sharnall's death, and of Martin's death.

Chapter Twenty One.

The foreman of the masons at work in the under-pinning of the south-east pier came to see Westray at nine o'clock the next morning. He was anxious that the architect should go down to the church at once, for the workmen, on reaching the tower shortly after daybreak, found traces of a fresh movement which had taken place during the night. But Westray was from home, having left Cullerne for London by the first train.

About ten of the same forenoon, the architect was in the shop of a small picture-dealer in Westminster. The canvas of the flowers and caterpillar picture lay on the counter, for the man had just taken it out of the frame.

"No," said the dealer, "there is no paper or any kind of lining in the frame—just a simple wood backing, you see. It is unusual to back at all, but it *is* done now and again"—and he tapped the loose frame all round. "It is an expensive frame, well made, and with good gilding. I shouldn't be surprised if the painting underneath this daub turned out to be quite respectable; they would never put a frame like this on anything that wasn't pretty good."

"Do you think you can clean off the top part without damaging the painting underneath?"

"Oh dear, yes," the man said; "I've had many harder jobs. You leave it with me for a couple of days, and we'll see what we can make of it."

"Couldn't it be done quicker than that?" Westray said. "I'm in rather a hurry. It is difficult for me to get up to London, and I should rather like to be by, when you begin to clean it."

"Don't make yourself anxious," the other said; "you can leave it in my hands with perfect confidence. We're quite used to this business."

Westray still looked unsatisfied. The dealer gave a glance round the shop. "Well," he said, "things don't seem very busy this morning; if you're in such a hurry, I don't mind just trying a little bit of it now. We'll put it on the table in the back-room. I can see if anyone comes into the shop."

"Begin where the face ought to be," Westray said; "let us see whose portrait it is."

"No, no," said the dealer; "we won't risk the face yet. Let us try something that doesn't matter much. We shall see how this stuff peels off; that'll give us a guide for the more important part. Here, I'll start with the table-top and caterpillar. There's something queer about that caterpillar, beside the face some joker's fitted it up with. I'm rather shy about the caterpillar. Looks to me as if it was a bit of the real picture left showing through, though I don't very well see how a caterpillar would fit in with a portrait." The dealer passed the nail of his forefinger lightly over the surface of the picture. "It seems as if 'twas sunk. You can feel the edges of this heavy daubing rough all round it."

It was as he pointed out; the green caterpillar certainly appeared to form some part of the underlying picture. The man took out a bottle, and with a brush laid some solution on the painting. "You must wait for it to dry. It will blister and frizzle up the surface, then we can rub off the top gently with a cloth, and you'll see what you will see."

"The fellow who painted this table-top didn't spare his colours," said the dealer half an hour later, "and that's all the better for us. See, it comes off like a skin"—and he worked away tenderly with a soft flannel. "Well, I'm jiggered," he went on, "if here isn't another caterpillar higher up! No, it ain't a caterpillar; but if it ain't a caterpillar, what is it?"

There was indeed another wavy green line, but Westray knew what it was directly he saw it. "Be careful," he said; "they aren't caterpillars at all, but just part of a coat of arms—a kind of bars in an heraldic shield, you know. There will be another shorter green line lower down."

It was as he said, and in a minute more there shone out the silver field and the three sea-green bars of the nebuly coat, and below it the motto *Aut Fynes aut finis*, just as it shone in the top light of the Blandamer window. It was the middle bar that Sophia had turned into a caterpillar, and in pure wantonness left showing through, when for her own purposes she had painted out the rest of the picture. Westray's excitement was getting the better of him—he could not keep still; he stood first on one leg and then on another, and drummed on the table with his fingers.

The dealer put his hand on the architect's arm. "For God's sake keep quiet!" he said; "don't excite yourself. You needn't think you have found a gold mine. It ain't a ten thousand-guinea Vandyke. We can't see enough yet to say what it is, but I'll bet my life you never get a twenty-pound note for it."

But for all Westray's impatience, the afternoon was well advanced before the head of the portrait was approached. There had been so few interruptions, that the dealer felt called upon to extenuate the absence of custom by explaining more than once that it was a very dull season. He was evidently interested in his task, for he worked with a will till the light began to fail. "Never mind," he said; "I will get a lamp; now we have got so far we may as well go a bit further."

It was a full-face picture, as they saw a few minutes afterwards. Westray held the lamp, and felt a strange thrill go through him, as he began to make out the youthful and unwrinkled brow. Surely he knew that high forehead—it was Anastasia's, and there was Anastasia's dark wavy hair above it. "Why, it's a woman after all," the dealer said. "No, it isn't; of course, how could it be with a brown velvet coat and waistcoat? It's a young man with curly hair."

Westray said nothing; he was too much excited, too much interested to say a word, for two eyes were peering at him through the mist. Then the mist lifted under the dealer's cloth, and the eyes gleamed with a startling brightness. They were light-grey eyes, clear and piercing, that transfixed him and read the very thoughts that he was thinking. Anastasia had vanished. It was Lord Blandamer that looked at him out of the picture.

They were Lord Blandamer's eyes, impenetrable and observant as today, but with the brightness of youth still in them; and the face, untarnished by middle age, showed that the picture had been painted some years ago. Westray put his elbows on the table and his head be-tween his hands, while he gazed at the face which had thus come back to life. The eyes pursued him, he could not escape from them, he could scarcely spare a glance even for the nebuly coat that was blazoned in the corner. There were questions revolving in his mind for which he found as yet no answer. There was some mystery to which this portrait might be the clue. He was on the eve of some terrible explanation; he remembered all kinds of incidents that seemed connected with this picture, and yet could find no thread on which to string them.

Of course, this head must have been painted when Lord Blan-damer was young, but how could Sophia Flannery have ever seen it? The picture had only been the flowers and the table-top and caterpil-lar all through Miss Euphemia's memory, and that covered sixty years. But Lord Blandamer was not more than forty; and as Westray looked at the face he found little differences for which no change from youth to middle age could altogether account. Then he guessed that this was not the Lord Blandamer whom he knew, but an older one—that octogenarian who had died three years ago, that Horatio Sebastian Fynes, gentleman, who had married Sophia Flannery.

"It ain't a real first-rater," the dealer said, "but it ain't bad. I shouldn't be surprised if 'twas a Lawrence, and, anyway, it's a sight better than the flowers. Beats me to know how anyone ever came to paint such stuff as them on top of this respectable young man."

Westray was back in Cullerne the next evening. In the press of many thoughts he had forgotten to tell his landlady that he was com-ing, and he stood charing while a maid-of-all-work tried to light the recalcitrant fire. The sticks were few and damp, the newspaper below them was damp, and the damp coal weighed heavily down on top of all, till the thick yellow smoke shied at the chimney, and came curling out under the worsted fringe of the mantelpiece into the chilly room. Westray took this discomfort the more impatiently, in that it was due to his own forgetfulness in having sent no word of his return.

"Why in the world isn't the fire lit?" he said sharply. "You must have known I couldn't sit without a fire on a cold evening like this;" and the wind sang dismally in the joints of the windows to emphasise the dreariness of the situation.

"It ain't nothing to do with me," answered the red-armed, coal-besmeared hoyden, looking up from her knees; "it's the missus. 'He was put out with the coal bill last time,' she says, 'and I ain't going to risk lighting up his fire with coal at sixpence a scuttle, and me not knowing whether he's coming back tonight.'"

"Well, you might see at any rate that the fire was properly laid," the architect said, as the lighting process gave evident indications of failing for the third time.

"I do my best," she said in a larmoyant tone, "but I can't do everything, what with having to cook, and clean, and run up and down stairs with notes, and answer the bell every other minute to lords."

"Has Lord Blandamer been here?" asked Westray.

"Yes, he came yesterday and twice today to see you," she said, "and then he left a note. There 'tis"—and she pointed to the end of the mantelpiece.

Westray looked round, and saw an envelope edged in black. He knew the strong, bold hand of the superscription well enough, and in his present mood it sent something like a thrill of horror through him.

"You needn't wait," he said quickly to the servant; "it isn't your fault at all about the fire. I'm sure it's going to burn now."

The girl rose quickly to her feet, gave an astonished glance at the grate, which was once more enveloped in impotent blackness, and left the room.

An hour later, when the light outside was failing, Westray sat in the cold and darkening room. On the table lay open before him Lord Blandamer's letter:

Dear Mr Westray,

I called to see you yesterday, but was unfortunate in finding you absent from home, and so write these lines. There used to hang in your sitting-room at Bellevue Lodge an old picture of flowers which has some interest for my wife. Her affection for it is based on early associations, and not, of course, on any merits of the painting itself. I thought that it belonged to Miss Joliffe, but I find on inquiry from her that she sold it to you some little time ago, and that it is with you now. I do not suppose that you can attach any great value to it, and, indeed, I suspect that you bought it of Miss Joliffe as an act of charity. If this is so, I should be obliged if you would let me know if you are disposed to part with it again, as my wife would like to have it here.

I am sorry to hear of fresh movement in the tower. It would be a bitter thought to me, if the peal that welcomed us back were found to have caused damage to the structure, but I am sure you will know that no expense should be spared to make all really secure as soon as possible.

Very faithfully yours,

Blandamer.

Westray was eager, impressionable, still subject to all the exaltations and depressions of youth. Thoughts crowded into his mind with bewildering rapidity; they trod so close upon each other's heels that there was no time to marshal them in order; excitement had dizzied him. Was he called to be the minister of justice? Was he chosen for the scourge of God? Was his the hand that must launch the bolt against the guilty? Discovery had come directly to him. What a piece of circumstantial evidence were these very lines that lay open on the table, dim and illegible in the darkness that filled the room! Yet clear and damning to one who had the clue.

This man that ruled at Fording was a pretender, enjoying goods that belonged to others, a shameless evil-doer, who had not stuck at marrying innocent Anastasia Joliffe, if by so stooping he might cover up the traces of his imposture. There was no Lord Blandamer, there was no title; with a breath he could sweep it all away like a house of cards. And was that all? Was there nothing else?

Night had fallen. Westray sat alone in the dark, his elbows on the table, his head still between his hands. There was no fire, there was no light, only the faint shimmer of a far-off street lamp brought a perception of the darkness. It was that pale uncertain luminosity that recalled to his mind another night, when the misty moon shone through the clerestory windows of Saint Sepulchre's. He seemed once more to be making his way up the ghostly nave, on past the pillars that stood like gigantic figures in white winding-sheets, on under the great tower arches. Once more he was groping in the utter darkness of the newel stair, once more he came out into the organ-loft, and saw the baleful silver and sea-green of the nebuly coat gleaming in the transept window. And in the corners of the room lurked presences of evil, and a thin pale shadow of Sharnall wrung its hands, and cried to be saved from the man with the hammer. Then the horrible suspicion that had haunted him these last days stared out of the darkness as a fact, and he sprung to his feet in a shiver of cold and lit a candle.

An hour, two hours, three hours passed before he had written an answer to the letter that lay before him, and in the interval a fresh vicissitude of mind had befallen him. He, Westray, had been singled out as the instrument of vengeance; the clue was in his hands; his was the mouth that must condemn. Yet he would do nothing underhand, he would take no man unawares; he would tell Lord Blandamer of his discovery, and give him warning before he took any further steps. So he wrote:

"My lord," and of the many sheets that were begun and flung away before the letter was finished, two were spoiled because the familiar address "Dear Lord Blandamer" came as it were automatically from Westray's pen. He could no longer bring himself to use those words now, even as a formality, and so he began:

My Lord,

I have just received your note about the picture bought by me of Miss Joliffe. I cannot say whether I should have been willing to part with it under ordinary circumstances. It had no apparent intrinsic value, but for me it was associated with my friend the late Mr Sharnall, organist of Saint Sepulchre's. We shared in its purchase, and it was only on his death that I came into sole possession of it. You will not have forgotten the strange circumstances of his end, and I have not forgotten them either. My friend Mr Sharnall was well-known among his acquaintances to be much interested in this picture. He believed it to be of more importance than appeared, and he expressed himself strongly to that effect in my presence, and once also, I remember, in yours.

But for his untimely death I think he would have long ago made the discovery to which chance has now led me. The flowers prove to be a mere surface painting which concealed what is undoubtedly a portrait of the late Lord Blandamer, and at the back of the canvas were found copies of certain entries in parish registers relating to him. I most earnestly wish that I could end here by making over these things to you, but they seem to me to throw so strange a light on certain past events that I must hold myself responsible for them, and can give them up to no private person. At the same time, I do not feel justified in refusing to let you see picture and papers, if you should wish to do so, and to judge yourself of their importance. I am at the above address, and shall be ready to make an appointment at any time before Monday next, after which date I shall feel compelled to take further steps in this matter.

Westray's letter reached Lord Blandamer the next morning. It lay at the bottom of a little heap of correspondence on the breakfast-table, like the last evil lot to leap out of the shaken urn, an Ephedrus, like that Adulterer who at the finish tripped the Conqueror of Troy. He read it at a glance, catching its import rather by intuition than by any slavish following of the written characters. If earth was darkness at the core, and dust and ashes all that is, there was no trace of it in his face. He talked gaily, he fulfilled the duties of a host with all his charm of manner, he sped two guests who were leaving that morning with all his usual courtesy. After that he ordered his horse, and telling Lady Blandamer that he might not be back to lunch, he set out for one of those slow solitary rides on the estate that often seemed congenial to his mood. He rode along by narrow lanes and bridle-paths, not forgetting a kindly greeting to men who touched their hats, or women who dropped a curtsey, but all the while he thought.

The letter had sent his memory back to another black day, more than twenty years before, when he had quarrelled with his grandfather. It was in his second year at Oxford, when as an undergraduate he first felt it his duty to set the whole world in order. He held strong views as to the mismanagement of the Fording estates; and as a scholar and man of the world, had thought it weakness to shirk the expression of them. The timber was being neglected, there was no thinning and no planting. The old-fashioned farmhouses were being let fall into disrepair, and then replaced by parsimonious eaveless buildings; the very grazing in the park was let, and fallow-deer and red-deer were jostled by sheep and common mongrel cows. The question of the cows had galled him till he was driven to remonstrate strongly with his grandfather. There had never been much love lost between the pair, and on this occasion the young man found the old man strangely out of sympathy with suggestions of reform.

"Thank you," old Lord Blandamer had said; "I have heard all you have to say. You have eased your mind, and now you can go back to Oxford in peace. I have managed Fording for forty years, and feel myself perfectly competent to manage it for forty years more. I don't quite see what concern you have in the matter. What business is it of yours?"

"You don't see what concern I have in it," said the reformer impetuously; "you don't know what business it is of mine? Why, damage is being done here that will take a lifetime to repair."

A man must be on good terms with his heir not to dislike the idea of making way for him, and the old lord flew into one of those paroxysms of rage which fell upon him more frequently in his later years.

"Now, look you," he said; "you need not trouble yourself any more about Fording, nor think you will be so great a sufferer by my mismanagement. It is by no means certain that I shall ever burden you with the place at all."

Then the young man was angry in his turn. "Don't threaten me, sir," he said sharply; "I am not a boy any longer to be cowed by rough words, so keep your threats for others. You would disgrace the family and disgrace yourself, if you left the property away from the title."

"Make your mind easy," said the other; "the property shall follow the title. Get away, and let me hear no more, or you may find both left away from you."

The words were lightly spoken, perhaps in mere petulance at being taken to task by a boy, perhaps in the exasperating pangs of gout; but they had a bitter sound, and sank deep into the heart of youth. The threat of the other possible heirs was new, and yet was not new to him. It seemed as if he had heard something of this before, though he could not remember where; it seemed as if there had always been some ill-defined, intangible suspicion in the air of Fording to make him doubt, since he came to thinking years, whether the title ever really would be his.

Lord Blandamer remembered these things well, as he walked his horse through the beech-leaves with Westray's letter in his breast-pocket. He remembered how his grandfather's words had sent him about with a sad face, and how his grandmother had guessed the reason. He wondered how she had guessed it; but she too, perhaps, had heard these threats before, and so came at the cause more easily. Yet when she had forced his confidence she had little comfort to give.

He could see her now, a stately woman with cold blue eyes, still handsome, though she was near sixty.

"Since we are speaking of this matter," she said with chilling composure, "let us speak openly. I will tell you everything I know, which is nothing. Your grandfather threatened me once, many years ago, as he has threatened you now, and we have never forgotten nor forgiven." She moved herself in her chair, and there came a little flush of red to her cheek. "It was about the time of your father's birth; we had quarrelled before, but this was our first serious quarrel, and the last. Your father was different from me, you know, and from you; he never quarrelled, and he never knew this story. So far as I was concerned I took the responsibility of silence, and it was wisest so." She looked sterner than ever as she went on. "I have never heard or discovered anything more. I am not afraid of your grandfather's intentions. He has a regard for the name, and he means to leave all to you, who have every right, unless, indeed, it may be, a legal right. There is one more thing about which I was anxious long ago. You have heard about a portrait of your grandfather that was stolen from the gallery soon after your father's birth? Suspicion fell upon no one in particular.

"Of course, the stable door was locked after the horse was gone, and we had a nightwatchman at Fording for some time; but little stir was made, and I do not believe your grandfather ever put the matter in the hands of the police. It was a spiteful trick, he said; he would not pay whoever had done it the compliment of taking any trouble to recover the portrait. The picture was of himself; he could have another painted any day.

"By whatever means that picture was removed, I have little doubt that your grandfather guessed what had become of it. Does it still exist? Was it stolen? Or did he have it taken away to prevent its being stolen? We must remember that, though we are quite in the dark about these people, there is nothing to prevent their being shown over the house like any other strangers." Then she drew herself up, and folded her hands in her lap, and he saw the great rings flashing on her white fingers. "That is all I know," she finished, "and now let us agree not to mention the subject again, unless one of us should discover anything more. The claim may have lapsed, or may have been compounded, or may never have existed; I think, anyhow, we may feel sure now that no move will be made in your grandfather's lifetime. My advice to you is not to quarrel with him; you had better spend your long vacations away from Fording, and when you leave Oxford you can travel."

So the young man went out from Fording, for a wandering that was to prove half as long as that of Israel in the wilderness. He came home for a flying visit at wide intervals, but he kept up a steady correspondence with his grandmother as long as she lived. Only once, and that in the last letter which he ever received from her, did she allude to the old distasteful discussion. "Up to this very day," she wrote, "I have found out nothing; we may still hope that there is nothing to find out."

In all those long years he consoled himself by the thought that he was bearing expatriation for the honour of the family, that he was absenting himself so that his grandfather might find the less temptation to drag the nebuly coat in the mire. To make a fetish of family was a tradition with Blandamers, and the heir as he set out on his travels, with the romance of early youth about him, dedicated himself to the nebuly coat, with a vow to "serve and preserve" as faithfully as any ever taken by Templar.

Last of all the old lord passed away. He never carried out his threat of disinheritance, but died intestate, and thus the grandson came to his own. The new Lord Blandamer was no longer young when he returned; years of wild travel had hardened his face, and made his heart self-reliant, but he came back as romantic as he went away. For Nature, if she once endows man or woman with romance, gives them so rich a store of it as shall last them, life through, unto the end. In sickness or health, in poverty or riches, through middle age and old age, through loss of hair and loss of teeth, under wrinkled face and gouty limbs, under crow's-feet and double chins, under all the least romantic and most sordid malaisances of life, romance endures to the end. Its price is altogether above rubies; it can never be taken away from those that have it, and those that have it not, can never acquire it for money, nor by the most utter toil—no, nor ever arrive at the very faintest comprehension of it.

The new lord had come back to Fording full of splendid purpose. He was tired of wandering; he would marry; he would settle down and enjoy his own; he would seek the good of the people, and make his great estates an example among landowners. And then within three weeks he had learned that there was a pretender to the throne, that in Cullerne there was a visionary who claimed to be the very Lord Blandamer. He had had this wretched man pointed out to him once in the street—a broken-down fellow who was trailing the cognisance of all the Blandamers in the mud, till the very boys called him Old Nebuly. Was he to fight for land, and house, and title, to fight for everything, with a man like that? And yet it might come to fighting, for within a little time he knew that this was the heir who had been the intangible shadow of his grandmother's life and of his own; and that Martin might stumble any day upon the proof that was lacking. And then death set a term to Martin's hopes, and Lord Blandamer was free again.

But not for long, for in a little while he heard of an old organist who had taken up Martin's role—a meddlesome busybody who fished in troubled waters, for the trouble's sake. What had such a mean man as this to do with lands, and titles, and coats of arms? And yet this man was talking under his breath in Cullerne of crimes, and clues, and retribution near at hand. And then death put a term to Sharnall's talk, and Lord Blandamer was free again.

Free for a longer space, free this time finally for ever; and he married, and marriage set the seal on his security, and the heir was born, and the nebuly coat was safe. But now a new confuter had risen to balk him. Was he fighting with dragon's spawn? Were fresh enemies to spring up from the—The simile did not suit his mood, and he truncated it. Was this young architect, whose very food and wages in Cullerne were being paid for by the money that he, Lord Blandamer, saw fit to spend upon the church, indeed to be the avenger? Was his own creature to turn and rend him? He smiled at the very irony of the thing, and then he brushed aside reflections on the past, and stifled even the beginnings of regret, if, indeed, any existed. He would look at the present, he would understand exactly how matters stood.

Lord Blandamer came back to Fording at nightfall, and spent the hour before dinner in his library. He wrote some business letters which could not be postponed, but after dinner read aloud to his wife. He had a pleasant and well-trained voice, and amused Lady Blandamer by reading from the *Ingoldsby Legends*, a new series of which had recently appeared.

Whilst he read Anastasia worked at some hangings, which had been left unfinished by the last Lady Blandamer. The old lord's wife had gone out very little, but passed her time for the most part with her gardens, and with curious needlework. For years she had been copying some moth-eaten fragments of Stuart tapestry, and at her death left the work still uncompleted. The housekeeper had shown these half-finished things and explained what they were, and Anastasia had asked Lord Blandamer whether it would be agreeable to him that she should go on with them. The idea pleased him, and so she plodded away evening by evening, very carefully and slowly, thinking often of the lonely old lady whose hands had last been busied with the same task. This grandmother of her husband seemed to have been the only relation with whom he had ever been on intimate terms, and Anastasia's interest was quickened by an excellent portrait of her as a young girl by Lawrence, which hung in the long gallery.

Could the old lady have revisited for once the scene of her labours, she would have had no reason to be dissatisfied with her successor. Anastasia looked distinguished enough as she sat at her work-frame, with the skeins of coloured silks in her lap and the dark-brown hair waved on her high forehead; and a dress of a rich yellow velvet might have supported the illusion that a portrait of some bygone lady of the Blandamers had stepped down out of its frame.

That evening her instinct told her that something was amiss, in spite of all her husband's self-command. Something very annoying must have happened among the grooms, gardeners, gamekeepers, or other dependents; he had been riding about to set the matter straight, and it was no doubt of a nature that he did not care to mention to her.

Chapter Twenty Two

Westray passed a day of painful restlessness. He had laid his hand to a repugnant business, and the burden of it was too heavy for him to bear. He felt the same gnawing anxiety, that is experienced by one whom doctors have sentenced to a lethal operation. One man may bear himself more bravely in such circumstances than another, but by nature every man is a coward; and the knowledge that the hour is approaching, when the surgeon's knife shall introduce him to a final struggle of life and death cannot be done away. So it was with Westray; he had undertaken a task for which he was not strong enough, and only high principle, and a sense of moral responsibility, kept him from panic and flight. He went to the church in the morning, and endeavoured to concentrate attention on his work, but the consciousness of what was before him would not be thrust aside. The foreman-mason saw that his master's thoughts were wandering, and noticed the drawn expression on his face.

In the afternoon his restlessness increased, and he wandered listlessly through the streets and narrow entries of the town, till he found himself near nightfall at that place by the banks of the Cull, where the organist had halted on the last evening of his life. He stood leaning over the iron railing, and looked at the soiled river, just as Mr Sharnall had looked. There were the dark-green tresses of duck-weed swaying to and fro in the shallow eddies, there was the sordid collection of broken and worthless objects that lay on the bottom, and he stared at them till the darkness covered them one by one, and only the whiteness of a broken dish still flickered under the water.

Then he crept back to his room as if he were a felon, and though he went early to bed, sleep refused to visit him till the day began to break. With daylight he fell into a troubled doze, and dreamt that he was in a witness-box before a crowded court. In the dock stood Lord

Blandamer dressed in full peer's robes, and with a coronet on his head. The eyes of all were turned upon him, Westray, with fierce enmity and contempt, and it was he, Westray, that a stern-faced judge was sentencing, as a traducer and lying informer. Then the people in the galleries stamped with their feet and howled against him in their rage; and waking with a start, he knew that it was the postman's sharp knock on the street-door, that had broken his slumber.

The letter which he dreaded lay on the table when he came down. He felt an intense reluctance in opening it. He almost wondered that the handwriting was still the same; it was as if he had expected that the characters should be tremulous, or the ink itself blood-red. Lord Blandamer acknowledged Mr Westray's letter with thanks. He should certainly like to see the picture and the family papers of which Mr Westray spoke; would Mr Westray do him the favour of bringing the picture to Fording? He apologised for putting him to so much trouble, but there was another picture in the gallery at Fording, with which it might be interesting to compare the one recently discovered. He would send a carriage to meet any train; Mr Westray would no doubt find it more convenient to spend the night at Fording.

There was no expression of surprise, curiosity, indignation or alarm; nothing, in fact, except the utmost courtesy, a little more distant perhaps than usual, but not markedly so.

Westray had been unable to conjecture what would be the nature of Lord Blandamer's answer. He had thought of many possibilities, of the impostor's flight, of lavish offers of hush-money, of passionate appeals for mercy, of scornful and indignant denial. But in all his imaginings he had never imagined this. Ever since he had sent his own letter, he had been doubtful of its wisdom, and yet he had not been able to think of any other course that he would have preferred. He knew that the step he had taken in warning the criminal was quixotic, and yet it seemed to him that Lord Blandamer had a certain right to see his own family portrait and papers, before they were used against him. He could not feel sorry that he had given the opportunity, though he had certainly hoped that Lord Blandamer would not avail himself of it.

But go to Fording he would not. That, at any rate, no fantastic refinement of fair play could demand of him. He knew his mind at least on this point; he would answer at once, and he got out a sheet of paper for his refusal. It was easy to write the number of his house, and the street, and Cullerne, and the formal "My lord," which he used again for the address. But what then? What reason was he to give for his refusal? He could allege no business appointment or other serious engagement as an obstacle, for he himself had said that he was free for a week, and had offered Lord Blandamer to make an appointment on any day. He himself had offered an interview; to draw back now would be mean and paltry in the extreme. It was true that the more he thought of this meeting the more he shrank from it. But it could not be evaded now. It was, after all, only the easiest part of the task that he had set before him, only a prolusion to the tragedy that he would have to play to a finish. Lord Blandamer deserved, no doubt, all the evil that was to fall on him; but in the meanwhile he, Westray, was incapable of refusing this small favour, asked by a man who was entirely at his mercy.

Then he wrote with a shrinking heart, but with yet another fixed purpose, that he would bring the picture to Fording the next day. He preferred not to be met at the station; he would arrive some time during the afternoon, but could only stay an hour at the most, as he had business which would take him on to London the same evening.

It was a fine Autumn day on the morrow, and when the morning mists had cleared away, the sun came out with surprising warmth, and dried the dew on the lawns of many-gardened Cullerne. Towards mid-day Westray set forth from his lodgings to go to the station, carrying under his arm the picture, lightly packed in lath, and having in his pocket those papers which had fallen out from the frame. He chose a route through back-streets, and walked quickly, but as he passed Quandrill's, the local maker of guns and fishing-rods, a thought struck him. He stopped and entered the shop.

"Good-morning," he said to the gunsmith, who stood behind the counter; "have you any pistols? I want one small enough to carry in the pocket, but yet something more powerful than a toy."

Mr Quandrill took off his spectacles.

"Ah," he said, tapping the counter with them meditatively. "Let me see. Mr Westray, is it not, the architect at the minster?"

"Yes," Westray answered. "I require a pistol for some experiments. It should carry a fairly heavy bullet."

"Oh, just so," the man said, with an air of some relief, as Westray's coolness convinced him that he was not contemplating suicide. "Just so, I see; some experiments. Well, in that case, I suppose, you would not require any special facilities for loading again quickly, otherwise I should have recommended one of these," and he took up a weapon from the counter. "They are new-fangled things from America, revolving pistols they call them. You can fire them four times running, you see, as quick as you like," and he snapped the piece to show how well it worked.

Westray handled the pistol, and looked at the barrels.

"Yes," he said, "that will suit my purpose very well, though it is rather large to carry in the pocket."

"Oh, you want it for the pocket," the gunmaker said with renewed surprise in his tone.

"Yes; I told you that already. I may have to carry it about with me. Still, I think this will do. Could you kindly load it for me now?"

"You are sure it's quite safe," said the gunmaker.

"I ought to ask *you* that," Westray rejoined with a smile. "Do you mean it may go off accidentally in my pocket?"

"Oh no, it's safe enough that way," said the gunmaker. "It won't go off unless you pull the trigger." And he loaded the four barrels, measuring out the powder and shot carefully, and ramming in the wads. "You'll be wanting more powder and shot than this, I suppose," he said.

"Very likely," rejoined the architect, "but I can call for that later."

He found a heavy country fly waiting for him at Lytchett, the little wayside station which was sometimes used by people going to Fording. It is a seven-mile drive from the station to the house, but he was so occupied in his own reflections, that he was conscious of nothing till the carriage pulled up at the entrance of the park. Here he stopped for a moment while the lodge-keeper was unfastening the bolt, and remembered afterwards that he had noticed the elaborate iron-work, and the nebuly coat which was set over the great gates. He was in the long avenue now, and he wished it had been longer, he wished that it might never end; and then the fly stopped again, and Lord Blandamer on horseback was speaking to him through the carriage window.

There was a second's pause, while the two men looked each other directly in the eyes, and in that look all doubt on either side was ended. Westray felt as if he had received a staggering blow as he came face to face with naked truth, and Lord Blandamer read Westray's thoughts, and knew the extent of his discovery.

Lord Blandamer was the first to speak.

"I am glad to see you again," he said with perfect courtesy, "and am very much obliged to you for taking this trouble in bringing the picture." And he glanced at the crate that Westray was steadying with his hand on the opposite seat. "I only regret that you would not let me send a carriage to Lytchett."

"Thank you," said the architect; "on the present occasion I preferred to be entirely independent." His words were cold, and were meant to be cold, and yet as he looked at the other's gentle bearing, and the grave face in which sadness was a charm; he felt constrained to abate in part the effect of his own remark, and added somewhat awkwardly: "You see, I was uncertain about the trains."

"I am riding back across the grass," Lord Blandamer said, "but shall be at the house before you;" and as he galloped off, Westray knew that he rode exceedingly well.

This meeting, he guessed, had been contrived to avoid the embarrassment of a more formal beginning. It was obvious that their terms of former friendship could no longer be maintained. Nothing would have induced him to have shaken hands, and this Lord Blandamer must have known.

As Westray stepped into the hall through Inigo Jones' Ionic portico, Lord Blandamer entered from a side-door.

"You must be cold after your long drive. Will you not take a biscuit and a glass of wine?"

Westray motioned away the refreshment which a footman offered him.

"No, thank you," he said; "I will not take anything." It was impossible for him to eat or drink in this house, and yet again he softened his words by adding: "I had something to eat on the way."

The architect's refusal was not lost upon Lord Blandamer. He had known before he spoke that his offer would not be accepted.

"I am afraid it is useless to ask you to stop the night with us," he said; and Westray had his rejoinder ready:

"No; I must leave Lytchett by the seven five train. I have ordered the fly to wait."

He had named the last train available for London, and Lord Blandamer saw that his visitor had so arranged matters, that the interview could not be prolonged for more than an hour.

"Of course, you *could* catch the night-mail at Cullerne Road," he said. "It is a very long drive, but I sometimes go that way to London myself."

His words called suddenly to Westray's recollection that night walk when the station lights of Cullerne Road were seen dimly through the fog, and the station-master's story that Lord Blandamer had travelled by the mail on the night of poor Sharnall's death. He said noth-

536

ing, but felt his resolution strengthened.

"The gallery will be the most convenient place, perhaps, to un-pack the picture," Lord Blandamer said; and Westray at once assented, gathering from the other's manner that this would be a spot where no interruption need be feared.

They went up some wide and shallow stairs, preceded by a foot-man, who carried the picture.

"You need not wait," Lord Blandamer said to the man; "we can unpack it ourselves."

When the wrappings were taken off, they stood the painting on the narrow shelf formed by the top of the wainscot which lined the gallery, and from the canvas the old lord surveyed them with penetrat-ing light-grey eyes, exactly like the eyes of the grandson who stood before him.

Lord Blandamer stepped back a little, and took a long look at the face of this man, who had been the terror of his childhood, who had darkened his middle life, who seemed now to have returned from the grave to ruin him. He knew himself to be in a desperate pass. Here he must make the last stand, for the issue lay between him and Westray. No one else had learned the secret. He understood and relied implic-itly on Westray's fantastic sense of honour. Westray had written that he would "take no steps" till the ensuing Monday, and Lord Blandamer was sure that no one would be told before that day, and that no one had been told yet. If Westray could be silenced all was saved; if Westray spoke, all was lost. If it had been a question of weapons, or of bodily strength, there was no doubt which way the struggle would have end-ed. Westray knew this well now, and felt heartily ashamed of the pistol that was bulging the breast-pocket on the inside of his coat. If it had been a question of physical attack, he knew now that he would have never been given time, or opportunity for making use of his weapon.

Lord Blandamer had travelled north and south, east and west; he had seen and done strange things; he had stood for his life in struggles whence only one could come out alive; but here was no question of flesh and blood—he had to face principles, those very principles on which he relied for respite; he had to face that integrity of Westray which made persuasion or bribery alike impossible. He had never seen this picture before, and he looked at it intently for some minutes; but his attention was all the while concentrated on the man who stood beside him. This was his last chance—he could afford to make no mistake; and his soul, or whatever that thing may be called which is certainly not the body, was closing with Westray's soul in a desperate struggle for mastery.

Westray was not seeing the picture for the first time, and after one glance he stood aloof. The interview was becoming even more painful than he had expected. He avoided looking Lord Blandamer in the face, yet presently, at a slight movement, turned and met his eye.

"Yes, it is my grandfather," said the other.

There was nothing in the words, and yet it seemed to Westray as if some terrible confidence was being thrust upon him against his will; as if Lord Blandamer had abandoned any attempt to mislead, and was tacitly avowing all that might be charged against him. The architect began to feel that he was now regarded as a personal enemy, though he had never so considered himself. It was true that picture and papers had fallen into his hands, but he knew that a sense of duty was the only motive of any action that he might be taking.

"You promised, I think, to show me some papers," Lord Blandamer said.

Most painfully Westray handed them over; his knowledge of their contents made it seem that he was offering a deliberate insult. He wished fervently that he never had made any proposal for this meeting; he ought to have given everything to the proper authorities, and have let the blow fall as it would. Such an interview could only end in bitterness: its present result was that here in Lord Blandamer's own house, he, Westray, was presenting him with proofs of his father's illegitimacy, with proofs that he had no right to this house—no, nor to anything else.

It was a bitter moment for Lord Blandamer to find such information in the possession of a younger man; but, if there was more colour in his face than usual, his self-command stood the test, and he thrust resentment aside. There was no time to say or do useless things, there was no time for feeling; all his attention must be concentrated on the man before him. He stood still, seeming to examine the papers closely, and, as a matter of fact, he did take note of the name, the place, and the date, that so many careful searchings had failed ever to find. But all the while he was resolutely considering the next move, and giving Westray time to think and feel. When he looked up, their eyes met again, and this time it was Westray that coloured.

"I suppose you have verified these certificates?" Lord Blandamer asked very quietly.

"Yes," Westray said, and Lord Blandamer gave them back to him without a word, and walked slowly away down the gallery.

Westray crushed the papers into his pocket where most of the room was taken up by the pistol; he was glad to get them out of his sight; he could not bear to hold them. It was as if a beaten fighter had given up his sword. With these papers Lord Blandamer seemed to resign into his adversary's hands everything of which he stood possessed, his lands, his life, the honour of his house. He made no defence, no denial, no resistance, least of all any appeal. Westray was left master of the situation, and must do whatever he thought fit. This fact was clearer to him now than it had ever been before, the secret was his alone; with him rested the responsibility of making it public. He stood dumb before the picture, from which the old lord looked at him with penetrating eyes. He had nothing to say; he could not go after Lord Blandamer; he wondered whether this was indeed to be the end of the interview, and turned sick at the thought of the next step that must be taken.

At the distance of a few yards Lord Blandamer paused, and looked round, and Westray understood that he was being invited, or commanded, to follow. They stopped opposite the portrait of a lady, but it was the frame to which Lord Blandamer called attention by laying his hand on it.

"This was my grandmother," he said; "they were companion pictures. They are the same size, the moulding on the frame is the same, an interlacing fillet, and the coat of arms is in the same place. You see?" he added, finding Westray still silent.

Westray was obliged to meet his look once more.

"I see," he said, most reluctantly. He knew now, that the unusual moulding and the size of the picture that hung in Miss Joliffe's house, must have revealed its identity long ago to the man who stood before him; that during all those visits in which plans for the church had been examined and discussed, Lord Blandamer must have known what lay hid under the flowers, must have known that the green wriggling caterpillar was but a bar of the nebuly coat. Confidences were being forced upon Westray that he could not forget, and could not reveal. He longed to cry out, "For God's sake, do not tell me these things; do not give me this evidence against yourself!"

There was another short pause, and then Lord Blandamer turned. He seemed to expect Westray to turn with him, and they walked back over the soft carpet down the gallery in a silence that might be heard. The air was thick with doom; Westray felt as if he were stifling. He had lost mental control, his thoughts were swallowed up in a terrible chaos. Only one reflection stood out, the sense of undivided responsibility. It was not as if he were adding a link, as in duty bound, to a long chain of other evidence: the whole matter was at rest; to set it in motion again would be his sole act, his act alone. There was a refrain ringing in his ears, a verse that he had heard read a few Sundays before in Cullerne Church, "Am I God, to kill and make alive? Am I God, to kill and make alive?" Yet duty commanded him to go forward, and go forward he must, though the result was certain: he would be playing the part of executioner.

The man whose fate he must seal was keeping pace with him quietly, step by step. If he could only have a few moments to himself, he might clear his distracted thoughts. He paused before some other picture, feigning to examine it, but Lord Blandamer paused also, and looked at him. He knew Lord Blandamer's eye was upon him, though he refused to return the look. It seemed a mere act of courtesy on Lord Blandamer's part to stop. Mr Westray might be specially interested in some of the pictures, and, if any information was required, it was the part of the host to see that it was forthcoming. Westray stopped again once or twice, but always with the same result. He did not know whether he was looking at portraits or landscapes, though he was vaguely aware that half-way down the gallery, there stood on the floor what seemed to be an unfinished picture, with its face turned to the wall.

Except when Westray stopped, Lord Blandamer looked neither to the right nor to the left; he walked with his hands folded lightly behind him, and with his eyes upon the ground, yet did not feign to have his thoughts disengaged. His companion shrank from any attempt to understand or fathom what those thoughts could be, but admired, against his will, the contained and resolute bearing. Westray felt as a child beside a giant, yet had no doubt as to his own duty, or that he was going to do it. But how hard it was! Why had he been so foolish as to meddle with the picture? Why had he read papers that did not belong to him? Why, above all, had he come down to Fording to have his suspicions confirmed? What business was it of his to ferret out these things? He felt all the unutterable aversion of an upright mind for playing the part of a detective; all the sovereign contempt even for such petty meanness as allows one person to examine the handwriting or postmark of letters addressed to another. Yet he knew this thing, and he alone; he could not do away with this horrible knowledge.

The end of the gallery was reached; they turned with one accord and paced slowly, silently back, and the time was slipping away fast. It was impossible for Westray to consider anything *now*, but he had taken his decision before he came to Fording; he must go through with it; there was no escape for *him* any more than for Lord Blandamer. He would keep his word. On Monday, the day he had mentioned, he would speak, and once begun, the matter would pass out of his hands. But how was he to tell this to the man who was walking beside him, and silently waiting for his sentence? He could not leave him in suspense; to do so would be cowardice and cruelty. He must make his intention clear, but how? in what form of words? There was no time to think; already they were repassing that canvas which stood with its face to the wall.

The suspense, the impenetrable silence, was telling upon Westray; he tried again to rearrange his thoughts, but they were centred only on Lord Blandamer. How calm he seemed, with his hands folded behind him, and never a finger twitching! What did *he* mean to do—to fly, or kill himself, or stand his ground and take his trial on a last chance? It would be a celebrated trial. Hateful and inevitable details occurred to Westray's imagination: the crowded, curious court as he saw it in his dream, with Lord Blandamer in the dock, and this last thought sickened him. His own place would be in the witness-box. Incidents that he wished to forget would be recalled, discussed, dwelt on; he would have to search his memory for them, narrate them, swear to them.

But this was not all. He would have to give an account of this very afternoon's work. It could not be hushed up. Every servant in the house would know how he had come to Fording with a picture. He heard himself cross-examined as to "this very remarkable interview." What account was he to give of it? What a betrayal of confidence it would be to give *any* account. Yet he must, and his evidence would be given under the eyes of Lord Blandamer in the dock. Lord Blandamer would be in the dock watching him. It was unbearable, impossible; rather than this he would fly himself, he would use the pistol that bulged his pocket against his own life.

Lord Blandamer had noted Westray's nervous movements, his glances to right and left, as though seeking some way of escape; he saw the clenched hands, and the look of distress as they paced to and fro. He knew that each pause before a picture was an attempt to shake him off, but he would not be shaken off; Westray was feeling the grip, and must not have a moment's breathing space. He could tell exactly how the minutes were passing, he knew what to listen for, and could catch the distant sound of the stable clock striking the quarters. They were back at the end of the gallery. There was no time to pace it again; Westray must go now if he was to catch his train.

They stopped opposite the old lord's portrait; the silence wrapped Westray round, as the white fog had wrapped him round that night on his way to Cullerne Road. He wanted to speak, but his brain was confused, his throat was dry; he dreaded the sound of his own voice.

Lord Blandamer took out his watch.

"I have no wish to hurry you, Mr Westray," he said, "but your train leaves Lytchett in little over an hour. It will take you nearly that time to drive to the station. May I help you to repack this picture?"

His voice was clear, level, and courteous, as on the day when Westray had first met him at Bellevue Lodge. The silence was broken, and Westray found himself speaking quickly in answer:

"You invited me to stay here for the night. I have changed my mind, and will accept your offer, if I may." He hesitated for a moment, and then went on: "I shall be thankful if you will keep the picture and these documents. I see now that I have no business with them."

He took the crumpled papers from his pocket, and held them out without looking up.

Then silence fell on them again, and Westray's heart stood still; till after a second that seemed an eternity Lord Blandamer took the papers with a short "I thank you," and walked a little way further, to the end of the gallery. The architect leant against the side of a window opposite which he found himself, and, looking out without seeing anything, presently heard Lord Blandamer tell a servant that Mr Westray would stop the night, and that wine was to be brought them in the gallery. In a few minutes the man came back with a decanter on a salver, and Lord Blandamer filled glasses for Westray, and himself. He felt probably that both needed something of the kind, but to the other more was implied. Westray remembered that an hour ago he had refused to eat or drink under this roof. An hour ago—how his mood had changed in that short time! How he had flung duty and principle to the winds! Surely this glass of red wine was a very sacrament of the devil, which made him a partner of iniquity.

As he raised the glass to his lips a slanting sunbeam shot through the window, and made the wine glow red as blood. The drinkers paused glass in hand, and glancing up saw the red sun setting behind the trees in the park. Then the old lord's picture caught the evening light, the green bars of the nebuly coat danced before Westray's eyes, till they seemed to live, to be again three wriggling caterpillars, and the penetrating grey eyes looked out from the canvas as if they were watching the enactment of this final scene. Lord Blandamer pledged him in a bumper, and Westray answered without hesitation, for he had given his allegiance, and would have drunk poison in token that there was to be no turning back now.

An engagement kept Lady Blandamer from home that evening. Lord Blandamer had intended to accompany her, but afterwards told her that Mr Westray was coming on important business, and so she went alone. Only Lord Blandamer and Westray sat down to dinner, and some subtle change of manner made the architect conscious that for the first time since their acquaintance, his host was treating him as a real equal. Lord Blandamer maintained a flow of easy and interesting conversation, yet never approached the subject of architecture even near enough to seem to be avoiding it. After dinner he took Westray to the library, where he showed him some old books, and used all his art to entertain him and set him at his ease. Westray was soothed for a moment by the other's manner, and did his best to respond to the courtesy shown him; but everything had lost its savour, and he knew that black Care was only waiting for him to be alone, to make herself once more mistress of his being.

A wind which had risen after sunset began to blow near bedtime with unusual violence. The sudden gusts struck the library windows till they rattled again, and puffs of smoke came out from the fireplace into the room.

"I shall sit up for Lady Blandamer," said the host, "but I dare say you will not be sorry to turn in;" and Westray, looking at his watch, saw that it wanted but ten minutes of midnight.

In the hall, and on the staircase, as they went up, the wind blowing with cold rushes made itself felt still more strongly.

"It is a wild night," Lord Blandamer said, as he stopped for a moment before a barometer, "but I suspect that there is yet worse to come; the glass has fallen in an extraordinary way. I hope you have left all snug with the tower at Cullerne; this wind will not spare any weak places."

"I don't think it should do any mischief at Saint Sepulchre's," Westray answered, half unconsciously. It seemed as though he could not concentrate his thought even upon his work.

His bedroom was large, and chilly in spite of a bright fire. He locked the door, and drawing an easy-chair before the hearth, sat a long while in thought. It was the first time in his life that he had with deliberation acted against his convictions, and there followed the reaction and remorse inseparable from such conditions.

Is there any depression so deep as this? is there any night so dark as this first eclipse of the soul, this *first* conscious stilling of the instinct for right? He had conspired to obscure truth, he had made himself partaker in another man's wrong-doing, and, as the result, he had lost his moral foothold, his self-respect, his self-reliance. It was true that, even if he could, he would not have changed his decision now, yet the weight of a guilty secret, that he must keep all his life long, pressed heavily upon him. Something must be done to lighten this weight; he must take some action that would ease the galling of his thoughts. He was in that broken mood for which the Middle Ages offered the cloister as a remedy; he felt the urgent need of sacrifice and abnegation to purge him. And then he knew the sacrifice that he must make: he must give up his work at Cullerne. He was thankful to find that there was still enough of conscience left to him to tell him this. He could not any longer be occupied on work for which the money was being found by this man. He would give up his post at Cullerne, even if it meant giving up his connection with his employers, even if it meant the giving up of his livelihood.

He felt as if England itself were not large enough to hold him and Lord Blandamer. He must never more see the associate of his guilt; he dreaded meeting his eyes again, lest the other's will should constrain his will to further wrong. He would write to resign his work the very next day; that would be an active sacrifice, a definite mark from which he might begin a painful retracing of the way, a turning-point from which he might hope in time to recover some measure of self-respect and peace of mind. He would resign his work at Cullerne the very next day; and then a wilder gust of wind buffeted the windows of his room, and he thought of the scaffolding on Saint Sepulchre's tower. What a terrible night it was! Would the thin bows of the tower arches live through such a night, with the weight of the great tower rocking over them? No, he could not resign tomorrow. It would be deserting his post. He must stand by till the tower was safe, *that* was his first duty. After that he would give up his post at once.

Later on he went to bed, and in those dark watches of the night, that are not kept by reason, there swept over him thoughts wilder than the wind outside. He had made himself sponsor for Lord Blandamer, he had assumed the burden of the other's crime. It was he that was branded with the mark of Cain, and he must hide it in silence from the eyes of all men. He must fly from Cullerne, and walk alone with his burden for the rest of his life, a scapegoat in the isolation of the wilderness.

In sleep the terror that walketh in darkness brooded heavily on him. He was in the church of Saint Sepulchre, and blood dripped on him from the organ-loft. Then as he looked up to find out whence it came he saw the four tower arches falling to grind him to powder, and leapt up in his bed, and struck a light to make sure that there were no red patches on him. With daylight he grew calmer. The wild visions vanished, but the cold facts remained: he was sunk in his own esteem, he had forced himself into an evil secret which was no concern of his, and now he must keep it for ever.

Westray found Lady Blandamer in the breakfast-room. Lord Blandamer had met her in the hall on her return the night before, and though he was pale, she knew before he had spoken half a dozen words, that the cloud of anxiety which had hung heavily on him for the last few days was past. He told her that Mr Westray had come over on business, and, in view of the storm that was raging, had been persuaded to remain for the night. The architect had brought with him a picture which he had accidentally come across, a portrait of the old Lord Blandamer which had been missing for many years from Fording. It was very satisfactory that it had been recovered; they were under a great obligation to Mr Westray for the trouble which he had taken in the matter.

In the events of the preceding days Westray had almost forgotten Lady Blandamer's existence, and since the discovery of the picture, if her image presented itself to his mind, it had been as that of a deeply wronged and suffering woman. But this morning she appeared with a look of radiant content that amazed him, and made him shudder as he thought how near he had been only a day before to plunging her into the abyss. The more careful nurture of the year that had passed since her marriage, had added softness to her face and figure, without detracting from the refinement of expression that had always marked her. He knew that she was in her own place, and wondered now that the distinction of her manner had not led him sooner to the truth of her birth. She looked pleased to meet him, and shook hands with a frank smile that acknowledged their former relations, without any trace of embarrassment. It seemed incredible that she should ever have brought him up his meals and letters.

She made a polite reference to his having restored to them an interesting family picture, and finding him unexpectedly embarrassed, changed the subject by asking him what he thought of her own portrait.

"I think you must have seen it yesterday," she went on, as he appeared not to understand. "It has only just come home, and is standing on the floor in the long gallery."

Lord Blandamer glanced at the architect, and answered for him that Mr Westray had not seen it. Then he explained with a composure that shed a calm through the room:

"It was turned to the wall. It is a pity to show it unhung, and without a frame. We must get it framed at once, and decide on a position for it. I think we shall have to shift several paintings in the gallery."

He talked of Snyders and Wouverman, and Westray made some show of attention, but could only think of the unframed picture standing on the ground, which had helped to measure the passing of time in the terrible interview of yesterday. He guessed now that Lord Blandamer had himself turned the picture with its face to the wall, and in doing so had deliberately abandoned a weapon that might have served him well in the struggle. Lord Blandamer must have deliberately foregone the aid of recollections such as Anastasia's portrait would have called up in his antagonist's mind. "*Non tali auxilio nec defensoribus istis.*"

Westray's haggard air had not escaped his host's notice. The architect looked as if he had spent the night in a haunted room, and Lord Blandamer was not surprised, knowing that the other's scruples had died hard, and were not likely to lie quiet in their graves. He thought it better that the short time which remained before Westray's departure should be spent out of the house, and proposed a stroll in the grounds. The gardener reported, he said, that last night's gale had done considerable damage to the trees. The top of the cedar on the south lawn had been broken short off. Lady Blandamer begged that she might accompany them, and as they walked down the terrace steps into the garden a nurse brought to her the baby heir.

"The gale must have been a cyclone," Lord Blandamer said. "It has passed away as suddenly as it arose."

The morning was indeed still and sunshiny, and seemed more beautiful by contrast with the turmoil of the previous night. The air was clear and cold after the rain, but paths and lawns were strewn with broken sticks and boughs, and carpeted with prematurely fallen leaves.

Lord Blandamer described the improvements that he was making or projecting, and pointed out the old fishponds which were to be restocked, the bowling-green and the ladies' garden arranged on an old-world plan by his grandmother, and maintained unchanged since her death. He had received an immense service from Westray, and he would not accept it ungraciously or make little of it. In taking the architect round the place, in showing this place that his ancestors had possessed for so many generations, in talking of his plans for a future that had only so recently become assured, he was in a manner conveying his thanks, and Westray knew it.

Lady Blandamer was concerned for Westray. She saw that he was downcast, and ill at ease, and in her happiness that the cloud had passed from her husband, she wanted everyone to be happy with her. So, as they were returning to the house, she began, in the kindness of her heart, to talk of Cullerne Minster. She had a great longing, she said, to see the old church again. She should so much enjoy it if Mr Westray would some day show her over it. Would he take much longer in the restorations?

They were in an alley too narrow for three to walk abreast. Lord Blandamer had fallen behind, but was within earshot.

Westray answered quickly, without knowing what he was going to say. He was not sure about the restorations—that was, they certainly were not finished; in fact, they would take some time longer, but he would not be there, he believed, to superintend them. That was to say, he was giving up his present appointment.

He broke off, and Lady Blandamer knew that she had again selected an unfortunate subject. She dropped it, and hoped he would let them know when he was next at leisure, and come for a longer visit.

"I am afraid it will not be in my power to do so," Westray said; and then, feeling that he had given a curt and ungracious answer to a kindly-meant invitation, turned to her and explained with unmistakable sincerity that he was giving up his connection with Farquhar and Farquhar. This subject also was not to be pursued, so she only said that she was sorry, and her eyes confirmed her words.

Lord Blandamer was pained at what he had heard. He knew Farquhar and Farquhar, and knew something of Westray's position and prospects—that he had a reasonable income, and a promising future with the firm. This resolve must be quite sudden, a result of yesterday's interview. Westray was being driven out into the wilderness like a scapegoat with another man's guilt on his head. The architect was young and inexperienced. Lord Blandamer wished he could talk with him quietly. He understood that Westray might find it impossible to go on with the restoration at Cullerne, where all was being done at Lord Blandamer's expense. But why sever his connection with a leading firm? Why not plead ill-health, nervous breakdown, those doctor's orders which have opened a way of escape from impasses of the mind as well as of the body?

An archaeologic tour in Spain, a yachting cruise in the Mediterranean, a winter in Egypt—all these things would be to Westray's taste; the blameless herb nepenthe might anywhere be found growing by the wayside. He must amuse himself, and forget. He wished he could *assure* Westray that he would forget, or grow used to remembering; that time heals wounds of conscience as surely as it heals heart-wounds and flesh-wounds; that remorse is the least permanent of sentiments. But then Westray might not yet wish to forget. He had run full counter to his principles. It might be that he was resolved to take the consequences, and wear them like a hair-shirt, as the only means of recovering his self-esteem. No; whatever penance, voluntary or involuntary, Westray might undergo, Lord Blandamer could only look on in silence. His object had been gained. If Westray felt it necessary to pay the price, he must be let pay it. Lord Blandamer could neither inquire nor remonstrate. He could offer no compensation, because no compensation would be accepted.

The little party were nearing the house when a servant met them.

"There is a man come over from Cullerne, my lord," he said. "He is anxious to see Mr Westray at once on important business."

"Show him into my sitting-room, and say that Mr Westray will be with him immediately."

Westray met Lord Blandamer in the hall a few minutes later.

"I am sorry to say there is bad news from Cullerne," the architect said hurriedly. "Last night's gale has strained and shaken the tower severely. A very serious movement is taking place. I must get back at once."

"Do, by all means. A carriage is at the door. You can catch the train at Lytchett, and be in Cullerne by mid-day."

The episode was a relief to Lord Blandamer. The architect's attention was evidently absorbed in the tower. It might be that he had already found the blameless herb growing by the wayside.

The nebuly coat shone on the panel of the carriage-door. Lady Blandamer had noticed that her husband had been paying Westray special attention. He was invariably courteous, but he had treated this guest as he treated few others. Yet now, at the last moment, he had fallen silent; he was standing, she fancied, aloof. He held his hands behind him, and the attitude seemed to her to have some significance. But on Lord Blandamer's part it was a mark of consideration. There had been no shaking of hands up to the present; he was anxious not to force Westray to take his hand by offering it before his wife and the servants.

Lady Blandamer felt that there was something going on which she did not understand, but she took leave of Westray with special kindness. She did not directly mention the picture, but said how much they were obliged to him, and glanced for confirmation at Lord Blandamer. He looked at Westray, and said with deliberation:

"I trust Mr Westray knows how fully I appreciate his generosity and courtesy."

There was a moment's pause, and then Westray offered his hand. Lord Blandamer shook it cordially, and their eyes met for the last time.

CHAPTER TWENTY THREE

On the afternoon of the same day Lord Blandamer was himself in Cullerne. He went to the office of Mr Martelet, solicitor by prescriptive right to the family at Fording, and spent an hour closeted with the principal.

The house which the solicitor used for offices, was a derelict residence at the bottom of the town. It still had in front of it an extinguisher for links, and a lamp-bracket over the door of wasted iron scroll-work. It was a dingy place, but Mr Martelet had a famous county connection, and rumour said that more important family business was done here even than in Carisbury itself. Lord Blandamer sat behind the dusty windows.

"I think I quite understand the nature of the codicil," the solicitor said. "I will have a draft forwarded to your lordship tomorrow."

"No, no; it is short enough. Let us finish with it now," said his client. "There is no time like the present. It can be witnessed here. Your head clerk is discreet, is he not?"

"Mr Simpkin has been with me thirty years," the solicitor said deprecatingly, "and I have had no reason to doubt his discretion hitherto."

The sun was low when Lord Blandamer left Mr Martelet's office. He walked down the winding street that led to the market-place, with his long shadow going before him on the pavement. Above the houses in the near distance stood up the great tower of Saint Sepulchre's, pink-red in the sunset rays. What a dying place was Cullerne! How empty were the streets! The streets were certainly strangely empty. He had never seen them so deserted. There was a silence of the grave over all. He took out his watch. The little place is gone to tea, he thought, and walked on with a light heart, and more at his ease than he had ever felt before in his life.

He came round a bend in the street, and suddenly saw a great crowd before him, between him and the market-place over which the minster church watched, and knew that something must be happening, that had drawn the people from the other parts of the town. As he came nearer it seemed as if the whole population was there collected. Conspicuous was pompous Canon Parkyn, and by him stood Mrs Parkyn, and tall and sloping-shouldered Mr Noot. The sleek dissenting minister was there, and the jovial, round-faced Catholic priest. There stood Joliffe, the pork-butcher, in shirt-sleeves and white apron in the middle of the road; and there stood Joliffe's wife and daughters, piled up on the steps of the shop, and craning their necks towards the market-place. The postmaster and his clerk and two letter-carriers had come out from the post-office. All the young ladies and young gentlemen from Rose and Storey's establishment were herded in front of their great glittering shop-window, and among them shone the fair curls of Mr Storey, the junior partner, himself. A little lower down was a group of masons and men employed on the restorations, and near them Clerk Janaway leant on his stick.

Many of these people Lord Blandamer knew well by sight, and there was beside a great throng of common folk, but none took any notice of him.

There was something very strange about the crowd. Everyone was looking towards the market-place, and everyone's face was upturned as if they were watching a flight of birds. The square was empty, and no one attempted to advance further into it; nay, most stood in an alert attitude, as if prepared to run the other way. Yet all remained spellbound, looking up, with their heads turned towards the market-place, over which watched the minster church. There was no shouting, nor laughter, nor chatter; only the agitated murmur of a multitude of people speaking under their breath.

The single person that moved was a waggoner. He was trying to get his team and cart up the street, away from the market-place, but made slow progress, for the crowd was too absorbed to give him room. Lord Blandamer spoke to the man, and asked him what was happening. The waggoner stared for a moment as if dazed; then recognised his questioner, and said quickly:

"Don't go on, my lord! For God's sake, don't go on; the tower's coming down."

Then the spell that bound all the others fell on Lord Blandamer too. His eyes were drawn by an awful attraction to the great tower that watched over the market-place. The buttresses with their broad set-offs, the double belfry windows with their pierced screens and stately Perpendicular tracery, the open battlemented parapet, and clustered groups of soaring pinnacles, shone pink and mellow in the evening sun. They were as fair and wonderful as on that day when Abbot Vinnicomb first looked upon his finished work, and praised God that it was good.

But on this still autumn evening there was something terribly amiss with the tower, in spite of all brave appearances. The jackdaws knew it, and whirled in a mad chattering cloud round their old home, with wings flashing and changing in the low sunlight. And on the west side, the side nearest the market-place, there oozed out from a hundred joints a thin white dust that fell down into the churchyard like the spray of some lofty Swiss cascade. It was the very death-sweat of a giant in his agony, the mortar that was being ground out in powder from the courses of collapsing masonry. To Lord Blandamer it seemed like the sand running through an hour-glass.

Then the crowd gave a groan like a single man. One of the gargoyles at the corner, under the parapet, a demon figure that had jutted grinning over the churchyard for three centuries, broke loose and fell crashing on to the gravestones below. There was silence for a minute, and then the murmurings of the onlookers began again. Everyone spoke in short, breathless sentences, as though they feared the final crash might come before they could finish. Churchwarden Joliffe, with pauses of expectation, muttered about a "judgment in our midst." The rector, in Joliffe's pauses, seemed trying to confute him by some reference to "those thirteen upon whom the tower of Siloam fell and slew them."

An old charwoman whom Miss Joliffe sometimes employed wrung her hands with an "Ah! poor dear—poor dear!" The Catholic priest was reciting something in a low tone, and crossing himself at intervals. Lord Blandamer, who stood near, caught a word or two of the commendatory prayer for the dying, the "*Proficiscere*," and "*liliata rutilantium*," that showed how Abbot Vinnicomb's tower lived in the hearts of those that abode under its shadow.

And all the while the white dust kept pouring out of the side of the wounded fabric; the sands of the hour-glass were running down apace.

The foreman of the masons saw Lord Blandamer, and made his way to him.

"Last night's gale did it, my lord," he said; "we knew 'twas touch and go when we came this morning. Mr Westray's been up the tower since mid-day to see if there was anything that could be done, but twenty minutes ago he came sharp into the belfry and called to us, 'Get out of it, lads—get out quick for your lives; it's all over now.' It's widening out at bottom; you can see how the base wall's moved and forced up the graves on the north side." And he pointed to a shapeless heap of turf and gravestones and churchyard mould against the base of the tower.

"Where is Mr Westray?" Lord Blandamer said. "Ask him to speak to me for a minute."

He looked round about for the architect; he wondered now that he had not seen him among the crowd. The people standing near had listened to Lord Blandamer's words. They of Cullerne looked on the master of Fording as being almost omnipotent. If he could not command the tower, like Joshua's sun in Ajalon, to stand still forthwith and not fall down, yet he had no doubt some sage scheme to suggest to the architect whereby the great disaster might be averted. Where was the architect? they questioned impatiently. Why was he not at hand when Lord Blandamer wanted him? Where was he? And in a moment Westray's name was on all lips.

And just then was heard a voice from the tower, calling out through the louvres of the belfry windows, very clear and distinct for all it was so high up, and for all the chatter of the jackdaws. It was Westray's voice:

"I am shut up in the belfry," it called; "the door is jammed. For God's sake! someone bring a crowbar, and break in the door!"

There was despair in the words, that sent a thrill of horror through those that heard them. The crowd stared at one another. The foreman-mason wiped the sweat off his brow; he was thinking of his wife and children. Then the Catholic priest stepped out.

"I will go," he said; "I have no one depending on me."

Lord Blandamer's thoughts had been elsewhere; he woke from his reverie at the priest's words.

"Nonsense!" said he; "I am younger than you, and know the staircase. Give me a lever." One of the builder's men handed him a lever with a sheepish air. Lord Blandamer took it, and ran quickly towards the minster.

The foreman-mason called after him:

"There is only one door open, my lord—a little door by the organ."

"Yes, I know the door," Lord Blandamer shouted, as he disappeared round the church.

A few minutes later he had forced open the belfry door. He pulled it back towards him, and stood behind it on the steps higher up, leaving the staircase below clear for Westray's escape. The eyes of the two men did not meet, for Lord Blandamer was hidden by the door; but Westray was much overcome as he thanked the other for rescuing him.

"Run for your life!" was all Lord Blandamer said; "you are not saved yet."

The younger man dashed headlong down the steps, and then Lord Blandamer pushed the door to, and followed with as little haste or excitement as if he had been coming down from one of his many inspections of the restoration work.

As Westray ran through the great church, he had to make his way through a heap of mortar and debris that lay upon the pavement. The face of the wall over the south transept arch had come away, and in its fall had broken through the floor into the vaults below. Above his head that baleful old crack, like a black lightning-flash, had widened into a cavernous fissure. The church was full of dread voices, of strange moanings and groanings, as if the spirits of all the monks departed were wailing for the destruction of Abbot Vinnicomb's tower. There was a dull rumbling of rending stone and crashing timbers, but over all the architect heard the cry of the crossing-arches: "The arch never sleeps, never sleeps. They have bound upon us a burden too heavy to be borne; we are shifting it. The arch never sleeps."

Outside, the people in the market-place held their breath, and the stream of white dust still poured out of the side of the wounded tower. It was six o'clock; the four quarters sounded, and the hour struck. Before the last stroke had died away Westray ran out across the square, but the people waited to cheer until Lord Blandamer should be safe too. The chimes began "Bermondsey" as clearly and cheerfully as on a thousand other bright and sunny evenings.

And then the melody was broken. There was a jangle of sound, a deep groan from Taylor John, and a shrill cry from Beata Maria, a roar as of cannon, a shock as of an earthquake, and a cloud of white dust hid from the spectators the ruin of the fallen tower:

Epilogue

On the same evening Lieutenant Ennefer, R.N., sailed down Channel in the corvette *Solebay*, bound for the China Station. He was engaged to the second Miss Bulteel, and turned his glass on the old town where his lady dwelt as he passed by. It was then he logged that Cullerne Tower was not to be seen, though the air was clear and the ship but six miles from shore. He rubbed his glass, and called some other officers to verify the absence of the ancient seamark, but all they could make out was a white cloud, that might be smoke or dust or mist hanging over the town. It must be mist, they said; some unusual atmospheric condition must have rendered the tower invisible.

It was not for many months afterwards that Lieutenant Ennefer heard of the catastrophe, and when he came up Channel again on his return four years later, there was the old seamark clear once more, whiter a little, but still the same old tower. It had been rebuilt at the sole charge of Lady Blandamer, and in the basement of it was a brass plate to the memory of Horatio Sebastian Fynes, Lord Blandamer, who had lost his own life in that place whilst engaged in the rescue of others.

The rebuilding was entrusted to Mr Edward Westray, whom Lord Blandamer, by codicil dictated only a few hours before his death, had left co-trustee with Lady Blandamer, and guardian of the infant heir.

TUNES PLAYED BY THE CHIMES OF
ST. SEPULCHRE'S CHURCH AT CULLERNE.

At 6 o'clock.   **Bermondsey.**

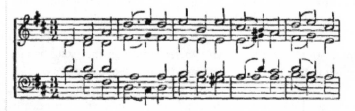

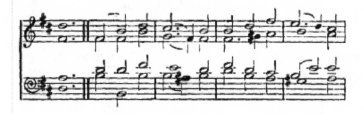

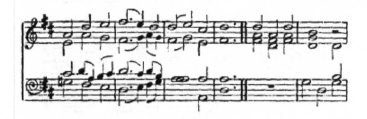

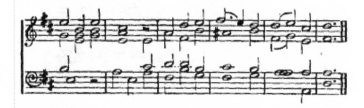

At 9 o'clock.   Sheldon.

At 12 o'clock.   Mount Ephraim.

CPSIA information can be obtained
at www.ICGtesting.com
Printed in the USA
LVHW102051190723
752798LV00031B/1093/J

EARTH
in Motion

by Christian Downey

PEARSON
Scott
Foresman

DK

How Earth Moves

Earth is always moving. In fact, Earth is spinning as you read this. Why can't you feel it? You are moving with Earth. When Earth spins, everything on it spins too. Earth's movement is smooth and steady.

How do you know Earth is moving? One way you can tell is that the Sun and the stars seem to be moving in the sky. Another way is by observing the change in seasons. This change is more obvious in some places than in others. The change in seasons is partly due to how Earth moves through space.

Scientists use many types of equipment to see how objects seem to move in the sky.

Earth as seen from space

The Rotation of Earth

Earth spins around its axis. The **axis** is an imaginary line that goes through Earth from the North Pole to the South Pole. A **rotation** is the spinning of Earth around its axis. One complete turn around the axis is one rotation. It takes Earth almost twenty-four hours, or one day, to make a full rotation.

Earth spins from west to east, but objects in the sky appear to move from east to west. You can see why this happens with a simple experiment. Hold your hand in front of your face. Move your head to the right. Did you notice that your hand seemed to move to the left? This is how the movement of the Sun and other stars appears to people on Earth. Earth moves from west to east, and the Sun and other stars appear to move from east to west.

The Sun appears to move through the sky during the day.

Shadows

In the morning and evening, when the Sun seems low in the sky, shadows look long. In the middle of the day, when the Sun appears to be overhead, shadows look short. Earth's rotation also causes day to become night and night to become day. Any place that is turned toward the Sun experiences daytime. Nighttime is when that part of Earth is turned away from the Sun.

The Sun shines too brightly for us to see stars during the day. Look at a clear sky for several nights. You may notice that stars seem to move from east to west in the sky.

Daylight

Every place on Earth has a different number of daylight hours at different times of the year. This chart shows the changes in daylight hours over a year, in Chicago, a city in the Northern Hemisphere.

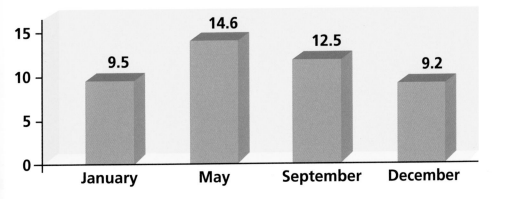

Revolutions of Earth

Earth rotates on its axis. It also revolves around the Sun at the same time. A revolution is the movement of one object around another. Earth has made one revolution when it has made one full trip around the Sun. An orbit is the path Earth takes around the Sun.

Earth completes one full revolution around the Sun in about 365 days, or one year. Earth travels a long distance at a fast speed during that time! Earth travels a total of about 940,000,000 kilometers in a year. It moves at a speed of about 107,000 kilometers per hour.

The sizes and distances in this diagram are not true to scale.

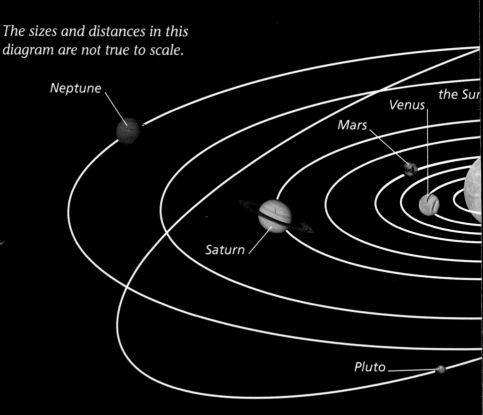

Neptune

the Sun

Venus

Mars

Saturn

Pluto

The orbit of Earth is an ellipse. An **ellipse** is a sort of stretched-out, flattened circle. Earth's distance from the Sun changes at different parts of its orbit. Sometimes Earth is farther from the Sun than at other times. Sometimes it is close.

Gravity pulls two objects together. It can work from far away. Gravity is the force that keeps Earth revolving around the Sun. Earth would move out into space if gravity did not keep it in place. Gravity would cause Earth and the Sun to crash into each other if Earth stopped moving.

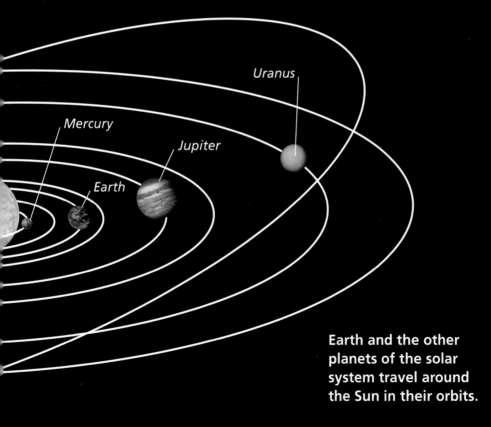

Uranus

Mercury

Jupiter

Earth

Earth and the other planets of the solar system travel around the Sun in their orbits.

Earth's Axis

Earth's axis is always tilted in the same direction. This tilt means that different areas on Earth get direct sunlight at different places in the orbit.

Earth can be divided into two halves, the Northern and Southern Hemispheres. When one hemisphere is tilted toward the Sun, the other is tilted away. The hemisphere that is tilted toward the Sun has warmer weather and longer days. It is summer there. While that half of Earth is warm, the other half is colder. It is winter in the other hemisphere. Earth's axis is not tilted toward or away from the Sun during spring or fall. During spring and fall in both hemispheres, the weather is less extreme. Hours of daylight and nighttime are more balanced.

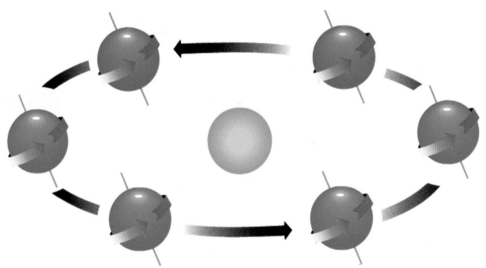

Different hemispheres tilt toward the Sun at different points in Earth's orbit.

When it is winter in the United States...

...it is summer in Australia.

The Southern Hemisphere is tilted toward the Sun during part of the year. It gets more direct sunlight. That means it gets more heat. Temperatures there are higher, and it is summer. While the Southern Hemisphere is tilted toward the Sun, the Northern Hemisphere is tilted away from the Sun. It gets less direct sunlight. So it gets less heat and has lower temperatures. It is winter. That means that while it is winter in the United States, it is summer in Australia! Temperatures in the spring and fall are milder in both hemispheres.

Patterns in the Sky

The Moon is the easiest object to see in the night sky. The Moon appears to shine brightly. But the Moon's light comes from sunlight reflecting off its surface. The Sun acts as a light bulb, and the Moon acts as a mirror.

The Moon orbits Earth. The Moon's orbit, just like Earth's orbit, is an ellipse. There is gravity between the Moon and Earth. This holds the Moon in its orbit. The Moon's revolution around Earth takes a little longer than twenty-seven days.

The Moon turns around its own axis as it circles Earth. As it rotates one time on its axis, it also revolves one time around Earth. Because of this, the same side of the Moon always faces Earth.

light from the Sun

The Moon spins around on its axis as it revolves around Earth.

The Moon's Phases

The Moon appears to be different shapes at different times of the month. Only half of the Moon ever faces the Sun. Sunlight reflects on the surface of that half. A full Moon appears when the lighted half faces Earth directly.

Most of the time, we see only part of the lighted half of the Moon. The different shapes that the Moon seems to have are called phases of the Moon. Each phase lasts a short time. A set of phases begins with a new Moon. This is when the part of the Moon facing Earth cannot be seen. It is followed by a crescent. This is a sliver of lighted Moon. Then a larger part of the Moon is visible. We call this the first quarter. Soon the entire half of the Moon is visible. This full Moon appears as a full circle. After that we see the Moon in the phase called the last quarter. It looks similar to a half circle. The phases begin again with the new Moon.

crescent Moon

first quarter Moon

full Moon

last quarter Moon

Eclipses

An eclipse happens when one object in space comes between the Sun and another object and casts its shadow on the other object. This happens when the Moon crosses Earth's shadow, or when the Moon's shadow reaches part of Earth.

A lunar eclipse occurs when the Moon passes directly through Earth's shadow. This can only happen when the Moon is full. The Moon and the Sun must also be on opposite sides of Earth for this to happen. During a lunar eclipse, Earth blocks all or part of the Sun's rays from reaching the Moon.

A partial eclipse happens when only part of the Moon is in Earth's shadow. Not every place on Earth can see every eclipse. A lunar eclipse is only visible from the places on Earth where it is night.

sunlight

lunar eclipse

During a solar eclipse, the Moon blocks
the Sun from view.

A solar eclipse occurs when the Moon passes
between the Sun and Earth and casts its shadow
on Earth. The Moon may block part or all of the Sun
from view. When the Moon blocks the Sun, a shadow is
cast. But the shadow covers only a small part of Earth.
A solar eclipse can only be seen from the places on
Earth that are in Moon's shadow.

A solar eclipse is an amazing sight. However, it
is never safe to look straight at the Sun. Any direct
sunlight can damage your eyes, even causing blindness.

Stars

Scientists think there may be 1 billion trillion stars in the universe. That would be a 1 followed by 21 zeroes! That's a lot of stars! The Sun is the star closest to Earth. It gives Earth light and energy. Some stars are bigger and hotter than the Sun. Other stars are smaller and cooler.

The brightness of the Sun keeps us from seeing stars during the day. If stars are very far away, they may not seem as bright. You can see more stars with a telescope than you can with just your eyes.